I0524480

The
Angel
Brings Fire

Book Two : *Doubt Me Not*

(Second Edition)

by

Marcus B. Shields

Copyright © Marcus Shields / Telostic Corporation, 2010-2014.

All rights reserved.

ISBN : (978-0-9939221-2-1)

For additional information about *The Angel Brings Fire*, surf to :

http://abfbook.telostic.com

For my father, Roy Allan Shields

Who could write great prose... 'with a chisel'

Table of Contents

Prologue

Since *The Angel Brings Fire* is a multi-volume series, it is strongly suggested that the reader should enjoy Book One, *Angel of Mailànkh*, before starting the narrative provided in Book Two, *Doubt Me Not*.

That said, it is recognized that for various reasons, some readers will have happened upon this volume of the series, without having convenient access to Book One.

We have therefore provided the following brief synopsis of the events of *Angel of Mailànkh*, so that the reader can make sense of some of the characters and themes brought forward from the beginning of the novel.

Marcus Shields

Author

Angel of Mailànkh revolves around the discovery of an extremely powerful female alien being on Mars, self-described as "The Storied Watcher" a.k.a. "Karéin-Mayréij", who may or may not be an "angel" and who may or may not be Earth's only remaining hope of stopping a Doomsday comet named *Lucifer*.

The Mars lander *Eagle* is crewed by Commander Sam Jacobson (46 year-old Caucasian), U.S. Air Force Majors Brent Boyd (38 year-old Caucasian) and Devon White (35 year-old African-American), as well as Professor Cherie Tanaka (32 year-old Eurasian-American), while Cosmonaut Sergei Chkalov (33 year-old Muscovite Russian) remains in the *Infinity* mother ship, in orbit around the Red Planet.

After a short time *en route*, Chkalov discovers that Karéin has somehow managed to stow away on board the *Eagle*. As a result of this, the Russian and the alien are isolated from the *Infinity* and the rest of the crew, on Jacobson's order.

While confined in the *Eagle* lander, the Storied Watcher learns of Earth's impending destruction by the comet; she resolves to take matters into her own hands, and barges, unannounced, into the *Infinity's* main crew compartment. While there, fearing that there may soon be no-one left on Earth, the alien passes her secret gift – a supernatural power called *Amaiish* or *The Fire* – to the human astronauts who she encountered and befriended on Mars.

Unfortunately, matters are proceeding apace, and Earth's several attempts to stop the comet, prove singularly ineffective.

Realizing that she is the only hope to save the planet and the billions of lives upon it, Karéin-Mayréij resolves to destroy Lucifer in a suicidal 'death-run', powered indirectly by the enormous energies of Earth's Sun.

And thus she does; for as she closes in on the comet, Karéin-Mayréij releases a final, annihilating burst of energy, which destroys *Lucifer* and saves Earth. But this feat is achieved only at a terrible price, because not even an angel, could hope to survive such an explosion.

As her mind goes blank, the Storied Watcher – as well as her grateful but heartbroken friends from the Mars exploration mission – knows that her work is done, even if her life has been sacrificed, in so doing.

Or... *has* it?

Aftermath

Picking Up The Pieces

The first rays of the early morning sun shone dimly through the skylight in the secluded bunker-complex, filtered first by the tall pines in this isolated, mountain-sylvan setting.

It wasn't the White House; but then, it was as safe as one could get, anywhere on a planet that had come within a hair's-breadth of disaster.

All stood, as he entered.

"This meeting will come to order," announced the President of the United States.

Surveying the occupants of the room – those who really counted, minus the several glowering Marine guards and other assorted functionaries – the President noted with considerable satisfaction and relief that only a few were missing.

Under the circumstances, this was a real accomplishment. After all, scant days ago, they all might very well have ended up forever missing, from the scarred face of Planet Earth.

"Very well, you may be seated, now," he said. He suppressed a smile as all complied, acknowledging the authority that had lately seemed close to irrelevant.

It felt good to be back in control.

"First of all, I'd like to say what's on everyone's mind," the President explained. "There's no doubt that we have all just come through the most serious crisis that the human race has ever faced, but, thanks to both our own resourcefulness and the help of the Almighty, we have prevailed. I have to tell you that just a few days ago, I thought that I'd never live to see another one of these meetings... I know we couldn't tell the public that, but, well – I think you all know what I mean. I'm just thankful that we got through it, somehow."

Mutely, all nodded their agreement.

Despite his long and mostly successful political career, and despite all else that had happened, the President tried, whenever possible, to run his meetings as he would have done a top-level business conference – quick and to the point.

Though he reveled in the trappings of office and always found time to, for example, console the widow of a dead soldier, he had never really felt comfortable with the endless give-and-take of Washington deal-making, with the need to accommodate this-one-or-that-one. Business was simple: everyone worked towards the same, easy-to-understand goal. Except for the situation just past, politics was like a rowboat with all the paddles pulling in different directions – too complicated and chaotic.

"That having been said, I suppose we should start with a status report. so we're all on the same page as concerns the emergency," he said. "Jeremy, that's your ball park. Proceed."

Franklin, the President's wizened, gray-haired Emergency Measures Coordinator, leaned forward and spoke up.

"Thank you, Mr. President," he replied. "Here's a summary of what we know, and where we're at, currently, sir. First of all, although obviously I need not repeat the synopsis of the events of the last few days here – God knows, they'll be forever etched on our memories – I think I should try to separate fact from fiction, or, perhaps, to separate what we know for sure from what we're merely guessing at."

All eyes focused upon him, Franklin continued, "As we all know, the 'Lucifer' comet disintegrated at the last possible moment, shortly after it entered the Earth's outer atmosphere. How or why, we're not completely sure – I'll elaborate on that later, but right now, we have to deal with the mess it left behind. Which is, unfortunately, a very considerable one."

"I've heard that Los Angeles, Spokane, Boise, Memphis, Des Moines, Boston and Detroit got hit," interrupted the President. "Do we have firm damage assessments from those cities, yet?"

"St. Louis, too, and communications are still very bad everywhere," answered Franklin, "Especially from outside the Western Hemisphere, since it appears that the comet's fragments cut some of the transoceanic cables, and, of course, most of the satellites are out – frankly, it's a miracle that *anything* in Earth orbit survived what went on up there."

He paused for a second, then went on, "But to answer your question, sir, from what we know currently, Boise and Memphis have basically been wiped off the map – nearly *total* destruction, worse than a megaton range H-bomb landing right on top of them. The outright impact damage to the other ones is less severe but LA in particular is in a very bad state, simply because of the number of people that are, or were, in the area at impact time. Reports are trickling in from all over about impacts from comet fragments, mostly small-size ones, but remember, there were thousands of the damn things – please excuse my language, Mr. President – and even a rock the size of a small car can take out a skyscraper, if it's falling as fast as the remnants from 'Lucifer' were. My own guess is that it'll be at least four months before we even *know* the full extent of the damage, let alone be able to start repairing it."

"Well," remarked the President, trying to sound philosophical, "Although we all mourn the loss of our fellow Americans in the affected areas, things *could* have been worse – I don't have to explain how."

"Excuse me," demanded a voice from far down one side of the table, "But is it over, yet? My people are telling me that chunks of the comet are still raining down, all over the place."

"Yes, and yes," Franklin answered. "I have checked with NASA, or what's left of it – Mission Control in Houston also took a fairly severe hit, but it's still operational, after a fashion. What they tell me is that over 99 per cent of the mass of the comet has now been accounted for, but due to some really complex stuff having to do with the atmosphere, some of its fragments got blasted back into orbit but are now slowly falling back to Earth, one by one. It's a process that may take weeks or months, but it's not a serious danger any more. At least, that's what they tell me."

"So," Franklin concluded, "What we have to deal with, basically, is the aftermath of, as the President said, the most serious crisis that we have *ever* faced. Right now, our best guess is that we have electricity working in no more than 50 per cent of the nation's households, oil refineries are down to 30 per cent of normal output and both the rail and Interstate transportation networks are all but knocked out. That's about it."

Turning to the immaculately-tailored, blow-dried, fiftyish man next to him, the President said, "Bob? You hear that? That's something we'll have to move on, pronto. The last thing we need on top of the damn comet, is the economy grinding to a halt. I'd like an action plan from you on that front, end of day Wednesday. Got that?"

"Understood, Mr. President," replied the Treasury Secretary. "For what it's worth, although there's no doubt that what Mr. Franklin says is true, I can tell you that the stock-market's still in business – thus far. I was on the phone all day yesterday talking to Chambers of the Fed, as well as to the major bank chairmen – excuse me, Madam Secretary, chairpersons – to shore up confidence. So far, so good. But don't bet any money on it lasting."

He half-smiled at the pun.

"Okay," the President acknowledged. He leaned over to the right, searching the table, then said, "DeWitt? Art? You there? Oh, there you are. Time for the security report. Go ahead."

A brush-cut, leather-faced Caucasian man – looking as if he might just have stepped out of a Marine training camp – leaned forward and spoke.

"Thank you, Mr. President," said the Secretary of Defense. "We had isolated outbreaks of panic, riots and looting just before and after the comet began its final descent – apparently things are still not under control in the Los Angeles area and in a few other places, for example Atlanta and Miami – but the National Guard's in place where it needs to be, and the situation is being dealt with. In the medium term, we'll need to know when you plan to rescind martial law, and if you want to do so on a nation-wide basis or just selectively, leaving it in place for the troubled areas."

"What about the armed forces themselves?" asked the President. "I saw the attack on TV, too. A lot of brave soldiers..."

His voice trailed off.

"There can be no doubt of their sacrifice, sir," replied DeWitt, in a wavering voice. "America's armed forces lost a lot of heroes and heroines on that fateful day – I'm now in the process of identifying candidates for the Distinguished Service Medal, the vast majority of whom will receive it posthumously; let me just say that it's a very long list, Mr. President. I know I speak for everyone here when I say that we owe the very survival of our planet, and of the human race, to these young men and women. Their bravery will not go unremembered."

Pausing a second to regain his composure, he continued, "Regarding our military stance and force levels right now, we have of course sustained very heavy losses – over 90 per cent of our nuclear weapons were expended in the effort to stop 'Lucifer', and both the Air Force and Navy lost well over 60 per cent of their available combat aircraft in the same campaign, most with full crews. The Army – no slight on it, of course – is in much better shape, since the theater of operations was outside its reach. But I can assure you, Mr. President, that we remain fully able to meet and deal with any likely threat, since all of our potential adversaries have suffered the same, or worse, losses in the last few days. For example, that the Russian Air Force has basically ceased to exist; they elected to get a lot closer to the comet than we did, to launch their final attacks. I have great respect for their bravery and I've sent my personal commendations, and condolences, to Senior General Kulikov in Moscow, already."

A voice, dignified and sad-sounding, said from the far end of the table, "General, neither I nor anyone else here, wants to dispute the bravery or importance of the role that our armed forces played in stopping the comet, but, well... there *was* that other, unexplained factor... was there not?"

"I was waiting for you to jump in, Fred," smiled the President, "But no harm done, I was about to ask the same question, myself." He turned to regard a white-haired, bemedalled figure.

"General," asked the U.S. leader, "We all saw – and some of us *heard*, don't ask me how – something very unusual flying towards the comet, just before, thanks be to God, it was destroyed. Has the military, or NASA, or anyone, been able to figure out what that was? Whether it played any part in 'Lucifer''s destruction? My point here is, we're bound to get questions on this front, once the dust settles."

"Before I answer that, sir," replied Harry Anderson of the Air Force, "I would remind everyone here that what we're about to discuss should be considered a state secret. *Strictly* off the record. Does everyone understand?"

They all, even the President, nodded in the affirmative.

"Okay, Mr. President, in that case, I'll turn the floor over to General Symington of Space Defense Command, who has accompanied me here today specifically to answer this kind of question. Jack?"

Another multi-medaled military man, who had been sitting quietly behind Anderson, now rose to his feet and addressed the group.

"Thank you, General Anderson," Symington said. "As the General said, I'm here to give you what we know about the last few moments of the 'Lucifer' object's trajectory towards Earth. Right at the outset, I think I should mention that our understanding of what happened up there, is very incomplete, and it may remain so, possibly forever. Not only because of the confusion of the battle, but also because, frankly, many of those who got closest to it, didn't expect to live to see another day, so record-keeping sort of fell by the wayside, in many cases."

"What I *can* tell you now," he continued, "Is based primarily on debriefings that we've been able to conduct with the few Air Force crews that managed to survive the attack, plus with remote interviews with observers on the ISS1 and ISS2 space-stations, plus with long-range telemetry from various military and NASA sensors on the ground – unfortunately, most of the near-Earth orbital satellites were either destroyed by the comet's debris field as it approached, or were not in a good position to record the events, even if they survived."

Stopping for a second to clear his throat, Symington explained, "As you know, the Earth's military forces – foremost among which were of course our own, but all of the others, as well – implemented a co-ordinated, last-ditch attack against the comet, which we knew had already been weakened to some extent by our earlier attacks. As it started entering the outer atmosphere, we launched our final volley, which included what amounted to a suicide run by the brave crew of the 'Salvador Two' spacecraft, which had been equipped with a payload of high-yield thermonuclear weapons – 'Salvador Two' had been trapped in Earth orbit due to an engine failure that prevented it from intercepting the comet further out in space."

Symington now paced around the periphery of the room, behind those seated at the table, as he spoke on.

"Shortly before the final destruction of the comet," he said, "We observed two significant attacks on it, either of which may have been the agent that finally destroyed 'Lucifer' and that therefore saved Earth. One, was the detonation of 'Salvador Two''s payload – we estimate that, given the explosive yield of this spacecraft's bombs, it *could* have caused the comet's breakup; but what we can't figure out, at least this is what my sources at NASA are telling me, is how it could have so completely shattered 'Lucifer'. The scientists' opinion is that had it been only 'Salvador Two' that finally split apart the comet, the remaining pieces would have still been very large, so large, in fact, that their impact shortly thereafter would still have been cataclysmic, far worse than what we actually suffered."

All eyes were trained on him.

Symington said, "Now, the second attack vector, is one that we're having a hard time explaining. Something – some new kind of weapon, which up to now we have never seen, or heard of – was observed flying directly at the comet at very high speed, – then it disappeared for approximately three-tenths of a second, then the comet simply blew apart. This unknown object shone brilliantly, so much so that it burned out the sensor arrays of some of the telescopes that we aimed at it, and, well, here the story starts to get really *strange*."

Melodramatically, he waited a second, then elaborated, "As Dr. McPherson has alluded to, there are reports from the ground all over Earth that observers heard various things, ranging from 'music' of some sort to incomprehensible voices, as the object approached the comet; but, none of the audio recordings of the period have recorded any of these sounds, so we're forced to conclude that these reports may be the result of mass hysteria, hallucinations, or something of that type."

"General," the man from the end of the table interrupted, "I'm sure you *know* what I'm going to say next. You're leaving something out."

"I was getting to that," Symington replied, matter-of-factually. "What Dr. McPherson is referring to, is the theory that this weapon – in other words, the thing that destroyed the comet – was, in fact, the alien from Mars, that is, the one who identified herself as 'Karéin-Mayréij', also known as 'The Storied Watcher'."

He expected a gasp from the audience, but none came.

"I can see," said Symington, smoothly, "That this theory is not new to anyone here."

"Of *course* not," commented a middle-aged, black woman. "HHS has been getting inquiries about this from all our state offices. Apparently a cult has developed about the alien in some of our churches, especially around Los Angeles and elsewhere in the Southwest, I'm still checking with my contacts in my community to try to find out exactly how and where it started. The idea is that she was some sort of 'angel' sent by God to save the Earth, maybe even the Second Coming, who knows. Right now, we don't know what to say back to them... we have no official position."

"That's true, Madam Secretary," added a portly, bald-headed, bespectacled man who had heretofore been seated quietly next to the President, "But I would remind you that the other half of the churches down in Dixie – the half that supports our party when it comes around to votin' – have this idea that the alien was the devil, and that she *sent* the comet to kill us all."

"For God's sake, Mr. Horn," protested the woman, "Surely nobody here can possibly believe that. I saw the recordings of what she said while she was on the Mars mission space ship. She said she was here to *help*, not to harm. And how could she have created the comet, anyway, when *we* – that is, Captain Jacobson and the crew of the *Eagle II* – were the ones that woke her, on Mars, weeks *after* we saw the comet, in the first place? The whole idea's absurd."

"Not too much more absurd than the idea that a single flesh and blood being could cause an explosion thousands of times more powerful than our biggest H-bombs," commented Anderson. "*You* tell *me* the physics of that, let alone the biology."

"Don't blame me, or our Southern ministers, Ma'am," said the bald-headed man, looking at the HHS Secretary. "Weren't our idea, anyway; word has it that it first started to show up with the Muslims and at least some of our friends in Israel, in the Middle East – they're real fired up about her, claim that she's 'the new Jezebel', or something like that. At least, that's what my contacts tell me."

"Team, team," exclaimed the President, motioning for order. "I appreciate the honesty, but there'll be time for speculation, later – this is a Cabinet meeting, not a theology class. Let's let the General finish, shall we?"

"Thank you, Mr. President," said Symington, as he re-took the floor. "But actually, this kind of debate has been going on within the Armed Forces, as well. Just to speak to Madam Secretary Jones' point, yes, it's true, the idea that the alien could have been responsible for either sending the comet against Earth – or, that she later could have been responsible for destroying it – *does* seem highly unlikely. However, we have some very strange reports of her somehow 'flying through space' just prior to the comet's arrival at Earth – I was personally involved in one of these conversations, and I can tell everyone listening here today, that in speaking with this being, I was acutely aware that I was dealing with a completely unknown quantity – so *anything* is possible."

"Why don't we just *ask* her?" inquired someone, not McPherson, from the far end of the table.

"Good question," replied Symington, "But unfortunately, that option appears to no longer be available to us. As you may or may not know, we asked the alien to *rendez-vous* with a spacecraft just before the 'Lucifer' impact, so that we'd get a better chance to evaluate her, and she verbally agreed to do that – but she never showed up, that's the bottom line. She simply vanished into thin air, there's been no trace of her since the time that she left Captain Jacobson's ship for the last time. So, unfortunately, she will probably remain a mystery, forever."

"I've spoken to some of the crew-members of the *Eagle* and *Infinity* mission to Mars about that," interjected McPherson, forcefully. "They claim that she died in the explosion that destroyed 'Lucifer'... that she told them she was going to sacrifice herself, to save Earth. That she had to choose between saving herself, and saving *us*."

"Do *you* believe that, Mr. McPherson?" asked the black woman.

"I honestly don't know *what* I believe," explained the scientist. "I have been going over the recordings of what happened on Mars, then on the *Eagle* and *Infinity* on the trip back to Earth, again and again – sometimes I find myself half-believing what Commander Jacobson's crew told me about the alien, although I get the feeling that there may be more to the story, that is, things that they're holding back from us. But you're right, General Anderson, I have no way to reconcile their story with what we know is scientifically possible. Which is not to say that it's *impossible*, I should remind everyone here of that. It's just that we don't know... now, we may *never* know."

"Well, if they're not telling you everything they know, I'll fix that," said Symington. "Commander Jacobson and at least two of his other crew members are under my chain of command."

"It's just a feeling," cautioned McPherson. "They've always answered all of my questions, truthfully, as far as I can tell. I wouldn't want you to think that there's been any *intentional* deception involved, here. I think what I'm trying to say, Jack, is that you and I both spoke directly with 'Karéin' – I don't know about you, but there was something... *mystical* about her, above and beyond the obvious fact of who she was and where she was from. I think that Commander Jacobson and his people have a special insight here, just because they were much closer to her, while she was with them. Don't ask me to explain what kind of insight that might be... I can't."

"Hmm... 'died to save the world and then just vanished'," mentioned someone from the back of the table. "Sounds like a familiar story... I remember hearing something like that in Sunday-school..."

"It's a *terrible* loss," sadly noted McPherson. "We learned *so* much from her, in the brief time that we had access to her. I just can't believe that she's gone."

"Maybe so," offered the short, bald-headed man, "But speakin' just for myself, I'm not really that sad to see the last of her. Would have been *disruptive*, if she had stayed."

"What do you –" started McPherson, only to be cut off by the President, who said, "It's an interesting issue, for sure, but there's another side of it that I want to ask you, General. So far, we've been working on the assumption that the alien may have had some kind of a role in the destruction of the comet. Fair enough, we can debate that one until the cows come home, but what I'd like to ask is, what if she *didn't*? Doesn't that imply that somebody else has a very effective weapon, that we previously had no knowledge of?"

"Indeed," replied Symington, "And Mr. President, I can see that we think alike, because you took the words right out of my mouth."

McPherson glowered silently from his vantage point at the end of the table. He noticed that the HHS Secretary was not amused, either.

Symington continued, "The first thing I want to say on this topic is that the weapon we're referring to, if that's what it was, was definitely *not* our own, Mr. President. I've checked carefully with the other Joint Chiefs of Staff and neither the Navy, nor the Army, nor the Marines, have anything like it. I checked with the Black program managers and, although we *have* been working on a number of what we call 'exotic high-energy explosive devices', none of these are even at the prototype stage yet. Nukes are the best we got, and whatever that was, it certainly wasn't a nuke, sir. *Nothing* in our inventory has the kind of explosive yield needed to do what we saw happen up there. If we had such a bomb, we would have used it long ago, when the comet wasn't nearly so close to Earth."

"John?" interrupted the President. "Has NSA or CIA got anything on this, that the Joint Chiefs don't know about?"

A nondescript, neatly-groomed, 40-something Caucasian man said in a flat, Midwestern accent, "We're still investigating, sir, but the short answer is, 'no'. We have our own programs, separate from those of the military, but none of those correspond to what we saw on that night, either. We have also been conducting an extensive investigation into the question of what other nation might have such a weapon, but so far, we don't have much information and what we do have doesn't add up, I'm afraid."

"Well... that's *good*," interrupted the rotund, bald Billy Horn, as he removed his glasses, staring straight forward. "You see – and here, I'm suggestin' something, Mr. President – I believe that we're best off tellin' everyone that this weapon *is*, in fact our own. *Whatever* may be the truth of the matter."

"I beg your pardon?" retorted Fred McPherson, leaning forward. "I thought I just heard from both the military and the intelligence community that it *wasn't* our own. That we don't have a clue what it really is, in fact. Do I have something wrong, here?"

"Not at all, Mr. Science Adviser," replied Horn, in his characteristic Southern drawl. "But what I'm gettin' at is, whether or not we did, in fact, invent this thing, we'd get a whole heap of goodwill from everyone out there in TV-land, if we take credit for usin' it to save the Earth, isn't that a fact, now? And, furthermore, seems to me that just *sayin'* that we have it will intimidate our adversaries, in these unsettled times in which we live, nowadays. Leastaways, it'll give us time to work on the real thing, until whomever actually did make it first, tries to call our bluff. If they dare. Which, I predict, they won't. Poker's *our* game, not theirs."

"I had hoped," commented the HHS Secretary, "That the Earth had gotten past this kind of thing, what with what we've all just been through."

"Amen to that," added McPherson.

"Crises come and crises go," replied the short, bald man. "Human nature, doesn't change. I'm just pointin' out the obvious and the inevitable, that's all."

Again motioning for the floor, the President said, "Thanks, Billy – you've certainly got an interesting idea there, one that we'll have to discuss off-line, later."

The little bugger's a weasel, the President thought, *But without his instincts, and his ability to rouse the Bible-bangers, I'd never have got here in the first place...*

"Certainly, sir," replied Horn. "And upon gettin' the go-ahead – should it please you, Mr. President – I can have our field-workers discreetly plant the idea with our most loyal voters... Suthen Baptists down in Alabama, for example. The word'll spread fast enough. And they would *never* doubt what the guv'ment of the Yew-Nighted States would tell 'em."

He replaced and straightened his glasses, showing his trademark, opaque half-smile, ignoring the looks of disgust on the faces of McPherson, Jones and a couple others in the room.

"So," the President continued, "General Anderson, I want you and the Joint Chiefs to launch an immediate, top-priority program, first to get to the bottom of this – that is, who has this damn weapon, if it really exists – secondly, to make one of our own. Whether or not anyone else has it. And I want CIA and NSA's full cooperation on this – no holding back, no secrets. Whatever you need for budget, you'll have it. Is that clear?"

"Very, sir," replied Anderson, DeWitt and Symington, as if one. The National Security Adviser just nodded.

"Sir," interjected the Treasury Secretary, "I don't want to speak out of turn here, but about the budget for this project... won't we have to consult OMB about that? And the Congress? As Jeremy is no doubt aware, the expenses associated with reconstruction after the comet are likely to be significant, on their own... balancing the next Federal budget will be a challenge, regardless..."

A balding, Caucasian man with shifty-looking, squinty eyes, perhaps 10 years senior to the President, spoke up from the chair next to the latter's own. "Understood, Mr. Secretary, but the consequences of the United States being caught at a military disadvantage against this kind of weapon would be far worse. At the risk of inviting the inevitable jokes and comparisons, ladies and gentlemen, we cannot allow a... a... comet-wrecker gap!"

"That's why I wanted you to be Vice-President, George," said the President with a wry smile, "So I didn't have to be the one to say things like that."

The Vice-President smiled back courteously, and the meeting continued on, long into the morning.

No Rest For Survivors

Several days had now passed since the epochal events leading up to the comet's none-too-soon demise, and the crew of the ISS2 space-station – not least among them, Commander Sam Jacobson and his former crew of the *Infinity* and *Eagle* mission to Mars (Cherie Tanaka, Brent Boyd, Sergei Chkalov, Devon White and, latterly, Alan Humber, Chief Mechanical Engineer of the station) – had finally recovered, more or less, from the emotional exhaustion of that time.

Although they had all been through crises of one kind or another at various times in their previous lives, there was nothing that could have prepared them for *this*, that is, the near-destruction of Earth, along with everyone and anyone that any of them held dear. Nor could anything have prepared them for how the threat had, finally, been overcome.

It had been far *too* close, and Earth had only been saved, at the last moment, by *her*. Of that, all of them – even Humber, who had never personally encountered the alien enigmatically entitled "The Storied Watcher" – were certain, although they had all been close-mouthed about the details, when the military men later came after them for the debriefings.

But Humber *had* participated in the Mars-girl's final ritual, some kind of other-worldly ceremony that he knew nothing about yet supported intimately, and he had *connected* with her, if only for a fleeting moment. His psyche and his being, call it his soul if you must, understood; his intellect did not. So he pumped and prodded the others for whatever they knew about the girl that they had freed from that stony tomb on the Red Planet.

At first, none of them had wanted to discuss the matter – they were all too overcome with grief at her loss – but slowly, Humber had come to understand the story of how this being had so quickly adapted to, no, *become* a near-facsimile of, the human race, how she had befriended the crew, how she had made mistakes and had tried to atone for them; and, how, finally, she had to accept the bitter cup of a task that would ultimately claim her life. Inwardly, he resented that he would never meet her; but, had she not done what she did, there would no longer *be* an Earth.

It reminded him of sermons he used to hear, around Easter time, after he finally found an Anglican diocese willing to put up with his lifestyle. He tried not to think of the obvious implications; but, at least according to those who knew her, the girl *had* called herself an 'angel'. Now, he would never know the truth of it.

Apart from these remembrances of things past, there was quite enough to keep everyone on the station busy, these days. ISS2 had been sent far out of its normal near-Earth orbit earlier during the 'Lucifer' crisis, had r*endez-vous*'ed with Jacobson's two Mars mission spaceships and had then been counter-boosted on a trajectory back towards its home planet. Unfortunately, the booster rocket had exploded in the process, also causing the loss of several of Humber's best staff, and the station now had no way of applying braking thrust.

At the time, estimates suggested that the best case would be that they would simply go flying past Earth, possibly to live a few more months before falling into the Sun's gravity well; the worst-case would be a quick, meteoric descent into the Earth's atmosphere. When Ariel Cohen, ISS2's commanding officer, had presented this set of facts to the station's crew, none of them had paid much attention, given the likely possibility that the Earth itself was about to be hit by the comet.

Devon White, ever the jokester, had tried to cheer them up by saying, "Y'all gotta look at the bright side, folks: first we're fine and Earth's toast, now it's the other way 'round... kinda evens out in the long-run, y'all think?" They had all appreciated the man's sense of humor, but the relief had been short-lasting. Now, it was different. Now, there was something to live for.

Humber turned a corner – as much as one could, in the perpetually-curved area whose centrifugal force substituted for gravity, up here – then peeked inside the conference room, in which were Sam Jacobson and Cherie Tanaka of Jacobson's former expedition, along with Ariel Cohen and three of his subordinates. The Chief Mechanic noticed that the Mars mission commander had, uncharacteristically, grown a beard, or at least the beginnings of one.

The stress of recent times must have worn off some of the man's former Air Force and NASA spit and polish.

"Fashionably late, as ever," Humber quipped. "Sorry blokes, call of nature on the way over here." It was as good an excuse as he could think of, off the top.

"No problem, Alan," replied Cohen, amicably. "We had just been chatting idly, anyway... but now that you're here, we can get down to business. Hard to talk about engineering, without an engineer."

Sheepishly, Humber took a seat next to Tanaka. He shot a quick, idle, appreciative glance at the woman's attractive, Eurasian countenance and felt stupidly guilty for doing so. He had just finished a long video-chat session with his partner back on Earth. Charlie and the kids had the right to expect fidelity, what with what they had both just been through.

Have to be straight with the me boyfriend, whether it's Cherie or that beefy Captain of hers I'm ogling, he thought. *Put that one in your pipe and smoke it, mates.*

"Recovered from the party yet, Alan?" said Jacobson, evidently playing White's role *in absentia*. "Don't know how you smuggled that Scotch on board, but I'm damn glad you did so. Just the tonic that we all needed..."

"I'm back to what you might call 'minimum functionality'," answered Humber. "Body's fine, but the mind, well... maybe we should have stretched 'er over a few more hours, or days. Who knows, we may need another parting shot, not too long from now."

"As good a way as I can think of to get on the topic, thank you for that, Alan," interjected Cohen. "You don't sound too optimistic, there. Can you fill us in on the details?"

"Please do," added Li-Ho Chen, Cohen's frustratingly humorless second-in-command. Humber secretly hated the man, ever since the incident in which Chen's scrounged, self-crafted rocket propellant mixture had exploded in ISS2's booster rocket, sending two of the chief engineer's friends and subordinates to an undeserving, unnecessary death. The *least* that Chen could have done would have been an apology; but, evidently, the concept of that was foreign to him.

However much Humber fervently wished to make his feelings known, though, there was no point in saying so, not until they were all safe on Earth, at least.

"There ain't much in the way of details to report, Commander," Humber replied, straightforwardly. "We're out of propellant, that's about it, and the rocket's still a write-off, despite the fact that me lads, those that remain of them I mean, have been working night and day on it since... well, since the *incident*. We've also been kicking a few other ideas around, notably using the engines on Captain Jacobson's Mars-expedition ships to apply braking thrust with... but ISS2's just too big, I'm afraid. Too much mass. The *Eagle* and *Infinity* might slow us a bit, but not enough to stop us where we want to stop."

"So where does that leave us?" asked Cohen.

"On the same trajectory as we have always been on, since the initial boost, I'd suspect," commented Tanaka.

"The Professor is correct on that front," noted Humber. "We have some time before we're in Earth's immediate vicinity – I'd suggest that you get a good look at it, since as matters stand now, it's likely to be your last look. You'll have no more than a day or so, before we're on our merry way again."

"Wait a minute," said an East Indian woman who had earlier been listening passively. "Will we be captured by Earth's gravity? Would we not end up in orbit, eventually?"

"I'm afraid not, Shivani dear," replied the Englishman. "We won't be getting that close, and our angular momentum's too great – don't ask me for any of the astro-mechanical details, that's not my specialty, but I've had some of the others go over all the figures on the computer and they all basically confirm the same thing. Incidentally, I'm not sure we'd *want* to get into too close an Earth orbit, even if we could; Mike Theodikas and meself have been doing some long-range scanning of the area and it's still crawling with the remnants of our dear old friend 'Lucifer'. Were we to hit one or two of 'em, that'd be it for old ISS2, I'm afraid. Chunks of ice and rock three times the size of a London double-decker, that sort of thing. They're still raining down on Earth every so often, scientists say that'll continue for *months*, and until it's over with we probably don't want to cruise anywhere near the area."

"So... where do we end up?" asked Cohen, fitfully.

"Still working on that, Commander," answered Humber, "We don't have that one completely figured out, because we're unsure of how much Earth's gravity is going to affect the trajectory – we may only find out after we go whizzing by, as it were. It seems that the possibility of actually impacting with Earth's atmosphere is now off the table; the computer is giving us a 60-40 chance of crashing into the Sun a few months or so after our fly-by, with the alternative being a long, parabolic course on its other side, almost as far as the orbit of Mars, in fact. Which would take well more than a year and a half to fully complete, by the way."

"That would seem to be a more desirable outcome than the first option," Cohen said.

"Not really," retorted the East Indian woman. "We have barely enough breathable air reserves to make it to Earth, with maybe a two or three week margin of error. We'd start running out long before we got anywhere near the Sun, if Mr. Humber's speed and timing estimates are correct."

"The Sun's starting to look better all the time," observed Humber. "Wouldn't be fun, but it'd be a lot quicker and warmer than slowly suffocating, I suppose."

"What about a rescue as we near Earth?" inquired Jacobson. "I mean, maybe by cramming everyone we can into the *Eagle* and *Infinity*, or by some of those 'Arks' evacuation mission ships. Have we considered that option?"

"I have already talked to Sylvia Abruzzio at Houston about that, Sam," interjected Tanaka. "And it's actually a miracle that I got to talk to her at all – they took a near-miss from a major 'Lucifer' fragment, thank God it landed in the sea instead of right on top of them, Sylvia herself only barely escaped the resulting *tsunami*. A lot of the rest of them weren't so lucky, they lost over a hundred of their people, with many more injured, for example Hector Ramirez will be in hospital for weeks. It took two and a half days for them to get communications back and running but finally Mike and I were able to raise them this morning."

"What about McPherson?" asked Jacobson, idly. "Oh, and Symington, our General friend?"

"I don't know," she replied. "Sylvia said something off-hand about him flying off in some kind of special military helicopter, accompanied by the

General, about a day before everything... happened. She wasn't too pleased about it, apparently, because there were still some last-minute, uncompleted tasks for the 'Arks' mission, and Fred kind of left her hanging. I get the feeling that there were some hard feelings, there..."

"I feel as badly as you do about Hector, Cherie," said Jacobson, "And as for the other two, well, that's working for the government, I guess. But what did Sylvia have to say about the idea of near-Earth rescue?"

"I'm afraid the upshot of our conversation is," answered Tanaka, "That we have only the *Eagle* and *Infinity* at our disposal. Most of the 'Arks' ships were destroyed along with the comet – very sad, of course, but no surprise there – and of the few that survived, none have enough propellant or shielding to even get safely back to Earth from where they are now, let alone to try to match our velocity and then brake all the way back to Earth. Plus, the priority is to try to get them back to Earth, somehow, not *rendez-vous* with us. Plus, there are no heavy-lift boosters left on Earth to lift anything new into orbit, none that NASA knows of, anyway, although they're hunting intensively for one... they were all used in the run-up to the 'Lucifer' event. As they should have been."

"Nothing that I didn't expect to hear," replied Jacobson, philosophically. "Ah, well, we've been through worse, so far. We'll figure something out."

"I certainly hope so, Commander," said Humber, "Because right now, what that solution may be, is something that escapes yours truly."

"What about the other two stations?" asked Cohen.

"Mike was able to raise a station-to-station link with ISS3 the day after, and with ISS1 yesterday," replied Humber. "Thanks be to the old wanker upstairs, they're still functional, although there have been some casualties on both of 'em due to this or that. But the outlook for them is pretty grim, none the less, they're both basically in the same boat as we are... enough air for the time being, not enough to last as long as they expect to have to last, on their own. ISS1's worse off than the other one, of course, old technology and so on. Docking with either of those stations, even if we could – and, we can't, they're both way off – wouldn't buy us much. Probably just more folks to draw straws, methinks."

"As expected," said Cohen, evenly.

"Commander Cohen," said Chen, who had been observing the back-and-forth as does a cat watching the occupants of a bird cage, "If the situation is as serious as the Chief Engineer says it is, then should we not be discussing some... extreme case options, sir?"

"What do you mean?" asked Tanaka, knowing full well what the taikonaut meant.

"It goes without saying that I do not prefer such a course of action," replied Chen, evenly, "But in the event that we cannot, ultimately, stop the station's trajectory and assume a parking orbit around Earth, then in my opinion we must consider the option of saving only so many of ISS2's crew as can be safely accommodated in Commander Jacobson's two ships, then using them as an escape vector back to our planet."

"Leaving the others...?" shot back Humber, needlessly.

"Leaving them," answered Chen, "To the same fate that will overtake all of us, if we do not face and accept the facts."

He stopped for a second, confronted by a stony-faced silence amongst the others, then said, "I should also point out that the select few may not include myself – only those whose value can be justified on scientific, cultural or other grounds. We should work to avoid this outcome, but to deny its possibility would be both unscientific and irrational."

"You have a point there, Li," said Cohen. "But I'd prefer, for the moment at least, for us to concentrate on thinking creatively about how we can save everyone."

The Chinese man just nodded, politely.

"We'll leave that until later," said Cohen. "Alan, any bright ideas about getting us some engine power, somehow?"

"Well," explained Humber, "We know that the on-board supply of conventional volatile chemicals – potassium, nitrates and so on – has already been almost completely exhausted by the lead-up to the booster incident, and the rocket itself was wrecked in the explosion. And we know that Commander Jacobson's ship's engines are still in working order, but there's nowhere near enough propellant remaining in them to fire them long enough to appreciably slow us, the whole station, that is. But perhaps we can try to scrounge up some lower-energy substances and refine them so we can at least try to ignite them in the *Infinity*'s combustion chamber... the reverse thrust would be pretty weak, but if we can find a way to keep it going over hours, days if need be, it might do the trick. That's the best I can come up with, off the top of my head."

"Before you do that," said Jacobson, "I think you'd better check with Brent Boyd – he's the propulsion system expert, so I'll defer to his wisdom, but based on what I know of *Infinity*'s engines, those of *Eagle* too, this plan worries me. I mean, we wrecked *one* rocket, already, with scrounged-up fuel... the last thing we want to do is wreck another set of them, the only ones we have left functional. They weren't meant for continuous firing, furthermore, only a limited number of quick boosts. And... I know that theoretically the *Eagle* and *Infinity* are under your control, Ariel, but I can't help thinking that they're still *my* ships. If you know what I mean."

He looked anxiously at the Israeli for signs of agreement.

"No problem, Commander," answered Cohen. "In fact – subject to future events, of course – I'll give you the final veto on whether we actually go ahead with this scheme. In view of the last episode," – he shot a quick glance at Chen, who just sat impassively, looking straight forward – "I think we want to make this a last resort. Or, second to last, anyway."

Jacobson looked visibly relieved. Thinking none could see, Tanaka grasped his hand, under the table, just within Humber's corner of the eye-shot.

"Yeah," added Humber, "And the other thing is, remember, we have no idea if firing Sam Jacobson's ships' engines in this way, even if we *can* pull such a bloody rabbit out of our hats, is going to actually slow us enough to stop at Earth. More likely that we might just end up with a slower flyby, but a flyby none the less."

"Point taken," said Cohen. "Okay. One more subject. Shivani, I know that this isn't exactly what you were hired to do up here, but I think you're probably in a better position than anyone else to assess what the state of the crew is. Remember, I mentioned that we were going to a debrief on this, after the comet incident, however it turned out?"

"Psychologically," replied Parmar, "The crew is in reasonable shape, other than for a few of them who are on stress-related bed rest. But as we near Earth, if we cannot find a solution to the braking problem, I cannot predict how they will react, then. In terms of environmental support, we have more than enough food and adequate water, if we are careful. You already know the consumable air situation, although I should point out that if we do, in fact, find some way to slow down ISS2, I will have to correlate the air reserves with our estimated time to Earth arrival... it will be of no use to get there and find out that our air is about to run out."

"Especially if NASA tells us that it will be another six weeks before they can get any rescue ships up to re-supply us or get us back down to Earth," added Tanaka.

"Indeed," noted Parmar. "I am afraid that we had not factored that issue into our calculations, at all. The assumption had always been that the 'Arks' ships were to re-supply us. But with their own mission being changed... I do not know, Cherie. It is all guesswork, right now."

"Well, let's get going on it, then," said Cohen. "Each second of delay is a potential pascal or two of lost thrust. "Anything else?"

All shook their heads in the negative.

"Meeting adjourned," said Cohen.

Meteor

Over and over it careened, this fragile ark, this dull-glowing cocoon of strange, latterly unknown, other-worldly energy, as it hurtled toward the blue-green planet, illuminating the sky with a fire only slightly brighter than the many hundreds of other fragments of a now-dead comet, as all fell into the Earth's fatal gravity well.

Now and again it flickered and briefly failed in small places, allowing demonic bursts of the raging incandescence that surrounded it to inflict hateful burns on what was inside. But mostly, inexplicably, it held firm, as it had so many times, in eons past human understanding, when all else had seemed lost.

The numbed, shocked, unconscious, all-but-lifeless mind of the not-really-a-meteor's inhabitant saw and sensed nothing, as she and it fell ever faster Earthward. Over Shenyang in China went the thing, lighting up the sky like some unexpected firecracker; shortly thereafter, it passed over the straits between Honshu and Hokkaido.

As the drag of this rocky, small planet's stratosphere started to brake its speed, had she been aware, the one within it would have seen the vast reaches of the Pacific opening up beneath her. Lower and lower now the fire-bubble fell, until, just as it descended into the troposphere, it cleared the cloud layer, revealing the western coasts of North America, with the mighty north-south mountain range looming to the east.

The meteor shower that accompanied this strange projectile was also now overcome by the gravity of the planet that, scant minutes ago, might have been denuded by 'Lucifer', as the humans called their erstwhile nemesis.

Instead, on *this* day, it would be the defeated shards of that almost-apocalyptic body, that would instead fall, flaming, to their demise. But as they did, the larger of them were still able to strike back, one last time. One by one, the larger of the fragments crashed down, striking cities, roads, power plants, railways and the occasional unlucky traveler, in a last orgy of destruction.

Finally, it was time, as the blue-green planet's gravity at last overcame the momentum imparted by the greatest nearby explosion that humankind had ever witnessed.

Four brightly glowing fireballs – three natural ones, after a fashion, one something else entirely – cleared the lower reaches of the Rocky Mountains and landed, thundering for all within many miles to hear, somewhere beyond. One fell in a lake; one hit a highway, wrecking six abandoned cars and cratering the roadway in impressive fashion; one hit the side of a mountain, promptly burying itself in the resulting avalanche; but the last one, glowing differently, in some indescribable way, crashed through the tree-tops of an evergreen mountain forest, charring all these as it roared by.

The special meteor etched a furrow of charcoal black upon the heart of the woodland, snow all around hissing and steaming at the brief touch of fire. It came to rest between two large, granite boulders, not far from a half-frozen stream that perhaps, somewhere, would feed the Snake River.

The fire upon the meteor was soon snuffed out by the wintry touch of this place, revealing only a faint, bluish-silver something-or-other – to the untutored eye, most akin to a very large soap-bubble – that, last reserves of energy spent, itself slowly faded away.

Leaving a frail-looking young woman-like thing, long, once-blond, now gray-and-black hair and otherwise immaculate European or maybe East Coast North American skin, filthy with congealed blood-stuff and charred wounds, garbed only in the burned, torn remnants of what might at one time have been a military uniform of some sort, lying face-down, cold, still and, most of all, alone, at the head of the furrow that the meteor had created.

No breath came from her nostrils, nor her lips; nor did her pulse carry forth, nor did any of the outward signs that would have told a passing human, had there ever been any in this remote place, that she was alive.

And only by the least of margins, in fact, *was* she still, alive, after the greatest fall that any of her race had ever encountered. Her body had been wounded in a thousand ways, some, for example a broken rib-cage and ruptured internal organs, familiar to humans; but she had also suffered terribly in other ways that the dominant race of this planet might never understand. Only the Fire within, the Demon that she had known since childhood uncounted eons ago, kept her alive, but then only by the most meager margin.

Dark, sinister red blood oozed from wound upon wound, vaporizing unlucky pine needles and assorted vermin on the forest floor, until its potency was spent in the soil several inches below.

Snow was falling, covering her in its cold, pristine mantle.

Thus laid this woebegone creature, for hours, days unremembered. Her brutally-abused body at first struggled mightily, merely to stay alive, then to heal the worst of the savage wounds she had sustained; until, at last, some inner strength – or, who can say – some higher purpose, returned the blur of semi-consciousness, to her.

The dense air of this world, fragrant with a thousand unfamiliar scents, filled her lungs, as the pain returned with each breath, despite the innate, ongoing ability to repair the trauma, no doubt fatal to any lesser being, that had been inflicted upon her.

Through sharp-fanged teeth, the fallen-girl spit more blood out of her mouth, along with a mouthful of dirt, water and plant-stuff. She tried to focus her eyes on the small pillar of steam that shot up as the ground sizzled and burned.

Where am I? she thought, wordlessly.

Is this the afterlife? No, it cannot be – it hurts so much. Was my life that bad, that I deserve to suffer thus? Great Spirit, have pity on me, have mercy.

After an hour or so, whimpering and crying in pain, she managed to roll over on to her back, facing upward to the sky (rather, those small patches of it that were visible, through the canopy of towering pines, spruces and cedars) of this unfamiliar place.

Grey clouds, blue here and there. Lots of the one that is good to breathe, she thought. *Much better than that other place, much more water... not nearly as cold, but why do I feel such a chill?*

The newcomer tried to sit up, but the stabbing pains in her chest warned her not to.

Her hair fell back into the dirt as she stared blankly into the clouds above, the snowflakes bringing a minuscule, but welcome, taste of water to her lips.

Dimly, she realized.

This is not my reward, or my punishment. My journey is not over. I am still, barely, alive.

With a small, pitiful whimper, the girl-creature folded her hands on her chest and lay back, trying to call upon inner vitality that healed where none else could, that gave life where only death would otherwise follow.

She did not know how, or why, she had this strength. Only instinct could be her guide.

Another day passed, with white flakes falling lightly on her face, the cold numbing her near-motionless body. More days came and went, with the fallen-creature – lying as if in repose, yet dimly aware of her surroundings – covered near-completely in the snow's soft, white blanket.

Finally, breathing steadily now, the newcomer's senses – vision, hearing, smell, taste and several other, less familiar ones – began to inundate her with information of the surroundings.

She tried to sit up again and did so, even though the duress of newly-healed bones and tissue was scarcely less than when they had been torn and broken. Though none could hear, wailing in pain, she cried rivers of hot, alien tears, into the soft snow of the dark, silent forest.

The fallen-girl tried to think, to remember where she was, to remember what had happened, to remember why she was here. She moaned with frustration, as her mind responded with only a haze of pain and a fog of ethereal faces and strange scenes, almost near enough to touch but fleeting, escaping her comprehension as she strained to recall the details of each one.

There was only one strong, clear memory : a feeling of power, purpose, peace and contentment, followed by a blinding light, then... *nothing.*

Who am I? she reflected, in a language she could not name, as foreign as foreign could be, in this place.

How shall I be called?

Re-Opening The *Santa Esmerelda*

Taking his last, deep breath of cold, early spring mountain air, Osvaldo Jiminez turned the key and heard the familiar 'creeeek' sound of the hinges, as he opened the back entrance to the *Santa Esmerelda* Grill And Licensed Establishment, As Certified By The State Liquor Board Of Idaho.

It was pretty much as he had left it, when he closed up in the wee hours of the night, last night. No, on second thought, it was *exactly* as he had left it. And not far off the week before, or the one before that, in fact. He wished he had to zip off to Gooding to replenish supplies, but the truth was, he hadn't sold enough food or booze this week to justify the trip, even if he had been able to get on to the road.

As he stepped inside the loading-dock-cum-pantry, he shot an idle glance at cordillera looming in the far, northern distance.

Like the Sierra Madre, he found himself thinking, *but back home, you had to go way to the top, to find the white stuff. Here, well, it follows you to your driveway. One day I'll find a way to mail some of it back to them, so they can feel it for themselves.*

It was drastically different from San Luis, what with these huge mountains – unlike at home, you could never really get to the top of them – and their dark, brooding forests, beyond the farms and ranches of the area.

But he and Gloria were settled, here. They were used to it, by now, and the boys would speak English just like a *gringo*, after being in an American school right from the start.

It was not their heart's home, but it was *home*, none the less.

Nothing much ever happened at the *Santa Esmerelda* and customers were scarce – then again, he had been told that, when he and his wife had scraped together the down payment for the place, so he had no reason to complain, so he didn't. By far the majority of those who stopped here were truckers who, for whatever reason, went off I-84 and decided to take Route 26 to Shosone or beyond; or, for the western-bound ones, those that were heading to Boise via Gooding and then the Interstate. Mostly, they pulled in for a coffee and maybe a sandwich or two; a few would occasionally park their rigs in the big, gravel-surface lot behind the restaurant.

Jiminez liked those ones, because it was an extra ten bucks for the privilege. The tourists tipped more generously, and there were quite a few local farmers who liked his house-special Tex-Mex pancakes; but without the truckers, he'd have closed the place long ago. They'd also pay good money for a cold beer and a hungry-man's breakfast, when they wanted that.

As with everything else about life here, far off the beaten track in *El Norte*, things were slow and he had to watch his pennies, quarters and Yankee one-dollar bills. But it *was* progress, compared to the *barrios* of San Luis Potosi where he had grown up. Despite all the costs of running a business, he had still managed to send some money back home, every month. He was proud of that.

He even had his "Red-White-and-Blue Card", procured from a high tech friend (a necessity, in order to copy the super duper computer chips that the cards all had, now) of a friend for the extortionate price of two thousand seven hundred and fifty crisp new American dollars. It was like that credit-card on the TV commercials, though: it got him past the Yankees' new, Gestapo-like "Alien No-exceptions Total Incarceration" act and even bought him the privilege of membership in Gooding's fine, upstanding Chamber of Commerce, via the Santa Esmerelda.

Everything had a cost. You either paid and got ahead, or you didn't, and stayed in the *barrio*.

Shuffling his feet unenthusiastically, Jiminez straightened a few chairs in front of their assigned tables, noted which of the latter still needed polishing and yanked on the draw-strings for the Venetian blinds on the front picture-windows. A beautiful view of Route 26, with nary a car, truck or bus sullying its pavement, revealed itself.

Well, it *was* only 6:04 a.m., after all. The only ones to be pulling in now would have been on the road for all or most of the night and, considering what had been going down over the last few days, he didn't expect much traffic, anyway; you'd have had to have been *nuts*, to have been traveling at a time like that. He'd have to make coffee just on the off chance that one or more of them would show up, although he hated throwing the stuff out, unsold, when they never did.

He heard a knock on the front door, followed by a Plains, or maybe Chicago, -accented female voice.

"Ossie? Mister Jiminez? Ya in yet? If yer there, open up, my key's in the bottom of my purse somewhere."

Jiminez took his time getting to the door – this was one of the very few times when someone had to wait for *him*, not the other way around – and turned the handle, after disengaging the deadbolt and the other half-dozen security contraptions that held the door shut.

"*Buenos Dias*, Karlie," he stated. "Did you sleep well?"

He could have addressed her, or treated her, pretty much any way he pleased, but, fancying himself a gentleman, Jiminez was usually courteous, except maybe when he caught the waitress under-reporting her tips.

"Sorta," the tall, average-looking, late teenage girl replied, stifling a yawn. "Still haven't got over the last few days, I guess. But I'm hardly the only one. I called her last night and Momma hasn't slept in a week and half her friends back home are in the hospital from stress, that is, those of 'em that could get a bed, there's a lot of people hurt real bad around there. But it's gettin' back to normal. Bobby says he's gonna take me campin' up to the mountains in a week or so to get my mind off it, when things settle down a little, you know."

"Hmmph," grunted Jiminez as he apportioned the daily cash float into each bill's slot in the till. "You *gringos* aren't used to danger, to the chance of things coming crashing down, with no warning and nothing you can do about it. Down where I come from, *senorita*, we have earthquakes, hurricanes, *banditos* and your American Border Patrol to deal with, each and every day. We get used to it – '*si la Santa Maria lo quiere, va que pasar, si no, no va que pasar*', as we say. We don't worry about such things."

He lied, of course.

"Yeah," she echoed, as she put on her uniform and apron. "But I think even you all ain't used to no meteor, or comet, or whatever it was. I just thank the Lord that He saved us from it. Ya know, Bobby and I hadn't been in church for round 'bout eight years, but we went last Sunday, the place was packed – everybody went in there to hide, in the basement I mean, when those big ones came flying overhead awhile ago. I never really believed the stuff, but there was nowhere else to go, considering that Momma was caught back in Peoria, and considering... And listen, Mr. Jiminez, about some of the things that I said, just before we closed down three days ago... I wanted to say 'sorry'... I didn't really mean them... I was *scared*..."

Jiminez shrugged. "I just said my rosaries to the Blessed Virgin, like I always do," he said, laconically. "Now that she answered that one prayer, maybe she will bless this restaurant and make us all rich, no?"

He grinned broadly, his gold tooth catching the rays of the morning sun, a smile half-matched by the waitress' own, as she straightened tablecloths and inspected cutlery. "And don't worry about what went on, back then. It was, how you say, 'a bad time', for all of us. Things will be better, now."

"I hope," replied Miss Karlie Tillman, "Because the landlord ain't givin' us any breaks on the rent, and we're a bit behind... I think I told ya before, Bobby's found it hard to get construction work over the last few months, people didn't really see any point in buildin' things, because, well... you know. Lately, with that over with, things have been pickin' up, but he don't get paid until end of the month..."

"Well, we should soon get more traffic by here, on the highway," observed Jiminez, avoiding her drift. "After you left last night I was listening to the radio and he – who is he, again, I think the U.S. Emergency Measures *jefe* – said that they are lifting the ban on private road travel, as of yesterday, five o'clock. I talked to some of my store owner friends in Gooding the other day and they were starting to run low on some of the supplies, so the trucks will have to start coming by to get them back up again. If we have too many tables with customers for you to handle yourself, Karlie, is that other girl – ah, I forget, oh, wait, Laurel, yes, that's her name, can she come in, too? Does she still need work?"

"I'm not sure, Mr. Jiminez," the waitress replied. "Last I heard from her, she was goin' back to Denver to be with her family just before... anyway, she phoned me and said that she couldn't get there because the Army had closed all the roads. But I don't know where she called me from. Maybe she's back in town, now, maybe she just waited it out and went on to Denver. I'll call her on my break, if ya want."

"Sure," answered Jiminez. "It's up to you. More tips or less running around, with all these customers shouting at you."

He swung his hand expansively at the empty restaurant, as they both waited for someone, *anyone*, to drop by.

Coming Down The Mountain

Wobbly-legged, the fallen-girl-being had now managed to stand up, breathing in the unfamiliar, spruce-tinged scents of this mountain-side forest. She strained to think, to remember, but very little returned to her. Half-memories, tantalizing but incomplete, taunted her as she slowly stumbled forward, not really knowing or caring where her footsteps led her.

I am a wanderer, a foreigner in a foreign land, she thought. *Yes, I remember that much.*

The sun had come up now and its rays flickered through the tree-tops. She saw the warmth given off by small animals – furry, four-footed ones and flying, feathered ones, darting through the trees – and smelled the faint radiation that the creatures gave off.

Her mind strained to find something familiar about this place, its sights, sounds, smells and energy-signatures.

I learned about this planet, she thought. *I studied about it. But in what Temple, what library, did I read the scroll?*

By surprise, an instinct from deep inside, made her try to leap upward, to soar into the sky. She forced herself into a short trot, then tried to escape the substantial gravity of this world; but her reward for this exercise was an unceremonious 'thud', as she landed face-forward amongst the snow and tree-needles.

Again, the alien-girl cried in frustration, as she slowly raised herself up on hands and knees, wiping the snow and dirt from her face.

What moved me to do that? she wondered. *I have but two legs, no wings. I am chained to the ground.*

She would have to walk.

Moving downhill, following the slope of the land, the girl shivered, arms crossed in front, while stepping cautiously forward. She tried to move quietly and inconspicuously – no need to alert carnivores to the presence of a weak, disoriented, lonely, out-of-place female-thing – as, shivering involuntarily, she tried to understand why the cold seemed so painful.

This is but a fraction of the cold I have known, she realized. *Far better than many other places, much warmer. Why does it hurt so?*

Hunger now building within her, extending her four fang-like incisors, the alien-girl tried to eat some of the needle-like things that covered a nearby tree-branch; but there was precious little nutrition there, so she spit the stuff out. She tried gnawing at the fibrous trunk of one of the trees, making deep gashes as her fangs scored it, but the results tasted no better and her teeth retracted again.

Compared to the forests that she remembered, this place seemed forbiddingly bereft of foodstuffs, not to mention shelter. There weren't even any of the little crawly- or squirmy-things that had sometimes sustained her, even though she hated to end the lives of those inferior creatures in order to prolong her own.

After perhaps another hour of weak steps down the slope of what she now knew had to be a large hill, maybe even a mountain, the girl-from-the-sky came upon a bush of frozen berries that might have been red in color, when – *if* – warmer seasons came to this place.

Cautiously, she tested one and tasted the poison within it.

I know this venom, said a dim memory. *It can kill. But it cannot kill, me.*

Greedily, she wolfed down the rest of the berries, feeling the toxin that they carried within them course through her veins – a lethal brew that would have quickly ended the life of any of those who inhabited this planet.

Gratefully, the alien-girl felt her body neutralize the poison, converting its molecules to other compounds, even a few proteins that could nourish her. She looked around for more bushes and found a few, but most of the berries seemed to already have been eaten by someone or something else.

The hunger-demon had been put back in its cage for a while, but it would be back to haunt her, soon.

As the cold-demon again started to bite at her fingers, only slightly less at her thinly-covered toes, she realized, *I should be able to survive out here, but I cannot. Things are not working as they should. I cannot even remember what I should be able to do, but whatever that is, I am unable.* Worry invaded her mind.

I have to find help, she thought.

Again, the sky-girl started down the side of the hill-or-whatever-it-was, guided by faint memories of valley-dwellers on unknown other worlds. Long hour upon hour, she traveled over many leagues, losing count of time, cold, fearful, hungry and alone, not knowing if she moved ahead or backward.

Once or twice, she had to quickly hide in the nearest available cover, when she heard some animal, maybe a carnivore, howling out a weird dirge to its fellow-beasts. To her dismay, the girl looked at her arms and noticed that despite trying to do what her instincts told her, they were still completely visible.

Luckily, whatever this creature was hunting must not have been herself, because after a few minutes the sound went away. Judging from the paw-print tracks that she had crossed on her downhill journey, there must be more than one type of large animal in these woods, at least one with claws on its feet and another with hooves. She did not see any heat-energy in any of the tracks, though, which meant that whatever made them had not gone by recently.

Finally, with the hunger again stabbing her and the cold numbing her feet and hands, all at once, she stopped in her tracks. There was a path through the woods, about as wide as a creature of her size would need to walk upon, made by no animal. And it included a stick of wood, off the path by about an arm's-length or so, with a written inscription upon it.

Great Spirit, thanks be, thought the pitiful, slim figure, wiping away a tear. *there are people, beings who think and comprehend, here.* A second later, she checked her enthusiasm with the knowledge that not all would be friendly, nor had they been, in the past.

The alien-girl attempted to read the inscription, trying to read the letters out loud, spelling them with the sounds of a language whose name she could not remember.

"Geh-err-ahh-enn-deh Teh-ee-teh-ohh-enn Teh-err-ahh-ihh-ell", she heard herself say.

What does that mean? she wondered. *'Teh-err-ahh-ihh-ell'... I hear the sounds of the letters in my head... I think that means a road – but how do I know it is so? Not the language that I think my own thoughts, in...*

Now she tried to read the smaller lettering, below the larger inscription on the top of the sign.

"Heh-eww-yee too-sihks forr emm-ihh-ell-ess" and an arrow, pointing that way, to the left, she thought. *The middle ones, they look like numbers... yes, they*

are numbers, they must be... but three digits, that many leagues? Great Spirit, I cannot travel that far in this cold, without food or shelter... have pity on me...

But each second of indecision would prolong her stay in this cold forest. So, hoping but not really believing, the fallen-girl set out down the path, following its twists and turns as it wound its way down the valley between the place she had come down from and that mountain's fellow-peaks.

On she went, each step hurting just a little more as the cold worked its evil and she prayed for deliverance, trying to remember the language she had just called upon.

The Only Game In Town

"Daddy, when are we going to *stop*?" demanded the little girl, cherubic in her pigtails and Buster Browns, except for a puckered-up, pained face. "I have to *go*," she implored.

"As soon as we find somewhere that's open," replied the exasperated man. "Unless you want me to stop by the side of the road and you go off to the bushes, sweetheart."

"Maybe that'd be best," commented the mother. "They all need to stretch their legs, you know. It's been two hours since Boise, what with all the roadblocks and detours."

"Yeah," the father replied. "I wouldn't mind a stretch myself... okay, then, looks like the woods are about to end, a half-mile or so further on, we'll pull over around there, then all who need can do their business before we get going again. But let's not be too long about it – this means *you*, Hayley – because we're already way past due on the trip and we still have to stop for lunch, somewhere. Grandma will be starting to get worried, I'd bet."

"I thought you called...?" asked the mother.

"Couldn't get through," explained the man. "cell-phone service is still hit or miss, you know. Remember that guy I talked to in the Boise gas station, the only one that had any gas to sell? He was telling me that all those meteors, one of 'em must have hit the local cellular repeater tower, and they've had quite a few other big ones land in the woods or the mountains. NeoNet's still down, isn't it?"

"Yes, it is," confirmed the wife. "Well, sort of. I tried to fire up the back seat player and hook up so the kids had something to watch, but no luck, I couldn't even get a log-in prompt. There was some kind of a message from the government saying about 'priority traffic only' or something like that..."

The husband was about to remind her of something called "off-line mode", but instead, he suddenly announced, "Hey, what's *that*, up ahead? Sign's all lit up... forget the woods, kids, we got us an open restaurant! Catherine, you got any cash left?"

The woman rummaged around in a purse, producing a rhinestone-encrusted wallet in short order. "About thirty or so, Mark," she stated. "We gotta find a working ATM, or there'll be nothing left for dinner."

"Don't worry about it," the man assured. "I still got another forty or so, I think."

"I'm hungry, too," added a teenage girl's voice, from the back seat of the van.

"We'll have to hope that we can find somewhere selling groceries, dear," the woman said. "If we make it to a city, soon – I sure hope your father's right about going off the Interstate and taking this road we're on. If we don't, well, make sure you all get a full helping while we're here – what's this place, anyway? The *'Santa Esmerelda'*? Mark, that sounds Mexican, doesn't it? The kids don't like spicy food..."

As the van slowly pulled up to the front of the establishment, the husband mentioned, "You know, Catherine, considering what we've all been through since we set out on this damn trip, having too many chili peppers in my taco sauce, doesn't seem like a very big problem. At least not from where I'm sitting, right now. You all saw what happened in Spokane. Bloody miracle that we've made it *this* far."

All were aware, so none followed up on this.

He turned off the ignition. "Well, we're here, for better or worse," he said. "If there's only one bathroom, you go first, Trisha, followed by Sammy if he has to."

"Why is it always *me* that has to wait until last?" complained the teenager.

"Because you're supposed to be setting an *example*, Hayley dear," wearily answered the mother, as if she had repeated these lines a hundred times before.

Turning to the man, she whispered, "Let's go easy on them, get them each a treat, Mark. They've been through a *lot,* so far."

Mutely, the man nodded agreement. "Everybody out of the bus," he demanded. As he stepped out, he noticed two trucks and three other passenger vehicles parked on the gravel, facing the restaurant.

"Popular place," he observed.

"When you're the only game in town..." his wife replied. "Trisha, time to put the book down, it's lunchtime, dear. You'll have lots of time to read when we get back on the highway. Here, Sammy, I'll help you with your seat belt."

"Only game in about six counties, I'd bet," the man noted. "What's that she's reading about? The temperance movement? Just don't believe everything you read, there, sweetheart. Temperance or not, this joint's licensed, thank God... I hope they have some beer left..."

"It's for my school assignment, Daddy," an eleven- or twelve- sounding voice said. "Mrs. Ditchens said I had to have it done by the time we get back. Remember, she gave me an extension because we were going on our trip."

"Well, fine... you can do all the writing you want at Grandma's place," the husband said. "Come on, let's get in there."

As they swung open a heavy, pine door, they beheld something like a shotgun marriage between a truck stop and a Tex-Mex franchise restaurant, with bright, Diego Rivera-style decorative patterns on the wall murals and tablecloths, but a traditional, sit-down lunch counter complete with bar stools arrayed in front of it. Four tables were already occupied, three by families much the same as theirs and one by a single trucker. Two more of his kind were sitting at the counter, sipping coffee.

It looked and smelled welcoming, relaxing, if you could overlook the tattoos on the trucker with the shaved head at the end of the counter.

Not much difference between driving a bike and a rig, I guess, at least not the kind of guy who drives them, the husband thought.

A tall, youngish waitress with long, blond hair, dressed in a neat smock and faded jeans, apparently not much older than their eldest daughter, greeted them. "Mornin', sir and ma'am," she greeted, in a Chicago voice. "I'm Karlie. Ya need a table?"

"For sure," the husband answered. "And one other thing, my kids need to use..."

He looked around, but they were already gone, as the washroom door on the corridor just inside the entrance-way swung back and forth.

"Don't worry, Mister," counseled the waitress. "Two stalls in each bathroom, two for the girls, two for the boys. And we got lotsa TP, too... we stocked up before all the bad stuff started happenin'. Ossie – Mr. Jiminez, I mean, he's the owner and the chief cook – he saw it comin', so we got plenty of everythin', all that's on the menu, it's available, still."

"Beer? Anything like that?" asked the husband.

"Sure 'nuff!" exclaimed the waitress. "And cold, too. Power wasn't off long around here and we had lotsa ice in the big downstairs freezer."

"I guess I'm driving after lunch," remarked the wife, patiently.

"Are you taking credit-cards?" requested the husband. "A lot of places we've visited on our trip so far are cash-only, what with all the computer stuff being down."

"No problem," replied the girl, cheerily. "Ossie says it's okay as long as yas leave your name and number and let us run your card through that thing with the ink paper on it. He always keeps it around, says it reminds of him of his old *cantina* down in Mexico. They mostly still don't have NeoNet down there, ya know."

Gratefully, the husband remarked, "That's great – let your boss know that you'll both get an extra tip for being so understanding. Most other places aren't, which is ridiculous, I think, considering that a few days ago nobody was worried about money, at all..."

Nodding, the girl said, "Can I show you to your table?"

"Please do," said the mother, as she headed inside, no small relief in mind.

Road Through The Forest

For many long hours, the fallen-girl had stumbled numbly though the wintry landscape, with the teeth of the frost-demon biting more painfully each minute, lighting up her nerves with cold fire, though she could hardly feel her toes. Shivering, she scarcely noticed the surroundings, concentrating only on following the trail, wherever it might lead.

Eyes half-shut, this creature who – had she remembered the fact – could easily evade the most lethal, hidden traps that the greatest wizards of long-gone worlds could devise, failed to notice a tree-trunk half-buried in the snow. She tripped over the thing, landing face-first in a drift.

For a second or two, she considered just remaining there, curled up against the elements.

Maybe I will just go to sleep, came a pitiful thought. *Sleep for many ages, yes, that is what I do, is it not... or, sleep forever... do I not deserve some rest?*

But after more tears of pain, despair and frustration, something inside made the newcomer raise up her head and take a second glance. The path was rising; it was going up an embankment, about fifty arms-lengths from her.

Something *big* – five to ten times her size, at least, with two or more wheels on it – whizzed past, following the path of the embankment.

It is a road, she joyfully realized. *Whereupon, those who inhabit this world, travel.*

Her mind raced.

Now, she mused, *it is up to me, to my arts of adaptation, to learn how to live among them.*

Drawing on strength fueled only by hope, the girl-thing crawled up the embankment and weakly rose to her feet. She stood beside a paved roadway that cut a path between the dark forest from which she had just emerged, and its counterpart on the other side of the road.

Her vision-senses lit up, inundating her mind with a riot of information. There was some kind of dwelling, not too far off, maybe a thousand paces, down the roadway. Several of the wheeled-things were parked in front of this building, which had a brightly-illuminated, glowing sign near the roadway to advertise its presence.

That glow, she pondered. *It is the gas that gives off light, when one wills the little energy-shine-particles to flow into it. These beings must know science.*

Staying on the gravelly side of the roadway, the fallen-girl walked cautiously towards the building, stopping twice along the way to stare at more of the wheeled-things as they shot by her, shivering again as the tailwind from these vehicles reminded her of the painful chill in the air.

At last, she was in the ante-yard in front of the dwelling-place. She walked by one of the wheel-vehicles, much smaller than the big ones that were parked off to the sides of the yard (one or two of the larger vehicles were also visible around the back, as she stepped down the driveway) and looked inside, hoping to detect clues about the beings she was about to encounter.

There was a reading-scroll of some kind, a strange one with its pages opening up in a fan-arrangement. The stranger stared absentmindedly at the picture on an upward-facing book-page. It showed a smiling creature with puffed-up, white hair and elaborate, frilly clothing, carrying one of the same reading-scrolls in one hand and something that might have been a weapon or magic-instrument in the other.

The newcomer tried saying the inscription that accompanied the picture, out loud.

"Ess-ahh-err-err-ihh-ee ahh enn-ahh-teh-ihh-ohh-enn," she whispered.

The name of a Temple, perhaps? Or of this creature? These beings look very familiar, just like... she thought.

The fallen-girl ran her hands over her own face, feeling each feature and texture, trying again and again to make sure.

Suddenly her heart skipped a beat as she heard a gruff voice coming from behind her. Wheeling in place, she turned, to confront one of what could only have been the dominant species of this world – a creature remarkably similar to herself, in fact, but considerably taller and heavier, with thick fur underneath its chin.

The heady scent of body odor and male pheromones invaded her nostrils, but she quickly suppressed the resulting urges.

"Ee-oo ok-kay lay-dee," it said, with a rising tone at the end of its statement.

I know this tongue, I have used it recently, I know not how, mused the sky-girl, in her own, alien language. *If I could just remember, just recognize the meanings that go with the sounds...*

Instinctively, she fell to her knees, head down, using the submissive posture learned from untold ages past.

The male-creature just huffed, shook its head from side to side and started towards the entrance to the dwelling. Cautiously raising her own, the girl observed him, then slowly followed behind. At the last moment, as the entrance-door was about to shut behind him, the male-creature noticed her and held it open.

Thank the Spirit, the sort-of-girl reflected. *They are friendly. And not too unlike me, it seems.*

She hesitated, afraid of the being's demeanor, but, reminded by cold and hunger, persisted and slowly stepped forward.

The male-thing grunted something like what it had said before, only there were more words, now.

Wait, thought the fallen-girl, as her mind raced to unlock the code what she was hearing. *I think I can... I think it is... that word, 'ok-kay', it means 'alright' or 'I am well'... yes, that must be it... what tongue is this?*

With a shrug of its large shoulders, the male-being started to close the door, but, at the last moment, the girl managed to navigate it well enough to sneak inside.

She was now in an entranceway, her senses bombarded by sounds and smells that were at once both utterly alien, yet strangely familiar, as if she had somehow been here before. There were about eleven of these beings in various places inside the common-area of the building; most were eating or drinking and discoursing with each other, but, fortunately, they did not seem to be paying much attention to her. The fallen-girl, listening to the chatter and straining her mind to comprehend it, had no idea if she would be welcome here, but, thank the Higher Powers, it was warm and dry.

She saw one of these beings, apparently a female and wearing garments different from the ten or so others in this place, striding toward her, carrying a beverage-pot.

Silently, the girl prayed for understanding and readied herself.

I must try to use the make-you-be-friendly-skill, she thought, *whether or not it, too, has left me.*

Forgive me, beings of this world.

Find Me A Table

"More coffee, Mister?" inquired the waitress as she passed by the booth.

"Yeah, sure, I guess," replied the husband. "Kids don't look like they'll be finished anytime soon. I might as well."

From the behind the husband's back, near the front door, they heard a voice, apparently that of a trucker, exclaiming, "You comin' in there, lady, or what?"

"Excuse me, Karlie – Karlie? That's your name, right?" interrupted the wife.

"Shore is," confirmed the waitress, as she tipped the last contents of the carafe into the husband's cup. "Whaddya want to know?"

"I was just wondering, how far is it to Pocatello from here?" asked the wife. "We really should get there by sundown."

"Well," explained Karlie, "Normally, I'd say, couple of hours, maybe... but what with things the way they are nowadays – stuff all over th' roads, cops divertin' traffic here and there, that kinda thing – I'd leave at least another hour or so, ma'am. Road was closed altogether a day ago, but then we started to get some truckers in here, they told us it's open now. I dunno about goin' west, though... haven't had a chance to talk to anybody 'bout that..."

"It's about the same, we came from there, detours, and such," mentioned the wife. "They're diverting traffic around Boise, and Spokane, well..."

She looked around, then added, "Better not to talk about *that*, around the kids..."

Knowingly, the waitress nodded.

"Is it dessert time yet, Mom?" demanded the ten-or-so boy, seated next to the wife.

"Your sisters are still eating dinner, Sammy," replied the wife. "Trisha, come on, eat *up*, dear, we won't be stopping for food again, until we get to Pocatello, if anything's open there."

"Should be," interjected Karlie. "Lot of places there are still closed, but Ossie got a call from one of his friends who's got a pizza place down on Jefferson Avenue, they got mobbed when he opened up again, called to see if we had any spare flour... oh, sorry, ma'am, looks like I gotta go get the door..."

"No problem," said the wife.

A beefy-looking trucker sporting a plaid work-shirt passed by, saying, "Hey, Karlie, I'll just get my own place, okay?"

"Ya, sure, Mike," apologized the waitress. "Sorry, I got tied up. Get ya some coffee in a sec. Somebody at the door?"

"Yeah," grunted the trucker. "Some girl. Real space cadet, too – maybe stoned, maybe had a few too many, dunno. I tried to be the gentleman, for once, and I opened the door for her, but she just *stood* there and stared at me when I told her to get in... finally she did, though. Looks damper and dirtier than I ever did, even after changin' my rig's brake linings. She's standin' just inside the doorway, waitin' for something to happen, I guess."

"Lord love a duck, here we go *again*," muttered the waitress, as she strode forcefully towards the doorway.

"Damn hippies," she shouted over her shoulder. "Every so often we get a few of 'em in here, they got communes or somethin' up in the mountains, but I didn't think they'd be out on the roads hitchikin', nowadays."

The waitress came up to the side of the table-seating-podium directly in line with the doorway and stopped for a second, nonplussed at what she saw : a young, twenty-something-at-most, apparently-Caucasian female, about a half-head shorter than Karlie herself, with intense cerulean eyes and long, dirty, early-gray hair that might once have been blond, cut into a short bang over her forehead.

Enviously, the waitress could see that this bedraggled creature must otherwise have been a *very* pretty girl, were she not filthy from head to toe and dressed in the tattered, burned and soot-marked remnants of what might have been a uniform of some sort.

"My, my," said the waitress. "We get some *dirty* ones in here, but I ain't seen nothin' like *you* in a year or more. If ya wanna eat in here, you'll haveta get cleaned up, first. Washroom's over there."

She pointed to the right.

The hippie-girl looked up at Karlie with big, uncomprehending, blue-green eyes. She let forth some kind of childish whimper, almost like what a puppy would make, and tried to smile, revealing an immaculate set of white teeth, strangely out of keeping with its otherwise disheveled appearance.

"Whatsa matter with you, girl? Don't understand English?" demanded the waitress.

The girl-in-rags shook her head back and forth, mimicking the gesture of the being that she had followed into the restaurant.

"I *told* you she was out of it," came a male voice from a table somewhere inside the restaurant.

"No kiddin', Mike," shot back Karlie.

Turning to the girl, she said, "Ya don't look like ya got money, anyway, and we don't *do* charity. Ya sure ya can pay?"

The girl-in-rags furrowed her brow, as if pondering a response. But the waitress interrupted her with a gesture of circles drawn on an open palm. "Money? Pesos? Ya know what I mean, girl?"

The girl-in-rags again shook her head.

"Well, I told ya, we ain't no church basement here. Time to leave. Ya know, go, *vamos*, scoot?" ordered Karlie, impatiently. She pointed towards the door.

The girl-in-rags fell to her knees, clasped hands extended in front, whimpering.

"For Gawds sake," groaned the waitress. "Every time we get one of these, nothin' but trouble... *every* time. Ossie! We got a *problem* at the door!"

Jiminez, wiping flour from his hands with a towel, appeared through the swinging doors leading to the kitchen.

"What is it, Karlie?" he said, followed, a second later, by "Oh," as he noticed the filthy-girl, huddled on her knees on the floor.

"She ain't got no money and she don't speak English," explained the waitress. "I told her to get out, but she don't understand... I don't think."

The restaurant-owner advanced until he was beside the girl, then bent over, saying, "*Me entiende? Si no tiene dinero, no puede comer aqui. Comprende?*"

The ragged-girl did not move.

Jiminez shook her shoulder, saying, "Does not speak Spanish either... but she looks like a *gringo*... strange..."

Now, the girl-in-rags looked upwards with big, wide-open green eyes, staring the restaurant-owner straight in the face.

For a second, Jiminez looked stunned, as if he had seen a ghost; then, he said, slowly, "Hmm... well, Karlie, maybe... maybe we should let her sit down. Yes, maybe she can pay. At least, we can get her a coffee, she looks cold, she feels cold. Put her in that booth over there, next to the family with the van."

Confused, the waitress replied, "But Ossie – I thought ya told us, 'no freebies'..."

"Yes," responded the restaurant-owner, heavily. "But I think it will be alright to make an exception, this one time. These are... how you say in *Ingles*, 'strange days'. Get her a coffee, *por favor*."

"Yeah, sure, Ossie," warily replied the waitress. "But she's a *mess*. I should show her to the ladies' room, first, dont'cha think?"

"Please do," agreed Jiminez. "Whew, I felt *faint* there, for a second... *Gracias a Dios*, it must be the late nights that I have been working..."

"Wouldn't surprise me," noted Karlie, sympathetically. "All that stress we've all been under, too. Come on, hippie-chick girl, get up," she ordered, motioning with her finger.

The girl-in-rags rose unsteadily to her feet.

"Here," said the waitress. "I'll show ya where it is. But no stealin' TP, ya hear? Hard to get nowadays. I'll know if ya try to hide any."

She held out her hand. For a second, the girl-in-rags hesitated, but then, timidly, she extended her own hand and grasped that of the waitress.

For a split-second, Karlie's own mind raced with a cacophony of unfamiliar, incomprehensible thoughts, as if a momentary daydream had suddenly overcome her. But the effect was over as quickly as it came, and, not wanting to show weakness, the waitress regained her composure and led this woebegone being to the ladies' room, opened the door and pointed inside.

The girl followed obligingly inside and sat down in the dark, on the closed toilet-seat.

Shaking her head with exasperation, Karlie switched on the light inside the washroom and closed the door.

"And don't fergit to wash yer hands, ya hear?" she cautioned, as she went back to wait on her paying customers.

Ladies' Room

Why did the female one lock me in this cell? wondered the fallen-girl. *Her words did not seem angry, at least, not after the other one came... the one whose mind I calmed... I heard something about my hands, yes, I think that word means 'hands' in this language...*

She looked around, noticing the switch-thing that made the glowing orb just below the ceiling – she could feel the particle-shine-power pulsing through it, rapidly changing direction – as well as various other knobs and activating-devices.

Advancing to a white, basin-like device with a circular hole in its precise center, cautiously, she experimented with one of the two levers on either side of a silver spout in the middle, above the hole.

Water poured out, cold and fresh. She drank several handfuls, then tried the other lever, the one on the left side. This time, the water was hot. Gratefully, she wet her face with it and tried to clean off some of the grime that encased her, involuntarily absorbing every small portion of warm-energy as the liquid passed over her body, falling into the white basin and on the floor in shards of ice.

She felt the nerves of her cruelly-frozen feet start to answer back.

Good, mused the girl. *My body repairs itself. Thank the Powers Above that I have not lost that ability.*

Looking up, she saw her own image in a reflective-glass plate, affixed to the wall just above the basin. Though the fallen-girl cringed reflexively upon seeing the damage that she had sustained, she was none the less immensely relieved to discover that the creatures around here, looked almost exactly like her, or the other way around... *probably, the other way around*, she realized.

Probably that ability at work, she said to herself. *I am whatever I need to be. It is the way of things. Except for the teeth. I had better keep those in. None of them seem to have them.*

The seeming-girl saw her hair and did a reflexive double-take.

Was it not yellow, before? she pondered. *Shiny, golden color. I liked it that way.*

Concentrating, she strained to remember how to invoke the trick that could make it change, to pick from a kaleidoscope of different colors. But her hair remained a salt-and-pepper gray with hints of black underneath.

This art, too, has left me, she thought, sadly.

Throwing another lever, the fallen-girl heard a 'whoosh' as water drained out from below.

The one I sit upon... I recognize it... a device for getting rid of body wastes... not much in the way of decoration, but at least I can stay in this prison with some dignity, she realized.

At length, the still-dazed, out-of-place creature, sat down in a corner, back to the wall. She tried to recall memories of the language that was used around here, waiting patiently for her jailers to return, whenever they chose to do so.

Failure To Communicate

"Mom, is the ladies' room free now?" pleaded the daughter. "It's been *twenty minutes* or more."

"Someone's still in there," replied the mother. "You should have gone when we first got in here, Hayley."

"I didn't have to, then... not really. But I *do*, now. How long can any one person spend in there, anyway?" complained the teenager.

"Miss? Miss!" exclaimed the mother, as she saw the waitress passing by, plates stacked and clattering in her outstretched arms. "My daughter has to use the women's room, but there's been someone in there the last two times she checked. Can you just see what's going on... ask them to hurry up, if you don't mind?"

"No problem," promised Karlie. "Ya know who's in there? Tell 'em to get goin'?"

"No," explained the teenager. "I went and knocked, two times, asked if whoever's in there could hurry, but there was no answer. The light was on, though. I'm pretty sure someone's in there."

"Okay, I'm right on it, soon as I get these back to Ossie," sighed the waitress.

She headed off towards the swinging doors.

Your Table Is Ready, Miss

"Hey, hey, *you* in there! Washroom's for *everybody*, ya know, not just you. Can ya get a move on, please?" exclaimed Karlie, as she stood by the womens' room door, knocking briskly upon it.

There was no answer.

The waitress rapped the whitewashed chip-board door a little harder. "I'm givin' ya one more minute, lady, then I gotta shoo ya outta there. Nothin' *personal*, ya know. Better get done whatever yer doin'."

Impatiently, Karlie's toes tapped out each passing second of the one-minute countdown. Still there was no answer.

"Okay, don't say I didn't warn ya," she warned, turning the handle.

As soon as the waitress could see inside the washroom, she let out a groan.

"*You*, again," she complained. "Whaddya think yer doin', just *sittin'* there? This ain't a lounge, sister, other folks get to use it, too. Come on, get up... *here*."

She extended her hand and motioned "up" with her index finger.

With the same big, only-partly-comprehending eyes, the girl-in-rags arose, unsteadily at first, then standing up straight, in front of the waitress.

For a second, that same strange, unfamiliar sensation impacted like a *tsunami*, upon Karlie's psyche, as she caught the girl-in-rags' glance; she felt lost, overwhelmed, as if in the presence of someone important, a queen or the President, perhaps, that is if a girl could really *be* the President, despite what the minister at the church used to tell her.

But the feeling only lasted a second or two, and then the waitress was able to say, "Well, at least ya got a little cleaned up there, girl... I was wonderin' if you'd even figure out how to use the sink, but I guess I can seat ya now, without bein' afraid of havin' to do too much wipin' it off afterwards. Come on."

Karlie put her hand over her shoulder and again made the 'come hither' motion with her finger.

Mutely, the girl-in-rags followed, as the waitress led her out of the washroom and into the main seating-area of the restaurant, past the muffled guffaws of several truckers as they observed her disheveled garb, the remnants of pine-needles in her hair and her blank, disoriented stare.

"Better put ya over here, where they won't bother ya. Not that you'd understand the jokes, anyway, girl, would ya?" muttered Karlie, as she motioned for the girl to sit in a booth one place closer to the door than the one accommodating the family from the van.

The girl-in-rags sat down, visibly appreciating the cushioned bench, and looked directly forward at the middle-aged woman and teenage girl sitting on the opposite bench in the next booth.

"Hey, *you*," Karlie added, taking a side-step to avoid the teenager who was heading rapidly for the washroom area. The waitress reached for a carafe at the serving-station, then deposited a cup and saucer in front of the fallen-girl.

"Ossie said to pour ya a coffee, so that's what I'm doin'. Ya want milk, cream or sugar?"

The girl-in-rags just smiled, earnestly and vacantly.

"Well, *whatever*," shrugged the waitress. "*You* decide, then. Here, I'll leave ya two of each."

She plunked small, sealed plastic demi-cups of ten per cent cream, two per cent pasteurized milk and two packets of finest white sugar, down in front of the girl-in-rags, along with a folding, plastic-encased menu.

For a second, the fallen-girl's glance shifted rapidly from the coffee-flavorings that had been placed in front of her, to the waitress' eyes, back and forth, several times.

Then, in a small, hesitant voice, she half-whispered,

"Oh-kay."

Only slightly taken aback, Karlie replied, "Ah, I *thought* so... ya *can* talk, after all. Well, fine, then. I gave ya a menu... when ya decide what yas want, just wave, I'll take yer order. Be back in five."

The waitress sauntered off to deal with a trucker who gestured for service, as the other's stare followed her.

As the girl-in-rags cradled the plain white porcelain cup in her hands, a slight, inscrutable smile came to her face. The wisps of steam coming from the coffee within, diminished more rapidly than they should have.

Cautiously, she brought the beverage to her lips, took a little taste, puckered her face a bit, then drank more deeply, repeating this process with both the milk and cream. Then, observing some of the other guests adding these substances to their own coffee cups, she did the same with what was left of the cream and milk. But as for the sugar, the moment when its first grains passed from her finger-tip to her mouth, the girl-in-rags greedily threw back the packet's entire contents, licking her lips with satisfaction.

Then she returned to her far-away, saturnine demeanor, staring absently and mutely at the strange beings who surrounded her, listening to the sounds of their chatter, trying to pick out the words and meanings.

Breakfast At The *Santa Esmerelda*

"She looks *stoned*," giggled the teenager, rather too loudly, while taking a seat next to her mother. "I said 'hi' as I passed by but she just smiled at me."

"Shhh!" corrected the mother. "It's very rude to say something like that, when you don't know for sure. Next time, try to tone it down a bit please, Hayley."

"But that sure *is* a weird stare she's got, like she doesn't have a clue," observed the father, as he munched on a piece of bacon. "I hate to say it, Catherine, but your daughter may be right," he added.

Turning his head around and quickly turning back, as he had been doing intermittently for the entire time, the boy asked, "Mom, that lady is just *looking* at you and Hayley. Is she sick or something?"

"Let me have a better look at her," said the mother, craning forward. A look of concern came to her face.

"Mark, have a look at her *clothes*," the woman whispered. Those black spots... they have to be burn-marks, and all the ripped places, she must be hurt underneath them – looks like she's been in a car-crash or something. Wait a minute... *now* I get it..."

"Get *what*, Mommy?" inquired the little girl seated next to her father, on the opposite side of him from the boy.

"She must be in shock," explained the mother. "I remember the symptoms from my First Aid training at the school back home. Mark, what do you think we should do?"

"Nothing," suggested the husband, matter-of-factly. "None of our business, anyway. And even if you're right, what are we *supposed* to do? There's no hospital around here, and you know how crowded the ones in the cities are, with more serious cases. To say nothing of the fact that she probably can't pay for her lunch, let alone a few nights in a hospital bed... if you don't believe me, just ask her if she's got any medical insurance."

He smirked stupidly and bit into another piece of bacon.

"Well, remind me not to appoint *you* lifeguard for our swimming-pool," the wife sarcastically replied.

Meanwhile, the waitress had returned and was now standing beside the girl-in-rags' table, pointing to the menu.

"So, girly, what'll it be?" she asked. "Ossie tells me I gotta feed ya, too."

"Oh-kay," answered the girl, looking up at the waitress with a pleasant, uncomprehending smile.

"No, for Gawds sake, lady, I meant, 'just pick something to *eat*'," complained an exasperated Karlie. "Yer hungry, right? Aren't ya?"

The waitress rubbed her own stomach with her hand.

Instantly, the girl-in-rags responded in kind, then pointed, as if picking at random, at one of the menu items.

"Yeah, sure, scrambled eggs and toast, good as anythin', I suppose," said the waitress. "Ya want ketchup, jam, marmalade, anythin' like that?"

The girl-in-rags' glance went from the waitress' face to the table and menu for an uncomfortably long time, as if she was pondering something or trying to solve a difficult mental problem. Finally, she looked up and voiced,

"Yess, pleesse, Karr-lee."

"Wow, *now* we're talkin', aren't we!" exclaimed the waitress. "Okay, then, girly, one Number Five, comin' up shortly. Sure hope ya got seven-fifty on ya, excludin' tax 'n tip, that is. Be back in a minute with yer order."

As the waitress left, the little boy in the next booth turned around and said, looking straight at the girl-in-rags, "Lady, would you like some of this sugar? I like eating it too and Daddy doesn't use it in his coffee."

The boy held up a couple packets, thrusting them over the partition between the two booths.

"Sammy, don't bother her – " the husband requested; but it was too late. With a friendly smile on her face, the girl-in-rags had somehow snatched the sugar-packets from the boy. She quickly ripped them open and shot their contents into her mouth, seemingly savoring every grain.

"Yeww thankk?" uncertainly stated the fallen-girl. Seeing uncomprehending stares, she thought for a second, then corrected with, "Thankk yeww."

Ignoring a gesture from his father, the boy again turned to face the girl-in-rags, and said, "Hi, I'm Sammy. That's my sister Hayley over there and Trisha is beside my Dad. Oh, and Mom is here too. What's your name, lady?"

The girl pointed at the boy. "Yeww?" she asked.

"Sammy," the boy replied, nodding affirmatively.

Now the girl pointed at the teenager. "Yeww?" she inquired.

"She's Hayley," explained the boy.

"Ahh, Hay-lee," replied the fallen-girl.

Then the boy pointed at the girl-in-rags, herself, asking, "You?"

She looked panicked, as if searching for something to say. Then, forcing out each syllable one by one, she pointed to herself and said,

"Sa-ree An-aht-ee-hen. Mee".

"Wow, that's an unusual name," spoke up the wife. "Well, I'm Catherine Porter, this is my husband Mark... you've already met the kids, I guess."

"*Told* you she was a hippie," joked the husband, under his voice. "Sounds like a Turkish hippie."

"Or a chicken farmer hippie," giggled the teenager, *sotto voce*.

"I'm sorry if our son bothered you... he won't do that again, *will* he, Sammy?" demanded the wife. "And Hayley, *behave* yourself, please."

The little boy shook his head and again sat down beside his father. The teenager smirked and went back to her food. By now, the father had turned around, to look at the girl.

"Yeah, but... there's a name on her uniform, or whatever she's wearing," he observed. "Looks like... 'Tan –', 'Tanak', I think... is that her last name?"

For a second, the girl-in-rags looked confused, but then she saw the lettering on her garment and elaborated, hastily, "Yess, Sari Anatihen Tanak. Nayyme maii."

She smiled broadly, as if pleased with having deciphered a puzzle.

"Hmm... maybe Russian," commented the husband. "Her accent sounds funny. Maybe *that's* it."

"Anyway, Miss... Miss Tanak," continued the wife, "Now that we're talking, we just couldn't help noticing that you look a little, well – please don't take this the wrong way – *unkempt*. Are you okay? I hope you haven't been in an accident or something like that?"

The girl-in-rags' brow furrowed, as the deep-in-thought look came over her again.

Eventually, she said, taking a deep breath, "Krashh... ai... krashh."

"Omigod," exclaimed the wife.

Leaning over the table so that the girl-in-rags could not see her face, the wife whispered, "Mark, I *told* you. She can barely *talk*, must have had a concussion. She needs *help*."

Turning to the girl, she asked, "Miss Tanak, where? Are you badly hurt? Do you need a doctor?"

"Dok-torr?" replied the girl, uncertainly. "Noh, noh dok-torr ai," she added.

"Okay, then, I guess you don't," allowed the mother. "But where did you crash your car? Is it near here?"

The girl-in-rags hung her head, looking at the table-cloth for a second, deep in thought. Then she said, "Wooods. Trees, inn... krashh ai."

"Is it far from here? A long way?" inquired the wife.

After a few painful seconds of contemplation, the fallen-girl added, "Waii lonngg wakk ai. Heere. Farr too."

"Mark," said the wife, "Her stuff, or what's left of it, is probably back there, wherever her car is... we should give her a ride..."

"Look, we *can't* –", started the husband, but he was interrupted by the return of the waitress, who deposited a steaming plate of toast and scrambled eggs in front of the funny-looking-girl.

"Here ya go," announced Karlie. "Brought ya some extra jam, too, in case ya can't make up yer mind which one to use."

The girl-in-rags looked up at the waitress, smiling earnestly and bending over the food, smelling it as would an animal surveying a just-discovered carcass, much to the amusement of the teenager in the next booth. She sampled a small piece of egg with the tip of her finger, chewing it with a stare into space, as if she was concentrating on identifying the taste on her tongue.

"Look at *that*," whispered the teenager to her mother. "It's like she's never had a plate of eggs before."

"People in shock do a lot of unusual things, Hayley dear," replied the mother, quietly. "Don't be surprised if she does more things like that."

"Well, it's just *weird*, that's all," commented the teenager.

For a second the girl-in-rags' face puckered up upon experiencing something unexpected, but, slowly, she began to chew more enthusiastically. She fumbled with the fork and knife, shooting occasional glances to nearby tables to observe whatever was going on there, but soon started using her utensils to divide and wolf down the food. As if desperate from hunger, she was now eating furiously, frantically, shoveling the egg and toast into her mouth, paying no attention to anything except consuming every last morsel in front of her.

"Mom... mom!" exclaimed the half-shocked teenager. "Talk about *weird*... you should see those *teeth* she's got... they're..."

The girl-in-rags stopped eating, momentarily. Wide-eyed with evident concern, she held her hand over her mouth, staring straight at Hayley, then closed her eyes for a second. Then she resumed her repast, slurping down the last of the coffee.

"What are you talking about, dear?" demanded the mother, between mouthfuls.

"That girl – her *teeth*, they were like a vam – ", stammered the teenager.

"They were *what*?" inquired the mother, taking a quick look at the one-called-'Sari', who was about to finish off her meal, jam-containers and all, at a record pace.

Noticing the woman's glance, the girl-in-rags returned a polite, perfectly normal, smile.

"I don't see anything except a hungry young woman. It's not *nice* to stare at someone who's had a bad experience," cautioned the mother. *Sotto voce*, she added, "You might make her trauma worse, dear. Send her back into shock. They told us about that in the First Aid training."

"Uhh... it's nothing... nothing, I guess," retreated Hayley. "Must have been my imagination."

The teenager shook her head and whispered, to no-one in particular, "That was *too* strange."

"Wow," interrupted the returning waitress, "Ya shore *was* hungry, wasn't ya girl? I ain't even seen any trucker finish it off that fast. Well, anyways, hope ya liked it."

The strange-looking girl looked up, grinning stupidly, giving a "heh-heh-heh" grunt of satisfaction.

Taking another look at the scraped-clean plate, the waitress offered, "I see yas *did*." Karlie picked up the plate and drained coffee-cup. "Want any more?"

The girl-in-rags looked up, blankly, and smiled again.

"I'll take that as a 'no'," replied Karlie. "Okay, then, I'll be back with yer bill," she stated.

"*This* is going to be fun," said the teenager, maliciously.

"Hayley –", complained the mother, as the waitress returned with a scribbled paper bill.

"Here it is," explained the waitress. "I need eight dollars and thirty-five cents from ya, that includes state tax, hospitality tax, war tax, media piracy tax and whatever other taxes they got nowadays. Time to pogey up there, chickie."

The fallen-girl took the bill in her hand and held it up in front of her face, carefully examining each inscription on the paper three or four times, while mumbling something in an incomprehensible tongue. Then she placed it neatly on the table and looked up at Karlie with the now-familiar, pleasantly inoffensive smile.

"Jaysus, I *knew* this was gonna happen," groaned the waitress. "Look, chickie, ya gotta *pay* for eatin' here. Ya know, *money*, pesos, that kinda thing? Ya don't have any money, do ya?"

Karlie took a dollar bill and an assortment of change from the purse on her belt and held this in front of the girl, pointing to the money and saying, "You got any of this?"

"Why don't you ask her for a credit-card?" chortled the teenager.

"Monn-ee?", innocently asked the fallen-girl. "Monn-ee? Mon-ee noh mee."

She turned to avoid the waitress' glance, hands folded in front on the table, staring straight forward with eyes down.

Two truckers guffawed, in the background. One of them joked, "I guess there goes your tip, Karlie."

"No shit," complained the fed-up waitress. "Okay, fine, then, this was Ossie's idea, anyway – no skin off *my* back. If ya can't pay, I'm not gonna force yas, but ya gotta leave. Let's *go*, girl."

She pointed towards the door.

The girl-in-rags moved involuntarily backward an inch or two, evidently frightened.

"Pleesse, Karr-lee," she whimpered, in a pathetic voice, "Koldd. *Koldd*," while making a shivering motion and embracing her trunk in her arms.

"Just a minute, Miss," interrupted the mother. "Leave her alone, for a second. I need to talk to you."

"Catherine," started the husband, but he was stopped in mid-voice by a warning look on the part of the wife, who quickly got up and took the waitress a few tables down the row, toward the interior of the restaurant.

"Miss," explained the wife to the waitress, "I think your guest at the table next to ours has been in a bad car accident. I think she's still in shock, I had some First Aid training and I think I recognize the symptoms, disorientation, trouble speaking, that kind of thing. She's in no state to help herself or even understand what you're telling her. You *can't* just throw her out of here – it would be *inhuman*. I bet it's illegal, too. 'Good Samaritan' laws and all that. We might get *sued*!"

"*Look*, lady," countered Karlie, wearily, swallowing her chewing gum, "I don't make up the rules here, Ossie does, and the rules say, 'if yas don't pay, ya don't play', ya understand? She might or might not be in a bad way, but we get plenty like her in here, if we gave free tables to every stoner that dropped by, we'd have to rename this joint 'The Santa Esmerelda Flophouse', ya know what I mean? Besides, what do ya want me to do with her, exactly? Just let her stay here all day? All *week*?"

Catherine shot a quick glance at the girl-in-rags, cowering in the corner of her booth like a trapped animal, then another at her own husband, then a third at the waitress. After a long second of contemplation, the wife said, with forced sympathy,

"No, of *course* you can't, Karlie. Here."

The wife pressed a ten-dollar note into the waitress' hand. "Will that cover it?" she asked.

"Shore," replied the waitress. "The bill, I mean. Ya need a receipt?"

"No, that's okay," said the wife.

"I can let her stay here another hour or so," offered Karlie, "But then I gotta free the table. And even in doin' that, I'm bendin' the rules. If Ossie asks, tell him that yer payin' for whatever else she orders. It's no sweat, I just won't get her anythin'."

"Sure," agreed the woman. "Thanks, Karlie."

Returning to her booth, the wife snatched the bill from the girl-in-rags' table, as she sat down.

"Catherine, you *know* we're rather short of cash," argued the husband. "And furthermore –"

But the eyes of all the rest of those occupying the family's booth were focused on the space just outside it. The girl-in-rags had got up and was now on her knees, hands clasped in front, looking directly at the family but especially at the mother.

"Thankk-yeww-thankk, Kath-arr-hinn," she whimpered.

"It's okay, lady," reassured the boy. "Sometimes I'm hungry, but I don't have any money, either."

The fallen-girl smiled kindly at him, slowly rising to her feet and standing impassively in front of the family, to the muffled laughter of the truckers in the back of the restaurant.

"Won't you... uhh... please sit down, Miss Tanak?" implored Catherine, motioning to a half-free spot to the left of the teenage girl.

"*Mom*," protested the teenager.

"Hayley, darling, *try* to be polite," remonstrated the mother. "There's plenty of space in this booth. Move over, please, dear."

Grudgingly, the teenager shifted a few inches closer to her mother. Tentatively, uncertainly, but gratefully, the girl-in-rags sat down next to Hayley, directly across from the boy.

"Could we have our bill, our *own* bill, that is, Miss?" shouted the husband to the waitress.

The wife shot him a dirty look.

"No problem, Mister, have it for yas in a minute, soon as I get these jokers their pancakes, okay?" replied Karlie, elbowing a trucker slightly as she left the table he shared with another.

"What's that *smell*?" complained Hayley.

"Yeah," added the little girl on her father's other side. She leaned forward, towards the girl-in-rags, taking a deep breath. "It smells like burnt toast, Daddy," she noted. "Or like the ashes in our fireplace, after the fire goes out."

"Yeah... yes, I guess it does, Trisha honey," answered the father, uncertainly.

The fallen-girl pointed to a burn-mark on her garment, taking it between two finger-tips.

"Boorn," she explained. "Boorn mee. Fai-err, bigg."

"Well, Miss... Miss Tanak," mentioned the husband, "It's nice to make your acquaintance – sorry to hear about your accident, but it looks like you got through it without serious injury... except for the burns, of course. More than I can say for a lot of others we've seen on the roads since... since, well, I'm sure you know what I'm talking about. What brings you to this part of the country? Where were you going, when your car went off the road?"

As he spoke, the girl-in-rags had focused her eyes on him intently, staring with determination at his mouth, as if lip-reading. Then she adopted the pensive look they had seen earlier.

She started to talk, but fumbled for words. At length, all she was able to communicate was, "Sarr-ee, Markk... ee-memm-berr noh... nott. Noh ree-memm-berr..."

She looked despondently down at the table, a tear in her eye.

The wife whispered to the teenager, "Memory loss. Another clear sign of post-traumatic shock."

"Yeah, I guess," responded Hayley, as the waitress appeared from around the next booth.

"Here it is, Mister," announced Karlie. "I brought ya the credit-card thingie to fill out... figured yas didn't want to use cash, right? Did yas like the food?"

"Right," replied the father, taking the credit-card slip and pen. Scribbling on the ink paper, he said, "And the food was great, thanks. Hope that's enough of a tip, I suppose the last few days, we've learned not to worry as much about how much money we spend... compared to before, that is."

The waitress took the slip. "Wow, yeah, Mister, thank ya, thanks a lot, ya hear?" She cupped her hand in front of her mouth, half-turned towards the truckers and loudly called, "A lot more than I get from *some* people 'round here, that's for sure!"

The obligatory chuckles issued from three tables, further in the restaurant.

"Glad to do someone a good turn," said the father, amicably. "Well, I guess that's about it – time to get going, you cowboys and Indians. Sammy? Out you go."

The little boy shuffled off the bench, followed by the father, clutching various coats and hats, followed in turn by the youngest child, Trisha.

"Sari? You mind?" asked the wife, with a friendly smile, motioning with her finger. After a second of blank stares, the girl-in-rags realized and got up off the bench. She stood nearby, watching each move intently, as the rest of the family donned their winter-garments and headed for the door.

As they went out of the restaurant, the wife half-whispered to the husband, "Mark, do you think she'll be okay? I'm really *worried* about her. Even if things were back to normal – and they're *not* – she doesn't look like she's in any state to cope with..."

The husband cut her off.

"Oh, *shit*," he muttered. "I just *knew* that something like this was going to happen," he angrily added.

"What –," retorted the wife, now in the parking-lot.

"Oh," she said, turning around.

The fallen-girl had followed them out, tagging behind the man and wife by about six arms-lengths. Evidently sensing the man's mood, she held her clasped hands in front of her chest, begging, although this time she did not get down on her knees.

"*You* handle her," complained the husband. "Not my problem... not *our* problem."

"Thanks a *lot*, Mark," answered the wife.

With a sigh, Catherine turned to the girl-in-rags and said, "Now what are we going to do with *you*."

She paused for a second, looking at the girl's big, sad eyes, the traces of a tear detectable within them.

"*Look*, Sari," the woman tried to explain, "We'd *love* to take you with us, but we're heading east, a long way from here. To Michigan – Dearborn, that's 'home', for us. It's probably way off your own route."

"Mihh-shee-gann," the girl-in-rags repeated, hopefully, a half-smile coming to her face. "Ai Mihh-shee-gann gohh."

"You mean you're going to Michigan, too? Is that what you're trying to say? Frankly, I find that a little hard to believe, Sari, and I doubt that Mark will believe it either," retorted the wife.

"Look, here," she added, now at a loss, as she pressed several bills of thin-plastic money into the fallen-girl's hand. "*That* should get you started, at least, it'll get you another meal, somewhere," she said, not really believing her own words. "It's not a lot, but we don't have much spare cash, these days. I guess it'll have to be enough..."

The girl-in-rags had been studying Catherine with laser-like intensity, as the latter had been speaking. To the other's surprise, the fallen-girl now spoke, slowly and deliberately, in hardly accented English,

"Kann ai goh yeww withh, Kath-arr-hinn? Ai werkk. Werkk doo yeww forr. Pleesse. Pleesse."

She looked down at the ground and said, in a small, pleading, voice, "Noh-wayre goh too. Forr mee."

"Sari, I *can't*," countered the mother, heavily. "I'm sorry... I have to go." Morosely, she turned towards the car.

The girl's face now wore the saddest of expressions, one that would have melted the heart of any human being. She quietly handed the money back to the wife, saying, "Ai oh-kay iz. Youu thiss need, forr kiddz. Morr thann mee, Kath-arr-hinn. Bai sell-eff ai soor-vaiv, howw havve all-wai."

She paused a bit, then said, as the wife was almost in the car, "Thankk-yeww forr food, Kath-arr-hinn. Luvv mayyn, tayyk yeww weeth. Dayy somme, pai youu forr bee mee kindd. Againn meet wee."

The girl-in-rags could not directly see the tears in the wife's face, as the van pulled out of the lot, turning east down the road thereafter; but that did not stop her from knowing, all the same.

Sensei Is Gone

"Yo, Cap'n!" shouted Air Force Major Devon White in his usual, cheerful, anything-but-military-regulation manner, as he finally caught up to ex-Commander Sam Jacobson, by propelling himself awkwardly forward in the weightless environment of this part of the station.

"Y'all move too fast for me there... especially in this zero gravity stuff – damn, I'd give *anything* to get my feet on the ground and run the 440 again," the astronaut added, his handsome, African-American face beaming a familiar, bright-toothed smile.

"Um-hum," replied the former Mars mission leader, "I know what you mean, there. I've been spending more than my share of time in the pseudo-grav area, too, but for me it's more just wanting to be out of space, back on Earth, out of *here*. Combination of cabin fever and too much time on my hands, I guess."

"Yeah, no shit. *Sir*," echoed White. "Well, anyways, the reason I wanted to catch y'all is, we're all waiting for you in your cabin. Today's touchy-feely session, you know. We even got Sergei to show up, this time."

"Can't make it today, Devon, sorry," answered Jacobson. "I was heading towards the boardroom, I got another meeting with Cohen – something about the configuration or capabilities of the *Eagle* and *Infinity*, I don't know exactly what. I could have sent Brent, instead, but probably better him than me to practice that... well, *that* stuff. I'm still having a hard time getting used to it, if you know what I mean."

"Don't we all," responded White, knowingly.

He looked around, furtively, for signs of an open intercom link, or a surveillance camera, and commented, "Especially without *her* to be our instructor, right? I'll tell them that y'all is dealin' with commander-type issues, I guess that outranks our little get-together, don't it? No sweat, anyway, not like we got a final exam coming up or anything such like that."

"Heh," grunted Jacobson, ruefully, "And even if we *did*, who'd be there to tell us if we passed or failed? Seems to me that the only authority on this lost art, is no longer with us, Devon."

"Yeah... no shit," confirmed the astronaut, reflectively. "You *know* how I feel about *that* whole thing. Well, okay, I guess I should let y'all get on your way. Give my regards to Commander Cohen, oh, and tell him that Mike and me almost got the comms stuff all up and runnin', if we can't talk to somebody it's likely to be because they're choosin' not to answer, not because the line's dead. Okay?"

"You got it, Devon. Give my regards to Broadway and the chorus line in my cabin," joked the ex-Commander of Earth's first mission to Mars.

He propelled himself forward, each meter sending him thankfully closer to the closest of space-station's revolving, pseudo-gravity drum-areas, while his former subordinate turned back to attend his own meeting, of the most select few.

Conference In The Cabin

The short man, awkwardly dressed in two pieces of a three-piece suit that never seemed to quite fit, no matter how many of the best tailors in Washington had been put to the task, took off his thickly-rimmed spectacles and brushed back what little was left of the hair on the top of his head.

He was still in a suit, however incongruous that looked in a log cabin, somewhere in the Rocky Mountain backwoods.

"Real pretty out here-aways," he offered, in his characteristic, south-of-the-Mason-Dixon drawl. "Nice clean air. But I won't be sorry to get back to the big town, back to the way things used to be."

He stubbed a cigarette, unapologetic about being one of the last to maintain that ancient habit.

"So," he pleasantly inquired, "What y'all got for me today, gentlemen? And ladies, or lady – sorry, I forgot there. Please *do* excuse that, and the fact that I seem to be a bit over-dressed for this fine occasion."

"No problem, Mr. Horn," replied a thirty-something, average-looking brunette in a white-and-blue fleece jacket and yellow jump-pants. "A lot of us, myself included, had to get out here on short notice, too."

"Anyway," she continued, "Polls are still okay, or, steady, at least. Well, let me *slightly* revise that. There's some slippage in California, especially around L.A., due to the riots, although that's a write-off for us, anyway – same story on the East Coast, New York and all... but we don't count on there, either. Midwest, Northwest and Southwest are still on board, despite the damage caused by the comet fragments, 'rally round the Chief' idea and so on are keeping us afloat there."

"The only real issue that I need to bring to everyone's attention," she cleared her throat, then explained, "Is in Dixie, the Bible Belt, specifically. I'm seeing a serious split developing in the Faith Foundation and the some of the other religious lobbies... it seems that somewhat less than half of them have camped on to this 'Mars-girl was the devil' thing, while the other half either hasn't bought it or just wants to pick up with the traditional issues, outlawing birth control, 'no-knock' raids for pirated movies, school prayer and so on. Could be a problem for us. I need not remind you that the off-year Congressional races are less than a year away, now."

"Why should that be a concern of ours?" asked the Vice-President, as he stirred the ice in his Scotch-on-the-rocks. "They're in *our* camp, anyway – they're sure not going to support the *Democrats*, whether or not they're fighting with each other over some damn theological argument."

He snorted in mildly suppressed contempt. "Besides, we got the 'inside track' with all the voting machines, anyway – you *know* what I mean. Just say a prayer or two with Billy's friends, they'll be fine," he cackled.

"What *I'm* worried about," cautioned the woman, "Is that they'll ask the President – or even yourself – to take a public stand on this issue. We're already getting inquiries from a few people in the Faith Foundation, for example... and if the Administration has to say what *we* believe, inevitably, we'll make one side or the other, upset with us. It's one of those 'no-win' situations, I'm afraid."

"Meanin'," added Horn, "That they might just stay home and not vote, at all. I'd remind y'all, Mr. Vice-President, that them folk are all that stands between us and the heathen hordes of the lib-rals."

"I *know* that," retorted the Vice-President, getting up from the wall-side divan upon which he had previously been reclining, in a gesture to show that he was a good, bald head taller than the political Adviser.

"And I've paid my dues to your religious constituency, Billy– but it's *money* that keeps us in power, not posturing on some goddamn 'how many angels sit on the head of a pin' kind of debate. Money for our candidates, but especially, money in the pockets of our supporters; you *know* who I'm talking about, the *big* boys, the *rich* boys, the ones I drink this fine *Scotch* with, the ones that *own* the Yew-Nighted States of America. I'm getting calls, more each day, asking when we're going to lift the state of emergency and let our friends get back to business. Take the Gulf oil rigs, for example – National Guard is still sitting on 'em, to protect them from *what*? A comet that's been and gone? These people count their income by the day, hour and minute, and they're *not* used to waiting, my friend. Frankly, I'm much more concerned about *them* pulling out from under us, than I am a few Bible-bangers arguing endlessly amongst themselves as to whether some Mars-girl was Jesus, Moses, the Virgin Mary or the devil, or the other way around. Money *talks*, and bullsh... well, just my personal opinion, of course."

"Why," replied Horn, with unctuous courtesy, "So taken, sir. And," – he sucked back a puff from his cigarette – "Far be it for *me* to be puttin' off anyone's golfin' trip or yachtin' party. I just wanted to remind everyone that there's a lot more of *my* folk, down at the Tupelo Bingo Hall and such-wise, than there are at the Silver Springs Country Club and the like. That *does* make a difference, if I do say."

"The Vice-President has a point, though," interjected the woman. "It's still early days, yet, but I'm seeing signs of dissatisfaction here and there, too, mostly from our middle- and upper-echelon supporters – stuff like 'when are we going to be able to take our vacation trip to Hawaii', 'when are the shares in my portfolios going to be unlocked so I can get back to trading', that kind of thing. I guess the whole idea of shared sacrifice, 'we all pull together', is fading fast, and politically, we have to be positioned to assure the country that we will be getting back to normalcy as soon as possible."

"Yeah," agreed a trim, middle-aged, soberly-dressed man with a clean-cut, though pock-marked, Hispanic face. "But we have to be realistic here, all the same. Standard methods of communication are still out in much of the country – I asked the phone companies yesterday and their estimate is six months until we get the cell network fully operational again, for example – and the reason that we still have the Guard, or State Patrols, out in some of these places is, the rule of law broke down completely just before The Event, or The Expected Event, however you want to call it."

The others watched intently as FBI Director Cesar Ochoa continued, "Petty crime is way up and we're tracking a big upward trend in violent crime, especially gang activity, as well... damn gangs are pretty much running large parts of many of the urban areas, South L.A., for example, is a no-go zone unless you've got a tank platoon to cover you. The minute that we pulled our resources out of these places to concentrate on the national emergency, these assholes – sorry, Ms. Feldner – moved right in to fill the vacuum. It's going to take us *months* and a *lot* of manpower and budget to clean 'em out again. As for 'normalcy', well, we've closed down our entire white-collar crime enforcement unit, so God knows what's going on with the stock-market – we're counting on SEC and Treasury to fill in for us, there. If they can."

"Who *cares*," commented the Vice-President, sipping the last mouthfuls of his Scotch. "Damn waste of time, trying to over-regulate business from doing what business is going to do, anyway."

He smiled, cynically. "Maybe that comet did *some* good, after all, now didn't it?" he snorted.

The woman gave a pained smile, looked at the short man and stated, "Listen, Mr. Horn... word got to me via the grapevine about that idea you had, you know, the one about the 'new weapon that we used to save the world'... I just wanted to say that in my opinion, we should go to press ASAP with this one. We've done a few exploratory polls – strictly deniable, no way to trace them back to us, of course – asking the question 'how would you feel about the Administration, if you knew that it was solely the United States that destroyed the comet', and the responses have been *very* encouraging."

"How's that?" asked Horn. "We've been winnin' for the past few years anyway, as I recall."

"When we extrapolate these results against the entire population and then run them against a state-by-state analysis, Electoral College I mean," explained the woman, "We're looking at a sweep that would make Johnson in '64 or Nixon in '72 look like a tight horse-race. We'd pick up New York for sure and we'd have at least a 50-50 for California... we might take every state in the Union. I'm sure I don't need to explain how well we'd do elsewhere. We're talking *coat-tails, long* coat-tails, here, gentlemen."

"It's a *lie*, you know," interjected the Vice-President. "Not that that matters. As long as we don't get *caught*."

"Well, now, Mr. Vice-President, sir, I wouldn't put it quite *that* way," argued Horn, his poker-face bedecked with a typical half-smile. "'Lie' is a mighty *strong* word. As y'all know, the government of the U.S. of A. is a substantially large institution, with many nooks and crannies containin' things, weapons of war n' all to protect us in just such a situation as we have recently been through, hidden away in 'em."

"My personal opinion," he went on, "Which I will if necessary say to our good friends in the press, is that our military dusted off one of these and used it to salutary effect on poor ol' Lucifer, there. Just *what* weapon? From *where*? And where is it now? Ah, that's 'national security', my friends. Can't say nothin' about it, I'm afraid... you all just gotta *trust* us.. I'm pretty sure that'll work for us. Always, has, in the past."

"FBI," mentioned the Hispanic-looking man, "Will simply refuse to comment. We'll say we don't know anything. Despite what people may think from those TV shows, we don't go poking our noses into places they have no right to be in."

"That's why we selected you for the job, Cesar, for your excellent sense of discretion," said the Vice-President. He continued, "Billy, you could teach us all, myself included, a few lessons in public relations."

He chuckled, and hoisted the bottle of finest vintage Chivas Regal for another drink. This time, the short man got the ice from the bucket, joining the Vice-President in an impromptu toast.

Learning From Donny

The trucker grunted, rolled over, as much as one could, in the always-too-narrow confines of the cab behind the driving-compartment, and tried to go back to sleep. But the rays of the mountain morning sun illuminated him mercilessly.

"Wha... wow, you girl... *oh*," he muttered, as he squinted and tried to rub the sleep from his eyes.

"I see you got up before me, girlie," he noted.

"Wake I now one hour for," replied the fallen-girl, in her strange, impossible-to-place accent. "You good sleep, Don-nee?"

"Never better, since all that fun last night," he grunted with a dirty grin, his long, muscular arms reaching for a cigarette, shaking his head to get the ashes of the last one out of his beard. "Y'all wore me *out,* girl. Not many can, y'know. Had three girls at once in Vegas, one time."

"Good at that, I am," she chimed, primly. "Have many many years of, oh, word what is, 'experience'. But three one time... two oh-kay but three, hard to that do, imagine I not can. Hmm, actually, *can.* Back somewhere from before long time. Lots of, how say you, 'flexibility', takes it."

She giggled.

Suppressing a chuckle, the trucker lit up, taking a deep puff. Noticing that the girl was staring strangely – she seemed to be looking at the fire burning on the tip of the thing, not at him or the cigarette itself – he asked, "What's the big deal, Sarrie? Just a smoke, you know."

"Oh, nothing is," she demurred, turning down her eyes. "Just not normal me for. Not oozed it to."

"Yeah," said the trucker, "I'm one of the last ones, I guess, most of the other guys in my line of work gave up years ago, or they're smokin' stronger things, but I'm not into the hard stuff, 'cept for Mr. Jack Daniels, that is, if that counts. I ditched the grass when they put through the 'death penalty for more than three grams' law. I liked it, but not *that* much."

His Okie drawl became softer, more reflective, and he explained, "See, I picked up this ol' habit in the Army, back when I was posted to the Pakee-stan thing a year or two ago, lookin' for them loose nukes – never found 'em, of course. A smoke here or there was about the only vice they let us do in the field, there weren't no booze, no girls either, fuckin' baghead place, nothin' but camels 'n ten year-old kids who'd blow themselves up just to take you with 'em... I was one of the first white guys to get one of them 'special invitations you can't refuse' that they started sendin' out, you remember, after they had the problems with the blacks goin' over to the other side in Koid- Kood- whatever-the-shit-Istan they call it, higher-ups decided that the ghetto-folk was a 'security risk', drummed near all of 'em out of the Army, so us white trash was the lucky 'uns that got to pick up the slack... ah, if it kills me, well, no great loss to the world, I s'pose. I *was* damn lucky to get out of that rathole, most of my company didn't. If my number comes up, well, that's life."

"Just it that smoke you like taste," offered the fallen-girl, pleasantly. "But the fire, enjoy it I do," she added, again staring strangely at the burning ashes at the tip of the cigarette, just before the trucker noticed that they were about to fall.

Donny flicked the cigarette over a nearby bottle-cap, but the other one's left hand caught the ashes as they fell, lovingly capturing them as one might an inadvertently discarded silver dollar.

The glow left the tobacco-refuse instantly, upon contact with the fallen-girl's open skin, which did not seem to be harmed in the least.

"Man, yer a *weird* one, chickie," he commented. "Y'all sure *do* got a thing for fires, there, just don't light one in mah truck, y'hear? But speakin' of that, we're burnin' daylight... I guess I'd better get this rig up and runnin'. Places to go and people to see, you know."

He fumbled for his pants, recognizing the fake-Western buckle of his belt after a few seconds.

"Don-nee," the fallen-girl inquired, "Where going we are too-day?"

"We?" he replied. "Oh, *I* get it. Well, I'm goin' East as far as Wichita, remember, I told you last night, before...? I can take you as far as the state line, but that's about it, girlie. Nothin' *personal*, you know, but I got two buddies doin' time in the big house for 'transporting workin' girls across state lines for immoral purposes', and I have nooo intention of joinin' them as guests of Uncle Sam."

She stared at him.

"And with that accent of yours," warned the trucker, "They might get me on the 'illegal alien' thing, too. They was crackin' down hard on 'em before the Big Thing, let up a bit while it was goin' down, y'know, but I bet you good money they'll be back at it soon. I got my papers to get 'cross the state line – don't want to lose 'em, that happens and I might as well just drive this here rig off a cliff, or something."

"What mean you, Don-nee?" the girl-in-rags asked, uncertainly. "Understand I not. What is 'big house'? It a place is many families it in? And, not I 'illegal alien'. I from here not, but have no broken laws any, not I know of. On road before day three you I met, tried ride get big wheel thing with seats man-ee, but no card crediting me had, saw then I some po-leece-man, and asked them if could I go down road, him past. One smiled and he said, 'shore, but fifty mahls too next truk stopp'. If broke laws I, they prison me dunn-jon in, no?"

"*Jaysus*," he laughed, "You just fall out of a *tree* or somethin', girl? Everybody knows that the 'big house' is the local State Prison. And y'all probably hit some State Troopers there, from what I hear they got their hands full just with cleanin' up after that comet thing – "

Fear instantly clouding her beautiful, innocent-looking countenance, the fallen-girl gasped.

"*Com-met*? Com-met!" she cried. "I see it, coming right me at, it is! Heading for it, hate it, fighting it! Scared, scared very, scared!"

She looked as if she had seen a ghost.

"Hey, *hey*," exclaimed the trucker, reaching out for her. Quickly, the girl moved into his arms.

"Didn't mean to frighten ya, there, Sarrie girl," he consoled. "I kinda forgot that a lot of people still have bad memories about how we just dodged tha bullet awhile ago. I'm mostly to myself in the truck, y'know... only chat with other guys drivin' rig, and they're more or less same as me, more worried 'bout not gettin' gas."

"You do not scared, too, Don-nee?" she queried, looking up at him.

"Nah," he laconically answered. "Same as with the smokes, more or less... when my number's up, it's up, nothin' I can really do about it, anyways. I don't worry 'bout it. After bein' the only one of my squad to make it out of Lahori – or whatever they call that damn baghead place – I kinda got fatalistic about the whole livin' and dyin' thing. Not that I take *chances*, y'know... which is why you get off at the state line, okay?"

"When that," she quietly inquired, looking down.

"Day or so," explained the trucker, indifferently. "Could do it in way less than that, back in the old days, but what with all the junk on the roads since the Big Thing, I gotta drive slow enough to get this rig 'round whatever's on. Just about hit a cow 'bout five miles back, remember?"

Regaining a measure of her composure and looking at him suddenly with far-away, cerulean eyes, the fallen-girl replied, with an air of reluctance, "Yes, remember. Oh-kay, guess I then, Don-nee. I stay not if you trouble it brings. But you thank for hug. Needed that."

"And when we get there, I forgot... I'll give ya the forty bucks I promised," he added. "Won't even deduct nothin' for all those vacuum wrapped 7-11 sandwiches you ate behind my back after you thought I was asleep, last night, either. I always pay well for good service, whether it's for coffee at the truck stop or..."

He grinned lecherously, only to find his smile met with one of knowing, at-least-equal salaciousness.

"For-tee?" she noted, uncertainly. "Thank youu. Must a *lot* be, that. And work easy is, too. Fun, me for."

The girl-in-rags smiled again, arching an eyebrow.

Shore knows her stuff, got me goin' full speed ahead, hard as the rock of whatever-that-is with just one kiss... must've got trained in them cat-houses by Vegas before them Bible-bangers closed 'em all down, mused the trucker. *A girl* that *good usually costs two hundred-fifty, maybe three hundred or more... hope she's workin' this route when I get back on my Westbound run.*

"Well, then, let's get goin'," he announced, "We're burnin' daylight, and what with all them potholes and washouts, probably take me better part of a day makin' it to the state border."

Now fully dressed, Donny climbed into the driving compartment and started the engine.

There was a familiar, throaty "roarrr", and they were on their way.

Here Comes The Sun

Looking over his shoulder, Humber saw the wiry, intense-eyed, olive-skinned figure of Commander Ariel Cohen dive through the zero-G, through the airlock separating the previous modular section of the ISS2 space-station, from the one which they both now occupied. The man cruised from side to curved side of the compartment, looking closely at the status of the white plastic panels that encased the space they were in.

"Blue Ten is now inhabitable, I see," mentioned Cohen, pleasantly. "Congratulations."

"Yeah, but just don't go poking any screwdrivers into the duct tape over those holes in the wall," answered the tattooed Englishman, in his trademark Midlands accent. "We did the minimum that we had to, just to get convenient access to Eleven and that blighted booster."

"That one's still de-pressurized?" asked Cohen.

"Very much so," replied the Chief Engineer. "After we had the EVA to recover the... well, *you* know... we had another couple to do a real damage assessment – I was on the second of those trips, meself, along with Brent Boyd, he insisted on going along. Place is still a mess, broken, burnt bits of rubbish floating everywhere. We got it fixed up so that we should be able to pump in minimum levels of air in there, but Shivani doesn't think doing so is worth the risk of one of the patches slipping and us losing it."

"To say nothing of what happens to anyone in there at the time," observed Cohen, evenly.

"Yeah," agreed Humber, his eyes looking down, or in any direction that counted as 'down', to avoid his superior's gaze. "Like what happened to the last ones."

"Alan," said Cohen, sympathetically, "There's obviously nothing we can do to change what has happened in the past, but you and I have to try to put that behind us. If we can. I came down here today – alone – to see for myself how we're doing, and what our chances look like, from here on in."

"So?" asked Humber.

"So... what *are* our chances, Alan?" requested Cohen. "Honest opinion, please."

"You *really* want an honest assessment, Commander?" shot back the engineer, fingering his earring with poorly-suppressed frustration.

"Please," replied the Commander. "You have my word that nothing you say will be repeated to *anyone*. Chen, especially."

"Slim and none," offered Humber, now staring the other man in the eyes. "No, let me re-phrase that. None. Bottom line is... we're *fucked*, mate, that's about the lot of it."

"Go ahead," demanded Cohen. "I need to know, one way or another."

"You *see*, it's like this," explained the engineer, slowly and deliberately. "Booster's shot, *kaput*, pick the language you want to – Hebrew for you, I suppose, whatever – it's gone, utterly beyond repair. I looked it over carefully in my last EVA and I can tell you, there isn't a *chance* that the bugger won't blow up, again, the first time we fill it with propellant – ignoring the fact that we don't *have* any – and push the button. If it weren't for the fact that it contains some unburnt propellant still in it, as well as some salvageable metal, I'd recommend we just jettison the whole thing."

"That doesn't sound like much of a survival plan," commented Cohen.

"You got *that* right, Commander," said the Englishman. "Because I don't *have* one. Nobody does. Boyd and I sat down and crunched the numbers – we also had help from Chkalov, you remember he was the Russian on Jacobson's ship, as well as from Helmut Weiss from Space Science and a couple others – on every possible alternative propulsion system on this station, everything from trying to physically move the maneuvering thrusters so that they're all on the inbound side of the ship to rigging up solar sails, and the results are always the same : we *can* slow us down a mite, some options do it better than others, but they all fall *far* short of being able to put us into a stable orbit around Earth, or even around the Earth and the Moon. Irony is that when the damn booster blew, it gave us quite a push, much more thrust than what we got on the outbound leg, in fact, so we're heading for Earth, or at least Earth's *vicinity*, a lot faster than we thought we were going to, beforehand."

"Meaning?" pressed Cohen, already knowing the answer.

"Meaning," replied Humber, heavily but professionally, "We're on our way to the neighborhood of the Sun, at a very smart clip, mate. No matter *what* we do, I fear. If it's any consolation, as Shivani has correctly pointed out, we'll no doubt be out of air *long* before we become a spark to a flame, as it were. Not sure which one I'd pick, if I had a chance, really..."

"I see," calmly noted Cohen.

"What I *can* offer you, Commander," offered the engineer, "Is that I can slow us down – not enough, as I said, to park us, but enough to prolong our Earth-area pass-by by, say, maybe as much as a day or so. Might give us more of a window to evacuate the lucky few, I suppose. That's about the best I can do."

"Have you checked these assumptions over with anyone else, other than Weiss and Jacobson's people?" asked the station commander.

"Aye," confirmed Humber. "With one other person in my own crew – Shoji Abe, specifically – just to get a 'disinterested' second opinion. If this matters, Brent Boyd is a bit more optimistic that I am regarding how much braking thrust we might be able to get out of the *Infinity*'s engines, but he and I agree that either way, we're looking at a difference of a few hours before we leave Earth proximity, at best. In the long-run, the results will be more or less the same."

Cohen regarded the other man intensely, for a few seconds. Then he again spoke.,

"Fair enough, Alan. I asked you for an honest answer, and I suppose that I got one. It's not the greatest of news, though, wouldn't you agree?"

"No, I guess not," muttered Humber. "Please believe me, if there was *any* way – any way at *all*, you know, Ariel – "

"No need to apologize," Cohen quickly replied. "We're all dealing with the same set of facts, the same outcomes. At least now, we have the knowledge that whatever happens to *us*, they'll be okay, down on Earth. That's something, isn't it? Quite an ironic role reversal, compared to a short time ago, wouldn't you think? Sorry. I was just thinking out loud about what I can tell the crew."

"I suppose," mentioned Humber. "What will be, will be. Except for a miracle."

Cohen looked away.

"Yes," he mused, "Except for a... *miracle*."

Brothers Against The Devil

"So... what do you have to report, Brother?" demanded the first man, his tough, leather-skinned face showing intense, interrogatory eyes.

Straightening his otherwise immaculate tie and nervously running his other hand over his crew-cut, lest even one hair be out of place, the second man replied, "Nothing so far, I'm afraid, Brother. Our sources are in constant contact – the 'inside track', I guess you'd say – but it appears that even the *Government* thinks that she's dead; that is, the threat is behind us. They're still looking, though."

The first man smiled, unctuously. "Of *course* they are," he commented. "That's because all they have is science. *We*, on the other hand, have more; we have faith in our Father God and His Only Son, our King and Commander."

"Praise the Lord," responded the second man, reflexively. "But... I was just wondering... I mean, how long do we keep looking, sir? The three contacts that I have been speaking with – two in the Air Force and one at NSA, and after all they're certainly in a position to have the best and latest intelligence on the subject – they're of the opinion that the devil-girl just disappeared without a trace. We can't prove that she *doesn't* exist; we'd need a body for that, wouldn't we?"

"That's probably true, my son," the first man explained. "Maybe we *will* need one, in the long-run. Or we will get one... somehow. But use your faith – pray for answers, and they will come to you. When you close your eyes and ask Father God, 'Lord, how can I fight Satan and his accursed agents on Earth', what does He tell you, Brother Martin?"

The second man closed his eyes for a few seconds and pondered. Then, uneasily, he said, "He tells me, 'There is work yet to be done', Brother."

Looking up anxiously, he asked, "Is that what He says to you, too, revered Brother Harold?"

"Indeed it is," replied the first man, through pursed lips, revealing just a hint of teeth in a controlled half-smile. "Keep searching, Brother. The Lord will guide you to our goal, if you remember to keep your mind and body clean in the pursuit of His enemies. I'll want another report in one week, or whenever you get something substantial to tell me."

"Thank you, Brother Harold," replied the second man. "I'll do that. Praise the Lord."

He stood up and bowed.

"His name be praised," intoned the first man, nodding the signal of dismissal.

The second man turned and walked smartly towards the door, saluting briefly as he passed the hulking, crew-cut plainclothes guards, each glowering under sunglasses with a discreetly stowed submachine gun.

Seeing the door closing, the first man reached into his desk, finding a handful of capsules in a bottle. Throwing them back with a deep gulp of distilled, purified water, he reclined into his chair, lazily watching the patterns on the ceiling dance and jig in front of his blurring, enlightened eyes.

Message To The Motherland

The cosmonaut entered a command code, followed by the nearest ASCII approximation of his originally Cyrillic password that the keyboards of the space-station could muster.

A screen flickered to life, first in random, multi-colored static, then in the display of a space control center, resplendent in various video-screens, computer consoles, tracking maps and the like.

Very much like the Americans' "Mission Control" in Houston. But this was *not* Houston, and the language was not American English.

"*Zdravtsvoitsye*, Sergei Mironovich," started the portly, Ukrainian-looking man at the other end of the special, encrypted communications-link. "It is good to hear from you again, after the recent interruptions. We were concerned that something might have happened to you, or that Commander Cohen had restricted your ability to use this channel."

"*Spasiba*, Ground Controller Poschuk," replied Sergei Chkalov, "But I am fine, personally, and, as a matter of fact, Ariel Cohen – we are, as the Americans say, 'on a first name basis', both knows about, and has approved, my discussing matters privately with Pletsesk, that is, with all of you. Equally with Chen, speaking with the Chinese space center. I would remind you that Cohen does not report to the American chain of command, although one could be forgiven for thinking that, by the way their military commanders try to issue him orders. He is not stupid... he is aware of political matters."

"Yes, undoubtedly," agreed the remote voice. "But that has been known for some time. In any event, Sergei Mironovich, we have other matters to discuss. Specifically, the state of the space-station in general, and the current plans... as you may be aware of them."

"I am afraid," explained Chkalov, "That the prognosis for ISS2, and myself, of course, is not very good. Although Commander Cohen has not yet made a public announcement to this effect, rumors up here say that the propulsion and braking situation is now hopeless – the rockets are damaged beyond repair. Not even my former commander Jacobson's ships, that is, the *Eagle* and *Infinity*, can add enough thrust to fully stop us; they might, at most, slow us down. So we will simply pass by the Earth, it seems. I have heard unofficially via some of the more senior officers that the most likely outcome will be for the station to eventually assume a parabolic orbit with the Sun... if, in fact, our velocity is, in fact, sufficient to stop us from being pulled into the Sun's gravity well. This would be of little difference, considering that our available air would run out long before we might burn up. One of my colleagues – you may remember Devon White – joked about us being the 'Flying Dutchman' of space, about our corpses being perfectly preserved for a future salvage crew; we all had a good laugh, about that."

The man down in Russia paused a second, then asked, "And how do you feel about that, Cosmonaut Chkalov?"

Chkalov shrugged. "I am not happy, Ground Controller Poschuk," he said, "But such were the risks that I assumed when I first flew into space, and – I realize that this may not make much sense to you – I have, lately, learned to have some of Major Devon White's faith. So I am at ease."

"'Faith', Sergei Mironovich? I do not remember you as a religious man. You did not even attend the blessing given by the Patriarch of Moscow, when he – "

The cosmonaut interrupted, "I was not a religious man then, and neither am I now, Ground Controller. No... it is something else, something else entirely. It is just that since I met *her* – that is, the being who we found down on Mars, the one called the 'Storied Watcher' – I have come to understand that there is a purpose to things, one that will be whether or not mortal humans such as ourselves want it or not. Beside that, in meeting this 'Karéin', I have fulfilled all of my most cherished dreams... I have done all that I set out to do, Vladimir Modlin. If it is to end soon, I will accept that. With no regrets."

They both remained silent, for a few seconds. Then Poschuk re-started the conversation. "I was meaning to ask you about that. Any news of her?"

"I was about to inquire the same of you, Ground Controller," replied Chkalov, rapidly. "Since the events leading up to the destruction of the comet, no-one here has seen or heard anything of her. Many believe that she is dead, now."

"Is that what *you* believe, Cosmonaut?" asked the other man, evenly.

"No, Vladimir Modlin," said Chkalov firmly, through clenched teeth, "I do *not* believe that she is dead. No, I take that back. I *know* she is yet alive. I am certain of it."

"How?" demanded Poschuk. "Have you seen her? Contacted her?"

"Not... exactly," replied the cosmonaut.

"Then how do you know, Sergei Mironovich?" said the other man.

"I just... *know*," answered Chkalov. "I have a special kind of contact with her. With all due respect, you would not understand how, if I tried to explain it. I am not sure I could do so, anyway."

"Please try," pressed Poschuk, with obviously faked amicability.

"I would prefer what I say to remain off the record, Ground Controller," requested Chkalov. "Is anyone else listening to our conversation today?"

"No, just the two of us, Sergei," responded Poschuk. "You have my personal assurance that I will not forward anything you say to me, in this context."

"Very well then. If you must know," said Chkalov, "We – that is, Karéin and I, were... *intimate*, shortly after I discovered her in hiding, on Jacobson's descent ship, and several times thereafter. You have to understand, Vladimir, that although I tried to avoid her advances, she is very... *difficult* to resist, in a way that no female on Earth could possibly be; I can personally attest to that. Although I probably would have consented, whether or not she had used her abilities on me."

"You slept with an *alien*?" gasped Poschuk. "You are indeed a pioneer, and a brave one at that, Sergei Mironovich," he said. "But the fact that you had sexual relations with this... being – how would *that* let you know that she is still alive? Perhaps you just want to have some fun with her, once more?"

"If I would be honest with you, Ground Controller," retorted the cosmonaut, "Yes, I *do*. But that is not how I know... not exactly. We are *joined* now, in a special way that, as I said, you could not really comprehend. Therefore I know that she is still alive. I do not know where she is, but I know she is still alive. I just know."

"I see," offered the other man, unconvincingly. "Would it be of interest to know that *we* think so, too? And, that we believe the Americans have her?"

Google-eyed, Chkalov exclaimed, "Are you *sure*, Vladimir Modlin? *How*? I mean, how do you know all of this? It would be my heart's fondest wish, if it were true. Have the Americans told our government as much?"

"Not... exactly, Sergei Mironovich," explained Poschuk. "I am not at liberty to give you the details, at least not now; 'the walls have ears', as the expression goes – yes, this *is* a private channel, but we cannot be sure that the Americans, or the Chinese, or someone else, might be listening, even now."

"I *can* tell you", he went on, "That thanks to your own recommendations just prior to the 'Lucifer' event, we had equipped some of our armed forces' attack craft with instruments designed especially to identify and track the alien, should she ever have made another appearance, as evidently she did; so we were able to get what we believe was a much more precise estimate of her energy output, her trajectory, *et cetera*, than the Americans had; unfortunately, most of the brave pilots who carried this instrumentation died in the 'Lucifer' event, but they fulfilled their purpose, they sent back the data, before... and we know that there was much to do about this being that was not revealed to the public, either in America, Russia or elsewhere. We therefore have a combination of scientific, observational, technical, circumstantial and human intelligence, all of which points to the same conclusion – that the Mars-girl is somewhere in the United States, perhaps already safely under the tender care of the Americans' CIA, NSA and other intelligence-agencies."

"And how does Moscow feel about *that*?" asked Chkalov.

"You can imagine," replied the other man. "The same could be said for the attitude of certain other nations, for example the Chinese People's Republic, which, it has come to our attention, has already lodged a protest with the American government. For their part, the Americans are trying to pretend that they know nothing about the whereabouts of the alien. We, of course, know otherwise."

"Is anything to be done?" asked the cosmonaut.

"You should wait and see, Sergei Mironovich," stated Poschuk. "Plans are currently underway, because such a situation would be intolerable, in the long-run. Of course, I cannot speak more of this subject, now."

"I understand, Vladimir Modlin," noted Chkalov.

"Until next time," concluded the Ground Controller. "Pletsesk out."

You Can Call Me, "Bob"

Wistfully, and with genuine affection, the fallen-girl waved good-bye to the trucker, as he closed the door of his cab. The truck's engine growled a low chord as its driver guided it around a lonely clump of trees, to a government roadblock astride the Idaho-Wyoming state line.

Walking quickly forward, she saw a man in a gray-green uniform, wearing a funny-looking, wide-brimmed hat, accost the truck driver, who opened the window of the cab, handed the uniformed man a bunch of papers and then sat waiting impassively.

After a minute or two, the soldier-or-whatever motioned for the trucker to get out, which he did, leading the uniformed man and a couple of his fellow soldiers to the back of the truck, which was opened and, evidently, carefully inspected. A bit later, Donny came back out, said something to the uniformed men and got back in his cab, restarting the engine. The rig started to head off to the east, disappearing in a cloud of dust.

"Bye-bye, Don-nee, bye-bye," whispered the fallen-girl, suspecting but not caring that he could not hear.

Alone I am, again, she mused, silently wiping the traces of a tear. *The stranger, the drifter from afar, whose only companions are sky, memory, the inner fire, and duty.*

What duty?

None payed any special attention to this woebegone girl-thing, lost as she was at the edge of a large crowd of dirty, down-and-out people of all shapes and sizes, milling about the roadblock.

Their loss; as, if they had so done, they would have seen a creature outwardly human, but in fact something *far* more, much more, facing an unknown future in a strange land – no, a strange *world* – as, she somehow knew, had been her lot so many times before.

Her face wore the serene, saturnine half-smile that others had seen before in another place, as her eyes and other senses scanned the scene with cool, analytical precision, trying to make sense of the cacophony of images, smells, vibrations, sounds, radiation and unfamiliar thought-patterns; she sampled the latter and her smile broadened ever so slightly, as she felt another of the old skills – one with no outward sign, but a vital one, none the less – gradually returning.

So that *is how they put the words together,* thought the girl-in-rags, bemusedly. *Catherine and Donny must be very tolerant, to have listened to my pidgin Eng-lish, without laughing.*

Upon a seconds' more of reflection, she remembered, *But I* knew *how to put the words in the right order, all along. I knew how, once. Not long ago, either.*

What made me forget?

A hundred or more men and women, mostly white but not a few blacks and Hispanics, and – though she did not yet know them as such – a number of native Indians, as well, families with and without children and countless others in a modern-day *Grapes of Wrath* scene, milled about this forlorn place, while the Prairie skies occasionally stung the eyes with gusts of wind-borne grit. By a range of measure that meant much to the inhabitants of this place, but which was far less significant in her own reckoning, it was considerably warmer here than it had been, back at the restaurant or in the truck.

The fallen-girl closed her eyes for a second, called upon a deep thought, and tried to adjust her metabolism accordingly.

This had once been simply a nondescript section of Interstate highway, back in the halcyon days prior to 'Lucifer'; nowadays, however, a collection of hastily-constructed tents, temporary buildings and even a Quonset hut – most, but not all, painted in the green-and-khaki of the military – had suddenly appeared astride the imaginary line separating Idaho from the next state.

The girl-thing's senses, sweeping from north to south in a wide arc, detected the life-signs of soldiers far off in either direction, undoubtedly there to stop anyone trying to end-run the Interstate barrier that she was now approaching. She also felt the presence of metal things buried in the ground, perhaps two hundred meters on either side of the highway, with a sign erected in the midst of these places.

"Warning, Mines!" it says, she mused. *I thought that was where these people retrieve elements from the earth... another one of these many words with more than one meaning, no doubt...*

A voice crackled out, all static and feedback, from a trumpet-shaped thing on top of a wooden pole, itself on top of what looked like a prefabricated hut or shack at the side of the road.

"Attention!" it barked out. "We need to remind all of you in the crowd that on the order of the Emergency Measures Authority, no-one without the correct documentation is to approach the border processing checkpoint! If you don't have your papers, there's *nothing* we can do to help you. Those with proof of citizenship or special authorization to travel, you may come forward. No exceptions!"

"I'm trying to get back home!" shouted a male voice from the midst of the crowd. "My papers are there. How the hell am I supposed to – "

"You *heard* 'em," said another voice. "No exceptions. Goddamn country's like Roossia, or Irat, or whatever that damn place is, these days..."

Though she was more than a hundred meters from the checkpoint, the fallen-girl's eyes focused sharply, effortlessly on the faces and figures immediately in front of its gate. She heard arguing, shouting, clearly – although some of the words were still new to her – a dispute of some sort.

There was more shouting, then some shoving, then, cringing involuntarily, she saw a soldier take out a weapon and use its butt to club a man over the head, sending him to the ground in a shower of blood. A nearby woman – the victim's mate, probably – wailed pitifully and dragged the wounded man away, cursing the soldiers as she went.

The bystanders moved back, helped along, undoubtedly, by seeing the soldiers' guns lowered, pointing forward. One of them fired a shot into the air, and the half-panicked crowd surged to the girl-in-rags and then past her, but she just stood there impassively unafraid, her glance moving from fearful face to face as each trotted or ran past.

An average-looking, forty-something white guy with a slight paunch around the waist and a couple of days'-worth of stubble on his face, at least a full head taller than the fallen-girl, with thinning hair combed back in a futile effort, stopped suddenly. He was wearing a too-tight, badly-creased business-suit that looked like 'three months since its last dry-clean'.

The man shouted out, "Hey, *you* there – you *stoopid* or something? They got *guns*! You better get your pretty little ass – "

"They are your own soldiers?" she replied, faking innocence. "They would harm you? You have broken no law... nor have I...?"

The man looked quickly over his shoulder, visibly relieved as he saw the soldiers retreating gradually to the checkpoint.

"Oh, yeah... yeah, you're right, there, Miss," he said. "Whew! Well, better safe than sorry, you know, especially these days with all the 'special' laws after the Big Bang..."

The rest of the crowd, seeing the same thing, gradually slowed down, milling aimlessly about, as the fallen-girl stood in front of the man, her glance sweeping over him, up and down.

I need someone who I can trust, she mused. *And I need to know, if this art still works, with those with whom I hold not close. I shall not trouble you for long, so friend, I hope that you and the Gods can forgive me.*

"Hi," she offered, fetchingly. Her gaze caught him straight in the eye.

Be my friend, she sent. *I am a nice person. Trust me. Love me.*

"Hel-*lo*," the man in the shabby business-suit, stammered. "Bob – Bob K. Billings, Junior, here, that's my name. Tucson, Arizona, but I can't get back to the damn place... can't even get across a state line, these days. How about you?"

"I am Sari Tanak," she primly replied. "Why did you come here, Bob K. Billings Junior? What brings you to this place?"

"Sari... Tanak... sounds *foreign*," he commented.

"It is," she deadpanned.

"Well, you can call me, 'Bob'", he explained. "Anyway, since you asked, I'm in sales, see, hardwood and ceramic floor tiling, that kinda thing. Part-owner of my store's franchise, we do business all over the Southwest, even some jobs as far as California, one or two in St. Louis, too, but I guess there won't be much more to do there... not for a while... what about you?"

"Use my first name, just 'Sari', Bob," the smiling fallen-girl requested. "I am just a wanderer. I go from place to place. I do not have a home."

"Hmm... that's too bad," replied the salesman. "But what do you do for a living? Not to be nosy, but..."

"Well, I got some money from the last man who I was with," the girl-in-rags stated, matter-of-factually.

"Ah, I *see*," Billings knowingly answered. "Forgive me for being blunt about this, but, well, you're a *working* girl, then?"

"Yes, I always do good work in exchange for money," she affirmed, with an enigmatic, slight smile.

Sizing her up, he offered, "Yeah, I'll bet you do. I'll *bet* you do. But don't take that the wrong way. I'm not the judgmental type, don't you know."

Can't imagine why I didn't see it at first, he reflected.

But God, she is *cute – what* is *it, that little-girl haircut? Weird, that salt-and-pepper hair looks like she's almost a grandma, but her face and figure says she can't be more than 20, probably not even that... is it those turquoise eyes? That small-boobed, "never-been-you-know-what" teenager physique? Maybe not a '10', but '9 and a half' for* damn *sure, and that's with her clothes on. Could stand to use a bath, for sure, but if those banking-machines were just on-line...*

He paused for a second, then continued, "Just for the record, I had a gf back in Tucson, and a kid, too, but he's from my ex-wife, not the girlfriend, you know? They're stuck down there, I'm stuck up here, and that's about the long and short of it."

"I am hungry," she said. "Is there anywhere around here, like a, how do you... a 'restaurant', where we could buy some food and talk some more, Bob?"

"'Fraid not," answered the salesman. "Closest thing is that charity mess-tent that the Salvation Army – well, I *think* it's the Sally Ann, maybe it's one of them other religious nuts, I dunno – is running, you see it there?"

He pointed at a tarpaulin-covered structure, a few score meters off to the left, with a lineup of people trailing out the front door-flaps of the tent, with hymnal-sounding music echoing outwards.

"We could go there," suggested the girl-in-rags, trying to sound helpful. "Would for-tee dollars of money be enough for dinner? Would it also buy us a warm place to sleep, tonight?"

"You sure don't beat around the bush, do you, Sari there girl?" he retorted, half-nonplussed, half-aroused.

"Beat the – " she started, but he interrupted, saying, "But, just so we don't have any... *misunderstandings*, here, I'm afraid that I don't have a lot of cash on me – you gotta appreciate, I live off my credit and debit-cards, normally, but when the Big Bang came down, well, I kinda got stuck out here when the computer-networks all went down, which is why I'm here telling you this, right now. Like, I can't pay you what you're probably worth, my dear, and – not that the girlfriend would mind that much, she's not really the jealous type, anyway and we've kind of been on the 'outs' recently, but I don't think the Bible-bangers running that place would cotton up to us sacking down on their turf, even if they had any place to put us up in, which I pretty much doubt, anyway. So I guess it's just chit-chat, for now. Is that alright by you?"

"I am not sure that I completely understand," replied the fallen-girl, "But I am alone and I would welcome company, even if it is just someone to talk with. If you want to lie with me, we can leave that until later. Oh-kay, Bob?"

"You *got* it," he agreed, mentally kicking himself for giving up so easily. "Let's go."

In The Big Tent

The girl-in-rags and the salesman slowly wandered over to the tent, which was a huge thing, easily twice as big as any one of the others excepting the Quonset hut (which, apparently, served as a barracks of some sort, judging from the soldiers coming in and out of it), joining the queue of miserable humanity – already a hundred or more people long – that lead into the building.

From inside, issued the Deep South-tinged sounds of revival music, along with a man, maybe more than one, haranguing the audience about something or other.

"May I be excused for disturbing you, woman," the fallen-girl asked of an African-American woman, who was taller and next in line ahead of her, "But is this the right waiting-line for food? Where we can get something to eat?"

The black woman turned around, looking startled at first, as if seeing something completely unexpected.

"Whaaa... who y'all – look... oh, nothin'," she stammered. "Oh... yeah. Well, that's what they's tellin' us, anyway... only place to get fed 'round here, but y'all gots to listen to th' religious stuff, before y'all get whatever they's servin'. Don't make no difference to me, ah'm used to it, ah used to sing in th' choir, anyway."

"Does it cost money? To eat, I mean," inquired the girl-in-rags.

"Not shore... somebody tell me they just take donations, or somethin'... the usual," stated the African-American woman.

"Woman," asked the strange-girl, "Why are you here?"

"What kind of question *that*?" the other shot back, with a suspicious tone. "Ah ain't done *nothin'* wrong. Y'all from the po-lice, or th' army? That uniform y'all wearin' don' look 'zactly like either of 'em... y'all been in a war, or somethin'? Shore *do* look beat-up..."

"Excuse me," Billings interrupted, "But my lady-friend here is from somewhere else, like, she isn't quite right with English, yet – don't get mad with her. I think what she meant was, 'Madam, how come you're in the line-up here, why couldn't you just get across the state line and on your way'. Right?"

"Yes, Bob, *that* is what I meant to say. Thanks. Sorry," quickly added the fallen-girl, reflexively giving an odd half-curtsy with a faint smile.

"Well, if y'all *gots* to know," explained the black woman, "Prolly same reason as two of y'all... no papers. Was headin' from De-troit to L.A., South L.A. in fact, to be with mah folks after the Big Bang, and that's also where mah kids' Daddy is, too. Made it clear past Missouri, but they tell me lot of roads was blocked south of St. Louis so we goes north, made it through Salt Lake but th' car died just into Idaho, couldn't get it fixed, couldn't find no mechanics – couldn't get credit-cards to work and used up th' cash earlier."

"Yeah, *tell* me," grunted the salesman. "I know *that* feeling."

"Had to leave it down there," continued the African-American. "Weren't worth much anyway, 'cept ah put two hundred dollar worth of new tires on it three weeks ago, just mah luck, ah guess. They tell me there ain't no buses goin' anywhere *near* L.A., whole place is locked down on account of them gang-bangers doin' they stuff, so now ah'm ass out of pants here in Idaho, just want to get home... had to hitch-hike and walk all th' way to the state line, so they tell me ah gots go back, to *where*, ah don' know, right now, all ah'm worried about is gettin' food for mah kids... they ain't eaten in a day or more, y'all know."

A small boy's voice from just ahead of the woman in the line asked, "Who y'all talkin' to, Momma?"

"Just a lady," replied the woman, looking backward and downward. "A *white* lady."

The fallen-girl immediately sensed a feeling of defensiveness, of wariness.

"Ah'm *hungry*, Momma," spoke another voice, that of a teenage girl. "When we gonna *be* there?"

"Soon, Melissa honey," replied the black woman. "We gonna be in the tent real soon now and they'll have lots of nice stuff, just like in the church basement back home."

"I am Sari Tanak," announced the fallen-girl, pleasantly.

"Whitney Claremont, that's mah name," stated the woman. "Them two," – she pointed to a boy, perhaps 8 or so, and a somewhat older girl – "They mine, this here's Melissa Arlene and the other's Curtis Ray."

"Nice to meet you," offered the salesman. "Bob Billings, here."

The girl-in-rags bent forward and to the left, staring at the youngsters.

"Hi, children... I have spoken to your friends, young ones who look like you... in a school, I think," she said, hesitatingly. "They sang me a song..."

Her voice trailed off, as she stared vacantly for a second or two.

"Hah, ah don' think so there girl, ain't *no* white-folk where we live back 'n De-troit, and none where they Daddy is, in L.A.; ain't *nobody* but us go there – not even them Latinos, but they always tryin'. Y'all would last about twenny minutes, ah figure," retorted Claremont.

"Ah," replied the fallen-girl. "Maybe I was wrong. I do not know. I do not remember much, unfortunately. Bad bump on the head... or something like that..."

"She's probably right about that, Sari," interjected Billings. "Twenty minutes on an average day, ten on a bad one, a half-hour if you're lucky... I learned long ago not to do sales-calls down there – no offense, Mrs. Claremont, but you *know* it's the truth – whole place is a 'no-go zone' for, well, anyone who doesn't *belong* there, you can like it or hate it, but it's the truth – "

The girl-in-rags interrupted him, with an odd, steely, determined look on her face.

"I would last longer than that, Bob," she firmly stated. "I can survive anywhere. *Anywhere*. Places where you would die and be consumed, in a half-*second*. Or less."

The salesman was about to dispute the point, but a voice shouted from behind them, "Enough chit-chat, there! You're holding up the line!"

"Oh... whoops," he cautioned. "Come on, let's get *going*, Sari... don't want to make any new enemies here – everybody's enough on edge as it is."

The fallen-girl just nodded and shuffled forward, following the black woman and her two children, who were sniffling and sneezing in the dust kicked up both by the crowd and the gusting Prairie wind. The sweat of hundreds of unwashed people from inside the tent intermixed with the wind-borne particles, making a particularly unwholesome brew to offend the nostrils.

A new voice sounded over the loudspeaker just outside the entrance to the tent.

"Ladies and gentlemen, the Klan of Jesus Christ welcomes you all to our sanctuary, where you can hear the good news about our Savior and how He saved us from the recent peril," it exclaimed. "We will be taking a collection – have your money ready – each one gives what he can. Please identify yourself at the door and take a name tag, before you sit down," it continued, with the sound of evidently-recorded gospel music in the background, intermixing uneasily with the live performance going on further inside.

Finally, they had reached the entrance, nothing more than a vertical slit in the canvas, really, with the resulting flaps thrown to either side.

Billings, Claremont and the girl looked inside and beheld two men, one – a clean-cut young white man, maybe 24 at most, in a conservative business-suit (minus the jacket) on the right, and a larger, menacing-looking guy on the left, helmeted and wearing riot squad gear, wielding an automatic weapon.

"Praise the Lord and pass the ammo, eh?" joked Billings.

"Sho' nuff," muttered Claremont, *sotto voce*. "Like ah say, don't bother *me* none. Po-lice cruise our 'hood all the time, y'all be fine long as y'all don' sass 'em."

She paused for a second, then added, "Most of the time, that is. *Most* of the time."

The fallen-girl said nothing, but the other two noticed that she had fixed a distant, laser-like stare on the gendarme, sweeping her gaze up and down his equipment, as if sizing him up. Her stance lasted only a second or two, then she smiled to Billings and nodded.

The clean-cut man addressed Claremont. "Welcome to the Hallelujah Klan of Jesus Christ, Ma'am," he announced. "And to your two little ones, too – they *are* yours, is that right? Ah, good. Do you have your contribution handy, Ma'am?"

The black woman handed something to the man. He looked into his hand and said, "That's *all*? Sorry, but minimum contribution's at *least* five dollars per adult, two-fifty for children. The Lord needs everyone to do their part, you know. I'm afraid you'll have to..."

With a tone of desperation, Claremont asked, "Please, Mister, that's all ah *got* – been on the road for a *week* now, can't get money from them machines... mah kids is *hungry*. *Please*, sir, can't y'all jus' – "

"Are we gonna get something to eat, Momma?" asked the teenager, worriedly.

"I'm sorry, Ma'am, but those *are* the rules, nothing I can do," rebuffed the clean-cut man.

He motioned to the guard, who started towards Claremont.

"Wait a minute," interrupted the girl-in-rags. "I have some mon-ee. I have for-tee dollars. Would that be enough?"

A look of gratefulness, mixed with suspicion, appeared on the mother's face, as she noted, "Ah gots three here – Miz 'Tanak', that yo' name, right? So ah'd need seven... normally would never take money without payin' y'all back same day, but mah *kids*..."

"I can pay for you and your children, and Bob and myself too," offered the girl-in-rags, kindly.

"Here, take it," she added, pressing a ten and two fives into the black woman' hand.

"Thank... thank y'all, thank you *very* much," stammered a relieved Claremont. "And y'all can call me 'Whitney', ah guess... we *folks* now, 'much as there be 'round here."

"Yeah," mentioned Billings. "By the way, I have a *bit* of cash on me, anyway, but we can settle up when we're inside."

"Well, that's enough to get you in, then," stated the admittance-officer. "You may all proceed – go to the far end of the tent, on the left. Mike, let 'em pass."

The pseudo-policeman stepped back and slung his weapon over his shoulder.

They shuffled slowly into the tent and a look of mild irritation appeared on Billings' face, as he realized that the fallen-girl was following Claremont and her two children while the queue dispersed in every direction.

Looking for the obviously rare commodity of available festival chairs or seating-places on the various wooden benches – the latter mostly closer to the central stage, upon which a tall, gaunt-looking man in a sweat-stained business-suit was exhorting the crowd with some kind of religious message – Billings tagged along, resigned to the fact that he would now no longer have his new companion's exclusive attention.

After a prolonged search, dodging resentful glances from those already ensconced within the tent, all they were able to find was a pair of apparently unoccupied fold-up chairs near the tent's far corner, along with enough space on the dirt floor to accommodate those lucky enough to find a seat.

"I do not mind being on the floor... I am well-used to the feel of the ground beneath my body," mentioned the girl-in-rags, to all of them. "Here, Whitney, why don't you put the children on the chairs, so they can see the man who is giving the performance."

"This like the circus, Momma?" asked the little boy. "When we gonna see them elephants? Or the clowns?"

"Ah don' think there gonna be elephants, Curtis dear," replied Claremont, patiently. "This here's all about preachin', ah think."

"Aww," whined the boy, kicking his feet to dig into the dirt until motioned to stop by his mother.

"Well, thankfully," interjected Billings, "We're too far back to hear all of it, anyway – ha, ha, that loudspeaker of theirs seems to be cutting in and out, you hear the static, too?"

"I can hear it, easily," remarked the girl-in-rags. "That man – the one on the platform – he is saying something about demons being all around us, a 'Devil', too, oh yes, that is the king of the demons, yes, of course – making people do bad things. I'm afraid that this does not make a lot of sense to me, though... he says, 'watch out for the 'Devil-Girl'? Do any of you know who *that* is?"

"'Fraid not," replied Billings. "I spend as little time as I can, in church."

"Them preachers tellin' us, least-aways some of 'em, that that means that ho' from Mars, y'all know, the one that they s'pposedly dug up there, just after the comet first got seen," explained Claremont. "Some of 'em think that she the Anti-Christ, or somebody real bad... but others was tellin' us that she an angel, on the Lawd's side, that is."

"That figures," snorted Billings. "Damn preachers can't agree on what the time of day is, either."

"Well, as for me, ah never believed *any* of it, on either side... them guys don't know *shit* 'bout what they talkin' bout, and ah think that whole Mars-girl story was made up, anyway, faked, you know, just something to take everybody's mind of the comet," offered Claremont. "Probably done with mirrors, somethin' like that. Sorry, Curtis, Melissa, y'all forget ah say a cuss word, there. Momma just *tired*."

"Hmm," commented the girl, uneasily. "I hope that I do not meet this 'Devil-Girl'... she sounds like a *powerful* demon, and I am *scared* of those."

Forcing a slight smile, Claremont managed, "Hah there girl, ah guess y'all a *bit* religious, after all."

"*Ah* think she *was* an angel," opined the teenager. "The Lawd sent her to save us, to kill the comet. But she *daid*, now; she die doin' it, just like Jesus die for us. Pretty much mah whole Sunday School class back home think the same thing, too."

"Well," stated Billings, trying to stretch out his frame, as much as one could, in the crowded confines of this pandemonium of humanity, "I'd probably lean more towards your mother's explanation of recent events, young lady. I was just passing by – didn't catch the whole thing – but there was something on TV the other day about some kind of hot-shot new killer weapon that, rumor has it, our very own Ew-Nighted States Air Force used to blow up poor old 'Lucifer'."

"Yeah?" inquired Claremont, with a bored look on her face.

"Of course," continued the salesman, "They then said that they couldn't tell us stupid voters anything more about it, 'lest it slip into the wrong hands', you know, standard BS from the Feds. I'm just glad that the whole damn thing's over with, now, frankly... they'll be arguing about what went on up there for years to come, conspiracy theories just like the 9/11 and the Miami Dirty Bomb incidents, but it's no concern of yours or mine... we got much more immediate things to worry about, like, for example, where do you get something to eat around here...?"

"I think that I saw a table with food on it, to the right, when we came in," noted the fallen-girl. "We could go there and ask..."

"Wouldn't be a good idea to give up these places, tho'," interjected Claremont. "Ah'd go up and beg if ah had to, no money that is, but we'd likely not have anywheres to sit when we get back."

"Don't worry about that," Billings reassured. "I'll pay – I owe Sari anyway for the entrance fee and you can pay me back whenever. What do the kids like to eat?"

"Well, times bein' what they is, *anythin'*, that's what they'll eat," replied the mother, shooting a 'no talking' look at the boy, who was about to say something. "Ah save y'all a seat," she added.

"Okay," agreed Billings. "Let's go, girl, before it all gets eaten out in front of us."

"Oh-kay," replied the girl-in-rags. "We will bring your children back something good, Whitney. I promise."

The two got up and wound their way slowly through the densely-packed crowd, a sweating, mostly filthy mass of formerly respectable humanity. Twice, Billings momentarily panicked, his mind racing as he lost sight of the fallen-girl, who was shorter than most of the people in the throng – but each time, she was somehow able to rejoin him, suddenly appearing as if coming out of nowhere.

He felt an irrational, surging sense of relief when she was again with him.

Barely know *her... I haven't even done it with this chick yet,* he thought. *But I can't* stand *to let her out of my sight... damn peculiar...*

They were moving past the center stage, now, as they approached what seemed to be a chow line, in the corner of the tent opposite to where Claremont and her children were encamped. Again, the tall man, his suit even more stained with perspiration than before, his bushy white mane flying hither and yon, was exhorting the crowd.

Billings was about to move on, but he had to double back to get the girl-in-rags, who was standing near the edge of the stage, staring with what looked like fascination at the preacher and his histrionics, although the man took no notice of her or, perhaps, couldn't see her for the crowd.

"I *tell* you, brothers and sisters, heed my voice!" he screeched. "You *think* you've been saved, but you think falsely, without hearing the voice of God! Just *who* do you think sent that comet, anyway? Why do you think it was called 'Lucifer'? Think, my children, *think*! Don't you remember your Bible-lessons from Sunday School?"

The tall man paused for a second, leaning forward to address the crowd, directly. "Our own Savior said that you see the signs, but you do not understand. But I tell you, I speak in the voice of Holy Jesus, and *I* understand! God Himself speaks to me, and I pass His inerrant message on, to all of you – now, hear the truth, and take it to heart, lest you, too, fall victim to the filthy Muslims' Anti-Christ, who, even *now*, walks among you!"

The fallen-girl looked from side to side, closely observing those in her vicinity, as a gasp issued from those in the crowd who were paying attention.

The preacher roared, "Yes – it *is* true, with Almighty God as my witness, I *swear* it! The one that the Mars-expedition, may God forgive their souls, unwittingly freed from the prison in which the Holy Spirit put her; yes, the accursed Devil-Girl, she is not *only* the demon who sent the 'Lucifer' comet to destroy God's kingdom on Earth, but, dear brethren, *she is the Anti-Christ, himself*! Do not let her supposed gender mislead you, for the one who the dirty Muslims – I can hardly bring myself to say it – call their 'God', but who we know as the Deceiver, Satan *himself* – can make his foul offspring assume any disguise – the Bible tells us this quite plainly."

"I ask you," he inveighed, with a sarcastic chuckle, "Is it just a *coincidence* that this being, who claimed all the while to be here to help us, that just as the comet – the one she sent, *herself* – was nearly upon us, she *vanished*, into thin air? What did she *do*, head off for a nice vacation on some sunny planet, somewhere? Who among you, believes that she's really gone?"

A few from the crowd muttered something, but nobody spoke out loud. Billings noticed that the fallen-girl's countenance had changed; she was staring, laser-like, at the tall man. But he had evidently not caught her glare, because he continued on, exclaiming,

"I think *not*, brothers and sisters. You want to know what *I* think? I'll tell you what. I think she's right *here* – on Earth, that is – and *she*, or, let's call her by her real name, that is, the child of the Evil One who God cast out of heaven before He made Adam and Eve, is down here right now, planning Hell's next attack on us all. You know, God had a child; He's called Jesus Christ, our Lord Sab-ay-oth and Savior! Well, *Satan*, mocking God as he always does, had a child, too – and *she's* the fang-toothed Jezebel, probably fathered by that heretic 'Muhammad' and his harem of whores, that Captain Jacobson and his sad, unbelievin' crew let free, on Mars. It's all in the *Bible*, my friends, all foretold in Revelation and elsewhere, including how the accursed Muslims are gonna try to convince God-fearin' Christians, that their *false* God, is the *real* God. Remember how Jesus warned us about the Muslims and their filthy false prophets? It's all coming true, right now, right here."

The tall man, hands in the air, was yelling, his voice rising into a frenzy in lock-step to the hymnal chorus issuing from behind.

"Thanks to the grace of God," he fulminated, "And the bravery of His chosen warriors in the U.S. armed forces, America, as God's divinely-blessed nation, was able to stop the Evil One's comet, *but do not let down your guard, children*! Unless we do God's work and eliminate the living vessel of Satan, another tribulation, and another, and another – each worse than the one before – will be inflicted upon us! Unless you'd like to have to get down and kiss the ring of the Muslim king of Arabia, and know that you're going to Hell for doin' it, you'd better join our holy crusade, to send the Devil-Girl and all her stinking Muslim followers straight back to the Infernal Pit, where they'll burn for eternity, like the Bible says they should!"

His head unexpectedly buzzing with the tune of a long-forgotten song that had somehow come back to him just now, Billings finally pushed his way through the cluster of bodies in front and grabbed hold of the fallen-girl's hand.

"Sari," he shouted over the din of the music and the preacher's bellowing, "Let's get going, okay? You can listen to this crap anytime, but if we don't get over to the mess-table we're going to be fighting over cold coffee and crusts of bread!"

The girl-in-rags did not reply; she seemed transfixed, staring absentmindedly at the tall man. But, to Billings' relief, she did not put up any resistance to being pulled in his direction, and soon the two of them were in the queue that lead up to the food-serving tables.

The line moved quickly, much more so than the one to get into the tent in the first place and in a minute or so they were in front of yet another clean-cut, white-shirt-and-tie church type.

"So, what's on the menu?" asked Billings.

"Depends on what you got," replied the churchman, as if reading from a well-rehearsed script. "Two-fifty per plate for the porridge, five for the vegetables and potatoes, seven-fifty if you want the chicken with it, soda pop or coffee are two bucks extra."

"Wasn't this some kind of 'feed the poor' thing?" grumbled the salesman. "I'd pay the same, but get a lot better, at any truck stop."

"Then go to it," retorted the man, indifferently. "It takes *money* to pay for the Lord's work, that's the bottom line, mister. But make up your mind... we got lots of people in line behind you."

"Well," Billings said, quickly turning around to address the fallen-girl, "It looks like chicken's out... that'd run me dangerously close to being broke..."

"No problem for me," she answered. "I do not really like meat, anyway. But no dessert? Nothing sweet to eat?"

"A 'veggie'... dessert? Hah, girl, you can *wish*, around here... but yeah, I guess the kids will be a bit disappointed... well, okay, so, I figure we can get one plate of potatoes and two of the porridge, plus a soda and a coffee that we can share. Not a great meal, but it'd give us some left over for tomorrow – ", Billings offered, then, turning to the churchman, he continued, "Okay, that'll be it... here, whatever your name is there, here's a ten and a five, I need one back..."

Lazily, the serving-man produced a tattered, one-dollar bill from a box that was evidently on a chair or box beside him, behind the serving-table.

It was a this point that the salesman noticed another fully armed gendarme, hiding in the nearly pitch-black shadows of a fold in the tent, just behind the churchman.

Billings whispered to the fallen-girl, "Whoa, Sari, check *that* out... man, they got enough security here to guard a bank vault, and with what they're making on this crap food, I don't blame 'em... did you see that guy, there?"

"Yes," she confirmed. "At least for my eyes, it is not as dark in there as that soldier must think. He looks rather foolish – his body is hidden, but his boots are sticking out, under the... the... canvas, yes, that's the word, right? You are correct, they certainly *do* have a lot of soldiers with guns here; maybe those running this place are afraid of you and me? I do not know why that should be, but I suppose they have their reasons..."

"Listen, sister," warned the salesman, "With things the way they are, not to say how bad they might yet come to be, it wouldn't surprise me a *bit* to see people killing each other for a few bucks, or a hot meal... oops, pick that stuff up, there, we gotta get going..."

This sentiment was reinforced by a 'move on' shrug by the churchman, so the two quickly grabbed the food and headed back towards their seating-places, dodging other refugees hither and yon. Billings almost lost one of the porridge-plates when he was unexpectedly body-checked by a portly-looking farm-wife, but the girl-in-rags, her hand shooting out, cat-like, somehow managed to seize the contents before they were lost. A couple of people stared in apparent amazement at how the girl was able to juggle two soft-drink cans, while doing all of this, but Billings encouraged her to keep moving ahead, and the others' faces were soon lost in the crowd.

They arrived back in the far tent-corner, to see Claremont with her two children dozing off, leaning on either side of her body.

"They been *real* tired, lately," wearily offered the woman. "Lotta stress, ah guess."

"Hate to have to say this," mentioned Billings, "But you'd better wake them up, anyway. We could only afford to buy porridge, mostly, so everybody would at least get something to eat... and, well, this stuff's not that appetizing when it's lukewarm... it'd probably be even worse cold."

But Claremont did not have to act; the boy opened his eyes and demanded, "It dinnertime, Momma? Ah'm still hungry."

Upon hearing this, the girl sat up too.

"You two can have whatever you want – I will eat whatever is left," added the fallen-girl, as she deposited one plate of porridge and a can of soda pop in front of Claremont's daughter.

"Here, Melissa Arlene," she said. "What is it, that one uses for an in-voh-cation – ah, yes. 'Bon Apetit'. That is... French, right?"

"Shore is, Ma'am," replied the teenager, smiling happily, as she dug into the meal. "Took a year of it in Monsieur Pichet's class, back home... he from Louisiana, well, actually, from N'Orleans, but he had to move when it sank, second time..."

"Jus' *eat*," commanded the mother. "Listen, Miz... Miz 'Sari', y'all *shore* y'all don' want nothin' to eat, just now? Way mah kids is, y'all might not be left with anythin' at all, later."

"Do not worry," answered the girl-in-rags. "I am sort of hungry, too, I would not want to deceive you about that, but I can go for a long time without food, if I have to."

She stopped, with a pensive look on her face, then added, "A *very* long time."

Unhappily, Billings, getting the hint, deposited the other plate of porridge in front of the boy.

"I guess the three of us share the veggies, then," he muttered.

Examining his third of what was allocated to the adults, he complained, "Man, not great stuff here... looks like they didn't even fully peel the potatoes. You'd think with all the volunteers that they got working here, they could at least give us a proper meal for our money."

"I have had worse," stated the fallen-girl, philosophically. "There was one place where I had to eat nothing but *stones*, for many long... but anyway..."

For this, she was rewarded by a querulous eyebrow and a shrug on the part of the salesman. "I'll take your word for it," he grunted, trying to force down the food.

Examining the adults' plate, the young-looking woman commented, "Ah... carrots. Nice. I *like* carrots. I just wish that there was dessert. Sweet things to leave a nice taste in my mouth, I mean."

"Well, we're sure not going to put on any calories with *this* stuff," complained Billings. "God, when I get back to Tucson, I'm heading right for the freezer – best T-Bone I can haul out, if the power didn't cut out and – "

Morosely, he picked at the mushy collection of vegetables.

"Yeah, Momma, there gonna be dessert?" chimed in a little voice.

"'Fraid not, Curtis," answered Claremont. "Leastaways, not 'till we get back to De-troit."

In between mouthfuls, she looked at the girl-in-rags and inquired, "So, Miz... Miz 'Sari', where y'all from? Y'all looks like y'all was in the Army, look like y'all been in a war or somethin', what is those, anyway, on the uniform ah mean, bullet-holes? If y'all in the Army, why they not let y'all through the checkpoint, girl? Don' wanna be nosy, but y'all a deserter, maybe, them ripped off pockets there, they got your colors? Wouldn't make no difference to *me*, honey, ah would have run mahself... all them soldiers they threw at the comet, ain't *none* of them come back..."

The fallen-girl's face first wore a startled look, and for a few seconds, she did not respond, as if trying to think of what to say.

Then she replied, "No, I am not... I mean, I was not in the Army, I do not think so."

"Air Force, then, maybe?" interjected the salesman. "That looks kind of like an Air Force uniform; saw 'em once, took my kid to the rocket museum in Houston, they had them there, I think. Except that they don't have a lot of women in any of the Armed Forces these days, you know, the whole 'back to tradition' thing, after they stopped letting in the min – "

Seeing a resentful look from the black woman, Billings cut himself off.

The girl-in-rags took over, saying, "The... 'Air Force'? In an airplane, you mean? Maybe... I guess. But I *was* in a battle... all I remember is, I was badly wounded, I almost died; there was a big flash, then, nothing. I woke up on the ground, I was very cold, so I walked through the woods to a restaurant, where a nice family bought me something to eat, because I didn't have any money, at the time. After that, I made my way here. I wish I could remember more, but it is all, how do you say, 'just a blank', right now."

"Hmmph," grunted Billings. "Yeah, doesn't surprise me, really. Heard of this kind of thing a lot, you know, the whole 'post-traumatic' crap, guys go into a war, get shot at or just shot, makes 'em crazy in the head for a while, you know, memory loss, flashbacks, but they usually come out of it, later. I knew one guy from the Iran thing who had it, also there were a couple of vets on our block back home that got *seriously* messed up in that Pakistan nonsense a couple of years ago; one of 'em got help and he came out okay, but the other guy... well. I'm sure you'll be fine, too, Sari, you just need a little time to relax."

"I hope that you are right, Bob. There is *so* much to remember," said the fallen-girl, quietly, with another far-off look.

"So, Mister Salesman there, what *y'all* doin' here? Where y'all goin' from here in? Y'all gots anywhere *to* go?" inquired Claremont, wiping some stray porridge from her son's cheek.

"Who, me?" responded Billings. "Oh, yeah, well, I'm from Tucson – I'm in the floor tile business, wood, ceramics, even those new composites that you never have to shine, you know, that kind of thing. Just before the big Lucifer stuff was about to go down, I went off on a last-minute sales trip, call on my big accounts, one last time – "

"Shit, man – Curtis, Melissa, y'all don't listen to that – y'all was still tryin' to *sell* stuff, when the world was fixin' to end? What *wrong* with you?" blurted out a nonplussed Claremont.

With a short, peevish stare, Billings retorted, "Didn't *expect* you to understand – don't blame you, really, but, see... well, the thing is, I've *always* been a salesman, it's all I really wanted to do. *Love* the job. Lots of sales guys don't, but I do. So when it looked like everything was going to be... *over*, I wanted to kinda go out, the way I had lived my life, doing my rounds, while I had a life to live. If *that* makes any sense."

"It makes *perfect* sense, Bob," counseled the girl-in-rags, sympathetically. "We are all searching for what it means, to be alive; all the more so, when it appears that our time may be coming to an end."

She grasped his hand, for a few seconds, and he stared back at her, utterly smitten.

"No, *ah* gets it," allowed Claremont. "Most of mah family was in church, 'cause that's where they felt most at home when, well, y'all know. But y'all can't get through? Ah'd of thought a *white* businessman... no offense, y'understand, but... they'd give y'all th' wave, and bye-bye... they always used to do it like that."

"Wish it were so," sighed the salesman, "But not anymore. I showed up here around sundown last night, went up to the checkpoint, argued with 'em, pleaded with 'em, even offered to bribe 'em, *nothing* worked – no papers, no go, that seems to be the rule these days, they won't even let the *Indians* back to their reserves, just across the border – or so one of 'em told me. I left most of my damn credentials back in Tucson – easy mistake to make, considering that I didn't expect to be alive to need them – so now I'm basically stuck, until they get the computer-networks running again. At least that's what I hope will happen, and soon."

Shaking his head briefly, Billings continued, "My only other option is to try going south, see if the Utah border's as tight, maybe try Nevada, too, somehow make it home from there. But I heard from a guy in camp that things aren't too great down there, either, word has it that there's a lot of refugees coming out of L.A. and Spokane... Southwest state governors want nothing to do with them, 'not our problem', the usual, so, this guy tells me, they're moving National

Guard, plus a whole lot of mercs, to the Idaho border, California and Oregon ones as well. I sorta understand what they're saying – what with all this global-warming crap, down in Arizona we've been under real strict water-rationing for *years*, like, 'don't flush your toilets more than once a day', that's how bad it's gotten – so now try to imagine *thousands* of refugees showing up all at once in the desert with 110 plus degrees in the shade for months on end, you're just asking for trouble, big time. Goddamn *mess*, no doubt about it."

"Y'all got a car, though?" inquired Claremont. "'Cuz there ain't no buses. I aksed them when the next Greyhound was comin', they say, 'not until further notice'. Maybe never... don't have the money for it, anyway."

"Oh, yeah, *sure*, I got a car," replied Billings, ruefully. "Latest, finest Patriotic SUV, well, I guess it's the latest you could get before they passed that 'American Cars For Americans' law and put on the thousand per cent tax on anything not designed in Detroit. I got GPS, NeoNet, electro-shock anti-theft, computer smart cruise, mobile entertainment setup, all the toys, gotta impress the customers you know. Mint condition, works fine... or, it *would*, if it wasn't out of gas. Well, almost – LCD display was reading "E" and I realized the jig was up, if you run it completely out it has trouble starting back up again, so I had to leave it at the side of the road, about ten miles back from the border on Route 30 towards Montpelier."

"How y'all get back *here*, then, Mister Billins'?" asked Melissa.

"Copped a ride from a trucker," explained the salesman. "I was hoping to get a jerry can from back up the highway, then bring back enough gas to get back to the last station I passed... that was before they locked the damn border down. At least I didn't get hit by the same thing that knocked out a lot of them, around the time the comet thing went down... you know, when they set off the nukes, it totally screwed up those new "complete computer control" cars. Doesn't matter, anyway; I tried to hide it by the side of the road, parked it in some bushes, that is, but the car's probably stripped down to the chassis, by now."

Claremont grunted, "Nah, ah don' think so, Bob, not out here, folk have all got more important stuff to handle... but if y'all left it down in *mah* 'hood in Detroit, well..."

She paused for a second or two, then, with a knowing grin, pointed at the girl and said to the salesman, "Y'all and she y'all *together*?"

Billings shot a quick glance at the fallen-girl, as she did in reverse to himself.

Rapidly, he stammered, "Uhh, no – ", only to hear her contradict, in the same breath, "Yes, we certainly are!"

The teenager giggled, upon hearing this, almost spitting out a mouthful of porridge.

At first, Billings was surprised by the girl-in-rags' claim, but something within him checked an urge to correct her. Instead, with nary but a happy wink in her direction, he involuntarily straightened his jacket and went back to work on his meal, his mind daydreaming of pleasures as yet extant only in his imagination.

Students Without A Teacher

Uneasily – the necessity of the act almost checked by years of instinct about minding one's own business – the cosmonaut peeked around the corner, seeing his former crew-mates, minus one, seated in Captain Sam Jacobson's personal quarters.

"Oh, *there* you are," noted Cherie Tanaka, her slender, Eurasian countenance brightening measurably. "We were starting to worry that you'd skip another one, Sergei."

"Y'all don't know what you're missin', bro'," chimed in Devon White. "Couple days ago I actually moved a book."

"Yeah, now if we could just get him to *read* one," quipped Boyd.

"That's comin', man," replied White with a grin, "As soon as I can open it with my mind and not my hands."

Chkalov replied with a smile of his own.

"Forgive me," he apologized, "I have been very busy with a few... things, recently. It was unfortunate that Sub-Commander Chen called me away for a propulsion check, a few minutes before you all got together for the last meeting – I tried to, how do you say in English, 'beg off', but he was most insistent and I suppose in some sense he is my superior officer, now. Also, I could not think of a good excuse at the time, one that would not attract undue attention. I promise I will not miss any more sessions, if this is at all under my own control."

"Don't worry about it, Sergei," commented Jacobson. "But you'd better close the door. Don't want to raise any eyebrows... well, you know."

"Very much understood, Captain," answered the Russian, as he moved inside the room and activated a control panel button, resulting in a slight 'swoosh' as the door to the quarters slid into place.

"Regarding that," he continued, "While, as I am sure you can appreciate, I cannot get into the details of what was communicated between me and them, I should let you know that Moscow, as well as certain other nations on Earth... *suspect* that something is now 'different', about us. Before you say anything, sir, please accept my word that it was not by information intentionally provided by me, that they have come to this opinion. But I thought you should know about this, regardless."

"Look," cautioned Jacobson to the rest of the group, mild alarm in his voice, "Did any of *you* say anything? To Houston, or Earth, I mean. I believe Sergei, but..."

Boyd and Tanaka shook their heads.

White replied, "Well, to be honest, sir, I *did* tell my son, that 'Daddy's going to be a superhero', or somethin' like that, when I talked with him and my wife, day before yesterday... but I doubt that he'd have told anybody, even if he did, he's just a kid, y'all know, they're always makin' things up, and anyway, I didn't say anything specific, so I hardly think..."

"Hmm... I doubt that they could really have inferred anything from *that* kind of statement, even if they were secretly monitoring Devon's transmissions to his family. Which they promised us, that they wouldn't do," said Tanaka.

"You're probably right about that, Professor," added Boyd, "But, of course, they could have been spying on our video calls to Earth, all along – or they could be listening to us, right *now*, couldn't they?"

Each looked at the others.

"I suppose they *could*," offered Jacobson, "But, apart from the same assurances that they gave to all of us that they wouldn't do that, well, they don't have much of a motive to spy on us. Do they?"

"We were all exposed to *her*, you know," mentioned Tanaka. "Perhaps that's reason enough."

"Maybe so," replied Jacobson, staring momentarily off into space. "Maybe so."

"Or," suggested Boyd, "They might have been informed by somebody else on the station. *That's* always a possibility."

"But... who?" countered Jacobson. "Who else would know – oh, wait a minute. Yeah, you're *right*. There *was* someone else who had a glimpse of it, wasn't there?"

"Of course," said Tanaka, knowingly. "*Alan*. You mean Alan, Humber, don't you? We – I – invited him into our 'circle', just before – "

"You are quite right about that, Professor," interjected Chkalov. "I do not know exactly how to say this in English, but, when we all joined hands on that day, I... I *felt* his presence. My eyes were closed, but I knew that he was there. I do not think the Russian language has a good word for this experience, either."

"I suppose it's possible," commented Tanaka, "But from what I know of Alan, he's not the type to gossip, especially not about something like *this*, and especially when, from his point of view, he really knows very little in the way of hard facts, regarding what he'd be gossiping *about*. It just seems unlikely to me, that he'd be how they came to know this."

"If not *him*, though, who else?" inquired Boyd.

"Your guess is as good as mine," replied the woman. "Other than for us, and maybe Alan, nobody here knows our little secret. At least, nobody that *I* know of."

"Captain," uneasily queried White, "I don't wanna be out of turn in askin', but, well... has Commander Cohen asked y'all about anything like this?"

"No offense taken, Devon," stated Jacobson, "But the answer is, 'no'. Now, to be completely honest with you, Ariel *did* question me quite extensively about Karéin, but it was more like 'how did it feel to have an alien living on your ship', 'what did she tell you about her history', that kind of thing, even 'does she have a sense of humor', to which I replied 'yes', by the way – I can't blame him for being curious, after all, particularly when he met her, himself, if only briefly. We never got into the *Amaiish* thing, though, not regarding either her or us. Maybe Cohen wasn't interested in it or maybe he just forgot to ask, I don't know, but as I'm sure you all can appreciate, I didn't go out of my way to bring up the subject. So if Ariel *does* have someone watching us, I very much doubt he would have done that on his own authority. It's always possible that he might have been told to do so by NASA, I suppose."

The group all felt silent, a couple of them reflexively looking to and fro, in a subconscious effort to see the bogeymen under the bed, inside the closets.

Eventually, Jacobson spoke up again.

"Well, if that's the case, they already know all they need to know, so we might as well get going, I guess."

"Yeah," echoed several, at once.

"Now, for Sergei's benefit," started Tanaka, "I think I should summarize what happened, the last two times. Basically, we concentrated on trying to even out the abilities between each of us; that is, as Devon mentioned, he was having trouble with telekinesis, while I had to get some tutoring from Sam on the self-healing thing... let's just say that I have the scars to prove it. By the end of last week's training, I was sort of hoping that the ISS2 fire detectors would finally catch on to what we were doing in here."

"Well, Rome wasn't built in a day, you know," offered Boyd.

"True, but after last week my hands were starting to look more like Rome after Nero," Tanaka retorted.

White chortled at this.

"Anyway, we obviously lacked a tutor for the mental powers, as you weren't here, Sergei, so we have some catching up to do in that department. However, since we didn't know you'd be able to make it for this session, we decided to try a new tack today which is – "

"A 'new tack', Professor? I'm afraid I do not understand... I have spent many years speaking English, but – " asked the cosmonaut.

For a second, Tanaka looked at him, with a startled, stunned, almost paralyzed, expression.

"Y'all *okay* there, Professor?" inquired White. "Y'all look like you just saw a ghost."

"I – no, I'm fine, don't worry," stammered the woman. "It's just that, Sergei, for a second there, you sounded exactly like *her.*"

"Yeah, I guess you *did*, a bit," added Boyd. "Perfectly understandable, really."

"No, Brent, it's more than that... dammit, for a second, he *looked* like her, too, *exactly* like her," Tanaka explained. "I could have sworn that I saw *her*, sitting in place of him. Ah, I guess my mind has been playing tricks on me."

All, save the woman, looked knowingly at each other, then at her.

Finally, Boyd said, "Maybe, Professor... maybe not. She affected us in ways that we may never fully understand. Perhaps you just had a glimpse of that."

"Captain," interjected Chkalov as he turned to address Jacobson, "It is not like that... not really. There is something else that I must tell you. I hesitated because I did not believe, myself. But now, I think I do."

"Umm humm," said Jacobson, patiently.

"She is *alive*, sir," the cosmonaut announced, to gasps of joy and silently, apparently fulfilled prayers.

"You *mean –* " started Boyd.

"Sergei," demanded Jacobson, guardedly, "Just *how* do you know this? Have you been in contact with her?"

"Yes. Uhh... no," answered Chkalov. "I did not talk to her, or, how would you say in English, 'think' to her, not directly. What I mean is, Captain – you see – I *felt* that she is alive. I felt her presence, her life-force, her intellect, as surely as if she were standing here, in front of us, now."

"You know, Sergei," mentioned Jacobson, speaking slowly and cautiously, "We all *want* to believe that, but, well... as you are no doubt aware, our minds can easily play tricks on us, where things like this are concerned. I still see my late half-brother occasionally out of the corner of my eye, at times when my thoughts wander to how much I miss him. Maybe, in a way, the person we have lost, *is* there, at times like that – "

"*I* believe him, Sam," interrupted Tanaka.

"Me too," added White.

"I haven't completely given up hope," said Boyd. "That's as far as I can go right now, I'm afraid."

"Devon," gently asked Jacobson, "I need hardly remind you of this, but wasn't you who told us that she was...?"

"Yeah, man, I suppose I *did*," muttered White, avoiding his former commander's stare. "But that wasn't what I meant... not exactly. Like, all at once, I got this powerful strong vision in my head, that she had, well, done what she was out to do, that she was happy, that she was at rest. That she had 'transitioned over to the other side', whatever that means, but those were the *exact* words that came to me. *Shit*, man, even *I* don't know what it means, but I don't think it means that she's dead, at least, I don't feel like that now, but I gotta admit, I *did* think so, then. Don't ask me why I think that, or how. But I think that Sergei's right."

"Ah, the challenges of being a prophet," joked Boyd.

"I *know*, man, but if y'all want the job, you're welcome to it," replied White, unhappily.

"Look," commented Jacobson, "We could ponder and re-ponder this endlessly, I suppose, and let me just state for the record that I certainly *hope* that Sergei is not just imagining things, but in the complete absence of any hard, objective evidence of Karéin's survival, I think that's pretty much where we have to leave it... that is, if we're going to have any time to do any of our 'exercises' today. Anybody got anything to add to that?"

Chkalov looked as if he was about to say something, but no sound issued from his lips.

"Right, then," stated Tanaka. "I guess we *should* get going, then. Well, as I was going to say, before we got side-tracked, what we decided to try today, was the idea of 'pooling our resources', 'two heads better than one', that kind of thing; in other words, seeing if we can get a second person, then a third, a fourth and so on, to reinforce the first person's use of *Amaiish*, so we can accomplish bigger and better things – sort of the same idea as you would get by having two people, rather than one, lift the end of a sofa that you're trying to get into your apartment."

"My first apartment wasn't big enough to have a sofa, so I wouldn't know," quipped White, "But y'all can get on with it, anyway, Professor. I've been imaginin' *lots* of stuff these days... that won't be too much of a stretch, I don't think."

With a shared chuckle from five untutored more-than-human beings, the session began, an other-worldly power flowing from one to the other and back again, over and over, in paths that none yet understood.

Something On Hill 1442

"How many is that, now, Cardenas?" shouted the U.S. Army Captain, surveying the forested scene, remnants of snow still marking the pine needles that snapped and crunched under the many pairs of military boots that now roamed all over this place.

Stopping momentarily to catch his breath after running up the hillside towards his superior officer, the First Lieutenant replied, "Uhh... seventeen, I think, Captain Butz, sir. Yeah, seventeen, not counting the one or two that they think fell in the lake, but those aren't our job anyway, of course, sir, them boys with the special gear gotta get 'em. My teams are all over here but we haven't found this one, yet."

The other soldier perched his foot on a rock and took off his hat, the cool mountain air providing a welcoming relief to the sweat of having to use muscles not much worked since the last field assignment, some years prior.

"Fair enough, Lieutenant," he allowed. "You get any word yet from Bingartner's company, over there on Hill 1431?"

"Yeah," affirmed the junior officer. "'Bout ten minutes ago. He's got a negative over there, sir. Just a rock – a *big* one, it's taking two squads to roll it down to the trucks they got standin' by. Lotsa gruntin' and moanin', but they'll get it there, eventually. Oh, and also I got a call from Annie Wilder's company on 1442 – they got a track, but no rock at the end of it, must've bounced over a cliff or somethin', they're still lookin'."

"Goddamn waste of time, I say," complained the Captain. "And just between the two of us, I *said* so to H.Q., when they sprang this whole damn exercise on us. There's a million more important things for us to do – folks without a place to stay, nothing to eat, and suchlike – and them desk boys from the Pentagon got us looking for *rocks*, for God's sake. *Rocks*. I'd like to get *them* up here, see how many Rockee-Mountain hills *they* want to climb in them nice shiny shoes of theirs, before they give up."

"Know what you mean, sir," replied the Lieutenant. "Heard over the comms link yesterday that things was out of control in L.A., for example – Guard is hollerin' for troops, and they can't get any, along with most of the rest of the Army, we're off doin' stuff like *this*. I got family in California and things aren't much better there, they're locked down most of the time, can't even go to get groceries without payin' off the gangs, 'cause there's no law, no Guard, no *nothin'*. And anyway... even if they need these rocks for something later, well, they're not gonna just grow legs and walk away, are they? I mean, we can always come back here and finish the job, when things settle down a bit. Hope I'm not speaking out of turn, sir, but that's how I think."

"You won't get any dispute from me on that front, soldier," commented the Captain, "But I'd keep it to yourself, if I were you, regardless. Them boys up the food chain don't like to hear how little they really know about being a soldier; me, I did tours in Iraq, Iran, Paki-stan, Cuba, the whole works... I'd bet you not *one* of them fancy-ass Pentagon 'adviser' boys ever got his boots dirty...."

"Of course, sir," quickly stated the Lieutenant. "I wouldn't – oh, *wait* a minute – ", he added, while unhooking the walkie-talkie from his belt, as the device buzzed and shone an 'incoming' indicator light.

At first, the Captain listened with only mild interest to the resulting conversation, as the discourse went on between the other man and whomever had called.

"Yeah, Cardenas here, with the Captain on 1430... nothing here, must be deeper in the woods... you got anything, Annie? Oh, really, yeah... huh? Say again? Well, why the hell would they tell you *that*? I can't just do *that* on my own authority, you know that. Umm-humm... look, I'll just let ya talk directly with the Captain, he'll sort it out. Sir?"

"What do they want?" muttered the senior officer, as he took the communicator and held it to his ear.

"Hello, Lieutenant Wilder, that's who I'm talking with? This is Butz here." he said. "Yeah, you too. Well, anyway, what's up over there – you're on 1442, right? So what's up, Lieutenant?"

A puzzled look came over the Captain's face, as he listened to his subordinate, over the radio link. After about thirty seconds, he said, "Yeah, understood, Lieutenant. I don't understand it either, but I'll find out – in the meantime, those are our orders, and I want you to put them into effect, you understand? I'll have the rest show up at the perimeter as soon as we can call the teams back and get 'em all accounted for. Butz out."

"So, sir?" inquired the Lieutenant.

"Peculiar," answered the Captain. "Listen, did you get any communications, over the walkie-talkie I mean, from anybody higher up, while your team was searching, Cardenas?"

"Yes sir, once or twice," explained the soldier. "I was *gonna* tell you about it just now, but then you asked about Bingartner's team... anyway, these guys that called me, they had the ID code and the mission profile, so I figured that they were authorized, although when I asked 'em who they were, they just said 'National Security Special Investigations' or something like that. They asked me to point the camera in the walkie-talkie at the rocks we found, and the tracks they came with, must have remotely triggered it to take pictures, 'cause I saw the flash go off, each time. But after that, they just said 'thanks' and went away, nothin' else ever came of it."

"Well, obviously something *has* come of it, Lieutenant," retorted Butz, "Because apparently they have seen something of interest to them, over on Hill 1442... they told Wilder to throw a defensive cordon around it, deny access to anyone other than them – whoever they are. They asked her to tell me that we're off the search, for now, we're supposed to reinforce the perimeter, once we get our teams back with us."

"Did they say what was so interesting, sir?" asked the soldier.

"Nothing specific," replied the Captain, "Except, Wilder tells me that they have a 'special team' on its way, something about a quarantine, why they'd do that there and not for all these other rocks, I can't – "

Suddenly, the percussive "thump" of helicopter turbine engines sounded overhead. First one, then a second; then, a dozen or more.

Both men looked up, seeing the fleeting shapes of the aircraft pass above the trees, moving quickly *en echelon* towards a nearby hill.

"Speak of the devil," offered Butz. "Those boys sure don't waste any time, do they?"

"Wow, no," shot back the lieutenant. "Can't have been more than ten minutes since they called Annie and got her pictures... so what do we do now, sir?"

"We do what we were told, like good soldiers, Lieutenant," commanded Butz, stoically. "We get our boys and girls and gather up where we were told. So get on the horn, call Chuvali, Johnson and that other guy – you know, the new one that came in from the 283rd – and tell 'em and their search parties to meet the two of us at the bottom of the hill."

"Understood, sir," said the soldier. "I'll get right on it, sir."

"Oh, and one other thing," commanded Butz, looking straight at the other man.

"Yes, sir?" asked Cardenas.

"Next time you get a call from someone telling you to do things I don't know about... make sure I *do* know about it, you hear, Lieutenant?"

"Yes, *sir*," replied the soldier, saluting awkwardly as he put the walkie-talkie back in its belt-cradle.

Now You See Me, Now You Don't

They had fallen into a fitful sleep upon half-filled stomachs, a state of affairs that would not have so affected any of them as much as a month before; but half a loaf, under these circumstances, was much more than none.

As the first rays of the morning sun issued through the tent's openings and dispelled the shadows from a select few spots within, Billings' eyes opened lazily, un-coöperatively, at first, his field of vision falling on the girl-in-rags, who was evidently already awake and alert, her own gaze sweeping back and forth over the rest of the inhabitants and furnishings of the tent in the same peculiar, analytical way that he had seen before.

Momentarily, a feeling of resentment came over him, as he realized that she had laid down beside him, but nothing had come of it other than a warm embrace; however, this wouldn't have been a good place for anything more, given the hundreds of other snoring, somnolent bodies hither and yon, to say nothing of Claremont and her two kids.

"Didn't sleep well?" he offered.

"No, in fact I had more than enough," she softly replied. "I do not really need a lot of rest, anyway. Somehow, the whole idea of sleeping seems... *new*, to me... odd, would you not say?"

Billings shrugged.

The fallen-girl regarded the black woman's family. "But we should keep our voices low – I think that the children are still asleep," she cautioned.

"No, ah ain't, lady," came a boy's voice. "Ah was just pretendin', 'cuz ah didn't want to wake y'all up."

"Hmm... I wonder why I could not..." started the girl-in-rags, stopping in mid-sentence. "Well, it seems that others are waking up, too," she added, noticing several bodies in the vicinity groggily coming to.

"Curtis, y'all go to bed... now... oh, sorry, guess it's mornin'," grumbled Claremont, as she wiped the sleep from her eyes and slowly sat up.

"Melissa?" she asked.

The teenager was still snoring away.

"Interesting that they didn't try to charge us rent, or something, for conking out in here," commented Billings. "I suppose it would have been more trouble for them keeping control over a crowd this size outside, rather than inside."

"But, Bob," asked the fallen-girl, "I thought that the army men, you know, the ones outside, at the... check-point, they are from the big army, the main one, not the Temple that runs this place?"

"You got a point there," answered the salesman. "They must be working together, or something. I guess. These days, who knows."

Now, they heard the other child's voice.

"Good mornin', Momma," she yawned.

"Mornin', Melissa Arlene, honey," replied Claremont, lovingly. "Y'all slept in a bit, there, girl."

"Only woke up cuz ah gots to go to the bathroom," explained the teenager. "Y'all take me there, Momma?"

"Me too," added the boy.

"Well, ah guess ah gots to take the young'uns to do they business," said Claremont. "But where is it? Didn't see no outhouse 'round here."

"There's *got* to be one," mentioned Billings. "What with this many people crowded in here, if not, things could get... *messy*, real quick. Look, Whitney, I kinda feel the call of nature, too, so why don't I take your kids with me. Wherever it is, we'll find it."

"Don't usually trust 'em with nobody else," replied Claremont. "But y'all paid for dinner, so ah 'spose y'all okay. Just don' let 'em take too long in there – that mean *y'all* 'specially... right, Curtis Ray?"

"Ah won't, Momma, ah promise," agreed the boy, quickly.

"Alright, kids, let's go," commanded Billings, taking the teenager in his right hand and the boy in the left.

"We will keep a place free for you," called out the girl-in-rags, as the three of them headed off to the front of the tent, trying to avoid stumbling over the shapes of sleeping refugees as they navigated the tent's still-dark interior.

After an unusually long time, a half-hour or more, Billings returned with the children in tow.

"Curtis?" demanded Claremont, sternly. "Ah thought ah *told* y'all..."

"Not his fault," interrupted Billings. "Effing nonsense going on up there – I couldn't find an outhouse anywhere inside here, not even a Port-A-Potty, so I had to take the kids up to the front entrance and ask where we could go. At first they tried to give me this crap about 'they'll just have to hold it' or something like that, but eventually I was able to talk sense into them – "

"Told 'em that ah was gonna pee on they shoes," smirked the boy.

"Yeah, well, *that* certainly got their attention," remarked Billings, with a wry grin, "So they let us go outside, they got three or four portable johns – "

"A 'john'? Does that mean a 'toilet?" asked the girl-in-rags.

"Y'all *shore* from out of town, girl," grunted Claremont.

"Yeah, bathrooms, whatever you want to call it," continued Billings, "But here's the *weird* thing – they let the kids go by themselves, I guess they figured they won't run away or anything, but as for me, they had some guy with a gun, you know, Sarl, the same kind we saw at the lunch-counter there, escort me to and from the facilities. I was going to ask him if I had a choice about coming back in here, but it didn't look like a good idea to do that."

"What y'all sayin'?" asked Claremont. "Y'all mean we *prisoners* in here?"

"Not sure, exactly," replied the salesman, "But there's something funny going on, that's for sure. Anyway, even if we were free to go, where'd we go *to*?

The state line blockade's still up, even more soldiers stationed there, I was able to see that when I was going back and forth between the tent and the outhouse, so we definitely can't get across, any better than we could have yesterday."

"All this sound *real* familiar," complained Claremont. "Back in De-troit, when they throw yo' ass in jail – cover yo' ears, kids – they charge you money for each day, y'all in there. No different here, 'cept they makin' us pay for our *meals*, too."

"I am confused about this," inquired the girl-in-rags. "We have committed no crime, at least none that I am aware of. If we have not broken any laws, then why are we in 'jail'? Do we not get a chance to plead our case in front of a... a magistrate, or a wise man, a law-keeper?"

"Don't know," answered Billings. "Those are all good questions, but like I said before we made our little trip there, I'm afraid it's very much no longer 'business as usual', these days... my vote would be for us just to sit tight and see what they have in store for us – I can tell you that they aren't letting *anybody* out the front door, and I don't feel like arguing with an M-116 to dispute the matter. Anybody feel differently?"

"'Don't make no sense to fight The Man, 'cept when he not in your 'hood for the night', that what we say back where ah come from," noted Claremont. "So me and mah kids, we'll wait here for awhile."

"Momma, ah'm hungry again," whined the boy.

"Ah *knows*, Curtis Ray, but y'all and your sister just have to wait for awhile, 'till them preacher-boys up there figure out what they gonna do with us," responded Claremont.

"That, and we almost out of money, anyway," she added, with a sub-tone of desperation.

At exactly that moment, the preacher-men were, evidently, ready to speak, because the crowd heard the crackle of static, as the loudspeakers came to life.

"Hello and hallelujah, fellow Christians," sounded a male voice, only barely distinguishable as such over the noise of the sound system. "The Lord's new day has come, and with it, some instructions for everyone who hears this voice," it pronounced.

"Do we get a vote?" muttered Billings.

"Never did back in *mah* 'hood," replied Claremont, indifferently, though with a barely-suppressed, malicious smirk. "Only thing diff'rent is, ah guess they doin' it to th' *white-folk* too, now."

"You are now all under the care of the Hallelujah Klan of Jesus Christ, as authorized by the U.S. federal government to ensure orderly processing of internally displaced persons on the Idaho-Wyoming border," announced the loudspeaker voice. "We want to assure everyone here that you will all be well looked-after, as long as you do not disturb the peace or attempt to leave our controlled area without permission; these measures have been put in place because the government does not currently have the resources to feed and house all of you, right here, and the military has told us that it does not want any more mob scenes at the border crossing outpost."

"When the Army has received the necessary tents and food and water supplies," continued the announcement, "You will be released from the authority of our church and transferred to the facilities of the Department of Homeland Security, which will be erected nearby this tent. In the meantime, in the next hour we will be taking a head count of everyone here, so we can allocate rations and sleeping-spaces with the most efficiency. Families with children will be given priority, as long as they conform to familiar Christian norms."

"So... we are imprisoned, held captive against our will?" asked the girl-in-rags, as the man's voice droned on, saying something about trash disposal.

"*Looks* that way, I'm afraid," confirmed the salesman.

A determined, steely look came over the fallen-girl's face, as, through clenched teeth, she growled, "I do not *like* that."

Not just Billings, but also Claremont and her children, now felt a sudden, powerful wave of excitement, like some unknown stimulant being applied to their nerves and minds.

"Somebody playing electric rock music on the AV?" asked a perplexed Billings. "I thought these Bible-bangers don't approve of..."

"Ah don't hear nothin'... no, wait..." interjected a confused Claremont.

"*Ah* does, Momma... oh, wait, it gone now," commented the little boy, as the countenance of the one they knew as 'Sari', slightly relaxed. "Hey, Momma, that feel *good*, where it come from?"

"*Weird*," remarked Billings. "Well, we'd better listen up – might miss the part about the potty breaks..."

The voice over the loudspeaker concluded, "We will feed you and keep you safe from harm, as long as you do not dispute our authority, which derives not only from your government, but also from God Himself. However, we will deal with rebellion swiftly and harshly – remember, you are being kept in this facility for your own good, so we cannot allow the un-coöperativeness of a few malcontents to endanger the common good of everyone. More announcements will be made to inform you of the rules, as necessary, and remember that your name must be recorded and counted for you to receive food and water. Glory be to God and His divine teachings. That is all."

A few voices from the crowd mumbled something or other, but, whether for reasons of hunger, fatigue or simply nowhere else to go, none stood up or shouted defiance.

"I always *suspected* that this country was becoming a goddamn theocracy," complained Billings. "Now I'm *sure*."

He surveyed the crowd.

"None of 'em want to get out of line, they all just want a nice free meal," he muttered. "So much for 'land of the free and home of the brave', I guess."

"They sayin' it just for a while, 'till they get things sorted out," offered Claremont.

"Yeah, *sure*," retorted the salesman. "Just like income tax was supposed to be 'temporary', too. I tell you, I'm not going to put – " he was starting to say, but at that moment, he was interrupted by the unannounced presence of two of the clean-cut, business-suited religious types he had previously seen, accompanied by a glowering, riot gear-clad gendarme.

The armed man shone a bright flashlight blindingly at the group.

From somewhere unremembered, a sudden instinct of alarm overtook the girl-in-rags.

The light rushes toward me! It will consume me! Run away! Hide! Evade! I cannot hope to live –

Noiselessly, reflexively, she stumbled backwards.

Small as a little mouse, you are a shadow, you are a wisp of fog, come the darkness over me, echoed the silent thoughts of a young-looking female, as she was suddenly... simply, *not there*.

"Oww – that's *hard* on the eyes, why don't you just turn on the lights?" protested Billings.

"That's too bad, sir," answered the first of the two clean-cut men, a red-haired guy of perhaps his early twenties with a crew-cut, as he motioned the soldier to shine the flashlight at the ground.

"Generator problems," he explained. "Blew a fuse when we tried to turn on the lights, while we were doing our announcement, a few minutes ago. But don't worry, we're working on it, we should have the lights working soon. So... how many do we have here, today?"

"Five," stated Billings, unenthusiastically. "Me, Mrs. Claremont and her two kids here, and the girl, 'Sari' – she's with me."

"The who?" responded the red-haired man.

"Brother David... do you see a *girl* with them?" he said, turning to the other clean-cut man, a slightly taller, dark-haired and probably younger one.

"Well, she's right – " shot back a mildly-annoyed Billings, as he turned around, looking where he had last seen the girl-in-rags.

"What the H... she *was* right *here*," stammered the salesman. "I dunno. Maybe she had to go answer the call of nature, or something. But she's with us, I can assure you."

"Listen, sir, we've seen this kind of thing before, so please be assured that we won't fall for it here, either," pompously pronounced the red-haired man. "We've already had three or four families claiming that they had people with them that just happened not to be there at the time, but if this girl you say is with you isn't here to be counted right now, then I'm afraid she doesn't get on the list, which means no extra food rations for the rest of you. It's a *sin* to try to cheat the Lord out of his bounty, you know."

"Whatever," said Billings, throwing up his hands while shrugging.

The first interrogator turned to the other man. "Okay, Brother David," he said, "I count four, here. Ready?"

"Yep," affirmed the other man, in a stupidly upbeat way. "This'll be family number 232."

Addressing the salesman and the mother, he demanded, "Names, please?"

"Ah'm Whitney Claremont," replied the woman. "These here is mah kids, Curtis Ray 'n Melissa Arlene. Say 'hi' to the nice man, y'all."

Two young voices chimed "Hello, Mister," in well-rehearsed unison, as they reflexively hid behind their mother.

"I'm Bob K. Billings, Jr.," interjected the salesman.

"You're not with... *her*, right, Mr. Billings?" asked the second man, as he busily scribbled something on to a clipboard.

"No," said Billings. "As I told you, I'm hanging out with Sari, Sari Tanak is her name if you want to know... Whitney and her kids and I are just friends," he added.

"Well, that's *good*," unctuously commented the dark-haired man. "There might have been, you know, *problems*, if you had claimed to have been married to her. Or, even worse, just... *with* her."

Billings just shrugged, all the while thinking, *If there's a God, he'll arrange for me to wring your pencil-thin neck, you strutting little...*

Claremont, however, answered back, saying, "Y'all don't gots to worry 'bout *that* – mah kids and me, we Baptists. They daddy in L.A., but we *married*, Mister."

"*Good*," said the red-haired man, smoothly. "Are you all U.S. citizens, Mr. Billings?" he requested.

"Born and bred here, Phoenix, specifically, but I live in Tucson these days," replied the salesman.

"De-troit," added Claremont. "But ah ain't gots no papers right now, they back home."

"Well, *that* may cause problems, too, but of course you're in the same situation as many of the rest in here," said the taller man. "Anyway... as Brother Harvey has explained, we can't include your, what did you say was her name, 'Tanak', in our head count for food allocation purposes. But in case we make an exception later, what's she look like? What's she wearing?"

"She 'bout eighteen, twenny or so, mah height, no, maybe bit bigger, ah'd say, blue or green eyes, gray hair like a grandma, cut straight in front, but it not really gray, got some dark stuff in it too, not bad-lookin'... for a *white* 'ho, that is," explained Claremont.

"Not bad-looking at all," commented Billings, with a lecherous smirk. "She's wearing some kind of really banged-up uniform, at least that's what I *think* it is. Looks like a gas station attendant, or maybe a car mechanic... after a few dirty lube, brake and filter jobs, that is."

"Gas station... mechanic... got that," said the red-haired man, as he scribbled something into an electronic notebook. "Thought they had phased out the women doing that by now, but I guess... ah, well, it's what we all *believe* inside that counts, not how we appear to others, isn't it? Is this 'girl' a citizen, Mr. Billings?"

"I guess," evaded the salesman. "I *think* so. But I'm not really sure, to tell you the truth."

"Very good," concluded the first interrogator. "So, I think we're finished here. Except, if this girl you say is with you, comes back, please ask her to report to the table up at the front of the tent for registration, okay? The Department of Homeland Security and the Immigration Service have told us that it's important to keep track of everyone in here. Not fair that illegal aliens get the food and water meant for *real* American citizens, is it?"

"Not arguing with you there. And, sure," replied Billings, evenly. "About the aliens, that is. *Hate* 'em, that is. Why, so does Whitney... right, Whitney?"

"Oh, yeah, ah don' like them aliens, no *way*, Bob," muttered Claremont, unenthusiastically. "Smelly food 'n such. Don' speak English too well, neither."

As the two men and the soldier-type headed off to the next group of refugees, perhaps ten feet away, Claremont turned to Billings and whispered, "Where she *go*? She be right there *behind* us not five minute ago – there ain't *nowhere* to hide round here, just people everywhere. And you know, she sound like she not from here..."

"Got no idea where she went, or how she slipped away without any of us noticing," replied Billings. "And what do *we* care if she's from –"

"Where *who* went, Bob?" asked the girl-in-rags, with a light tap on Billings' shoulder.

He turned around to see her wearing a cheery, slightly bemused smile, with an insouciantly-arched eyebrow.

"Who – what – oh, *there* you are," breathed the salesman, with a perceptible sigh of relief.

"Sari, where the *hell* did you – sorry, let me re-phrase that... it's just that you weren't here when the Bible-bangers showed up, taking the head count. So now you're off the chow list, I'm afraid," he said.

"Oh, blazes," replied the fallen-girl, matter-of-factly. "Does that mean no dessert, either?"

"Girl, y'all a regular *Hou-dini*, there," commented Claremont. "For the life of me ah can't figure how y'all was there one minute, and not the next. Somethin' y'all scared of, with them 'Klan of Jesus Christ' folk? They don' seem too bad to me, least, not any worse than the Man be normally."

"Momma," interjected the teenager, with the sound of complete astonishment in her voice, "She just... *vanish*. Like, she... she *disappear*, right into the air, that's what ah see."

"Yeah, Momma, she *magic*," exclaimed the boy.

"I just stepped into the shadows, Melissa, dear," claimed the girl-in-rags, bending slightly down to look the teenager more or less in the eye. "There is nothing 'magic', about it."

Stopping to think for a second or two, she added, "I do not really *like* magic acts, anyway. But I *do* know some tricks. If we have a chance, I will teach you one or two... oh-kay?"

"That be *dread*, lady!" excitedly exclaimed the boy.

"Curtis Ray, Melissa Arlene, y'all don't need to be doin' no tricks in here," commanded the mother.

Turning to the fallen-girl, she explained, "Ah don' want too much *attention*, y'all know. Bad for folk like us."

"Ah, yes," knowingly responded the girl-in-rags. "Too much attention – bad for me, too, I think. So I am afraid that the 'not-magic lessons' will have to wait until we get out of here."

"*Aww*," whined two young voices, which were quickly 'shussed' by their mother.

"But," added the young-looking woman, "Something tells me, that presently... you will learn a *lot*, from me."

None of the rest knew what to say back, so the troupe of unlikely partners waited on their captors, while the girl-in-rags sat enigmatically surveying the scene, as does an owl studying a darkened forest.

I'll Pass On The Pie

The shortish, 50-something, bald-headed man reached for a checkered hand-cloth and fumbled for his eyeglasses, touching and recognizing the thick glass of one lens with silent gratitude.

He should have had the procedure of taking them off and wiping them clean down by heart, after all these years, but somehow, he had never completely got the hang of it.

"Another big slice of pecan pie with the whipped-cream toppin', Mister?" asked a waitress, passing by the 50s-motif Formica table-top, in the booth where the man had sat down, alone, a half-hour earlier.

"No, that's fine, young lady," the man replied, with well-rehearsed, reflexive, if superficial, courtesy. "Two are right enough for me, I'm afraid... or so my doctor says. I'll tell y'all if I need anything else, still got lots of your fine black coffee here. Oh, and... I'm waitin' for a friend; when we get to talkin', you can bring him a coffee too, one cream, one sugar, then, we'd be obliged if y'all could let us speak with each other in private, until we ask for anything else, that alright?"

"Shore 'nuff, Mister," nodded the waitress, hustling off.

At that moment, the portly man, wiping the sweat from his forehead but not even attempting to do anything for the stains it had marked his over-tight shirt with, looked up and waved to another, just inside the doorway. A newcomer, twenty years younger and a head taller, crew-cut, in a conservative business-suit, fully buttoned despite the oven-like heat of rural Georgia, headed rapidly for the booth, extending a hand.

"Many regrets at being late, Mr. Horn," apologized the taller man. "My driver ran into a couple roadblocks, on the way over here."

"No offense taken, Brother Martin," smiled the shorter man, wiping his lips, "But I believe y'all should have had a pass, for them? If they aren't honorin' it, well, I'll have to have a talk with my distinguished friends in Homeland Security... tell 'em that you're a V.I.P."

"Weren't Federal roadblocks that slowed us up, not the 'national security' kind," explained the second man. "State Patrol, I think – lookin' for a gang of darkies that 'been holding up cars on the Interstate, bad stuff, according to the troopers, so far these fuckin' niggers have killed six or seven white citizens, including two girls raped until they were dead, as well as who knows how many wetbacks."

"Lord *preserve* us," intoned the short man, by rote.

"May be more than one gang, too," added Brother Martin. "Things have been just out of *control* down here, since The Event, my folk can't even go to church without an escort by our guards, and we've had to hire over a thousand more rent-a-cops from GrayWar just to handle our other properties... we would have done more, but guards and bouncers are in mighty short supply these days."

"*Most* unfortunate," offered the first man, smiling to the waitress as she quickly deposited a cup off coffee, plus condiments, on the table-top, then quickly departed. "Although, I 'spose, that also makes it a good day to be lookin' for work, if you are a man with aptitude for firearms. But give it *time*, Brother, give it *time*. Up where I come from, they're workin' as hard as they can to teach them black boys, the Hispanics 'n Injuns too, to get back in their place, you know."

"Well, I *hope* so," noted the taller man.

"So, Mr. Horn," he stated, "I suppose we're both here for the same reason, aren't we?"

Smiling past the Brother, Horn replied, "Yes, undoubtedly we are."

He paused for a moment, then continued, "Why don't y'all go first?"

"I was about to say just the same thing," answered the taller man, reflecting Horn's insincere smirk, "But since you beat me to it, I suppose I should. I'm afraid I don't have much to say; our people have been keeping their eyes and ears open, everywhere we got someone on the lookout that is, which is most of the country plus Mexico and a few in Canada, but we do not have any positive evidence. Yet – "

Horn arched an eyebrow. "Yes, Brother?" he asked.

"It's just a *feeling*, sir," mentioned the taller man. "We have been praying, you see..."

"That's nothing *new*, for y'all, I do believe," commented the portly man.

"Very true," replied Brother Martin, earnestly, "But our hearts tell us, when we listen for the voice of the Lord... that she is *here*, in our very own United States of America."

"Well let me give y'all a bit of friendly advice," offered the bespectacled man. "Little bird tells me that you'd be best off concentratin' in the western half of the country."

Immediately, the second man sat straight up, a gleam of hope in his eye.

"How so? If you don't mind me asking, sir."

"Oh, nothin' *specific*," explained Horn, sipping deeply for the last dregs of his coffee. "Just that, that's the most likely place, based on some... circumstantial evidence, courtesy of the heroic men – and, I s'pose, these days, a few women too – in our Armed Forces."

"At first, you see," he went on, "Based on reports from that there space-ship that first dug her up on Mars, the spy-folk told us that she just, well, flew off, somewhere. That's still what a lot of 'em think. But more recently, the theory is that in fact, she landed, somewhere on Earth. As I said, we neither have a living alien, nor a body... yet."

"My superiors will be most interested to hear this information," replied the taller man, gratefully. "Although a few of them, I must admit, had hoped that the Lord would spare us from the tribulation of dealing with... But, Mr. Horn, you haven't ever said anything to us, I mean, you know, to my senior Brothers, regarding what to *do* with her, if and when we find her...?"

"Y'all are quite right about that," answered the short man, running his hands over what little was left of the hair on top of his head. "Especially as we don't know what she's capable of, if that's anythin' at all. But in the absence of any better strategy, I'd say y'all should just do what comes... *naturally*, if you catch my drift."

"The Holy Bible says, 'thou shalt not suffer a witch to live', you know, Mr. Horn," offered the younger man, evenly. "If Scripture is right, and it always is, then she is far worse than *any* witch."

"Indeed it does," responded Horn. "Indeed it *does*. Now, in that light, I have some more advice, and y'all should pass this on to those higher up in your church – strictly off the record, of course."

"Of course," quickly replied the other man.

"Alright," continued Horn.

Smoothly, he stated, "Now, y'all see, here's the thing. Both I and my friends in the Government, well, we understand that your church, as well as many others, have read the Bible to mean that this, this – *whatever* she is, is *evil*. That may be the case, and if so, far be it for me to tell you otherwise. But from our perspective, we have other reasons."

"Such as?" inquired Brother Martin.

"See, the way things was before, I mean before the whole 'Lucifer' thing," elaborated Horn, "Well, the good ol' Ew-Nighted States of America was fightin' to be on top, yes, them yellow China-men and the Rooshians and them sand niggers from India, has been challengin' us, but it was a contest that we were *familiar* with, one that we thought we could win. Still *can* win – except for now, we have this new, disruptive, unknown factor. One which, or so the scientists tell me, could smash a comet into little bitty pieces just like you or I could break a Christmas tree ornament. So..."

"So...?" pressed the other man.

"What I'm drivin' at, not to put too fine a point on it, Brother, is that both yours truly, as well as a lot of other people in the Government – 'specially in the Armed Forces – would just as soon see this 'devil-girl' *disappear... permanently*, if you understand what I mean. That way, things'd be back to the way they was. Nice and predictable, with Uncle Sam on top, with nobody to upset the apple-cart."

"I have no doubt," noted the younger man, "That my senior Brothers would like that outcome, as well, but for reasons of Scripture."

He paused for a second, then added, "But... other than for our long-standing relationship, that is, yourself and your church, foot-soldiers for getting the vote out and such, why are you going to the trouble of telling me – *us* – this, Mr. Horn? No doubt the Government could do a better job of eliminating this problem themselves, than we ever could. True, we have the sword of the Lord and His righteous fury; but you have the entire U.S. Army, Navy and Air Force, not to say the intelligence-agencies. Our resources pale in comparison to that."

Horn shrugged, nonchalantly.

"And, also – you should know this far better than I," argued the Brother, "If the Devil-Girl had the ability to use the fires of Hell, so as to do all she has been credited with, she would be *terrifyingly* powerful, maybe too much for even the Government to deal with, at least without risking Armageddon. Maybe only our Lord and Savior Himself, could defeat her, but as yet, our prayers to Lord Jesus for Him to come down and save us, have not been heard. To put it bluntly, sir... why do you need us?"

"Y'all hit one of the reasons on the head," agreed Horn, wiping the sweat from his brow. "That is, our previous relationship... I'm obliged to tell your superiors what's goin' on, no doubt about that."

"But, you see," he continued, "As far as eliminatin' this problem once and for all – if and when we find her – it – well, that gets *complicated*. We got quite a few of them pointy-headed scientist types who are of the opinion that the creature should be captured and studied, not sent to an early grave; that could be dealt with, but the more immediate problem is that in the absence of firm evidence that she's actually here, the President hasn't yet made a decision."

"If and when he does," went on the short man, "I'll have to also contend with a school of thought within our Armed Forces that the Devil-Girl can be – y'all don't laugh, now – 'recruited' into the Air Force, or somethin' like that, so the Ew-Nighted States of America can make good on all them promises our illustrious President has been makin' about this excellent new weapon we supposedly have –"

"No military man with a *lick* of common sense would believe that," exclaimed the taller man, rather more loudly than was appropriate. "She's the spawn of *Satan* – she would never work for God's chosen country – Russia, China, those Christ-denying Jews or Muslims, maybe –"

"I know, I *know*, Brother," responded Horn, with unctuous fake patience, "But they're basin' this idea on the fact that supposedly, she *did*, at one point, follow the orders of that space-Captain, what was his name, yes, 'Jacobsen' or something like that, apparently she said that she owed him her allegiance, who knows, I don't think it's worth a handful of red Georgia clay, but *they* do, that's the point."

"And, as to her abilities, well, that *is*, indeed, a bridge that we will have to cross, when we come to it," he added. "But – and y'all must understand that this is just a *feelin'* that yours truly has, just like your own insight courtesy of your Father God up there – I think she's much less than she's made out to be. I mean, stories of her flyin' round in outer space, smashin' comets, *et cetera* – so much hogwash, I say. I mean, if the Devil-Girl was really *that* powerful, then why wouldn't she just fly down here and set herself up as ruler of all us lesser mortals, or some such thing? It make any sense to you, that she wouldn't, that she'd just come down here for a lil' ol' sight-seein' vacation?"

"No, it sure doesn't," answered the younger man. "But she may just be biding her time. Scripture tells us that the Devil is patient. That he will wait until the right moment to strike, when the guard of God's faithful is let down."

Horn sat back, with a sigh.

"Anyway, Brother," he continued, "*You* know that she's got to go, and so do *I*; but a lot of people in the Government *don't*. I'd just as soon we never get to the point of havin' to worry about what to do with her, in the first place. So... what I'm askin', and I want y'all to make sure your higher-ups know this, is – if, and when, y'all locate this creature, if you can do the deed before she falls into the tender clutches of our Federal Boys in Black, please do so, forthwith. If she unfortunately ends up in our custody, we'll have to make other plans."

"What are we supposed to do, in that case?" complained the Brother. "You know the Government as well as I do. They'll have her locked away in some facility – "

"The best I will be able to do, in that eventuality," said Horn, drawing back a breath and reclining, "Will be to open a few doors for y'all, give you access that might otherwise be difficult to procure. But whomever y'all send, in that case, he should be ready and willin' to meet his maker, because there likely won't be *any* gettin' out, afterwards, on account either of our quarry herself, or on account of the Yew-Nighted States Army, Marines and Air Force. Do I make myself clear, Brother Martin, sir?"

"Quite clear, sir," replied the younger man, evenly. "We will do our best, and, as to your second point, I don't think you need worry about us finding volunteers for that task. You know, a week or so ago, in my local branch of the Klan of Jesus Christ, we had a sermon on 'Would you Have Struck Down Judas

Iscariot To Save the Lord' – and after all, what matters the life of one martyr, when he will go to his reward knowing he has been the Hand of the Lord, against the Devil?"

"Oh, let me echo that," agreed Horn, with a cynical smile. "To say nothing of being the one to save America from its most dangerous military threat. I can think of no cause more noble... can you, Brother?"

"None, at all, sir," firmly answered the younger man. "I can only pray that I should be so lucky as to receive the call to do this... and that I should neither quaver, nor fail, while fighting for our Blessed Lord and Savior."

"Then, I believe our business here is done with," concluded Horn. "Time for both of us to be on our respective ways."

The younger man got up and extended a hand to the other man, still sitting. "I will report what you have told me here, to my superiors... strictly off the record, of course."

The older, stout man just nodded, with one of his obligatory, insincere smiles.

The younger man turned and headed for the door, not looking back.

Horn called to the waitress for the bill, as he got up himself.

"Charge today, sir? Machines are down, but we're still takin' cards, 'long as you leave your phone number and address," she mentioned.

"I'll just be payin' cash, thank you very much," he answered. "Since I don't believe I'll be back here, anytime soon."

He dusted a few crumbs from the many creases of his over-used suit, left enough to pay the bill, plus a generous tip, on the Formica of the table-top, then headed out, no faster than had the other man, shortly before.

He did not notice another man, dressed in an equally tight-fitting, over-warm business-suit, who had been quietly sipping on a soft drink, away in the corner.

But as Horn left, this stranger removed a small, discreet earphone and opened a leather-bound notebook, inscribing a few entries in it, in flowing Cyrillic script.

A Lottery You Had Better Win

"What's he called us all together here, for?" asked Tanaka, as she and Jacobson waited, floating weightlessly in the space-station's forward observation bay, staring occasionally at the small, bright disc of the nearing Earth, surrounded by a panoply of stars all about.

"As if you didn't know," casually answered the former Mars mission commander. "You've been working with Shivani... you know the situation..."

"I was hoping that Ariel and you had come up with some kind of secret, miraculous plan, something that the peasants didn't deserve to find out about, until now," muttered the woman, her Eurasian brow wrinkled with worry.

"Ever the optimist, aren't I?" she added.

"Only miracle we'll get today," offered Jacobson, "Is that I've finally figured out that 'flying with no engine' trick that she taught you... see?" replied Jacobson, as he moved slightly forward, though far out of reach of any hand-hold.

"Wow! Well... congrats, Sam," exclaimed Tanaka. "Practice makes perfect – but I'd advise you not to try it any more, with everyone else showing up, around here. Did I ever tell you, the first three times I did it, that is, with her in the *Infinity*'s central core, I only moved an inch or so; then, the fourth time, I went flying forward so fast that I got a nice bruise on my shoulder, when I hit the bulkhead. She told me that it's sometimes like that, your abilities mostly grow gradually, but every so often, they develop in quantum-fashion... I sure got a quantum *headache* from that one, I remember..."

"Yeah," agreed the astronaut, "But I'm getting *used* to the buzz that comes with the headaches. Funny, you know, Air Force and NASA have all these elaborate checks and tests against alcohol, drugs, whatever, but they never figured on how to stop people from getting high from the use of an alien power... just another one they'll have to go back to the old starting board for..."

"True, but – oh, that'll have to wait for later, Sam, *there* he is," interjected Tanaka, as Ariel Cohen's spare, Mediterranean figure appeared at the podium (really, a collection of spare science office parts, hastily strung together with computer fiber network cables).

"Hello, crew of ISS2," announced Cohen. "This is your Commander speaking to you today, both to the majority of our crew, assembled before me in the forward observation bay, plus, by intra-station video, for those individuals who had to remain at their posts for load balancing or other technical reasons. How is everyone, today?"

A few members of the crowd forced smiles and mumbled unenthusiastic-sounding acknowledgments.

"I *see*," noted Cohen, evenly, "That news of today's topic has preceded me. Well, we're all a family, I suppose, so that's not a major problem; but, as some of you already know, what I have to tell you, is a *very* serious issue. Michael – yes, now, please – okay, there it is."

A holographic depiction of the inner solar system from the orbit of Mars to the Sun, appeared to Cohen's side. It showed Mars, Earth, Venus and Mercury, all correctly arrayed in relative orientation to each other. About an eighth of the way from Earth to Mars, there was a small, red dot, with a dashed line from it, almost – but not quite – intersecting with the orbital path of the Earth and Moon. After crossing the plane of Earth's orbit, the red line went toward the Sun, but stopped abruptly at a point slightly more than half the way to the orbit of Venus.

"Reminds me of another one that we prepared, for someone else," whispered Tanaka to Jacobson.

Somberly, the man nodded.

"That we have to discuss now, not that anyone – least of all myself – wants to, is what we are going to do, to cope with the situation that you all see depicted in the 3-D display that Michael Theodikas has put up, in front of us," explained Cohen. "The exact physics of the trajectory are available on ISS2's computer-network, for those of you who are curious, although I should point out that they have been reviewed and verified not only by several people up here but also by a number of experts on the ground, down on Earth."

"To use an American expression," stated Cohen, taking a deep breath, "The bottom line is, based on our velocity after the explosive burn of our one remaining booster, plus the unavailability of any other braking system, ISS2 will not be able to achieve a parking orbit around Earth."

Several in the crowd gasped.

Tanaka muttered to Jacobson, "As if they didn't know before."

Her former commander replied, "They may have *known*, but they didn't *believe*, until the Captain said it. Goes with the position, I'm afraid."

"So," continued Cohen, "it falls upon me to explain the consequences of this state of affairs to all of you. Here are the facts, as far as we know them at this point. At our current velocity, we will arrive in circum-lunar space approximately thirty days from now – I will discuss the practical considerations surrounding that, in a few minutes."

"Then," he said, slowly and precisely, "Due to the 'slingshot' effect of Earth's gravity well, we will have a very short time in Earth's vicinity, no more than a few days at most, before we pass by our home planet. After this, our trajectory, as much as we have been able to calculate it so far, brings ISS2 toward Venus, then... well, after that, we don't really know; but by that time, it will be too late, anyway."

Trying to make the best of it, he added, "If it's of any interest, some of you may get to be the first humans to fly near to Venus... you will get a good, close look at it."

Silence enveloped the station, as Cohen explained,

"As most of you know, although ISS2 was, as part of its involvement in the 'Arks' project, provided with much more than its normal on-board supply of air and water, even taking these extra life-support resources into account, we simply don't have enough air and water to sustain our present crew for the duration of the trajectory we have so far been able to project... and, if it makes any difference, even if we did, our preliminary calculations indicate that after Venus, we would eventually pass so close to the Sun that no human being could survive the ionizing radiation that ISS2 would be subjected to. We have no shielding that could *possibly* protect us from it, ignoring the fact that our air would run out months before."

"Are we going to burn up?" asked a female voice from the crowd.

"Not really," Tanaka heard a different voice, which a second or so later she recognized as Humber's, interject from behind Cohen.

"We'll just become another planet of ol' Sol, luv," Humber tried to joke. "But with a healthy glow, from all those hard X-rays and gamma rays... kids on Earth should be able to see us light up the sky, every six months or so. On second thought, we'd be more of a comet, I guess."

A comet, thought Tanaka. *Funny you should put it that way.*

"Thanks, Alan," said Cohen, turning reflexively to his left to address Humber.

"And as my First Engineer here has so ably pointed out, no, we aren't going to collide with the Sun. But we still have to face the facts."

Cohen explained, "Both Alan and the rest of my team have worked day and night to avoid the outcome that I'm about to describe, but, unfortunately, there is no way to do so, with the resources available to us. We have thought of *all* the possible alternatives, some reasonable, some outlandish, but we have found nothing that stands more than a marginal chance of success. So, we now have to make some very difficult decisions, in order to avoid the loss of our entire crew, which would be the inevitable result of doing nothing. Before I explain the plan to you, I think I should point out that you were all aware of the risks, under the 'Arks' program; this one is not significantly different."

He continued, "Now, the first fact that we have to face, is that we have no plausible way of stopping ISS2 at Earth – thanks to Alan's tireless work, we now believe that, by careful use of the maneuvering thrusters, we *can* slow us down near Earth and thereby have more time in its vicinity; but, we *will* still eventually fly by the planet. Therefore, the only practical solution, is to try to get as many of us as we can, off the station, before it gets too far away for the escape vehicles to reach Earth, or, at least, get close enough to it so that they can in turn be rescued."

"We plan," Cohen went on, "To use Commander Jacobson's former two ships – the *Eagle* lander, and the *Infinity* mother ship – as our primary evacuation vessels. These will be accompanied by ISS2's two emergency escape modules, which have already been rigged with makeshift, low-energy booster engines, to give them a delta trajectory from ISS2's own, when we arrive close enough to Earth to make doing so theoretically possible. The challenge here, is to balance the human occupancy of all of these escape ships, with enough internal volume devoted to air and water to give those on the ships, a reasonable amount of flight time, before they get back to Earth, or to another rescue ship."

"So," he concluded, "Taking all of the above into account, the management team has come to believe that the highest number of occupants that can be safely accommodated in the *Eagle* and *Infinity*, for evacuation purposes, is," – Cohen coughed, momentarily – "Twenty-two, assuming a fifty-fifty ratio of male to female evacuees, with the understanding of the relatively lower average weight of women compared to that of men. Now, this is, obviously, a much lower count than the current crew of our station, which means that we must have some equitable way to allocate spots on the evacuation ships; for this purpose, we have devised a lottery, which is available to everyone on ISS2 with the exception of the management team..."

Someone interrupted, "Who's the management team, again?"

"Myself, Commander Sam Jacobson of the recent Mars mission, Sub-Commander Chen, and also Alan Humber and Mike Theodikas," replied Cohen, evenly.

Tanaka shot a pained look at Jacobson and was about to say something, but the man just stared forward, stoically.

"The lottery will be run by the computer, using a randomizing function, and its neutrality and validity will be verified by the management team," noted Cohen. "Your names will be automatically added to the draw, unless you inform us otherwise in writing by eight o'clock Solar Time tomorrow evening. We will be announcing the results at nine o'clock tomorrow, with the names of the winners being posted on the ISS2 internal network. After that, we will begin an intensive training and preparation phase, for the evacuation crew; this is because special measures regarding load distribution and environmental resources consumption will have to be implemented, for the 'lifeboats', if I can call them that, to have a good shot at reaching Earth orbit – "

"Commander," interjected the voice of Brent Boyd, from behind Tanaka and Jacobson, "Neither the *Eagle* nor the *Infinity*, have the *slightest* chance of surviving an Earth atmospheric re-entry. Just what do you plan to do with these ships, and with the crews in them, when they get into orbit? I mean, how are the people supposed to get down to the surface of the planet?"

"We're still working on that one, Major Boyd," answered Cohen. "Our current hope is that Earth will send up a ship to get them."

"But they don't *have* – oh, forget it," argued the former Mars mission pilot. "Never mind."

"On the latter point, I want you to be of no illusions," stated Cohen. "Due to the 'Lucifer' incident, Earth has virtually no space-worthy ships left right now, although we are in constant contact with NASA, if the situation changes, as we hope it does, we will be the first to know."

"What happens to those of us whose names aren't on the list?" demanded a male voice from the crowd.

"That's another one that we have not finally decided the plans for," answered Cohen, in his typically professional, detached, manner. "But as I suspect that some of you have already inferred from Alan's description of what's likely to happen to those who remain on-board ISS2 after the evacuation vessels have left, it's obviously not something that most of us would willingly choose to endure."

He paused for a second and then said, "Speaking just for myself, when matters reach 'the point of no return', I think my own preference would be to take something, a pill, that kind of thing, to 'go down with the ship', as it were. But as Commander of this station, I'd only want to do that after all the rest of my crew have made their own... *arrangements*. However, as I said, we're still working it out. Any input that any of you could give us, suggestions and so on, would be welcomed."

The silence was awkward and palpable.

"Just get me a surfboard and point me at the airlock, man... just like that old movie, sure looked like a fun way to go," called out someone from the back, to a few muffled guffaws.

It *had* to have been White, and neither Tanaka nor Jacobson had to turn around, to verify that fact.

"Well," commented Cohen, slowly, "I know that this hasn't been a pleasant discussion, but the management team and I all believe that it would have been much worse to have kept everyone in the dark, about the real situation. Now, at least we are all working with the same set of facts and choices. It's up to us to make the best of them... and to make the best use of whatever time remains to those of us, who will stay behind on ISS2."

He paused a for second or two, then asked, "Are there any other questions?"

None spoke up, and all went silently back to their quarters.

Doubt Me Not (Prologue)

"So what is it tonight?" sarcastically inquired Billings. "The same fine cuisine?"

"Probably same as last night and tha night before, 'an th' night before that... ah kinda lost count," answered Claremont, with an indifferent shrug. "But after the money ran out, ah'm just glad they still feedin' mah kids, even if it *is* just that porridge stuff, or whatever it is."

"Well, that may be true," stated the salesman, irritably, "But I'm getting *awfully* tired of that tasteless crap, and of being stuck in here, especially with no end in sight. I asked the buggers twice yesterday, and as usual I couldn't get a straight answer, just some put-off line like 'you'll be told soon', that kind of thing. Goddamn *disgrace* that this can happen in our own country, if you ask me."

"Y'all say a bad word, Mister," taunted the little boy next to him.

Billings glowered.

"Maybe *you're* used to going a week without a bath," he muttered. "I'm not."

"Ha, Mister Whitey, y'all just *not* used to it," retorted the black woman. "Back where ah come from, it just regular business, that's all. Y'all just do what they say, what you *want*, that don't come into it, that's just the way it is. Don't believe *me*, if y'all don' want to – just ask them Injuns over there. Same for them."

"Maybe," he grunted. "But we've been over *that* one, before. Several times."

"It certainly *is* interesting listening to the two of you," commented the girl-in-rags, who had just come out of one her Sphinx-like sessions of quiet, cross-legged meditation. "If I did not know better, I would have to think that you came from two different countries... not the same one."

"'*Lot* of people say we do," mentioned Claremont.

"You know, Sari," asked Billings, "I was *meaning* to ask you about that... like, when we first met, a few days ago, you mentioned that you weren't from the States, which I kinda could tell right from the start. But I never *did* get a chance to ask you, where *are* you from? I mean, I can't quite place your accent –"

The fallen-girl at first looked puzzled, then, a defensive tone took over her voice.

"I am from – I do not really *remember* where from," she answered. "Bad bump on the head. I *told* you... remember?"

"Yeah, sure, but for God's sake, you *must* remember *something*," Billings interrogated. "I mean, I've *heard* of amnesia, but not like *this*, not a complete blank... I once dated a doctor – pity it didn't go all the way, I'd be set for life – but, anyway, she did a lot of head trauma cases, she said that somebody with a concussion might forget who they are, for a while, but they'd at least have some memories of childhood, a trip to the beach, Mom and Dad's faces, that kind of thing... She'd never seen anyone with a total memory wipe. Seems strange that you'd have one."

He is supposed to be my friend, mused the girl-in-rags. *It sometimes wears off, yes, I remember that it does, but in a day or two? Where am I, that my skill is so fleeting? Or perhaps his mind is strong, it finds the fortress-of-the-will defense, all by itself... admirable... you* impress *me, Bob Billings, salesman...*

"There is a first time for everything," she evaded. "Perhaps I am the first one of my kind."

Should I use it again, on him? worried the fallen-girl, staring distantly at Billings. *No. I violated him once, of necessity. It is not right that I do it again. I should* earn *his trust in the way that ordinary people do. And his mind might rebel. It might backfire.*

"Yeah, maybe you *are*," answered the man. "Look, I didn't mean to pry, it's just that I found it interesting, what with you being in that uniform and all, I thought that you might be Russian or something, or – "

"Shh!" interrupted Claremont. "They *sayin'* somethin', on them loudspeakers up there."

After a short crackle of static, a bland monotone sounded over the PA system.

"Attention, attention," it barked. "An important announcement follows."

There was a pause.

"Well, get *on* with it," muttered Billings.

"Please pay close attention, because these orders will not be repeated," pronounced the voice. "By the decree of the Government of the United States, you are directed to report for resettlement into long-term holding-facilities, where you will be accommodated until the Department of Homeland Security can assess each detainee's credentials, on a case-by-case basis. The Klan of Jesus Christ has been delegated the responsibility for organizing your departure from this temporary facility and has been granted provisional authority to exercise all due force during the transition from short- to long-term detention.

"Please be advised", warned the loudspeaker, "That our Guard is heavily armed and well-trained in riot control measures, so, if you do not want to get hurt, we suggest that you do as you are told; rebellion or attempts to escape will be *harshly* punished."

"About what I'd *expect*," complained the salesman. "concentration-camps, American-style. Maybe it'd have been better if the damn comet had just taken us out, after all – "

The girl-in-rags' expression, already dark, took on a strange combination of hurt, disgust, but, also, astonishment, or perhaps sudden awareness.

"You do not know what you are *saying*, man, if I had been just two *seconds* late –", she exclaimed; then she stopped, abruptly, as if shocked by what she had heard herself say, staring vacantly into space in absent-minded contemplation.

"*Quiet*, y'all!" demanded the black woman. "He yellin' somethin', again!"

"As the first phase in the implementation of these measures," continued the voice, "You are directed to fall in to the three waiting-lines that we have established at the entrance to the tent, within ten minutes of hearing this order. Line One, is for men; Line Two, for women; Line Three is for children under sixteen years of age. The lines will each march to separate nearby temporary accommodation barracks, from where you will be sent to permanent facilities, when these are available."

Claremont's face wore an expression of stunned panic, while the announcement went on,

"We are pleased to inform you that in these new buildings, you will each be assigned your very own uniforms and a fold-up cot, complete with pillow and blankets, and all new tents also have portable toilets, so you will have much better living facilities than those that you are now in. Bring only essential items with you and be aware that we will be inspecting backpacks and other containers for prohibited items such as non-Christian literature, alcohol, illegal drugs, tobacco or weapons. There is to be no talking, either to each other or to Church staff, during this process and failure to comply with this directive will result in the un-coöperative being *swiftly* apprehended, immobilized and placed in special punishment facilities. Glory be to God Almighty and to His Favored Nation on Earth, the United States of America! Amen."

"What the *fuck*," protested Billings. "They have no *right* to do that, none at all – let me see that government order they talk about..."

"Mah *children*, they fixin' to take mah *children!*", cried a panicked Claremont. "Ah ain't done *nothin'!* Ah ain't *lettin'* 'em!"

"They mean to imprison us, do they not?" demanded the girl-in-rags. "When we are but victims... when we trusted them. Truthfully, I have tried very hard not to offend anybody, around here –"

"Maybe worse than that," mentioned Billings. "Maybe make us work in some factory, enslave us, that is, maybe just shoot us, who *knows*. I've read the stories of the Nazis, the Commies, them Iranian nut-balls, this is *always* how it starts, they make you line up, the off you go, never to be seen again. I just can't believe it's happening h*ere*."

He turned to the girl-in-rags.

"Listen, Sari," he apologized, "I'm *sorry*, I really am, for having lead you in here. Hell of a price to pay for a meal, I guess."

The fallen-girl took hold of his hand and smiled warmly.

"Do not blame yourself, Bob," she consoled. "And all is not lost, anyway. I have been in much worse situations, in previous lives, I know that somehow, I will –"

"Momma," whimpered the boy, as he tugged on Claremont's dirty dress, "Ah don' *wanna* go away from y'all! Don't let them *take* me, Momma!"

"Me neither, Momma," added Melissa. "Curtis, y'all and me, we better hide... ah sees them comin' – look, over there, they already goin' after that family eight or so 'head of us. We don' gots but about ten minutes, maybe less –"

"That's *crazy*," interjected Billings. "I don't blame you for wanting to, kids, but there's nowhere to hide in here, all we got is tables and chairs, and besides, they'd still get your mother, Sari and myself. Best we can do is try to make a break for it... any of you want to try?"

"It take us least a few minutes to get under the tent," countered Claremont. "They got it staked down good. Kids might make it 'fore us, though..."

"But there are armed guards stationed in several places outside the tent," cautioned the girl-in-rags. "They would *surely* catch anyone trying to sneak out from under it."

"How *y'all* know that, Missy?" demanded Claremont. "Ain't *none* of us been outside lately..."

"I just *know*," retorted the girl. "I can see them, hear them, smell them. Well, *sort* of."

"Look, let's leave that for another time," interrupted Billings. "They're getting closer by the minute. If we don't make a break from it now, how the hell are we supposed to get out at all, will you explain *that* to me, please? Our only chance is while things are all confused, while other people are keeping them busy."

There was a scream from three ranks of the crowd ahead of them, followed by a commotion.

A heavily accented male voice yelled, "Dishonor my wife, you *dogs* – "

They heard a gunshot, then another, then two or three more.

A different voice, passionate, driven, shouted, "This is a *Christian* country, devil-worshiping bitch! Let that be a lesson to *all* of you!"

"What was *that*?" asked Claremont's daughter, uneasily.

"Just what it *sound* like, Melissa Arlene, child," replied the mother, as if hearing something as familiar as the song of birds in the morning. "Just like in the hood."

As the crowd started to move back rapidly towards the periphery of the tent, pushing all five of Billings' troupe involuntarily with them, they saw a blood-spattered Middle-Eastern-looking woman, the top half of her *chador* ripped clean off, hanging her head in shock and shame as she was dragged toward the front of the tent by two huge, glowering, riot-helmeted security-guards.

"*Jesus*," breathed Billings. "I never really believed it – but they're willing to *kill* – maybe we better just do what they say –"

And I am too weak to do much of anything, mused a frustrated fallen-girl, hanging her head in shame.

She looked up, and hissed, through clenched teeth, "But now I *know* by what principles, those people behave. And I will *not* forget."

"Ah don' care!" wailed Claremont. "They *ain't* takin' mah children! Ah'll *die* first!"

"What we gonna *do*, Momma?" whimpered the little boy, starting to cry.

"Well whatever we decide, we had better do so quickly," warned Billings. "They're almost here."

"Everyone come close around me," demanded the girl-in-rags, a weird look of serene determination on her face. "I have a plan."

"Yeah, Missy?" inquired Claremont, huddling down with the rest of them. "What yo' bright idea?"

"For this to work," explained the girl-in-rags, her eyes bright with confidence, experience and some other, faint light, "You must all trust me. You *must* trust me with your *lives* and your *fates*."

"Girl, we hardly *know* y'all," protested Claremont.

"Yes," replied the one named 'Sari Something-or-Other'. "And what is more, I tell you, I am of a kin and essence *much* greater than anyone here yet suspects. But the time is short, I must describe the plan now, or lose my chance. I want each of you to allow yourselves to be taken, as they commanded – "

"Ain't no *way!*" retorted the black woman.

"Just *listen* to her, Whitney," replied Billings, swiftly. "At least let her finish."

"Do *nothing* that would mark you as a, a, 'troublemaker', yes, that is the word... obey all of their commands, which is exactly what I will do, myself," ordered the fallen-girl. "But keep careful track of the time. I will come first for Whitney, a few minutes before midnight; I will take her to a safe hiding-place, then, at exactly midnight, using weirding arts that you know not yet, I will come for the children and will take them safely out of wherever they are being kept. I will bring them back to where I have left Whitney and then ten minutes after that I will free Bob."

"Say *whaat*?" shot back a befuddled Claremont.

"I will tap each of you two times on the head, so you know it is me," continued the girl-in-rags, "But keep *absolutely* quiet, or we might get caught. I will sneak all of you out of these prisons. After that, we will all be free to do as each of us chooses."

She stopped, in vacant thought for a second, then added, "For this to work, you must all stand as close to me as possible, you must always be touching me. It will be *very* dark, even darker than the blackest night, when you are next to me, it will be hard to see where you are going. Do not say *anything*, not a sound, not even if it seems that your captors are looking right *at* us – it will seem like they *must* be able to see us, but they can not. Just let me lead you, and you will be oh-kay."

"Sari, I'd love to believe you, but that's *nuts*, they'll probably have those barracks where they're taking us, even more locked-down than *this* one, and you saw what might happen if they catch you trying to escape," argued Billings.

The gendarmes were now no more than a row and a half, in front of their group. A woman was wailing about her children.

"Do you have a *better* plan, Bob?" disingenuously countered the fallen-girl.

"No, but, you'd have to be Houdini to – " protested the salesman.

"Mister," interrupted the little boy. "Houdini, he a magician, right? Mister?"

"Yeah, son, he had all *sorts* of magic tricks, to get out of being locked in boxes and... for God's sake, they'll be here in *ten seconds!*" Billings retorted.

"Well, *she* magic too, Mister," replied Curtis, matter-of-factually. "Ah believe her. Ah *seen* her do magic. Melissa did too. Right, Melissa?"

"Yeah, ah guess," confirmed the black girl, dejectedly wiping a tear. "She just disappear, then she show up again. But we never gonna find out how, now... Momma, let me hug y'all one last time, please..."

"You there!" shouted a gruff, male voice. "You're next! Fall in line!"

"Remember," whispered the girl-in-rags, as a faint, exciting tune sounded in the back recesses of the psyches of those who she addressed. "Before midnight, then twelve o'clock, then ten minutes, then another ten. Be ready, and say nothing when you feel my touch. I will come to your aid, believe in that; and, believe in *me*."

"Sari, you know I'd like to, but I doubt –" started the salesman, hastily straightening his tie as the gendarmes strode forward.

She looked the man straight in the eye, using no craft save the strength of her conviction.

Firmly and plainly, she said in a low, haunting voice that might have sounded like an oath,

"Friends of this beautiful blue world, *doubt me not*," as the soldiers of the church calling itself "the Klan of Jesus Christ", motioned them all to get up.

Purely Hypothetical

The President reflexively straightened his posture, as his advisers – mostly in U.S. business class mufti, but not a few dressed in medal-bedecked military garb, as well – filed into the White House West Wing Cabinet Room.

It had only been a few days that he'd been back, after all the recent "excitement", and no matter how assiduously that he tried to settle in, somehow something or other *always* seemed to be out of place.

But they were here, now. He'd have to leave the re-decorating for later.

"So, let's get right to it, gentlemen. And ladies," he announced, casting a friendly glance in the direction of his senior polling Adviser and the Secretary of Health and Human Services.

"Mr. President," started a gray-haired, uniformed military man, depositing a ring-bound report on the desk. "I understand that you've already seen this on your computer terminal, but just so that we have it handy to refer to, I've made you a hard-copy... here it is."

"Let me have a look," said the American leader. "Yeah, same one. Okay, go ahead. Anything new, since this was printed?"

"Negative," replied the military man. "Although we're obviously still conducting tests. However, as you already know, sir, the results so far are mighty interesting, or, to put it another way, mighty *suspicious*."

"You mean the results from, where was it again, that mountain in..., in...", said the President.

"Idaho, sir," interjected the Science Adviser.

With mild irritation, the President noted that McPherson, as was his wont, had not bothered to properly button up his collar; the man's tie was hanging down like that of a 40's newspaper reporter.

He wouldn't have gotten away with that as a junior staffer, but McPherson had been running the President's data mining systems since the latter's first Congressional campaign, and for this man, loyalty counted first, above all.

"Okay. Idaho, it *is*, then," noted the President. "Fred, I appreciate all this science stuff – radiation levels, chemical analysis, and so on, but you know, it's all Greek to me, I left that stuff back when I left DuPont, more years ago than any of you can count," he added, to polite chuckles from the group. "I'd appreciate it if you could give me your take on it... what's it all mean, you know what I'm asking."

"Well," answered McPherson, with a tone of unease, "You have to understand, Mr. President, that what we have right now, is far from conclusive – our formal term for the site is the 'Hill 1442 Anomaly', and that's for a reason, because all we have is some unusual readings, in terms of burn patterns at the impact site... no 'smoking gun', as they say..."

"Mr. President, I'll fill you in on the Air Force's perspective, when Mr. McPherson has given you his," interrupted Air Force General Harry Anderson.

"Of course," replied the President. "So, Fred... what, *exactly*, are the facts, here? Don't be worried about giving me opinions – nobody's going to keep score, here."

"Getting things wrong and correcting them later, that's the essence of the scientific technique, sir," said McPherson, with a slight smile.

"Anyway," he continued, "What we have now is an unusual impact site... the joint Air Force and NSA team checked hundreds of these, all of which we considered were within the theoretical boundaries of where the alien could have fallen. What we've got at the end of the trajectory for this one, is is a large indent in a boulder, accompanied by the same kinds of burn-marks, where whatever it was that landed, probably ended up. Yet, despite extensive digging, we couldn't find so much of a *trace* of a meteorite at the site. Even if the object shattered upon striking the boulder, there should have been traces of it deposited in the surrounding area. It's as if something crashed to Earth, left a trail of smashed trees and so on in its wake, then just disappeared."

"Or," commented a second military man, "Just got up and walked away."

"I'd remind you, General Anderson," countered McPherson, "That it's entirely possible that the meteorite, or whatever it was that touched down there, was simply consumed in the final collision with the boulder at the head-end of the impact path. There are many well-documented examples of exactly that kind of thing happening."

"Or," intoned the second military man, "It could have been protected by something like a force field, couldn't it have? Mr. President, if I may."

"Sure," replied the President. "Fred, I assume you're finished?"

"More or less, sir," said McPherson.

Anderson got up and paced slowly back and forth, in front of the desk.

"The issue, Mr. President," he stated, "Is that, as Mr. McPherson has so ably explained, we have a great deal of circumstantial evidence, that all points to one, almost undeniable, conclusion."

"Which is?" inquired the President.

"Which is," replied Anderson, calmly and deliberately, "That the alien has landed, and now walks among us."

A gasp, shared by neither McPherson nor the military personnel, issued from the Executive Office functionaries in the back of the room.

"That's *wildly* speculative, General," interrupted McPherson. "We have no proof at all of that hypothesis."

"I thought that you had finished – " shot back the General.

"Fine," complained the Science Advisor.

"The point is, Mr. President, sir," interjected Arthur DeWitt, addressing the American leader, "That in the military, we have to deal with *capabilities*, not *intentions*. If we start from the assumption that the alien may have, indeed, survived the 'Lucifer' incident and may subsequently have landed on Earth – possibly somewhere in our very own United States of America – the Joint Chiefs and I have to consider that we may be faced with a creature of *great* destructive power, with unknown motives and objectives, wandering at large, among us. If that's the case, we have to locate this being, determine its capabilities, then, if possible, neutralize it and keep it in captivity until we can fully understand its intentions. If that's not feasible, we may have to eliminate it and the threat that it represents."

"That's about what I *expected* the military to say, Mr. Secretary," retorted McPherson, icily.

"Mr. Science Advisor," commented Symington, addressing McPherson with an unusual tone of sympathy, "I know how you feel... I spoke directly with her, too – it was the most fascinating experience that I've ever had, there's no doubt about that. And – a move which I sincerely regret, now – I even invited her here to Earth, in those dark days just a few weeks past."

"But," continued the General, "Both you and I have to put our personal feelings aside here and think of what a radically challenging situation this might represent, if this 'Karéin' really *does* have anything even remotely like the amount of power needed to shatter a comet – that's far, far more energy than the biggest H-bomb that we've ever deployed. As a matter of fact, it's probably more than *all* of the United States' nuclear-armed adversaries, put together. No sane person would ever trust an ordinary human being with such destructive power; all they would have to do is have a bad day, lash out for one reason or another, and it could be the end of all of us. Can you, as a scientist, honestly and objectively tell me that you'd want an alien being, with largely unknown goals and motivations, with *that* kind of ability, wandering around the streets of America, completely out of our oversight or control?"

Looking straight ahead, away from Symington, McPherson slowly said, "No, General, I suppose I can't. Although I'd point out that you could say much the same thing about – no offense meant, sir – our own President, with his 'finger on the button', as it were. *That* genie's out of the bottle, for better or worse, and we just have to trust our President to use his powers wisely; maybe now, there's another, bigger genie, that we also have to trust. Maybe not. I don't know. We're way outside the realm of the known, here, I'm afraid. And anyway, this entire discussion is purely hypothetical. There might be impact craters similar to the one that we found in Idaho, all over the world, each of them with a perfectly natural explanation. No landing, no alien, everything back to normal."

The room went silent for a few seconds.

Now, another voice, that of the Vice-President, spoke up. "Mr. President," he said, trying involuntarily to smooth back non-existent hair, "I hate to be the one here to raise the grubby business of the political aspects of all of this, but, as our friend Billy hasn't yet stepped up to the plate, I guess I'll have to."

"Y'all play my part, sir, with my untold gratitude," chimed Horn. "I cede the floor."

The Vice-President smiled, in his usual, unctuous fashion.

"If this creature really *is* here, and if she really *has* dropped out of a nice blue Idaho sky right into the good old U.S. of A.," he suggested, "Maybe could get her on *our* side, you know, pay her whatever she wants to tell the voters that 'we're the ones who rescued her', a few photo-ops and carefully scripted interviews, the whole media baffle-gab thing, we'd sweep the whole damn *country*. Democrats might as well not even show up – we'd have the voting machines, as well as the Supreme Court, locked up tight, and now we'd have the issues, too. They might as well not show up, anyway."

While a few chuckled at the temerity of the proposal, a Brooklyn accent, unheard up to now, interrupted.

"Excuse me, Mr. President," said the short, bow-tied, professorial-looking, elderly man behind the voice, "But there would be *complications* associated with any such strategy, on our part."

"What do you mean, Jacob?" asked the American leader.

"State Department has already received formal requests from every one of the major military powers, and a few lesser ones as well, for us to turn over every last record or detail that we have, related to this Mars-girl, to them," explained Hyndman. "Russians and Chinese in particular have been very demanding, they're saying things like 'we know you have information that you're withholding from us'. I think we have to consider the foreign-policy implications of trying to use this creature, if of course she really exists, for our own purposes – doing so, if we don't try to get the United Nations stamp of approval, might touch off a diplomatic crisis, and it could be far worse if we end up harming her – "

"*Fuck* the United Nations," barked the Vice-President. "This is about *power* – and if we've got her, and they don't, possession's 99 per cent of the law, all it might take is a little wining and dining and we'd have the most powerful weapon in the history of mankind... I'll take that over pandering to the Russkies and the Chinamen, any day."

McPherson's eyes rolled.

"According to what Jacobson and his crew figured out, she's several hundred thousand years old, you know," he protested. "I'm sure she's had a few bribe attempts before, and I'm sure she knows what's typically behind them. And don't think that I'm buying your idea that she's really alive, when I say that."

"That may or may not be the case," retorted the Vice-President. "But she may be more amenable to our kindness, if she's made aware of the other... 'alternatives' that we can offer. The same kind we gave to those guys we captured in Pakistan a few years ago. Remember?"

As several among the crowd winced at the memory, a flat, colorless, male Midwestern voice added, "I think I should remind you, Mr. Vice-President, that CIA has no experience base in punitive interrogation of creatures like this. We have no idea at all of what techniques – "

"Start by breaking her legs," said the Vice-President, coolly. "Always worked for me when I was with Black Ops in Iraq."

"We're aware of that, sir," replied the CIA Director with his own unctuous half-smile, "And I can assure you that we have some very... *advanced* abilities in that department, such that no *human being*, no matter what his or her training or self-control, could withstand for so much as a minute. But, while you're probably right that more... 'primitive' techniques would presumably work on the alien, we have to consider these as only a last resort."

"Could have fooled *me*," interjected the inner-city accent of the HHS Secretary, unhelpfully. "From the way this discussion is going, a lot of us are thinking it's your *first* option."

"Certainly not, Madam," said the CIA Director, "But for operational reasons, not moral ones – morality's something that we can't afford, on our side of the Potomac. In my opinion, Mr. President, it would be very inadvisable to harm or unduly antagonize this being, unless and until we're *absolutely* certain of what its real abilities are – as both Mr. McPherson and the General Staff are both no doubt aware, if this 'Karéin' turns out to have even a small fraction of the destructive powers that have been attributed to her, she could pose an *enormous* risk to our way of life."

Nods and mumbles of agreement came from DeWitt and several members of the uniformed military.

"Far better," continued the Director's dispassionate cant, "To make her comfortable, keep her in a controlled environment, where we can engage in some long-term study, using scientific methods. CIA has, in fact, already prepared a secret facility to be used for this purpose, buried deep underground in the Arizona desert. Our main problem is, unlike others that we have kept in this location, in addition to the question of what coercive and brainwashing techniques would be applicable, we are in uncharted territory on many other fronts... for example, what her primal fears or desires would be, what she might take as payment for services to us, what types of sedatives or other drugs she would respond to, or – "

McPherson, no longer able to contain himself, half-shouted, "You *have* to be joking! A 'threat' that probably doesn't even *exist*, and if it – she – *does*, all we can think about is killing her, or drugging her and putting her in a zoo, or using her to win a few votes, instead of using her to unlock a treasure-trove of scientific knowledge that could otherwise take the human race a *thousand* centuries to learn. I'm terribly ashamed to be hearing what's going on here, and so should *you* be, Mr. President, in all due respect, sir."

"Hear, hear," issued from several in the crowd.

"We've never been ashamed about doin' whatever we desire, to protect the Ew-Nighted States," countered Horn. "Up to and beyond a few late-night sessions that our victims don't walk away from, when we deem it necessary."

"Gentlemen, *gentlemen*," exclaimed the President, motioning for calm, "There's no need for any of us to get worked up about this – let's take a step back, here."

He paused for a moment, eying the Science Adviser, the Secretary of Defense and Anderson in turn.

Then he said, "Now, Arthur, I understand that it's your job to assume the worst, but Fred *has* a point – there's no doubt that this 'Hill whatever-the-number-was Anomaly' thing is suspicious, but we shouldn't jump to conclusions, at least not until we have hard evidence, that is, a little green woman showing up at a 7-11 somewhere, or something like that – "

The tension in the room eased a bit, as a few giggled at this *bon mot*.

"However," continued the President, "At the same time, we still have to think through what we'd do, in that admittedly unlikely situation. As well as how we're going to find out what the truth is, one way or another. So, I'm going to direct the Science Office and the joint DoD and Homeland Intelligence Task Force to undertake an intensive search for any traces of the alien, starting with the impact site – "

"Already underway, sir," interjected Anderson. "Nothing to report, I'm afraid. Other than the tracks that were mentioned earlier, that is."

"Okay," noted the President. "But keep me informed of any developments, even minor ones – Fred, you have to appreciate that the Arthur and the Joint Chiefs *do* have a point, too... if and when something *does* turn up, we are going to be faced with a potentially explosive situation, so I want as much advance warning as possible of it coming to pass. And I agree with both the Vice-President and the Secretary of State, even if they're saying the same thing for different reasons; it's going to be much more difficult to manage this situation, if the word gets out that this creature is here and in the United States."

"So," ordered the U.S. leader, "In the event that we do locate this 'Karéin', dead or alive, I want both the fact of her presence, and the whole operation, kept *absolutely* secret – Billy, I'm putting you and Jerry Kaysten in charge of a suitable cover-story for the press, you know, 'plausible deniability', that kind of thing. If it looks like anybody from the media gets on to what's happening, I want him or her placed in preventative detention, and that goes for any other ordinary citizens that might have had contact with the alien... the less people know about all of this, until we figure out how we're going to cope with it, the better. We can use the cover-story for this new weapon that I went on TV to talk about, to justify the disappearances. Just make sure that whomever we pick up, is kept in comfortable surroundings."

The President paused to think for a moment and then commanded, "In that context, Arthur, I want it clearly understood by you and the Joint Chiefs, and CIA, too, that *no* move is to be made against this creature, without my *express* permission – *if* she does still exist, and *if* she has, God knows how, survived the fall to Earth, and *if* she is amongst us, and *if* you somehow do find her, I want you to keep track of her, but do not under *any* circumstances try to capture or attack her, until we have had a chance to try to communicate with her. You got that?"

"Understood and acknowledged, Mr. President, sir," said the Secretary of Defense.

"Yes, sir," replied the CIA Director, in his characteristic monotone.

"Then I think we're done, aren't we?" concluded the President, not expecting an answer, as the throng of his courtiers and subordinates filed silently out of the Cabinet Room.

Just into the corridor, after DeWitt had gone his separate way, Symington turned to Anderson and mentioned, "Well, we've got our orders now, don't we?"

"Certainly," replied the General, "And you can be sure that we'll be implementing them... *creatively*. The President's the C in C, of course; but it's *our* job to defend the country, and sometimes in the heat of battle, well, we have to make things up as we go, make split-second decisions, don't we?"

"Yes, *sir*," echoed Symington, as he straightened his four-star hat and continued silently down the corridors of the White House.

Ghost In The Barracks

Stalking silently through the night as a phantom from some half-remembered dream, the newcomer guided herself swiftly from room to room inside the "Daughters of the Faith" building, as the Klan-folk had named it.

With relief, the fallen-girl noted that her sense of smell was no longer being overwhelmed by the odors of the ragged, never-cleaned clothes that she had worn since falling to this world, nor by the heady smells of hundreds of bodies equally unwashed.

She had not protested when they ordered her to remove this uniform from she-knew-not-where and had then marched her into the showers, along with Claremont and a hundred or so new "recruits for the faith", as the church-woman had called them. A sense of relief had come upon studying the others, as it was apparent that she was anatomically identical to the females who inhabited this place.

Without cause, they would keep us captive, mused the young-looking female, *But they gave us clean new clothes – plain gray, but comfortable, none the less – and did not force themselves upon us, at least not yet. More than many others would have done for me, in ages and places long ago and far away...*

This building, despite having been hastily constructed over a few short days, still had an elaborate system of interior doors, each checked every ten minutes or so by a male, uniformed guard, in the corridor that connected all the rooms together.

Silently, the fallen-girl waited in the shadows, no more than an ethereal shadow herself, as the guard passed by; then, she quietly opened the door to the last room that Claremont could have been in.

Invisible to human eyes except for perhaps a brief ripple in the air – hard enough to see, in daylight, well-nigh *impossible*, in this benighted place – she made haste from cot to cot, silently thanking those who snored for the covering noise.

Finally, the newcomer encountered a covered figure, whose size and shape was a perfect match. She lightly pulled back the blanket by a few inches and tapped twice on the somnolent woman's exposed head.

"Whaaa..." grunted an African-American woman, in an unfamiliar voice, as she slowly arose, propping up her fore-body by outstretched arms behind.

The woman looked straight at the girl-called-'Sari', and groggily requested, "Anybody there?"

Then the woman looked side to side, uncertainly.

"Who touch me?" she demanded, again looking right at, but not seeing, the fallen-girl.

"Ain't nobody there? Damn, ah thought... *shit,* must be seein' things. Come on, Charlene, better get yo'self some sleep."

The woman reclined, pulled the covers back over her head and closed her eyes.

Curse it, thought the fallen-girl, *I did not smell her aura correctly – yet another thing that does not work the way it should, down here. But at least she did not see enough of me to raise an alarm... where* is *Whitney?*

More cautiously now, her feet alternatively tip-toed and floated across the plywood-planked floor, as the fallen-girl examined sleeping figure after figure. Finally, three from the last cot, she came upon another well-blanketed shape that looked very similar to Claremont's body dimensions.

The one-called-'Sari' leaned over, concentrating, trying to match mental patterns.

I forgot how difficult that this is to do, when they are sleeping, she reflected. *Their thoughts do not smell like the ones they have when they are awake.*

It was as close a match as she was likely to get. The fallen-girl tapped the sleeping woman's head, twice.

Instantly, a familiar face sat up and said, softly but still too loud for comfort, "Sari, girl? Y'all there? Can't see *nothin',* girl, where y'all hidin'?"

"Shhh," intoned the fallen-girl, as she slowly dropped her light-bending cloak, coming slowly into view as does the image of a lens being brought into focus.

"You will wake someone up," she cautioned.

Her eyes staring with astonishment, Claremont gasped, "Oh mah *Lawd,* girl, them kids wasn't *kiddin',* was they? What the hell *is* you, girl, some kinda ghost or somethin'?"

"Not a ghost," whispered back the one-called-'Sari', "I am *quite* alive. But if we keep talking like this we soon might *not* be, if we alert a guard. Come next to me, take my hand, Whitney. And remember, when I use my hiding-trick, you will have a hard time seeing things. Just let me lead you, oh-kay?"

"Yeah... shore, okay," stammered Claremont, *sotto voce,* as she stood up, quickly donning the cheapish slip-on running shoes that had been issued to the women of the facility.

The girl known as 'Sari' took the black woman's hand, smiling warmly and whispering, "Here we go... what do they say down here... ah, yes. 'Lights out', and no talking."

Claremont saw the surroundings, already dimly lit but still easily visible to a fully opened human iris, quickly fade to near total blackness, with only the dim edges of something-or-other at all discernible.

"I will lead, you follow – little steps, one by one," whispered the fallen-girl, as they clumsily navigated between the sleeping-cots, stopping momentarily to see if the 'creek' sound of the inner door awoke anyone; but, fortunately, it did not seem to.

Both of the fugitives tiptoed towards the fire-exit door at the back of the building, and, once almost upon it, the one called 'Sari' turned, and said quietly, "Now *this* is the only, ahh, 'tricky' part... the door is not locked, but there is an armed guard outside. I will push the door open, and when it does, you and I must make haste to go down the steps from the back door as quickly as possible – we do so in no more than two or three seconds, before he has time to turn around and start up the steps himself. Take hold of my waist and match me, pace by pace. We will continue until we are far outside the military compound, too far for their looking-glasses to see us. And remember, it will be even darker outside, you will hardly be able to see *anything*. Oh-kay?"

"Got no choice, Missy," muttered Claremont. "Ah guess we screw up, we get shot... normally ah not do that for anythin', but this is for mah *kids*, so ah 'spose it worth the risk. Go ahead, ghost-girl."

The fallen-girl led the woman to the door, until both of them were almost flat against it. Then, without any apparent effort, the portal swung wide open, casting a beam of interior light out upon the wooden steps and Prairie grass beyond.

Instantly, Claremont and her rescuer hurried down the stairs, almost reaching the bottom one before the guard had even a chance to turn his head to notice the breach.

"What the – " exclaimed a guard, staring at the doorway, now behind the two.

"Sisters? If you're in there, you should *know* it's past curfew – if the commandant catches you sneaking out to smoke – "

This be crazy, thought Claremont, as she dutifully marched behind the fallen-girl. *He* gots to *see us, if just from the shadow –*

But, unknown to the black woman, the guard was now behind them too, investigating the activating-latch on the door.

"Psst, Sari girl, how we doin' – " whispered Claremont.

"Shh!" shot back the girl, as quietly as possible. "We are still close..."

"Who's *that*?" suddenly shouted the guard, turning to look out into the dark wilderness.

Claremont would have panicked, would have broken with the one-called-'Sari' to run off in any direction, but, somehow, she could not; she tried to move her lips, to make a sound, but, as if silenced by some weird drug, neither a peep nor a whisper came out.

The guard said a few curses, confusedly scanned the surroundings two or three times, then closed the door and, automatic rifle at the side, resumed his post.

On they continued, further and further, up one hillock and down another, then another. Then, finally, the fallen-girl announced, still quietly but no longer whispering, "I think that you will be safe here, Whitney, but try not to make too much noise, and stay low."

The surrounding landscape, at least, that much of it that any human being could see in the unlit darkness, faded into view. They were on the safe side of a small gully, with a row of uneven terrain between it and the compound.

Claremont rubbed her eyes.

"Curtis was right, that was *dread*, girl," she intoned. "Can't still see but *shit*, guess it just dark here, well, *naturally* dark. Listen, girlie... y'all *gots* to tell me how y'all does that."

"Why must I tell you, Whitney?" guardedly answered the fallen-girl. "Why can you not just accept my gift?"

"Because doin' that ain't *normal*, ain't accordin' to God's law," retorted the black woman. "Ah only knowed one person who could ever do things like that, never met any else in thirty-seven years –"

"Who?" interjected the newcomer, with a tone of unexpected joy. "*Who* is like me? Where are they? Can you get me to them?"

"Was mah grandmother, on mah mother's side," answered Claremont. "Voodoo. That was how she do it. She could make things appear, and go away, out of thin air..."

"Voo-doo?" inquired the fallen-girl. "What is that? A religion, a temple?"

"Black magic," explained Claremont. "The *old* magic, from the bayou, down by N'Orleans. As old as Mother Earth herself, and against the teachin's of God and Jesus; although, Grand-Mere Rubie always tell me, she still went to church, and she was buried a Christian, none the less."

A look of terrible disappointment appeared on the fallen-girl's face.

"Magic – even worse, the Black Arts," she groaned. "No kin of mine," she added, quietly and dejectedly.

"Hear that a *lot*, before, Missie," consoled Claremont, sympathetically. "But we don' choose our kin, y'all knows that... we get whatever the good Lawd choose *for* us. Neways, y'all better get goin' – y'all gonna be late to pick up the kids."

"Yes... of course, the children," replied the one-called-'Sari'. "I must make haste. It cannot be more than a few minutes to midnight."

"And, Sari..." started Claremont.

"Yes, Whitney?" answered the fallen-girl.

"They all ah *gots*, y'understand?" implored Claremont. "Please, *please*, keep 'em safe. Even if y'all can't get 'em out... ah wants to see them again, so *bad*, but if it too hard... ah'll understand why."

The black woman was taken aback by the fearsome aspect that now illuminated the newcomer's face, glowing plainly in the Stygian blackness all around.

"Woe betide the fool," she weirdly growled, "Who knows not who I am, and who lays so much as a *finger*, upon those who I love."

Then she faded completely from sight, leaving a half-awed companion, waiting silently in the starlit Prairie night.

Sword Of Freedom

"Karlie," complained the big, muscular trucker as he finished the last of his first cup of coffee, "Can't you switch that damn thing to some sports, or somethin' else? Guys on the CB told me that NBA's back in business... or was it NCAA, can't remember, but whatever, it's *gotta* be better than that talkin' head stuff."

A husky voice from elsewhere in the room added, "Both of 'em, I hear. Bask'tboll, anyways. NFL and baseball, no dice... stadiums are wrecked, they say. So ya gotta just watch them hoops, pardner."

"Love to, Verge," replied the waitress, as she poured the man's refill. "But Ossie says some kinda big thing's comin' on in a few minutes, maybe even tha President. He said we could put on whatever ya like when its done. Hey, I forgot, just black fer you, right?"

"Yeah, nothin' in it," the trucker grunted. "And probably nothin' in the speech, either. Been twenty years since I heard them stuffed shirts say anythin' that mattered to me."

"What was that?" idly asked the waitress, while clearing a table.

"Rebate on diesel," answered the trucker, to chuckles from the left and right at the lunch counter.

"Hey, you *gringos*, hold it down there, will you," interrupted Jiminez, wiping his hands on his apron as he appeared suddenly from behind the swinging doors leading to the restaurant's kitchen.

"I think it's on in a minute. Yeah. Karlie, turn it up, *por favor*."

"Ossie, yer more of a patriotic American than I or my buddies are, ya know," cracked the trucker. "I don't pay those guys any attention."

"I *have* to be, Veer-jil", responded Jiminez. "You *gringos* don't have to worry about being thrown in jail, just because you speak English with an accent. Since they passed that *carajo* law – "

"Shh!" motioned the waitress. "I think he's on now."

Fifteen or more pairs of eyes now focused on the nano-LED television screen – not the latest holographic gimmicks in it, but a good, clear, picture, none the less – that Jiminez had propped up uneasily in the top-left corner of the demi-roof covering the restaurant's lunch-counter, a week or two after he had originally bought the place.

They beheld the elongated, gray-haired, clean-shaven, blue-suit business-executive face of the President, sitting in the familiar confines of the Oval Office, more or less as those with the least interest in politics had seen many times before.

"Greetings, fellow Americans," sounded the familiar, fatherly voice of the man. "This is the President speaking."

Pausing for a brief second to absorb the lines passing invisibly in front of him on the teleprompter, the President said, "By the grace of almighty God and by the valiant efforts of America's armed forces – I'll have more to say on that, in a few minutes – as you all know by now, the 'Lucifer' comet that only a few days ago threatened the entire human race with extinction, has been destroyed."

"I should tell you, however," he went on, "That despite our triumph over this menace, our nation has, none the less, suffered from the after-effects of this incident. Although the comet itself *was*, indeed, destroyed, some of the resulting parts of it that fell into the atmosphere were large enough to cause widespread devastation."

He paused again, this time for effect, then explained, "I must tell you that St. Louis, Los Angeles, Boston, Spokane, Detroit and Des Moines have all suffered various amounts of 'Lucifer'-related damage, while Boise and Memphis have sustained much more serious impacts; these two urban areas have been almost completely destroyed, as have also been other cities, elsewhere in the world. Our thoughts and prayers go out to all Americans who have had loved ones lost or injured. Our emergency measures and reconstruction forces are working day and night to provide comfort and assistance to citizens in all of the affected areas, especially south-western Tennessee and western Idaho. We ask for your patience, as we undertake these measures, as the United States has, with the 'Lucifer' incident, encountered the greatest natural disaster that we have ever faced."

The American leader stated, "In the meantime, we ask all of you to comply with the federal and state authorities in your area as they try to repair damaged infrastructure such as roads, power grids and phone lines. Due to factors beyond the government's control, we will have to maintain martial law in some areas, for the foreseeable future and, be aware that the police and National Guard *will* strictly enforce the law. Organized criminal activity, especially gang activity, will not be tolerated and will be swiftly and effectively suppressed, with 'shoot-to-kill' rules in effect where called for. We expect the economy and road system to be back to normal in six months to a year, with everyone's co-operation; Social Security payments will be re-started in the next week and you should be able to access your bank-accounts by early next month. We will overcome this challenge, working together, as Americans always do."

"He talkin' about a different country?" joked one trucker, from the back of the room.

"Shhh!" shot back the waitress.

The President continued, "Now, as I mentioned earlier, I think it is important that all Americans understand what happened in the last hours and minutes leading up to the destruction of 'Lucifer'. For reasons of national security, we had decided not to reveal this information before, but lately, it has become apparent that a number of negative and misleading rumors regarding the event have become increasingly widespread. So the Cabinet and I believe that it's important that all of you have the facts."

"And the truth is," – he coughed slightly, then continued talking – "That although the heroic, self-sacrificing attacks launched by thousands of our airmen, sailors and soldiers undoubtedly helped, the ultimate destruction of 'Lucifer' was accomplished by America's use of a previously secret weapon, one of far greater destructive power than we have ever previously revealed. Some of you saw it in action; what I'm referring to here is the 'bright light' that you saw approaching the comet, just before it was destroyed."

"Wow," exclaimed someone, to a chorus of gasps from around the room.

"We got us a *death ray!*" triumphantly shouted another guy.

The President elaborated, "This weapon, which was jointly developed by NASA and the Air Force, using the best minds and resources available, has been named 'Sword of Freedom'. Now, as I'm sure you can appreciate, I'm not at liberty to explain exactly how 'Sword of Freedom' works, except to say that it leverages techniques that are quite different, and obviously much more powerful, than those employed by any of the devices in our current nuclear arsenal."

Stopping for a second to take a breath, he said, "As to why we did not reveal 'Sword of Freedom' earlier, there were a number of reasons, but mainly, not only was the weapon experimental – we were not sure that it would actually work – but also, if we were to have tested it prior to 'Lucifer's arrival, the resulting explosion might have caused almost as much devastation as the comet itself. I want to take this opportunity to assure both our allies – and our potential adversaries – that the United States pledges only to use this weapon as a last resort, to further the goals of freedom and liberty that we all hold so dear."

"Yeah, *sure,*" commented a trucker. "Just like the gangsta' with the biggest gun uses *his.*"

"Yee-ha! America, on top again!" exclaimed another. "Gotta *love* it! Look out, you Paki bagh – "

"Will you just *listen,* Billy-Ray?" pleaded the waitress.

"I also want to assure everyone listening to this broadcast," stated the President, "That we will neither threaten anyone with our 'Sword of Freedom', nor will we share this potentially devastating technology with any other nation or group, lest it be used inappropriately. To that end, I have imposed a total communications blackout regarding 'Sword of Freedom'; your government will neither answer any questions from this point forward regarding the weapon, nor will we allow anyone involved in its development to return to civilian life. Anyone who has worked on "Sword of Freedom' will be well looked-after in one of several private, high-security facilities that the government has established, so if someone near to you has to leave suddenly when asked to by Federal agents, please be assured that nothing bad is happening, only that they are, necessarily, being affected by this security measure."

"Doesn't the Pledge of Allegiance say that they can't do that? What about the... uh... Const-, Constitu-, whatever that is," whispered the waitress.

"They can do anything they *want, señorita*," whispered Jiminez, back to her. "Ask any immigrant who gets caught without his *Carte Rojo y Blanco*, these days."

Semi-simultaneously, a voice from somewhere in the back of the room muttered, "Or ask anybody who gets caught puttin' movies off NeoNet on his cell-phone... my brother's doin' twenty-five years in the State House for that, didn't even get a *trial*, told him some shit about 'summary conviction by the Recording Industry Defense Council' –"

"Shhh!" demanded Carlie.

The U.S. leader went on, "I know that it's a great sacrifice that we are asking the scientists and Armed Forces personnel involved to make, but we simply cannot take even a slight chance that a hostile power or group might gain access to a power that could conceivably destroy our entire planet. We will retain the weapon only as a safeguard against, God forbid, the appearance of another dangerous comet or meteor. My fellow Americans, I know that many of you may have questions about this subject, but, for everyone's own good, you will just have to trust us here. There is no other way, if we are all to stay safe."

"Heard it all before," muttered a guy at the lunch counter. "'Trust me, I'm from the government...'"

"So, in summary," said the President, "Each and every person on the face of our planet, should know that he or she owes his or her life to the selfless bravery of America's armed forces. We seek no special advantage or privilege for this great accomplishment; all we ask is that the other nations and peoples of the world not try to duplicate the 'Sword of Freedom', lest this awesome power fall into the wrong hands. Should anyone attempt to do this, the United States must reserve the right to take appropriate measures to safeguard both ourselves, and the rest of the human race, from the danger of an arms-race with this extremely dangerous type of technology."

"Didn't work for the nukes," commented another trucker, in a Southern drawl. "Damn Rooshins and Injuns is probably workin' on same thing right now. Chinks 'n Japs, too. Even them Frenchies."

Jiminez nodded, affirmatively. "Just a matter of time, *señor*," he remarked, quietly. "Just a matter of time. Like the last *ultima* weapon."

The waitress looked on, worriedly.

"My fellow Americans," concluded the President, "After the defeat of 'Lucifer', we, and the rest of the world, have a historic opportunity to put the divisions of the past behind us, as we rebuild our economy to be even bigger and better than before, safe in the knowledge that America again has unquestioned military superiority over any potential adversary. We will use our power wisely, to ensure peace, freedom and prosperity for all. God Bless each and every one of you, and God Bless America."

The man's picture faded from the screen, as the seal of the Presidency conversely slowly made its own appearance.

"Glad *that's* over with," grunted the beefy trucker at the lunch counter, throwing back the last of his coffee with a half-grimace at the taste of the dregs of the stuff.

"Karlie," he complained, "Can ya just give us the ball-game now, and some *fresh* coffee for a change, instead of this junk?"

The waitress sighed, as she grabbed the cup from the table and headed for the kitchen.

"Ossie," she sighed, "It's Verge, again. Fetch me another bag o' beans."

Came For One, Left With Two

Now the one-called-'Sari' was next to the building with the sign saying "Children-of-God", hiding in the shadows, calculating her options.

With interest she observed that, unlike the military compound several hundred meters off in the distance towards the road, neither this building, nor the other two, were that well-guarded; there were, indeed, a few gendarmes patrolling here and there, but evidently her erstwhile captors had not counted on large-scale disobedience, or attempts to escape. There had been many more soldiers outside the tent in which they had previously stayed; these must now have been berthed somewhere else.

Thus as always, she reflected, *the power to control their own destinies lies within them, but they have not the will to use it. The strange bond between those who rule and those who are trod upon.*

But children, at least, cannot be blamed for doing as they are told, she thought, while considering the plan of action to free Claremont's two. She had had the advantage of already being inside the first building when she rescued the mother, but here, she would have to both break in and break out.

Ordinarily I would just wait until someone came normally in to or out of the building, then just follow them, mused the young-looking female, *but there does not seem to be much movement and this night I do not have the luxury of time. I will have to steal in.*

Carefully studying the building, she forced her eyes – at the price of slight, transitory discomfort – to use the special-seeing that showed the warmer places distinctly from the rest of the scene. But the ability gave no hint of how to enter;

there was a door at the front, another at the rear, and there were a few windows high enough on the walls to be at least a meter over her head, but otherwise the place was sealed tight.

An unrequited thought arose from the un-remembered depths of her psyche.

Use thy mind to tear it open, to rend the wooden planks apart, it suggested. *Or burn a hole through. Use the stare, the glare when everything shines and that upon which thou gaze, melts and burns. Nothing can withstand thee!*

For a trice, the newcomer stood silently in the dark, benumbed, perplexed.

What dream speaks this to me? she wondered.

What nightmare?

The sound of a door slamming shut inside the building snapped the fallen-girl out of her reverie, returning her eyes to the practice of seeing as humans do.

She resolved to try the window, pushing her body against a nearby storage-crate. Something rattled within it, and instantly she stopped. Fortunately, after a minute or so of waiting, without any sign of guards, the girl was able to resume moving the object, more slowly and carefully, until it was directly below the window.

This would be risky, as she would have to stand out of the shadows. Instinctively she raised her dark-cloak, trying to force it only around the back side of her body, so that she could use all of her seeing-powers to survey what was inside the window.

Her gaze, switching back and forth between the human-seeing, the warm-seeing, as well as between two or three other types of illumination, revealed a scene of perhaps a hundred children lying on cots; all girls, apparently, ranging from no more than toddler age to a few teenagers.

The one-called-'Sari' tried to open the window, but it did not budge. She applied all her strength to it, but realized that it was locked from the inside – a strange way to keep a jail, but then, any child who managed to open the thing would have been confronted by a dangerously long drop to the ground outside, absent the crate upon which the fallen-girl was now standing.

Frustrated, she now stole quietly around to the front doorway. Hiding again in the shadows, she tried the latch, but the door was again locked from the inside, and even though she could hear its gears and could sense how they worked, she had no way of moving or manipulating them.

I cannot lock on to the little latches and catches, she mused, in frustration. *The mind-hand force is not working, either... even for something this small. How feeble am I!*

The young-looking female crept away, circumnavigating the building, looking desperately for some other way in.

The inner instinct-strategy voice came back.

Just leap into the air, fly like a night-bird to the top of the roof, it counseled.

Motivated by she knew not what, the 'Sari'-girl took three quick steps and leaped upwards, latent instincts urging her on.

She landed, fortunately upright, with a soft 'thump' about a meter or so further forward, irrationally disappointed but not really surprised, and just stood there, enveloped in a dull mantle of ennui and confusion, for many long seconds.

Who am *I*, she silently cried, *that I dare such impossible things.*

Eventually, she tried the back door. It was locked, as well.

Curses, she reflected. *They leave the doors to a jail for adults wide open, but lock those for children. Perhaps*, she mused, *adults have a better appreciation of what punishments await those who try to escape.*

But the one-called-'Sari' could not abandon this quest, so again she stood upon the crate, forcing her cloak into a hemisphere over her back, but open at the front, facing the window.

She tapped on the portal; once; twice; thrice.

Suddenly, a young Hispanic girl's face appeared, staring with surprise, on the other side of the window.

The child turned to the others, still evidently sleeping, and whispered, rather more loudly than necessary, "Hey, there's a *lady* at the window!"

A couple of other children grunted.

The fallen-girl heard one of them say something about "Full of sh..."

She tapped again, and whispered, "Little child – little girl – open the window for me, if you please. I mean no harm."

But the child just stood there and stared.

Again, the 'Sari'-girl requested, "Please, little one... open it for me. The lock, the latch."

She pointed at the locking-mechanism at the bottom of the window-pane. After an agonizingly long few seconds – being acutely aware that from the outside, although her figure would certainly not be discernible, the window-area would look different from its normal appearance – the child inside seemed to understand and started to fiddle with the apparatus.

Now, two more children, a fair-haired one of perhaps five and an African-American one maybe twice that age, had arisen from their cots, to see what was going on.

"You gonna get in *trouble* with the Mistress, Serena," whispered the black girl.

"She looks like a nice lady, though," argued the Caucasian child.

"Where are the lights and the stars?" asked another voice. "Is it really *that* dark outside?"

The one-called-'Sari' heard a 'click'. She applied her strength to the window and, to her immense relief, felt it immediately give way, manhandling it upwards. She moved effortlessly up to the window-sill, propelling herself inside the room as would a gymnast showing off a well-practiced routine.

The fallen-girl now stood among the children, her cloak instinctively vanishing as she entered the building, her eyes repeatedly blinking between the inside door and the figures before and all around her.

"*Wow*, lady," said the fair-haired child. "Your eyes are really nice and *shiny*."

"Hi, children," replied the newcomer, in as friendly a voice as she could muster. "My name is 'Sari', and I have come here looking for two children, who were taken away from me. Do you know where I might find them?"

"You not *s'posed* to be in here, lady," whispered the Hispanic girl. "If they catch you, they'll be mad. *Really* mad."

"I know it," replied the one-called-'Sari', crouching in front of the child, smiling and hoping that her incisors were still behaving and staying put. "Which is why I am trusting all of you to keep my being here, a secret, just for us to know. Oh-kay?"

"Okay, I guess," said the little blond girl, her eyes still staring solemnly.

"Missy, your kids, what they names?" requested the black girl.

"Curtis Ray and Melissa Arlene," the fallen-girl replied. "Claremont, that is. That is their – uhh – clan-name – I mean, their last name, their... fam... fam... *family* name, yes, that is it."

"Hah," snickered the black girl, trying to suppress the loudness of her giggle.

"Well, Melissa, she snorin' in the last bed near the wall of this here room," she said, pointing to the far left corner of the room, "Ah had to whack her three time with mah pillow to get her to roll over."

"Oh, that is *wonderful!*" softly exclaimed the one-called-'Sari'. "But what about Curtis? Is he here?"

"No, lady," interjected the Hispanic girl. "They don't let boys and girls be together. He's in one of the other rooms... I guess."

"I see," replied the fallen-girl. "Well, I had better wake Melissa, I suppose."

Walking lightly over the floor to the far corner, she left the three young girls staring in her direction as she side-saddled onto the bed and gently tapped the figure of Claremont's daughter on the shoulder.

"Go... *away*, Shameeka," muttered the teenager, groggily. "Ah ain't snorin' no more."

"Melissa, it's *me*," countered the 'Sari'-girl, patiently. "Remember – I *promised* that I would come for you."

Now the Claremont child sat up straight, staring in amazement.

"Who – what – oh, man, it y'all, Sari – that really y'all?" she exclaimed, excitedly. "How y'all get *in* here? This whole place locked *tight!*"

"*Shhh*," admonished the young-looking female. "There is already too much noise as it is – "

"Mistress comin'!" warned the voice of a seven-or-so year-old girl whose ear was at the door.

As the children rushed quickly back to their cots, Melissa turned to the fallen-girl and worriedly whispered, "Sari, where y'all gonna *hide* – ain't nowhere 'round here, y'all too big to even fit under mah bed –"

"Do not worry about me," reassured the newcomer, "Just make sure that whoever comes in, does not take special notice of you. I must find Curtis, then I will come back and get both you and him out of here. Oh-kay?"

"Okay, ah guess," reluctantly replied Melissa, as she pulled up the covers and lay down her head. "It *yo'* life, not mine... sorry, didn't mean it that way, Miz Sari..."

"No problem," answered the one-called-'Sari'. "I will hide, now."

She scanned around and went to the largest natural shadow that she could find, standing straight up against the wall behind the young Claremont's cot.

The fallen-girl activated her dark-cloak.

A ray of light entered the room as the door opened with a '*creekkk*' sound, followed by the thump of adult feet and a second ray, that of a flashlight.

"Child-REN!", boomed out a commanding, matronly voice. "You were *clearly* told, 'no talking after lights out time', but I heard voices from in here – remember, Lord Jesus will punish naughty little girls who disobey their Mistress with the strap on your bare bottoms... now won't he?"

The one-called-'Sari' heard a few giggles, but, evidently, they were too soft for the intruding woman's ears.

"Well," continued the woman's voice, "I had better *not* find any of you out of their beds, and no talking – I *mean* it."

The matron started walking down the center aisle between the two double rows of cots. Halfway towards the far end of the room, she stopped.

"What's *this*?" she shouted. "*Who* of you opened the window! It's *strictly* against the rules! I sincerely hope that none of you have tried to escape – "

The woman hurried over to the window and looked down, not looking behind to see a shimmer, a slightly-darker-than-all-else shadow, briefly interrupt the light from the door as it slipped noiselessly out into the hallway.

"Someone moved that under the window... but still too far for a child to jump," the woman muttered.

"Alright!" she ordered, producing a clipboard and pen from her side. "Lights on. Everybody out of bed. I need to make sure that *all* of you are still here."

While the youngsters in the first room that she had entered, sounded off one by one, the one-called-'Sari' – or, rather, an all-but-invisible *facsimile* of the same – stole down the hallway, listening for a second or two at each door for the sounds of sleeping children.

At the third door down the hall, the fallen-girl stopped, comparing what she heard here with the sounds that had come, a few minutes earlier, through the window.

It was a match.

The newcomer opened the unlocked inner door as little as possible – just enough to let her slim, lithe figure sneak through – and came inside, dropping the dark-cloak as she transitioned from the lit hallway to the unlit sleeping-quarters.

"You want us to get up, now?" offered a groggy boy's voice. "But it's still *dark* outside, Miss Mistress, ma'am..."

"Shhh," responded the 'Sari'-girl. "I am not one of the ladies who run this place. I am just a friend of Curtis Ray Claremont – I have come to get him out of here. Do you know where he is sleeping?"

"Who? Curtis?" replied the boy, propping up his half-somnolent head on a palm and elbow.

"No, sorry, I don't know anybody like that, lady," he mentioned. "Is Curtis *your* boy? But you had better be careful – they told us that if our Moms and Dads tried to come in here, they'd give both them and us a whipping, fifty strokes each. One kid who talked back to them got the strap five times on both sides of his face, and it was a real big man usin' it, blood all *over* the place, they hauled him out in front of everybody so we'd all learn a lesson, that's what they said... that kid was cryin' a *long* time, tonight."

Pausing for a short second to take this all in, the one-called-'Sari' replied, "No, I am not Curtis' mother – I am just a, uhh... *friend*. And they will not be able to do *that* to him, or to me, *that* is for sure. I will look for him... you just go back to sleep, oh-kay?"

"Yeah, okay, lady, but if they ask, I didn't talk to you, you understand?" answered the boy.

The fallen-girl nodded as she turned around, raising a vestige of her cloak, just enough to blur the outline of her figure while hurrying from bed to bed, trying to smell the Claremont boy's sleeping thoughts.

One row of cots... two... three...

She had now reached the window. The whole room had been checked, but there was no Curtis.

The young-looking female quietly exited the room, hastening to the next door. It, too, seemed to lead to a sleeping-chamber.

Following the same procedure, slipping into this second place with the stealth of a stalking feline, here, fortunately, she did not wake any of the boys. She went from cot to cot, bending over each to feel the thoughts of the sleeping children therein, but there was still no sign of the Claremont boy.

Her mind calculated the hour. Panic began to sink in.

Where is *he*, she mused. *I saw him taken here, with the other boys; there were only two sleeping-rooms, for the girls, and I have already checked the two for the boys...*

Again en-cloaked, the fallen-girl crept down the hall towards the front door. Almost at this portal, she heard a faint, muffled whimper from a door to her right, bolted from the outside to prevent egress from the room beyond it.

She stopped and concentrated, straining to smell the thoughts from this inappropriate distance.

Very faint, but it feels like... she reflected, as the mundane sense of smell was confronted by an unpleasant odor, at the same time.

Hesitantly, the young-looking female said softly, "Curtis?"

"Yo, Sari! That *y'all?* Oh, man, ah thought y'all *never* come," exclaimed a voice from behind the door.

"*Shhh*," warned the fallen-girl. "You are Curtis, Curtis Claremont, correct? What are you doing in there, away from the other boys?"

"Shore am," replied the boy's voice. "Got put in here for bein' two seconds late to line up, when they get us ready for bedtime. That, and a worse lickin' than ah *ever* got from Momma. So, y'all gonna let me out?"

"Right now," confirmed the 'Sari'-girl, quickly undoing the bolt and opening the door.

As she slipped inside the room and closed the door, to her dismay, she beheld not only the Claremont boy, but also *another* young male child who might have been a bit older than Curtis, one with tan skin, dark, straight hair and slightly slanted eyelids.

A handsome young lad... his mind smells honest and noble, she reflected. *I envy his parents... no, more than that... voices, what say ye, now?*

The second boy, who had evidently been crying not two seconds before, rubbed the tears from his eyes, looked at Claremont and asked, "Curtis, is this your Mom? You never told me you were adopted."

For a second, the 'Sari'-girl just stood there, nonplussed.

Then she replied, "No, I... uhh... am not Curtis' mother; I am just... 'Sari'. That is, I am a friend of Whitney, who *is* Curtis' mother."

"Yeah, that right – but Sari, we gonna get goin', now?" requested the African-American boy. "Ah'm sick of this place, and ah gots to pee. Don' want to use that bucket in the corner. 'Specially after Tommy puked in it."

"Tommy?" inquired the fallen-girl, in the second boy's direction.

"Tommy Singing-Bird George, that's my name, Ma'am," explained the brown-skinned boy. "Got put in here for talking back to the Mistress. Didn't *mean* to throw up, honest, lady, but I never got beat up really bad, before. Well, okay, maybe once or twice by my Daddy on the reserve, but not like they did to me, today..."

He paused, then quietly added, while looking at his feet, "Guess I just can't take it... Uncle always said I was just a runt, never amount to much..."

"You should not have had to 'take' *anything*," immediately consoled the fallen-girl, sympathetically, bending over the second boy. "Hurting those who cannot fight back, is the mark of cowardice and unworthiness, not strength or merit. And putting a stop to such things, is my special vocation."

For a second, a far-off look appeared on her face, and she repeated, as if in a trance, "To bring them to the Fire, to the Light... yes – *that* is why I am here, I know..."

Shaking her head in an apparent effort to clear her mind, she demanded, "But anyway, Curtis, we must be going."

"Yah!" chimed the Claremont boy. "Okay, Tommy, y'all get up, and stay right next to me –"

"Now, *wait* a minute, Curtis," reprimanded the one-called-'Sari'. "I came in here to rescue *you*, and Melissa, then Bob Billings – I already have your mother waiting outside. But *him* – sorry, Tommy – he was *never* part of the plan. I am afraid that your friend will have to stay behind."

"Uh-uhh," retorted the boy. "Either he come with me, or ah don' go. He my friend, y'all know, mah homie, Miz Sari; and where ah comes from, we don' *never* leave our homies behind. *Never*."

"Curtis," pleaded the fallen-girl, "Please, try to *understand* – I cannot... besides, where are his *parents?* Are they not also in here? It would be shameful to remove him from his kin, and besides, I cannot rescue *everybody* in this camp!"

"No *way*," dug in the Claremont kid, folding his arms defiantly in front of him.

"My Mom's back on the reserve, over the state line," commented Tommy. "Dad's there too, but they don't live together... I don't see my Dad that much. I was on a bus to go meet them before all the bad stuff happened, but I got caught here... they wouldn't let me go back home."

"I could *make* you, force you to come with me, that is," the fallen-girl glowered at the first boy. "You have no *idea* how strong I can be, Curtis."

There was something in her voice that transparently lacked sincerity.

I want to take him along – ohh, think, *for once, whomever-I-am,* she silently self-argued.

Why does my heart speak so at odds with my reason?

"I'll *yell*," taunted Curtis, with a smirk on his face. "So many of 'em will come, that not even y'all with that magic hidin' trick of yours, will get past 'em!"

"*What* magic trick?" interrupted the Native American boy. "She's a magician, Curtis? I never met a *real* magician – on the reserve, we have medicine-men, but they usually just mix up stuff to put on your knees, when you scuff them... nothing really *magic* about it... 'least, I don't think there is..."

Curtis turned to address Tommy and said, matter-of-factually, "She the real thing, Tommy, the real deal. She can *disappear*. Show him, Sari. He have to know, anyway, for when we all go out."

From some unknown corner of her subconscious, the fallen-girl's mind perceived,

The one who vanquishes the Demons of the Dark, She who flies above the clouds, the Great One... and she cannot outsmart a small boy...

She looked at the frightened, all-alone face of the Indian-boy, and something stabbed at her heart, a remembrance from long ago, perhaps, or maybe just long-suppressed maternal instincts.

"Tommy," she quietly inquired, "When they take you back to... wherever they will take you – who will look after you?"

"Nobody," answered the boy, with the hint of a whimper in his voice. "I got nobody who's my friend out here; 'cept for Curtis, that is. I kinda miss my Mom and my Dad, I guess. But I've learned to pretty much be by myself, you know?"

The 'Sari'-girl looked Tommy straight in the face.

"*I* am all alone, here, too, you know," she commented. "With no-one to love me."

The fallen-girl turned away for a second, hoping that the boys could not see her wipe a tear in the half-light.

With a frustrated groan, she relented, "Oh, all *right*, then, Curtis, you win; but it will be up to *you* and your mother to figure out what to do with your friend, when we are all outside. It is not *my* fault, all of this, oh-kay?"

Curtis nodded, with a triumphant grin.

The newcomer now addressed the second boy. "Pay careful attention, Tommy," she instructed. "I will show you what we will look like from the outside, that is, as if you are someone looking at the three of us – actually, the *four* of us, when we go back for Curtis' sister – when we will be traveling close together."

Instantly, the 'Sari'-girl vanished from view, with only the slightest shimmer in the air to reveal her location.

"See?" she offered. "I am still here, right in front of you; but you can not see me. It will be like this if someone looks at all of us, as long as you stay right by my side; but my magic trick doesn't stop sound, so be absolutely quiet, and we will all get out. Oh, and one more thing. It will look *very* dark from inside my trick, you will hardly be able to see anything except yourself, myself, Curtis and her sister, so just follow where I lead you. Do you understand?"

"*Wowwww*," breathed the awed boy. "Yeah, sure, I guess," he stammered.

"Let us go," commanded the young-looking female. "Come straight forward, and when it gets dark, take hold of my waist. Then we will turn around, and we will head for where Melissa is waiting for us."

Curtis confidently advanced, stopped for a second in amazement as he saw his forearm disappear into the faint shimmer of the fallen-girl's cloak, then vanished himself as he edged up next to her.

"Come on," he requested in Tommy's direction, mixing juvenile excitement with as much quietness as he could.

Slowly, the other boy inched closer, closer still, until he was almost at the boundary of the cloak.

He extended a finger and gingerly thrust it at her.

"*Too* cool," he remarked. "It doesn't hurt when it goes away. Lady, how do you *do* that?"

"Later, Tommy," she cautioned, worriedly. "We are wasting valuable time. And just so you have been told... the truth is, I really do not *know* how I do it. I just wish it, and it happens. How, exactly, do you make your fingers work, when you want to grasp something?"

"Yeah, I guess," replied Tommy.

He stepped forward and vanished into the shimmering something-or-other, half-suppressing a gasp as his eyes were instantly confronted by near-total blackness.

"Chill, bro'," sounded Curtis' voice, rather too loudly. "Y'all just do what she say, and we doin' the jet just *fine*."

Clumsily, the threesome turned and headed for the door.

Out To The Prairie Night

Mercifully, the Claremont girl had asked few questions – just an understandable one about why there was now an 'Injun' child in the troupe – when the one-called-'Sari' had visited her bed, the second time.

So, to the bemused stares of the more adventurous of the girls in Melissa's room, the four of them, the 'Sari'-girl first, dropped through the window.

The Claremont girl was last. Uncertainly, she released her grasp to fall into the young-looking woman's arms.

There was a stumble, a 'thud' and a muffled curse in an unfamiliar tongue.

"Hey, what *give*, Sari," complained Melissa. "Y'all 'sposed to *catch* me!"

"Sorry," sheepishly apologized the fallen-girl. "You must weigh more than I had expected you to. And my sense of balance is not at all what it should be. Everything here feels... *heavier* than it should, that is the only way how I can explain it."

"Heavier than *what?*" inquired the tan-skinned boy. "Nothing's changed around here, lady. Gotten bigger, I mean."

"Maybe she gettin' sick or somethin'," commented Curtis. "When ah got th' flu, my legs got real weak, couldn't hardly get up from bed..."

"Yeah, and y'all puked all over me when ah bring y'all that chicken soup," grumbled the Claremont girl.

"Children, *children*," interrupted the one-called-'Sari', "I can *assure* you that I am *not* sick... it is something other than that. Anyway, we dare not tarry. Everyone cluster around me, the way how I told you before. Melissa, do you remember what I said, earlier on?"

"Yeah, ah did," replied the teenager, as she hurried over and stood beside her brother.

"But ah don' think – *holy sh* –", she stammered, as the lights went totally out, all around her.

"Y'all ain't *never* been in here before, Sis," giggled Curtis.

"*Shhhh*," pleaded the fallen-girl. "Remember, they can still *hear* us. No talking until I say that we are safe. Let us go."

Stumbling, foot over foot, guided only by the being that they had entrusted for reasons that none of them understood or questioned, the troupe moved forward, then a hundred or so paces to one side, then far forward again.

It was only a relatively short trip, no more than five or so minutes, in fact, but it seemed longer due to the Claremont boy's incessant whispers of "are we there yet", or words to that effect. The joke, however, seemed lost on the 'Sari'-girl, who simply warned with a "*Shushh!*" at each turn.

"Maybe she never had to drive no kids nowhere," whispered Melissa, as their feet felt the incline of the ground rise, marginally but perceptibly.

"Maybe not, but ah still gots to *go*," complained Curtis. "Don't think ah can hold it too much longer –"

"Melissa, baby girl? Curtis? That *you*? Oh, praise the *Lawd!*" they heard a woman's voice, rather more loudly than would have been called for, exclaim from in front of them.

"Momma?" called out the Claremont girl. "*Momma!* Miz Sari, can ah go now?"

"Yes, I think that we are far enough to be safe," allowed the one-called-'Sari'. "But stay low, until you get into the gully just ahead of us... that is where your mother is staying. Here, I will drop my hiding-cloak."

Instantly, ebon blackness became only the darkness of a Prairie night.

"Me here too, Momma!" half-shouted Curtis, as the boy hurtled over the embankment to Whitney's grateful arms.

The black woman started softly crying.

"Sari – cain't repay y'all for this, not now, not never," she sobbed. "But ah want you to know that it's appreciated, girl – anythin' y'all want, now and anytime, you just ask. Ain't got much, girl, but ah *owes* y'all, and ah'll do whatever ah can. *Whatever.*"

She broke down completely, holding her children close.

The fallen-girl came noiselessly to her side, resting a hand on the woman's shoulder.

"Whitney," she consoled, while faint hints of strange, far-away music played in the night, "I bind my fate to your own, just as the threads of a garment are interwoven with great strength, even if their arts or colors are different or individually weak. If you will take my love and kinship freely given, I will defend you and your dear children from even the most terrible perils... and I will *never* leave a friend in need."

"Lady, you sound like the old folks we got back on the reserve, when they talk about our ancestors, like, how we can always turn to ourselves or the spirit-people for help," commented a half-awed Tommy. "Like, how we're different from the... *others*, I mean, everybody off the reserve. Uhh... no offense, Mrs. – Mrs. – Curtis' mom, I mean."

"You are right about one thing, young man," noted the one-called-'Sari'. "I *am* rather older than perhaps I appear to be."

"Whitney," added the black woman, not looking up. "Whitney Claremont. That's mah name."

"Tommy Singing-Bird George, that's me," responded the Native American boy. "I kinda tagged along with Curtis, 'cause we... well, we were both in *trouble*, I guess."

"Why don' that *surprise* me none," teased Melissa.

"Ah should box yo' ears, both of y'all," breathed Claremont, "But ah won't, maybe never... ah just never thought ah'd see y'all again, but ah prayed, don't mind sayin' that, and the good Lawd brought y'all back. Ah'm just so happy y'all here."

"Whitney," mentioned the one-called-'Sari', "You flatter me, saying things like that... if your 'God' comes into it, then forces larger than me are *indeed* at work here. But whatever the truth of that, I must again be going – there is yet one of our friends who is still kept captive, and I am already late to rescue him."

"Yeah, ah s'pose so," agreed Claremont. "Bob probably wonderin' where y'all got to, 'specially what with the way he was always makin' eyes at y'all, girl."

The one-called-'Sari' gave what amounted to a smirk, for her, still visible even in the nearly unlit surroundings.

"All the more reason, then, for me to bring him back here," she promised while suddenly vanishing from their sight, her passing evident only by the slipstream of a swift breeze upon the grass.

Decisions On The *Flying Dutchman*

"This meeting will now come to order," intoned Commander Ariel Cohen.

They all sat down, or, rather, gently floated down.

"I understand why he's trying to save on energy," muttered Tanaka in Jacobson's direction, "But I still miss the damn gravity, especially as we might not ever get to experience it again."

Jacobson just nodded, looking forward.

"Well, by now we all know the outcome of the lottery, who's 'in' and who's 'out', so to speak," remarked Cohen, in the same, business-like tone that he started all of his discussions with. "So the work order here is really to agree on the implementation plan. Li, I believe that you've been doing some work on that front?"

"Yes, Commander, I have," replied Chen, pushing a memory chip towards Cohen, who obligingly inserted it into one of the omnipresent modular openings in the surface of the meeting-room's table.

A slide presentation instantly appeared on the nearest view-screen.

"This," stated Chen, standing up and awkwardly navigating in the half-G environment over to the screen, "Is what Ms. Parmar, Captain Jacobson and... Mr. Humber, have been able to come up with."

Humber sat there impassively, staring past Chen to concentrate on the slide show.

Pressing an icon on the touchscreen, Chen explained, "We have had to slightly adjust some of our assumptions as to the recommended time for launch, based on more precise trajectory readings as we neared the Moon and considering factors like the optimal energy-conserving trajectory. We therefore estimate that the best time to release the *Eagle* and *Infinity* on their final trip to Earth orbit is about a week from now."

"So," continued Chen, "Based on this information, we have been able to do some balancing of weight and size factors since we now know the exact characteristics of those who were selected in the lottery, and happily we have been able to accommodate one more woman – I believe that is Ms. Daladier, the novelist from the European Union – in the escape vessel."

"Good for her," mumbled Humber.

"Personally I was encouraged by that news, when Li told me a short while ago," added Cohen. "She was one of the ones who met the alien... it is good that she will carry that experience back to Earth."

"That is true, sir," mentioned Chen, "Although, as you also know, there is another who fits into that category – Cosmonaut Sergei Chkalov, of Captain Jacobson's original Mars mission crew. And in this respect, Chkalov's inclusion in the 'lifeboat' mission is quite important for another reason... subject, of course, to your veto, Commander, the planning committee feels that he would be by far the best candidate to pilot the *Eagle / Infinity* combination, with his second-in-command being Ms. Ang-San Thant. Do you concur, sir?"

"Uhh... isn't Ang just a space scientist?" inquired Tanaka. "I thought she was on board doing telescopes, remote sensing, that kind of thing?"

"Yes, Professor, that's true," interjected Humber, finally coming to life. "But she was the best pick we had other than Sergei, from the twenty-two – excuse me, twenty-three, now – that we had to work with. That's what you get with a truly random lottery, I guess."

"And she is taking intensive training right now from Cosmonaut Chkalov," added Chen.

"Wonderful," offered Jacobson.

"So who else are on the crew end of the mission?" asked Cohen.

"We have Mr. Giles Sejour from ESA on environmental controls and Mr. Kwame Anindo from SASC on navigation," replied Chen. "And they, too, are currently undergoing training."

"You know that neither of them have any experience *whatsoever* in those fields," Cohen noted.

"That's why we're training 'em, Commander," replied Humber, with a sardonic grin.

"There's your 'random sample' for you again, Ariel," commented Jacobson. "But, okay, I think everybody here understands that we have to work with the crew sample that made the cut into the mission.

Cohen just nodded and fell silent for a short while. Then he spoke up again. "Well, alright, Alan, that's set, then," he said. "And now that we have these plans decided upon, we need to start thinking about the... *alternative* situation."

"What 'alternative'?" asked Tanaka.

"I think Ariel means, 'what happens to the *rest* of us, that is, those of us who stay up here... am I right?" remarked Jacobson.

Cohen nodded in the affirmative.

"Ms. Parmar and I have also done some preliminary work on that issue," replied Chen, coolly. "We have a high-level plan, but none of the details have been discussed yet."

"Well, go ahead, Li," requested Cohen.

"Obviously this is subject to change, as well as subject to your approval, sir," said the taikonaut. "However, Ms. Parmar and I have had to consider the issue of how to plan for the... inevitable. That is, the eventual exhaustion of on-board life-support resources."

"I suppose we should have the figures," said Cohen, impassively.

"We estimate," explained Chen, looking down at a display screen, "That given the overpressure that will be applied to the escape modules, although this will be somewhat offset by the net loss to ISS2 in terms of personnel using the remaining supply of air," – he took a second to compose himself – "That assuming no extraordinary use of oxygen, I mean, no strenuous exercise on the part of the crew, no on-board fires, no unexpected leaks, no – "

"Just get *on* with it," managed Cohen.

"After we leave Earth-local space and resume our inward trajectory, we will have, approximately, between forty-five and fifty-two days' worth of oxygen supply left, before the crew begins to experience the first signs of hypoxia," stated Chen, professionally.

"And how long after *that?*" asked the Israeli.

"I can help you there, if 'help' is an appropriate word here," interjected Tanaka. "Although you should remember your NASA emergency situation training, Commander. Anyway, once the available oxygen content dips below approach fifty per cent of normal, the crew – especially older people or those with pre-existing respiratory ailments – will start to experience severe shortness of breath, light-headedness, headaches, dizziness, that kind of thing, sometimes retinal hemorrhage and vomiting. You also typically get pulmonary and cerebral edema after a few hours and in the latter case, people can hallucinate or start acting incoherently or irrationally. When it gets below about thirty per cent of normal, most people will fall unconscious in an hour or two. Then you just never wake up."

"Not nice, but I've heard of *worse* ways to go," offered Cohen.

"It's not something I'd like to try," retorted Tanaka. "From those few who have survived an experience like this – and they frequently end up with irreparable brain damage – it's apparently like being slowly strangled, or maybe drowning, bit by agonizing bit. Perversely, people with good respiratory systems are actually the ones who are likely to suffer the longest. I know I don't want to have to deal with this kind of fate, myself."

"Which leads," commented Jacobson, philosophically, "To the next inevitable question, namely, 'what do we *do*, when we get to the point of no return'. I've heard talk of a pill – ?"

"We have a problem with that option, unfortunately," mentioned Chen.

"What *kind* of problem?" asked Cohen.

"Ms. Parmar and I have done an inventory of our existing supply of the necessary ingredients – barbiturates, narcotics, also chemicals that could be mixed to produce similar compounds," said the taikonaut. "The problem is that since an issue of this... *magnitude*, was never anticipated when ISS2's current crew complement was embarked, an adequate supply of these 'suicide pills' – I believe that is the term in English – was never uplifted to the station. So, based on the factors that I just described, Ms. Parmar and I believe that we could create enough of these special pills to perhaps deal with a third of our remaining crew, once the evacuation crew has departed."

"I find the word, 'safely' rather contradictory, in this context, don't you?" complained Cohen.

"Well, you have to consider that an inadequate dose might make matters *worse*, not better," countered Tanaka. "And there are a large number of complicating factors – the body mass of the recipient, how quickly you want it to work... oh, for God's sake, *listen* to me. I don't know if it matters, but I had to take the Hippocratic Oath one time, you know, 'do no harm', that sort of thing," she muttered.

"We're all just trying to find the best one of a lousy set of options, Cherie," consoled Jacobson.

None of the rest could see his hand grasp hers, below the table, though all noticed the appreciative look that the ex-Professor of the Mars-expedition shot back at her former commander.

"Now *that's* quite funny, mate," joked Humber, with a sardonic laugh. "I smell another lottery coming up, sort of like the 'booby prize', right, Commander? I mean, 'fail this one' and you're bloody well shit out of luck, or shit out of breath, wouldn't you say?"

Cohen was about to reprimand the engineer, but Jacobson cut him off, saying, "You know, Alan, you sound just like Devon, there – always something funny to say, no matter what the circumstances. But I don't think most of the crew could handle another lottery... Ariel, any thoughts?"

"I wish I could think of what to suggest," forced Cohen. "This situation is just so far from what I expected, when I accepted command of ISS2, that I am at a complete loss, right now. As you know, we have no firearms on board, and although we could perhaps sharpen certain medical instruments to achieve the desired... effect, there is no knowledge base about how such a process would work in low or zero gravity. Much human suffering might be involved."

"There's always the airlock," half-quipped Humber.

"Much quicker, but very painful," commented Chen, looking impassively forward. "In my basic space flight training, we were shown animal simulations of what would happen to any living thing who would spend so much as two or three seconds in a total vacuum environment. I resolved never to have this happen to me."

"Figures the Chinese would do that kind of thing to cats and dogs just to prove a point," muttered Humber, with just enough volume to be heard. "You're lucky you aren't with ESA, the Animal Rights folk would have your hide... but you *didn't* learn your lesson, as two of my mates –"

"Alan, that's *way* out of order," warned Cohen.

Tanaka, staring into space as if trying somehow to see far beyond the walls of the station, said to no-one in particular, "But you're *wrong*, you know. Not *any* living thing. There *was* one... a living, thinking being who was *fine* out there, completely at home out there. She once said that we'd fly along with her, that she'd teach us how to do it. Remember, Sam?"

"Yeah," agreed Jacobson, heavily, with an arched eyebrow warning Tanaka to be circumspect.

"She *did*. As clear as if it was yesterday... but just like a daydream, somehow. Surreal. *Unreal*."

"Well, real enough to a bunch of us," noted Humber. "I saw her meself... so did the Commander here. And Mr. Chen, too. Although I have to admit that this feeble mind has a hard time accepting the idea that she was just floating around there, without so much as a winter coat on... you're right, Captain Jacobson, *damn* unreal."

Great Sensei from Long Ago and Far Away, where the hell are *you*, silently thought Tanaka. *You taught me* so *much*.

Cohen motioned for silence, then said, "I think we're getting a bit off-topic, here, everyone – but, it's also evident that we need to give the issue of how we deal with those members of the crew to whom we cannot issue the appropriate... medication, a bit more thought. In any event, we certainly *do* have more time to think that one through. You know, it's ironic that the business of space travel involves very complex and exacting infrastructure to ensure that we all stay alive up here; yet, we cannot figure out how to do the opposite. One would think that it would be easy, no?"

"You'll get no argument from me on *that*," dejectedly confirmed Tanaka.

"Meeting dismissed," said Cohen.

AWOL With A Very Strange Girl

Occasionally studying the patterns of the planks in the ceiling, Billings tossed and turned in bed, secretly wishing for a cigarette to take his mind off the uncertainty and anticipation, even though he'd given up the damn things decades ago.

He had been sorely tempted to cuff the officious church-nut bastards when they ordered him to surrender his clothes, but had wisely thought the better of it, so encouraged, no doubt, by the SMG-toting Gestapo guard just outside the barracks entrance.

Despite this humiliation, and the fact that the water was effing freezing-cold, the shower – his first, it seemed, in days or weeks – had felt good, and the nondescript uniform that he had been given afterwards fit surprisingly well, if you didn't count how stupid his original shoes looked with prison duds.

Plus, he had seen where they had stuffed his sweat-stained, heady-smelling traveling duds, specifically, in a pile in the hall closet, just down from the door to the barracks in which he now lay prone.

He'd get those back, somehow. They made up his best suit, the one that he had planned to wear on his last sales trip, the one where he was going to meet his Maker.

Like most sales-calls, that one hadn't turned out in the way he had planned... thank God.

Meanwhile, he lay on the cot, waiting for – well, *who*, exactly?

What were you thinking of, Bob my boy, he told himself. *She was just another chick you met along the way. Okay, a cute one, a very cute one – the kind you only scored with once in a blue moon, okay, let's not kid ourselves, like you never scored with – but no workin' girl's going to spring you out of this jail, my friend. If she gets out herself it'll only be because of some 'special favors', you know what I mean, that even those 'Thugs for Jesus' goons can't turn down. Don't know why you ever listened to that space-cadet plan she was babbling on about.*

Let's write that one off to wishful thinking, in both senses of the word, he realized.

"Psst – hey, *you, cholo!*" whispered a voice with a thick Latino accent, from the cot next to the salesman.

Billings pointed to himself to demand confirmation, although a second later he realized that the other man probably couldn't see a finger in this darkness, anyway.

"Yeah, *tu*," the voice repeated. "Listen, they get all your *stuff* off of you? You know, the *shit, hombre*?"

"I think you got the wrong guy there," replied the salesman, quietly but irritably. "I don't *do* any of that crap. At least, I haven't in *years*. And anyway, these Bible-bangers took away every last thing I had on me – wallet, credit-cards, even my bubble gum. If I had had any of that stuff on me, it'd be gone by now... nowhere to hide it in the shower, for God's sake."

Maybe he's too stupid to tell that I'm lying, Billings hoped.

"Oh, well, sorry, man," the voice responded, "I thought you were my buddy Julio. Julio, you there, *cholo?*"

There was no reply and after a second or two he again addressed Billings. "But in case you into it, *hombre*, there definitely *are* places to hide the shit, if you do enough time in the big house, if you know the game, you know what I mean? Swallowed a double Trojan of it just before they gave us the old 'strip and dip', and Julio, he hid his right up his – "

"Alright, for Christ's sake, I get the picture," complained Billings, his voice rising intemperately. "But like I said, I don't got any."

After a few seconds of uncomfortable silence, he said, "By the way, my name's Bob Billings. From Tucson, 'till I got caught in this goddamn little rathole. I do sales for a living. You got a name there?"

"Yeah, man," answered the voice. "I got a name. Enrique Vasquez, but my *compadres* back in Houston just call me *'Perrito Loco'*."

"What the hell's *that* mean?" inquired Billings, immediately regretting having done so.

"It means 'Crazy Little Dog' in English, Mister Sales Man," explained the Latino, with a light, but ominous-sounding chuckle. "You see, I'm not too big... but I make up for it with attitude. *Lots* of attitude, man, 'specially when I'm on the shit. Which is most of the time, except now... which is why I need to get some, *pronto*, you understand, Mister Sales Man?"

Jesus Fucking Christ, thought Billings, silently, *What fit of insanity made you start talking to this junkie street thug.*

"Well," mentioned Billings, trying desperately not to let the slightest hint of fear sound in his voice, "You could always just wait until you gotta take your next crap, I suppose. Although with the way they've taken the doors off the stalls in the men's room, you'd have a hard time fishing it..."

His voice trailed off.

"Fucking *great* idea, man, except that I need some matches and a needle for this stuff, and that ain't happenin' 'round here. Julio, he's got the shit that you can do easy, but I can't find him, man, *I can't find him!*", half-shouted Vasquez, his fist striking the side of the bed in suppressed rage.

Now that's just great, mused the salesman, in near-panic. *I've got a gang-banging junkie about to OD on me, one cot over. If he doesn't succeed in strangling me when he flips completely, when the guards come out shooting from the hip, well...*

"Shut the *fuck* up, you Mexican pussy," complained a white trash-sounding voice on Billings' other side.

"You gonna wake up them butch nuns and get them fuckin' guards on our asses. Last one I mouthed off to just about broke my jaw an' he said that they'd shoot any man talkin' after midnight, if he didn't have that gun, ah'd have – "

"*You* shut the *fuck* up, *puto*," growled Vasquez, ominously. "You want to find out why they call me *loco*, man? I'll fuckin' *show* you, *puto!*"

Billings winced and closed his eyes, his mind racing feverishly, trying to decide if it would be better to roll off the cot to the left or right.

I'd last six seconds in a fist-fight with either of these guys, on a good day, he thought, *Even if I was twenty years younger and fifty pounds lighter... plus, they make any more noise, those guards are going to shoot at the commotion...*

He decided to roll towards the backwoods voice, but his movement was stopped midway, by a tap on the shoulder.

Billings froze instinctively, trying to avoid giving the guards that he knew must already be there, any reason at all to fire in his direction.

He opened his eyes, only to see a Stygian blackness, darker by far than the already dim barracks surroundings.

And a face. *Her* beautiful, innocent-teenager face, beaming relief and a host of other, welcome emotions, along with worry and consternation, all somehow at the same time.

"Bob," whispered the one-called-'Sari', in her typically plain, yet inexplicably appealing voice, "What is going *on?* You and your friends are making a... how do you say – a 'racket', here. It will be hard already to get you out, and – "

"Sari? Sari!" exclaimed the salesman. "Holy *shit*, girl, I never expected to see *you* in here – how the hell did you *do* it, I mean, the doors are all locked and guarded – and I can't see – "

"Hey, Mister Sales man, where you *go*, there," both of them heard a *loco*-sounding Hispanic voice ask.

They heard a soft 'thump', as if a head had hit a pillow.

"Man, oh mannn, I *need* some shit, man, I'm seein' things and hearin' things, I start hearin' a toss-up's voice and he just *disappear*, he get some pussy in here? What the fuck! Man, I need some *shit!*"

"Look, you fuckin' little wetback, I told y'all –" they heard the backwoods voice warn, as a pair of feet behind them hit the floor.

"*You* shut up, farmer boy," growled another voice, from the opposite row of bunks. "Let the little dago punk OD by himself. You'll get them damn guards, yourself –"

"Bob," quietly stated the fallen-girl, "We *must* exit from here. This commotion will attract far too much attention. Roll over towards me. We will crawl out along the floor."

Clumsily, Billings complied, landing on the floor next to the 'Sari'-girl's crouching figure.

He looked to his side, right into her girl-next-door-cute, friendly face, feeling her lithe, teenager-style physique beside him... *so* close, *so* appealing.

For an instant, the urge was overwhelming, unnatural, unreasonable; he longed to grab her, throw her beneath him, have his way with her. But a sudden burst of common sense made him think the better of it.

"Bob," she whispered affectionately in his ear, "I feel the same way, but now is *not* the time. I remember these words of wisdom, from somewhere – 'let not the fires of passion consume you, in a burning house'. Let us go."

He wondered if she could see the smirk on his face, as he awkwardly shuffled alongside her, blind to all except the faint outlines of the floor-boards, inexplicably trusting his very *life* to this intriguing creature who he had met scant days ago.

For an instant, Billings had to suppress an urge to laugh, as his mind tried to picture the absurd scene of a middle-aged salesman and a seventeen-something sexpot girl doing a four-limbed baby crawl, right in front of a room-full of fellow prisoners, all the while expecting not to be noticed.

But in a trice, he had to return to reality, as one of them – maybe him, maybe the girl – ran right into what must have been a human foot.

"You kick me, *puto?*" shrieked the Hispanic voice. "You dis' me, man! *Nobody toca al Perrito Loco!*"

"Bring it *on*, little man, ah'm waitin' fer ya," they heard the other voice say, dismissively. "I'm a-gonna shove my foot right up your fuckin' –"

"Bob! To the right!" desperately implored the fallen-girl, and Billings complied, dragging himself on three limbs as his hand clenched her robe to avoid losing contact.

"I fuckin' *kill* you – *Carajo*!!!" yelled Vasquez.

Billings felt a sharp pain in his left side, like he had been kicked, then felt a heavy weight impact his back, then heard a "crash", as if a man had fallen forward.

"Keep going, Bob! Straight ahead!" commanded the 'Sari'-girl, not bothering to whisper, this time.

Totally at a loss as to what else to do, the salesman complied, charging forward as quickly as he could.

He heard the sound of door-hinges, and instantly, his eyes perceived – as much as anyone *could*, inside this strange cloak of shadow – bright light flooding into the room from in front of him and the girl. There were footsteps, along with curses and the sounds of punches and kicks from inside the barracks.

Her voice again a whisper of panic in his ear, the one-called-'Sari' said, "There are people coming! To the right, *quickly*, Bob!"

He moved as far over as he could, body-checking the poor girl into what must have been the door-jam.

"*You* in there!" shouted an unfamiliar voice. "Get back to your cots! You have five seconds, or we start firing – *what the* –"

Billings' left breastbone shot a wave of pain, as for the briefest of time he saw a military boot impact with it, then pull away.

"I *hit* something –" exclaimed a male voice, followed by a haughty, female one, saying, "There's nothing *there*, Brother Duncan – get in there and teach them God's harsh justice!"

For an agonizingly long second or so, Billings and the 'Sari'-girl fought clumsily to un-entangle from each other, but the effort was successful and they somehow managed to make it into the lighted area.

She pulled him hard to the right, then the left, then back to the right, as if trying to navigate around obstacles invisible to the salesman.

He felt a wall, as she pressed him tightly against it.

"There are too many guards here," breathed the fallen-girl. "I do not think that we can move around them and not be noticed. We will have to hide somewhere, where they will not look."

She whispers so quietly that I can't really hear *what she's saying*, noted Billings' subconscious. *But how do I understand what she means?*

"We went right, didn't we?" he replied, as softly as possible. "How about the closet down the hall and around the corner. They threw all our clothes in there. It's fairly big and dark –"

He felt the stifling grasp of a petite, but very strong, hand over his mouth.

"Who's there?" they heard a suspicious-sounding, female voice demand, from behind them.

They waited.

From inside the barracks, there were sounds of furniture being thrown about, followed by shrieks and yells. A rapid-fire barrage of shots rang out, then a second fusillade, then screaming, which soon died down to barely-audible moaning.

"What is it?" a second, male, voice asked.

"I thought I heard talking," answered the first voice. "From right beside me."

"I don't see anything, Sister," countered the male voice. "Nothing at all, and nowhere to hide. Excuse me."

There was the crackle of static, then a far-off voice saying something or other.

"We have to get in there, Sister," added the male voice. "One of our brother guards is injured. Oh, and three of the captives are dead, plus a few more shot."

"Good riddance," replied the woman's voice, "The Lord throws the chaff into the fire. Let's make these unbelievers clean up their mess. We must also do a new count."

"Praise be," said the male voice.

There was the sound of footsteps receding towards the barracks-room.

The fallen-girl's hand slipped from Billings' mouth.

"Sari... I think we can go. Let's get going... Sari, you okay?" he uneasily inquired.

The salesman heard soft crying. Then the fallen-girl replied, "Yeah, I am alright. No, I am *not*. But we have to move. Hold my robe. Here we go."

They shuffled down the corridor, staying almost pressed flat against the wall. Eventually, they turned a corner.

He head the 'Sari'-girl whisper, "Stand up... we are by the door, but there are still two enemies that can see it. When they leave, I will open it – follow me quickly."

Billings wondered if she could see him nod.

They sat there for at least a full minute, possibly more. Then the salesman felt himself being pulled from the side, into a noticeably-darker area.

He heard the sound of a latch closing, as he fell backwards onto a soft pile of assorted clothing, all smelling profusely of accumulated dirt, human sweat, other, less agreeable body-fluids, and other refuse.

The cloak vanished, and the two were presented with just ordinary darkness, faintly illuminated by a sliver of light issuing from the gap between the door-bottom and the corridor beyond.

As soon as his eyes refocused, he beheld the 'Sari'-girl staring morosely, aimlessly, at the ground.

He moved his hand to touch her cheek. It was wet with tears.

"What's wrong?" he asked.

"Three dead... killed, on *my* account," she sobbed. "Dead. Gone, their short lives ended far too early."

"Their short... *what*? Don't be ridiculous," implored Billings, as quietly as he could. "You had *nothing* to do with it – if anyone, it was *me, I* picked a fight with that stupid little Mexican junkie. Besides, who are they to you, anyway?"

"You do not *understand*, Bob," she retorted, introspectively. "I do *not* want people to die because of me, because of things I become involved with. I have the blood of *thousands* on my hands, already."

She gasped back tears.

"Uhh... *okay*," replied the salesman. "Whatever you *say*, Sari. But you don't look much like a serial killer, you know. I mean," – he tried to force a chuckle – "Unless you started offing them when you were still in grade school, you could hardly... well, if you don't mind me asking, just who *did* you kill, anyway?"

God damn, thought Billings, *Here I thought she was just an underage hooker and she turns out to be a nut case or a druggie – the girl's not big enough to even give me a bad hickey, let alone kill anyone...*

There were footsteps in the hall, approaching, receding. Both fell silent for a second or two.

"Why do you want to know?" the fallen-girl eventually countered, looking away from him. "What good would it do?"

"Oh, just so I can be sure I don't fit your profile, like, your preferred victims, that sort of thing," he replied, half-seriously. "I mean, if it's white, middle-aged salesmen from Arizona, then we'd have a *problem*, wouldn't we?"

She turned her head and caught him in a laser-like stare that paralyzed him with malevolent sentiment.

Through clenched, glistening teeth (*what the hell is* wrong *with those*, thought Billings, *damn, but don't the ones on the sides look* sharp), she muttered, "I do not remember who I did it to, or why. I only remember that I *did* it. And that I was a different person – a very *dangerous* person, when I did it. But I still live the memory, and suffer by it."

She hung her head and looked as if about to cry.

Billings moved next to the fallen-girl and put his arm around her shoulder, pressing her to himself.

"Sari," he started, as compassionately as he could muster, "We *all* have skeletons in the closet. Me, too... when I was a few years younger, I did a lot of stupid things, to women, business partners, myself, even my kids, any one of which could easily have landed me in the slammer. But I got away with it. Well, except for that *one* time... look, at some point, you gotta move on. I did. You can, too."

"I envy you, Bob Billings of Tucson, Arizona," she replied, with a far-off stare. "Your past is something that you can, how you say, 'live down'. If only mine were as short... as simple."

More footsteps issued forth from outside, and both fell silent for a minute or so. Then Billings spoke up again.

"If this helps, at all," the salesman said, "Every time that I remember one of the bad things, the negative things, from my past, I mean... what I do, is try to remember the *good* things. You know, accomplishments, like getting married, having a kid – that is, as long as you don't just walk off and leave 'em with the ex – so they cancel out the stupid things I did. Sort of like a cosmic account balance sheet, I guess... you know, 'assets versus liabilities'. I figure I'm still in the black. If barely."

He grinned and her her countenance brightened in turn.

"That is an interesting way of putting it," she offered. "Maybe I, too, have done something good, something that might excuse crimes of the past. Do you think I have done something good, Bob? Anything at all?"

She looked at him plaintively, as if asking for redemption.

"I can think of at least one," he replied. "You've got me *this* far out of this accursed place. And who knows, maybe you were a nun, Mother Theresa, that kind of thing, in a former life. Thing is, Sari... I just can't *picture* you as a bad person. And I'm a pretty good judge of character. Made my livelihood doing that. So do I believe that you're a killer? Sorry, no, I don't. At least, believing *that*, is better than thinking I'm stuck in this shithole with a psycho, wouldn't you say?"

In the half-light, Billings saw the 'Sari'-girl manage a faint smile and nod affirmatively.

"Anyway," he whispered as he began rummaging through the haphazardly-strewn clothing, holding his nose as shut as he could manage, "I've got something else to do, than worry about your past, girl – I've got to get my stuff back."

"Your, 'stuff'?" she asked. "That means drugs, things to make you imagine things, see colors that aren't really there and so on..."

"No, not for me," he explained, "I mean, my wallet, keys, and so on. Wallet's got my credit-cards, the whole shootin' match. Bastards checked all my pockets for it when they stripped me, but I've been around the town a few years, had the wallet, plus my car keys, zipped into an inside pouch in the ass of my pants... they usually don't grope you down there, an old trick I learned down Mexico way to deal with the street people, times were that I mostly didn't have to use it, but these days, well, I *knew* that things were going to be bad, so I thought ahead. Here, help me – there are a *hell* of a lot of clothes here."

He felt her hand planted suddenly over his mouth, the action made less oppressive by her gentle rubbing of his lips, something that would, in any other circumstances, have been unbearably erotic.

It stayed there for perhaps thirty seconds, as they heard footsteps and confused discourse in the hallway. The chit-chat was too far away for Billings to make out, but after she released her grip, the fallen-girl filled him in.

"From what I heard," she mentioned, "They have now found about what has already happened, in the two other buildings. That is good, in a way – they will be confused, they will run from one to another."

"The two other... you mean the *Claremont* kids?" stammered the salesman. "You've already *been* there – but how the *hell* –"

"What color were your pants, Bob?" the one-called-'Sari' interrupted. "What did they look like?"

"Brown... well, okay, sort of half-brown, half-tan, 40 waist, nice pleat in 'em when I set out, that's gone now, of course... but you're going to have to work from feel, can't see colors in here anyway. Grab each pair by the crotch and squeeze, you feel something hard, bingo, you get it?"

"Uh.. oh-kay," she replied. "Let me see... that one is black... two that are, how you say, 'blue-jeans', those are the wrong kind, no?"

"Definitely," Billings stated, as he fumbled through the pile, reflexively wiping his hands on each new piece of clothing as he finished with the previous one.

"Arrow on the mark," announced the fallen-girl, in an unsurprised monotone.

"Oh, come *on*," retorted the salesman, "We've only looked at a *fraction* of the – what the – "

He felt the pants as she handed them to him.

"God *damn*," he muttered. "That's *gotta* be them. Man, they smell as bad as I remember them, but I might as well put 'em on, that way I don't have to carry the stuff out in the open. My hat's off to you, Sari – Olympic record in finding needles in haystacks."

"I just looked for the light brown ones," she replied. "There are only three or four pairs of them."

Billings offered, "But how did you – oh, never mind, girl, I've seen cats and bats with worse eyesight..."

"Well, I *need* that ability, especially when I make things dark, as I must again, now," she commented. "But you must stay absolutely quiet, for a few seconds – try not even to *breathe*. I need to listen, to tell if anyone is around. Ready?"

"Yeah, sure," he managed, gasping a deep breath and holding it.

The 'Sari'-girl stood up and put her ear to the door. All was still.

After about ten painful seconds, Billings could sustain himself no longer, and he exhaled, asking, "Well?"

"I think that we are oh-kay," she answered. "Stand up and take my hand – walk right behind me, as much as you can; we will stay as close as possible to the wall. When I squeeze hard on your hand, it means you should immediately stop and be very quiet. I will open the door."

A mantle of ebon blackness enveloped Billings as he stood next to, then behind, his new companion.

Not a psycho, he told himself. *Not a nut case. Keep it* together, *Bob my boy, she's just a pretty girl with some slick tricks... but this is really,* really *weird. CIA, FBI, Men in Black... some super-duper secret stealth-ninja-type thingie that they implanted in her – one of those bio-chips – yeah, that's* gotta *be it. How else could she do this?*

But if she's got a stealth chip in her, what if she's got a tracking chip, too? One of those GPS things they had in Popular Mechanics, they track you with the satellites. The Feds will be up your ass the second you get out of this fucking little Bible-banging jail. The Jesus-people said that the Feds were on their *side, didn't they? And oh, yeah, it's a sin to tell a lie. Right. Suure.*

But didn't all the satellites get blown up, when the Big Thing went down? Maybe just most of them? Maybe you'll be okay. Until they put a few back up there and turn 'em on again, at least.

He heard the door-hinges protest slightly, then the darkness lessened slightly, but perceptibly, as the two stepped out into what must have been the hallway.

"Around the corner... flat against the wall... not much further now..." she directed, in her curious, half-audible demi-whisper.

He felt the fallen-girl's hand squeeze his, suddenly.

He froze, his back flat against the wall.

There was the sound of boots – many boots – running toward them.

"Sister, you summon us? What for? We have our hands full here!" shouted a male voice.

"I don't know what's going on," a female voice, different from the one they had heard earlier, called back. "Only that there has been an incident in the Daughters barracks – maybe the Sons one, too. They request reinforcements. Do any of you have detective training?"

"Aye," confirmed a second male voice. "Before I was born again, I was with the Arizona State Troopers. We did a lot of wetback-tracking, that kind of thing."

Along with screwing me over speeding tickets on the Interstate, you assholes, thought Billings.

"Me too," added a third voice. "From the City of Memphis police."

"Well then, get yourselves over there, quickly, Brothers," the female voice ordered. "The rest of you, too. My Sisters and I will take care of things, here."

"Are you sure that's a good idea, Sister?" questioned the first male voice. "The barracks is all men... granted, the little Mexican monster is dead and the white man that he was fighting with won't be getting off his cot any time soon, but there are others in there that might be just as... *rebellious*."

"I think we can handle the situation, until you get back here," replied the female voice. "They have *seen* what happens to the disobedient. Besides, I still have two Brothers stationed across from my office. They have orders not to warn before opening fire. Remember what Father Abraham said to the rich man, when he called out to Lazarus, Brother?"

They heard a rough, contemptuous laugh issuing from several of the voices, all at once. The second male voice said, "You're right, Sister... they have all the example they need. And we can give them more, if we have to."

"Amen to that, Brother," concluded the woman. "Now you should go."

When you hear the boots heading off, leave the wall and follow quickly behind me, Billings heard.

No, I didn't *hear that,* his confused mind shot back. *No sound came to my ears. Didn't hear so much as a* whisper. *But I got the message, anyway. This is getting more creepy by the minute –*

He felt her tug on his arm, as the sound of jack-boots started to echo across the floor-boards.

The salesman stumbled forward, faster and faster, in response to her insistent prodding, unused to proceeding at this accelerated pace, while able to see neither where he was going, nor where he was coming from.

There was the sound of a lock being unlatched and then that of an outside door opening. The surroundings ahead, as much as he could make out anything in this strange place, looked even darker.

"You three head off to the Sons' quarters, the rest of us will go to the Daughters'," commanded a gruff voice.

"Right, Brother, we'll meet you back here in twenty minutes, then?" asked a male voice.

Billings' feet marched clumsily forward. He stepped ahead, one, two, three paces, but on the fourth, where he had expected to put down a step, he trod upon air.

Desperately, he tried to keep his balance, but to no avail – the salesman fell, impacting with most of his weight right into the middle of the 'Sari'-girl's back. The two of them hurtled forward, impacting suddenly with something that quickly gave way.

There was the sound of an object striking the ground, a few feet in front of them. Billings felt the fresh smell and taste of Prairie grass in his mouth.

"What the –" they heard a male voice shout. "Brother Grant, you fell –"

"No, I was *pushed!* Hit from behind! Someone *attacked* me!" yelled another voice.

"Brothers, *guns!*" barked the first voice.

"Help him up," added a third. "*You* there!" it gruffly ordered. "Whoever you are, *freeze!* We're going to shoot, in one second!"

Billings heard the 'click-click' sound of safety locks being disengaged.

"*Shit,* Sari –" he swore out loud, before a hand, itself smelling of grass, dirt and something else, something acrid, pungent, a faint scent of things burning, dissolving, hit and covered his mouth.

A thought, easily recognizable as her voice, yet without the slightest hint of a sound, resounded in his mind.

Crawl, idiot, crawl beside me, crawl forward, if you want to live!

"They must be over there!" shouted a different voice.

"Fire!" commanded a second.

For a second, Billings froze, certain that his insignificant, mundane little salesman of something-or-other life was now playing out its final second or two.

You're supposed to see your whole life in front of you, he silently cursed. *But all I see is, 'you dodged the Big Thing and got your sorry ass shot by a bunch of Holy Rollers', fucking great thing for your tombstone Bob my boy, so this is how it ends, fucking great...*

Billings heard the whistle of bullets passing over his head, not more than chest-height above where he was now.

The stupid fuckers are shooting in the wrong direction, he realized.

She must have tackled one of them from the back when I stumbled into her – how can they possibly *not see us?*

He felt an insane urge to laugh, but somehow mustered the presence of mind to control it.

Billings felt the 'Sari'-girl tug hard on his arm, pulling him to one side. Desperately, he crawled forward, trying to keep up with her. The sweat poured from every part of his body, as the salesman suppressed a pleading desire to gasp for breath, hoping that adrenaline would substitute for years of neglected physical fitness activities.

More bullets whizzed through the air. It sounded like they were shooting in all directions, in a kind of crude 'reconnaissance-by-fire' exercise.

After an agonizing few seconds more, he noticed that the grass they were traveling through was higher. It was wild now, uncut.

I sure hope I didn't piss my pants, he thought. *That's right where I hid my wallet, isn't it?*

Every muscle in his body protesting, the salesman felt the fallen-girl drag him further and further away from the compound, as, mercifully, the sounds of military orders, gunfire and chaos receded until they were barely audible.

"Sari," he whispered, "You gotta let me *rest* a second. I can't keep going like this. I'm not a great candidate for the turtle races at summer camp, girl, I guess."

"Alright," she quietly allowed, "But only for a few minutes, oh-kay? If they have the dark-eye-glasses, the ones that can see as I do – uhh, what I mean is, the ones that can pierce the night – they might still notice us, until we arrive where the others are. Oh, Heavens *forgive* me, Bob, I did not even think to ask – are you wounded? Were you hit by any of those gun-bullets?"

"Am I..." Billings started to reply, slumping with exhaustion, both nervous and physical, for a second.

Then he felt the pain come to him, as he reflexively touched his lips with one of his hands.

"What the – shit, this *hurts*, Sari," he complained.

"You *are* gun-shot, then?" she worriedly inquired. "Oh sweet starlight, Bob, I do not think that I can fix *that* yet –"

"No, *not* shot," countered the salesman. "It's my damn *lips*, they feel like I've just sucked on the hottest chili peppers on the *planet*. Parts of my face, too, same thing. It's burning something *awful*. Maybe I went face-first into some goddamn kind of poison they put on the lawns, back there? Did any get on you, girl? 'Cause I sure hope not."

"No, I am fine," she knowingly replied. "Here, let me have a look."

The 'Sari'-girl approached, closer, closer still. Her face, gentle and sympathetic, was now scant inches from his.

Billings stared into her beautiful, strangely large blue-green eyes, hypnotized, entranced, relaxed, despite the fury of pain spreading slowly across his face.

A finger extended to one of the open sores that had now broken out on Billings' mouth, this one just below the lip. She brought her fingertip to her nose and breathed in, deeply.

"Curses," she muttered. "I fell down, cut my hand on something, I was bleeding slightly... it is healed now, but some of it must have ended up on you, when I had to stop you from speaking... oh Bob, I am *so* sorry. I did not *mean* to hurt you."

She let out a soft sob.

The pain was becoming excruciating. Billings' face felt like it was on fire.

"No offense taken, Sari," he grunted, "But I've *got* to get to a doctor. If it keeps on like this, I'm going to pass out."

"Even if there were some doc-tors around here, and even if they would not just hand us back to the men with the guns," she argued, as her face came right up next to his, her breath fragrant in his nostrils, "I do not think they could help you with *this*. They would not know what to do."

"Well, what the hell am I supposed to *do*, you little weirdo popsy, just sit here and watch my face burn off?" growled Billings, ashamed in the same second of having said it, but knowing that the pain was speaking, not him.

"Look, Sari, I didn't *mean* that... but, God, get me to a *doctor*, even if it means going back," he moaned. "No matter how much training they have, they can't torture me like *this!*"

"Do not worry, Bob Billings from Tucson," she counseled, in a knowing, bedside-manner voice. "I can *fix* it, right here, right now. But there is something that you must know, first."

"For God's sake, what is *it*, girl," gasped the salesman.

"When my tongue heals your lips," she counseled, "Do not fight the feeling, the urge, that will come upon you. Give in to it – do what you want, without thinking, without worrying. When your need overtakes you, it will do so to me, in the next second, as well; I can resist it no more than can you. It is my first gift to you, and yours to me. Accept, and enjoy. I assure you that I will do this happily and willingly."

"Whatever, for Christ's sake, Sari," he was barely able to say. "Just get *on* with it."

"Oh-kay," confirmed the girl, her countenance beaming, as her tongue expertly licked the places on his face where the sores had appeared.

With each touch, Billings felt coolness, relief, release from pain. He could almost think again, as tears of gratitude formed in his eyes.

"Sari," he apologized, "Listen – I'm *really* sorry I said that stuff a few minutes ago – it's just that it hurt *so* much –"

"Shhh," she purred. "Still one place for my mouth-water to go, lover Bob. Still one place for my tongue to find."

He felt her tongue wash over his lips, as the same cool healing vanquished the sores that had agonized him. But the feeling was followed not a second later by arousal of a kind that he hadn't felt since, well, maybe since the first time that he had done the good-old in-and-out with Maria Tuscodero, back in high-school days, after weeks of blue-balls frustration.

Back then he had thought, '*this* is as good as it gets'.

How wrong you were, Bob. It's like his chick has got 180-proof Viagra for spit – God, I feel like every porn star ever born, rolled into one, shrieked his over-stimulated mind.

Jesus, and I was worried about getting it up? How the hell am I going to get it down?

Momentarily, he tried to think rationally, to reason it out.

She said she was a killer, right? And this is just as weird as the blacker-than-black darkness, Bob – super pheromones, bio-engineering, we've still got guards on our tail, don't let it...

He tried to regain control, to no avail. This was crocodile-brain stuff, caveman-style.

Who I if I get shot or get my throat slit – more than worth it... I want *her – I* need *her – I got* to have *her! Right* now!

Billings grabbed the unresisting fallen-girl, pushing her below him, cursing like a sailor as he fumbled for his zipper, seeing but not caring in the slightest that her incisors glistened malevolently, illuminated by a glow from both her wicked grin and from he knew-not-where, inside the ebon cloak that enclosed the two.

Somehow, he felt his clothes leave his body, as, rock-hard, he was pulled effortlessly inside her. She moaned and whimpered softly, driving the poor salesman yet more insane, with a primeval urge that washed over him like some perverse *tsunami*.

You can last a few seconds more, she's soaking wet but give her time, Bob, rub her the right way – the least you can do, he tried to convince himself. *Relax, don't do it...*

He felt her hands cupped on either side of his head, pulling it close to her own. Their lips were almost touching, now, and as she gave a little whimper, he smelled her breath, entrancing, bewitching.

"How do you like my medicine, Bob my love?" she quipped, as her tongue, guided by unimagined experience, probed deeply into his mouth.

As desire – brutal, animal, senseless – overpowered him, Billings tasted deeply, and collapsed under a tidal wave of passion.

Well, if she takes me down, at least I'll go smiling, he thought.

Across The Fields

"*Bob*," implored the fallen-girl, poking the somnolent salesman in the side, "I would rather lie peacefully here in your arms, too, but we must be on our way, now."

She poked him again, then complained, *sotto voce*, "Well, at least stop *snoring*, man. I told you, I *can* stop light... but I cannot stop noise."

"Whaaa...", mumbled Billings, the pleasant haze of recent indulgence in the sins of the flesh slowly fading from his mind as he slowly came back to life.

"Oh, sorry, Sari. Ha, ha – hey, 'sorry, Sari'. Funny, right? Heard a line like that in a movie, one time..."

Had the surroundings not been as dark as the deepest depths of night, Billings would have seen a mild smile break upon the fallen-girl's lips, but instead, he just heard her repeat, "Hmm, yes, *funny*, I, how does one say, 'get it'... I wish that I knew something funny that rhymed with *your* name, Bob. Oh, wait, I have it... 'let us put our minds to the job, Bob'. *That* is funny, right? Anyway, we have wasted too much time here already. We must again be moving."

"You seemed like you *enjoyed* 'wasting' all this time, you know," muttered the salesman. "And, 'ha, ha'. Don't give up your day job, whatever that is, for the Comedy Channel, girl."

She leaned over and kissed him twice, once on the ear, once on the cheek.

"*Of course* I did, lover Bob, our mating gave me beautiful pleasure," she earnestly affirmed. "And I really *do* want to have you again, feel your manhood rubbing me in the right places, swelling up so big inside me, flooding and warming my wet space. But you need to get up, put on your clothes, right *now*. I can hear voices, in the distance – they are saying something about a 'search party', that is when they hunt for us, no?"

Billings fell silent for a time, listening.

"I don't hear *squat*," he argued. "But okay, fine... give me a few seconds. Hard to find the front and the back when you can't see anything, you know."

"I have good ears," the 'Sari'-girl replied. "And they hear people coming, slowly, but they are *definitely* nearing us, so hurry. When you are ready, you can stand up. I will make my dark cloak bigger so that we can walk normally... not crawl."

"Listen, Sari," started Billings, as he fumbled for his belt-buckle, "I don't exactly know how to *say* this, but... but... well, what I mean is, I'm afraid that things kind of got the better of me a few minutes ago, like, I didn't use any *protection*, if you know what I mean. So I'm a bit worried that if you're not on the Pill..."

"The... 'Pill'?" asked the fallen-girl, her tone displaying slight worry. "That is something that you eat, as a cure for a disease? Other than for where my blood injured you – sorry – you do not look sick, Bob?"

"Let's talk while we walk," Billings requested.

The 'Sari'-girl grasped his hand and led him in what must have been a direction away from the encampment, although as usual he could see no further than the end of his arm.

"A disease?" he said. "Heh, not *exactly*, unless you count it as 'the Egyptian Flu', that is."

"The... 'Egyptian Flu'?" replied the fallen-girl, sounding concerned, now. "That sounds *serious*. Why did you not tell me that you had it, before we mated? Can it be spread through male seed?"

"Jaysus, girl, where did *you* come from," sighed Billings, as the two strode on through the tall Prairie grass. "It's *not* a disease – that's a *joke*, you know, 'catch the Egyptian Flu and you become a mummy'... look, what I was *trying* to say is, I don't want you to get pregnant, have a baby. I already got too many kids to pay support for, anyway. And if you're not using something for protection, with the state of the hospitals these days, it might take months and a trip to Mexico or Canada for you to get an abortion, *if* you can find a clinic that the morality police haven't shut down yet, and there were precious few of those even before the Big Thing went down – thank God we aren't in Dixie, last one got firebombed out twenty years ago, the girls all end up in my town or Phoenix, but we only got one or two places left ourselves, and a lot of 'em end up getting the butcher treatment in back alleys, damn shame but I kept my mouth shut.... Look, you appreciate my concern, don't you?"

The fallen-girl stopped for a second, turned and looked Billings directly in the face, her visage barely perceptible in the strange, out-of-nowhere demi-luminescence that passed for light in their ebon cocoon.

In a sad-sounding tone, she offered, "Somehow I do not think that you have to worry about that, Bob. Though part of me wishes that you *did*. It would be exciting, it would be *wonderful*, to have a child. To be a mother, again."

"What do you *mean*?" the salesman uneasily inquired. "If you've already *had* a kid, then that means you can have another. Especially without the Pill..."

"No," she countered, in the same, quiet, reflective tone, "I remember that I had children, once... a very *long*, long, time ago. Far away. They must be grown up now. But I cannot, anymore. At least, not here, not by you. Though I wish I could, Bob. I really *do*."

"Damn... for a minute, I thought you were – look please don't take this the wrong way, but you gotta admit, it can have some *advantages* – one of those girls who can't have kids, you know, the whole infertility thing, something in the water that does it, I heard... but you're not making any *sense*, you know, Sari," said Billings. "For one thing, you're not *nearly* old enough to have had a kid more than K-12 age, anyway. At least, you sure don't *look* more than, say, twenty or so... and how can you be so sure? You got one of those implants, you know, the ones that go in the – the – your womb, I mean, they stop you from conceiving..."

"Implant? No – *nothing* can go in my female parts, or anywhere else inside me, for that matter, and keep working," answered the girl, firmly. "My body would destroy it, disintegrate it, in no more than a few seconds. And as for the children... well, maybe it was just a dream. Maybe just a wish. I do not *know*, Bob. *Nothing* about my past is clear to me, nothing. But I do know that we have to get moving, again. Let us go."

"Fine," muttered Billings, "But just remember, I'm not paying for it. If and when."

"As I said, I do not know why," she shot back, as she pulled him in what he hoped was the right direction. "But you do not have to worry about being the father of my child. Although I would cleave to you, Bob Billings, and love and care for your own, if things were the other way around."

She sounded hurt. Her head hung down, as they stumbled forward.

I never could *understand women*, he thought. *Not even the normal ones, and this one's anything but.*

Now it was Billings' turn to stop their movement. He took hold of the girl's shoulders, turning her to face him, sensing that she did not resist his grasp.

"Sari, *Sari*," he protested, trying to muster up his most sympathetic voice, "I didn't mean it that way. It's just... just that these are really, well, really *difficult* times. Everything's up in the air; I mean, who knows where each of us is going to end up a week from now, a year from now. You can understand why a man – hell, you too – wouldn't want new *obligations*, can't you?"

Mutely, she nodded, with doe-like eyes observing him.

"Okay, so... so, let's leave it at that, and hope for the best, right?" he asked.

"Oh-kay," she replied. "Hope for the best. But..."

"But... what?" demanded Billings, nervously.

"But... do not think that this will keep my tongue out of your mouth forever, lover Bob Billings," she noted, matter-of-factually. "Desire still burns in my breasts, in my thighs. It will need release, your man's touch, how do you say... 'sooner rather than later'. I waited patiently, when we were in the tent, you know."

Amen to that, thought the salesman, to inner delight. Somehow, he fought off a sudden, brutal urge to throw her on the ground again, congratulating himself for this amazing feat of self-control.

At the insistence of her tug, they started moving again, and after a few minutes, Billings observed that the ground had started to become more uneven.

"Careful," cautioned the fallen-girl. "We are going down a slope."

"Yeah," replied the salesman. "Just about tripped there. Wouldn't want to do *that* again... and by the way, sorry about back there, with the guards, I mean. It's damn hard figuring out where to put my feet, in this, this, black hole you've got us in. I was meaning to ask you, how does it work? Like, how do you turn it on?"

"What do you mean, 'turn it on'?" the 'Sari'-girl guardedly answered.

"Well, I felt enough of your body, in the buff – no offense, you understand – to know that you *can't* be hiding some kind of super-duper CIA type contraption under your clothes, Sari. So you have to be making this black stuff somehow, but how? Bionics? Implants? I mean, it's not the kind of thing that you can learn at the local YWCA; and the way you whispered to me, back there, without making a sound –"

"I am sorry, but I do not understand a lot of this, Bob," countered the fallen-girl. "'In the buff'? What is *that*? Is 'buff' another word for 'grass'? And what is 'super dooper'?"

"Naked, and, like, strange, wonderful, powerful, that kind of thing," stated Billings.

He suppressed a curse, as his toe caught on a root or something, and he almost lost his balance.

"Ah," the girl-called-'Sari' replied. "Well, you are right in that... I carry nothing with me except the clothes that I wear. About the dark-trick, the truth is, I do not *know* how I do it. I kind of think, 'let it be dark', and I imagine how big I want the darkness to be, around me. It always just works... that is about it, I suppose."

"But where'd you learn it? Have you been able to do it since you were a kid, or did somebody teach you? Where?" pressed Billings. "You gotta admit, it's damn peculiar. Almost *magical*, I'd say."

She stopped, turned to him and spat out, "No – *not* magic, not at all. If it was, I would not use it. Not *ever*. How you say – 'no way'."

Her tone was defensive, nearly angry.

"Hey, whoa, *down* girl," cautioned Billings, as he shuffled step by deliberate step down what appeared to be an embankment. "I can see it's a sensitive subject for you... sorry if I'm being nosy. It's just that, well, I wouldn't have had a *chance* of getting out of that rathole without this little 'hiding in plain sight' trick of yours. Anybody with half a brain would be interested in how you do it, where it comes from. Please don't get mad when I get curious... okay?"

"That was not what I meant, Bob," the fallen-girl, her voice easing, explained. "I do not mind you asking things about me, as long as you understand that there is not a lot I can tell you. I have no idea where I learned how to do this thing, if I even 'learned' it, at all, maybe it has always been something that I can do... I mean, if I were to ask you, 'explain exactly how your mind tells the muscles in your hand to grasp something, or let it go', you would not be any more able to do that, than can I, when you ask me about the dark-thing... right?"

"I guess you got me there," admitted the salesman.

"And about the whispering," she continued, "I was just trying to communicate messages with as little noise as possible, I mean – to use your expression, Bob, 'for God's sake', there were men with bang-guns all around us, can you blame me? Maybe your ears are better than you *think* that they are... you just heard a really soft sound, is that not possible?"

"Yeah, *right*," retorted Billings. "But I bet it wouldn't have shown up on any tape recorder. More magic there, Sari?"

"Oh, will you *stop* about the magic, Bob," groaned the fallen-girl. "The idea of me using it, is irritating, that is all."

"What you got against magic?" inquired the salesman. "It's all hokum, anyway. What's the point of getting worked up about it?"

Again, she stopped, and looked at him with big, searching eyes.

"No, Bob," the 'Sari'-girl retorted, politely but firmly. "It is *not* all, how you say, 'hokum'. Some of it is *very* real, and *very* dangerous – weirding spells that can kill you, or worse, in the blink of an eye, and the summoning of sinister beings who would annihilate everything, and every*one*, nearby. Several times I have very nearly lost my life, to such things. Behold, thus why I do not like magic..."

"Oh, come *on*, Sari – how can you *possibly* know that," half-joked Billings. "The only 'magic' that I've ever seen is the kind they do at the State Fair. With mirrors, sleight of hand, dry ice, trap doors and so on. None of it's *real*."

"I just... *know*, Bob," countered the fallen-girl, looking forward, evading his glance. "You will have to trust me on this, I suppose."

"I suppose," he shrugged, huffing and puffing as his feet felt the ground-level out. "But you gotta *admit*, girl, there's a lot about you that you don't seem to be able to explain. I'm not the nosy type, you understand, but, well, if we weren't so, so *friendly* with each other... This black cloud we're traveling under, it's science-fiction stuff – I mean, my life, just like the lives of everybody I've ever hung around with, it's been *normal*, up to now, up to the Big Thing, that is, just gettin' up in the morning, going to your lousy job all day long, having a beer at the end of the day; you're the most exotic thing that I've ever encountered... you're really exciting, but just a little scary, too. Oh, and take that as a compliment, please."

She turned and gave him a wry-looking smile, while continuing to lead him forward, hand in hand.

"I'm glad that you think that I am special, Bob," she remarked. "Considering that I have no idea of who I am, or where I came from, or where I am going, or anything, really, it is good to know that *someone* cares for me. And that he should never fear me, that I would never hurt a lover, a friend."

She squeezed his hand and looked at him with an honest, trusting stare.

"And, perhaps," she reflectively added, "Your 'normal' life, may soon be changing into something much different... something more, ahh, 'interesting'."

Billings was about to tell the joke about the ancient Chinese curse, but at that moment, the 'Sari'-girl stopped, all of a sudden.

"Wait a second, please," she commanded, followed, a second later, by a soft exclamation : "Oh, yes! I hear them!"

"Who?" asked Billings.

The coal-deep blackness faded to reveal the unlit expanse of a Prairie gully, with three or more ghostly shapes just visible in the distance.

"Whitney? Curtis? Melissa?" called the fallen-girl.

"Yo, Sari!" shouted a child's voice. "Y'all *late*, lady!"

"Hush, boy!" cautioned the 'Sari'-girl, as she and Billings broke out into a trot. "We are coming, but keep your voice down... we were pursued back there. I think they are no longer after us, but they might still be."

After a few seconds more, Billings could perceive four figures within a stone's throw ahead.

"Whitney? Mrs. Claremont?" he asked. "That you?"

"One an' the same," replied a familiar, African-American ghetto voice. "Got Melissa and Curtis – y'all 'member, the one who cain't keep he mouth shut – wid me too. Sari got 'em back for me, after she spring me out. That *y'all*, Bob?"

"Yeah," confirmed the salesman. "Bob Billings, who has no reason at all to be standing here talking to you – God, Whitney, you should *see* how she got me out of that jail back there. Or, rather, I guess you *won't* see it... ha ha, *none* of 'em saw it, or us. Pretty damn slick mumbo-jumbo, I gotta admit, but how she did it, well, *you* tell me."

He stopped for a second and re-surveyed the scene.

"Hey," he continued, "I can make out you, Curtis and your daughter, but... who's the *other* one... looks like a kid?"

"He Tommy George," replied Claremont. "He Injun."

"Tommy *Singing-Bird* George, Ma'am," corrected the voice of the second boy.

"Did I mention that the 'Bird' part of your name is very, how do you say, 'poetic', Tommy – somehow, it reminds me of home," interjected the one-called-'Sari'. "Like how people were called, where I was born."

"You said you didn't remember where you came from – " noted Billings.

"I do not," she answered. "But he just *reminds* me of it. Wherever, 'it', is."

"Well, that's nice, I suppose," grunted Billings, "But what's *he* doing here? Not that I *mean* anything by it, kid, you understand – just that you weren't part of our group..."

"Tommy 'n me, we homies," countered the Claremont boy. "We blood brothers. Got caught doin' stuff together back in the barracks, got thrown in this room, then Sari got us both out. So Tommy, he chillin' wid us, now."

"Nice to see y'all, too," commented Claremont, sarcastically.

"*Swell*," muttered Billings. "Just what we *need*, another kid tagging along with us – but, for God's sake, that's *nuts*, Whitney, if you *knew* what we somehow escaped from back there, 'cloak of shadows' or not, it'd be *suicide* for her to go back and try to get this kid's parents, the whole place has gotta be in an uproar by now – "

"My Dad's back on the reserve, Mister," mentioned the AmerIndian-boy.

"Fine. Yeah. Whatever," answered the salesman. "Well, look, anyway, we should be on our way, soon. Sari's right – we might have lost those gun-totin' goons back there, but we might *not* have, and I don't want to hang around here to find out. We've spent too much time yakking as it is. Let's get going."

"Goin' *where*, Mister Bob?" queried Claremont. "Ah don' even know where we *is*, right now. Not to say how we get anywhere's else."

"I can answer some of that," offered the girl-called-'Sari'. "I guided you to the north, from the campsite – this was because they had the bang-things in the ground just back from the, how you say, 'state line', so I thought that the gunmen from the jail-houses would not go through those, to try to overtake us. Then, when I knew the bang-traps were behind us, I turned to the left. We are probably a third-part of a mile from the encampment, to the... the 'west', yes, that is the word."

"Well, unless you've got a better idea, I'd suggest heading back to my SUV," recommended Billings. "Assuming that it hasn't been totally junked by now – God willing, they'll just have stolen my stereo, maybe the cash I had hidden under the front passenger seat, too – we'd at least have wheels. Although I very much doubt we'd have enough gas to even make it back to Montpelier... ahh, I don't *know*. Probably a stupid idea, they might be patrolling the roads for us. But I can't think of anything else to do. I mean, we can't all just *walk* back home, can we?"

The fallen-girl sat down on a nearby rock and quietly stated, "At least all of you *have* homes to go *to*, Bob. Unlike me."

She sounded depressed.

Billings, joined almost immediately by Curtis Claremont, sat down beside her.

"Hey, *hey*, Sari," consoled the salesman, extending his arm around her shoulders, "You're always welcome with me, at my place in Tucson, I mean. Don't ask me *how* I'm going to explain you to my girlfriend, but we'll cross that bridge when we come to it."

He felt her nuzzling his cheek, and was barely able to control himself. But fortunately one of the others spoke up.

"An' y'all can *always* come stay wid us, Miz Sari," added the boy. "Right, Momma?"

"Yeah, ah s'pose, there no doubt, ah owes y'all, lady," affirmed Claremont, wearily. "Owes y'all a *lot*. We ain't got much, but y'all can lay yo' head at our place, long as y'all want. An' ah don' know which of us gonna have more trouble 'splainin, Bob wid he girlfriend or us wid our homies tryin' to 'splain why we keepin' a *white* girl wid us, but like Mister Sales Man say, that a problem for later. Curtis, Melissa – yeah, and y'all too, Tommy, guess ah gots to be yo' mamma, leastaways till y'all get back to yo' own – get yo' stuff up off the ground, we all best be goin', now."

"But that's farther away from the reserve," objected the Indian-boy. "Can't we go east? To the reserve, I mean. They'd let you in, if I said that you were with me."

"How far would that be, Tommy?" asked the girl-called-'Sari'.

"Dunno, exactly," replied the boy. "It's north of Route 30, in Wyoming, that is. I think I heard my dad say, one time, that it was... was... maybe thirty miles, to the state line? Or fifty... or..."

"Look, kid," said Billings, "We all appreciate that you'd like to get home, so would I, so would Whitney, so would her kids, and Sari, well... but unless you want to head off on your own – something that I advise you not to do, by the way – you'd be far better off getting in the car with the rest of us. If and when this nonsense with the border ends, it'll be a simple matter for me to drop you off at this 'reserve' you talk about. Okay?"

"Okay, Mister, I guess," unenthusiastically replied the Indian-boy.

"What about *us*, Mister Billins?" asked the Claremont girl. "Y'all gonna drop us off, too?"

"No. Well, *maybe*... for God's sake," complained an exasperated Billings. "You're all from Detroit, right? A few miles inside Wyoming, that's a detour, Michigan, well, that's a hell of a lot *more* of a detour, you understand? Look, we can worry about all of this, when we actually get into a working car. Which, need I remind you, we may not even be able to do. That make sense to everybody?"

"Of course it make sense," interjected Claremont. "Y'all just get us to somewhere that we can make a few phone-calls, talk to mah folks, y'all know? We be all right, after that. Come on, Melissa. We been talkin' too long, now."

"Yes, Ma'am," replied the teenager.

All the troupe, except for one, got up, dusted themselves off. And stood in place, each waiting for the other to ask the obvious question.

"So, let's get going," commanded the salesman.

"Which way, Mister Billins?" inquired the Claremont boy.

"That way," pointed the girl they knew as 'Sari', hoping that they could see the gesture.

"Follow me," she added.

"How you *know*, lady?" asked the Indian-boy. "It's *really* dark out here, even without that weirdo trick that you did for us, back there. The sun's already gone down and I only learned a bit about how to tell north and south, east and west by the stars and the wind, when I was back on the reserve. My Dad and the other hunters from our tribe can do it, but I can't. Are you *sure* that's the way?"

"*Very* sure," replied the fallen-girl, confidently, her eyes glowing dimly, eerily. "It is an art that I have known since times long-forgotten. The unseen forces, the metal-pulling ones, that is... they tell me."

"Uhh, *riight. Really* sure?" wondered Billings.

"You will just have to *trust* me," she answered. "Do you trust me, Bob Billings, my love?"

He stopped and thought for a long second, then replied, "Do I trust you... yes, I do, Sari Anati – Anyt – Anywhatever Tanak. I mean, I trusted you with my *life* back there, don't know why I did, considering the odds... so did they, but you got us all out, somehow. So lead on, girl. Oh, and one other thing."

"Yes, Bob?" said the fallen-girl, patiently.

"Well, it's a hell of a time to *ask*, isn't it?" muttered the salesman, with poorly-faked malice.

The one-called-'Sari' wheeled to address the rest of them.

"I think that is how Bob says, 'yes', would you not say?" she primly stated, arching an insouciant eyebrow.

"Way a lot of boys do, when they *like* you, Miz Sari," observed Melissa, with a knowing grin invisible to all but the one who would lead them onwards.

The 'Sari'-girl giggled goofily.

"Come on, then; let our feet be worthy sisters to the Four Winds," she ordered, as they strode forth into the cool Prairie night.

Target Not In Sight

"How far we gots to go, Miz Sari?" requested the teenager.

"Do not ask me, Melissa," replied the 'Sari'-girl, as she determinedly strode forward. "Ask Bob – I did not arrive here, or rather back there, with him."

"Don't ask *me*, either," complained the salesman, huffing and puffing as he did his best to keep up with the rest of the crew.

"Granted, she dropped that weirdo super-dark thing of hers and I can see as well as I normally could, out here," he added. "Which is to say, 'I can still hardly see *anything*'. We might have gone right *by* the damn car by now, for all I know."

"I do not think so, Bob," argued the fallen-girl. "If I am dividing the number of our footsteps into what you call a – a – 'mile', yes, that is it, we still have eight or more of these 'miles' yet to go. We still are not very far from the encampment, you know, and –"

Her voice stopped suddenly.

"We are being *watched*," she warned. "Gather around me – quickly!"

"I don' see *nothin*'..." complained the elder Claremont.

"Yeah, lady, it's pitch black out here," remarked the Indian-boy.

"Can you not see that thing over there, shining right *at* us –" exclaimed the 'Sari'-girl, jabbing her finger at the horizon, in the direction from which they had just come. "It looks warm, almost hot. It is lighting up all of you just like a candle inside a lantern. Now move next to me, or they will *see* us!"

"Sure, whatever, Miz Sari," complied the Claremont girl, with a shrug. "Come on, Curtis... she ain't never lied to us before. Ah cain't see nothin' neither, but y'all and ah wouldn't be out here in the first place, if'n she didn't get us out of that jail back there."

The teenager shuffled over to a place very close to the fallen-girl's side, accompanied indifferently by her younger brother.

"Look, Sari girl, like mah daughter, see, ah trust y'all, but there ain't *nothin'* out there –" observed Whitney Claremont. "And if we stickin' as close to y'all as we was back there, we bein' all over each other's feet, soon as y'all can say –"

From the far distance, a ghostly voice commanded, "You out there! Prisoners! We see you! Halt *immediately* and surrender, or we'll open fire!"

"*Shit!*" exclaimed Billings. "They must have one of those damn night-sights, they use infra-red, see by heat, that sort of thing!"

"They can see in the dark, you mean, Mister Salesman?" asked Tommy.

"You have five seconds!" warned the voice.

"Look, Sari, I think the jig may be up," he started. "If they can track us in the dark... how the hell do we..."

Billings hesitated, for a second; but then he felt himself being pushed – or was it pulled – toward the fallen-girl, as if an invisible force, akin to a strong wind at his back, was gently nudging him forward.

"No *way*, Bob," she contradicted. "After all I the work that I have put into getting all of you out, they will *not* recapture you, *that* easily."

Immediately, she started singing, or maybe chanting, something under her breath, a rhythmic, humming sound unlike anything that Billings had ever heard.

"What you think you *doin'*?" asked Claremont. "That a prayer, girl?"

"Gather around me, *now!*" ordered the newcomer. "I can block *that* kind of light, too. But you must be close, I cannot cover all the distance between where you are now, and me."

Billings' ears – no, wrong word, his *mind* – started to hear some weird kind of music, made up of unfamiliar chords, yet uplifting, exciting, reassuring, none the less.

Music? What the hell? thought the salesman. *Some kind of stupid psycho-warfare crap by those Bible nuts back there? But it doesn't* sound *at all like the stuff they had playing in the tent, no, it's much more like, maybe one of Led Zeppelin's undiscovered tracks – or Boston's...*

A bullet whizzed overhead.

"Okay, comin', ah gets the message," muttered Claremont, as she joined the 'Sari'-girl's side, next to Billings.

"Bob, y'all hear *music* playin'? Sound like it right here, but we ain't gots none of them little computer music player boxes, leastaways mah kids don't, couldn't afford all that networkin' stuff –"

"*Quiet*, Whitney!" demanded the fallen-girl. "Ebon curtain coming down."

The one-called-'Sari' was ever true to her word. A shroud of blackness enveloped them.

She called out, "Tommy, move in here with us!"

"I don't *see* you, lady," the boy stammered. "You all just disappeared."

Another bullet whistled overhead, followed by another, and another still.

"Tommy!" cried the fallen-girl. "They are trying to target you! Just run forward!"

Without further argument, the Indian-boy dashed in the direction of the 'Sari'-girl's voice, running headfirst into Billing's midriff, just above the belt. Caught completely off balance, the salesman let out a muffled curse as he fell backwards, leaving only the lower half of his body within the six-foot-or-so radius of his newfound girlfriend's strange black stealth aura.

He now saw conventional searchlights scouring the area about thirty feet behind them, towards where the gunfire had come from.

A smile came to Billings' face. He yelled out to the direction of the searchlights.

"Hey! Fuck *you*," the salesman taunted. "Catch us if you can!"

A bullet whizzed by, nowhere near.

"For the sake of the Blue Sun of the Black Night, Bob, *shut up!*" pleaded the fallen-girl. "And move your – your – damn head back inside here!"

Reluctantly, Billings retracted his upper-body back into the protected area and stood up, dusting himself off as best he could.

"Why Sari, girl, ah ain't never heared y'all cuss, befo'," maliciously commented Claremont.

"I suppose that I am learning all sorts of new habits, these days," muttered the newcomer, semi-apologetically. "Not necessarily *good* ones. Come on, let us flee. If they persist in firing, there is still a small chance that they will hit us – my cloak can stop light, not bullets. Each person hold one other as we go. We need to put some distance between us and these dangerous people."

She took a fast first step, and the others followed, their feet empowered by something that felt like an ethereal tailwind.

Soon the searchlights were far behind, still washing over where they had latterly tarried, in a gesture of futility.

A Charge Out Of You

"Can't y'all carry me, Momma?" asked the boy, plaintively. "Ah can't hardly *walk*, no more."

"Ah *knows*, Curtis Ray, but y'all in the same boat as all the rest of us," replied Claremont, firmly but sympathetically. "Melissa? How y'all holdin' up, child?"

"'Bout as bad as Curtis, Momma," answered the elder sibling's Detroit accent. "Mah feets killin' me. It was easier on the grass, but we been' walkin' this road for *hours*."

"Oh-kay, then," announced the one-called-'Sari', "We can stop, for a few minutes... we should be alright, for a while. I have seen no sign of the gun-men since I dropped my hiding-cloak, and that was at least four of your 'miles' back behind us. But we should not tarry too long, even so."

"You got *that* right," managed Billings, gasping for breath but trying to hide the fact. "Who knows, they might have helicopters... airplanes... maybe even those remote-controlled drone-spy things. They got radar, night sights on 'em – I can *personally* attest to it, got nabbed twice for speeding down home, in the dead of night."

He leaned back against a nearby rock, strategically chosen for its ability to accommodate exactly two persons, side by side, and was elated when the fallen-girl got the hint and reclined next to him.

The two looked up, staring in wonder at the glory of the Milky Way, resplendent above them like some diamond-studded sash across the waist of the sky, here far away from the maddening, distracting lights of civilization.

"Beautiful, aren't they?" idly asked the salesman.

"You have *no* idea, Bob," commented the 'Sari'-girl, faint echoes of wonder leaking from the tone of her voice. "I never tire of the glory that they display, no matter how many times that I see them from this perspective... I am a tiny, unimportant being, staring at their majesty; stars and worlds without end, millions upon uncounted millions, like little shining jewels to the eye, but each in fact complex and fascinating, such as one could never guess without going there."

She paused for a second, then continued, "I suppose that I never *will* visit most of them, and that makes me sad, but it keeps me humble, I guess. Yet not many places are more full of life, of people who think and dream and have a chance of being great, as is the 'Earth'... it is hard to compare one with the other, really; every world has its own unique charms, its own reasons to be preserved and cherished. Some the places up there are dark, terrible, evil and forbidding; thankfully, those are few and far between. Most are beautiful in their own way, even if they are too hot, cold or otherwise impossible for the likes of you and Whitney to inhabit. Life is resourceful and will adapt as it needs to survive, but here on Earth, everything is in abundance and the environment is... *mostly,* pleasant. One does not know how much one has, until one loses it..."

He did not get up, but Billings turned his head at the fallen-girl and remarked, "Wow – for a second there you had me thinking... ah, hell. I mean, I'm sure there *are,* other planets, other civilizations *et cetera,* but, how would *you –*"

Innocently, she replied, "Because I just *know,* Bob. I do not know how, but I do. And I know that I am in a *good* place and that I intend to stay here, on this 'Earth', if I can. There's no desire whatsoever to leave, on my side of our little rock."

She giggled, weirdly.

"As if you *could,*" uneasily offered Billings. "Leave, I mean."

The 'Sari'-girl smiled pleasantly back at him, a hint of sharp teeth barely visible in the starlit Prairie night.

"Alas, I can only walk and run... right now," she stated, neutrally.

There was another pause, then she reflectively added, "Right... *now.*"

"Mister Sales Man," interjected the Indian-boy, "I don't wanna bother you, but... well, shouldn't we have found your car yet? We've been going down the road for a *really* long time."

Billings spat on the ground.

"Yeah, kid, we *should* have," he replied. "About an hour ago. Or more. I'd like to think that's just because I hid it so well, but my guess is that I forgot where it is... or, somebody has already stolen the damn thing, towed it away, I mean. Would be just my luck for that to happen, I suppose."

"What we gonna *do*, Momma?" whimpered the Claremont girl. "Now that Mister Billins wheels is gone."

"Hush, child," retorted Claremont. "Y'all don' *know* that. Bob still gonna find it. Just take *time*, that's all."

Billings winced. He thought that none could see him do it.

"Let us not jump to conclusions, everyone," cautioned the girl-called-'Sari'. "If Bob's memory does not fail him and if I have been counting our paces correctly, we still have a short distance to go before we would be near the –"

She stopped, abruptly.

"Something is coming! From the west, down the road!" she warned.

"Ah don' see –" started Claremont.

"How can you not... *see*, way down the highway, at least three of them, they look hot-color," exclaimed the fallen-girl, to darkened looks of puzzlement amongst the others.

"We should *hide*," she ordered. "Follow me – there is a rock over there, south of the road... some bushes too, lots of cover. Come on!"

Reluctantly, the group shuffled on behind the newcomer, assembling in crouched formation behind a large rock no more than a few seconds before a vehicle of some kind roared past them, then another, then one more.

Off to one side, the Indian-boy whispered to his African-American friend, "Curtis, what's a 'hot-color'?"

The Claremont boy gave a palms-up, 'got-no-idea' gesture.

"Interesting," commented Billings, *sotto voce*. "They look military – like, the Army, I mean. Convoy, of some sort."

"Yeah," agreed Claremont, "They goin' towards that jail they set us up in. If they the Army, maybe they gonna free everyone else in there? Y'all know, like, 'Uncle Sam back in charge'?"

"Who is this 'Uncle Sam' person, Bob?" interrupted the 'Sari'-girl. "I keep hearing about him. Is that another name for your deity, or your President?"

"Neither," grunted Billings. "Well, *sort of*, for the President... he's more like a symbol for the whole good ol' U.S. of A. – a trademark, you know? And as for what happens to the camp, more likely, they're going to give those stupid Bible-bangers a big friendly slap on the back for doing such a fine job – for God's sake, Whitney, pun not intended, since way before the Big Thing, you know, it's been damn near *impossible* to tell where the religious nuts begin and the government ends, or *vice versa*. Wouldn't surprise me a *bit* to find out that the

Jesus people decided to make their move in all the confusion of the last few months. After what we all went through back there, you'll have to convince me otherwise."

"Maybe," offered Claremont, indifferently.

"So how long we waitin' here?" asked her son. "Don' like all them bushes. They might be spiders. I don' like spiders."

"Or scorpions," noted Tommy, unhelpfully. "Dad told me about the ones down south on another reservation – one sting and you're dead in ten minutes –"

Claremont glared at the child.

"I do not hear any more cars," announced the girl-called-'Sari', "But I should make sure. Here, Bob – help me up, please... I will climb to the top of the rock. I should be able to see quite a bit further from up there, it is two or more man-heights to the top."

"Well, okay," answered Billings, hoping that the fallen-girl couldn't feel the lechery in his grasp upon her shapely waist, as he tried to get her foot on his shoulder.

"But you just said that we'd be too easy to spot... oh, yeah, I *forgot*," he muttered, as the 'Sari'-girl vanished completely from his eyesight, though he could still feel her body next to his.

Then she was gone, evidently clambering up the side of the rock-formation.

"So what do you see?" inquired Billings. "Any more cops or robbers? Cowboys or Indians? Oh, sorry, kid – didn't mean any offense."

"No problem, Mister," cheerfully replied Tommy. "I get called that all the time. I'm used to it."

"'Cops' or – oh, I think that I understand," came back a familiar voice, from the top of the rock. "No, nothing like that, but it has taken me longer than normal to look around, I must drop my cloak for a second, sneak a glance, then put it back up again... I am sure, now – I do not see any vehicles. Except, what is *that* –"

"Sari?" asked a worried Billings.

"I think that there is a vehicle, something metal, at least, behind a group of bushes, about fifty man-lengths beyond this big rock," she explained. "Yes... *definitely*. A big one, not like those 'Army' things that just went past, but larger than an ordinary car."

"*Yeah!*" exclaimed the salesman. "That's *gotta* be it! God *damn*. And here I thought – well, maybe ol' Bob's luck *is* coming back, after all. Let's skedaddle!"

"Skee – *whaa?*" came back a confused reply, from the rock-top. "Does one not need snow to do that...?"

To the accompaniment of at least three young voices all laughing at once, Billings shouted to the fallen-girl as he strode briskly across the road, checking both directions for signs of any more traffic.

"Not *that* kind of skiing, my dear," he chuckled. "Just a fast trot towards what's going to get us out of this miserable chunk of nowhere. All them that wants a ride out of here, you better get over here with me, *pronto*."

Claremont, her two children and the Indian-boy rapidly followed the salesman across the road, towards the vehicle.

"Just another one that I guess I must learn," he heard the 'Sari'-girl complain.

Billings glanced momentarily behind him, only to see the newcomer appear out of nowhere at the bottom of the rock.

"Glad you could join us, Sari," he called back to her. "Come on!"

As she rapidly came up to his side, he remarked, "You know, you were right on *top* of that thing... how'd you get down so fast?"

"That is simple enough, Bob," she replied, matter-of-factually. "I just jumped down."

"Yeah, but it's ten feet or more from up there to down here," he argued. "If *I* tried something like that, you'd need a stretcher to carry me away."

"Well, sorry to have to say it in this way, Bob," she mentioned as they trotted forward, "But you... uhh.. *weigh* more than I do. There is a rule of the natural forces concerning that – something like 'the more heavy the object, the faster it's going, the more force when it impacts'..."

"Makes sense, I guess," muttered Billings.

Inwardly, he thought, *no gymnast, however well-trained, would try something like* that.

And I didn't even hear a sound, *when she landed.*

"Yo, Mister Billins!" they heard a young voice call out. "This one yours? Sure is a nice big car, Ah ain't *never* seen wheels like this! Hey Tommy, check out them tinted windows – ain't *nobody* seein' us in there, we could moon peeps in th' street – "

"Curtis *Ray*," grumbled the boy's mother.

As they came closer, they saw that the three children were already clearing the underbrush from the vehicle.

Billings stopped and stated, "Yeah... *that's* the one, alright. And yeah, it's nice enough, I suppose – I mean, I spend so much goddamn time on the road, I figured I might as well do that comfortably... listen, you three, go ahead and clear her off, but don't fiddle with the door-handles, you could get a nasty surprise from the anti-theft... that's assuming, of course, that anything's still *working* on the crate."

To the sound of giggles, the branches and leaves came off the vehicle rapidly, revealing a dirty, but clearly high-end, SUV, all in silver and black finish.

Billings advanced and peered inside. He let out a sigh of relief.

"Sensor's still on – that's a good sign," he noted. "We still got some battery. But – "

"But *what*, Bob?" inquired the fallen-girl.

"Well, we may have juice in the starter, but when I parked her, the gas gage was already reading 'E' for 'Empty' and the main hybrid drive battery was 90 per cent depleted, so don't get your hopes too far up... if we're lucky, we can make it back west to town and hope that one of the stations is open now, none of 'em were when I stopped here, which is why I did; I mean, we obviously can't go back east, now *can* we?"

"'Spose not," commented Claremont. "They just put us in jail, again. So ah guess we goin' west. Hey, Mister Bob... y'all think we could take a detour to L.A., since we headin' west, anyway?"

The salesman shook his head as he reached embarrassingly low into his pants and retrieved a precious car-key.

"Whitney, we've already been *over* that," he countered. "Even if I *wanted* to – which I don't – last I heard, the damn place's a no-go zone for fifty miles on every side. Don't know if I got a chance to tell you, but when I was in the barracks with all the other poor bastards they put in there, I overheard two low-lifes talking about it in the showers... seems that there's something like a full-scale war going on all over good old Cali-for-ni-ay between the Bloods and the Crips, or the Crips and the skinheads, or the *Maras* and the *Zetas*, or whatever the hell they call each other these days."

"Yeah, ah knows," muttered the woman. "But that ain't much diff'rent from how things is, usually."

"One of these assholes in the shower was trying to get the other one to help him 'off' somebody from the other gang who was also in the barracks by the way," added Billings. "But, back to the story, cops aren't even bothering to stop it, they're waiting until all of the gang-bangers kill each other off. Which may be some time from now... and which is why I *ain't* going to L.A., sister."

He grunted as he wiped the last of the dust off the front windshield with a branch of leaves.

Claremont did not reply; instead, she sullenly shrugged her shoulders.

Billings typed a code into a recessed keypad on the driver-side door and turned a high-tech digital key.

He jumped into the seat.

"*Amazing*," exclaimed the salesman. "Nothing's out of place. They didn't even get the stereo... hah, old Bob's better at hiding things than he let on."

He fumbled under the driver's seat, and yelped joyfully.

"God *damn*," inveighed Billings. "Money's still here! Well, at least we can buy some gas now. Come on, get in, all you."

At the touch of a button, the other doors unlocked too.

Each one obliged and entered the vehicle, with the 'Sari'-girl in the front and the rest in the rear seats. A chime sounded repeatedly when Billings inserted his key in the ignition.

He looked back, then to his side.

"Sari," he grumbled, "Haven't you forgotten to *do* something? I can't get going, you know."

"Forgotten *what*, Bob?" the fallen-girl answered, with an innocent-looking-smile. "I am sitting down... I am ready to go."

"Your seat belt isn't fastened," the salesman complained. "It won't start up. The car, I mean."

"My *what* belt?" protested the newcomer. "Oh, you must mean *this* one, here. Oh-kay..."

As the catch on the belt engaged with a click she added, "Although I do not think that it will help very much – it is a 'safety' thing? I can assure you that I will have no trouble handling high-speed impacts..."

"Thanks," said Billings. "And I'm sure you *are*, but apart from the fact that the car won't start if you don't do it up, if we get stopped by the cops or the Army, I don't want to give them the *slightest* reason to throw us in the clink or impound this beast. It's against the law to drive without seat belts, has been for thirty or more years – how could you not... anyway. You all ready to get going?"

Three small voices cheered an enthusiastic "Yep!" from the back seats. Billings turned the key.

There was a 'chug, chug' sound.

The car shuddered. And did not move.

Desperately, the salesman tried again, and again, pumping the gas. Each time, the results were the same.

"*Shit*," cursed Billings. "I was *afraid* of this. We got enough juice in the starter and hybrid drive batteries to light the anti-theft and the instrumentation, but not the car itself. I *knew* I should've replaced the damn things, but with how it was few months ago, I figured, it probably wouldn't matter, anyway. I'm afraid that we're stuck, folks."

The children groaned. "What we gonna do *now*, Momma?" whined Melissa.

"'Juice', Bob?" inquired the 'Sari'-girl. "Electricity, that kind of energy, you mean, right? It is stored in this 'battery', and it somehow became depleted?"

Billings nodded unhappily.

"Well, can we replenish this 'battery'?" she asked. "Then the motor will start?"

"Laws-a-mighty, girl, where y'all *from*," sighed Claremont. "Ain't y'all never seen a car before?"

"Yes, of *course* I have," defensively shot back the fallen-girl. "Why, I *rode* in one... well, oh-kay, a truck, actually, to get to where we all met. It was a big one, with many wheels..."

Billings had slumped over the steering wheel for a second, deep in thought.

"Well, we can try a push start," he suggested. "Get the alternator turning. That is, if we can get this crate up to the road. Everybody out. Except *you*, Sari. You know how to drive a car?"

"I... uhh... *sure* I do," uneasily replied the newcomer, forcing a faked confident smile. "The round thing, that steers it, right? I saw somebody use one of those. But where is the... uhh... the 'shift'? Does one not need a 'shift' to make the engine work? The truck that I was in, the man who drove it, he was always moving this stick back and forth..."

"J.H.C., girl," muttered an exasperated Billings, "How can you *not* know how to... never mind. Look, why don't you help me push. Melissa, do you want to steer? Come on, get up here."

The 'Sari'-girl hung her head and moped in disappointment.

"Yessir!" chirped the teenager. "Ah done drove three cars already, but ah don' got my license, that okay, Mister Bob?"

"Yeah, fine, no problem," agreed the salesman. "Here, we'll keep it in neutral, so you don't drive off on us... just give it a little gas, when we get going... you understand?"

Melissa shook her head up and down, enthusiastically, as she took her place in the driver's seat.

The rest of them gathered behind the vehicle.

Billings mentioned, "Now, I realize that she's a big one, so take this easy... we all put our shoulders to it, and push at once. One... two... *three!*"

The SUV rocked, but did not roll.

Billings looked around. "Sari, where the hell *are* you – we *need* you, girl, get over here!"

The fallen-girl shuffled over and leaned against the back of the vehicle.

"Let's try again, guys," commanded the salesman. "One... two... *three!*"

The troupe behind the car gave a mighty push. The SUV inched forward, forward more, more still; then it rolled backwards, almost pinning the Indian-boy underneath one of the wheels, before the vehicle came to a rest.

"It too *big*, Bob," complained Claremont. "We keep tryin', somebody get hurt."

The 'Sari'-girl had disappeared, without warning.

"Where she go?" asked the Indian-boy.

"Prolly gave up," offered Curtis. "Cain't blame her. She pretty strong, but not strong enough to move *this* big a set of wheels."

"This isn't *working*," spat Billings. "What with the incline and the uneven ground, we'd need a couple more full-grown men just to get her up to the road. Hate to say it, but I guess we'd better get ready to start walking again."

A groan issued from the three children.

"Momma, ah *way* too tired to walk anymore," complained Curtis.

"Child's got a point," observed Claremont. "Even if we keep walkin', we not likely to get anywhere to sleep. Can't we just bunk down here, Bob?"

There was a 'sproingg' sound from the front of the SUV.

The black woman could just see that the hood had apparently been opened.

"*Sure* we can," replied Billings, in a sarcastic tone. "If you want to take the chance of being noticed... we're not too far off the road, you know, if another one of those convoys comes by. We can try to cover her up again, I suppose, but we'll have to leave at least one door uncovered, the side away from the road, of course. We'll have to keep the lights off, which won't be hard, considering that we might not have enough charge to turn 'em on anyway."

They heard a 'click', then a soft, pained moan, from around the front of the vehicle.

"Who's *that?*" shouted a worried Billings. "What's going on up there?"

"Just me, Bob," came back the voice of the 'Sari'-girl. "I am trying something."

"You okay?" demanded the salesman. "I thought I heard the sound of somebody getting hurt..."

"I am fine," called the fallen-girl. "I just wanted to see this 'battery' that you've got. You know, the one that holds the electricity."

"Look, keep your mitts off of it, Sari," commanded Billings. "You could *hurt* yourself – all you'd have to do is ground yourself to either of those terminal posts on it... it might not have enough of a charge to get the car started, but still have enough to give you a nasty burn. And I don't want you fiddling with the engine, you could make a bad situation worse. You got that?"

"Yes, Bob... whatever," muttered the newcomer's voice.

"Well Bob, y'all say we can stay the night, that make sense to me," interrupted Claremont.

She peered around the side of the SUV and called out to her daughter.

"Melissa, honey," she requested, "Y'all get down from there, Mister Billins say we gonna put the branches n' such back on, then we gonna hide out here till mornin'. Come on, child."

A voice answered, "Just a sec, Momma... 'Sari round the front, she say she tryin' somethin'. She want me to turn the key."

"*Lawd*, child," complained Claremont. "Don't y'all know that Mister Bob's battery *daid*? Car can't go without no juice, you know. Y'all get down, right now."

"Try it now, Melissa," ordered a voice from the front of the vehicle.

The teenager turned the key.

There was another strange sound from the front of the SUV, and this time, Billings hurried around the side, just in time to see sparks and a faint puff of smoke coming from the right side of the engine area, followed by the 'Sari'-girl, moaning as if punched in the gut, falling flat-backward to the ground just as Melissa tried the ignition again.

Roaarrrrrr.

The SUV shuddered as its engine turned over, coming to life with a throaty growl.

"Sari!" shouted the salesman. "Whitney! Melissa! Come help me! Something's *happened* to her!"

He was rapidly joined by the others as they all crouched over the newcomer. Billings grabbed her shoulders and tried to get her fore-body to sit up, and as he did so, he noticed a sheen of cold sweat on the poor creature's brow.

"Sari! Sari! Can you hear me?" he shouted.

"Ohhhh..." whimpered the fallen-girl, reflexively licking her lips as if trying to come out of a trance.

Gradually, her eyes fluttered open. She forced a smile.

"Hi, Bob," she breathed. "See? I started it. Well, oh-kay, Melissa did. But I helped her."

"Whew," exclaimed Billings. "For a second there I was afraid something really... *bad* had happened there, girl. What the hell were you *doing*?"

"Well," she explained, proudly but nonchalantly, "You said that it was short of electricity, right? The 'battery', I mean. So I thought that I would try to help it a little, put some more into it. But I was not expecting that thing to... to make the little bits of energy to... flow back *at* me. I mean, the charge path, the flow, it changes all the time, like, *thousands* of times per second. Why would anyone set it up that to act in that way? The flow is supposed to go all the same direction, like a river −"

"Y'all talkin' *shit*, girl," commented Claremont. "Ah cain't understand a word you sayin'. What this all about 'puttin' more 'lectricity in it? There ain't no other battery hidin' round here."

"Easy, there, Whitney," cautioned the salesman. "She might have got a bump on the head there, when she landed. Sari, do you think you can walk? The car's running, but I don't know how much gas we have left, and we shouldn't wait around here any longer than we have to, before we get on our way."

"I... I feel a little faint, Bob," noted the fallen-girl. "Oh-kay, maybe a *lot* faint. Can you help me up?"

"Of course," agreed Billings. "Uhh, Sari, I don't like putting it this way, but you didn't... *cut* yourself when you fell down, did you? Because, you remember... wouldn't want any more of that stuff on me, or them..."

"*What* stuff?" inquired Curtis, to no reply.

"Cut... what? Oh, right. No, Bob, I do not think so," the 'Sari'-girl replied, softly. "I just feel completely... *drained*, that is all. Like you would if you had to work all day, or maybe all week, without any sleep, that's the best way I can describe it. But I do not think there is any physical damage. I hope not."

"Well, thank God for *that*," remarked Billings. "Here, Whitney, you take her other side."

Claremont did so, unenthusiastically. Gradually, they got the fallen-girl upright. Even in this light, they could see how much of her color had departed.

"Miss Sari, you look really pale, like a ghost," observed the Indian-boy.

"I will recover," she mentioned, as they shuffled toward the car's side door, dragging the newcomer's rubbery-feeling feet on the ground. "Sooner or later. Sooner, if I have something to eat... I am *really* hungry. Is there any food around? Candy bars? I would even eat one of those, how do you say... 'pep-per-onee' things, they stink, but anything, now..."

Melissa shook her head.

"Ah already looked everywhere ah could in Mister Bob's car," noted the teenager. "Oh, sorry, Mister Bob. Would have told y'all if ah found anythin'. Really would."

"Yeah, *sure* you would," mumbled Billings. "But don't worry about it. Unfortunately food wasn't one of the things I stocked up on... thought I could just buy myself one last supper, when it came down to that..."

The 'Sari'-girl sighed.

"So there is nothing to eat, then," she whimpered, stumbling upon trying to enter the car. "Oh, I am *so* weak now..."

Billings and Claremont gently deposited the strange female in the rearmost seat, taking the entire row as they laid her face-up.

"Try to get some rest, Sari," requested the salesman, bending over the fallen-girl as does a father with a sick child. "Just keep the seat belt on, try to sleep. I'll wake you if we make it to a gas station, or, better still, a restaurant. Okay?"

He found a blanket and covered her with it, leaving only her head peeking out.

She managed enough strength to raise her hand and grasp his. Looking at him with big, doe-like eyes, the one-called-'Sari' offered, "Oh-kay, Bob. You trusted me; so I will place my trust in you. Lead us on, lover Bob."

The salesman just stood there, transfixed, for some reason, by – *what*, exactly? Was it her eyes, her smile, the warm touch of her hand, or something else altogether?

He wanted to kneel down, lay his head on her chest, fall into a peaceful slumber with this mysterious creature.

She jump-started the fucking car with just her hands – *not even a booster cable*, a little voice told him. *What the hell* is *she?*

But God, I'd marry her, run off anywhere with her, without a second's hesitation. Girlfriend down south or no. Can't say 'no' to her... don't know why...

At length, he heard Claremont's voice saying, "Yo, Mister Bob, y'all gonna get us out on the highway, afore we gotta get out 'n push again?"

Billings opened the side-door, wheeled in place and jumped into the driver's seat.

"Well, here we go," he announced, as he guided the SUV, his pride and joy from the fondly-missed, simpler times back not so long ago, up to the open highway, off into the night.

Footprints In A Forest

The smartly-uniformed young Air Force lieutenant's hands played expertly over the keyboard of the windowless meeting-room's teleconferencing system.

Facing its operator, the system's marvelous, combined holographic-and-conventional LCD projection display showed "Primary Secured Channel", then, for a split-second, "Secondary Channel"; then it again displayed "Primary Secured Channel".

"Connection security verified," pleasantly stated the soldier, turning the display to face a senior government official. "You can start the conference whenever you want, Mr. Secretary, sir," he added.

"Very well," said Arthur DeWitt, in his usual, non-nonsense undertone, gesturing for the subordinate to leave the room.

The young man instantly complied, closing the door behind him with only the slightest 'click'.

"Go ahead, Ms. Chu. I also have Mr. McPherson of the Science Office, here with me," announced DeWitt. "Oh, and General, this is our fifth and final call of the day – we've already heard in from the other field teams, that is the ones doing elsewhere from the Northwest. Nothing interesting to report from them, other than widespread damage, of course. I just brought you in so you'd get an idea of the quality of information that we're receiving."

"Understood," called a ghostly male voice.

"The situation up here is pretty confused," started a distant, female tone on the loudspeaker in the center of the meeting-room table, "There are a lot of contradictory stories. Also, it has been hard for us to keep the team from being pulled off to assist local law-enforcement – unfortunately, we've seen some of the gang-related violence that's been going on in the urban areas, percolating even this far north."

"Yeah?" asked the Secretary of Defense. "How so?"

"Well, sir," continued the woman over the long-distance link, "It shouldn't be a surprise that the 'Lucifer' thing killed a lot of gang leaders all over the country, and in regions like this where there's now a power vacuum at the top, there are murders everywhere... apparently thousands of the *Maras*, maybe tens of thousands of them, got across the Rio Grande – the Wall got knocked down by comet debris in several places – and the seconds-in-command of the Crips and Bloods are shooting it out amongst themselves and with the Latino gangs for the top job, control of the synth drug market, that kind of thing."

"Looks like Ochoa's got his hand's full," remarked DeWitt.

"Very much so, sir", stated the remote voice, "Not just with the urban gangs, but we've got bikers, skinheads and just common criminals, running wild on the Interstates, entire campgrounds of people turning up robbed, hurt or dead. They've basically taken over several small towns and they're openly defying the authorities to dislodge them. The locals are depending on us to fill in the manpower gaps for investigations –"

"That's to be expected," interjected the other voice. "But do you have any results for us? Any leads?"

"That's General Anderson, am I right?" said the first voice. "I'm on my cell and we've been told that most of the repeaters around here are still out... can you hear me okay, sir?"

"Yes, he's on the bridge," commented Fred McPherson.

"Coming in fine," replied the second voice.

"Hi, General Anderson sir, Special Agent Minnie Chu of FBI here," politely stated the first voice. "I should mention that it's pretty difficult for us to assess the evidence that's come our way so far, without knowing exactly what we're looking *for*, sir. I mean, and this is an opinion shared by the rest of my team, 'report all evidence related to impact anomalies', that's a pretty vague set of marching orders... if you told us what the precise target is, we could –"

"*We'll* be the judge of that," interrupted DeWitt. "Just the facts, if you please."

"Of course, sir," answered Chu. "Well, as I said, it's hard to separate factual evidence from some of the wild stories that we have been hearing up here, everything from flying saucers to sightings of the Virgin Mary to invasions by 'black-shirted armies of the United Nations', that kind of thing. It takes a significant amount of time to go through all of these, just to listen to what the people involved have to say. The Psy-Ops people from the Army have advised us to at least appear to treat all these stories seriously, to avoid giving the locals the impression that we're covering anything up."

"So what *else* is new," commented McPherson. "Go on."

"Yeah," confirmed Chu. "There's really only *one* thing that we thought was worth further investigation. There are multiple impact sites up here, we checked every one of them; NASA was excited to see that some of them contain comet fragments, so they've taken over those locations. Only one site was different; that is, Hill 1442. What we – I mean, the forensics teams up on that mountain and down here on the highway – have been able to determine, is that the tracks coming down from 1442 were *not* made by anyone in the Army and National Guard units that were detailed to do the search."

DeWitt arched an eyebrow.

The FBI team-leader continued, "We interviewed all the soldiers involved – took shoe sizes and weight impressions for them, and so on – and none of them match. Also, the tracks are on the *reverse* side of 1442, that is, we're pretty confident that nobody from the military search teams went up that way when the first climbed the mountain. It was difficult following them because they wander all over the place... Forest Service liaison people mentioned that this pattern is typical of what they find, when they're tracking people who get lost in the woods, and so on. They were concerned that somebody might still be out there, possibly hurt – maybe they got injured by whatever landed on the mountain – and they sent out search teams, but didn't find anyone. The tracks eventually give out near the road, so what we figure is that whomever was up there, just got back into their car and drove away."

"Did you get a description of anyone *unusual*, appearing in this area, Agent Chu?" inquired Anderson, with interest in his voice rising.

"Very definitely," explained the woman, half-suppressing a chuckle. "At least three truckers whom we interviewed, as well as one USPS employee, gave us stories of little green men landing, with flying saucers, the whole works. Two more of the locals – one was a logger, the other was a farmer, I believe – saw a whole family of, what do you call them again, now I remember, that 'Bigfoot' thing, according to them these shaggy-haired monsters are stealing sheep, family dogs, and whatnot."

DeWitt let out a frustrated sigh.

"Oh, and did I mention," Chu went on, "That the postal worker claimed that he was *abducted* by these same, 'space-aliens'. He had quite an imaginative story about the 'experiments' that they supposedly subjected him to... took us over an hour and a half before we could get him to stop talking. As for the rest of the interviews, we didn't hear anything out of the ordinary, just tales of refugees of one kind or another passing through, pretty much par for the course when you consider how unsettled the conditions still are, out on the Interstates and so on."

"I *told* you this was a waste of time, Mr. Secretary," complained McPherson. "What did you *expect* to hear, after a near-apocalyptic disaster on the 'Lucifer' scale, anyway?"

"Alright, Agent," said DeWitt, patiently. "That's all you have for us, right? Thanks for the report, and keep up the good work. I think we can call this a –"

"But, *sir*," interrupted the woman's voice, over the static of the wireless link, "There *is* just one other thing, probably just an instrumentation error, but its something that the forensics teams thought was peculiar. Up on Hill 1442, that is."

McPherson, who had been staring into space, came to life.

"What?" he retorted. "Isn't that one of the hills where they sent the special teams – "

"Yes, it is, and I know how unlikely this is going to sound, sir," mentioned the woman's voice, "I wasn't even going to raise it, because we think the readings we got might just be the result of some kind of local contamination, waste dumping, that kind of thing. But, remember those tracks I told you about, earlier? If the equipment isn't malfunctioning, that is if the readings are correct, a few of the footprints on the trail seem to be... *radioactive*."

The lines went quiet, for a long second, as McPherson stared at DeWitt, his gaze met with an equally knowing one.

"Please elaborate, Agent Chu," managed the Defense Secretary. "General, did you copy that?"

"Very definitely," gasped Anderson, from wherever he was. "And... '*my God*'. Is it *possible*?"

"Sir?" asked the FBI agent. "You sound *concerned* –"

"Uhh... nothing, Ms. Chu," prevaricated Anderson, partly regaining his composure.

"Please continue," he requested. "And... let's not jump to conclusions, just yet."

"Right... well, the emanation is very faint, so weak, in fact, that we missed it the first time, a regular Geiger counter won't detect it," explained Chu. "We didn't want to waste any more time on this particular site, but one of the special teams people *insisted* on bringing in more sensitive gear to look it over. And there's something else strange about it."

"What's that?" asked McPherson. "Wait, don't tell me, let me guess."

"What do you *mean*, sir?" countered the woman.

"I'm guessing that the energy pattern is one that you aren't familiar with... that is, not alpha particles, not beta, not gamma, not X-Rays, not *anything* that's in the books, right?" requested the Science Advisor. "A very real signature, but one that you can't identify?"

"Yes, *exactly*," confirmed Chu. "How did you know, sir? I don't want to be argumentative here, but FBI was given *very* categorical assurances that our communications were not to be monitored –"

"I didn't *have* to listen in on you," shot back McPherson. "Because I know what kind of radiation it is, already."

"And," added DeWitt, "We both know where it came from, where it *must* have come from... don't we, Fred?"

"Yes," replied McPherson, reflectively. "Indeed we *do*, General, indeed we *do*."

He paused for a second, then softly offered, "I can't *believe* it. How in God's name could she – *it* – right *here?* In the U.S.? What are the *chances?* I mean, we're in completely uncharted territory, here, ladies and gentlemen. The world... just got a lot more complicated, there's no doubt about that."

"General Anderson," interjected the Secretary of Defense, "I assume we have to tell the President, immediately – and, that the contingency plan is now in effect. Do you concur, sir?"

"I concur," stated Anderson, over the conference link. "You and Mr. McPherson get going, from your end. I'll call CIA and the President. Do you copy?"

"Copy that," confirmed DeWitt.

"Excuse me," demanded the ghostly voice of the woman, "But what are you talking about? I feel that FBI has the right to know."

"You want to know?" asked Anderson, rhetorically.

"What we mean, Madam," he said, "Is... '*the hunt is on*'."

Commonality Of Interests

Mr. Billy Horn, Chief Unlisted Political Adviser to the President of the Ew-Nighted States of America, Arguably the Most Important White House Aide You Never Heard About, pondered the incongruity of the setting, and of the occasion, as he leaned his formidable girth back into the dusty, small-town Dixie bus-stop bench.

Damn uncomfortable, he reflected, *but made durable to save our taxpayers' precious money. Or, at least, that's what we tell them dumb-ass citizens, 'round votin' time.*

He threw a couple more peanuts into his maw.

He'd have far preferred to have met in the same restaurant as before, or just any other restaurant; at least you could get a cup of coffee and you could ogle the waitress. But he had been around the track a few times, no doubt could be had about that.

Never the same place, or the same kind of place, twice in a row, he thought. Have to send the Missus off to another Eagle Forum convention and make the next one a cat-house... at least the waitin' won't drag like it does here.

A bus came and went, then another, then another, with the occasional stare from those within, seeing this nondescript Southern man waiting but never climbing on board.

Finally, to the sound of crickets chirping at the imminent onset of dusk, another, immaculate in a finely-pressed business-suit, sat down beside him.

"Nice afternoon the Lord has made, today," offered the other. "Best time's just before the onset of night."

"Nothin' better," replied Horn, nonchalantly. "Not even Sunday mornin'."

"So... you're the famed Mr. Horn, I presume, sir?" inquired the second man.

"Oh, well, y'all can presume that, I s'pose, Brother...?" said Horn.

"Leo," came back the reply. "Work with Brother Martin, whom I believe you have met?"

"Indeed I have," remarked Horn, looking straight forward, not addressing the other in the face. "And I prefer to be as, 'un-famous' as I can, if you get my meaning, sir?"

"Of course," agreed the Brother. "So shall I give my report first?"

"Please do," suggested Horn, through his usual inscrutable smile.

"Well, here is what – little – that we now know, sir," started the second man. "But what we *do* know, is very important. As I believe Brother Martin may have told you some time ago, those of faith have been vigilant ever since the Incident – we've been on guard, lest the Devil-Girl come up to Earth from Hell below. Now, may the Lord save us, it appears that exactly this, *has* happened. She *is* among us."

Horn threw another peanut in.

"And what," he evenly asked, "Makes y'all so *certain* 'bout that, Brother? A dream, a revelation from above, maybe? A prayer answered, though not the way y'all wanted it to be?"

"We have our sources, Mr. Horn," explained the other. "*Deep* within the Government. You might say that 'our ear is close to the ground', or something like that... use any words you want. But no, sir, this is not from a prayer – it's from the government that you work for, yourself. And there's more. We even know where she appeared."

"My, *my,* that's *mighty* interestin'," offered Horn. "And just where would *that* be, Brother?"

"I was hoping that you could tell *me*, sir," politely countered the second man, tightening his tie slightly. "Just as a measure of good faith, you understand. Our relationship is... a 'two-way street', you know."

"Alright," allowed Horn. "Y'all got a point, Brother. So... since you already know that it's in the Northwest, Idaho way, specifically, have your people seen anythin'? Heard anythin'?"

"We're praying every day," said the man. "But no... nothing yet. And yes, I can confirm that it was a hill, up in the Grand Tetons, I wasn't told the exact one, not that that is important. Our operatives have been asked to report *anything*, however insignificant, but although there have been a few strange stories, people seeing the blessed Virgin Mary, *et cetera*... but there's nothing corresponding to the descriptions that we have at our disposal. What about from your end, sir? Any further direction you could give us?"

Horn paused for a second or two, considering what to say. Eventually, he responded.

"I can tell you, Brother," he observed, "That my people, too – well, maybe that's too strong, people in the Guv'ment, because, y'all see, a lot of 'em and yours truly don't really see eye-to-eye on a lot of matters, 'specially *this* one – they are in what you might refer to as, 'panic mode', if you understand what I mean. They are well-nigh *certain* that this creature, whatever she, or it, *is*, is indeed out there. So they've set about to lookin', and lookin' as hard as they can, usin' just about every resource that they have at their disposal."

"And – " asked the Brother, "If we could just get a *fix* on her – even down to a few miles – we'd get her. We have *hundreds* who would welcome martyrdom, just to do the deed. We can have them there in less than a day, maybe a few hours, once the Government rescinds the ban on private air-travel."

"I'm afraid y'all bein' rather *premature*, there, son," warned Horn. "You see, although they *do*, indeed, have substantial proof of where she first showed up, well, the trail goes cold, right after that. Tracks go right down to a highway, so I'm told... then, just nothin', I'm afraid."

"Just... *nothing?*" half-stammered the other man, not hiding his dismay.

"Well, the Feds is re-interviewin' everybody up there, but there's a whack of 'em to go through, and what with things bein' in such a state after the Big Bang, many of the likely suspects, includin' maybe the object of our search, may have moved on down the road," noted Horn. "With each passing day, they, or she, might have got yet further from Point Zero, as it were. They'll keep at it, but don't get your hopes up, Brother; y'all better keep prayin'. Maybe the Good Lord will fill y'all in where our fine F.B.I., can't."

"Hmm... I *see*," stated the second man.

Pensively, he stared into space for a moment. "Not the greatest of news," he commented, "But at least we both know where we stand, now, don't we, sir?"

"I would say so," confirmed Horn.

He held the bag up in his left hand, still not looking in that direction. "Peanut?"

"Thank you, but no thanks," demurred the second man, pleasantly. "I'm trying to keep my sodium intake down. 'Purity of body', you know – where I come from, we take such things rather seriously."

"Ah, of *course*," said Horn with an unctuous half-grin. "I should have guessed. Well, then – ?"

"I'll report back to my higher-ups, and they will send you a letter explaining where we will next meet. Does that work for you, Mr. Horn, sir?" replied the Brother.

"I think it will," answered Horn.

He looked to the side, far away.

"Well, what do you know? There's my bus," he added.

"Have a good trip, sir," offered the man in the neat suit, as the Greyhound roared up to the sign-post.

Awkwardly, Horn dusted a mess of peanut-shells from the front of his shirt and then boarded the bus, making a reflexive wave to the other man just before the front door of the vehicle enclosed him within it.

The second man also got up, turned in the other direction and walked smartly away.

He did not hear the faint 'click' of a voice recording system being turned off; nor did he take note of the discreetly parked car in which the machine had been located, driving off to the north, its tinted windows concealing a man with a self-satisfied smile.

On The Road

Bob The Preacher-Man

"I'll tell you, Whitney," commented the salesman, relief palpable in his voice, "I never thought the old beast would get so far, just on fumes and a trickle charge... we've been pushing 'E' for twenty miles or more. And I don't mind saying that I've never been so glad to see a gas station, especially *this* time of night. Okay, maybe when I almost ran out of gas in downtown Philly... took a wrong turn, went into the wrong... well, you know what I mean, I guess."

"Yeah, ah knows," replied the black woman, indifferently. "Ain't no problem for me to hear it, just the way things is, Mister Bob. And the kids is just as glad to see that bathroom, as y'all is to see that gas pump, there. Yo' card work?"

"Nope," answered Billings. "Damn system's still down, had to give him fifty in cash, and that only got us less than a quarter of a tank, but I didn't want to spend it all in one place. I had quite a bit squirreled away in the car, but there's still only so much, and I learned the hard way about being in a strange town without 'liquidity', as they say. Sometimes you gotta grease a palm or two..."

"Um-hum," intoned the woman. "Listen, Bob... ah was meanin' to aks y'all somethin'..."

Billings' gaze came up from the dashboard, momentarily, looking at Claremont directly.

"Yes, Whitney?" he inquired.

"Well... thang is, y'all know that Melissa and Curtis, an' that Injun boy, too, is in there, gettin' snacks, after they do they business. So we got a minute or two, and ah figured that y'all 'n me – and *her*, if she want to be in this, the adults, ah mean, we oughtta decide where we's goin' from here. We got gas, we got money..."

Claremont looked over the seat. The 'Sari'-girl was sleeping blissfully, seemingly oblivious to the world.

"Just y'all an' me then," the black woman added.

Billings looked away.

"I don't want to seem unfair," he argued, "But that's not quite true... *I* have a car, gas, and money. So far, I'm the *only* one who has contributed anything in the way of wheels or U.S. dollar bills, to this little expedition. Now, please don't think that I don't understand or appreciate the situation that you're in, Whitney... it's just that 'money talks, and BS walks', that's the bottom line."

"What y'all meanin' to *say*?" Claremont shot back, suspiciously.

"What I'm saying," Billings explained, firmly, "Is that we go where *I* decide to. I don't owe *anybody* an explanation, and – I hate to put it this way, but for better or worse, here it is – those who don't like where we're going, well, they're free to head off on their own, and God bless 'em. Is that clear?"

The African-American woman stared resentfully at the man for a long second, then mumbled, "Yeah, it is... ah guess."

She let out a sigh, then added, "But ah just wish that some time, even for one day, y'all would understand what it *like*, always havin' to aks somebody else for favors, on account of always bein' on the bottom, lookin' up, 'specially when bein' there ain't yo' own fault. That pretty *hard*, Mister Business Man... pretty *hard*."

She went quiet.

Avoiding her stare, Billings offered, "Yeah, Whitney, I suppose it is. Can't argue with you on that. All I *can* say is, I didn't make the world, either. I just *live* in it, and I'll concede you the point that I probably got a head start over you and your folk. But that doesn't change what we're doing. Which is, incidentally, getting out of here as soon as we can."

Claremont nodded and looked away, then mentioned, "Well, ah guess we goin' where y'all goin', but it gonna be dawn, soon, an' the kids been up more or less all night, ah'm awful tired, too, otherwise ah'd offer to drive to take some of the load off, Bob. We gonna stop somewhere, or we sleepin' in the car?"

"Yeah," replied Billings, suddenly aware of the fatigue that had been creeping up on him since the death-defying excitement of the past few hours had slowly waned.

"You have a point there. We *should* get some sleep... but I'm really afraid that we're still too damn close to that little Jesus freak Gestapo outfit back there."

"Look, I got an idea," he started, fumbling for a map. "Let's see if we can get to I-15, or close to it, before the night's out – if we can find a motel that'll take a chance on my card, without it getting a confirm on the network, that is, we'll bed down there, get cleaned up. Looking at this, I'd probably settle for Logan, if anything's open there. You all also oughtta get out of these stupid uniforms as soon as we can, I got a change of clothes in the trunk, and Sari should be able to fit into the track suit I got for my girlfriend – got that when I went through Provo on the way up – but you guys will stick out like a sore thumb, that is if they're bothering to look for you..."

"Yeah," agreed the woman.

"Maybe we can stop at a Sally Ann in Salt Lake," continued the salesman. "If and when we get that far, because we might run into exactly the same goddamn nonsense at the Utah state line as we did trying to get into Wyoming. Also, when we're in the big city, you might be able to find out what's going on in Detroit, or... you were going to L.A., or something, right?"

Claremont shrugged.

"Ah s'pose," she grunted. "Or back to De-troit. Like ah tell y'all, kids' Daddy, he in L.A., or, leastaways, he *was*, last we talk wid him. But ah'm not shore ah want to take the kids down there in that 'hood, what ah hear, things still pretty *bad* down there, them gang-bangers' dealin' an' shootin' near every two *hour* or so. Ah guess we just 'long for the ride, till we find some way to chill wid our folk, find out who gonna take us in."

Billings looked at Claremont, half in resentment, half in pity.

"You know, Whitney," he offered, "Sometimes the problems of this world – *your* problems – just seem too big to handle. For *me* to handle, anyway."

A young voice and face appeared at the car door next to Claremont.

"Yo, Momma!" called Curtis. "We gots lots of junk food – man in there gave us a discount, he say ain't *nobody* been by for days, now... least, nobody with cash money, they only got cards, and he not takin' em. Y'all want some?"

"Might take a bag of them chips, there," replied the woman. "Come on, y'all get yo' sister an' Tommy in here. Y'all all done yo' business?"

"Yes Ma'am," came back two voices in unison.

"Okay, then," announced Billings, as the engine rumbled to a start, again. "Let's get going."

The 'Sari'-girl had come out of her slumber, now, although she still lay down.

"We are moving again, Bob?" she asked. "Is there anything to eat or drink? I am very hungry."

Melissa passed the fallen-girl a chocolate bar, which was wolfed down immediately, leaving naught but an empty wrapper.

"Do you have any more? *Pleease!*" demanded the young-looking woman, with a tone of semi-desperation.

Two more candy bars came her way, each disappearing as quickly as the first, but when she pleaded for a fourth, all she got back was a good look at the Claremont boy's stuck-out tongue. So the 'Sari'-girl settled back into the seat, arms folded regally on her midriff, eyes closed over a saturnine half-smile.

Billings checked in every direction, inside the vehicle.

To Claremont's accompanying harsh stare, he commanded, "Hey, you there, Tommy? Seat belt on, please – that's an *order...*"

"My own Dad never made me wear it in our truck on the reservation," complained the Indian-boy.

"Good for *him*," retorted the salesman. "But you *will* do it here, and not because I especially like your face, kid, but because of something I've been meaning to tell all of you."

He turned to fully face the rest of them.

"Now *look*," Billings explained. "There are a few things that we got to get straight, now that we've got a bit of food and gas, hence the ability to put some real distance between us and those Bible-banging goons back there. First, *I'm* in charge, while you all are in this car, understand? I tell you to do something, or, more importantly, *not* to do something, I don't want any arguments, you got that loud and clear?"

Four just nodded, but the one-called-'Sari', half-awake and propped up by the car door, softly replied, "I understand, Bob. I will do what you say, if I can."

"Good. And, second," continued the salesman, "I don't know if any of you have ever been in a situation like this before – maybe Whitney has, I can tell you that I've been here all too many times before – but we have to assume that we may have the Man out looking for us –"

"What 'man' do you mean, Bob?" innocently inquired the fallen-girl. "Someone in particular?"

Billings rolled his eyes.

"No, for God's sake, Sari," he grumbled. "The '*Man*', as in, 'the *police*man', as in, 'the police', 'the army', 'the Jesus-nuts' – pick whichever one you like. The point is, we have to assume that we're being looked for – maybe we are, maybe we aren't, but we can't be *sure* that we aren't, at least not until all of this confusion settles down and we can find out what was really going on back there at the state line. So we have to regard anybody from the police or army who approaches us, or stops us, as potentially hostile, that is, they might want to arrest us or throw us in jail for God knows what."

"Bob," asked the 'Sari'-girl, "Did you not say back in the camp, that those people who imprisoned us, did so illegally? That is, they were in the wrong. If that is true, then why would someone want to 'throw us in jail' a second time, simply for escaping being kidnapped? I remember seeing a book, with thin, glossy paper, in a truck in which I was able to ride, a few days ago... it said something about 'Land of the Free', or something like that. You mean that what the book said was not really true?"

"You obviously don't have very much experience with recent events in the good old Ew-Nighted States of America," retorted Billings, with a cynical chuckle. "Ever since those terrorist stuff, and the 'six wars overseas stuff', it's just gotten worse and worse... times were that you had some rights, 'can't put you away without a lawyer', that kind of thing. Well, I can tell you, sister, those days are gone *forever*. I learned the hard way about ten years ago that the cops can do *anything* they want, if you talk back to them – they just call you a 'suspected terrorist', 'suspected illegal alien', then you just *disappear*, that's the way it goes. They might just shoot you on the spot, but much more often, they beat the crap out of you, then you end up rotting away in one of those 'Special Detention' facilities that the Feds set up after the first Pakistan disaster... remember, around the time they outlawed publicly worshiping Islam?"

"Uhh... no, Bob, I'm afraid that I do not 'remember' very much at all," remarked the fallen-girl.

"No, I suppose you don't," he muttered. "Well, anyway, sometimes you get released after however much time, for reasons that they don't have to explain, and they usually don't, sometimes they just throw away the key, you might as well suck on a .45, at that point. I can remember when people, your friends, your folks, I mean, would ask questions, 'what happened to nice old Bob', that kind of thing, but these days everybody just shuts up and gets on with their life, if they know what's good for them. That's the way it is, I'm afraid."

His head hanging forward slightly, Billings paused for a second, then added, more quietly, "In my own case, I was *lucky*... When they got me, it was for sales fraud, or something like that, some asshole I screwed over – just business, you know – went to them and lied about me being involved in 'subversive funding', or some BS like that; but I had friends on the outside, regional sales manager took some damn *big* risks to save my hide. I'll never forget how much I owe that man... kind of thing you can't *ever* repay..."

His voice went silent.

Claremont unsympathetically grunted, "So y'all got a taste of what us folk gots to deal with, every day, Mister Sales Man. Ev'ry *day*. Sorry that y'all did... how it go, 'misery love company', somethin' like that?"

The 'Sari'-girl caught Billings in an unnervingly determined, knowing stare.

"I believe that I understand, now, Bob," she commented. "Although I would have appreciated having been told, a little earlier in our adventure together. My behavior differs according to who I perceive to be in charge."

"No shit," muttered Billings. "Sorry, honey – I kind of assumed that you'd have put the two and two together by yourself... thought the storm troopers with the guns would have tipped you off."

"You said a bad word," interrupted the Indian-boy.

The salesman scowled.

The 'Sari'-girl forced a smile, then admitted, "Yes, I suppose that I should have, how you say, 'taken the hint'. I guess that I am not infallible –"

She stopped abruptly, as if surprised by something that she had heard or said.

Eventually, she added, "You know, Bob, I have been in places like this, much worse in fact, many, many times before. More times than you could ever *possibly* appreciate. But you all," – she made a sweeping gesture – "*You*, are my family, now, the only family that I have. Fate has brought us together... for a *purpose*."

Again, the fallen-girl stopped, as if pondering a memory. "I will protect you. I will keep you safe. This I promise."

"Heh," interjected Claremont, "'Cept for that Hoo-deeny trick y'all can do, seems to me that y'all be doin' well just to look after *youself*, girl. No offense, y'all understand –"

"Oh, none taken, Whitney," answered the 'Sari'-girl, with a serene smile. "And I concede your point. I am *very* weak, right now, that is for sure. In time, I will be much, much... *stronger*."

"Well if *that* happen, ah mean, the Man come after us, Mister Bob," chimed in Melissa, "What y'all wantin' us to do?"

"I was getting to that," answered the salesman. "Sort of. I'll have to make it up as we go, but for now... if I tell you to hide, do so."

"Yeah, but there ain't nowhere to put us... *oh*," protested Claremont.

A mischievous giggle issued from the three children, as the 'Sari'-girl vanished momentarily from view, then instantly re-appeared a second later.

"Yeah, ah keep forgettin'... *that* how," muttered the black woman.

"Just remember," remarked the newcomer, "That you must be quite close to me, for it to protect you. I could try to cover you in the front seat, but the policemen might notice the seat being gone, too. Also, I do not think it a good idea to use my hiding-trick more than we absolutely need to. In previous... lives, I have found that eventually, just vanishing whenever one wants, can draw a *lot* of unwanted attention. You people evidently cannot do this, which makes it... unusual, interesting, that sort of thing. I do not exactly *like* this saying, but its words are wise – 'the best magic, is rarely-used magic', I remember hearing that, somewhere long ago."

"Amen to that. And third," noted Billings, "We can't hide *everywhere*, so at some point we're going to be seen, so we have to think up a story that explains why we're all in this crate, together. Any ideas?"

"Why y'all not tell people that y'all an' mah Momma goin' to Las Vegas, to get married, Mister Bob?" proposed Melissa.

The salesman slumped forward a bit and wearily shook his head.

"I appreciate the thought, Melissa, but, well, I don't think it would be too convincing... there are, uhh, just a few *problems* with that..."

"Then how 'bout y'all gettin' married to Miz Sari, Mister Bob?" asked Curtis' voice, to simultaneous giggles from the two other children. "We knows y'all *like* each other."

Billings turned to face the fallen-girl, his exasperated, half-embarrassed glance meeting her own.

The one-called-'Sari' spoke up. "It is a wonderful idea, Curtis," she acknowledged, warmly, "But I do not think that I would make a very good wife, at least not until I remember more of my own background – I mean, what if I am already married to someone else? What if I already have a family? I do not *think* that I do, but... by the way, Bob, is it against the rules here to have more than one wife or one husband?"

"Say *whaat*?" blurted Melissa. "Y'all don't *look* like no A-rab –"

"A-what?" asked a perplexed 'Sari'-girl.

The salesman looked crestfallen.

"Yeah, theoretically, it *is* against the rules, 'bigamy', they call it," he offered, "*If* they catch you at it. Damn! I guess I never thought of, I mean, the possibility that you might already have *commitments*. And anyway, if we were to use *that* as an excuse, we'd still have to explain what the other four of you are doing in the car with us. So..."

Claremont chuckled. "Ah knows what y'all mean, Mister Bob, but y'all got a better idea?"

"Give me a few minutes, I'll think of something," muttered Billings.

"I got an idea," sounded Tommy's voice.

"We're all ears," replied the salesman.

"Well, Mister," said the Indian-boy, haltingly, "I know we all just had a bad experience with them, I mean, those Christian people back there, but... well, the only time that I ever used to see groups of people like us, I mean, people who don't all... *look* like each other, being together, traveling together, was when a bunch of these 'missionaries' used to come visit our reservation, to try to 'save' us, whatever that meant. So maybe we could say we're like them, you know, you could be the Minister, and we'd be the people in your church, something like that?"

"You gotta be *kiddin'*, son," protested Billings. "Do I *look* like a preacher? I haven't set foot in a church, that is if you don't count that little setup back there, in thirty years... I couldn't quote the Bible to save my life, and I don't have one in this car, wouldn't you think that's the first thing they'd check? And I hate those people's guts! I appreciate the thought, but –"

"Had one in mah car," interrupted Claremont, "But don' got it no more... s'pose we *could* buy one at one of them thrift stores if we make it to town, they always got 'em in the used book sections. Mister Bob, ah think Tommy, he got a point... when them Holy Roller types come into our 'hood, that were 'bout the only time that we see our folk 'n white-folk goin' together, too."

"It sounds like these superficial differences are considered to be very important," remarked the fallen-girl. "It would be amusing, were it not so short-sighted... I wonder how they would react to people who are bright red, violet or green... or who have four legs and four arms?"

"Ha, you *funny*, Miz Sari," giggled Curtis. "Ain't nobody like *that*, 'round here."

"Yeah... around *here*," she replied, staring distantly out the window.

There was an awkward silence for a few seconds, then Claremont continued, speaking in the direction of the newcomer, "For 'zample, they used to have black folk in the De-troit po-lice aways back, some of them Latinos, too, but then they got kicked out – they said it was 'because of disloyalty' or some such talk – n' now they mostly white again, like it was when my own Momma was there, hundred year ago or so. Same thang wid the Army, ain't seen *nobody* from mah hood get in there for past twenty year or more."

"Yeah... they passed some damn law about that, a few years back, as I recall," noted Billings. "But didn't that Mars thing have an African-American on it?"

"Shore did, Mister Billins," chimed Curtis' enthusiastic voice. "He a *Major*. He first man on Mars!"

The face of the 'Sari'-girl wore an instantly-astonished look, but she said nothing and eventually again became lost in her private thoughts.

"Well, maybe he in there before they change the rules, heard of that happenin' once or twice," suggested Claremont. "But anyways, ah cain't think of any *other* way to 'splain how we all in this here car, unless we say y'all takin' us to jail yourself or somethin' like that. Why *not*, Bob? 'Bout the preacher-man thang, ah mean. We not gonna make y'all give no sermons, but if y'all wants to, ah can tell y'all how some of 'em go. All y'all gots to *do* is try not to take the Lawd's name in vain, not use no cuss words... that so hard?"

"Hell, yes," muttered Billings. "Oh, whoops."

He sat and thought, for a bit, then said, "Well, I guess I'm outvoted... and I can't think of something more plausible off the top of my head, I'm afraid. Also, maybe the Feds and that crew of Bible-bangers back there might cut us a bit more slack, if we say that we're 'one of them'... Hah, *me*, as a preacher, now *that*'s something... wait until I tell my bookie."

He laughed, cynically. "So what's the name of my church, folks? Protestant, Catholic, Rastafarian or Satanist?"

The teenager laughed out loud, until silenced by her mother's stern glare.

"Say-tann," inquired the 'Sari'-girl. "He is a *bad* god, is he not?"

Claremont's eyes rolled in exasperation.

"Something *mainstream*, then," retreated the salesman. "Something nice and hard to place. I got it – 'First Episcopalian Church of South Tucson', how does *that* sound? Minister Bob Billings, In Residence. Hell, I feel like a saint already!"

"Bob, y'all ain't s'posed to cuss no more –" protested Claremont.

"Sorry," replied Billings, maliciously. "I'll say ten 'Hail Mary's, followed by a Bloody Mary or two just to dull the pain."

"Bob," asked the fallen-girl, earnestly, "Is there *really* a 'First Episcopalian Church' in this 'South Tucson' place? What kind of religion is it, good or evil? Is it of the Light, the Dark or the Twilight? Does it have a big temple-building? What manner of clothing do its priests and priestesses wear?"

"The 'light'... *what*? Damned – sorry, darned – if I know," joked the salesman. "And is it a *good* church? That depends on the collection revenues..." he smirked. "Oh, and I guess we'll also have to decide what all the rest of you are doing in our fine religious establishment... who wants to be in the choir?"

Three hands went up, two black ones quickly and a tanned one with more hesitation.

"We already in our choir, Mister Bob," said Melissa. "Curtis 'n me, we won a singin' contest last year."

"A 'choir', that is a place where people sing, right?" asked the 'Sari'-girl. "I would like to be part of a choir, then. I like singing very much. A certain kind of tune, the right notes and rhythm... these make me more powerful..."

Billings gave the newcomer a puzzled stare.

"Stronger?" he stated, quizzically. "Whatever, I guess. Swell, then you can be the choir director –" he added.

"Miz Sari, sing us somethin'," demanded Curtis. "We ain't never heard y'all do that."

"Look, we can do this later –" requested Billings.

"Yes," added the 'Sari'-girl. "Bob is right. I would *love* to sing for you, but right now, I have many tunes in my head, but I cannot remember any of the words that go with them. Do *you* know any songs, Curtis? Maybe you could teach me the ones that you know, and once I figure out what the music-notes are for them, then I will sing along, too. Oh-kay?"

"Sure, Miz Sari," replied the boy, enthusiastically. "Y'all ever hear 'Compton Pimp Nigga-Killer' by .44 Steel-Jacket? He mah *fav-o-rite* hip-jumper! Ah listen to him 'n he homie when Momma not 'round."

He smirked in Claremont's direction, knowing how to push all the buttons.

"Whitney," sighed Billings, as he turned the key and headed out on to the highway, "Can you please look inside the glove compartment? I think I left my earphones in there... I'm hoping they'll work like earplugs, if I don't connect them to the stereo."

Lifeboat

The loudspeakers throughout the space-station announced, loudly and unmistakably, "Attention, all remaining lifeboat members, bring your evacuation gear and report immediately to Green 24! High atmospheric protocol is in effect, when entering the departure ships; seal the external hatch first!"

Ariel Cohen's visage showed an uncharacteristic scowl.

"I can't *believe* that you're doing this, Chkalov," he complained. "It's totally irrational, not to say, destructive. *Surely* you know what their chances will be, without you? Without someone who knows how to fly Jacobson's ship?"

"I understand your concern, Commander Cohen," explained the Russian, in a calculatedly polite voice, "But I assure you, I *do* have my reasons. And it may not be so bad, for the evacuation mission. I have spent every spare minute of the last three days teaching Ang-San how to operate the controls, how to manually correct the flight path, how to do everything that I would do. And in any event, Major Boyd and I have pre-programmed the trajectory into the *Infinity's* computer. All she has to do, is push a button and fire the engines when prompted to do so. Little has been left to chance."

"I'm not *that* stupid," retorted Cohen. "I know all *about* what's involved – I haven't yet seen a single mission where manual course corrections weren't required, especially for situations like *this*, with so many variables and 'unknowns'. Earth orbit is still filled with debris from the comet. Would you trust *your* life, to a half-trained pilot such as this?"

The cosmonaut looked distantly away, for a second.

Not turning to face the other man, he stated, "You know, Commander, in fact, what I will be doing, *is* trusting my life to a hypothesis, that is – by any rational way of thinking – in fact far *less* plausible, than would be my chances as a passenger on board the *Infinity*. Whether my former ship were to be flown by, say, Major Boyd, or someone even less trained than Ang-San."

"You're talking nonsense, Chkalov," shot back the commander. "*Nobody* is getting off this station alive, once those two spacecraft depart. There is no hope, at all, anyone who knows the facts understands that. Which makes your decision all the more irrational."

"Any more so, sir," answered the Russian, "Than your own decision, not to be considered for the lottery?"

One by one, the lucky few began to float into the compartment, clasping what few belongings that they had been allowed to carry.

Cohen did not reply, for a second or two, then he demanded, "I take it that your mind is made up, then?"

"Yes, it is," replied Chkalov. "And, Commander —"

"What?" asked Cohen, wearily.

"There *is* still hope, sir," offered the cosmonaut, calmly, with an eerie confidence in his voice. "Like there was for Earth, when all seemed lost."

His olive-tinted Mediterranean face briefly showed a quizzical look, then Cohen spoke up.

"Ah. I wish I could believe that," he mentioned. "But *she* – the alien, I mean – she's *dead*. White and the others *said* so. If you're holding out some kind of misguided idea that she will just show up and rescue us, well, that is – as the Americans say – 'wishful thinking', Cosmonaut Chkalov. You might as well think that we're going to be saved by God or His angels."

The compartment was now becoming crowded.

How can all these people possibly fit into Jacobson's little ships, mused Cohen.

Several of the newcomers looked as if they were trying to gain the station commander's attention.

"Maybe that is what I *do* believe, Commander," commented Chkalov, evasively. "Or maybe I believe that she *was* an angel. Where I come from, it is said that not even the Devil himself, can kill an angel."

"My own people," muttered Cohen, "Learned all about waiting for salvation by the angels, or the Messiah, in the *Shoah* of the 20th Century, you know. Go to the memorial site in Jerusalem, and you will find out how these hopes are remembered."

The Russian looked away, again.

"I cannot answer that," he noted. "For I am not a religious man. I do not know much of such things. But in *this* – this, I believe."

"In *what*?" complained Cohen. "You still haven't told me how you propose to —"

"Commander," interrupted a short, round-faced, Asian woman, "I hate to break in, but according the schedule, we have less than twenty minutes —"

As if grateful to be relieved from the previous conversation, Cohen's countenance brightened.

"Hi, Ang-San," he said. "I take it that you are ready? All prepared?"

"Perfectly, sir," answered the woman. "Well, let me... correct that. I am as ready as I will ever be. Thanks to a great deal of help from your friend here —"

Cohen shot an accusatory glance at Chkalov, which the other man studiously ignored.

" – I think I will have no problem getting us all there, assuming that nothing unexpected happens," added the Burmese woman. "Have we heard anything more from Earth, regarding the *rendez-vous*?"

"Only that they are still 'working on it'," answered Cohen, evenly. "The Russian Federation space-plane is almost ready, or so they think... however, there is no word on anything else to accommodate the rest of the people on the evacuation mission, above the twelve that the Russian craft can handle. I assume that everyone else here is aware of that factor?"

"Yes, they are, sir," offered the woman. "And not a single one has changed his or her mind."

"Well, there *has* been one, actually," grumbled Cohen. "But that is neither here nor there. Alright. You may as well begin the boarding process. Chkalov, could you open the hatch, please."

"Of course, sir," confirmed the Russian, floating over to a computer display.

Taking a microphone close to his lips, he muttered a code phrase, then he entered another on the touch-pad just below the display.

Whoosh.

The hatch leading to the only way off the ISS2 space-station sprung open, revealing a dimly-illuminated sanctuary, the interior of the only human ship ever to fly to and from another planet.

"Where's Jacobson and his team?" inquired Cohen, out loud. "It's surprising that they aren't here – if it was *my* ship, I would have wanted one last look... oh, *there* you are, Alan. Have you heard anything from Jacobson or Tanaka?"

An English Midlands accent issued forth from three ranks back amongst the crowd and replied, "Yeah – just spoke to the bloke, in his cabin, ten minutes ago or so, Commander; his crew and him are tied up in some daft kind of ceremony. I poked my head in and asked what was going on and Cherie Tanaka gave me a dirty look, although to be fair, as I went away she said I'd be 'invited for next time and check your assumptions at the door', whatever *that* means."

"Ceremony?" asked a suspicious Cohen. "What kind of..."

"Dunno," interjected Humber. "Looked like a wake or something... which I suppose kind of makes sense, if you think about it."

Puzzled, Cohen ordered, "Well, now is quite a time to be doing something like that – if, that is, Sam wants to get a glance at the *Infinity* and *Eagle* before they push off. Sergei, do you mind calling him up on the video? Tell him he has ten minutes to get down here."

"Certainly, Commander," replied Chkalov studiously, his hands playing pianist-like over the keypad once more.

The video-screen lit up.

"Yes? Ah, I *see*, Commander," repeated the cosmonaut, not looking up. "You are going to try – very well, then, go ahead without me... yes, but Cohen says that if you want to see the *Infinity* and *Eagle*... what? Alright, I will tell him. Chkalov out."

He turned to Cohen and explained, "Commander Jacobson wishes to inform you that he and the rest of his crew will not be able to attend... they are, how you say, 'tied up' doing something very important. He sends his regrets and wishes the lifeboat crew every success."

"Something 'more important'?" exclaimed Cohen, with an air of frustration. "Alan, come forward, please, could you?"

Clumsily – despite months up here, he had never really gotten the hang of it – the engineer navigated through the throng and appeared next to the station commander.

"Listen, Alan," half-whispered Cohen, "Keep an eye on Jacobson, will you? He seems to trust you, but I'm worried that the pressure of recent events may be getting to him... I hate to say this, but I've heard rumors of insubordination..."

"With all due respect, Commander, don't you think that's just a *mite* far-fetched," argued Humber, *sotto voce*. "I mean, considering where we're all going to be once Jacobson's little lifeboat pushes off into the briny black deep, sir, what's he got to *gain* by challenging your authority? I reckon we're all *fucked* anyway. All he – or anyone – could really accomplish is to make the last few hours or days, slightly more unpleasant than it's already going to be. Not much of a justification for mutiny, as I see it. Far more likely that they're all just going crackers or something."

Cohen muttered back, "That may be, Alan, but this nonsense with Chkalov – the only pilot that could have given them half a chance – it's *criminal*, and I can't help suspecting that Jacobson put him up to it, for some reason that I can't at all understand. He seems to trust you, much more than Li, for example. So will you do this for me, or won't you?"

Humber looked the man straight on, and replied, "Yeah. Sure, mate. But I think it's nothing. If it's more than that, I'll tell you. You have my word on that."

Cohen nodded.

One by one, the evacuees drifted through the hatch, into the twilight of the rescue ships beyond.

Silently, Cohen, Chkalov and Humber watched them depart, until all, except for the Asian woman, had entered the *Infinity*.

"Well," quietly noted Cohen, "I guess that it is time, Ang-San. I wish I could think of something memorable to say."

"I'm not the kind of person to do this, sir," spoke Thant, appreciatively, "But I wanted to, anyway."

She pushed off a wall and hugged her commander.

"Thank you, Commander Cohen, for getting us this far," the woman breathed, her eyes welling up.

A perfectly globular tear shimmered in the zero-gravity air like a ethereal silver pearl.

"I want you to know," she said, "That we will *never* forget you. And the rest of your team."

Uncomfortably, Cohen offered, "It's okay, Ang-San, it's okay. And thank you for the kind words. I want you to know that I have complete confidence in you."

He winced and continued, "If *anyone* can get them back to Earth, you can. I'm counting on you."

Cohen tried to force a smile.

She released him and nodded.

"I won't let you down, sir, I swear it. Well, I guess we should get going," she said.

Sadly, Humber waved to the woman.

"God bless, Ang-San," he said. "Remember us fondly, will you, my dear?"

"I promise, Alan," she replied, her voice barely audible, as Thant took a last, longing look at the three.

She started to close the hatch, then hesitated for a second, staring at them.

"What is it, Ang-San?" asked Cohen.

"What will you do, Commander?" she asked, plaintively. "What will you *do*?"

Cohen seemed at a loss for words, but, mercifully, Chkalov spoke up.

"There is still hope for us, Space Scientist – or, should I say, Acting Flight Commander – Thant," he stated. "We have a plan."

"A *plan* – ?" interjected a startled Humber.

Cohen motioned him silent, hoping that Thant could not see.

The woman stared at Chkalov, for a long second.

"May the Buddha be with you, Cosmonaut Chkalov, and all those who have sacrificed, so we might tell the story," she managed.

She turned and closed the hatch.

Coming to life, Cohen announced, "Okay, well, we've done all we can, here, gentlemen. Time to go. Attention, Environmental Control and Station Flight Control – departure oversight team leaving Green 24. Prepare for hatch and dock rupture in forty-five seconds from now."

"Affirmative, Commander," called a ghostly Chinese voice over the intercom.

"Yeah, time to get out of here, I guess," agreed Humber, already heading towards the junction with ISS2's next-inward section. "When you all get into 23, I'll shut the door."

Silently, Cohen, followed by Chkalov, pushed off from the nearest objects, propelling themselves towards Humber's path. After twelve seconds or so, all three men had gathered in the Green 23 subsection of the space-station.

Noiselessly, the inter-section door slid into place.

Cohen gazed through the small porthole in the top center of the door, towards the hatch that connected the Infinity – and, as all were only too aware, the last possible escape from a fateful end – with ISS2.

"Anybody got something profound to say, before the last dinghy gets lowered off the *Titanic*, mates?" half-joked Humber.

"I remember seeing that movie, once," mused Cohen. "They had an orchestra. It kept playing, all the while..."

"Aye," commented the engineer, with a rueful laugh. "'Nearer My God To Thee', as I recall. But I'm afraid I forgot to bring me bleedin' harmonica, Commander."

"Twenty seconds," warned Chen's voice, over the intercom. "Flight Commander Thant, confirm burn system arming."

"Ready," stated an even more distant voice. "Thrusters in two seconds from rupture, boosters at one kilometer. Computed course showing green. All other systems nominal."

Chkalov looked down at his wrist chronometer.

"*Pyat... Shest... Teree... Dva... Adeen,*" he intoned.

For the briefest of moments, blackness showed at the docking hatch, but it was instantly cut off by a sliding circular cover. There was a slight shudder.

"*Infinity* away," announced Thant's faint voice. "Thrusters... *now*. Velocity forty-seven, just under plan... reaching burn point in twenty-one point three seconds..."

"Well, at least she's got 'em off to a good start, away from the sinkin' ship, but she'll need –" began Humber.

His voice was suddenly cut off by the apparent impact of something *big*, reverberating through the entire station. Walls shook, alarm sirens sounded, and two nearby storage-compartment doors flew open.

"What *the* –" shouted the ISS2 station commander. "She must have fired the boosters *prematurely!* I *knew* that something like this was going to happen – Li! Damage report!"

"Checking, sir," sounded the taikonaut's voice over the loudspeakers.

"Negative, Commander," he continued. "No impact, as far as we can determine... I cannot see any hull breaches on the environmental displays. Mr. Theodikas is tracking the *Infinity* on the visual. That craft's main engines have not yet fired. Acting Commander Thant, please confirm."

A ghostly voice responded, "Confirmed... main sequence burn in thirteen... twelve..."

"Well then, what the *hell* –" exclaimed Cohen, as the siren fell silent. "There's *nothing* else that could have produced *that* kind of impact –"

Haphazardly, he glanced at Chkalov. The man was wearing a weirdly serene expression and nodded knowingly.

"Sergei?" Cohen demanded. "I need an explanation. What's going on?"

"There, Commander," replied the cosmonaut, "Are your angels."

Red Rover, Calling AF2

Plainly unhappy, the President turned his long, clean-shaven face from his stare out the oval, double-paned window, to address the rest in the aircraft's luxuriously-appointed main meeting-room.

"Are you *absolutely* certain that all of this is necessary, General?" he demanded. "I mean, hopping from place to place every day in Air Force Two. You know, McPherson says that I might as well be back in the White House, for all we know for sure about – "

"Sorry, sir," replied Anderson, firmly, "But the National Security Council, the Joint Chiefs, all of us, are of one mind on this. As matters stand now, we all believe that you'd be running a completely unwarranted risk to be anywhere where you could be positively identified. I know that Fred thinks she's no threat, but if she is, and she *does*, in fact, turn out to be hostile, the White House is the first place she'd come looking for you."

"Wonderful," muttered the American leader.

"So," explained the General, "I'm afraid we're on the milk run, for the foreseeable future; until, at the very least, we locate the alien and get some idea of its motivation and intent. We have the stunt doubles, even for the wife and kids, all in place at the White House and on Air Force One, fake agendas, the works, so our cover should be good for the time being. It's hard on *all* of us, Mr. President, but we're convinced that it's the right thing to do."

"Yeah, I suppose, Harry," said the President. "It's just hard to believe that all of this has been made necessary by a set of footprints on a mountain, somewhere... not the kind of thing I ever imagined I'd have to deal with when I won the election, I can tell you."

He got up and looked out the aircraft window, again, absent-mindedly studying the clouds below.

"Did you manage to get John on the line?" he asked.

"Just a second, Mr. President," replied the General. "Coming through now – he's at the field headquarters, link quality isn't great, but we still should be able to send and receive."

"Where's that?" inquired the President.

"Cheyenne Mountain – remember the old NORAD H.Q.?" replied Anderson. "He's in the alternate, secret, underground site, twenty miles from there. We figured that would be as safe as it gets, on the ground, that is. Comms gear isn't fully operational yet, unfortunately, due to the... hurried nature of the preparations."

Static sounded on the speaker, followed by a Midwestern voice.

"Hello? Mr. President? This is Bezomorton here, with the Project Red Rover field team," it sounded. "Mr. President, can you hear me?"

"You're faint, John," replied the President, "But I can still understand you. What's with this 'Red Rover' stuff?"

"That's the code-name for the operation to locate and neutralize the alien, sir," replied the voice over the intercom. "We wanted to pick a name that wouldn't give away any hint of what's going on, if it was leaked to the public. We can change it at your order, of course, sir."

"No, that will be fine," agreed the President.

He voiced a mordant chuckle. "'Red Rover, Red Rover, please don't come over'," he rhymed. "Kind of makes sense, wouldn't you say, George?"

"Depends if we win the game," commented the Vice-President, coolly. "Scotch for you?"

"No thanks, you go ahead, just coffee for me right now," answered the U.S. leader. "Okay, maybe a shot of Bailey's with it, then."

Briefly adjusting an earphone, a smartly-dressed young Air Force lieutenant dutifully delivered the beverages to the two leaders.

"Okay, John," asked the President, "What do you have for us, so far? Any more news?"

"I'm afraid not a lot, sir," cracked the voice at the other end. "We've had our best teams analyzing the footprints on Hill 1442 to try to see what direction they might go off in, but although based on the radiation signature, they definitely *do* check out as having been made by the alien, once they hit the highway, we draw a *complete* blank. One challenge here is, much of the original ground reconnaissance in the area was done by FBI, but since we have not, as yet, chosen to include their field staff in the project briefings, we're not getting much help from those guys in the Hoover Building –"

"For God's sake," angrily retorted the President. "Where the *hell* is Cesar? Get him on the phone and I'll straighten him out."

"We've been trying to reach him for the past day or so," explained Bezomorton. "But to be fair to the Director, we've mostly been dealing with the agents in the field, so he may not know all of what's going on. I've been told that he's personally in charge of one of the new 'Anti-Gang Strike Forces' that FBI set up a week ago, down on the L.A. front, they're working in co-ordination with the National Guard and the Army, but from what we've observed, it's nearly a full-scale war against the gangs in that area –"

"Yeah, so I've heard," noted the President.

"Definitely, sir," confirmed the National Security Adviser. "Gangsters are fighting back with heavy weapons, everything from machine guns to anti-tank missiles, that is, when they aren't fighting each other – local intelligence is saying that there are at least three major gangs contending for control of southern California, with six or seven smaller hangers-on whose allegiances seem to change by the day. They even shot down two State Patrol helicopters yesterday, with man-portable SAMs. We've left messages for Director Ochoa, hopefully we'll hear back from him soon."

"Well, when you do, he'll get a piece of my mind," muttered the President. "Same BS as always among you guys – too many cooks stirring the pot, while the country goes down the toilet."

"Hear, hear," interjected the Vice-President, as he swizzled a gulp of finest Scotch.

"Anyway, get on with it, John," requested the American leader.

"Finally," mentioned Bezomorton, "Based on what we *think*, and we're not sure by any means, are the decay characteristics of the radiation signature, it appears that the tracks were made at *least* a few days ago, possibly more, meaning that the alien could potentially be quite far away by now –"

Anderson nodded, with a knowing expression.

"You can say *that* again," he added. "You know, Mr. President, there is an interesting possible explanation of the evidence down there. With what John has just said, it seems a bit more plausible to me, now. Did McPherson ever share it with you?"

"Not sure... what do you mean, Harry?" inquired the President.

"Well, the point is, the tracks go to a road, then they just *disappear*, with no trace in any direction. On the ground, that is. Remember, sir, we're talking about a being here which – if the events recorded in and around the Mars mission craft and the space-station are to be fully believed – is capable of unassisted flight, possibly at enormous velocities. Your Science Adviser mentioned the possibility that she got as far as the highway and then just... took off."

"You mean she just flew away?" asked the President, arching an eyebrow. "To where?"

"Your guess is as good as mine," said the General. "But if she *did*, it presents a whole new set of challenges. Not the least of which is, she could be flying around, trying to find us... find *you*, right now."

The President gulped, reflexively straightened his tie and again looked out the window.

He forced a weak smile.

"Don't see her *yet*," he managed. "That's a good thing, I guess."

"If I may," continued the voice over the intercom, "Mr. President, while it's true that we cannot completely rule out the scenario that the General has just described to you, it's the unanimous belief of the National Security Council that it would be *most* unwise for us to rely upon it unless and until we have a positive sighting of the alien, preferably somewhere else in the world."

"Mr. President," interrupted Anderson, "Although I'm not sure that I believe either the premises or the conclusion of what John is saying here, if he's even *partially* right, then you should be able to see for yourself how urgent the task is, to intercept the alien, before it gets any more well-established. These few hours, days or, hopefully, weeks, may be the only chance we get to eliminate it, before it's too powerful for us to handle."

"'Eliminate it'," muttered the President. "I can just imagine what McPherson would say to *that*. Why don't we just try to *reason* with it... with her? Cut her a deal? I mean, for God's sake, Jacobson at one point had her eating out of the palm of his hand. If she'd do that for a junior officer, surely she'd do it for his boss's boss's, boss. If we got this 'Karéin' on our side, our military predominance over the rest of the world would be *unquestionable* – "

"I would remind you, sir," countered Anderson, "In the military, we have to deal with *capabilities*, not intentions. When Jacobson and his team first unearthed the alien, neither they nor we had any idea of what its capabilities might be; now, if the 'Lucifer' story is to be believed, we do, and as your senior military Adviser, I have to tell you that if I had known then what I know, or what I think I know, now, I would *never* have authorized this being having been brought back to life."

"Go on," requested the American leader.

"Well," elaborated the General, "What if you try to 'reason' with it, and it decides not to listen? What if *we* think that we have a deal with it, then the next day, it changes its mind and decides to vaporize you or the whole *country?* Your own opinion of this issue might be different three months from now, if *you* had to deal with a god-like and potentially hostile alien being, confronting you in the Oval Office. We *may* be dealing with the most serious crisis ever to confront the Republic. Okay, maybe the *second* most serious crisis. But the situation is the same either way."

"Point taken," stated the President. "But I want you to understand that I'm not ruling anything in, or out, General. I'm worried about the possibility that we underestimate this creature's powers, make a hostile move against it and then have the whole thing literally blow up in our faces. If you're scared about what it might be like to have a godly alien wandering around here with unclear intentions, just think of how much worse we could make it by *ensuring* that it gets mad at us. I have to weigh the chances of something like that, against the chances of what you've just outlined, Harry."

Bezomorton interjected, "I should let you know, sir, that both I and the other senior members of Project Red Rover have been carefully studying the recordings of the alien's behavior and activities, while she, or it, was on Captain Jacobson's ship, and it seems well within the creature's ability to do this kind of thing – you may recall that in its second presentation to us, it hinted at 'greater powers' that it supposedly had at its disposal. I've gone over the recordings again and again, but, unfortunately, we don't have first-hand evidence of many of its abilities – excepting the space flight, of course, that part of it was independently verified by the command staff of the ISS2 space-station – because Jacobson and his crew only enabled video recording at their own discretion on the trip back from Mars, so we do not have a complete record of everything that transpired on the *Eagle* and *Infinity*."

He added, "Furthermore, we have made several attempts to interrogate the Captain, also his subordinates Major Brent Boyd and Major Devon White, to try to find out what this 'Karéin' being was capable of, but their responses have been evasive; the kind of answers we got were 'she's dead, what difference does it make to you'. When we started to ask for a specific listing of her powers, all three of them clammed up, we got only vague, contradictory replies. We also tried to interrogate Professor Tanaka, who you may remember was the science-officer on the mission, but she refused to talk altogether, and the Russian, Chkalov, seems to have been given orders from his own Space Command not to talk, either, or at least that's what he told us –"

The President rolled his eyes.

"Not to quote George, but this is effing *ridiculous* as well," he complained. "I can't get FBI to talk to NSA or the National Security Council, I can't get my own party in Congress to pass an emergency budget, I can't get CIA to talk to Homeland Security, and now, I can't get a goddamn junior Air Force officer to tell the truth to his superiors... *I'm* supposed to be in charge, here – doesn't this Jacobson guy understand the chain of command?"

"I can remind him of it, if you'd like, sir," offered Anderson.

"Please do," requested he President. "I just don't *get* it... when he was on Mars, and on the way back, I had a chat with him, the rest of his crew too. They seemed like professionals, at the time – for that matter, 'Karéin' herself seemed like a rational being, not like a *threat*, I mean, she was certainly polite enough... Look, especially if those astronauts up there really believe that the alien's *dead*, why on Earth should they not want to tell us everything they knew about her, or it? You'd think that they'd want that kind of thing recorded just for posterity's sake, if for nothing else. This doesn't make sense, from my perspective."

The National Security Director, his voice faintly audible over the static, replied, "I agree, sir, it doesn't add up to us, either. *Unless*, possibly, close exposure to the alien affected the Mars mission crew in some way we don't yet understand – maybe she inflicted some kind of long-lasting mind control over them? Oh, and by the way, one of the former Mars mission crew – let me check my notes, yeah, that's him, Major White, made some kind of comment to the effect of, 'we're all on a ship to nowhere up here, so we're not too interested in listening to orders'... I think that kind of gives you an idea of what we're up against, in interrogating them. The bottom line is, they're up there, we're down here, and we really can't make them do or say anything that they don't want to."

"For Christ's sake," muttered the President.

"Well, from what Fred tells me, I suppose Major White has a point about his long-term survival prospects, but that's still no excuse for insubordination, in my book."

He paused for a second, then asked, "Listen, John, you didn't tell them that she's *alive*, did you?"

"Of *course* not," came back the remote voice, quickly. "But it *is* possible that they were able to put two plus two together, from the nature of the questions that we were asking. Jacobson, Boyd, White, they're all intelligent men, 'best of the best', that kind of thing, Mr. President; after all, you don't get given a berth on NASA's first flight to Mars, by being second in the class."

"Wasn't our *first* try at Mars," commented Anderson. "I need not remind you of what happened to the one before them."

"Yeah," grunted the Vice-President. "*That* fucking disaster cost us three million votes and God knows how many trillion U.S. greenbacks. A few years back, I suggested that we should have pulled the plug on the whole *program*, remember? Just think, if people had listened to *me*, we wouldn't have to be worrying about a Martian space princess troubling this fair land, and we wouldn't be having this discussion..."

The line went silent for a second, then Bezomorton, with some temerity, noted, "If they hadn't gone and then brought back the alien from Mars, there might not have been *anyone* to have *any* discussion, sir."

Anderson came to his assistance, saying, "And eventually, *somebody* would have got out there and dug her up, one way or another... I don't have to remind you, Mr. Vice-President, that the good old days of the last century, when we had undisputed control of Planet Earth, as well as of space, are gone forever. Half the regular Army and most of the Marines never made it out of Pakistan, and since the 'disloyal minorities' rules got passed last Administration, we can barely get enough, uhh, 'Caucasian' soldiers, to keep order here in North America."

The National Security Adviser added, "And let's not forget that it was the *Europeans* that first discovered the Anomaly and that the Russians only agreed to postpone their *own* flight to Mars, because we agreed to stick Chkalov up there with Jacobson and his boys. Frankly, for all the problems that we have now, I'd far prefer the current situation to one where this 'Karéin' showed up here, speaking Russian, or, worse, Chinese. *Sir.*"

The Vice-President grunted something or other and took another sip.

The President leaned back and let out a sigh.

"I think we're all aware of those facts, John, and Harry," he said, wearily. "Ahh, you're right... it's all just damn guesswork, at this point. Is she here or isn't she? Can she just fly away, or does she have to hitch a ride? Does she want to take over the world, or doesn't she? How the hell am I supposed to make an intelligent decision, with *this* kind of evidence?"

"We all appreciate the difficult position that you're in, sir," came back the voice from the vicinity of Cheyenne Mountain. "May I recommend that the optimal course of action is just for us to keep looking as diligently as we can. The worst that can happen is that the process goes on for some time, with no results; in which case, we could assume that this was all a false alarm. Things could then get back to normal."

"How long is 'some time', John?" requested the President.

"As long as it takes to be sure that we've left no stone unturned, sir," explained the National Security Adviser. "I can't give you a precise estimate, but personally I'd be surprised if we can't complete our work in the Northwest in less than a month or so. Give or take a week or so."

"A *month*," groaned the President, with a pained chuckle. "A I stuck on this plane. All the comforts of home, I guess... *wonderful*."

"Speak for *yourself*," shot back the Vice-President. "Booze is much better back at the White House... listen, can't we get some *real* Canadian Club up here, for God's sake?"

Welcome To The Fraternity

Jacobson and White had managed to get three or four laps around the pseudo-grav area, ignoring the constantly-upward curvature of the cylinder as they trotted in an endless loop up, around, down and around again, before they saw the wiry, Mediterranean visage of ISS2's commander peek through a hatch to the no-gravity areas beyond.

Well, at least it's bigger than the one that I had on Infinity, *but I'd give* anything *to be back with her*, Jacobson thought wistfully, as he realized how much he resented having sent his former ship off on its one-chance-in-five rescue-mission.

"Sam?" asked Cohen. "Mind if I have a word with you?"

"Oh, certainly," replied the Air Force captain.

"Just with me?" he inquired, casting a glance at the African-American ex-astronaut.

Cohen sized them up for a second or two, as he popped through the hatch, closed it and stood up beside them.

"No," he stated, "Ordinarily, I'd ask Major White to excuse himself, but given the nature of the question I've got... he may as well be here."

"Much obliged, I'm sure," muttered White, unenthusiastically, as Jacobson wiped the sweat off his brow.

"I'm sure that you two are aware that we're under oxygen conservation protocol... no strenuous activity, *et cetera*?" noted Cohen.

"Oh, yeah, sorry, we kind of forgot," apologized the black astronaut. "Keepin' spirits up, y'all know," he added, with a faked smile.

"Absolutely, Ariel," mentioned Jacobson. "I guess that's the end of our workout, Devon."

"So... that's it?" he asked, looking at Cohen with an arched eyebrow.

"No, not really," replied the station commander. "I need to ask you something about what's been going on with you and your crew, Sam. And I need an honest answer. A *complete* one, too."

Jacobson and White looked at each other, uneasily and knowingly.

"And what would *that* be, Commander?" asked Jacobson.

"Well, I'm not sure," said Cohen, "Because the reports that have come in to me don't make a lot of sense – I've been trying to piece it together without having to confront you in this way, but so far, I'm at a complete loss."

White looked at Jacobson and tried to give a 'what is he talking about' type of shrug.

"As both of you know," continued the ISS2 commander, "When the *Eagle* and *Infinity* left the station a short while ago, we encountered another one of those kinetic events – shudders in the structure, things flying loose here and there and so on. At first I thought it was a collision with your former ships; but that turned out not to be the case, and, like the other one that we encountered shortly after the alien left us, there doesn't seem to be any evidence of impact with an external object, certainly nothing of the size that it would have to have been to have caused the kinds of structural reverberations that we experienced. That's a *good* thing, I suppose, because if it had been that big, we might not be here talking to each other."

"Probably true... but I'm afraid I'm not following you on the rest of it, Ariel," replied Jacobson, evenly.

White just looked down at his feet, avoiding the Israeli's glance.

"Oh, I think that you're following me just *fine*, as you Americans say," countered Cohen.

"Look, I'll lay it on the line, here," he said, his dark eyes staring at the other two with determination. "Chkalov was there with me, and he blurted out some strange comment about 'the angels doing it' or something like that. I asked him to elaborate, I insisted upon it, but all he said was, 'you'll have to ask my former Commander'. So, here I am, asking you the same thing. I *really* need to know what's going on. No double-talk, no evasions."

"Uhh... *nothing's* going on," replied Jacobson. "Why would you think otherwise?"

Cohen's countenance darkened. "Commander," he pressed, "I hope that I've treated you respectfully since you arrived on my station, but I *don't* like being played for a fool, and I have my own sources of information. I've been monitoring this situation for some time and I know that *something's* going on – just not what. So I need to know what you and your former crew-members have been doing in the private meetings that you have been conducting, since the end of the 'Lucifer' incident. From what I was able to piece together from Chkalov, the shock that we encountered after your ships left, and these meetings, are connected, somehow. I need to know how. And I'm hoping that you won't play games with me, about this. *Sir*."

Again, the two former Mars mission crewmen regarded each other with palpable unease.

Finally, White spoke up.

"Y'all ain't that good a liar, Captain," he sighed. "Me neither. Might as well tell him, that's what I say. Stupid idea to try to hide it, anyway – what that man say, 'better inside the tent pissin' out, than outside pissin' in' – "

"Sam?" demanded Cohen, arching an eyebrow.

"Alright, *alright*," muttered Jacobson. "You know, Devon, I'm beginning to appreciate how Cherie felt, when she was the *only* one, and she didn't know if it was right to tell –"

"Tell *what*?" interjected Cohen.

Jacobson leaned back against a storage-box and folded his arms in front of him.

"Well," he remarked, "Before I do, Ariel, I need your assurance that you will not convey this information to *anyone* else, meaning especially, anyone on Earth, without the permission of both myself and of the rest of our group. So far we have been very careful about keeping the details of our little... *secret,* secret, and there are some good reasons for that. Do you understand?"

"I don't believe that I have to give any such guarantee," argued the station commander, "But just on the basis of our personal relationship, I'll do so, for now. However... what do you mean by, 'our group'? You mean your former crew members, from the Mars mission, I presume?"

"Yes," confirmed Jacobson.

"Y'all forgot Humber," reminded White. "And, *her*... if..."

Looking far away, the former Mars mission commander grunted, "Yeah, that's right, Devon. We discovered that Alan Humber has it, too. We think."

"Has *what?*" demanded Cohen.

Worriedly, he added, "A disease, you mean?"

"No, *not* a disease, the *opposite* of one, in fact... it's like this," elaborated Jacobson, his voice rising in confessional tone. "Do you remember how the alien, the same 'Karéin-Mayréij" who we encountered down on Mars, stowed away in the *Eagle,* then, later, managed to show up right among us, in the Infinity?"

"Of *course* I do," said Cohen. "I met her myself, as did a number of other staff of ISS2. An experience that I'll never forget, I can assure you of that. If only we had had more *time*..."

"Know what y'all mean, man," commented White, "*Really* do. I could have spent six lifetimes with that chick, she was *that* interesting, in ways that maybe nobody 'cept us loons on the *Infinity* could know. But we had all the time we needed."

"What Devon means – I think," continued Jacobson, "Is that in the brief time that we had Karéin living with us, she... well, she taught us how to *do* some things. Quite *amazing* things, actually. Cherie – Professor Tanaka, I mean – was the first. Afterwards, she taught the rest of us the secrets of her power, or a small fraction of them, anyway."

Now Cohen himself came to a semi-recline on the opposite side of the central area's pathway, mimicking the other man's posture.

"Such as, flying around in outer space, maybe? Wow," he gasped. "I'm beginning to see why you wanted to be... *discreet* about this."

Jacobson let out a soft chuckle.

"No," he replied, "Nothing *that* dramatic, Ariel, unfortunately. Wouldn't it be nice if – then we'd all just fly away, ha, ha. But what she *did* show us how to do, I can assure you, that's amazing enough as it is."

"Exactly what *can* you do?" inquired a fascinated Cohen.

"Well," explained the former Mars commander, "We can all *affect* things – move them around, push them, just by using our minds, and some of us have developed other abilities, for example, I seem to be able to heal cuts and scrapes in just a few seconds, no Band-Aid needed, as it were. We've been practicing, together, hoping that 'the total effect will be more than the sum of its parts', to use that cliché. Most of the time we're oh, *so* close, it's just beyond us, but occasionally, we all 'click', I don't know of any other way to explain it... and the last time we tried it, was just after our former ships departed the station. Which is what you misinterpreted as a space impact. The one that happened before, just after Karéin last left ISS2, we're guessing, was her exercising the same power... only on a *vastly* greater scale."

Cohen shook his head and ran his fingers across his face, as if wiping it after a morning shower.

"Telekinesis – that's... *incredible*, Captain," he commented, staring in astonishment. "And ironic, when you consider that in all likelihood, you're going to take this new knowledge to your graves, along of course with the same fate for the rest of us –"

"Well, just may be 'whistlin' in the dark', Commander," observed White, "But the whole plan is that we're gonna use this newfangled super-hero stuff to put the brakes on, when this old crate gets near enough to Earth. Maybe get us into orbit so we can get our asses off here, before the O^2 all gets used up."

"You're planning to do... *what*?" asked an amazed, but instantly-elated, Cohen.

"Wait... wait, just a *minute*," he stammered. " This is *crazy*. It's totally non-scientific. You're going to brake the station? With *what*? Doing something like that requires thrust, action-reaction, it's basic Newtonian physics. I just can't believe –"

"Commander," offered White, looking at the man deliberately. "Stand up."

Complying uneasily, Cohen replied, "Why?"

"All you gotta do," explained White, "Is just try to stand there. In one place, without movin'. Captain, y'all see anybody around here?"

Jacobson quickly glanced in every direction.

"Negative, Devon," he said. "Go ahead. Show our friend here."

"Show me *what*?" asked Cohen, guardedly.

He looked down at his feet as White stared at the man with laser-like determination.

From somewhere, music, like someone humming a martial tune – beautiful but powerful, all the same – sounded faintly.

The Israeli astronaut was being pushed backwards, centimeter by centimeter, thus propelled by some unseen force.

"I can get y'all at least five feet off the floor, too, if I want to, six on a good day," noted White, insouciantly. "More than that, and I get the mother of all headaches – think of eight bottles of Manechewitz on an empty stomach, the day after, that's kinda what it's like, Commander. And we're all out of Pepto-Bismol 'n Aspirin up here, don't you know."

"That... uhh... won't be necessary, Major White," Cohen said, quickly.

White complied, and the music stopped immediately.

Cohen commented, "Truly *incredible*... I suppose that you *do* indeed have these abilities... but is this *magic*? I mean, I can't *believe* that there is no scientific explanation... Captain, I promise that I won't reveal this without your permission, but how did the alien explain that she, now, you, were able to do this kind of thing? Can it be taught to others? Maybe if we extend the ability to the rest of the crew, they could amplify –"

"First of all, Ariel," the Mars mission commander stated, "The power, or, rather, the energy source, that enables this kind of ability is called '*Amaiish*', you may remember her talking about it as the 'Fire' in the televised interviews she had with NASA, while we were en route."

"Umm-humm," confirmed Cohen.

"Right. Well," continued Jacobson, "It turns out – and now, Commander, here comes the *really* secret part – that, apparently, most human beings have some ability to use this power, no, to tap into it, that's perhaps a better word... you see, we're not really *generating Amaiish* by ourselves, at least I don't *think* we are, it's out there in sub-dimensional space there somewhere, and what we're doing is kind of like plugging in to it like you would plug an electrical device into a wall socket... it's hard to describe, we're outside the boundaries of familiar human experience in all of this. If you hadn't already realized that."

Cohen just stared at the other two, stunned by what he had heard.

"What does one say in a situation like this... 'no kidding', I believe the expression is. Sam," he observed.

"Do you mean that we – I – could...? My *God*. This is... *historic*. If I knew English better, I'd use a bigger adjective, but..."

"Theoretically, yes," replied Jacobson, nodding sympathetically. "However, I hate to tell you this, but there's a catch. When Karéin taught us how to do it, she used some kind of secondary ability – which unfortunately none of us appear to have inherited – to instantly impart, 'unlock' would perhaps be a better word, the ability to tap into this energy source and thus do the super-hero stuff. When she did this, she required us to swear a very precise oath *only* to use this new power when appropriate and to make sure that anybody else who stumbled upon it, also promised to live by the same principles... the whole process was over with in a few minutes, but it was quite a moving experience, I can personally attest to that... not the kind of pledge that I'd ever voluntarily break."

"Even if that's true," argued Cohen, "She – the alien, I mean – is no longer with us... so there would be no-one to enforce such a pledge... isn't that right?"

Ignoring the bait, the Mars mission commander stated, "On top of *that*, Karéin specifically instructed us *not* to indiscriminately spread the knowledge of her 'Fire' to people who weren't aware of its potential to destroy, as well as to do positive things. She warned us that doing this could, in the long-run, be worse for the human race than the comet was... maybe it was hyperbole, but she didn't lie to us about anything else, so I'd have to give her the benefit of the doubt on this subject."

Jacobson looked away for a second, then continued, "The bottom line is, Ariel, that however much I'd like to share this ability with yourself and with others on board the station, I don't think that I *can* – I don't think that any of us know how to, either. We can *try*, if you want, because I trust you and I think that Karéin would have trusted you, too. After all, you're one of the very few human beings that she ever met in person, and she seemed to like you; she *told* me so, she said that she thought you were 'noble' in how you treated her and in how you were running ISS2. Just don't be too disappointed if you end up as the same old human being you started out with."

"Yeah, but Captain," remarked White, "How y'all explain *Humber*, then? He never even met *her* in person, not directly anyway, but the last two times he dropped in, and the Professor said that she could 'smell' it on him, or in him, whatever *that* means..."

"You're absolutely right about that, Devon," stated Jacobson, unhappily. "But you may recall that he was *with* us, in those last few minutes, in which we all tried to send our power, such as it was, to her. I can only assume that maybe Alan was exposed to so much of it that somehow it got unlocked in *him*, too – look, for God's sake, what do you want me to *say*?"

He threw up his hands.

"I have no real idea how this ability *works*, how I do it, what scientific principle, if any, that it's based on, or what its ultimate boundaries are, within any of us," the former Mars commander complained. "I'm guessing about everything and learning bit by bit, by doing. As are you. As are all of us."

Cohen looked crestfallen, but he managed to hide it with a forced smirk.

"Ah, for a minute you had me imagining myself as the Superman of Tel Aviv," he wryly observed. "But... fair enough, and here is what I hope will be my *only* example of pulling rank on anyone while we're all up here – I *would* like you and your group to at least try to teach me a bit of this... 'Fire', or whatever its real name is. If the effort is unsuccessful, there will be no harm done... is this request acceptable, Commander?"

"I see no reason not to try," responded Jacobson, politely. "Just don't be too disappointed, when it doesn't work. As is likely."

"Understood," replied Cohen. "But in the meantime, Captain, assuming that you can't extend this ability to anyone else on ISS2, I need to know how you plan to proceed on this plan that Major White explained a few minutes ago, the one to slow the station, that is. I can already see one rather major challenge, here: If it is going to require interaction with anyone else amongst the crew, or even a high-level explanation of any more of these 'events', it will be difficult to keep the confidentiality that you've explained is necessary. Have you thought of that? Or of what you're going to tell NASA, when ISS2 slows down magically, without a booster rocket? They will ask for answers, details..."

"You're probably right about that," agreed Jacobson, "But to tell you the truth, we're nowhere *near* worrying about those kinds of details... I guess we'll have to leave the public relations angle in your own capable hands. Just to give you an idea of what we're up against, yes, it's true, we *can*, when everything works perfectly, mind you, make our presence felt around here –

"Indeed," said the station commander.

"Yeah, the 'shimmy and shake' routine we somehow managed to set off recently, is evidence of that," noted Jacobson. "But we have no way of telling if we're having any effect at all on the station's trajectory – we can't even tell if we're pushing in the right direction, let alone if we're pushing hard enough. I guess what I'm saying, Ariel, is, 'don't get your hopes up'. What we're trying is the longest of long-shots."

"More like tryin' to throw the long bomb on fourth and fifty with ten seconds left on the clock, and we don't know which way's the goal posts," joked White.

"But we're the only game in town, y'all know," he added with one of his trademark bright grins.

Cohen shook his head.

"I can see," he ruefully observed, "That I have a *lot* to learn about all of this. Certainly more than I can handle, right here and now."

He looked at his wrist computer.

"I suppose I should be going," he added. "Captain? I'd like to have lunch with you, tomorrow, would that be possible?"

"Until we had this talk, Ariel," replied Jacobson, "The answer would have been 'no'... tomorrow's the day when our group usually meets in the mess hall and discusses individual progress on our set of mental exercises. However, I guess we're one big happy family now, right? So you're welcome to drop by. Just let me explain things to the rest of them, before you say anything. They're all quite careful about revealing this subject to 'outsiders'. But you're on the inside, now, Commander. Welcome aboard."

"Honored..." muttered Cohen. "It's nice to be 'welcome' aboard my own ship. And, just this once, you have my permission to finish off your track and field meet... just don't let me catch you at it again. It would seem that you don't need muscles to move around, anyway, any more, do you, gentlemen?"

He smiled, opened the hatch to the zero-G sections, gave the other two a last, searching look, then disappeared.

"You know," mentioned White to his former commander, "Y'all didn't tell him about the other, really *interestin'* stuff, did you, Captain? I mean, the laser beam eyes, how she lit y'all up like a Christmas tree and it just tickled, me 'n the icicles... all the other tricks..."

"I did not," confirmed Jacobson. "And neither should you, Brent, Cherie, or Sergei. It's true that we've been concentrating on the telekinesis thing, given the predicament that we're all in; but have you considered what the attitude of the rest of the ISS2 staff – or, may we be so lucky, the attitude of people back on

Earth, when and if we get back there – might be, if we start to develop these other abilities, as well? Use your *brains*, Devon... they used to burn witches for much less. And from what I hear on the comms channels, witch-burning, or something quite like it, is apparently coming back into fashion in some places in Dixie and the Bible Belt, these days. We've been away from Earth for quite a long while, you know. Apparently things back home may not be quite the way how we left them."

"*Tell* me, sir," shot back White, sarcastically. "Y'all remember how just before we blasted off, those Southern crackers was circulatin' some damn petition down there, demandin' that I be yanked from the mission, just on account of... well, *you* know. They're probably right *pissed* that I ended up winnin' the 'first-man-on-Mars' lottery. I sure wouldn't put it past 'em to be doin' any of what you said."

Appreciatively, Jacobson nodded and went on, "No, I think we'd be best off keeping all of this under wraps, for as long as possible. If and when we get strong enough to defend ourselves, then, *maybe*. I don't want to get strung up for alien abilities that are definitely there enough to get us feared and mistrusted, but that aren't powerful enough to do anything that we couldn't do just as easily with our fists, or a gun. Does that make sense?"

White's eyes surveyed those of Jacobson for a second.

Then the black man offered, "Yeah, I guess. But... I mean, we lived with *her* for all that time, and we knew what *she* was capable of. If we can do that for a girl from Mars, why can't they do it for us?"

"Because," said Jacobson, calmly, "Unlike her, you and I, my friend, aren't angels."

Ho-tel, Mo-tel, Holiday...

By now, the low rumble of the SUV's engine had lulled all but its driver into a peaceful, contented-as-possible sleep.

Around them, the dark, vast countryside of the Continental Divide wilderness rolled silently on, enveloping either side of the narrow ribbon of highway pavement in a gloomy embrace, while a narrow swath of what lay ahead was lit up by the vehicle's powerful hi-beams.

"Figures," grunted Billings, as he reflexively tried to wipe the fatigue from his eyes, concentrating on the white guideline of the meridian. "Just about got ourselves killed trying to get across the other state line, but here, we cruise past the Utah one on Route 89 without even a *toll-booth* to trouble us. Unless you count these snow squalls we seem to hit every few miles... you'd think that we'd get the white stuff elsewhere, but the rest of the road's not got any that I can see."

"Y'all shore?" yawned a now half-awake Claremont. "Ah didn't see no sign, mind y'all, weren't lookin'. Y'all not let me drive, Bob, well, after we go past that big lake and ah couldn't see nothin', figured ah'd get some sleep, much as ah can, sittin' up."

"Nah, I didn't see one either," replied the salesman, "But the GPS doesn't lie... according to what it says, we're way south of the state line, we should just about be to Logan, any minute now. Didn't expect it to work, they warned us 'satellites are going to be right in the path of the comet' or something like that, but I guess at least *one* of them must have dodged the bullet. Like we have, so far... I was worried about crap all over the road, but so far I've only seen a couple of cars off in the ditch, and there was a semi kind of half on the highway, but the headlights lit him up in enough time for me to swerve this crate.

"Glad that didn't happen in that snow squall we went through by the lake, we're still pretty high up, that's par for the course, or at least it was before things really got hot the last couple of years," he added. "But it's exhausting driving – gotta keep paying attention, all the time. I'll sure be glad when I can finally get some real sleep. I almost miss that garbage that your son was listening to, before he conked out... it's annoying enough to keep me from dozing off, I'll say that for it."

"Well, ah don' like it either, but he friends all listen to it, ah gave up tryin' to stop him... y'all see any of them army tanks? Po-lice?" asked Claremont.

"Nothing," asserted Billings. "Nobody except us, in fact. Might be a curfew, or... well, we're pretty far from nowhere, still. Even in the old days you might not see a lot of traffic – I used to take this road every so often when I did my northern sales run."

"Didn't y'all say they had a roadblock – at th' state line, ah mean..." lazily inquired the black woman.

"*Thought* so," explained the salesman. "But maybe they only got 'em on the Interstates, or the main ones. They can't block *all* the back roads, not enough troops, what with the stuff going on in the cities, I guess. Or maybe they're just late, or maybe they're just stupid. Who *knows* – I'll take it any way I can get it. Listen, Whitney, can you hand me another one of those Ne-wake pills from the bottle over there? Usually I don't like taking more than one per day, but I guess this counts as an emergency."

"Shore," replied the black woman, handing the man a small capsule.

He threw it back, not needing a chaser, and then she spoke up again.

"Listen, Bob..." started Claremont, but her voice was cut off by another one coming from the back.

"We there yet, Momma?" asked a sleepy Melissa.

"Not yet, honey child," replied the mother.

"As if we know where 'there' is," commented Billings. "Actually, I *think* I do... yeah, see that, up the road? Hot damn! That's Logan, folks, there's the Country Club. None of you golf, right?"

And indeed, the headlights of the SUV illuminated a large sign saying, 'City of Logan Private Golf and Country Club', alongside another, even bigger one, with a slogan painted in bright red, white and blue : 'America : White, Christian And No Place For Illegals'.

"Okay, we're on... what?" the salesman said to himself. "Yeah, 400 South... I saw the sign. Man, this place is shut *tight*... but never mind, I've stopped through here a few times on late runs... just up 300 to the lights, then south..."

He fell silent for a few seconds, then mentioned, "Lot of abandoned cars around here... creepy-looking, that's for sure."

He was almost whispering, now.

"Whitney," he muttered, "You see *that?* Half of those cars are stripped... and busted windows – look at what's left of that building over there, what the hell did *that*, maybe one of those meteors back when –"

Claremont shrugged and let out a *sotto voce* laugh.

"Remind me of home, sorta," she offered. "We *used* to seein' junk all over th' place, nothin' special for the kids 'n me. But... if y'all don't mind me aksin', Bob, where we goin'?"

"You'll see," replied the salesman. "Hah! Ol' Bob *never* forgets a town, not when he's been to half the damn businesses in it, trying to sell them floor-tiles. Place we're going to – just a few minutes more, now, there's the 91 sign, so we're on Main – well, he actually didn't *buy*, but that was alright, because if he's open, he's the cheapest damn place to stay this side of –"

"Y'all shore *is* some preacher-man, Mister Bob," smirked a small voice from the back seats.

"Yeah, I know, okay, I gotta *watch* that," agreed Billings, as he navigated the SUV down the silent, nearly-deserted streets of this mid-sized Utah town.

His gaze started to dart from side to side.

"You'd think I'd remember which side of the road it's on... yeah! *There* it is. Okay, folks, everybody get ready to get out of the bus... I think. Here we are at the beautiful downtown Logan Motel. Hmm... no lights on the sign, that's a bad sign, but maybe he's just gone to sleep."

He brought the SUV to a gradual stop, parking it in the second instance of a large number of empty parking spaces, with the headlights illuminating the door to the *faux*-Southwest stucco motel's business office. Other than for a couple of clearly-disabled cars, and one truck up on blocks behind a building, there seemed to be no other vehicles in the lot.

The salesman unhooked his seat-belt and turned to address the children and 'Sari'-girl in the back seat.

"Now listen," he commanded, "I know the guy who runs this place, that is, of course, if he still does, and I'm sure he won't ask too many questions, but some of you are still in those garbage-man uniforms they gave us back at the Jesus Freak Prison Farm, and I'd just as soon not have you drawing too much attention to yourselves, so I'm going to go out and see if I can get us a room for the night... okay, *two* rooms, one for you and the kids, Whitney, another for me and –"

"That would be very nice, Bob, thank you," came back the voice of the newcomer.

With the hint of a giggle, she added, "I suppose that this means that your priesthood does not make a habit out of... self-denial. But will this room have somewhere, where we can wash ourselves? I *did* have a shower back in the camp, but..."

"Ain't y'all never been in a mo-tel, there, girl?" asked an incredulous Claremont. "We don't get to very often, but yeah, they should have a shower 'n a bath... some of 'em got TV, Neo hookups, coffee makers, and them little fridges, where y'all can get candy bars, booze 'n such –"

"Tee-Vee?" started the 'Sari'-girl. "Mo-tel?"

"Well, not on *my* tab, thank you," interjected Billings. "Look, anyway, we can worry about this kind of thing when and if we can actually get in here. You all stay put for the time being, is that clear?"

Claremont nodded. The others all responded affirmatively.

"I'm going to tell him that you guys are all really tired and just want to get to bed – not much of a lie, there – so he'll only see you in the morning... that'll give us a bit of breathing room to decide what we all end up wearing," added the salesman. "Oh, and one more thing..."

He motioned to the black woman, to come closer.

As she bent over in his direction, he whispered, "Listen, Whitney, I didn't want to say this right in front of the kids, but there's a small chance that something *bad* might happen out there... probably just paranoia on my part, but damn, this place is spooky quiet right now, even compared to how dead I remember it having been, in the wee hours. So if you don't see me come out in fifteen minutes, I've told Sari where the spare key is – get her to find it for you, then take this thing and drive out of here, any direction, as fast and far as you can. Understood?"

Silently, Claremont nodded.

"Thanks, Bob," she then whispered.

"Okay, well, here I go," he stated, stepping gingerly out of the car, slamming the door shut behind him.

Billings stood in front of the door to the motel's lobby and knocked firmly on the portal. He waited for a minute or so, then pounded more insistently.

A man's voice, growling suspicion, sounded from inside.

"Get the *fuck* out of here! I've got a gun and I got no money!" shouted the voice.

"Hey, don't shoot, it's just *me* – Bob Billings from Tucson – out here!" called Billings, as he stepped immediately out of the line of sight of the front door.

"That you, Elmer?" he asked.

"Billings... Billings? I don't know... oh, yeah, the linoleum guy, right?" retorted the voice.

"Uhh... floor-tiles, actually. Hardwood and ceramic... look, I got a carload of people in my SUV out behind me, all we need is a place to stay for a day or so, we've been on the road all night. You open for business? It's Elmer, Elmer Pollack, right? And what's with the gun, for God's sake?"

"Yeah, this is Elmer in here," replied the hidden voice. "And as for business, well, there hasn't been *nothin'* in that department for weeks, around here – just every fuckin' thug and low-life in the state, and from everywhere else for that matter, trying to break in here and steal me blind. Already lost half the televisions in the suites and that was *after* I padlocked all the doors, assholes just broke the windows and helped themselves. So I don't think..."

"*Look*, Elmer, I know it's been a while," argued the salesman, "But can't you do me a favor, just this *once*? I got money, and we aren't going to be too picky about what we get – right now, my only alternative is bedding down two other adults and three kids in my car. What's your risk? I'll pay up front, if you want."

"What's *yours*?" countered Pollack. "Risk, I mean. Don't get me wrong, I'd be happy to let you all stay here – God knows I could use the business, *any* business – but I can't guarantee safety or security, man. You notice that nobody's out and about, on the streets? There's a *reason* for that. We've had rapes, murders, break-ins by the dozen... bikers from up somewhere, gangs from California, no cops anywhere in sight for a month or more, businesses like mine have had to take up arms to defend themselves. Damn shame, this used to be such a *safe* town. But not any more."

"Come *on*, Elmer," pleaded Billings. "Just tell me, what's your normal rate? For a single room, double bed, I mean?"

"Seventy-five," replied the voice. "You know that's as cheap as you're gonna get. Even Super Six is twice that."

"Your credit verifier up?" asked the salesman.

"Don't make me laugh," retorted Pollack. "Been down since the 'total communications requisition' they did just before the comet. They're saying it'll be back up next week, they said that on TV yesterday, but then they said the same thing three days ago and a week ago."

"Look, I'll make you a *deal*," offered Billings, hoping that the other man couldn't too easily hear the desperation in his voice. "I can't pay the whole thing in cash, but would you take fifty up front for two rooms, and I'll let you take down my credit number for three hundred when the net's back up?"

Silence enveloped the scene for a second or two, then the voice came back.

"Hundred up front. I'll never see the other three hundred, you know."

"Look, Elmer, I only got so much cash and the kids and I gotta *eat*, for God's sake," protested the salesman. "You serve breakfast, don't you?"

"Did, when we had any food," remarked the motel owner. "Well, *still* do, I suppose, that is if you like pancakes and that tofu vegetarian breakfast sausage junk, all we got left after the bacon, eggs and sausages ran out. I've been livin' on it for three days now. They keep tellin' me there's going to be another convoy in from Salt Lake any day, with supplies for the whole town. As if."

"Okay, look, why don't we do it this way," negotiated Billings. "I give you the fifty up front, then we buy breakfast from you, charge us anything you want for it, up to fifty. Make sense?"

Another pause, then the voice relented, "Yeah... sure, I guess. As long as you and these kids of yours understand, *no* guarantees. We got deadbolts, reinforced windows, but... when the lights go out, you're on your own, if you get into trouble, I ain't goin' out there to play 'here comes the Cavalry', know what I mean? Just about got my *own* ass whipped day before yesterday, surprised a biker trying to break open a mini-bar to get the booze. Thank God he didn't have his gun, and I *did* have mine."

And where'd you hide the body?, the salesman found himself thinking.

Let's hope we don't get a return visit from that late Hell's Angel's fellow riders.

"Done, then?" asked Billings, hopefully.

"Done," confirmed Pollack.

There was the sound of multiple locks being disengaged and the door to the motel's front office opened, just a crack at first, until its inhabitant – a clean-shaven, tall, balding, elderly but evidently still in-shape man, dressed in cowboy jeans, a plaid shirt and porting a substantially-large pump-action shotgun, cautiously peered out and verified Billings' identity.

The gun went by the door and the man extended his hand, which the salesman gratefully shook.

"Listen, sorry 'bout all that," mentioned the hotel owner, half-apologetically. "You just can't be *too* careful, these days. Almost found out the hard way myself, more than once, lately."

"So which ones should we pick?" requested Billings.

"If I was you, I'd leave the car 'round the back, keep it out of sight from Main Street... actually, garage is open, if you want to park it in there, that's okay by me, my truck got stolen two weeks ago – don't worry, wasn't in the garage, I was stupid, I parked it on Main and forgot to lock it, just that once – but take the top two over there, 14-A and 14-B, we've had a lot fewer break-ins on the second level than the first, I guess they figure they don't have to carry the loot down a set of stairs to get off with it. Also, most of the stuff in 'em still works, satellite's out for the TV, of course, but you can still get stuff off the local cable channel and the movie server still works. That's an extra ten, by the way," explained Pollack.

"Yeah... okay, no problem," said Billings. "And I doubt we'll be doing the video thing, tonight – we're all completely beat from the road, been driving most of the night. I'll introduce the rest of the group to you for breakfast tomorrow."

"Okay," replied the motel owner. "Here, just a minute," he said, disappearing inside the door.

A few second later he re-emerged with two sets of keys.

"Used ta be that you'd have to hit this little button doohickey on the plastic part of the key-chain, as you turned it in the lock," noted Pollack. "But when all the power went down it knocked out the computer thing that got the key and the doohickey workin' together and it never *did* work right after that, so I just turned off the computer lock system altogether. All you gotta do now is put the key in and turn it."

"Just like the good old days," grunted the salesman. "Before they got all the damn computers, everywhere, doing stupid stuff like your fridge telling you that you're out of milk. Never *could* get mine to tell me I'm out of Jack Daniels. Eventually it went berserk, some effing computer virus or something, it started to call in so many home-delivery orders for horse-radish, that my whole damn fridge was full of it – I had to disconnect the gizmo before I went broke. Something big happens like just did, and you find out very quickly how useful all that techno-stuff is... like, not worth a bucket of warm spit. Thanks, Elmer."

"No problem," answered the other man. "Tell you the truth, it's kinda nice to have somebody to talk with – somebody that ain't gonna try to slit my throat for five bucks, which is about the state of things these days. When you're in the motel business you gotta be careful *all* the time, of course, but after the damn comet it's been like the worst part of town, all *over* the place. But I got all my money sunk into this set of shacks, don't have a choice about hangin' on as long as I can. See ya in the morning."

"Can't find much to disagree with, there," offered Billings. "Good night."

Gingerly, he returned to the SUV.

"Well...?" asked Claremont. "Which one of us get the front seat? Y'all looked like y'all 'bout to get shot back there, Bob."

"No such thing," happily countered Billings. "I not *only* got us some nice clean beds to sleep in, but I even bargained him down a bit... two rooms for us, one for you and the kids, one for me and Sari. Hey, hey, whaddya *say* – has ol' Bob still got it, or *what*?"

A girlish giggle emanated from the back seat, somewhere.

"We shall find out about *that* later, Bob," said her pleasant, yet seductive, *faux*-teenager voice. "Once you have had a bath."

"Oh mah *Gawd*," echoed Melissa.

"What's so big a deal," observed the Indian-boy. "Happens all the *time* on the reserve. She's grown up, I mean..."

"Girl, y'all gots to be *discreet* 'bout such thangs," suggested Claremont. "Them boys won't *respect* y'all, if y'all too eager..."

"R – E – S – P – C – T, find out what it mean to me –" started the teenager.

"Don' be *smart*, child," admonished the mother. "She learn soon enough, for sheself."

"*You* respect my talents, do you not, Bob?" the 'Sari'-girl asked, with an innocence that might have been feigned or indeed genuine.

"Oh, yeah, indubitably," replied Billings.

"Uhh... I'll get the bags, okay?" he added, fumbling for the proximity unlock dongle.

Not at all to his surprise, it didn't work, so the salesman found his way to the rear hatch door, turned the key and hoped that the dark would hide the special stuff that he had hidden in the trunk.

"14-A and 14-B, up the stairs," announced Billings. "And no thieving from the mini-bar, unless you've somehow conjured up some money. Bob's paying for the *room*, not the floor show, don't you know."

No Failure For Jesus' Warriors

Imagine a room that might, under other circumstances, have been part of an art gallery or maybe a high-class dance hall, with immaculately-polished, marble floors, walls of finest mahogany leading up to a cathedral ceiling fifty or more feet high.

No window interrupted the symmetry of this place, and if there had ever been accouterments of any type, these were long gone, except for a single bank-president-style desk and chair, dimly lit by an atmospheric background glow at the far end of the room.

Two large, brass-bound doors at the other end boomed suddenly open. Through these came the hesitant steps of a portly, 50ish Caucasian woman with salt-and-pepper hair, modestly garbed in flowing robes, something like what a nun would have worn, but no Catholic habit, this.

The woman was accompanied by two much larger, riot combat-clothed guards – or, 'Soldiers of Christ The Warrior-King', as they were known around here – the face of each one invisible under a helmet and visor, each toting a loaded automatic rifle.

The woman looked from side to side as if trying to find a trace of humanity in either automaton. This was to no avail.

One guard cuffed her roughly on the shoulder, pointing forward.

"Go!" he ordered.

Straightening up as much as the worry would allow her, the woman walked slowly forward, the heels of her shoes making a faint 'click' on the cold, reflective floor, a sound that would otherwise have been inaudible except for the gloomy silence in this place.

She was now ten feet in front of the desk.

"Stop," called out a half-lit figure, reclining in the chair. "State your name."

"I am Commanding Sister Wilhelmena, of the North-West Realm," replied the woman, mustering an unsure dignity.

"'Commanding', Sister," unctuously parodied the figure. "'Commanding', is it? You know, that word carries with it, certain implications. For one, being in *control*. Wouldn't you say?"

"Yes, sir," tremulously answered the woman. "If it *is* 'sir', I don't know your title, sir – I mean, who do I –"

"*I'll* ask the questions here," growled the man in the chair, still not showing his face. "But I *can* tell you this much, woman. You don't *know* who you're speaking to. Let's just say, you're in front of someone *far* superior to anyone that a woman is ever likely to serve, in our Church. If I were you, I'd be very, *very* forthcoming, today."

Reflexively, the woman bowed.

"Yes, of *course*, sir," she said, uneasily.

"Right," the figure leered, leaving the word to hang in the air a few seconds. "So... let's get right down to it. My understanding, my dear 'Commanding' Sister, is that we recently had a few little *problems* in that camp you were assigned to, the one on the Idaho-Wyoming state line... remember?"

"*Problems*, sir?" the woman nervously replied. "I'm not aware of any problems, sir."

She noticed that the guards had now advanced to either side of her.

With mock sympathy, the man shot back, "Oh, just a few little issues with some of the people who we rounded up, and who we planned to bring into the fold... going *missing*, *that* kind of thing. You wouldn't know anything about that, would you, Sister?"

"Missing? Oh no, sir, we did a full count... they're all accounted for..." the woman tried to explain.

The man behind the desk made some kind of a motion, perhaps the wave of a hand or a finger.

At once, a guard slapped the woman hard on the back of the head, sending her flying forward.

She sprawled on the ground, then, after a second or two to try to regain her composure, convinced her wobbly legs to bear her upright.

"Now," said the figure, a few features of his clean-shaven, leathery-lined face visible in the half-light, "Let's try that again, Sister. Are you *sure* that you didn't lose anyone? Remember, it's a *sin* to lie to your Church superiors."

Wiping tears, the woman stammered, "Sir, why – why – I... I... as God is my witness, sir, I don't *think* that we lost any of the captives, but... but... we didn't want to bother Headquarters with just a little accounting error that was probably nothing –"

This time, she was knocked to the ground by a clenched fist. A guard strode to her side and gave her a brutal kick in the trunk, followed by a sharp blow to the side of the head.

Blood flowed from underneath her hair.

"Get up, slut, and *answer* this godly man!" he barked. "The next lie will be your *last!*"

"Don't you *know* that I'm a *man*, made your superior in every way by the infallible Word of God Himself and by the laws of our Church?" the shadowy voice behind the desk hissed. "Don't you *know* the position you're in? I can make it get worse, *much* worse, if I so choose. Talk, *now*."

Pain shooting through her ribs, the woman, shaking with fear and trying to stop the flow of blood from the back of her head, somehow managed to kneel in front of the desk.

"Sir," she whimpered, "We... we *thought* that we had a few more... but it must have been a *mistake*, sir, that's what I mean, a mis-count, marked down two when we only had one, that kind of thing... there's no way that we could have lost *that* many, we were locked down tight, there was no way at all that anyone could have escaped! I'm *so* sorry, sir, I didn't mean to lie. Please forgive me, sir, have mercy!"

"Ah, I *see*," replied the man, his voice dripping feigned sympathy. "You only *thought* you had more than you really had, is that it? And how many would *that* be, I wonder? I'd think really, *really* carefully about what you say, next, my dear 'Commanding' Sister. If you don't give a convincing answer, well, I'm sure you've heard the stories about how people... *disappear*, haven't you?"

Terrified, sweat pouring from her brow, the woman stammered, "Sir, I *swear* to you, this is the truth – everything that I know. We... we thought we had... it was three children – two boys, one girl, or maybe the other way around, and two, maybe three adults... one or two women, one man. That was the lights-out count, that my Sisters gave me, I mean. But then they just *vanished*, sir, as God is my witness! The windows, the doors, they were all closed, and the guards were up and down the halls, every minute... we didn't *mean* to deceive anyone, but *nobody* could have gotten out of those barracks! So we... we assumed that we never had them in the first place."

She took a heavy sigh, bending on her knees, crying, paralyzed with fear. "This is the truth, sir," she sobbed. "I swear on the Holy Bible!"

"*Now* we're getting somewhere, Sister," the man smoothly observed, with mock amicability. "Tell me... was there anything... *unusual*, about any of these prisoners that you say you may or may not have had, in your tender care? About any of the females, especially?"

The woman thought for a moment. Somehow, despite the nagging, growing pain in her torso, her tears ceased.

"Unusual? Uhh... no, sir, I don't think so," she whimpered. "But I didn't see any of these prisoners myself, I mean, if we even *had* them in the first place, sir... one of my Sisters said that there might have been a white man in his 40s, and a black woman, also middle-aged... oh, and..."

"And *what*?" growled the man. "Speak up and speak *fast*, woman. I'm becoming impatient."

"Well," the woman said, her voice trembling, "There was a black boy, maybe another boy... they said he was a Mexican or maybe black, or a mongrel, they weren't sure... we whipped them both a good lick, as the Bible says to, because they gave us lip... and one of the guards said that there was a pretty white girl, green or blue eyes, gray or white hair. But we had six or seven like every one of these in the camp, sir! It could have been *any* of them, or maybe we just counted wrong, like I said –"

She could just see him raise his hand and, terrified, she groveled.

"Please, sir, *please*, have pity on me! I'll do *anything!*" she cried, tears flowing profusely down her cheeks, darkening her dress as it mixed with blood.

"Shut *up*, woman!" the man shouted. But somehow, his tone was introspective, not immediately threatening.

"What did you *say*? A *girl*? A *white* girl? One that somehow just *vanished* from your supposedly locked-down compound?"

Silence enveloped the scene. The woman bowed her head and waited, saying a last silent prayer.

"Now think *very* carefully, whore," the man spat out. "How old was this white girl? What was she wearing? What did she look like? What was her name? Did she talk to anyone? What did she say? Everything, I want *everything*! Right now, or I'll let the guards *really* have some fun with you!"

"Sweet Lord God, *no*, sir!" sobbed the woman. "I swear, I tell you all I know... I can find out more, if I could just speak to the other Sisters, *please* sir – the girl, I don't know, we really didn't pay any more attention to her than to the hundreds of others that we had to process... I never saw her myself, but I heard that she was a teenager, maybe a bit older – might have been wearing workman's overalls, you know, the kind the auto mechanics have... the Sisters said that she had an accent and that her clothes were ripped and ragged, dark stains and holes in them all over, but then there were *many* like that, sir, she was no different from all the others, you know how it is out there, a third or more of the people we had were filthy immigrants from down South –"

"You're so stupid that you didn't notice anything at *all* different about this female?" mocked the Christian leader. "Father God, forgive us for putting the likes of you, in a position of responsibility... well, enough of *that*. So what did you *do* with her? Maybe give her a polite 'good-bye' and a free bus ticket to the next town?"

"We put all of them in the showers because they stank to high heaven – oh, Lord, forgive my intemperate language, sir!" whimpered the woman. "And we gave them uniforms so they'd be easy to tell from the new ones that were arriving all the time, at the state border, I mean. The man, they thought he had a suit, a white shirt, maybe he was a businessman or something, the black woman and the children, we never found out about –"

A man's gruff voice sounded above the woman's semi-prostrate figure.

"Want me to give her a bit more *persuasion*, Master?" he threatened, raising the butt of his gun.

"No... not right now," replied the shadowy figure behind the desk. "No, that will be enough for today. You've done better than I had expected, whore – that's *very* interesting information. I'll need some time to consider our next course of action."

Another figure emerged from the shadows, standing just behind the man in the reclining-chair. The interrogator whispered something to his master.

The Commanding Sister could just make out the words, "...pull the camp records, we need *every* name..."

Hopefully, she looked up.

"But take *her*, to the basement," the man behind the desk added, with a barely-visible, evil grin. "Keep her there until I call for her again. Maybe a few days... or weeks... or... however long, will reinforce her memory."

The woman wailed.

"You know, if I were this pathetic, disobedient, half-honest female," he paused for a second, then remarked, "I'd want that to be *sooner*, rather than later. I hear it's rather... *cold*, not much to do except think, and you don't serve regular meals down there, do you, Brother Jack?"

The guard grunted a guttural laugh, saying, "This bitch *will* tell you what she knows. We'll make *sure* of it."

He grabbed one of the woman's arms, as his compatriot roughly seized the other. She screamed in fear and pain, as they pulled her almost upright and turned for the door, dragging her away.

"*Please*, sir!" cried the woman. "Have *mercy!* I *beg* you!"

The man made a motion, and the guards stopped, for a second.

"Ah, the quality of our mercy," remarked the man at the desk. "You shall soon know all *about* it."

He waved his hand.

"Take her away," he ordered.

Minnie, Otis And Will

"Okay, park it *here*," requested the woman, stretching as much as one could with these oppressive, newfangled body restraint belts.

She ran her fingers through dark, Asian locks, trying to relieve some of the fatigue that had been building steadily over the past few days. Her shapely, attractive, almond-skinned face could not do as well to hide the tension.

"Why?" inquired the driver. "We're not even halfway to Boise yet. It's just a stretch of road."

"Park it anyway, Will," demanded the woman. "I need to get *out* of this thing for a minute or two. Get some air. Do some thinking."

The young, lanky agent in front of the wheel shrugged and pulled over, the black, nondescript SUV's tires crunching on the gravel shoulder.

Immediately upon the cease of motion, a door opened, and the figure of a slim, Chinese-American woman, neatly and conservatively dressed if you didn't count the creases and wrinkles of three days of highway travel, stepped out.

She paced a few steps away, facing the far-off glory of snow-capped mountains.

"Take your time, then," called out the driver, indifferently, as he removed his dark glasses. "I think I got Neo up with our priority code. Might be a ball-game on Disney-1846."

He flipped a switch and looked downward at a small video display.

The agent stood, stared and contemplated.

Another car door sounded and she was joined by a powerfully-built, black man, at least a head taller and a hundred and fifty or so pounds heavier, in a disheveled business-suit.

"Figured it all out yet, Minnie?" he asked in a friendly baritone.

Still staring out into space, she let out just enough of a wry smile for the man to notice.

"Nope. Have you?" she shot back, mischievously.

"Was countin' on yourself for all the psychic stuff," offered the black man.

"Yeah, well, we're going to need more than a bit of something like that, before we get to the bottom of this, Mr. Boatman," replied the Asian-American woman.

"Ah, you gotta have a little *faith*, there, Madam Agent Chu," observed the other. "If she's out there, somewhere, we'll find her. Find *it*. Just a matter of time. In my *opinion*, of course. But, also of course, that's an opinion from eighteen-plus years in the field. I seen some that stay out there a month, a year, ten years, sometimes. But we *always* find 'em, least if they're here in the good old U.S. of A."

"I know, Otis... I know," said Chu. "You're as good as they get. I know that, the Department knows it, too. But this one's... *different*, for God's sake. I don't have to tell you how. And..."

"And what?" asked the big black man.

Chu turned to face him. She kicked a stone out towards the wilderness.

"What I just can't understand," she said, "Is how we – they – the Army, the spooks, I mean, all those fancy 'special forces' guys that they sent up there... how they could *possibly* have missed her. It doesn't add up, you know. Alien being, new world... well, try to imagine how you or I would do, under the same circumstances. We'd be lucky to blow our nose twice, before we got put in a zoo, or just got shot. How could she have just *vanished* like that?"

The black man looked down, thought for a second, then looked up and said, "No, I guess it doesn't add up, does it? Not at all. But I'd remind you – not that I need to – that this is no ordinary fugitive. Who knows *what* she's capable of. If, that is, she really exists at all. I'll believe *that*, when I see it. Her. Whatever."

"Don't blame you for thinking that," replied Chu, leaning back on the vehicle. "But the higher-ups – going way up the food chain, you know I can't say exactly how high – *they* certainly seem sure about it, almost to the point of panic, I'd say. I know I shouldn't repeat rumors, but rumor has it that they've even got the President under 'special protection', whatever that means, lest she show up unannounced at his doorstep."

Abruptly, she stood back up.

"Damn," she complained. "Forgot how filthy these things get out here, what with the snow on the road. Oh well. Dress is just about shot anyway, I'll have to change in Boise."

She tried to brush herself off, though the effort was mostly futile.

"You know, Minnie," said Boatman, "If they're so sure of it, if this is such a 'national security crisis', that's what I heard, remember? Then why the *hell* have they got three FBI-agents, with no backup to speak of, out chasin' this little green girl in the backwoods of Idaho, instead of the Army, the National Guard, the CIA, a cast of thousands? Why wouldn't they just cordon off the whole damn state, nobody gets in or out?"

The woman shrugged.

"Doesn't make any sense to me," continued the black man. "My guess is that it's some kind of PR stunt, a diversion to take all the attention off of what's going on in the cities, you know things are *grim* in L.A., Chicago, Detroit, just about everywhere. You must have heard the rumors that the whole Mars thing, or at least the alien story, was just that – a story to take people's minds off everybody bein' blown to Kingdom Come... can't really blame them for doing that, I guess. Truth is, I think this whole chase is probably a waste of time, but then that's just me."

"I respect that," countered Chu, "But I have to believe what I heard from the high mucky-mucks... I can tell you, Otis, if you had heard the concern, no, let me rephrase that, the *fear*, in their voices... *that* sure didn't sound like the standard BS. No, there's *something* to this, for sure. I'm just not sure that it's really what they're telling us. But if it's anything like what they're saying... well. Maybe the low-key approach is to keep the rumors down; I mean, if they started something like locking down the whole region, people would *talk*, wouldn't they? There's enough panic going around, anyway. What bothers me more is, they haven't told us what we're supposed to *do*, when and if we track this girl, this thing, down."

"Welcome to the FBI," joked Boatman. "Making it up as we go. Standard Operating Procedure, or hadn't you figured that out?"

She turned her attractive, but 'it's business now, mister,' Asian countenance directly at him.

"I've been in the Bureau almost as long as you have, Otis, so that's no surprise. But... I think we had better *understand* each other on this."

"What do you mean?" he asked.

"The bottom line is," the woman explained, "I've heard through the grapevine, that some of the higher-ups, not all of them, mind you, consider the alien a threat... a serious threat. One that needs to be *eliminated*, as soon as possible."

The black man let out an impressed-sounding whistle.

"Whew," he commented, "That's some *heavy* manners there, Agent Chu. That what you plannin' to do?"

"I asked you first," Chu parried.

"Well, I don't *know*," replied the black man, in an introspective tone.

"Assumin' that this creature is *real*, and assumin' that we somehow manage to track her down – two real big chances to make an 'ass out of you and me', need I remind you – in the absence of a clear order from Headquarters, I'd have to say that I'd just follow her, try to learn as much as I can about her, report it back to H.Q., of course, then let *them* make that decision."

"But what if they tell you to... *terminate* her?" pressed the woman.

His big, brown eyes stared at Chu for a few long seconds, hoping to see a sign, finding none.

Eventually he stated, "You know, I'd have to tell you honestly, Minnie, I'd have a hard time doin' that, even with positive confirmation from Headquarters. It's not just that we might be eliminatin' something *unique*, somethin' we can never get back; it's also, well, that I'm an agent of the FBI, not a hit-man for the Vegas Mob. Goes against ninety-nine per cent of everythin' I believe in. Plus... if she's *really* the same one that they claim was flyin' all over the place in outer space and such, somethin' tells me that if we miss on the first shot, we're not likely to get a second one, you know what I mean?"

"That thought had crossed my mind," remarked the Asian-American woman. "Right after they first told me, I got on Neo and did some research on what kind of energy output would be required to do some of the things that they attributed to this being, if, as you say, it's really the same one and *if* – big 'if' here – any of the stories about her are true. Shooting at something like *that* with a service gun... it'd be like trying to stop an elephant, no, a Brontosaurus, with a peashooter. All you're likely to do is just make it mad."

"Yeah," agreed Boatman. "'Specially if you're just doin' it on orders, if you don't otherwise have any quarrel with the creature. If somebody did that to *me*, first time I landed on some other planet, and I had any way of fightin' back, I sure wouldn't be in too good a mood, afterwards. Truth is, I think, that encounterin' this alien-lady, when and if, is likely to lead to some really *unpredictable* consequences. 'Special assignments' always do... and this one's 'bout as 'special' as it gets, I reckon."

The two stared at each other for a few seconds.

Then, the black man continued, "To answer your question *directly*, Madam Agent, you know where I stand, in general, but I guess I'd have to make my decision based on the facts at hand, at the time... that's the best I can do. Does that work for you?"

She smiled appreciatively.

"Yeah, it does," she said. "As much as anything can. Thanks, Otis."

"You cleaned off your dress yet?" he asked.

"As well as I can, out here on this godforsaken road," she replied.

The woman motioned to the man in the car, needing three waves and a good rap on the window to get his attention away from the video-screen where, apparently, a touchdown was about to be had.

"Let's get going, Will," she demanded.

No 'Contraband', Officer

"Next stop Salt Lake, folks," announced Billings, as the throaty roar of the SUV propelled them back onto the road. "Boy, *that* was worth the stop – belly full of food, okay not *haute cuisine* but best we've had so far, some spare clothes from his lost-and-found and a good night's rest... all of which are scarce as hen's teeth around here. Well, at least *I* got some sleep, but our friend here seemed to be up all night. Sorry if I snored too much."

"Do not worry about it, Bob," the 'Sari'-girl stated, with an affectionate smile. "Actually I *was able* to sleep, myself. It is just that I do not need a lot of it, not nearly as much as the rest of you... people, seem to. If I have some time alone to relax, close my eyes and meditate, that is usually enough for me. I could hardly hear you when I did that last night. Oh, and thank you for showing me how to use the, what did you call it, 'teeth-brush'."

"Well *ah* could hear him," complained Melissa. "Even in the next room. An' it's 'tooth-brush', Miz Sari."

The newcomer stared off into the distance, with an absent-minded look.

"But you are sort of right about my having trouble sleeping," she noted. "Lately, I have been finding it difficult to close my eyes and try to go off to the dream world. I keep having a strange feeling, like a voice saying, 'Sari, you have spent far too much time asleep as it is, you awoke too late, many terrible things came to pass here while you slumbered, you should have been *there*, should have put a stop to them'. I do not know what it means, but anyway, it makes me feel guilty, so most of the time, I try to rest while still awake. Ahh, never mind... probably this is all just, how do you say, 'idle chitter-chatter', to the rest of you..."

The salesman turned his head and took a long, reflective stare at the one who had shared his bed, then looked back at the road ahead of them and offered, uncomfortably, "Oh, I'm sure it's just a, a, bad dream, we *all* get 'em now and again. Nothing to worry about, and, I'll try to be a little more quiet tonight."

Changing the subject, he commented, "I guess old Pollack's not such a bad guy, after all, eh? I sure *owe* that man, now. I'll cut him the best deal possible on the finest Italian marble stuff I got, next time I'm in town, that's for sure. I figure we'll be square, then."

"Y'all forgot to mention that Gideon's Bible that y'all lifted from the ho-tel room," lazily reminded Claremont.

"'Lifted'?" cynically retorted Billings. "*Never*... I just *borrowed* it, for an extended loan. Besides, what did I hear about 'spread the Word of the Lord', or some such nonsense? We're just spreading it – hey, I like putting things that way, spreading it all over..."

"Y'all mean like spreading sh –" interjected the Claremont boy, stopped instantly by a severe glare from his mother, although the boy was rewarded for his effrontery with a giggle on the part of the fallen-girl.

"What if your friend at the mo-tel does not *want* something new to cover up his floor, Bob?" she asked, in a tone that would have been mocking coming from anyone except her apparently naïve self.

"But I like the – how do you say it – 'tracking suit'? It is very flexible and it has nice bright colors," she continued. "Well... on second thought, maybe bright colors are not what I *should* be wearing, right now... I wish that I knew what 'Brigham St U' means, though. Just in case someone asks me what the writing on the shirt is all about. Oh, and what is written on this little hat you gave me – the 'A' with a little circle at the top. 'Anaheim', that is a city, isn't it?"

She coltishly donned a baseball-cap that had needed both a good dusting-off and a drastic size adjustment, down from the circumference of the salesman's much larger head.

Billings shrugged.

"About old Elmer, that's not *my* problem," he said. "I do what I can. If I was selling roofing materials, I'd give him the best of *those*, too... knowing all the while that he's already got a roof. Can't get him something I don't *have*, now can I? Oh, and by the way, it's a 'track suit' and the writing on it stands for 'Brigham State University', you know, professors, books, classes, that kind of crap. Don't ask me much about it, I got as far as first year community college, I'm not really the academic type."

"Ah," knowingly replied the fallen-girl. "Yew-nee-ver-sit-ee," she repeated, slowly and deliberately. "*Now* I remember... a Temple of Knowledge, of learning. I would like to visit one of these, if I could. There is usually much wisdom in hearing what learned people have to say, in trading one's own knowledge with theirs – each gains from the other..."

Again, the salesman shrugged.

"Sorry, but a bit out of our way, I'm afraid," he countered.

The 'Sari'-girl pursed her lips for a second in disappointment, then settled back into her seat.

"That a baseball-cap, Miz Sari," explained Curtis. "Y'all get 'em most anywhere, an' back home, they tellin' everyone yo' colors. Y'all knows, who yo' homie, who y'all chillin' wid, an' who from th' other gang."

"Ah," acknowledged the newcomer. "I would have thought that it was about sports. Well, what 'gang' does it indicate that I belong to, then?"

"We don' talk 'bout such thangs in front of Mister Bob and Miz Sari, Curtis Ray," cautioned Claremont.

The boy crossed his arms and pouted.

"You are *all*, in my 'gang' now," observed the fallen-girl.

"We gots a *choice* 'bout that, girl?" replied the black woman, apparently half in jest.

"Nope," cheerily remarked the newcomer. "And you should be honored, Whitney. It is a very, ahh, 'exclusive', club, to which you now belong."

"Well, there *is* a baseball team in Anaheim," offered Billings, trying to change the subject. "At least there *was*, until recently; but with all that's going down there now..."

"Man, am ah *sussed* that we stopped in there," interrupted Claremont, supporting the salesman. "Yeah, ah knows they put us through them showers back in that prison camp, but it weren't the same thang... seem like *years* since ah had a bath. 'Specially with bubble bath 'n such. Ah would have lifted that hair dryer they had – y'all not pay no attention to that, children – 'cept the cord was bolted to the wall. Oh well... did mah hair real nice. Finally got the kinks out."

"But it weren't *fair*, Momma," complained Melissa. "Between Tommy 'n Curtis ah hardly got *no* time to soak in there myself."

"Y'all had an hour," responded the mother, half-patiently. "More than y'all usually get at home."

The teenager crossed her arms in imitation of her brother, pretending to pout, herself.

"Ah, *kids*," quipped Billings. "I *hate* writing those checks for support, but it's better than having to feed 'em, dress 'em and just deal with 'em, each and every day. Uhh... current company excepted, of course."

A cynical chuckle issued forth from his gut.

"Yeah, but you were one yourself, not too long ago, Mister," said the Indian-boy.

"Not too long?" challenged Billings, with mock sincerity. "Ha! Longer than *I* can remember, that's for sure. I tell you, kid, you get over 40, first your memory goes and then... damn, can't remember what the other two things were."

The 'Sari'-girl giggled.

"That is a funny one, Bob," she remarked. "I never heard that joke before."

"*Laws*," interjected Claremont. "Can't imagine how y'all didn't. Everyone know *that* joke."

"Well, it is the *truth*," protested the 'Sari'-girl.

Idly, she stared out of the window, her eyes washing over everything outside, as she had done, on and off since the ride had started, as if it was the first time that she had ever been on a car trip.

Her gaze caught a large video-billboard, now dull and lifeless as the power supply had evidently been cut; although, the thing's main message was still dimly visible in burned-in pixels : '*America The Great – Free Of Burdensome Socialist Regulation and Excuse-Making Liberalism*', it depicted.

"Have any of you noticed all the signs beside this road?" inquired the newcomer. "Places to stay, things to buy... always telling one to 'hurry up over here', 'do not miss this one there', and so on. Why do they only speak of buying and selling? Why do they not have words of philosophy, or poems, or lovemaking, or something more interesting than just 'if you are a real man, then buy my four wheel drive truck', or 'your shirts will not really be clean if you do not use my detergent'? It was the same with the tee-vee that Bob and I watched last night after we got into bed, and after we... *well*..."

"Oooh," moaned Curtis, with a nasty, low, little-boy chuckle.

"That will be *enough*, Curtis Ray," growled Claremont. "It *they* business, not ours, boy."

Behind her back, the Claremont boy stuck out his tongue, earning a wink and a grin from the 'Sari'-girl, along with a giggle of her own.

"Do not worry about it, Whitney," she offered, pleasantly. "I have sort of figured out that one does not openly discuss *that* kind of thing, in this society, although you *do* talk about other natural functions, eating, even 'I have to pee', that kind of thing... it just seems strange that the only thing that you *cannot* talk about is people playing with each other's bodies and giving each other love and pleasure. But 'no harm done', as you say. I will try to avoid giving Curtis too much to speak of, in the future."

"Ha," chuckled Billings. "There's all too much talk about *that*, and a lot more than *talk*, for some of us, I can assure you. Once we get NeoNet back up... the moral nuts keep claiming that it's now 'clean', but if you know where to look... but... 'this' society'? What *other* one –"

"Well, it is just that I find all this chatter about merchant stuff quite distracting," interrupted the 'Sari'-girl. "They have these, what is the, yes, 'commercials', every ten minutes or so, sometimes every five minutes, even on the one that says that it is the 'channel for learning'. It is difficult to concentrate on what one is doing, when a voice is always *interrupting*, urging one to buy a new car or try out a new pill. Especially when most people seem barely to have enough money to buy *one* car, and there are other messages on the tee-vee telling you not to take too many pills. Does it not bother all of you about those flickering commercial pictures that show up right while you are watching another tee-vee show?"

"What y'all *talkin'* 'bout, girl?" asked an incredulous Claremont.

"I do not know how you could *miss* them," replied the fallen-girl, matter-of-factually. "It is like they are showing you the, uhh, 'main story', but every half-second or so, they flash a picture of a bag of potato chip food, or a car, or a 'luxury vacation', and these quick little pictures have the word 'BUY' somewhere on them, usually in big red letters. Did you not see these messages too?"

"Ah didn't see *nothin'*," countered the black woman.

"It's called 'subliminal advertising', my dear," noted Billings. "Started to show up big-time a few years ago after they passed the 'Unchaining the Airwaves for Business Act', if memory serves me correctly."

"Ah, one of these laws... I *see*, then," remarked the newcomer. "And everybody in these 'commercials' looks young, beautiful, with skin like mine," she continued. "They all have nice clothes, but that is not how the people that I have so far met appear to be – where are the old people, people with dark skin like Whitney and Melissa and Curtis, oh yes, and you, too, Tommy. Where are the poor people? I have seen many of them since I met all of you, but there are none on the tee-vee. Watching that tee-vee was like having a sales-man trying to interrupt my, uhh, moo-vie all the time with a really unconvincing story, and a boring one at that. How do you tolerate it? I would rather read a good writing-scroll... at least then I can start and stop reading when I *want* to."

"Ah just turn down th' volume," replied Melissa, matter-of-factually. "Only thing we can do, after they pass that rule few year ago sayin' that usin' the 'Mute' button on them remote-controls was 'gainst the law 'bout... uhh, ah don' remember, oh yeah, the law 'bout 'respectin' 'lectual property' or some such nonsense like that."

"Obviously you're new to the good old Ew-Nighted States of America," commented Billings, "But then, we already *knew* that. Anyway, as somebody once said, 'the business of America, is business'. It's what makes our economy run, and that's why we have to watch all those commercials... Melissa's right, I long for the good old days before they started doing things like adding penalty fees on your cable for skipping ads on your video recorder and so on."

"'Skipping' ads?" inquired the 'Sari'-girl.

A frustrated Billings sighed and ignored this question.

"But, hell – yeah, Whitney, I know, I'm supposed to be a preacher man, humor me here – if it wasn't for all that buying and selling, guys like me who make a living by cash-flow, for me it's selling hardwood floors, we'd all be out of a job, wouldn't we? They've tried the Commie thing, the Islamo-nut thing, okay, *that* one's still going strong, I gotta admit, but so far our wonderful capitalist system has outlasted all the other ones. Bottom line is, I mean, it's the only game in town. Anybody tries anything else, well, they find out soon enough that they don't have a choice about it..."

All of a sudden, the fallen-girl's countenance darkened.

A palpable chill, as if a blast from some ethereal Arctic storm had somehow issued forth from the SUV's climate control vents, ran through all of them, and it was all that Billings could do to keep the car from veering off.

"No, Bob, you are wrong about that, *very* wrong," she countered, her blue-green eyes staring at the back of his head with steely determination. "There *are* other ways, *many* other ways in which people can live with one another, care for one another, love one another. Or rule over each other, hurt each other, exploit each other. I have seen far too many of the latter and far too few of the former, but if what you say is what people around here really believe, then it is a conceit of your society, and a stupid one at that, to think that it is, how you say, 'the only game in town'."

"Uhh... *rightt*," mumbled Claremont.

"Many, many great empires have fallen, due to thinking like that – among other things," offered the 'Sari'-girl. "Maybe *yours* will too. In the long ages of time, *nothing* lasts forever... especially the vanity of kings. This I have seen, with my own eyes."

"*Whoa*, girl," protested Billings. "Don't take it so personally, Sari... I call it like I see it. May or may not be the way I like it, but from where I sit, that's the truth, whether you like hearing it or not. And what's all this talk about empires and kings? You don't look like much of a history professor –"

Now the Indian-boy, who was sitting directly next to the 'Sari'-girl, looked up at her, staring in what might have been worry, or perhaps something else.

"Lady, why you getting so mad?" he asked, interrupting the salesman. "Mister Billings is right... at least, about America. The way things are, that is. But you sound a little like our elders, too, when they talk about the old times, before the white people came here and, well, *changed* everything. When we would sit around the campfire, sometimes they would tell stories about how the Indians used to live, like, when everybody shared things, where everybody was in one family, or something like that. Is *that* what you meant, about these 'other places'? Which one do you come from?"

Again, the fallen-girl appeared to be staring out at the scenic Utah countryside past the road-side billboard with the big '*Dirty brown-skinned neighbors look like Muslims to you? Take no chances... report 'em to Uncle Sam*!' slogan on it, as her composure came back.

Eventually, she replied, "It is oh-kay, Tommy," she mentioned, "I am not upset. Sorry if I gave anyone the idea that I was. It is just – well, it is disturbing to me, to hear something that I know is absolutely wrong, to be stated as if it is a fact. And, as to your question, I do not really remember –"

Her voice was cut off by Billings' shout.

"Hey, *you* back there!" he warned, in an alarmed voice. "Looks like a roadblock up ahead! Now remember, everybody on their best behavior – we're just one big, happy church family, right? And let *me* do the talking, you got that?"

"Yes, *sir*," chimed the two Claremont children. Tommy just nodded, as did Claremont.

The rhythmic growl of the SUV's engine revved down to a low purr, as the vehicle slowed as it approached what appeared to be an extempore barricade, erected directly across the highway. On either side of this structure were two or three four-by-four pickup trucks with the words "UTAH STATE POLICE" marked clearly on several places.

A State Trooper, a big, beefy white man with a handlebar mustache, a prominently displayed sidearm and the obligatory dark glasses, stuck out his palm, motioning them to stop.

Another one of the police tapped him on the shoulder, thereby gaining the first Trooper's attention, and the two of them briefly discussed something, both nodding in agreement.

Billings brought the vehicle to a complete stop and the mustachioed Trooper sauntered slowly and deliberately toward the driver's side of the SUV. The salesman surveyed the scene, becoming instantly and acutely aware that several other State Troopers were cradling a variety of small arms – including automatic rifles and some very large shotguns – in evident readiness to fire.

"I see a *lot* of itchy trigger fingers out there," Billings whispered. "No talking back to them. *Please*. Does everyone remember the drill?"

"Yes," responded a number of voices in various accents and syntaxes.

But Billings noticed that one was missing. He turned his head to face backwards inside the SUV.

"Sari? Sari? Where *are* you?" the salesman demanded, as he noticed that the fallen-girl had vanished. Her seat-belt buckle was now disconnected.

Billings looked at the Indian-boy, but all he got was a shrug.

At that exact moment, "Excuse me, sir," commanded a no-nonsense voice, from outside. "Please step out of the car, *immediately*."

"Oh, of *course*, officer," replied the salesman, as pleasantly as he could stand to do.

He opened the driver's side door and got out, standing directly in front of the State Trooper, who looked an inch taller, a few score pounds lighter and a whole *lot* meaner, than Billings' own not insubstantial posture.

"What can I do for you today?" nervously asked the salesman.

"Just answer a few questions for us," stated the Trooper. "Oh, and by the way, we need to inspect your vehicle. Is this your car? You wouldn't be carrying any *contraband* with you today, would you, sir? Somebody from outside the Ew-Nighted States, who shouldn't be here in our fair country?"

"Contraband?" responded Billings. "Oh, no, nothing like *that*, officer. As a matter of fact, I don't even smoke – none of our church-members here in my SUV do – we've basically got nothing aboard except ourselves, our clothes, a little food, and of course our Bible. And we're, ahem, all Americans, sir. I'm from Tucson, the black lady and her kids are from Detroit, and the other boy, he's from, well, he's from Nebraska."

How the hell are we going to get out of this, thought the salesman. *I got proof of I.D.... but as for Whitney and those kids, not to mention my new little squeeze...*

"Well, I hope that's the truth, sir, because we're not being very tolerant these days of people carrying drugs or illegals; we're also lookin' out for quite a few other things, as well," laconically observed the Trooper. "Matter of fact, dependin' on the severity of the infraction, under the new emergency powers, we have the authority to, well, do just about *anything* that we want, if we should happen to find some contraband, or someone without his or her papers, in there with you. Of course, if you tell us honestly about any contraband, or illegals, that you might be carrying, well, then we have some *discretion* as to what course of action we might take. Mind if I ask you a few questions, sir?"

"Oh, certainly, Officer," replied Billings, trying not to sweat.

"That's *good*," stated the Trooper, without a smile. "That's *real*... good. So... let's go down the list."

He pulled out what appeared to be a portable electronic device of some sort, with a stylus. He hit a button and then started to mark off what must have been check-boxes on the thing's LCD screen.

"Do you have any subversive prop-a-ganda on you, or in your car, today, sir?" inquired the Trooper.

"Uhh... no, I don't think so, unless you count a Zane Gray novel," Billings tried to joke.

The man didn't laugh, and just sat there, staring.

"What I mean, sir, is stuff like there 'Ko-ran' Muslim book, you know, books or e-books that have anti-American concepts in 'em," eventually explained the Trooper.

"Oh... well, now that you put it *that* way," said the salesman, "The answer is, 'no sir'."

"That's *good*," repeated the Trooper. "That's *real* good." He shot a malicious half-smile.

"Any illegally copied ring-tones or movies, sir?" he continued.

"No," answered Billings.

"Any illegal, unpatriotic computer software, sir?"

"What?" asked the salesman.

"We get that question a lot, sir," observed the Trooper, with mock politeness. "I bet you don't know there's a law against that so-called "open software' stuff? There's places you can get it on NeoNet, but it's illegal to download it or use it. Takes valuable market opportunities away from our fine American commercial software vendors – we wouldn't want to undermine their ability to stay profitable and provide valuable employment, would we?"

"Wouldn't want to do *that*," unctuously agreed Billings, trying to look convincing as he shook his head. "Truth is, I wouldn't know an 'open' software program from a 'closed' one, Officer. They're all Greek to me, anyway."

He laughed, hoarsely.

"Okay. Now let's *see*," drawled the Trooper, as he leafed through a pocketbook-sized manual of some kind. "In the same category, you wouldn't have any of them 'data hiding' or 'cryption' programs on you, would you? None of them maybe on your car stereo or your mo-bile communee-kator? You got a cell-phone, sir?"

"Somewhere," replied the salesman. "But as for 'data hiding', well, not only don't I really know what you're talking about, officer, but the only data I ever try to hide is my belt size."

The Trooper just stared.

God, this guy must have special 'can't take a joke' training, thought Billings.

"Well, that's good," allowed the Trooper. "Lot of people don't know that the government outlawed those 'cryption programs about fifteen year ago, or so. They stop Uncle Sam from listen' in on that computer stuff to prevent subversive and anti-American agitation, and we *all* have to trust Uncle Sam, don't we, sir?"

"Oh, yeah," muttered Billings. "Trust the good ol' Uncle more than my own mother. Besides, like I told you, I can hardly figure out where the 'on' button is on those computers, anyway."

"Any illegal drugs, cigarettes or alcohol, sir?" asked the Trooper, unctuously.

"I... uhh... had a hip flask back there, I think," admitted Billings, his brow furrowed with worry. "I'll pour it out if you want... if there's anything left in it."

"Well, we'll have a look at it and tell you," answered the Trooper. "Any stowaways? Illegal aliens? Undocumented American workers?"

"Oh, *no*," the salesman quickly replied. "What you see is what you get, Officer. It's pretty crowded in the back seat, there... I doubt there'd be any space to hide anyone, anyway."

The man gave a menacing smile.

"We'll see about *that*, too," he said.

His voice rose. He shouted, "You there in the car! Everybody out, on the double!"

Slowly and uneasily, three other doors opened on the SUV.

Claremont and her two children stepped gingerly out of the passenger-side – the black woman from the front, Melissa and Curtis from the side door – while the Indian-boy inched slowly out of the rear door on the driver's side, his hands thumping the seat where, not thirty seconds ago, the 'Sari'-girl had been sitting.

The doors slammed shut after the car was emptied of its passengers.

'Momma', whispered Melissa to Claremont, "Where Sari go?"

"Shhh, child!" commanded the mother, *sotto voce*. "Y'all not be sayin' *nothin'* 'bout her, y'all understand?"

Melissa nodded, hoping that she had not attracted the attention of the police, who were still questioning Billings on the opposite side of the vehicle.

"Come around to this side of the car, please," ordered the Trooper.

Step by nervous step, the three children and the black woman complied.

"Okay," interrogated the State Trooper, "Now, while my fellow officers are searching this vehicle for contraband, I just need to ask you a few questions. Is that alright?"

His sunglass-obscured, weatherbeaten, no-sass face descended to Curtis' height, as he crouched down.

"Is that alright, son?" he repeated, more assertively.

"Yessir," replied Curtis.

The boy nodded, trying to make it look and sound as if he were not scared. The other two children just stood there, mutely.

"*Good*," replied the Trooper, unctuously. "Now, first of all, let's have the names. Starting with you." He pointed at Billings.

"Bob Billings," the salesman said.

The Trooper arched an eyebrow at Claremont.

"Whitney Claremont," she repeated, in an undoubtedly well-practiced monotone. "This here's Curtis Ray, he mah youngest, and th'other, she Melissa Arlene, mah daughter."

"That right?" asked the Trooper, addressing the Claremont children.

Both nodded affirmatively.

"The other boy?" continued the man. "He yours, too?"

"Oh, no, Mister Po-lice man, no, he not mine," answered Claremont. "Well, not 'zactly – ah just lookin' after him, Tommy, ah mean, 'till we get back south to our church. Cain't find he folks... well, y'all must *know* how things been these days..."

"Why, *certainly*, we do," replied the Trooper.

He turned to face Billings.

"So, tell me a little about what you're *doing* out here, Mister Billings," he demanded. "You know, things aren't... safe out here, these days. Why would you be going along an Interstate with a car full of kids? Road travel's still prohibited in a lot of places, you know."

"I'll tell you," shot back the salesman, "But first – I didn't know that we're not supposed to be on the highway? Didn't I hear something on the radio about 'the Interstates are now open', a day or so ago?"

"Yes, you did," confirmed the Trooper. "And yes, this one's open... that is, if *we* say it is. Whether you can keep going on it, well, that depends on what you tell me now," he added, with an inscrutable half-grin.

"Okay... fair enough," acknowledged Billings. "So here it is. I'm the Minister, Reverend I mean, of," – he suppressed a cough, looking at the ground for a second – "The First Episcopalian Church of South Tucson. Whitney here is one of our lay preachers... we went north to, uhh, minister to the flock, just before the Big Thing went down, got caught up there, unfortunately... this was the first chance we had where we felt that it'd be safe to head for home."

The salesman cleared his throat and continued, "Oh, and by the way, Tommy there," – he motioned towards the Indian-boy – "He's Native American. Not originally part of our group, but he was alone, well, as Christians, of course you can understand, we had to, uhh, take him under our wing, until we could find his folks –"

"You know," challenged the Trooper, propping a steel-toed cowboy boot upon a nearby rock as he turned his head to look Billings in the eye, "You don't *look* much like a preacher to me, if you don't mind me sayin' so. No collar, no tie –"

"Oh, no offense taken," bluffed Billings, trying to think on his feet. "We're, a, uhh, church of the people, we live in the real world. You know, minister to the heathens in their own language. Would you like to attend our next service? We'll be holding it on the first Sunday after –"

The Trooper held up a hand and shook it at Billings. "Just a minute there, Mister 'Minister'," he requested.

He called out towards the two or three other like himself who were searching the SUV.

"Find anything?" he asked.

"Not really, Bobby Jack," came back a gruff male voice. "Couple magazines, empty hip flask, snacks... nothin' interesting, unless you count a few Ne-Wakes –"

"I got a prescription. *Somewhere*," immediately protested Billings.

"Relax," shot back the first Trooper. "If we confiscated those, wouldn't be any truck drivers left on these roads. A bottle or two, you get away with; a *case*, that's another story. Anything else, Dennis?"

The voice called back, "Checked the trunk and the wheel wells, too. They're more or less clean – nowhere to hide them tamale-suckers in this thing, anyway."

"No contraband," commented the Trooper, the same, insincere smirk appearing on his visage. "That's *good* for you, preacher man. I *think*, that is," he said.

"Hey!" he shouted, while turning his head over a shoulder. "You find any Bibles back there? Maybe a Sunday program?"

"Nope," called the other voice.

The salesman looked in a panic at Claremont.

"Wait, no, sorry," corrected the other Trooper. "Yeah, sorry, missed that – they got a Gideon's under the front passenger seat."

Billings shoulders slumped with relief.

"That's an odd place for the Bible, don't you think, Mister Preacher Man?" offered the first Trooper.

"Yes, I'll grant you that," quickly babbled the salesman. "Word of God shouldn't be on a floor. It's a *sin*, I'd say. Must have slipped down from a seat or one of the storage-holders, I guess. Whitney, let's make sure not to let *that* happen again, okay?"

"Shore 'nuff, Rev'rend," answered Claremont, trying desperately not to look either Billings or the highway cop in the eye.

"Ah be keepin' it on me, from now on. Praise th' Lawd," she muttered.

"Well," grunted the Trooper, "I'm not sure that I believe your story, Mister," – he let out a contempt-laden laugh – "'*Reverend* Billings from South Tucson', but I suppose we got bigger fish to fry on these roads, at the present time. I *could* ask you for your papers, internal passports, *et cetera*, but for now, considerin' that your vehicle is clean, all I'll do is tell you to stay on the Interstate, no goin' off in all directions off the main road... and watch out for the bad-guys."

"For sure," agreed Billings.

"Unfortunately," explained the Trooper, "We got a whole passel of real *bad* folk on the highway, these days – bikers, gangs from Cal-i-for-ni-ay, even lots of wetbacks who been out in the desert, who ain't eaten in a week and who'd slit your kids' throats for two pesos. Ain't pretty, but that's the way it is. Just thought you'd like to know."

He showed another trademark half-grin.

"We're free to go, then?" anxiously asked the salesman.

"Not just yet," replied the Trooper. "Not just yet."

"Dennis, y'all got the picture on you?" he called to the other one.

"Yeah," replied the other voice, which they saw belonged to a thin, leather-skinned Trooper, taller than the first one, with red hair and the remnants of a few freckles.

"Heard on the DCB that they got a newer one on NeoNet, but the link's still dead in my cab. Yours up yet, Bobby?" he asked.

"Nope, so..." said the first Trooper, "This will have to do."

He flashed a police artist's rendition of a female suspect in front of the group. It showed a pretty Caucasian girl of perhaps her mid-twenties to early thirties, with blue eyes and blond hair, coiffured into a kind of elaborate, curly perm. She had a scar on her right cheek and was wearing damaged, camouflaged outdoors-hunting clothing of some sort.

Why does that girl look... familiar, mused the salesman. *But not the same as...*

"Have any of you seen this female?" demanded the first Trooper. "She's a fugitive from justice. If you have any information on her whereabouts, you have to tell me, right now."

Billings looked at Claremont, who was about to say something, but the salesman's glance – or, perhaps, something else – forced her silence.

The children looked back and forth among each other, uneasily.

"There are... uhh... a *lot* of people who potentially meet that description," offered the salesman. "Can you tell us anything more about her, like size, weight, height, age, occupation? Is she armed, dangerous? What's she wanted for, murder, shoplifting, tax evasion, or maybe jaywalking?"

The Trooper stared at Billings, with an icy demeanor.

"Funny, Mister Reverend Man," he said, "*Real* funny."

The salesman came to his senses and shut up.

"I *can* tell you this," growled the Trooper. "She's wanted for a lot of serious things... *very* serious things. Can't tell you more than that, about the charges. As for the physical description, we think she's about 28 or so, tall for a female, maybe five-nine to six feet, doesn't talk much or can't talk at all, mostly keeps to herself, maybe hides out in the woods and raids farms or small towns to steal food, possibly kills farm animals and pets for food, by night, skins 'em alive, drains 'em clean of all their blood –"

Instantly, a low, haunting melody, accompanied by a gust of wind, came from behind one of the parked pickup trucks at the barricade.

Ooo-ooo-ooo-ooo, howled *something* from *somewhere*, a sound both audible and more-than-audible.

Billings, Claremont and the children all felt the hackles of their necks rise in recognition, but through the feelings of awe, all of them managed not to reveal anything save a knowing glance, back and forth.

Two Troopers immediately ran over to investigate, as Claremont and Billings shot knowing glances back and forth.

The mustachioed one called to them.

"What you got over there?" he shouted.

"Nothing," came back a voice. "Must be one of them coyotes, I guess," it said.

"Yeah, we got a lot of them 'round here, nowadays," the first Trooper explained. "Wolves and foxes, even a bear or two. Some of 'em seem to have lost their fear of man, been coming right into farms and raiding sheep, chickens, anything that moves. We'll have to set that situation right, soon."

He smiled and patted his gun.

Billings smiled back and nodded, obsequiously.

The Trooper took a breath and continued, "But as to the fugitive, we think that she might have been hitching rides on the highway or perhaps on the freight trains, those of them that are back to running, of course. She may *appear* to be on drugs, incoherent, unable to put a sentence together, but don't let that fool you; she *is* armed and is *extremely* dangerous. If you encounter this woman, do *not* attempt to capture her or converse with her – contact the authorities *immediately*. Do you understand? All of you?"

"Certainly, officer," answered Billings. "Once we get back, we'll make sure to inform everybody that we meet, of this dangerous... person. Can't be too careful these days, *that's* for sure."

Now, Claremont mumbled something. It looked as if she was trying to talk, but somehow couldn't.

"Yes?" demanded the Trooper, staring now at the black woman. "If you've got something to say, speak up. You don't want us to have to take you back to the station to tell us your story, now do you, honey?"

"No," managed Claremont, as if forcing out every word. "Didn't see nothin'. Sorry if ah... got... yo'... thinkin'..."

"Figures," muttered another of the Troopers, a shorter, bull-necked man with a massive build. "Can't never get them niggers to say nothin' worth listenin' to. Take her back with us, Bobby Jack, you think?"

Claremont's face froze with fear, but it was instantly relieved.

"Naw," replied the first Trooper. "She don't know *shit* – oh, sorry, Reverend, I forgot, I'm in the presence of a man of God. Beggin' your pardon."

"Oh, that's quite alright," replied Billings, not missing a beat. "Being a church of the people, well, we're *always* having to forgive things, you know. Goes with the territory."

"That's nice," noted the lead Trooper. "Wish everyone out here was just as nice. But I guess they ain't, isn't that right, Reverend?"

"Alas," muttered the salesman.

"Well, I guess y'all had better be on your way," announced the mustachioed Trooper. "Remember what I told you. No short cuts."

He waved to the men at the barricade and soon a two car-wide path was opened in its midst.

"Absolutely," answered Billings. "We're staying on the straight and narrow, that's for sure. Okay, everyone – time to go. Whitney, let's not forget about that Bible. Kids, back seat, please."

He turned to the Trooper. "Been a pleasure. God Bless," he mumbled, turning quickly so that the man couldn't see the grimace of fear, combined with elation-at-successful-flim-flammery, on his face.

How the hell did we pull that *off*, thought Billings. *How many* more *times do I have to dodge comets, bullets, or psychos with guns, or all of 'em, on this fucking disaster of a trip.*

With relief, he headed quickly for the car, not looking back.

What Do You Think Of My Story?

After a confused second-cum-eternity of half-panicked clambering-in, the last car door slammed shut, and the group was again enclosed in the SUV.

Hearing the 'click' of the seat belts, Billings turned the key and the vehicle roared to life.

"'Sari'? *Sari*!" he called out. "You hiding in here somewhere? If you are, for God's sake, tell us, girl!"

They waited for five or six seconds, but there was no answer.

Billings looked like he was about to cry with frustration.

"*Damn* her," he cursed. "Where *is* she?"

"Maybe she gots to do the jet," suggested Curtis. "Them po-lice-men was searchin' *everywhere*. Even if they couldn't see her, they could still bump into her... and the darkness, too..."

"We *cain't* just leave Miz Sari here, Momma!" whined Melissa.

Through the SUV's tinted side-windows, Billings noticed that two, then three, of the Troopers had again turned their gaze towards the vehicle, as if having noticed the frantic discussion going on within it.

"*Shit*," exclaimed the salesman.

He waved to the Troopers, hoping that they could see the gesture.

"We gotta *go*. Right *now*."

"No!" cried the Indian-boy. "She *saved* us, Mister! You *can't* just leave her here, all by herself!"

"You don't *understand*, kid," shot back Billings, as he gunned the engine and slowly guided the SUV back onto the highway, praying that he wouldn't be followed. "We get stopped again by *those* guys, for whatever reason, especially like, we're a fake church that's having a bun-fight, we're toast. Well-done on both sides."

The salesman looked into the rear-view display and let out a sigh of relief, upon seeing the Troopers at the barricade staring for a second or two, then moving back slowly.

"What we gonna *do*, Bob?" pleaded Claremont. "Ah owes her. Y'all do, too. We *all* do."

"What am I going to do, Whitney?" retorted Billings, as the engine roared to full power, propelling the SUV up to full speed.

The barricade receded in the distance.

"I'll *tell* you what," he commanded. "I'm going to put a mile or so between us and this damn roadblock, turn a corner or two hopefully, then I'm going off-road, hide this crate... and wait. With any luck our cute little friend will come looking for us, and with better luck she'll find us before the cops do –"

He stopped talking for a second, as if concentrating on driving.

"What the matter, Mister?" said Tommy.

"Whitney, you hear a knocking sound?" asked Billings. "God *damn*, and nothing about the language, *please* – must be the engine, maybe the cylinders – if I don't pull over –"

His voice stopped again, as he looked out to the side window.

A broad smile came to the salesman's face.

"Why y'all so *happy*, all of a sudden... *oh*," started Claremont.

She was now looking out the driver's side, too.

A disembodied fist, attached to perhaps two-thirds of an arm, was pounding bizarrely at the car window.

Billings hit a button and rolled it down halfway.

"Thank *God*," he breathed. "We were *wondering* where the hell you went."

"Keep driving, Bob," instructed a familiar voice. "There is some cover up there, around the curve. You can stop for a second there, so I can re-enter your vehicle."

Counting every second, the salesman navigated around a bend and then, checking to ensure that neither traffic nor barricade was anywhere in sight, stopped at once.

"Open the door next to you, Tommy," he ordered. "And be *quick* about it... we don't want those guys thinking we're picking up any 'contraband', now *do* we?"

"No *sir*," smartly replied the Indian-boy, as he unlocked the catch and opened the door.

For the briefest of moments, there was a shimmer in the air. Then the 'Sari'-girl appeared, as if by magic, in the seat next to Tommy.

He gave her a hug, which was immediately returned with genuine affection.

Billings again gunned the engine and in a few seconds, they were cruising down the highway.

"I don't want to seem petulant," he offered, "But what was the meaning of all that? We all were afraid we'd *lost* you."

"I do not blame you, Bob," responded the fallen-girl. "You almost *did* lose me, or maybe a better way of putting it is, *I* almost lost *you*."

"*Do* tell," muttered the salesman.

"Well," she explained, "As we came to a stop, I heard two of the men outside saying, 'don't forget to ask them about the fugitive female'... that did not sound too good. So at first, I tried to hide in the car, but then all these policemen came – I thought that they would not look for someone clinging to the inside of the car roof, but one of them very nearly put his hand right on my head, and at that point I figured that it was only a matter of time until they discovered me, because there are only a few other places to hide in there. So I went backwards, little by little, and eventually slipped out by the back hatch, when they opened that to search your, how do you say, yes, your 'trunk'."

There's nothing to hold on to, except the inside light and the video display, silently thought Billings.

"But why didn't you just get back in the car, when the rest of us all did?" asked the Indian-boy.

"I tried to," continued the newcomer. "But you entered quickly, and the policemen were looking right *at* me, and the door closed just before I could try to jump in... I might have done so, anyway, but then you all would have been enclosed in my shadow and at least *some* of you would have instantly vanished, right in front of their eyes. I was stuck outside and then I heard Bob start the engine... when the car started to move, I had to make a decision, so I jumped on top, hoped that my shadow would not make too much up there disappear. Luckily, I think that I... 'got away with it', this time. Right?"

She gave one of her characteristic, almost-goofy smiles, the tips of her incisor teeth malevolently visible.

"Sort of," allowed Billings. "That's the good news. The *bad* news is, if you didn't know already, it appears that they're *looking* for you, or for someone who looks a lot *like* you. Which means, for those of you who aren't familiar with the law, that we're running the risk of being accused of 'harboring a fugitive'. Carries a long, *long* prison term, if they catch you doing it."

The 'Sari'-girl fell silent for a few long seconds, as if waiting for someone else to pick up the conversation.

Eventually, with a sad, upset look on her face, she mentioned, "I heard everything that you did, of course. But... are you *sure* that it is *me* for whom they are searching? I mean, the description that the police-man read out – that is *nothing* like me... I do *not* hide in the woods or eat animals, Bob, *you* know that! Why would they want to put me in a jail? I have done *nothing* bad, unless you count taking all of you out of that jail-camp where we all first met. That was not a crime, was it? Or *was* it?"

"No, not that I'm aware of," replied the salesman. "And, of course, there's certainly a *chance* that they're looking for someone else, or, more likely, they have you confused with that 'someone else'. But.. there *is* that comment that you made back at the camp, you know. I have to tell you, I've been thinking about that..."

"*What* comment?" inquired the fallen-girl, feigning ignorance.

"*You* know the one. When we were in the closet," pressed Billings.

"What she *say*?" interjected Melissa.

"That's between her and me," cautioned the salesman. "Except that, Sari, you have to admit, if what you said was true, *that* might be a reason why they'd want to talk to you... don't you think?"

The newcomer slouched dejectedly back in her chair.

"Those events happened a *very* long time ago, *very* far away from here... I think," she protested. "How would they know of what I told you?"

Her voice had a frightened, pleading tone, now, and she absent-mindedly wiped the trace of a tear from one eye.

"A few seconds ago, you were *happy* to see me... Whitney? Melissa? Bob? We *are* still friends... are we... not?"

"*Shore* we is," reassured Claremont. "Least, *ah* is. *Shit*, girl – no smart-talkin' now, children – ah ain't hardly *never* known nobody who the Man *ain't* lookin' for, for one reason or 'nother. It be 'cause y'all doin' synth drugs, or they *think* y'all doin' 'em, or 'cause y'all ain't paid the war tax, or y'all don' got yo' papers, they think y'all one of them 'illegal aliens', whatever... down where ah lives it just a fact of life, and we look out for each other when th' Man come callin'."

"I... *see*," observed the fallen-girl, her composure partly returning.

"Y'all bet, girl," continued the black woman. "Th' Man, he show up wid he guns 'n them dogs, we somewhere else, 'till he go away again. Ah gots to be *honest*, ah *was* gonna say somethin' back there, maybe a little white lie or two bout y'all – y'all know, 'she went the other way back there', that kinda thang – but somehow ah couldn't get no words out. Can't speak for Mister Bob, but y'all got nothin' to worry 'bout from *me* or mah kids, ain't that right, Curtis, Melissa?"

"Yes, Ma'am!" chorused two young voices.

"Sari," commented Billings, trying to both keep his eyes on the road ahead and to look the girl in the face as he addressed her, "Of *course* I'm still your friend. Please don't misunderstand what I'm saying – *nobody* here is going to abandon you. We'd just like to know what's going on, that is, if it really *is* you that they're out to hunt... you're quite right that their rendition of the perp, as it were, was off, but then that happens a lot – they don't seem to have a picture, a photo, I mean, so they've got to do this computer-enhanced artist stuff."

"So you *believe* me, that I have not done anything... *really* bad?" implored the 'Sari'-girl.

"Yeah, I believe you, but it might mean that they *are* looking for you and they just don't know what you really look like, or it might be that they're looking for somebody else altogether," cautioned the salesman. "But if it's the first of those two, I think you owe all of us an *explanation*. Just so we're all on the same page. If you've got anything to say, now's the time."

"Y'all know, Miz Sari," added Melissa, "Y'all ain't never told us 'zactly where y'all comin' from, how y'all got here. Maybe if we knew that we could back y'all up, if the Man come lookin'."

"I *told* you," protested the fallen-girl, "I do not *know* where I am from. Or what I am guilty of, if anything. I have no memories... oh-kay, only vague memories, of who I am. Why do you not believe me?"

"Well, why don't you start with the first thing that you *do* remember, going back as far as you can?" inquired Billings. "Listen, everybody, anything that she says, stays just with us, is that understood?"

"Y'all got that, Curtis, Melissa?" ordered Claremont. "An' y'all as well, Tommy?"

"Yes'm," replied the black children.

"Sure," said the Indian-boy.

The 'Sari'-girl fell silent for a long moment, as if thinking, considering, pondering. Her gaze darted from person to person within the vehicle, sizing up each in some strange way.

Eventually she spoke, softly, "If I tell you what little that I know, I will make myself... *vulnerable.* Especially as I do not know anything that *you* all might hold private. It is not a position that I like to be in; but I will risk it, to earn your trust. Or *re-*earn it, if I have lost it. I will tell you my most private secrets, friends. Do you swear to reveal them to others, only as I allow?"

All replied, "Yes."

"Oh-kay," she began, drawing a deep breath. "Although I do not exactly know why... I feel that I may be making a huge mistake in giving away all of this... but, here it is. If you want to know what my oldest recent memory is, well, this is not going to make a lot of sense, I am aware of that, but... I remember first being in a cave with sand, a desert, but the air was quite thin, so maybe it was up in the mountains, somewhere? It was *very* cold, but I became used to it soon enough, I guess... *thirsty,* oh, Gods Above, I was *so* thirsty, I needed water very badly, it was painful... then the next thing that I recall is another place, it was mostly white on the walls, but there were lots of instruments, dials, like on the car, here, but different, more elaborate... there were people, five or six of them..."

After a pause, she started speaking more rapidly.

"They were my friends, oh yes, my *friends!* Where are they now? Where are they now? They are *trapped* in there! I must *help* them!"

Her voice echoed worry, as she fumbled, as if hypnotized, to undo the seat-belt.

"What *that*... she look like she got a flashlight in her *haid*...?" whispered Melissa to Curtis, seeing an eerie, blue-green glow, barely perceptible but there none the less, issuing from the fallen-girl's eyes.

"Hey, hey, *easy,* there," cautioned Billings. "It can be *traumatic,* the whole recovered-memory thing. Take your time. No jumping out of moving cars, please."

She's got to be hallucinating, nervously reflected the salesman. *Or on drugs. No, not drugs, she doesn't have any. She must have seen the broadcasts from up there, too. Just deluded, yeah, that's it. Power of suggestion, that's all. Because the* alternative –

"You asked for the truth," she shot back, with grim-faced determination. "Well, you will *have* it."

The 'Sari'-girl closed her eyes, evidently trying to retrieve something deliberately locked away, then spoke up.

As if in a dream, she started breathing more and more rapidly, with excitement and panic building with each new word.

"*Had* to leave them, had to go," she moaned.

Faint bars and chords of ethereal, stirring, exciting music, began to infuse the atmosphere inside the vehicle.

And the humming, beautiful voice of the fallen-girl began to chant :

"Did not *want* to, *had* to, duty from above, oh,"
"By all that is holy, cannot run *this* time,"
"*Not* make the same mistake, *redeem* myself, oh,"
"*Whatever* the cost, whatever the risk,"
"Streaking through ebon night, cold as deepest Hell, oh,"
"Breathe I not, but it is oh-kay,"
"Far short I fall, need much, *much* more, oh,"
"Are you *mad*, shining-woman,"
"Dare not go *this* close, be *incinerated*, it fills the whole *sky*, oh,"
"Yellow and white and hot-color, more-than-purple everywhere,"
"Can not not open my eyes, oh,"
"Oh, the pull is *gigantic*,"
"Holds a mountain-range, like a whirlpool on a fish, oh,"
"How can I *possibly* keep on the path..."

Billings tried to open his mouth to demand "That's *enough*," but *something*, perhaps fascination, perhaps fear, maybe something else entirely, stopped him.

She continued, wailing on, as the music poured adrenaline into their bloodstreams :

"Do not *fight* it, welcome this Fire, *embrace* it, oh,"
"Oh, Great Spirit it *hurts*, it *burns*,"
"*Pain, pleasure, power*, oh,"
"*Nothing* like *this*, even a thousand centuries gone by,"
"Yes, oh *yessss*, die happy to have tasted, oh,"
"*C*ome on, come *on*, can *do* it, how *mighty* am I now,"
"At last – faster, *faster*, oh,"
"A clock-tick to go now, it is almost *upon* them..."

The fallen-girl's body twisted back and forth in some weird passion, sweat breaking on her brow.

Jesus H. Christ, silently mused the salesman, as he tried to refuse the improbable thoughts that bedeviled his rational mind.

I'm not just hearing it. I'm seeing it... I'm feeling it. My eyes are open, I see the wheel, the road, but I also see... what is it that I see?

They told me this is what LSD's like, or maybe it's what being insane is like –

He tried desperately to keep the car's wheels on the road.

"Who turn on the radio?" exclaimed Claremont. "Turn off that music –"

"Shut up and *listen*, Whitney," growled Billings.

Secretly, he wanted to record the tunes that were ricocheting back and forth in his head, but somehow he knew that notes on a page couldn't start to do them justice.

"Somethin' lightin' up her eyes, ah can tell even tho' they closed," whispered Curtis to Tommy. "And look at that 'lectric stuff under her skin – that not *natural*, slick –"

Sweat pouring down her forehead, the 'Sari'-girl's voice now reached a crescendo of passion, or maybe desperation, as she writhed in her seat, while the minds of those around her suddenly reverberated with a kaleidoscope of weird, unfamiliar and unrequited thoughts, sounds, music and images.

And she concluded, crying :

"There it is! The time is *come*, oh!"

"Beloved friends, I hear your prayer!"

"God of Earth, I lay me down, oh!"

"At peace, at last, oh!"

"Holy Flame *burn in me, oh!*"

"Ohhhhhhhhh!!!"

Eyes shut tight, the newcomer slumped back in the car-seat, drenched in sweat, chest heaving, gasping for breath, as if she had sustained a crushing body blow.

The strange tune that had been issuing from everywhere and nowhere, gradually subsided into nothingness. But there was a brief wisp of smoke with an acrid smell, akin to scorched polyester.

She bent over, gasping for air, head down over clasped hands and mumbled,

"I *hear*, friends, still up there,"

"Need time, need *time*, oh,"

"I will repay you, oh yes, ten times over,"

"Save yourselves, you are *strong* now, oh,"

"Just reach inside, call upon the *Fire*, oh..."

The fallen-girl stopped talking, hair hiding a face that showed near-total exhaustion, as, shaking and bent over her knees, she tried to regain her composure. Little beads of sweat formed at the tip of her nose and lazily careened, one by one, to the floor of the SUV below.

"Momma," whispered an awed Curtis, "What she *talkin'* 'bout? Ah seein' weird things in mah *haid*, like a dream, but not a dream..."

"Ah don' know, son, ah don' *know*," quietly replied Claremont, although Billings noticed a look of shock, or possibly realization, on the black woman's normally impassive face.

"Yo, Bob, y'all turn up the heat? It *warm* in here, all of a sudden," she stammered.

No... I think you know exactly what she's talking about, Whitney, mused the salesman.

"Mister Billings, can you stop the car, please?" requested the Indian-boy. "I feel *excited* all of a sudden, like I gotta get out and run around..."

"Me too," added Melissa. "Whew, Momma, what a *rush*! Like the first time when ah tried them synth..."

Quickly, she shut up.

Billings tried to concentrate on not rolling the SUV, out of stunned, finally-dared-to-admit awareness.

My God... right here, right now, in the car of Bob Billings, nobody salesman from nowhere, U.S.A.?

No, not possible. No way, he thought, hoping that no-one in the car would see the faint sweat now breaking out on his own brow.

It was all a trick, not real, everyone knows that it was something cooked up by the Feds to take our minds off the... all this 'sent by God to save us' crap, that was just the televangelists trolling for a new reason to send 'em fifty bucks – she can't possibly be... can she?

And I slept with her? he realized.

Now there's one for the history books, right, Bob old boy?

A half-mile or so passed by, with the only sounds in the SUV being the intertwining rhythms of the tires, the engine and the 'Sari'-girl's breathing, as it slowly came down to what was normal for her.

She slowly opened her eyes and again spoke up.

"Then, I remember lying down, on the ground outside, I mean," she stated. "It was cold – very cold, no, on second thought, it was not as cold as in the cave, only it *felt* much worse, that is the only way how I can say it."

"Snow was falling," continued the fallen-girl. "I was on a mountain, somewhere. The air, it smelled strange, heavy, there were many scents that I had not known of before... it does not smell any more, I suppose that I am accustomed to it by now. I hurt *terribly*, it felt like I was burned over half my body or more, my legs and arms did not work, all I could do was lie there and try to breathe, but many of the bones in my chest were broken, *pain, ohhh, the pain...*"

She gasped, as if seized by a cruel demon from her past, while tears streamed down her cheeks.

Considering how you got here, reflected Billings, his mind racing with a melange of awe and fear, *I don't blame you for being a little banged-up... I saw the replays from that day that I expected to be my last, girl, watched 'em over and over...*

"Like Bob say, take it easy, there, girl," advised Claremont. "Y'all gots *lots* of time."

"Thanks, Whitney," appreciatively replied the fallen-girl. "Sorry... I mean, you have no *idea* how much it hurt... somehow I know that I should have died from the wounds that had been inflicted on me, *you*, you people, you would *surely* have died from an ordeal like that... but slowly, I recovered. Finally, after a few days – I do not remember exactly how many – I again could stand up. So I shook off the snow that had by then covered me, nearly all over... I started to walk."

"You 'recovered'?" inquired the salesman, trying to bluff her into admitting making the whole thing up. "If you're crippled from a plane crash, internal injuries, cracked ribs, that kind of thing, you *don't* just 'get better', without a doctor –"

"You asked me to tell you the *truth*, Bob," retorted the newcomer. "I am trying to *do* that, as best I remember it."

"Fair enough," answered Billings. "Go on."

"So," elaborated the 'Sari'-girl, taking another breath, "I walked down the mountain... it took a long while, and I was cold, *so* cold... I was still dizzy, I had no idea if I was going the right way, had no idea where I was. And – I realize that this may not make a lot of sense to you, but anyway – I just could not *do* most of the things that I would normally do to warm myself up, to heal, to travel, to be in control... somehow, things just were not *working*, that is the best that I can put it. They still, mostly, *are* not working, either."

"What y'all mean, 'not workin'', girl?" grunted Claremont. "Seem to me that, 'specially after that night we spend in the ho-tel, an' y'all an' Bob, ah means, everythin' wid y'all workin' just *fine*."

Curtis, Melissa and Tommy giggled.

"You see," countered the fallen-girl, "When I am in a new place, I am usually much more powerful, more *confident*... but *this* time, I was just hungry, hurting and cold. This may sound crazy, but... well, I have memories of having been perfectly oh-kay in places that were a hundred, a *thousand* times colder than where I was on this mountain, but somehow, this time, it *felt* much worse, even though it should have been easy for me to cope with. It did not feel at all good... it *still* does not."

She stopped and thought for a second, then added, "I was freezing, and so much in despair, that I thought of just lying down to die, to let the numbness wash over me and give me peace, but... but... well, I *cannot* let myself die, do you understand?"

"Funny you say that," the salesman tried to joke, "But my doctor's told me not to die, either... it's bad for my health."

"No, I guess you do not understand... *do* you?" muttered the newcomer. "This is hard to say in Eng-lish, but I am not *allowed* to die, I have seen *thousands* come and go, but I cannot pass on to the Other Side as they do, I am here for a *reason*, I must keep on, keep trying, however much it hurts... but I am neglecting my story."

"At last," she told, "When my strength was almost gone, I finally came across a road. I looked down it and there was a, how you say, rest-o-ront some distance off, actually I did not know what it was, because I could not read, then – the injuries must have knocked *that* ability out of me, too – but I stumbled up to it and was able to enter through the door. Thankfully, it was warm in there, but I could not speak to the staff, I had... *forgotten* how to speak En-glish. The lady who was serving the food did not like me very much, I suppose I *was* pretty dirty and probably smelled bad, but there was a nice family who helped me out, who bought me a meal. They could not take me with them, that made me very sad, and the wait-ress said that I was not allowed to stay in the eating-house unless I paid her lots of money, at least that is what I *think* that she meant, so I had to leave."

"So that's all?" inquired Billings, trying not to sound nervous.

"No, not all," replied the 'Sari'-girl. "Appreciate my *position* – I was outside again, yes, I had had a meal, also I was 'cleaned up', as you say. I was very lonely, nowhere to go. This is another thing that you might not understand, but... I had just spent a long, *terribly* long time alone, by myself... I do not want to be alone, any more, no, I want to be with friends, want people to *like* me, to stay close by me, and me close to them... as I said, it is hard to communicate how I feel about this..."

She looked away for a few seconds, then continued, "I walked for hours and hours down the road, hoping to find another place to stay, but everything else was shut, all the doors were locked, the windows had big sticks covering them, and I did not want to break in anywhere because I was afraid that might make people upset with me. I was again becoming cold, but I noticed some people who also looked cold and hungry, by the side of the road. One of them stuck out his thumb in the direction of the road, a lot of vehicles passed by, but after ten or so of these, a car stopped and picked up these people. I assumed that this gesture meant 'please stop, help me', so I did the same thing, with my thumb, I mean."

"And?" asked the salesman.

"Well, almost immediately, some vehicles stopped for me, but I could not understand what the men driving them were saying – I still could not speak Eng-lish."

"Y'all speakin' it pretty well *now*, girl," offered Claremont.

"I must have remembered how to do it since then, I suppose," evaded the fallen-girl.

"Then," she went on, "A big silver vehicle with a lot of windows stopped, but when I tried to walk up the stairway that it had, the man driving it showed me some money, along with a little piece of plastic-stuff with two holes punched in it... he gestured that I needed to give him more money if I wanted to climb aboard, so I had to go back to the road. That disappointed me greatly as the seats on this vehicle looked really comfortable."

"Hah! Y'all missed th' bus," grunted the black woman. "Y'all in good company, girl..."

"What happened next?" asked Billings.

"Some trucks came by," explained the newcomer. "The first two of these just said something that sounded like they were angry, then they drove off. The third one tried to grab me and drag me in to his car with him, but I was afraid that he might want to arrest me for some law that I might have broken, so I evaded him and ran into the woods until he drove away."

The salesman let out a 'whew' sound.

"What y'all *mean*, y'all 'evaded' him?" asked the black woman.

"Same way as how I 'evaded' those people in the camp," smugly replied the 'Sari'-girl.

"Oh... *yeah*," muttered Claremont. "Ah keeps forgettin' 'bout that tricky-business that y'all into."

"Finally," concluded the newcomer, "There was a man driving a big truck, he was called 'Donnie', he had long hair and one of those little beards that only covered the part under his chin... he was nice, he somehow knew that I wanted a ride and a place to sleep, so I went with him. He even let me lie down in the little bed in the rear part of the cab with him – ohhh, *that* felt *so* good, just being warm and being able to touch someone, feel him touching me..."

This time it was Melissa's turn to giggle, but the reply from her mother was no different from that meted out to her brother.

You wouldn't be laughing, if you knew who you were laughing at, silently thought Billings.

A second later, he realized, *And there goes my 'first to...' place in the Guinness Book... damn...*

"Oops, I forgot about that," apologized the 'Sari'-girl, with a bemused smile.

She added, "When I was with Donnie, my understanding of how to speak your language started to come back, and I was able to piece together that he had to let me off at the inter-state border. That made me sad, again, because I *so* much want to have friends. And when he finally did make me leave his truck, at the camp, you know, Bob, the one where you and I first met, I said to myself, yes I did, 'the next people you meet, Sari, you will make them your friends and you *will* do *whatever* it takes, to *keep* them as your friends'. The rest, you already know about."

The group drove on in silence for another half-mile.

Then the fallen-girl asked, innocently, "That is all that I know, all that I remember. What do you think of my story, friends?"

"It's... *amazing*," offered the salesman, guardedly. "But I have to admit, a lot of it doesn't make *sense*. And there's certainly nothing there that I can see, that would be a valid reason why the cops would have a dragnet out for you."

You liar, he thought. *You know very well why, Bob. If only you had the slightest clue what to* do *with her, now.*

"Listen, everyone," announced Billings, while he brought the SUV to a slow halt, off the road by perhaps fifty feet or so, "I think I'll take Tommy up on that idea of his... we all need a few minutes to get out, stretch our legs, you know?"

He turned the headlights off but left the vehicle running.

"Whitney," he said, *sotto voce*, "Can you please step out of the car? I need to speak with you... *privately*."

Claremont did not answer, just nodding, wide-eyed.

She opened the passenger-side door and debarked.

"Should I come, too, Bob?" asked the 'Sari'-girl. "I did not say something that *scared* you, did I?"

Again, she sounded distressed.

"No, this is between Whitney and me, and it's... uhh, about Melissa, Curtis and Tommy, nothing earth-shatteringly important," lied the salesman. "I just have to get something straight with Ms. Claremont, that's all. We're *fine*, no need for you to get worried. Would you mind staying in the SUV and keeping an eye on the kids?"

Earth-shattering, reflected Billings, a second or so after he uttered the phrase. *Funny you should put it like that, Bob.*

"Oh-kay, well, I guess that I will just sit here in the vehicle," complained the fallen-girl, locking Billings in a laser-like, knowing stare.

The salesman waved with his hand and Claremont followed him another fifty or so feet into the wilderness, away from the SUV.

"Careful, Whitney," he cautioned, "Be on the lookout for things moving out here. Remember what those guys back there said about the coyotes, the wolves, and the..."

"Look, Bob," replied the black woman, "Y'all didn't get us back here just to chat 'bout the wildlife. What on yo' mind? Maybe go for a run 'round the block? Don' know 'bout y'all, but ah feel, dunno, sorta... like ah gots energy, like ah *high*, all of a sudden..."

"Yeah, definitely some adrenaline going on back there in the car, it was quite a story, after all," commented Billings. "Tell you the truth, I had a hard time keeping my hands on the wheel. But I'm thinking of the same thing that you probably are. About our guest back there."

"Y'all mean *her*, right?" asked Claremont.

"You got it," answered the salesman.

"So, what?" said Claremont, evasively.

"After that last explanation, assuming of course that what she said to us was the truth, well... I'm sure that you've figured out who – *what* – we have in the car with us, haven't you?" offered Billings.

"Why don't *y'all* tell *me*, Mister Sales Man," countered Claremont.

He propped his foot up on a nearby rock, taking care first to ensure that it didn't accommodate any snakes or creepy-crawlies, though the cold should have precluded that, anyway.

"Well, here's how *I* see it, " he remarked. "From the first time I laid eyes on our friend 'Sari' here, something told me that there was something... *different* about her. Might have been the accent, might have been how she's so naive about ordinary things that everybody learns within a week of living here in the good old U. S. of A., might have been the eyes that seem green one day and blue the next... might have been how I looked her in those eyes just once and after that I couldn't *bear* to be away from her, not for a *minute*, not for a *second* –"

"That don' prove nothin'," retorted the black woman. "She damn pretty... for a *white* 'ho, ah gots to give her that. Y'all wantin' to get it on wid some ho' half your age or less, well, ain't nothin' new 'bout *that* – look, ah'm not fixin' to *judge* y'all, Bob, but what y'all 'n she be doin', it perfectly *natural*. Nothin' *special*, ah mean. Hell, every slick in mah 'hood after th' same thang! Melissa nowhere *near* the right age for that, but ah still gots to look out that they don' fool wid her..."

"Come *on*, Whitney, you're a *bright* person," pressed the salesman. "Even *if* we dismiss all of *that*, look at the weirdo 'cloak' trick that got us out of the Jesus Freak prison back there at the border, or all the other semi-possible things that she's been pulling off – like, seeing in the dark, or jump-starting a car without even a hand crank, or how about jumping off a rock that's high enough to break our legs, no 'ifs ands or buts', if *we* tried that – and landing without so much as a *whimper*... then add it all to her own little life history that she just gave us back in my good old Patriotic..."

Claremont just stared.

"It all leads in *one* direction – *only* one direction, doesn't it?" pressed Billings. "To one, inevitable conclusion, about *who* we have in the back seat, rolling down the highway with us."

Claremont looked down and kicked a rock off into the distance.

"Yeah, ah knows what y'all thinkin', that is, who she is, where she *from*."

Her eyes briefly shot up to the sky, then came down to look Billings in the face.

"But ah just can't *believe* it," protested the black woman. "Ah mean, *shit*, Bob, that kinda stuff only happen in th' *movies*, on TV, none of it *real*, y'all understand what ah'm sayin'? She look just like an ordinary white girl, not some kind of, well, *y'all* know..."

She paused for a second, then looked straight at the salesman again, and proposed, "Maybe she just... uhh.. *haloocinatin'* or somethin'. Y'all know, *lots* of folk think they Elvis, or Santy Claus, Superman, or Supergirl, or whatever. Maybe she just on some weird new synth drug that do some funky shit wid her brain. Or... or... maybe them Men In Black dudes gone 'n messed 'round wid her, made her into one of them, what they call it, yeah, by-onic thangs. Ah seen shows 'bout that on TV. Hell, ah heard that all what they say was goin' on up there, it all *faked*, special 'fects shit, just to give all of us somethin' to take our minds off of... it all..."

Her tone pleaded for agreement, for confirmation of the normal.

Billings shook his head.

"No, Whitney," he argued. "Sorry, not *this* time. I can hardly *believe* it myself, to tell you the truth, and I keep trying to think up another explanation, but the pieces all fit, unfortunately. If it wasn't for the darkness thing, I'd have just written it off to coincidence or some kind of cheap magic trick. But, for God's sake – I guess this isn't news to you – I've seen her buck *naked*, several times, and yes, she *does* have a hell of a figure, but the point is, there's no *way* that she could be using some kind of machine to do that hiding-thing that got us out of the camp."

"Y'all don' *say*," chuckled the black woman.

"Let's just say," continued the salesman, "That I've checked in every *possible* place on her body – if you know what I mean – where she could be hiding some kind of secret agent gear, or drugs, for that matter, and I'm one hundred per cent sure of it. Which means that she *has* to be generating that hiding-field, *naturally*. Which is something that *no* human being could possibly do. No... *human*, being. Which means..."

The black woman managed a grin.

"Yeah, but when y'all was... y'all know, *wid* her... y'all find any lil' green antennas growin' out of her haid, or anywhere else?" Claremont inquired. "Ah seen some of them sci-fi movies, them space-aliens *always* gots some-such thang. Sometimes they just wearin' a human body like a coat an' they really some slimy monster inside. Or they try to suck the blood out of y'all, or turn y'all into a zombie, or shit like that..."

"No," replied Billings, "I can *personally* attest that every inch of her is, well... completely human-looking, and completely, nicely, *outrageously*, female. No, let me take that back; she's... uhh... way *better*-looking than any woman I've ever seen or been with, and let me tell you, ol' Bob's been with more than a few, I don't mind saying. She's very definitely all flesh – soft and warm, no false limbs, no implants, no false skins; and... and..."

Get your goddamn mind out of the gutter and back to the topic, Bob... but there were *the teeth, weren't there?* a voice told him. *She tried to hide them, but when she moaned as she was about to...*

"Yeah?" asked Claremont.

Billings looked down at the ground, avoiding looking at the black woman, then sending her a sheepish, school-boy look.

"Whitney," he offered, "This is... uhh... something that guys usually don't talk that much about, at least to women that they just know casually, but in view of what we're discussing anyway, I guess I *should* mention it to you."

Claremont laughed, both knowingly and cynically.

"Y'all mean she a good *lay*, Bob? Well, *shit*, slick, that ain't news to the rest of us, even mah kids and that Injun boy in the know. It all over yo' face... and hers. So what?"

"It's kind of hard to describe," he tried to explain. "But, well, when you get to my age, sometimes the spirit is willing but the flesh is weak, you know what I mean? And I don't do the 'get-it-up' drug thing, don't trust putting that crap in my body. But when I'm with *her*, God, how would I say it, I feel like a porn star... when we do it, I don't feel the slightest *bit* weak, thank you... quite the opposite, in fact, she makes me feel like I'm thirty again, no, twenty, maybe. And ever since I've been... *intimate* with her, each time we do it, I just feel healthier and stronger. I haven't felt *this* good, in charge of myself, aware of my surroundings, since high-school. I've stopped using reading glasses, for Christ's sake!"

Claremont stared at the man in suspicion.

"The point is, Whitney," elaborated Billings, "It's *more* than just the rush that you get from, uhh, doing it. It's something *more* than that. I don't know exactly what, but it's not *natural*, that's what I'm trying to say. I used to be 'Bob Billings, the nobody salesman from Tucson'; now, I'm 'Bob Billings Plus, the New And Improved'. It's intoxicating, amazing... words fail."

"Maybe y'all should stop," cautioned the black woman. "Maybe it some kind of weird shit she doin' to y'all."

"If it is," reflectively observed the salesman, "Then so be it. I *like* it. Wouldn't stop if I could. And I *can't*... or hadn't you noticed."

"Ah *had*," stated Claremont, impassively.

Her voice now rose a pitch, interrupting his thoughts with a tone of anxiety.

"Bob... not sayin' that ah does, but if ah was to say ah believed yo' theory there... do y'all think that mah children might be in any *danger*? Ah mean, runnin' 'round with the likes of *her*... what if she get mad with us? Don' remember 'zactly, but when she – if it *is* she – was up there with them space men, ah remember Curtis comin' in one day and he say, 'that Mars lady', she can do *anythin'*, she like Superman!' Y'all knows that song that go, 'you don't tug on Superman's cape'..."

The woman went silent for a second, then added, "An' y'all know, some of them guys back at the camp, they say she the *devil*, Bob... you heared it just like ah did. Wouldn't that 'splain the darkness thing...?"

Worry showed all over her face.

"Just as many of them, probably more, say that she's an 'angel', you know," countered Billings. "And I can personally attest that if she's that', she ain't like any of 'em that I recall from reading my Bible," he added, with a semi-cynical chuckle. "But come *on*, Whitney, even though I'm supposed to be playing preacher man on our little trip here, I can't *believe* all this religious mumbo-jumbo about her, and I don't think *you* really can, either. The truth is fantastic enough, without having to lard on all the crap about God, Jesus, the Devil or the Pillsbury Dough Boy, on top of it. Don't you think?"

"Maybe," uneasily allowed Claremont. "Mah Momma never tell me *nothin'* 'bout things like *this*. Don' got no easy way to figure it out, ah guess."

They both looked in the direction of the car.

The 'Sari'-girl seemed to be playing some kind of 'patty-cake' hand slapping game with Curtis and Tommy, while Melissa was hectoring her brother about something or other. They were all smiling and laughing.

The eyes of the black woman and the white salesman registered this not, but their minds somehow perceived a glow from inside that car, something good, warm, inviting, life-preserving, but at once just slightly outside their consciousness.

"I don't think she's any *direct* threat to us, Whitney," mentioned Billings. "If she were, she's already had many good opportunities to do us harm, and all she's done is risked her own neck to get us out of that camp, for example. On top of that, as you know, I've gotten to know her a bit more – ahem – 'intimately' than any of you have, and I trust her as much or more than I would any... *human* woman. It's just that..."

"Just *what*," queried Claremont.

"We have to think about the fact that the Feds are probably looking for her," he explained. "Now, we don't have any idea if they already know what you and I suspect, but if they *do*, well, that could be bad for us on any number of grounds. They might come at us with guns a-blazin', they might drop a bomb on us, or they might just arrest us all on some law they think up just for this purpose and let us rot in jail."

"Yeah," muttered the black woman.

"Or what if," continued the salesman, "They try to grab her, she fights back – she's damn strong and fast for a girl of her size – and we get caught in the crossfire. Look, I have no *idea* of what's on their mind or what their intentions are, but let's face it, they shoot people just on *suspicion* of distributing synth drugs or illegals – who *knows* what the hell they'd do to stop someone like *this*. I'm just trying to say that we're *way* out of our depth, here."

"So what y'all fixin' to do," asked Claremont, skeptically. "Turn her in?"

Billings stared at the woman, for a second or two, then retorted, "No, Whitney... I could *never* do anything like that. Not just because of the facts of the matter, or because she risked her pretty little ass to get us out of the Jesus Jail, but... truth is, I really don't *know* why. I only know that I couldn't, I wouldn't. But I'd understand it if you wanted to take Curtis, Melissa – and, I'd hope, Tommy, too – away from this situation. Just in case."

Claremont looked torn.

She stared off into space, thought a little more, then offered, "Shit, Bob, ah just don' *know* what to do 'bout this one. Ah mean, we's up that ol' creek without a paddle if we don't stay with y'all until we can get settled back with our homies, y'all know? No bread, no wheels, no papers, no homie nowhere 'round these parts, an' no way to get back to th' hood, might as well just check into jail right now... but if we keep on goin' down the road wid y'all, and wid *her*, well, who *know* what might happen."

She paused for a second, as if considering whether to reveal a private thought.

Then she requested, "Don' tell th' kids, Bob, but y'all know what else?"

"Of course," replied the salesman, sympathetically. "I mean, I won't."

"Well, it just that... what ah means is, if y'all right 'bout our friend 'Sari', well, this 'bout the only big thing that ever happen to me or my folks, y'all understand?" explained Claremont. "Ah don' want to take no big risks, y'all know ah'd never do *nothin'* to put mah kids in danger, but... if she *really* some 'space lady' or such, ah figures we could get us somethin' just by talkin' to the press, sellin' our story for one of them cee-leb-ritee books, right?"

Billings smiled.

"We ain't never had *shit* in our fam'ly before," noted the black woman, "'Cept for mah brother-in-law when he bangin' an' dealin', and he land he ass in the Big House for that... maybe this here's our big chance. Just thinkin' 'bout what's best for th' *kids*, that's all."

Billings let out a cynical chuckle, accompanied by a perfectly matched grin.

"Whitney, you sound just like a salesman, right there," he cackled. "Good for you, sister."

"And to tell you the truth," he added, "Something like that *had* crossed my own mind, too – the old 'fame, fortune, riches' thing. Get your picture on the front cover of *Us People*, or whatever. But I don't know. Just seems like a long shot to me – something tells me that what's likely to end up happening, is going to be something we can't even *imagine*, right now."

He took a deep breath.

"You know, there's *another* problem, that we have to contend with," he said. "A more immediate one."

"An' that would be?" replied Claremont.

"Well, I mean, right now, you and I are both pretty convinced about who she is and where she's from," said the salesman. "But I don't think *she* is, herself. What are we supposed to tell her? Or ask her?"

"Y'all think she not makin' up that story 'bout losin' her memory?" asked the black woman.

"Maybe she is," offered Billings, "But knowing her as I do, I think it's more likely that she isn't. So what we have riding along with us, is," – he held his fist up to his mouth, to baffle a nervous cough – "Let's call a spade a spade – no offense to current company of course – a cute, naive little *Martian* girl, who's wandering around the good old Ew-Nighted States of America like a wee sheep who's lost her way, and who doesn't have a *clue* who she really is. Who might have the power of a Superman within her, or whose only tricks might be what we've seen so far. All the while the Feds may be combing the country trying to put her in a cage, or worse."

Claremont folded her arms and shot back, "Well, Bob, even if y'all right – which ah'm not nearly so sure of – why would it be *our* job, to up 'n tell her all that?"

"Don't know that it is," replied the salesman. "But at the very least, you and I have got to agree on if we do or if we don't. If we start arguing about it, we get the worst of both worlds, wouldn't you say? For the record, I think we *owe* it to her... but on the other hand, who *knows* how she might react. Bad memories, that kind of thing... hell, let's just let it lie, for a while. Can you live with that?"

"Yeah, no problem," agreed the black woman. "And ah tell y'all what – ah ain't sayin' *nothin'* 'bout this to little Miss Martian there or nobody else, but ah ain't *lyin'*, neither, if any of th' kids guess what's goin' down theyselves. Curtis, he pretty bright, ah think he *suspects*, already, don' know if he on to the whole picture, but wouldn't surprise me none if he was. He ain't said nothin' to me directly, but sometime he look at her funny... y'all know what ah mean."

Billings nodded.

"I don't pay much attention to kids," he noted, "Intentionally. No offense to present company of course. But I have noticed that your son *has* struck up quite a close relationship with our guest, that's for sure... that Indian kid, too. I guess they're more open to believing in the really weird stuff than us world-weary adults are, so maybe Curtis and Tommy are clued in to all of this on some level, too. Anyway..."

Claremont raised a quizzical eyebrow.

"The bottom line is, Whitney," warned the salesman, "We'll have to play it by ear, from this point onward... I have no idea what we're going to do with our friend 'Sari', except to just wait and see what *she* wants to do. If and when she figures out who she is and what the hell, if anything, she's here to do. Until then, we have to try to *protect* her, as best we can. And..."

"Yeah?" asked the black woman.

"This is the *big* time, my dear," advised Billings. "The *biggest*, of the big times. No more Little League for us – we're in the World Series, now. We step up to the plate, we better not miss. I have a feeling that the pitches will be comin' at us real, *real*, fast, from now on."

Claremont shut her eyes and took a deep breath.

Slowly, she intoned, "May the Good Lawd guide our steps, Mister Sales Man. This ah do pray, on my dear Grandma's grave. May she forgive me for sayin' so."

They stood silent for a second, staring at each other in the cold Utah night. Then a loud call emanated from the SUV.

"Hey, Bob," shouted the 'Sari'-girl's pleasant voice, with an air of excitement.

"Come see!" she exclaimed. "I won a 'Gin Rummy'! Pretty good for someone new to these 'card games', do you not think?"

So Many Books, So Little Time

"Can't you hurry up just a *bit*?" demanded an exasperated Billings, tapping his feet as he reflexively looked again at his wrist-computer, subconsciously congratulating himself for having stashed the thing in the SUV's glove compartment, back... *before.*

"For God's Sake, Sari," he complained, "You've had us in here for *six hours*. I know NeoNet's probably fascinating for somebody who hasn't had the use of it before, but we gotta get going... and anyway, I should be able to connect up, in the car... any day now."

"Well, I have not been on your 'Neo-Net' for the whole time, you know, Bob," commented the fallen-girl, not taking her stare away from the 3-D LCD screen that she had monopolized for the last who knows how long, much to the irritation of the afternoon shift managing assistant of the Salt Lake City Civic Library's public access section. "I had some trouble at first, because I do not have, oh, what did they call it, yes, a 'Federal Face-Space' account, and they said that I had to have one to use the com-puters –"

"Yeah, I guess you wouldn't," Billings said, allowing himself a chuckle. "It's some kind of 'mandatory identification' thing, that's how they explained it to me, when I first got hooked up on to the network – you gotta go to some kind of government information portal and give it your Real National ID number, then fill out this personal profile with what you look like, photo ID I mean, your phone number, your address, what kind of breakfast cereal you like to eat, all that kind of crap, before they'll let you connect your computer to NeoNet –"

"Why is that?" she asked.

"Oh, they hand you some kind of BS about 'it's so that we can track down the perverts, the gangsters and the terrorists'," explained the salesman, "But really I think it's just so they can spy on what kind of movies you're watching and ding you for more taxes. Well how did you get on, then?"

"I invoked pity and told them that I forgot what my, uhh, 'special account number' was, and the librarian said not to worry, they have many visitors who have that problem, so she said that I could use one of the, uhh, 'floater' Face-Space accounts that they retain for this purpose," answered the newcomer. "This woman warned me not to tell the government that they were doing this because she could really get in trouble if they found out. Of course I agreed to honor her request. So I sent at least the first hour in that 'reference book' section, *you* know that. And about hurrying off, now... Curtis and Tommy are still down there. You will have to find them first, anyway –"

"Yeah, yeah, I know," countered Billings, "But if I go and try to read them the riot-act, they'll just say to get *you*, first... nice try there, girl. And I got done what *I* needed to... thank God, they had an automatic money machine down in the lobby, bastards charged me twelve per cent for the withdrawal. Finally, I got through and got enough cash to keep us going for awhile, topped up the credit-cards, too. Had a bit of a hiccup with the Real National ID at first, but after the second try it confirmed that I'm "me", or some crap like that."

"Hmm... good that you were successful," observed the fallen-girl, as her eyes moved rapidly from one information database page to another. "*Everything* here, seems to cost money."

"Besides," harangued the salesman, "Haven't you ever read a *book* before? I can understand why you want to surf the Neo, there's new stuff there every day, but most of these 'reference' books haven't been updated in *years*... nobody pays much attention to them anymore, least not where I come from. Come *on*, let's get going."

The 'Sari'-girl looked up and to the side, as if surprised by an unexpected thought.

"You know, Bob," she commented, "This may sound stupid, but... no, the honest truth is, I do not think I *have* read a 'book', well, not one exactly like you have here in this building... something tells me that the last time I encountered knowledge in written form, it was on a long piece of paper, yes... not a bunch of pages stuck together, where you open the one after the other."

Billings rolled his eyes and sighed.

"Although," continued the newcomer, "This 'Neo-Net' seems much more familiar to me, it is like I remember how one navigates within it, to go from one source of information to the other and so on. Odd, do you not think? I mean, I have been trying to remember where I would have learned that, but somehow it escapes me... ah, never mind. I suppose that you are right – if you allowed me, I would probably stay in this place for the next *week*, not bothering to eat, drink, pee or sleep... as it is, just in the short time that you have allowed me to spend in here, I have learned *so* much about this worl – uh, this... *place*... "

She sent him an awkward smile, with a half-cringe in her shoulders.

"I'm sure you *have*," replied the salesman. "Frankly, though, I find books kind of boring, if you want to know the truth."

"Oh, come *on*, Bob," persisted the fallen-girl. "There is *so* much knowledge available for free, here, like information about ingenious com-pu-ter technology, flying machines, boats that go under the water, the different countries, rich ones and poor ones, famous people who act in movies... I learned about geography and history, religions and cultures, who is the ruler of this nation or that; and how people work for money, how they dress, how they make love... I think that I know *much* more about the United States, than I did even a few days ago."

"Good for you," he grunted.

Now her tone was less bubbly; it was more studious, more analytical.

"You know," she observed, "There is a great deal of cruelty depicted in the history-books that I reviewed... so, now I can understand why you were afraid of those men back at the compound and the ones that stopped us on the highway – these rulers who tell everyone what to do, their armies – my! They have *so* many scary types of weapons, do you not think, even bombs that can destroy an entire *city*..."

"Well, you're unlikely to have one of *those* dropped on your pretty little head," remarked the salesman. "But getting shot by saying the wrong thing to a State Trooper who got up on the wrong side of the bed on any particular morning, now *that's* very much been known to happen. Which is why I wanted to get away from there, as fast as I could."

She nodded, then added, "Thank you *so* much for agreeing to take me here. It is a *grand* building, all these stairs and different levels, and all the glass that lets the light of the sun shine in. It has been *very* long since I can remember having been in such a big and impressive place."

"Uhh... yeah, *sure*, absolutely, Sari, I know exactly what you mean, there," replied Billings, trying to sound convincing. "Look, I'll tell you what – I got a whole personal library back in Tucson, mostly old English Lit books and novels with lots of old National Geographics in there, too, inherited it from my grandfather, actually, can't claim to have made much use of it up to now, so you're entitled to however much of it you want to take, if and when we get there. Sound like a deal?"

Impulsively, the 'Sari'-girl jumped up, and in a heartbeat had her arms draped all over Billings' body.

"Oh, *thank you*, Bob!" she gushed. "Would you *really* do that for me?"

Then she paused for a second or two, evidently pondering something, and added, "Knowledge, learning, the accumulated wisdom of those who have gone before us; that is the *real* power... right, Bob? In the long-run, much more powerful than... than..."

Her voice trailed off, as her glance, still friendly but now with an introspective quality, caught Billings' own.

The two stared at each other for a second.

"What are you thinking, Bob?" she requested.

"Uhh... *nothing*, Sari," he replied.

"*Liar*," she countered with a girlish grin, the tips of sharp teeth showing ever so slightly, despite her best efforts to restrain them.

"You are thinking about *power*, Bob... the kind that makes a 'cloak of shadows', right? About where it comes from. And *who* it comes from."

He looked down at his feet, then up at her, again.

"Listen," warned the salesman, "I don't think this is the right place to be talking about this, you understand?"

The fallen-girl surveyed the surroundings and her countenance darkened subtly.

"You are right," she agreed. "'Just our little secret', that is the saying, is it not? And I *promise* you, man, in time, you *will* learn more, *much* more... greatly blessed, are you. I hope you appreciate that, Bob."

Uneasily, Billings said, "Oh yeah, *that's* for sure. I mean, I sure *do*."

What the hell –? he thought.

With an inscrutable smile, she offered, "Let us go in search of the others."

He nodded, as the 'Sari'-girl took his hand. They headed down the spiraling stairs towards the ground-level of this massive, steel-and-glass building.

Secretly, Billings reveled in the scarcely-concealed glances of various library-goers, some regarding him with disapproval but others with envy, as he lived the middle-aged Hollywood movie star's dream of proceeding in front of a crowd, hand-in-hand with a fetching young trophy thing who could have been his daughter.

You're a pervert, Bob, he mused, *But you threw common sense to the winds, a long time ago on this trip. Waste of time to start doing it again, now.*

No you are not, came back a sudden, random thought, not his, he somehow knew.

You are just enjoying yourself. So am I. The more guilt you feel about love, the more diminished will be its wonderful gift.

Not stopping his gait, he turned and looked at the fallen-girl, who shot him a goofy-looking smile.

"What is the matter, Bob?" she insouciantly inquired. "Is your mind, ahh, 'wandering', perhaps?"

"No," he muttered without missing a beat, "*Yours* is. But I guess I'm getting used to that, by now."

They both laughed, just before Claremont and the children came into view.

"'Bout *time*," complained the black woman. "We was wonderin' if y'all had decided to pitch a tent up there or somethin'."

"Or *somethin'*," giggled Curtis in his malicious little-boy style, followed by the obligatory stern glare from his mother.

The fallen-girl bent over to address the Claremont boy.

"*Naughty* little boy," she tut-tutted, with a smile. "Always thinking about *that*. However, there are many worse things to think about, I suppose. Whitney, it was not really Bob's fault – *I* was the one who, how do you say, 'overstayed her welcome', just like it was me who wanted to come here in the first place. This Temple of Knowledge, it is *so* grand, *so* nicely-built, and there is *so* much information about your pla – I mean, about the whole world, in here... I could have spent weeks, just reading the books and going from place to place on this 'Neo-Net' computer thing."

"Ain't you never been in a library before, Miss Sari?" asked the Indian-boy. "We even got one back on the reserve – just one room, nothing like *this*, and no computer-network, either, but I read every book in it, even though we had TV..."

"Not that I remember, Tommy," remarked the 'Sari'-girl, staring off into space. "Maybe some time, long ago... I am not sure. But listen, if you read all of these books, do you remember enough of them to tell me some of the stories they told?"

She searched inside a pocket while saying this, then produced a pair of cheap sunglasses, which were quickly donned, along with the baseball-cap that she had temporarily removed when entering the building.

"Sure, lady," bashfully stated the boy. "Like there was this one about a guy who was chasing a big whale, and another one where they were knights and kings and they had swords and shields, that kind of thing. I'm not sure I remember the whole story for them, but I could give you an idea."

"Thank you," she answered, smiling at him, her eyes now shaded by the glasses. "I would like that very much. Swords and shields, men with armor... that sounds familiar, somehow. I have many stories in my head, too, some like that, some not. We could trade them with each other, just before bedtime, each night. Can we call it a 'deal'?"

"Deal!" enthusiastically agreed Tommy.

"I will start searching my memory for the first tale, now," promised the fallen-girl. "It may take me some time to piece everything together, though, so please be patient, Tommy. Oh, and, Bob... I was meaning to ask you... do these 'sun-glasses' make me look pretty, do you think? They do not make it any easier to see things, and they only block a little bit of the... uhh... what would you call it, the more-purple-than-purple..."

"You look *cool*, Miss Sari," chirped the Indian-boy. "Like a movie star. A real famous one. Like the ones you see in those magazines at the supermarket check-out, when they catch them trying to be like a normal person, wearing a baseball-cap and dark glasses so you can't tell who they really are, but the guys with the cameras, they *always* figure it out."

He grinned, self-consciously.

The newcomer bent over and, too quickly for him to flinch away, impulsively kissed the boy on the cheek, producing a heavy blush, as Tommy tried to conceal his excitement.

Curtis stuck out his tongue.

"Okay, folks," interrupted Billings, "If we're all agreed on the bedtime stories front, I think we'd better get going – we've been hanging around in here for quite a while, you know what I mean, Whitney?"

The black woman nodded, knowingly, as she donned her own dark spectacles.

"Yeah, y'all got *that* right, Bob," she offered. "Too much time in one place. Gots to get movin', y'all know."

The children looked back and forth at each other, with a mixture of light puzzlement and suspicion.

The troupe headed toward the doors and their home-away-from-home, parked far down at the other end of the University Boulevard Library's massive lot, with the children insistently pressing the fallen-girl for an advance glance at one of her personal stories.

Meanwhile, a man on the fourth floor above them leaned over a balcony, studying them with expert intent.

The others had all gone out of the front doors and Billings was about to do so himself, but he felt a tug on his arm and then whirled in-place, confronting the 'Sari'-girl, who had suddenly removed her sunglasses.

She stared upwards, toward one of the higher levels of the library's open-concept architecture.

"See that man up there, Bob?" she remarked, calmly but forcefully. "He was *watching* us, all the while. He is staring at you and me, now. I am not going to point. Just look up to the level three above the one that we now stand upon, in the middle of the balcony. He is holding something in his hand, it is pointing almost right at us."

"Uh, yeah, oh, yeah, there he is," replied the salesman, while trying to avoid talking about what he was thinking.

Damn, mused Billings, *He's one H of a long way away, and I can see him... perfectly. A week ago, there wouldn't have been a* chance *that I could do that.*

What's going on?

"But come on, Sari," he continued, "That guy might just be staring outside, and there are *dozens* of other people around here who he could be looking at, or ogling, or whatever. How do you know he's paying special attention to you and I?"

"I just *know*, Bob," she replied. "He is looking at *me*, specifically. I... *sense* things like this. Anything that might be a threat, something that could be dangerous. It is one reason why it is very hard to surprise me."

"Well, what do you want to *do* about it?" demanded the salesman. "Go up there and tell him that he can't look at a pretty girl?"

"No," she explained, "But I *can* tell that he was watching us, for a *purpose*. What that is, I cannot say. I am too far away from him to look inside his... well. But I can tell you that I do *not* like it. Having people with whom I am not familiar, and who I do not trust, trying to follow me, that makes me *nervous*, puts me on guard. I just thought you should know."

"Don't *blame* you," offered Billings. "Well then, let's get going. The less he sees of your cute little face, boobs or ass, the better."

She turned toward the door in lock-step with the salesman.

"I do not *like* being stalked by strangers, Bob," she noted with a faked smile, as she put the dark glasses back on. "But I *do* love it when my appearance pleases you. To be cherished, to be desired, to be needed, by at least one other person, that is proof of one's place in the universe... that is a wise saying from somewhere. Race you to the car, oh-kay?"

The two quickly exited out the glass doors, the fallen-girl deliberately staying a pace or so behind Billings, feigning exhaustion. They reached the SUV, laughing as would a pair of newlyweds on a honeymoon, much to the amusement of the younger children, the exasperation of Whitney Claremont and the secret envy of Claremont's daughter.

All climbed aboard and the SUV roared off in the direction of I-15, only a few blocks to the west.

"I'll take a few side-streets," said Billings. "Just in case we have any secret admirers. Other than myself, of course."

Meanwhile, the man on the fourth floor of the Salt Lake city-library's University Boulevard library spoke rapidly into a secured mobile voice-computer, trying as best he could to mask a faint but discernible Eastern European accent.

"Priority one report to Western Hemisphere Operations," he stammered, in hushed Russian.

Still half-whispering, the man reported, "Identified group including individual who meets the profile almost perfectly. Have already compared the photo taken locally with this device, with same taken of the individual on the mission. After many near misses, I was fortunate to get a clear shot and she is almost a perfect match in *all* respects – facial features, height, everything, but unfortunately I was not able to get close enough to get a good check on the radiation signature, at least not from a range of 75 plus meters, but I *did* get a positive response on the equipment, and it is precisely the same signature that the cosmonaut from the Mars mission sent back to headquarters some time ago. In contrast to what we had expected, she is now wearing a loose-fitting, red-and-green track suit, the top of which has the name of a Utah university on it, plus, when she is outdoors, red baseball-cap with a prominent 'A' on it; and her hair is not completely blond, but rather is a light gray, as if she were older than she otherwise looks."

He stopped for a second, took a deep breath, then stated, "I was able to review some of the reading material that she accessed during her visit here and it was mostly general geography, history and natural science, as well as certain reference books concerning religion, military technology, American laws and social etiquette; this, of course, fits the expected profile. The target seems to be traveling with a group consisting of a middle-aged man, dark hair, somewhat overweight, about a half-meter taller than the target and a black woman, also middle-aged, spare build, about the same height as the target."

"There are also three children, two Negro ones – a girl in her early teens and a grade school-aged boy – and there is another school-boy who may be Hispanic or Oriental, possibly," continued the observer-man. "I am unsure of the relationship between these others and the target – perhaps they are under her mental control? They are traveling in a silver-colored SUV with black trim, probably an import, Toyota, Nissan or similar model. Headed to the west on University Boulevard. I am proceeding to my own vehicle to stay in discreet pursuit."

He paused for another long breath, pondering what to say.

Then, talking as he quick-marched into the parking-lot, he concluded, "*Finally* we have some luck, comrades. Tell Chubatkin that I was right and he was wrong – far more likely to find a being like this in a library, than a homeless shelter; given her background, she would need knowledge of her new environment, much more than she would need food. Suggest we concentrate our resources in this area, as much as is possible without disclosing the mission, to maintain track. Please advise as to procedure from this point forward, considering the changed circumstances, especially policy in the event of imminent capture of either our team or the target, by American authorities. Misha out."

He snapped shut the lid to his super-duper mobile phone-computer, the best, un-tappable technology that SVR back in Moscow could supply, and headed rapidly for his own car.

This time, I got the right *one – the ultimate prize*, he said to himself.

Good News, With A Caveat

"Hector? *Hector*? Is that *you*?" exclaimed Tanaka, with something near to overt joy sounding in her voice. "God, I'm – *we're* – so happy to see you again. We heard otherwise, but until I saw you with my own eyes, I was still afraid that you were..."

"One and the same, Professor," acknowledged the familiar, Tex-Mex voice from down on Earth, accompanied by the same round, mildly-grinning face that had communicated with Jacobson's team right from the start of its Mars-expedition, seemingly now so far in the past however recent.

"As they told you, I had a little... bump or two, when our friend 'Lucifer' made its last kick at the soccer ball, as it were," said Ramirez. "But I'm one hundred per cent, right now – at first they thought it was something really serious, but in fact it turned out to be just a broken rib and some bruises."

"I don't know if you heard the story," he continued, "But I am kind of lucky to have gotten out in one piece, at *all*, and that's true of Sylvia, too. We volunteered to stay behind at Mission Control and we got away with it, but as you may already know, an awful lot of the rest of us... *didn't*. At least they went down doing what they lived for doing. As you know."

"Yes, Hector," replied Tanaka, softly. "We know."

After a second or two, the remote caller spoke up again.

"Anyway, that's all over with, now... well, okay, not *quite* all over with, since, as you can see," – his arm washed over the background of the Houston Mission Control Center in an expressive gesture, revealing a high-tech junkyard scene replete with jury-rigged cabling and the remnants of smashed furniture – "Things are still a little, ahem, *untidy*, around here. But we expect to be back up to full capacity within the month, and we have all of our major up-links to ISS2 operational, now. In fact, we have had a track on your trajectory going for three days. So..."

Tanaka, as well as her former Mars mission commander and the commander of the space-station, just stared impassively into the camera.

"So," explained Ramirez, "I guess the reason for this meeting is, we just have a few things to clear up about the trajectory that ISS2 is currently maintaining. Is that Commander Cohen that I see there? Hi, Commander, Hector Ramirez here – I know that you were mostly dealing with my counterparts down here since I was in charge of the *Eagle* and *Infinity* mission, and ISS1, but unfortunately Ling and Mary-Anne are still injured, so that job has fallen to myself. Okay?"

"Why, certainly," politely replied Ariel Cohen.

"Well, then," noted Ramirez, "We have been tracking your inbound flight path since... since the booster incident, and, as you are no doubt already aware, the outlook has not been too good..."

"*Tell* me," interrupted Tanaka, sarcastically.

"Yes, Professor, I can imagine what it feels like to be going over this again, from your perspective up there," offered the Mission Control scientist. "But just to try to stay on the facts for the time being, we both know that your inbound velocity was *much* too high – there was no chance of establishing a stable orbit around Earth –"

"All of this has been well-known for some time, sir," interjected Cohen. "Is there a *question* that you wanted to ask?"

"Well, yes, in fact, there is," answered Ramirez. "So I'll get right to it. Now, you said in last week's communication that you hadn't yet repaired or, therefore, fired, any of the remaining propellants for braking thrust, is that right?"

"Correct," answered the ISS2 station commander. "Since the departure of Captain Jacobson's two ships on that... ill-fated mission, we have essentially had only maneuvering thrusters at our disposal; they can't really do anything to stop us, anyway, and we didn't want to deplete them; if we did, we couldn't even change the relative attitude of the station. Sub-Commander Chen is trying to scrounge up chemicals that could potentially be jury-rigged into reactive compounds, but I have to tell you that this effort is likely to be futile. Almost all such materials were already used, in the abortive booster project that you referred to earlier."

"Then, if I may be so blunt, Commander," demanded Ramirez, picking his words slowly and carefully, "Why do we track you as slowing down?"

"As *what*?" shot back Cohen, with a startled look that might have been genuine.

Tanaka and Jacobson shot a glance at each other, hoping to at least partly avoid the camera in so doing.

"At first, we put this down to instrumentation-errors," continued the NASA scientist. "And the decrement in your velocity is quite small – on the order of about 1.1 to 3.1 per cent – but it's definite and it seems to have been increasing since we re-established radio contact with ISS2 after the incident."

"Are you sure?" asked Tanaka, trying to maintain a poker face.

"Definitely," confirmed Ramirez, "And from our point of view, this is the first good news that we've been able to relay to you, especially after what happened to the evacuation ships. If we know what's causing this thing, maybe we can amplify it, get it to slow you down enough to park you somewhere where we can get at least a few people off your station. Can you explain what's going on, Commander?"

Cohen looked unsure. He fumbled for an answer as the other two turned away from his pleading stare.

"I... uhh... no, Professor Ramirez, I really can't provide you with a valid answer about this... maybe solar winds?" he stammered. "Gravity distortions caused by the shock wave of the comet's destruction? Your guess is as good as mine, but I agree with you, this is about the first good news that we have had up here since the tragedy of the lifeboat expedition. I don't think I'll release the information to the rest of the crew until I have some more hard evidence about this... are you okay with that, Professor?"

"I guess that it will *have* to be," replied Ramirez. "But as soon as you know something, please communicate the details to us ASAP. If it's some kind of environmental thing – some kind of 'space drag', I don't know what you'd call it – then we will have to start investigating, determining how it might affect our plans to rescue you guys and those few of the 'Arks' project that still have, uhh, at least some life-support left. As you probably know already, there aren't too many of the latter, but we have to try..."

"Oh, certainly," agreed Cohen, carefully. "Was there anything else that we had to discuss, then?"

"No, that will be it," concluded the NASA scientist. "Best of luck to you and your team up there, Commander... we're pulling out all the stops to get you and your crew safely back home, you know. Especially Captain Jacobson, Professor Tanaka and the rest of the Mars mission – having them gone all the way to Mars and then get *this* close, but not... well, you know what I mean, I'm sure. And not that we're not looking out for everybody else up there on ISS2. Anyway, that's it from down here. We'll give you another call in two days, or whenever circumstances demand it. Okay?"

"Okay," agreed the Israeli, smoothly.

The "link active" light on the communications display went dark.

Cohen turned to face his NASA and USAF counterparts.

"It would seem," he offered, "That your little experiments may have had more of an effect, than you previously thought, wouldn't you say, Captain? I just wish that I could be adding something to them. A funny feeling, as you Americans say; I'm in charge up here, but I'm completely dependent on your exercise of an ability that I can barely comprehend."

His chin pensively propped up by a half-fist, Jacobson thought for a second and replied, "Well, Hector's report is as much great news to us as it is to you, Ariel – even though three per cent or so won't buy us much more than a few more hours watching the Earth go sailing lazily by us... but I suppose it's a start. I just hope that we can build upon it in the time remaining, as short as that is."

"Yeah," interrupted Tanaka, "But it isn't *all* good news," she warned.

Jacobson arched an eyebrow at the woman and asked, "What do you mean, Cherie?"

"Simple," she replied. "They're *on* to us now, Sam."

No Fun Being Number One

"Tensh-HUT!" barked the Captain of the Marine Guard, as the President entered the windowless, antiseptic chamber, far underground of the buildings at a certain U.S. Air Force Base, and far away from the publicly marked building locations.

"Commander-in-Chief on deck!" exclaimed the Marine.

"At ease," announced the President, as he removed a fine-leather bomber-jacket, its eagle-and-stars insignia prominently visible near the left breast pocket.

His glance swept across the room and around the elongated oval table, which accommodated dozens of senior military officials. The civilians, as usual, were mostly seated in the shadows behind the table, although a couple had still been alloted positions of honor on either side of the President's own.

The President surveyed the table, the Advisers and the surroundings.

"Where's Horn?" he demanded.

"Doing fund-raising, or organizing, or something like that, down in Dixie, last I heard," commented the Vice-President.

"Well, tell him next time, I expect him here," complained the President.

"Look," he continued, bending over the table, his palms supporting his torso upon it, "We all know why we're here, so I'll skip the formalities. But before we get into the National Security report, I want to state for the record what my own perspective is. Both I and my family have been participating in this charade for a week or so now and the novelty of it is, frankly, starting to wear a bit thin. It's only a matter of time until the media – we don't control all of it, need I remind everyone, in particular I hear that the damn BBC have been poking their noses where they shouldn't –"

"We threatened to revoke their credentials," said a voice from the back of the room. "But unlike our own news channels, they didn't cave... I'm afraid the good old 'it's for national security' thing doesn't resonate too well with them. We have agents following their reporters, but until we get your go-ahead to rough 'em up a bit so they get the message, sir, I'm afraid there's a limit to what we can do..."

"The answer is still 'no', Jack," shot back the President. "All *that* will do, is tip off the rest of them, that something really *is* going on."

Bezomorton, flanked by the white-haired Harry Anderson on one side and by DeWitt, on the other, now commanded the floor.

"I have an update on the Pakistan front, Mr. President," he stated. "As you know, given the gravity of the situation with the comet, as well as the... unfortunate outcome of our military intervention in that country, we had substantially reduced our asset deployment in the Indian Ocean and Arabian Gulf areas. In the last week or so, though, the Joint Chiefs have restarted our surveillance of the situation – basically we've cashed in the few chits we had remaining with the Indians, who have much better HUMINT than we do, and we've been able to run a couple of *Aurora-II* flights over Pakistan, that's been necessary because none of our few operational satellites can easily be moved into a good trajectory for reconnaissance of the area."

"And?" inquired the President, with a slight tone of weariness.

"Well," continued the National Security Adviser, "I guess the best way to put it is, 'things *could* be worse'. By that I mean, despite a very chaotic situation on the ground –"

The Secretary of State laughed, mordantly.

"By 'chaotic', I believe you mean, 'the Muslim Salvation League is now beheading all the Pakistanis who were stupid enough to believe that we were going to stick around, in the market square in Islamabad, don't you?" he mentioned.

A green-uniformed general wearing four stars on his shoulders and breast, interrupted.

"We all *knew* that unfortunate things like that were bound to happen, when the President made the decision to withdraw our forces," he retorted. "And I'd remind you, had we *stayed*, the likely alternative was that it would be *our* troops, being marched up to the chopping block... we were outnumbered two thousand to one – not even the U.S. Army can beat odds like that."

Silence was about the table.

Bezomorton again spoke up.

"May I continue, Mr. President?" he requested.

"Please do," answered the President. "Although I'm not sure I want to hear the rest."

"As I was going to say, sir," continued the National Security Adviser, "Despite some very difficult circumstances in which to sort out the intelligence, DIA, working with NSA and CIA, have been able to establish that *most* of the nukes are still safely in the hands of the Pakistani military. General Al-Sharif has given us a personal pledge that his officers will die before they'll hand them over to the MSA; they'll set off the destruction charges, there won't be anything left except little bits of U-235 littering the landscape. *However...*"

"Go on," muttered the President.

"The bottom line, sir," said Bezomorton, slowly and deliberately, "Is that we still have around twenty, that's the low end estimate, to thirty, that's the high end, that are unaccounted for. Of those, we believe that unfortunately, at least five or six – maybe more, as I said, getting exact numbers here is almost impossible – have, ahem, left the country."

A pall of silence fell over the group.

"Does *anyone* know where the bombs have gone?" demanded the President. "No, I take that back, you already answered that, didn't you. Okay. Do we know *who* has them? What groups, that is. As if I need to *ask*."

The CIA director's flat, unemotional voice, sounded.

"We have an intensive program to determine that, sir, " he mentioned. "Our best estimate is that currently, at least one weapon is in the hands of the Muslim

Salvation League, although it's unknown if they have the technical capability to detonate it. There is also unsubstantiated intelligence that the *Al-Jihad* organization may have come into possession of one, maybe two other weapons, but as I say, this is all hearsay, right now."

"For *Christ's sake*," growled the Vice-President. "Why don't we just vaporize the whole fucking *sub-continent?* Pakistan, Iran and every other shit-hole place where they could be hiding the damn things?"

"We don't have any, excuse the language, 'fucking bombs left'," shot back the Secretary of State. "We used them all on the *comet*... remember? And if you dropped some bombs on India, well what if they just –"

"Gentlemen, *gentlemen*," cautioned the President.

Slowly, the room again went silent.

"John, Arthur, Harry," commanded the U.S. leader, "We need to track these things down and eliminate them... *immediately*. No matter *where* they are. You understand?"

"Understood," quickly replied DeWitt.

The Secretary of Defense leaned back in his chair, motioning to Bezomorton and Anderson. The three men whispered back and forth for almost a minute.

Wearily, the President pointed at the FBI director. "So things are *great*, overseas. How's the situation domestically, Cesar?" he asked.

A brush-cut, clean-shaven Hispanic man, younger than most at the table by ten years or more, spoke up.

"Basically, sir," answered Ochoa, "I'm afraid I don't have very much good news for you either; the opposite, really. Until we can devote the entire attention of the nation's domestic public safety apparatus – and here, I mean not just FBI, but the Army, the Guard and local police forces, in a coordinated effort to wipe them out – the gangs will basically have the urban streets to themselves. The Bureau simply doesn't have anywhere *close* to the manpower, not even with help from local law-enforcement, to clean them out, not without losing half to three quarters of our people."

"I've been hearing that for a while," observed the President. "It's not news to me."

"Well, sir," replied the FBI director, his head slightly bent, gesturing with his hands, "Maybe *this* will be news – according to the last reports we have from Southern California, the *Maras* are now in control of much of downtown L.A.; they're setting up roadblocks across the freeways, and –"

"Please tell me," demanded the American leader, "That this isn't getting through to the news-media?"

"Don't worry about that," interjected the Vice-President. "We got those guys by the balls – told 'em that they'll 'disappear' if so much as a word of what's really going on, gets on the evening news."

"That's true, sir," explained the FBI director, "And we have NeoNet, at least the *official* news sites on it, locked down as well; but, unfortunately, we've had some incidents of people with portable camcorders, wrist-computers and so on, sneaking in and out of the L.A. area and then adding video clips to Neo from other end-points. Particularly from Mexico, news of what's going on in L.A. is all *over* the media there... it's only a matter of time, in my opinion, until it starts to leak back into mainstream America."

The President pointed to a tallish, thin man with blond hair, near to one end of the table.

"Listen, Jerry," he indicated, "I want you to stay on top of this... we need as little as possible about the situation, to leak out to the mainstream media, *especially* Disney News, okay?"

"I'm on it," quickly replied the Chief of Staff.

"Sir," continued Ochoa, "I think I need to point out that there's a situation of near *anarchy* on the streets of downtown L.A., extending for twenty miles from the core of the city. Office towers, car dealerships, banks, department stores, *everything*, have been systematically looted, with anyone – for example private security-guards or just ordinary citizens, defending their homes – who resist, being brutally tortured and murdered by the gangs. They're not just using pistols and assault rifles; some of them apparently have heavy machine-guns, bazookas, land mines, armored cars... you name it. The *Maras* have taken over some of the local cable television stations and are broadcasting 'live and in color' torture sessions as a sign that they're in the driver's seat... Southside has been divided between the Bloods and the Crips, with both of them fighting an ongoing war with each other – as well as with the 18th Street'ers and the *Maras* – for control of the whole show."

"*That* good, eh," mumbled the American leader, shaking his head.

"Oh, and, by the way, what's left of Hollywood is, apparently," – the FBI director coughed, briefly – "Under the control of the WAR, that is, White Aryan Resistance', movement."

"Well at least *somebody* down there's on our side," joked the Vice-President.

A few laughs issued out upon hearing this.

The President hung his head and ran his fingers through his hair.

"Okay," he started. "Blanshard? Yeah, *you*. How quickly can we get the Army down there and get them set up for a... uhh... police action. Can we go for, say, end of this week?"

The same bull-necked, green-uniformed man who had spoken a few minutes ago shook his own, crew-cut head.

"I hate to say this... but that won't be possible, sir," he replied. "We don't have a fully combat-effective division, much less one with heavy armor, anywhere west of the Rocky Mountains, as of yet. We *do* have scattered Army and National Guard units, none of them above brigade size and most of them quite a bit below, all over Oregon and the rest of California, although they're all already committed to other projects. I can try to scrape something together, but..."

"What are you *telling* me?" shot back the President, now totally frustrated. "That we don't have enough troops to even secure *one* goddamn city?"

"No," explained Blanshard. "It's just that right now, Mr. President, I have no idea where I can get the boots on the ground to give us a realistic chance of this plan working. It will take *time* to do this, however. Can I have two weeks?"

"You have three *days* to get me a plan," countered the American leader. "And no more than a week after *that*, to make it work. Start plans for taking back the other cities, as well. Coordinate the actions of the Army and the Guard under FBI's leadership. We want to minimize civilian casualties if possible, but failure is *not* an option, so you have my authorization to do whatever you have to, to restore order. Is that understood, General?"

The Army man nodded reflexively.

"Very well understood, *sir*," he said.

The President continued, "That's just *wonderful* news, team... so I think I'd like to change the subject, we can come back to that later, if anyone wants more punishment. Okay, now, as to our wild-goose, or should I say, wild-*alien*, chase. Anderson? Anything more to report?"

"With all due respect, sir," replied a blue-garbed Air Force general, as he opened a file folder in front of him, "It's not like we're not making progress, although I have to be honest – do we have the alien in custody yet? Unfortunately, no. Do we know exactly where she is? Again, I have to give you a negative on that. But we're getting closer, that's my gut feeling."

The President rolled his eyes.

"Look, Harry, I have no reason to doubt your sincerity," he remarked, "But no more than a short while ago, you guys told me that you knew for *sure* where she had landed, didn't you?"

"What about airplanes, helicopters, for Christ's sake?" argued the Vice-President. "I mean, if we know where she first showed up, can't we just send a few people up in the air to track her down?"

"We've tried that," explained Anderson. "And we're *still* trying, but there are a lot of constraints on us – not so much aircraft in flyable shape, we have plenty of those because they weren't the types that were used against the comet – but more that we're *very* short of trained pilots."

"Fine," complained the President, "But if we don't think that the planes are going to track this being down, then why haven't we just done it the old-fashioned way... you know, having *people*, that is, the police, the Secret Service, anybody, go out and look for her? How hard can *that* be?"

"I can comment on that, sir," spoke the FBI director. "The Bureau has had a direct role in Project Red Rover since its inception and we have been working the target area intensively, but we are concentrating on the civilized areas, we're leaving the backwoods to INS and the Army. There are various leads which we are following up. We've got good people working on this one, sir; you just have to trust us and give us *time*, that's all."

"Um-humm," muttered the American leader.

He turned to his right.

"What about CIA?" he asked. "Any news on your front?"

"We have agents, both working in the open and in deep-cover, in every major city and town west of the Mississippi," sounded the deadpan voice of the CIA director, seated to the President's right. "And we have a lesser presence elsewhere. If this is of interest, sir, we have already detained over two thousand young females whose physical features, that is, blond hair, roughly the same height as observed on the Mars mission, slim figure, *et cetera*, correspond to those of the alien; three hundred or so of these are still in custody for various reasons –"

"So *that's* where they all went," interrupted Ochoa. "Nice to find out *now*, our field-agents were wondering –"

"I take it that none of these little popsies are the real thing?" commented the Vice-President.

"No, unfortunately we don't have a match," answered the CIA director. "We had high hopes for two of them that we picked up from the Pacific Northwest, one from just outside what's left of Spokane, one from Eugene, since these females looked almost identical to the last recorded images we had of the alien, and one of them had a number of mysterious personal habits. But it later turned out that the first one was just a high-school cheerleader who was into Eastern religions and that the second one was a synth drug-addict."

McPherson sighed.

"Two for two," mentioned the FBI director, unsympathetically.

"Well," noted the CIA director in his frustratingly emotionless monotone, "In the case of the second girl, it was an easy mistake for our field-agents to make. As you know, some of these new synthetic drugs cause rather striking physical changes in addicts, among which are skin and iris discolorations and highly elevated physical strength, along with psychopathic paranoia –"

"Then why are we still *holding* all of these girls? I mean, if you *know* that they're not the one we're looking for?" interjected the President.

"While we released most of these young females after only a cursory interrogation – with, of course, the obligatory warnings 'not to say a word about what we have done with you – the Project has determined that there would be a public relations or national security risk, or both, in releasing the remainder of those who are still in our custody," answered the CIA director, matter-of-factually.

"For example, to give you an idea of the tests that we have had to employ, to be sure that we have located the right suspect given what we know about the alien's self-preservative abilities, we have had to subject our prisoners to substantially reduced atmospheric pressures and to electrical stimuli," he remarked.

"Another method," he elaborated, "Is to remove blood from the detainee for chemical analysis, since it was observed by Captain Jacobson's crew that at least some of the alien's blood was corrosive... regrettably, a few of the captives suffered certain side-effects, such as inner ear, brain or internal organ damage, from these tests. A larger number have displayed evidence of traumatic stress syndrome, or have obstinately refused our demands not to discuss what has transpired –"

"You *sons of bitches*," growled an angry McPherson, from behind the President. "If you ever catch her and try this Gestapo stuff on *her*, I hope she tears you limb from –"

But the Science Adviser was silenced by an up-stretched Presidential index finger.

Grim-faced, the President said nothing in reply, although the Vice-President let out a cynical chuckle.

After a second or two, the American leader again spoke up.

"Well, these reports are going about the way that I expected," he said, morosely. "Does anyone have anything to add?"

A hand went up from the far end of the table.

"Oh, yeah, *right*, Bob. Okay. Go ahead," the President ordered.

"I'm afraid the news on my front isn't terribly good, either, sir," said the man, reflexively straightening the front of his Italian suit-jacket, his blow-dried hair standing up like some kind of albino feline mane. "We're facing a liquidity crisis, both in the public and private sectors. The Fed is warning that they're seeing the early signs of a run on the banks. Bottom line is, I'm very worried that we could be looking at a severe recession, or worse, in no more than three to six months, unless we get prompt and swift action on the part of the federal government to stabilize the situation."

Now it was the President's turn to lean back. He sighed in frustration.

"Jesus," he complained, "The damn comet somehow seems *easy*, compared to *this*. Maybe we should call on this 'Karéin' to bail us out of our budget problems, as well. She couldn't do any worse than we have already, could she? And if she showed up and we caught her, well, there's two birds in one shot..."

A polite laugh issued forth around the table.

"Bob," requested the President, "Have you got a plan to deal with this?"

"Well," said the Treasury Secretary, taking a deep breath, "Desperate times call for desperate measures. I'm recommending, that we implement an immediate and complete freeze on foreign withdrawal of capital or other liquid assets from United States domestic markets, also limiting citizens' bank withdrawals for the remainder of the year to one-tenth of each person's last-recorded taxable marginal income –"

"You've *got* to be kidding!" angrily protested the Vice-President. "You mean currency controls? That's *communism*! Mr. President, our supporters will *never* go for anything like that, their money will be on the first computer transaction out of Wall Street, the second that they get wind of –"

"It's okay, George," cautioned the President. "Let's hear him out. Remember, we haven't made any decisions yet."

The Treasury Secretary retrieved a neatly-bound, fifty-or-so-page document from his portfolio case and pushed it across the table towards the President.

He said, "Thank you, sir. And, Mr. Vice-President, please be assured that not only myself, but indeed everyone else at a senior level within Treasury, completely understands what a serious set of measures we are contemplating here."

The U.S. leader took the document and skimmed its table of contents for a few seconds.

"Very well, Bob," he offered, with a resigned sigh. "The White House staff and I will have a look at it and get back to you."

He tapped his fingers on the table.

"Not too much good news today," he commented.

None replied.

"Well, it *could* be worse," he added.

"How's that?" asked the Secretary of State.

"We could already have *found* her," said the President.

"How would that be worse?" half-chuckled the Vice-President.

"Because then... we'd have to figure out what to *do* with her," replied the American leader.

Sing Me An Angel-Song

"If y'all don' mind me aksin'... where we goin' now, Bob?" inquired the black woman, idly looking straight ahead down the road, seemingly transfixed on the white line.

She did not seem to be paying much attention to the Utah scenery on either side of the speeding vehicle, as the suburbs of Salt Lake City receded in the background.

"South," answered Billings. "I'm hoping on being able to take any one of the five or so turnoffs to Arizona that I usually take to get home."

"So... we goin' to Tucson, that right?" asked Claremont.

The salesman pursed his lips for a second, considering what to say.

Then he replied, "Um-humm... unless you've got a better idea. Look, I know it wasn't *exactly* what you had in mind, Whitney, but we have to think practically, at this point. Out here – in this car, I mean – yeah, it's true, we have a bit of food, some money, mobility, all that, but you've already seen how things can get, well, *unpredictable* –"

"No shit," grunted the woman.

"You got *that* right, sister," acknowledged Billings. "Now, I don't want you all to expect the Taj Mahal when we get back there, but –"

"Excuse me, Bob," interrupted the 'Sari'-girl, "What is a... 'Taj Mahal'? Is that a really big imported tee-vee or a car or something, uhh, 'high-class'? It does not sound like an English word."

"For God's sake, Sari, where did *you* come from – never mind, don't answer that question," retorted the salesman, as he shot a knowing glance toward the black woman.

Worriedly, he noticed, in so doing, that Claremont's two children were sharing the same look.

"No, it's not a television," explained Billings. "It's a big palace in... in... India, Pakistan, somewhere like that."

"Anyway, what I was trying to point out," he continued, "Is that I've got a nice little shack back home... not a mansion, so I don't want to raise false expectations, but it's more than big enough to give everybody in this car their own bed to sleep in. Four-person Jacuzzi tub, home theater system, swimming-pool out the back – of course I ran over my water allotment last year so I couldn't quite fill it to start the season this year – ol' Bob likes to live *comfortably*."

"Gonna chill some good in yo' crib, Mister Billins'!" chirped Curtis, enthusiastically, a gesture that won the boy a warm smile from the fallen-girl.

"And more to the point," elaborated the salesman, "Back in Tucson, I have friends, connections, all my papers... it's home base, as it were. When we get back there we can all take a breather, make some phone-calls, see to our financial affairs, wait for things to settle down... after that, Whitney, you and the kids can decide how to get back to wherever you want to get back to. I mean, out *here*, I don't even know if the interstate buses are running. Down *there*, at least I know where the terminal is. That sound good to everybody?"

"It sounds good to me, Bob," the 'Sari'-girl cheerily agreed. "Ever since I first heard you talk about this 'Tucson', I wanted to see it. You told me that it is warm down there, right? That *definitely* sounds pleasant. I have some... bad memories of being cold, lately."

"I guess we's goin' too, as if the kids an' ah gots a *choice*," grumbled Claremont.

Billings shrugged, noncommittally.

"Well," muttered the African-American woman, "Ah s'pose we can leastaways call mah homies in De-troit an' L.A. when we gets there, see what theys up to. Ah just hope we got somewhere to *go*. Y'all know, when we was back at that library, Curtis hook me up on Neo-Net an' ah try to get some news... most of De-troit, mah old 'hood anyway, it locked down by the Man, ain't *nobody* gettin' in or out, an' there ain't no news at all 'bout anywhere in California south of mid-state, all y'all get is some stuff 'bout 'under control of Federal Authorities' an' a sign sayin' 'no goin' there 'till further notice'. Cain't even see them Neo sites 'bout movie-stars. First time *that* ever happen, that ah can remember."

The SUV came up to an intersection and Billings swung it to the left, scarcely bothering to pay attention to the "Stop" sign at the side of the road, nor to the nondescript car a half-kilometer behind them, which also took the same turn-off.

"Side road," explained the salesman. "Interstate turns off south-west... it'd be out of our way at the best of times, and these ain't that. Besides... I got a question for all of you."

"What *that*, Mister Billings?" asked Melissa.

"Well, any of you seen the Grand Canyon yet?" inquired the salesman, insouciantly.

"We goin' to the *Grand Canyon*?" exclaimed the Claremont boy. "Yo mama, Mister Billings, he *bad*!" he added excitedly. "We ain't *never* seen that!"

"The... 'Grand', Canyon," mused the 'Sari'-girl. "I read about that in the, the, 'atlas', yes, that is the book. It is a big ditch in the ground, right?"

"Much more than *that*," smiled Billings. "One of the Seven Wonders of the Natural World, or some such thing. Many miles long, and a mile or so deep, too. Quite spectacular, really – I never get tired of going there, even though I've been dozens of times, it's more or less on the route north from Tucson. There's a little town on the Utah-Arizona border we can stop in to top up the tank, bed down for the night and get some supplies for the last leg of our little motor tour... then we'll take Route 89 south. We get to see the Canyon either way, but if you want the whole show it's a bit of a detour. Then again, I guess we aren't really in that much of a hurry, are we?"

"No we ain't!" chimed the Claremont children, in unison.

"Uhh, Bob," asked Claremont cautiously, "Ah don' want to be the bad guy here, but how much money it cost to get in there?"

"Don't worry about *that*, Whitney," assured the salesman. "They got a special rate, as long as you're all in one car, no more than fifty bucks – or was it a hundred, don't remember exactly – but what the H, oh, sorry, I forgot I'm a minister now. Well, 'Hail Mary' or whatever it is. Anyway, it's my treat. I'm fine now that I got to raid the banking-machine. Funny, you know, near the end of the comet thing, I had all this money saved up – a few months before I was planning on going somewhere nice, maybe to Hawaii, then nasty old 'Lucifer' showed up –"

"Ohhh..." moaned the 'Sari'-girl, as if sustaining a body blow.

"You okay, Sari?" asked Tommy, worriedly.

Wiping a trace of sweat from her brow, the newcomer said to the boy, "Yes... I am oh-kay, Tommy dear. I just do not like that name, 'Loo-see-fer'. I do not really know why. It just reminds me of... danger, pain, something overwhelming. Ah, another of my 'bad dreams', I suppose."

"Well, they tell us in church that the name of the Devil," commented Melissa. "So ah'm not s'prised that y'all scared of it. The Devil, he *nasty*."

The Indian-boy reached over and squeezed the fallen-girl's hand.

She smiled appreciatively, as Billings and Claremont exchanged glances in the front seats.

"So," continued the salesman, "I was going to just give it away, the money that is, on the street before I left for the last road trip north, but the truth was, nobody was really that interested... I bet it'll be a cold day in... *heck*, before we see *that* again. I'll have to get back to work eventually when I get back home, of course, but I'm not worrying about it now. So don't you either."

"Thanks, Bob," replied Claremont, in a monotone that could have been from gratitude, or from envy, or from both of the two.

"People around here, that is, in this 'Yoo-Nighted States', sure *do* seem to be very concerned with money," observed the 'Sari'-girl. "Almost everywhere I have gone, and that is a lot of places, there has been money... but it is almost like it is a religion in its own right, here."

"Y'all got *that* right, girl," grunted the black woman, with a laugh.

"Do you remember that tee-vee advertisement back at the motel, that had that preaching-minister-man, 'Reverend Dime' – I guess he was kind of like what you are pretending to be, Bob – where he said, 'if you come to my church every Sunday, God will make you rich'?" elaborated the 'Sari'-girl.

"Then," she went on, "Just before the real tee-vee show returned, the last thing that I remember seeing was this 'Reverend Dime' lifting his hands, and many little slips of green paper money came showering down on him as he smiled right at me. I could not tell whether he wanted people to be worshiping *him*, or this 'God' that he claims to talk to, or the little pieces of green paper."

"Probably the latter," remarked Billings.

"Money is important," said the fallen-girl, "But it is just one way of obtaining or giving the things that you need to live... honestly, I do not understand why people here are so concerned if a can of 'so-da pop' costs two dollars, or two dollars and ten cents. In the long-run, I would not worry about the ten cents... I would just want to remember the sweet taste of the drink, on my lips."

"Easy for y'all to say," countered Claremont, "If y'all don' have to pay for feedin' a family an' keepin' a roof over they haids."

"Yes, you have a point about that," replied the 'Sari'-girl. "It has been a very... *long* time, since I have had to watch over children. I am used to looking out only for myself, I guess. It is honorable and dutiful of you to keep watch over Curtis and Melissa until they are grown enough to, how do you say, 'leave the nest'."

"Yeah, but it a *lot* of work," mentioned the black woman.

"It must be a nice feeling to have children, to *belong*, Whitney," continued the newcomer, "To have little ones who will love you until the end of your days..."

Her voice trailed off, and, wistful-eyed, she looked away into the wilderness, trying to avoid any of the others seeing her face.

"Aww, don' be so sad, Miz Sari," consoled Tommy. "Curtis, Melissa, and me, *we* all love you, too, for getting us all out of that jail up there. For taking a big chance on account of us, and you hardly *knew* us. Just 'cause you're not really our Momma doesn't mean that we can't love you, does it?"

The 'Sari'-girl wheeled in her seat, seemingly unencumbered by the seat belt and shoulder restraints, and suddenly hugged the Indian-boy, as if he were her own.

"No, it most certainly does *not*, dear Tommy," she breathed. "And I will *gladly* take all the love that you can give me, though you owe me nothing for having freed you. And... may I ask a really big favor of you?"

"Sure... what?" he inquired.

"Well," she started, uncertainly, "You see... uhh... it is like *this*... the thing is, Whitney has Curtis and Melissa to look after... so I thought that maybe..."

"Maybe *what*, Miss Sari?" Tommy answered, innocently.

The fallen-girl loosened her grip slightly and went on, looking down and forcing out the words, "It is kind of funny, really... when I think of all the very great challenges that I have faced, but I find it very difficult to ask this... what I wanted to say, is, until we return you to your real parents, Tommy... do you think that *I* could be the one who looks after you? Who takes care of you, makes you brush your teeth at night, who... 'tucks you in' to bed? Like Whitney does for Melissa and Curtis, you know?"

"Sure, I'd like that – I've really been missing Mom and Dad since everything happened," agreed the smiling boy, nestling his head against the 'Sari'-girl's shoulder, to her visible relief.

A contented smile was on her face, but instantly, Billings and Claremont shot a concerned stare back and forth.

"Uhh... Bob... y'all think that a good idea?" Claremont stammered. "Ah means... *considerin'*... what ah means is, there Sari girl, no offense but y'all got any *'sperience*, in raisin' kids? They can be quite a handful... like, y'all can't just be goin' off by yourself leavin' them somewhere, y'all gots to be watchin' over 'em all the time..."

Nervously, Billings cleared his throat.

"Uhh, well," he offered, trying to think as he spoke, "I don't want to burst your bubble there, Sari, but I think we all have to be *practical* about this... I mean, don't you think you're a little *young* to be taking on this kind of responsibility?"

Under arched brows, the fallen-girl shot the man a resentful-looking glance.

"I *told* you before, Bob, I am... *older* than I look," she argued. "And I have had *plenty* of experience in looking after children, teaching them, protecting them, caring for them. I have just as much, or as little, money as Whitney has, and besides, she has two of her own to look after – does it make sense for her to have all the responsibility, and me to have none?"

"But –" the salesman tried to interrupt, only to be one-upped by the 'Sari'-girl's continuing rant.

"And did I not hear you say," she pressed, "That you did not *want* to have any, yourself? Children, I mean. What is it about me that makes you and Whitney so hesitant to allow this? If Tommy wants to let me be his mother for a while, and I want to do that, why do we need someone else's permission? All I want to do is to protect him, give him a kiss 'good-night. How challenging can *that* be, compared to, say, freeing you all from a heavily-guarded prison-camp?"

Again, the two in the front seats regarded each other with a faint air of desperation.

Claremont leaned over and whispered to Billings, "Bob, what we 'sposed to say now? Y'all *know* why that a bad idea, if th' Man catch up with us and find out 'bout *her* – least he be safe wid me –"

"Did I mention that I have pretty good hearing?" observed the 'Sari'-girl, through half-clenched teeth.

"Oops," muttered the salesman.

"You have two already, Whitney," complained the newcomer. "I do not understand why I cannot look after just *one*, and he was not yours in the first place –"

"No, it ain't nothin' like *that*, girl, y'all *gots* to believe me, it just that... shit, ah don' *know*," pleaded Claremont. "It just that y'all bein' –"

"She bein' *what*, Momma?" inquired Melissa. "Besides, y'all knows, they lots of girls back in th' 'hood her age or younger, an' *they* got kids. Some got three or four. Y'all 'member Bessie-Anne, she had two, an' she only one year older'n me."

"Nothin', sweetheart," replied Claremont, avoiding everyone's stare.

"She... *nothin'*. Ain't no problem, no problem at all," the black woman said, desolately.

Billings, having pondered silently for a few seconds, then stated, "From where I sit, I just don't think it's a good idea – I *know* you're lonely, we all go through that sometimes, but you have to be careful not to take on responsibilities that might be too much for you to handle. Personally I think that Tommy would be better off having Whitney look after him, but if your mind is really *set* on doing this, you're right, neither Whitney nor I is in a position to – ahem – *force* you not to do it, so I guess we'll have to give it a try."

Sullenly, the 'Sari'-girl responded, "I think the phrase that one uses is, 'Gee, thanks for the vote of confidence', Bob."

The salesman shot a glance over his shoulder and tried to smile.

"*Look*, everyone," he said, "Let's not make a mountain out of a mole-hill here. All we're really talking about is, I don't know, make sure the little twirp brushes his teeth, read him a bedtime story, that kind of thing – I didn't hear anything about adoption papers or running off to Brazil with him, did you?

"Bra-zil... that is in the big continent south of here, is it not?" commented the fallen-girl.

Billings sighed.

Then he suggested, "So let's all chill out here. There's no harm done in letting 'Sari' fuss over the kid until we get to Tucson, then we relax a bit, re-assess the situation – not just *this* one, but what we're all doing, we've been on the go, non-stop, since back at the border-camp – then we make the best decisions that we can. Does that work for everyone?"

"Ah guess so," unenthusiastically muttered Claremont.

The fallen-girl said nothing, contenting herself with just holding the Indian-boy's head to hers, the both of them smiling happily.

"But y'all *knows*," commented Curtis, in his usual mischievous small-boy voice, "That if y'all gonna be Tommy's momma, that make Mister Billings he daddy."

"Hey, not so *fast*, kid, we're just –" complained the salesman. "I mean, we're not even *married* –"

The 'Sari'-girl giggled.

"Curtis has a point," she remarked. "And besides, it is only for a short while, until Tommy finds his, uhh, *real* parents. Come *on*, Bob, what could be the harm? I mean, you are *already* pretending to be a temple-priest, when by your own words, you are indifferent to most of what this 'Christian' religion stands for. You might as well pretend to be a *father*, too. Who knows, you might even learn to like it."

"Fat chance of *that*," countered Billings. "I won't even admit to having been a kid, myself. If Tommy knew what kind of a father I'm likely to be, I'd give you good odds that he'd kibosh the idea himself."

Tommy stuck his tongue out at the man and to the boy's delight, he saw the 'Sari'-girl do the same.

Claremont laughed so hard that she almost fell out of the passenger seat.

"Ah think they *gots* y'all, Bob," smirked the black woman.

"Okay, okay, I'll *think* about it," pleaded an exasperated Billings.

Trying to think of something to change the subject, he mentioned, "Say, does anybody know any songs that we could sing to pass the time, while we're cruising along here?"

"Why don't y'all just turn on the radio, Mister Billings?" asked Melissa.

"I did, just before we got going today," he explained. "Satellite-stations are still out and all I'm getting from the FM-bands are emergency bulletins, a bit of local news... nothing nationally except something about 'a statement from the Government on the economy', which is funny considering that as far as I could tell back at the library, NeoNet's still got news from overseas, I didn't bother to read it, of course. And anyway, I doubt that you guys would like my own tastes in music too much. Unless you like punk rock, that is."

"If y'all don' mind," commented Claremont, dryly, "Ah think ah'd rather hear the kids."

Billings nodded in agreement.

"So," he offered, "Who here knows a song that we can all sing? Something nice and non-controversial, please."

"How 'bout 'Kumbaya', Mister Billins?" proposed the teenager.

"What's a 'Kumbaya'?" inquired the 'Sari'-girl. "That is another word that doesn't sound like Eng-lish, to me."

"It isn't," replied Billings. "Or at least I don't *think* it is."

"It mean, 'come an' be with me, Lord'," noted Claremont. "That what my Momma say, when we used to sing it back 'n the hood. In church, that is."

"Ah... a prayer. A hymn to the Powers Above, to the Light?" asked the newcomer. "To your... 'God'?"

Claremont nodded.

"Okay, since you seem to know it," replied Billings, "Why don't you start?"

"Well, ah *couldn't*," protested the black woman. "Ah mean... ah ain't no good at singin'..."

"Yes y'all is, Momma," countered Curtis. "Y'all sing me to sleep when ah's just a kid, ah *'member* that song. When ah was just a *little* kid, if y'all know what ah mean."

"And ah learn it in the choir back in the 'hood, Momma... y'all 'member that," added Melissa.

"I know it too," said Tommy. "We used to sing it by the campfire, when the revival folk would show up on the reserve. Come *on*, Miz Claremont! I'll sing along with you."

With a pained, uncertain look, Claremont said, "Okay, if y'all *insist*... but no laughin', y'all hear? Been a long time since ah done any singin'."

"We *promise*, Momma," disingenuously giggled Curtis.

Slowly, the woman began to sing, in a low, throaty, reverent tone, an amateurishly sincere, simple and faithful African-American voice that would have instantly disarmed the judgment of the most cynical critic.

Kumbaya, my Lord, kumbaya
Kumbaya, my Lord, kumbaya
Kumbaya, my Lord, kumbaya
O Lord, kumbaya

The car's inhabitants, save for Claremont's steady voice, picking up expressiveness and impact with each word, all fell into a hushed silence.

Even the road noise seemed somehow to recede into the background.

Someone's laughing, Lord, kumbaya
Someone's laughing, Lord, kumbaya
Someone's laughing, Lord, kumbaya
O Lord, kumbaya

After a second or two, an awed Curtis managed to regain enough of his composure to whisper to his sister.

"Damn, Melissa, ah ain't *never* heard Momma sing like *that* before... it like her words goin' right inside me. Right *here*."

He pointed to his heart.

The shocked teenager numbly nodded in agreement.

"Whitney... *wow*," breathed Billings, hoping that none could see him wipe the traces of a tear. "I never *imagined*... well, kids, let's try to sing along. Although it's a hard act to follow. One... two... three..."

Again, Claremont began to sing, with her words hanging in the air like sparkling motes of hoarfrost shaken loose by a fresh winter wind, and one by one, the voices of the children – Melissa first, followed by Curtis, then Tommy – joined in, each of them adding brush-marks of ethereal color to the hymn.

Someone's crying, Lord, kumbaya
Someone's crying, Lord, kumbaya
Someone's crying, Lord, kumbaya
O Lord, kumbaya

The Indian-boy's pleading glance found the eyes of the 'Sari'-girl, and *another* voice now sounded from the rear seat.

It was strong, noble and crystal-clear, yet at the same time kind, gentle and carefully controlled, as if not to overwhelm Claremont; it was also beautifully, hypnotically, *impossibly* multi-tonal, singing perfect harmony with the black woman's own unexpectedly confident, inspired voice.

From nowhere, all heard the sound of *what?* an orchestra? playing along, as a kaleidoscope of feelings – relief, happiness, belonging, contentment and, not least of all – amazement, washed over the salesman, who struggled once again to keep the SUV on the highway.

Someone's praying, Lord, kumbaya
Someone's praying, Lord, kumbaya
Someone's praying, Lord, kumbaya
O Lord, kumbaya
Someone's singing, Lord, kumbaya
Someone's singing, Lord, kumbaya
Someone's singing, Lord, kumbaya
O Lord, kumbaya
Kumbaya, my Lord, kumbaya
Kumbaya, my Lord, kumbaya
Kumbaya, my Lord, kumbaya
O Lord, kumbaya.

Sweating, Billings abruptly pulled the vehicle to a stop on the side of the road.

"That was... *beautiful*, folks," he gasped. "But I need to catch a little fresh air, if you don't mind. Just five minutes' worth, if you don't mind... okay?"

"Uhh, no problem, Bob," agreed Claremont, herself sounding emotionally exhausted. "Ah guess we all could use to stretch our legs, too."

"Y'all gots a *really* pretty voice, Miz Sari," said Melissa. "As nice as ah *ever* did hear."

"So does your mother," offered the 'Sari'-girl.

A strange, saturnine smile, like one might receive from a visiting monarch or head of state, was on the newcomer's face.

"But how y'all sing that song right wid us?" demanded Curtis. "Ah means, y'all *said* y'all didn' know what a 'Kumbaya' was."

"I do not know," explained the 'Sari'-girl. "The words just *came* to me when I looked at Whitney. Sometimes I just *know* what to say."

"Miz Sari," continued Melissa, "Do y'all know any songs? Ah mean, from home, from wherever y'all from, that is."

The fallen-girl looked down at the ground for a second, then again raised up her head.

"That is an interesting question," she stated. "Because since we decided to sing that 'Kumbaya'-song – and a very nice one it is, to be sure, I will do my best to remember it, I promise you that – I have also been trying to recall the songs of my own childhood, or, at least, the melodies from 'back home', as you call it. But..."

Her voice trailed off in uncertainty.

"But what, girl?" asked Claremont. "Y'all can't remember *nothin'*, that what y'all tryin' to say?"

"No, not that," answered the newcomer. "It is just that... well, you see, they are in another language, one that I do not think that any of you would understand."

"That don' matter none, Miz Sari," interjected Curtis. "Y'all gots such a nice voice, it be 'nuff just to *hear* it, even if we don' really get what it mean."

"Why don't you try to translate it?" suggested Billings.

The 'Sari'-girl shot him back a glance.

"I guess I could *try*, Bob," she explained. "But doing this is difficult, more so than I think you can appreciate without knowing my – how do you call it, ah, yes – 'mother tongue'. It is not just that the words are different, but the way how you put together a sentence or how you express a thought, these are not at all like the way how you do it in 'Eng-lish' –"

"How can there be any other way, Miz Sari?" inquired the teenager.

"Well, for example in *Makailkh*, which is my language, one can tell exactly when something happened, or is going to happen, by the tone in which one says the words which describe the event, and if one says the words backwards, that means –"

Claremont laughed.

"Laws, girl," she guffawed, "We ain't aksin' y'all for a language-lesson in some crazy-ass thang from, well..."

She stopped herself.

"Curtis has a point there, bless his pointy little head," noted Billings, with a sound of exasperation. "Who *cares* what it means."

"Shore, sing us a song!" demanded Melissa.

"Uhh... oh-kay," allowed the 'Sari'-girl. "As long as you understand, it will not be *nearly* as good as it would be, in my own way of speaking. Like a painting done in bright colors, that you only see in the twilight, when all is gray. I hope that I can find the words in your language."

She walked right past them, facing out into the wilderness, as if addressing the song to the denizens of the Southwest desert.

The fallen-girl closed her eyes, concentrating, then opened them again, showing them resplendent in a startling, aquamarine green-blue.

As a burst of adrenaline, or something alike, raced through the veins of those nearby, the newcomer perceived a small figure, right next to her.

"Miz Sari," requested Tommy, "Can I stand beside you, as you sing, please?"

She smiled warmly, nodded and offered the boy her right hand, which he squeezed gratefully, looking up at her as does a child reunited with its mother.

Now, her face, looking as if illuminated from below, wore a strange, distant visage, like she had been suddenly transported to another place, another time.

"Hmmm... hmmmm... hmmm..."

The fallen-girl's voice began to sound at the fringes of their consciousness, but rapidly achieved a powerful, yet restrained, crescendo; it echoed out into the night, reflecting from the rocks and cacti, bathing them in a dignified, beautiful cadence, akin to but not the same as what the rest had heard just a few minutes ago in Billings' car.

She sang a tune gentle and melodious, like a folk-song but somehow reverberating with sounds akin to flutes, violins and a chorus, as some kind of ethereal accompaniment.

Where go you now, my one lost love
Do you fly by dim light of the Blue Sun?
Where go you now, my long-lost love
Do you lie in the Halls of the Dark-Shadowed One?
Long have I tread the path wild and well-paved
Beneath forest, mountain and marble-walled tower
Long living for the sweetest of dawns
When you and I shall meet again... my love.

As the hint of a tear appeared in one eye, her voice now trembled with passion, and the desert air seemed to respond, itself shimmering with emotion. Tiny wisps of multi-colored light now appeared above them, falling Earthward like improbable, meteor-like streaks of fire.

They all would have gasped at the majesty of it, but none could dare.

So this *is what it sounds like to hear an angel sing,* reflected Billings. *A thousand choirs and a thousand orchestras, couldn't do this justice – but where in God's name are those violins coming from –*

The 'Sari'-girl continued,

Long have I stepped the sky with wing-ed foot
Long have I worn face upon strange face, anew
Long have I looked deep to ebon night sky
Long have I treasured those long-gone days
Long have you been my fondest of dreams.
I will search you forever, my love, brave of old
I will go on to world known to none still
I will seek, though long age and age pass, on
Great Spirit, I pray thee guide my path
'Till I lie in my love's warm arms once again.
Where go you now my one lost love
Do you fly by dim light of the Blue Sun?
Where go you now, my long-lost love
Do you lie in the Halls of the Dark-Shadowed One?

Her voice slowly trailed off, as did the strange, musical background sounds.

For a few long seconds, the fallen-girl continued to stare out into the desert night, as if deep in contemplation.

"Wow, oh *wow*," breathed Tommy. "I saw it, Miz Sari, I *saw* it. I saw the dream. As if you and I were –"

"Sari?" started the salesman, finally able to let out his breath.

The newcomer turned to face the others, her visage wearing a soft, sad look. "Yes?" she replied.

"That was... very *nice*," commented Claremont. "Mah daughter shore right 'bout y'all bein' able to sing, ah's honored to be able to put mah poor old voice along with yours... but y'all seemed a bit far *away* there for a minute, girl. Somethin' botherin' you?"

The 'Sari'-girl pursed her lips.

She replied, "Yes, Whitney, you are right about that – but nothing is bothering me. It is just that singing that song brought back memories from long ago. Do not ask me from *where*, or *when*, but they are precious memories, of that much I am sure."

For yet another time, the salesman and the black woman shared a knowing glance.

"Ah... this is a burden that I will just have to learn to bear, I suppose," offered the newcomer. "It must be nice being one of you, that is, being able to remember who you *are*, where you come from and so on. For me, it is like looking into a mirror covered in dust; I can see the outline, but not the detail..."

"Y'all sound more than just 'nice', Miz Sari," remarked Curtis. "Don' mean to 'dis Momma, but that just the best singin' ah *ever* hear. It sound like y'all got a whole choir singin' behind you. How y'all *do* that?"

"I do not know," she softly replied. "I only know that it comes from within me."

"Whew," observed Billings. "I'll have to agree with Curtis again, that was quite *some* performance. You know, when we get back to Tucson, I may just match you up with a couple of talent-scouts that I know from around town – if we can get that singing on a recording, you might have one hell – oops, one *heck* – of a career ahead of you –"

"It would be nice to try," answered the fallen-girl, "But something tells me that it probably would not be preserved properly, not all of it, at least, on these, how do you say, 'em-pee-five' boxes that you use to store music inside of. Some of it is not sound, exactly – it is inside your head. I suppose that we would have to try it and see. Oh, and by the way, what is a 'talent-scout'?"

"Somebody who can get you into the music business," explained the salesman. "For a small fee, of course."

"Oh, of *course*," she replied, with an amused smile. "For a small fee. That is how you do *everything* here, is it not?"

"Well, you're getting a free car ride," noted Billings. "*That's* something, right?"

"*Sure* it is, Bob," replied the fallen girl, affectionately. She strode towards him, kissing him quickly on the cheek.

"Thanks. I owe you very much, my love," she added.

Billings blushed, wearing a sheepish, but smug, grin.

"Momma," interjected Melissa, "Ah got kinda, well, tired out listenin' to that, like as if ah watchin' a movie for awhile, an' ah gots to *go*, now..."

"That's okay, child," said Claremont. "See them rocks back there? Y'all go there, but no further, y'all hear?"

"Yes'm," replied the Claremont girl, heading slowly out into the desert.

"Come on!" called Curtis. "Momma, we goin' out there too, okay?"

"No, ah don' think –" warned the black woman.

"Do not worry about it, Whitney," countered the 'Sari'-girl. "I will go out there and look after them. The fresh air will do me some good, too, I think. Just call to me if we have to rapidly get back to the car, oh-kay?"

"Yeah, ah guess," muttered Claremont.

The 'Sari'-girl turned, and shot a long glance down the highway, following it all the way to the only visible bend, miles away along the route in which they had just come.

"What is it?" inquired Billings.

"Uhh... nothing, really," she replied. "It is just that an idea came into my head that we are being *followed*. I think that there is a car down there, somewhere."

The salesman looked hard in the same direction.

"I don't see anything," he argued. "Road's clear for five miles or more."

"Ah, you are probably right, Bob," said the 'Sari'-girl. "I sometimes have these *feelings*, you see. As if my mind is telling me, 'something is not right, here'. It is probably nothing."

"Well, 'better safe than sorry'," allowed Billings, sympathetically. "Especially in times like *these*. We'll keep this little stop to five minutes more, or so."

"Shore nuff," added Claremont.

"Let's go!" shouted Tommy. "I'll race you guys!"

"Not too far off the road, kids, okay?" cautioned the salesman, as the three children, followed obligingly by the 'Sari'-girl, rapidly disembarked on the off-highway side of the vehicle and began a foot-race in the direction of a nearby boulder.

The two left in the car heard the newcomer warn, "Careful, Tommy – I have heard that there are serpents, out here, and large insects, as well. Some have a venomous bite... watch where you step."

"Already playin' 'mommy'," wryly commented Claremont.

Billings looked at the black woman and added, "And Whitney, I think I said it before, but I had never *imagined* – I mean, you sounded better than Mahalia Jackson there. Between you and our friend in the back seat, my *God* – sorry for the cuss there Old Boy – if you made it a duet, you two could clean up the hit parades. *Where* did you learn to sing like that? You're *terrific!*"

Claremont shot the man a long, knowing glance, hoping to shield the ones outside from seeing.

"That just *it*, Mister Sales Man, that just it," she quietly explained. "Minute ah started singin', 'spectin' for it to be just mah plain old voice, things come in mah head – ah sees Momma, an' Grand-Mere Rubie, an' the Lawd Himself, all talkin' to me, sayin' 'come on, Whitney, just *do* it' – and then it just come out, like ah found some part of me that ah always had but didn' know 'bout."

Billings nodded.

The black woman continued, "Y'all knows 'bout gettin' scared of singin' as hard as y'all wants to, on account of bein' 'fraid of makin' a fool of youself? But this time, ah *weren't* scared, not at all, ah feels like ah'm doin' the Lawd's work, an' whatever come, that be okay. Ah bein' *perfectly* at ease. If *that* make any sense. Point is, ah never *did* learn to sing like *that*, before. That is, not until now. Not 'till –"

Billings half-slumped back in his seat.

He shook his head.

"Ah. I *see*," he observed. "Just like me, and after doing... with *her*... well, you know."

Claremont stared off long into the wilderness.

"Ah gots to admit, Bob," she offered, "Ah thought y'all was talkin' *shit* when y'all said that stuff 'bout feelin' hundred and ten per cent better than before after screwin' wid her, back there... but now ah ain't so sure. She havin' an *effect* on us, we both knows that. Ah'm *worried*, Bob. Not just for me, but for th' kids. Who *know* what she doin' to them?"

"I won't deny that," mused the salesman. "Just being *around* her is changing us, at least, it's definitely changing you and me. As for the kids, well, I haven't seen anything yet, but I'll take your point that it's a real possibility. But, for God's sake, Whitney, it's a *positive* change – I mean, things could be far worse, she could have given us some kind of Martian flu or crap like that."

"Well maybe y'all gots it an' y'all just don' know it... *yet*," said the woman, warily.

"Yeah, but I could turn the question right around," argued Billings. "Would you deny your children the ability to interact with her? It's likely going to be by far the most important thing that will ever have happened to them. Maybe they'll end up doing better in school... I don't know. It's all guesswork, but short of simply leaving her by the side of the road, what are we supposed to *do* about it?"

"Ah don' know, Mister Sales Man... ah don' *know*," wearily replied Claremont. "'Cept to say that it feel *wicked* weird, that's all."

"But a *nice* kind of weird," noted the salesman.

Claremont again looked to the far horizon.

After a second or two, she commented, "Ah *do* know one thing, though. She *cain't* be the Devil, Bob. Ain't no *way*. Not after ah hear her sing that song wid me, ah mean, and then that second one. In mah head, somehow ah *knowed* she believe in the same things that ah do. Ah could *feel* it, when we was singin' together. Same as before, ah don' know how to 'splain it, 'cept ah'm *certain* of it. She on *our* side, Bob. Side of the Lord Almighty, may He strike me *daid* if that ain't true."

They waited for a second or two, but no thunderbolts from above, troubled either the salesman or the black woman.

Billings let out a rueful chuckle.

"Good to know that you've concluded that, too, Whitney," he said. "Although me being on the side of the Lord – well, I suppose I *do* play a preacher-man on TV, as the saying goes. And you don't have to explain – I know what you're talking about. I would have mentioned it myself, but I didn't think that *you'd* understand."

They both sat in silence for a few seconds, then got up and disembarked, leaning on the car and watching the children.

"Race you back to the car!" they heard one of the children shout.

A "thump" sounded on the off-highway side of the SUV, made by Melissa, whose longer legs had outpaced the two junior children.

"Okay," announced the salesman, "Everybody back into the bus. Buckle up. Oh, and by the way, I hope you took the opportunity, if you had to –"

"Yeah, an' Curtis tried to peek, when ah went behind the bush," grumbled the Claremont girl.

"No, it was Tommy," answered back the Claremont boy. "Ah was tryin' to drag him back."

"Tom-mee?" intoned the 'Sari'-girl, doing her best imitation of Whitney Claremont's cautioning voice, as she stared intently at her new charge.

"Sorry, Miss Sari," sheepishly replied the Indian-boy.

"Alright, then," she allowed, "But *please* try to respect Melissa's privacy, next time. Oh-kay?"

"Okay," obligingly returned Tommy.

Billings looked behind him, and saw that the fallen-girl was the only one not yet in her seat; instead, she had one foot braced inside the SUV with the other on the ground outside, as if ready to leap inside.

"Well?" he demanded. "You coming, or not?"

The newcomer's saturnine half-smile transfixed both the salesman and the black woman next to him, as she effortlessly propelled herself into the vehicle.

"You are changing *me*, too, you know," she remarked.

A Lead For Ms. Chu

"You gettin' anything on the digital-bands?" asked the big, African-American man, as he awkwardly adjusted and re-adjusted his considerable bulk within a driver's seat that clearly had never been designed for someone of his size.

"Damn, they make these things for... I don't *know* who," he complained. "Haven't found a car I liked since they ordered the last of them reconditioned '2020s Impalas off the road. You know, the *gas* thing. After Pakistan and Iraq went down the tubes, I mean."

"On the radio – yeah... like music, country. Or maybe a ball-game?" asked the twenty-something agent in the back seat.

"And I know what you mean... sorta," he added. "My dad had an '2006 Malibu. Huge honkin' thing, but it could *move*. Ah, *those* were the days."

"You ever get *tired* of them ball-games?" inquired Boatman.

"No," replied the other man, with a smug grin.

"Not too much on the digital, I'm afraid," commented Chu, unplugging a headphone jack from a port on the vehicle's dashboard. "Funny how it keeps cutting in and out... I thought when they went all the way over to those channels it was supposed to fix that kind of thing."

"Nothin' *else* in this country works the way it should," grunted the black agent. "Why should those things be any different?"

The FBI team-leader nodded and went on, "Well, anyway, there isn't a lot thats going to help us get this over with and out of here. News-channels, at least when they were on, keep talking about some kind of financial crisis, interviews going on with 'the investment-experts' about how to avoid losing your money or some stupid thing like that –"

"I'd be interested, if I had any in the first place," mumbled the third agent. "But I work for the Bureau... remember?"

Chu arched an eyebrow and addressed Boatman.

"Funny you mention Pakistan, Otis," she remarked, "There was something on about 'we're *sure* that we have all the nukes accounted for', which of course means that they *don't,* and the rest of the news from there is depressing. They said something about the 'Muslim League is now in complete control of most of the country' – what a *mess.* Europeans, Russians, Chinese, *everybody's* bitching about this 'Sword of Freedom' thing that the President announced a while ago, they're threatening 'repercussions' if we don't let them see it, the report said something about 'a technology and investment embargo' against the United States if we don't –"

"So things is gettin' about back to normal," said the black man.

"Yeah, you got *that* right, Mr. Boatman," returned Chu, with a wry smile.

"Oh, yeah, and remember that space-station?" she noted.

"Which one?" asked the agent in the back seat, his frame stretched across two seats. It was impossible to tell if his eyes were open or shut, since his too-cool sunglasses encased them in typical fashion.

"Weren't there more than one of them? Or is there only one left now?"

"Don't know," replied the Asian-American team-leader. "All I got was something about a 'last-minute rescue-mission' or something like that. Apparently they had written all those poor guys on this... uhh... 'ISS2' off, already, but now there's hope for 'em – I didn't hear all of it, just got the last couple minutes of the announcement. Seems that the Feds and NASA are pulling out all the stops, 'strategic objectives to preserve our outposts in space', you know, standard baffle-gab..."

She glanced briefly at the LCD display in the front seat's special box, looked away briefly and then did a double-take.

"*Wait* a sec, Otis," she exclaimed. "Something coming through on the secure link."

Clumsily, Chu fumbled for the headphones, seized them, did some more fumbling to un-entangle a cord and then plugged its opposite end into a jack on the secret box.

She pressed a button and stared off into space, listening intently.

"Wow... now *that's* interesting," she breathed.

"What?" asked the third agent, now leaning forward.

Boatman stared sideways, checking the road in front of the vehicle every second or so.

"Just a second, guys, I want to listen to this again – I gotta be *sure,*" cautioned Chu.

"*Wow,*" she exclaimed. "I didn't think – I mean, that it was for real, but *now* –"

Again, she stared intently, a look of fascination, anticipation, something else, perhaps, on her face.

After twelve or thirteen seconds, she removed the headphones.

"Turn around, Otis," commanded the FBI team-leader, with an air of semi-repressed excitement.

"Okay, Agent Chu," responded the black man, as he did a precisely-practiced U-turn across the highway.

"So we're going south, now. Where to?"

"Not exactly sure," answered the woman, "But first stop is Salt Lake, one of the libraries there, specifically."

"Huh?" asked the man in the back seat, incredulously.

"What's the matter, not enough reading material around here? We planning to pick up a few paperbacks for the cottage?"

"Don't I *wish*," said Chu, steadily. "No, boys, we're going to have something a good deal more interesting to be looking at... DNA samples, specifically."

"Say *what*?" shot back Boatman.

A second later he added, "Hoo, *boy*. You mean –"

Chu nodded, looking at the other two.

"*Alien* DNA. Or so they tell me. They think we've got a good chance of finding it..."

"Holy *shit*," exclaimed the third agent. "You mean they *caught* her?"

"Nope, at least not yet," answered the woman. "But for the first time since the mountain that we've got a *real* lead, hard evidence, that is. HQ is telling us to get down to this library ASAP, so Otis, step on the gas, I don't care about 50 miles per hour anymore... we've *got* to get down there before CIA and the spooks show up themselves and lay claim to the find."

"You mean they don't know about it, yet?" incredulously inquired Boatman, as his big foot pressed down on the pedal, propelling the SUV forward faster and faster.

"I don't think so," explained Chu. "HQ didn't say specifically how we got keyed in to this thing, all the message said – you can listen for yourselves when we're done talking – is that 'this lead is based upon communications-traffic intercepted exclusively by the Bureau plus some on-line data mining of library check-in records, so it's not to be shared with any non-Bureau staff'... remember, we got a whole bunch of taps domestically, we *own* those, whatever the spooks over at NSA, CIA and the Secret Service, think."

"Sure, until they tap in to *our* taps," countered Boatman. "It's happened before, you know."

"Nothing I can do about that," philosophically offered the FBI team-leader, "But we've had this particular branch cordoned off by local law-enforcement using some cover-story about uncovering a synth drug distribution-ring in the reference section – if you can believe that – but it won't be long until the Agency and the rest of Red Rover gets wise to what's going on. So we have to get in there and get the evidence, *fast*. Brownie points for the Bureau... you know the rest."

"Don't I," chuckled the big black man, his eyes glued on the road ahead to stay on it at this breakneck speed. "You understand, don't you, Agent Chu, that we pull *this* off – even a little part of it – and we're on the inside track for movin' up fast, career-wise, I mean. Havin' this stuff would give the Bureau the upper hand in finding out where she's been. Might even put the Director in charge of the whole shootin' match. So *yes* ma'am, I *am* going to get us there as fast as this crate will fly, be of no doubt."

"Fukin' *ay!*" added the man in the back, with a huge grin. "Few steps up the ladder, hell, that's worth forty or fifty G's. I'll take that, thanks. And it sure as hell beats taking testimony from a bunch of nut-cases who keep chanting from the Bible to every question..."

"There's *more*," continued Chu. "HQ is saying that the alien may not be alone, that is, she may be traveling with one or more companions. We have a tentative profile on one of them from a remote interrogation that HQ did with some of the library staff – some guy named 'Billings', middle-aged, white, a bit too much on the waistline, thinning but still full head of dark brown or black hair."

"We know where he's from, where he's going? What he's driving? We get a Nat Real ID location fix on him? I mean, the car transponder. Aren't they all supposed to have 'em?" demanded the third agent.

"Not so far, Will," replied Chu, "Remember... even if we *do* narrow it down to say four or five suspects, he may have one of the old cards without the tracking chip, and anyway, apparently many of the RFID transponders are down – both the Real-Patriotic ID and the car-tracking ones – courtesy of our friend the comet, again. We may not get another fix on him until he uses his ID somewhere else... and remember that a lot of the authentication-terminals are still off-line."

"Swell," grumbled the younger man. "First damn time we really *need* them and the effin' satellites are all shot. This Billings guy could be *hundreds* of miles away by now. What if he lives in, say, Boston or something? The spooks will get him *long* before we do. Bye-bye promotion, bye-bye big old reward..."

"Yeah," agreed Chu. "We just have to hope that he's stopped somewhere – he was at this library yesterday afternoon, so part of the work order when we get there is to see if we can get a better description of him – I mean if he was at the Salt Lake library then maybe he's from Utah? Back at the Bureau they're running the name against all known citizens matching the profile... so far they don't have a positive match. There are *thousands* of men by that name, you know."

"I *don't* know," commented the black man, not taking his eyes off the highway. "If it were up to yours truly, I'd say it would be a better idea to spend as little time as possible at this here library, just get as much as we can about our friend Mr. Billings – specifically the plate on his car and his credit-card numbers – and go huntin'. I mean, the DNA's good, but it's just the tracks, not the bear. At the end of the day, tracks don't make a rug or a wall ornament... only the real thing does. Whoa!"

He swerved to dodge some debris.

"Yeah, I *hear* you, Otis," agreed the team-leader, "But the order to get all the goods that's there for the getting, came right down from – I don't know exactly *who*, but high up, might even be the Director's office. That's enough for me to want to do it right. And besides, how the hell can we make a one hundred per cent positive ID, without having a DNA match, anyway?"

"Uhh... how about the teeth, or the eyes?" offered Boatman. "Or if she just ups and flies away. That'd be good enough an ID for *me*."

"No *shit*," sarcastically confirmed Chu. "But, come *on*, guys, let's use our *brains*, here – why wouldn't she just have done that already? The impression I get from HQ is that she's trying to travel incognito, for some reason we can only guess at. Look, I'd like to corner her, too, don't get me wrong, but we *have* to follow procedures, here. Let's just get there, get it over with and report whatever we learn, as fast as possible. Best of both worlds, as it were."

"Best of both worlds," echoed the black man. "You got a way of puttin' things, Agent Chu," he said.

"I just wish we knew *what* worlds," complained the man in the back seat, as he again reclined, adjusting his sunglasses.

Many Things, I Can Teach You

"Well, wasn't *that* something?" asked Billings, already knowing the answer that he'd get from three googly-eyed children, as the SUV gathered speed down the highway, with one of the Wonders of the World receding in the distance.

"Sure was, Mister Billins!" exclaimed Curtis. "I ain't *never* seen nothin' that big before. Y'all could drop our whole 'hood in that big ditch, maybe all of Detroit, and there still be space for more."

"Cabin y'all got for me an' mah kids was good," acknowledged Claremont. "Y'all best be careful, Bob... we gettin' too used to all this-here high livin'. Might get down to *'spectin'* it, y'all know what ah mean?"

"Hey, I'm just glad that we're still 'livin', in the first place, you know?" observed the salesman, with a wry grin.

"I just wish we had had more time there," complained Melissa. "Like, to do things like go on them donkey-rides down the canyon, ah mean. Or them boatin'-expeditions, where y'all go down the river..."

"Next time, honey dear," answered the black woman. "Mister Billins already been nice to us, spendin' all that money, that is. We get back to the 'hood, ah start savin', we go back real soon. *Real* soon."

The Claremont children nodded obligingly, knowing that this was another promise that would likely never be honored, not that they would hold that against their mother.

After a few seconds of silence, the salesman again spoke up.

"Hey there, Sari," he mentioned, "You've been kind of quiet, lately, ever since... well, since that little incident at the cliff. Come *on*, girl... it's nothing to get your shirt in a knot about. We were just watching out for you, that's all. Nobody's upset. I hope you aren't, either."

"My... 'shirt in a knot'?" uncertainly replied the 'Sari'-girl. "It is actually quite loose..."

"That means, 'don't get mad about it', Sari," explained Tommy, looking up cheerfully at the newcomer.

She returned the smile and tussled his hair.

"Oh," she muttered. "I, uhh, 'get it'. But, no, Bob, I am not upset, no, that is not it, not exactly. It is just that I am, I suppose, a little... *disappointed* with myself, that is all."

Claremont let out an amused laugh.

"'Bout *what*, there, girl?" she asked. "That y'all didn't get to jump off a cliff without one of them, what they again, oh, yeah, one of them bungee-cords, an' get away with it? That a *long* way down, girl."

"I was not going to *jump*," replied the fallen-girl, with mild irritation.

Staring faraway out the side window, she remarked, "I was just holding out my arms, trying to re-imagine how feels to be akin to a bird, to feel free, to soar up to where the air is thin, free from the chains of gravity... up to the edge of Heaven, yet beyond..."

The 'Sari'-girl paused for a second or two, then added, "I was trying to *remember*."

"'Member *what*?" inquired Melissa.

"Never mind, child," interrupted Claremont, with a cautioning look recognized as such by both of her children.

Billings shot a knowing stare at the black woman.

The fallen-girl whispered something to the Indian-boy, who immediately looked up at her, wide-eyed.

He replied, obviously trying not to be heard, "Miss Sari, you mean you can —"

Regarding him straight-on, she nodded and extended her arm over his shoulder, hugging him near, then again staring out the vehicle's side window.

"I *could*, before," she said softly to Tommy, with the trace of a tear in her eye. "But nowadays, I am just a 'pale shadow' of my former self... that is what you would say, I guess."

The newcomer let out a sad-sounding sigh.

"That *real* funny, Miz Sari," offered Melissa, with a half-in-jest tone. "Y'all shore *can* tell a story."

"Hush," commanded Claremont.

"Right. Well, folks," stammered Billings, "bungee-cords or not, that's all behind us now, except for that old credit-card bill, you know?"

"Well, we *gonna* pay y'all back, Bob," grumbled Claremont. "Sometime."

"Ah, don't worry about it," returned the salesman, regaining a bit of his composure. "Tell you the truth, I've had worse from a bad night or two at the bar... that is before I, ahem, became a man of the cloth. You know, from multiple Bloody Marys to multiple Hail Marys, all in one nice little trip."

He cackled maliciously and continued, "Anyway, we're only about an hour away from the Maricopa, oh, for you guys from out of town, that's I-17, that is. We'll be home in no time, now."

"Home," introspectively noted the 'Sari'-girl. "A refuge from the world, that one little place that one calls one's own. That sounds *so* nice."

"Yeah," commented Claremont. "'Specially when y'all so far away from it, an' y'all think y'all *never* gettin' back. Ah sure Tucson real nice... but ah gots to admit ah wish ah was back in the 'hood, De-troit way. Ain't nothin' to write home 'bout – hey, that funny, right – but it where we *familiar*, where everyone knows us. No offense there Mister Sales Man, but Tucson just cain't be the same, ah don' think."

"None taken," answered Billings. "And besides, you might get to *like* it, and besides *that*, you'll be on your way when things... *settle down* a bit, when you guys have had a chance to chill out, get back on your feet, catch a breath... use any one you like, principle is the same. I got lots of room. All I ask is that you stay out of my bedroom and out of my liquor-cabinet... oh yeah and 'hands off' the gun-rack in the basement as well, truth is that I'm not even sure where I put the key to unlock the damn thing – whoops, there's another Hail Mary I owe – but just as well leave good enough alone, you hear?"

"Yes Mister Billings," replied three cherubic voices from the back seat.

"You mean that you have a gun? A weapon, a firearm, in your basement, Bob?" asked the fallen-girl. "Is it for hunting, or self-defense? But I do not know why you would have to hunt for food, I mean, there are these big stores all over the place where you can buy all the food you want, without having to clean it first... and did you not tell me that Tucson is a nice, safe place to live? Who would you need to defend yourself against?"

"Actually I have a bunch of 'em, three rifles and a .38 pistol," replied the salesman, matter-of-factually. "Tell you the truth, I'm not really sure why I got them in the first place, well, all except for the oldest rifle, it was a gift from the widow of a friend, who was over in Paki... *well*. It was more a 'fitting-in' thing, you see; all my buddies at the office had guns, and when they started to chat about what ammo's in the stores, how they did down at the range and so on, I kinda didn't want to be out of the conversation, know what I mean? In my business, you *gotta* be one of the boys. Or the girls, I guess."

Out of the blue, the 'Sari'-girl requested, "Can you teach me how to use one of these 'guns', Bill? How to load it and fire it, I mean."

Nonplussed, Billings argued, "Uhh... well, I don't know... I mean, what would be the *point*? Like, you're not planning on going on a bank-robbing spree or something like that, are you? What do you need a gun *for*, anyway?"

"I mean no-one any harm," she stated. "But right now, all I have to defend myself with is my arms and legs, my wits and my skills. In the back of my mind I keep hearing a voice saying, 'you are over-matched, Sari, you cannot fight a gun-bullet with a *Vrùn-Ch'é* kick, you must learn these weapons, you must *adapt'*. I can use the dark-trick, that is true; but all they would have to do is fire in my direction –"

"Look... can we maybe deal with this a bit later?" pleaded the salesman. "And honestly, I *have* to say, I'd prefer not to. Take the bloody things out of the cabinet, that is. 'I'm a lover, not a fighter', you know?"

"Well I guess that it is your choice, Bob," countered the newcomer. "Since these weapons are for you to dispose of as you see fit. But... could you not, at least, then, teach me how to resist them?"

"I'm not sure I'm getting you there," asked Billings. "What do you *mean*, 'resist' them?"

"Sorry if I was not making myself clear, Bob," said the fallen-girl, with an enigmatic half-smile. "I just meant that for each attack, there is a defense, for each weapon there is *always* a counter-measure. It is ever like this, in the arts of war. So I thought that if you could teach me what the trick is, to dodge these 'bullets', the projectiles that a gun fires, that is... or, if hit by a bullet, how one resists it –"

"Say *what*?" incredulously demanded Claremont.

She laughed, dismissively, and added, "Y'all talkin' *shit*, girl. First thang y'all gots to know 'bout a gun is not to argue with anybody who got one. Second thang is, y'all *cain't* dodge no bullet, y'all cain't outrun it, neither. Third thang is, y'all get hit, better be sayin' some prayers there. Them thangs, 'specially them new 'Dee-You' ones that them black-suited boys from the Guv'ment always shootin' wid, they do they sweeps of the 'hood every so often, they hit y'all in the right spot, it 'game over' right there; an' if they hit y'all in the *wrong* spot, well, it just take longer 'fore y'all *daid*, y'all *understand*, girl?"

"*Really*," answered back the 'Sari'-girl, with an arched eyebrow and a haughty look.

For a second or two, the humans in the car heard a whisper of a song of power, its ethereal chords bringing unexpected energy and excitement.

Claremont and Billings exchanged a quick, nervous glance.

"Only thing that I know of that will resist a bullet," noted Billings, "Is a good Kevlar Two flak-jacket. Oh, uhh, you wouldn't know what that is, *would* you? Well, it's kind of like a piece of body-armor, meant specifically to stop them, bullets that is. I don't happen to have one around at home, they banned selling 'em a few years ago when they had that big urban-terrorist thing in Philly, but anyway, from what I heard from the boys back at the office, they won't stop any of the newer bullets that the Feds have, not to mention the gangsters – something about 'special DU penetrator shells' or crap like that. And none of them ever *could* stop a shotgun, at close range."

"Hmm," purred the 'Sari'-girl.

"The bottom line is," continued the salesman, "'Don't get hit'. It's not the kind of thing that you're going to walk away from, *that's* for sure."

"Thank you very much for the explanation, Bob," politely concluded the fallen-girl, in a strange, analytical tone. "It has been *very* informative. The books in the librar-ee gave many numbers and figures, but the practicalities of such things are usually best learned from, ahh, people who have seen the heat of battle, with their own eyes."

She was staring straight ahead, with a steely gaze down the road.

"'Scuse me, Miz Sari," piped up Curtis, "But what y'all say there, minute or so ago? Sound like y'all talkin' Chinese..."

"Oh, sorry," apologized the 'Sari'-girl, "You mean when I said '*Vrùn-Ch'é*'?"

"Yeah," answered the Claremont boy. "How y'all say that again?"

"It is pronounced 'vay-ROON ch-ay', and you stop your voice for a very short time, in between the 'ch' and the 'ay'," explained the newcomer. "And I will save you, your next question. I do not know what language that this word originally comes from. I *do* know that it is not from my own native tongue, however."

The Claremont boy giggled and interrogated the 'Sari'-girl, saying, "That like Kung-Fu? martial-arts, ah means."

"It is a form of unarmed combat, using just your body," answered the fallen-girl. "It is very deadly, if fully mastered. But of course it, is of limited effectiveness against a weirding-armored enemy, or an opponent with magic weapons, or against someone who has a powerful weapon like a gun. And it is much more effective if one fully understands the weak points of the physiology of one's target – the joints, pressure-points, nerve-centers..."

"Like, some of them Kung-Fu guys, they can bust up bricks wid just they hands, an' if'n y'all use a sword 'gainst 'em, it just bounce off – is this 'Vroon' thang like that?" demanded Curtis.

"Yes... and much more, in fact," responded the newcomer, neutrally, to the delight of the two boys. "Many a dirk and arrow has been shattered on my skin, thus empowered by this art."

She studiously ignored the pained looks on the faces of the salesman and the African-American woman.

"Miss Sari," inquired Tommy, "Are you really *good* at this Vroon- Vroon-*whatever*, stuff? Like Bruce Lee, I mean."

"Tommy, I want you to pronounce the name of this art, *properly*," implored the fallen-girl. "Try it again : 'vay-ROON ch-ay'. Go ahead, if you please."

"Okay," complied the boy, looking up at the 'Sari'-girl with obvious affection. "Veh-vay... roon... cheh-ay. Is that any better?"

"It is a good start," replied the smiling newcomer. "But make sure that you do a little stop between the last two words."

"Sure... but why is that so important?" requested Tommy.

"Two reasons," she explained. "First, because certain words carry power – the great power of my ancestors – within them; *this* name is such a case. Second, because you are... my... *special* one, dear son; and I now have the responsibility of raising you to know the truth of these things, in the right way. You will come to know many such words as you grow into manhood, and learning the principle of this correctly right from the start, will eventually be a gift that you will very much value for as long as you will live."

The 'Sari'-girl paused for a second or two, and then sheepishly offered, "Ah, I suppose that all of this is a little, ahh, how does one say in Eng-lish, 'over your head'... right?"

But Tommy, staring now with what had to be love in his eyes, answered, "No, Miss Sari, it's not. I understand it *exactly*. You're just saying what the old ones tell us kids, when we're around the campfire, out on the reserve. About how we should honor our ancestors... how if we do that, we'll be powerful, no matter what the, uhh, 'others', try to do to us."

The 'Sari'-girl let out a little sigh and embraced the boy, trying a futile gesture to wipe away a tear, before any of the rest could see it.

After she had regained her composure, the newcomer asked, "But I *do* have a question for you... all of you. Namely... who is this 'Bruce Lee'?"

"He the best Kung-Fu fighter, *ever*," excitedly explained Curtis. "He could take on a whole *room-full* of bad-guys, just by heself, y'all oughtta see this movie ah gots back 'n the hood, ah think it called 'Kung-Fu Master of Death' –"

"Ah," acknowledged the fallen-girl, appreciatively nodding her head.

"Well?" pressed Tommy.

"Well, *what*?" responded the newcomer.

"Well how good *are* you, Miz Sari?" said the Indian-boy. "Are you as good as Bruce Lee? Can you even kill people, just with your bare hands?"

"To answer your question honestly," replied the 'Sari'-girl, slowly and carefully, "Yes, I *am* very good at this style of unarmed combat, and several other ones as well. I am what you would call a 'master' at all of them. I have not used any of these talents for quite a long while; but I am sure that yes, I *could* do what you are talking about. But I hope that I will not have to do anything like *that*, around here... I really *do*."

"He just *aksin'*, y'all know," quipped the Claremont boy. "In them movies, why, the good guy, he kill whole *bunch* of bad-guys. Ain't no big thang."

"Curtis *Ray!*" sharply reprimanded the mother. "That will be *enough*, y'all hear?"

"Yes'm," mumbled the boy.

"You should ponder, Curtis," countered the fallen-girl, as she sent a serious look in his direction, "That killing an intelligent being, except where it is absolutely unavoidable, is *not* 'fun' – it is the *worst* breach of the most universal, fundamental laws of justice and decency. Each time that one does it, a permanent wound of shame lies not only upon one's heart, but upon one's soul, as well. My own have many, *many* such wounds... and they hurt *terribly*, every time that I think upon it."

She sat back in her seat and fell silent, while Billings tried to ignore the sweat on his brow.

An uncomfortable silence was broken after a few seconds by Curtis' still-upbeat voice.

"Momma," whispered Melissa, "That mean that she done *killed* –"

"Shush, child," whispered back Claremont.

"Miz Sari," requested Curtis, "Could y'all teach *me* some of this Vroon-Vroon- whatever. Ah promise ah won't hurt nobody."

"*Vrùn-Ch'é*," patienlty instructed the 'Sari'-girl. "It is pronounced 'vay-ROON ch-ay', with a brief stop between the 'ch' and the 'AY'."

"Ah work on that," chirped the Claremont boy. "But how 'bout it, Miz Sari?"

"Miss Sari," added Tommy, "If you're going to teach Curtis, I'd like to learn too. If that's okay."

"I did not say that I *was* going to teach him, young man," evaded the fallen-girl.

"Now, *now*," spoke Claremont, "Ain't no good in teachin' fightin' 'n such. Ah don't think that such a good idea... right, Bob?"

Billings just shrugged and flared his fingers up in the air in an "I surrender" gesture, keeping his thumbs on the steering-wheel.

"Thanks for the *support*, Bob," sarcastically whispered Claremont.

The salesman shrugged, again.

The two boys, joined quickly by Melissa, stared at the 'Sari'-girl.

"Well, I suppose that I *could* teach you a few of the least... *demanding*, defensive maneuvers," offered the newcomer. "And perhaps it *would* be a good idea for you to start learning some of my... *arts*. We cannot know what, uhh, adventures, may lie ahead of us, after all."

Why don't I like the sound *of that*, nervously mused Billings.

"Oh, *yeah!*" interrupted an elated Curtis.

He immediately high-fived with the equally-excited Indian-boy.

"But I should warn you," cautioned the 'Sari'-girl, "That there is a *lot* of falling involved, off your feet, that is. As well as, some of it can be a little, ahh, *uncomfortable*, as your body is trained to do things that ordinary flesh and blood could never safely attempt. After a short while, it becomes, how do you say, 'second nature', then you can go on to the more... *interesting*, maneuvers. I cannot really see any harm in showing you a little of this technique. Oh, and... Bob? Whitney?"

"Whitney, *what?*" asked Claremont.

"Well, what I meant was... would you like to learn, too?" remarked the 'Sari'-girl. "If nothing else, it is good exercise. You will find your health improving in every respect, if you persist with this discipline. And even learning the most basic forms of *Vrùn-Ch'é* mind-meditation will help you resist other kinds of... uhh... *stress*. So it is well worth the effort."

"Uhh... sure, I *guess*," mentioned Billings, not being able to think of an excuse quickly enough. "As long as there aren't any smart-Aleck jokes when ol' Bob ends up on his butt. And God knows, blasphemy intended, I *could* use a bit of a work-out; I kind of fell of the diet wagon when our friend the comet showed up, didn't figure it'd make much of a difference if I showed up at the Pearly Gates with thirty or sixty extra pounds, but man, when I was doing the crab-walk away from that compound up north, I sure realized how out of shape I had gotten..."

"'Fell off a wagon'?" asked a perplexed 'Sari'-girl.

"Another phrase," answered the salesman. "It comes from the 'Temperance Wagons' that the Jesus-nuts used to drive all over these parts in the last century, when they were trying to ban booze – there was some old biddy named 'Carry A. Nation', if you can believe that, she used to get people to take the pledge and climb aboard, but each time it turned the corner near a saloon, off they'd fall –"

"'Carry A. Nation'," observed the newcomer. "Wow. That is an interesting name... I wonder if it was the one that I saw..."

Her voice drifted off for a second.

Then she requested, "Whitney?"

"What? Oh no, ah *couldn't*... ah means," uncertainly stammered Claremont.

"Come *on*, Momma," chided Curtis. "Ah go easy on y'all. That a *promise*."

"Yeah, Momma," piled on Melissa. "Y'all always sayin' we don' do stuff together, as a family. This be somethin' we *all* can do. An' 'member how y'all sayin' that we don' get enough exercise, after that pool up 'n th' hood done dried up, when they don' put no more water in it an' we cain't go swimmin' no more?"

Claremont shot a pained look at Billings.

The man offered, "Might as well, Whitney – if only to keep an eye on the kids. And to pick poor old Bob up off the ground, when he gets thrown by Little Kung-Fu Master of Death back there."

"Okay... fine," dejectedly muttered the African-American woman. "But ah gots to warn y'all, ah ain't no good at that kinda thang, can't dribble 'n hit a basket even if nobody checkin' me. Ain't never been much on sports."

"Join the club," noted the salesman. "Watching a ball-game on TV, that's about *my* speed, in the exercise department, I mean."

"So when do we start?" excitedly demanded Tommy.

"Yeah, Mister Billings, ah feel like stretchin' mah legs right now," added Curtis.

"Not until we get to Tucson, and we've got a nice private back-yard, or, better still, a nice basement rec-room to practice in," cautioned Billings. "Might attract a bit too much *attention*, I'm afraid."

Claremont nodded knowingly. "Lots of things we cain't afford, Mister Sales Man," she stated, "An' bein' *famous*, that near the top of th' list."

"Aww," whined three voices from the back seat.

"How about the next time when we stop for a, uhh, 'pee-break', Bob?" suggested the 'Sari'-girl. "There would be almost no-one out here in the desert, to observe us. And there would be substantial space in which to practice."

"But we just *did* that, a ways back," argued Billings.

"Mister Billins'," interrupted Curtis, "Hate to tell y'all, but I gots to 'go'... real *bad*. So if'n y'all don' want to have to clean up yo' car..."

As the salesman sighed, rolled his eyes and pulled the SUV off the road, the fallen-girl shared a smile with her new-found young charge.

"I will give you a *special* lesson, Tommy," she whispered to him.

For Your Eyes Only

"Link will be active in about thirty seconds, sir," instructed the young Air Force lieutenant, pleasantly. "When the green light comes on, you'll have two seconds, then the video from the station will show on the screen."

"Thanks," replied the President, looking up briefly and reflexively adjusting his bomber-jacket.

He turned around to address those behind him.

"Is this going to be televised?" he asked. "By the networks, I mean. We're not going to be live, right?"

"We were planning on releasing some out-takes to the media, later, Mr. President," mentioned a female voice. "But we turned down requests by the networks to get their crews in here, as well. They were pretty persistent, but ultimately we got rid of them."

Seeing the seconds tick down, she shut up.

"Yellow light, sir," warned the lieutenant.

"Five seconds... four... three... two... one," he counted, eventually giving a chopping gesture.

The link-light now glowed bright green and slowly an image appeared on the LCD screen that had been set up on one of the walls. It revealed the interior of a spacecraft of some kind, one that had once been immaculate white, but which had obviously seen better days, with small parts missing and the occasional tear in the covering-surfaces.

Five human faces appeared on the screen, evidently floating at random places in the zero-G : a burly, middle-aged, clean-shaven (except for the obligatory stubble) American man, a second man, much smaller and thinner with olive skin and a newly-grown mustache, an attractive, thirty-something Eurasian woman, a stone-faced, Chinese male taikonaut, and, finally, a lanky, clean-shaven African-American man with searching brown eyes.

"Greetings, ISS2," announced the U.S. leader. "This is the President of the United States addressing you, from the White House. How are you all doing up there, today?"

"Very well, sir," politely replied the second man. "I am Ariel Cohen, IDF/AF, Commander in charge of the ISS2 space-station. And may I say, sir, that it's good to hear from you, too. It is perhaps a sign that things are getting back to normal, down on Earth. Considering what we have all lately been through, one could be forgiven for having thought that they would never do so."

"How right you are about *that*," agreed the President. "And I would not want to mislead you on that front, Commander. We are still very far from business as usual, down here, on many different fronts. Oh, and before I get on to the main purpose of this call, I wanted to let you know, I have been asked by your King to convey the highest commendations on behalf of the Knesset to yourself; apparently they're planning a big party for you, when you get back to Israel."

"Thank you, Mr. President," answered Cohen. "I am of course hoping that I will be able to attend that event sooner, rather than later."

The President nodded.

"And," he continued, "I know that I'm speaking on behalf of everyone in the United States when I say that we're all very proud of what you all have accomplished up there, especially, the Mars mission crew – am I correct in saying that I'm seeing Mr. Jacobson, Professor Tanaka and... and... right, also, Major White? Do I have all of you?"

The first man spoke up.

"Yes, that's right, Mr. President," he stated. "I'm Commander Sam Jacobson and I have Professor Cherie Tanaka and Major Devon White, along with me, today. Majors Brent Boyd and Sergei Chkalov, the latter of the Russian Federation Space Force, are both unfortunately tied up with maintenance duties – as you can imagine, just keeping this station capable of life-support is a major task, up here – and the other gentleman that you see is Lieutenant-Commander Chen of the People's Republic Air Force. Commander, I hope I got that right...?"

"Yes," smoothly confirmed the Chinese man. "And may I say, Mr. President, that I am authorized to convey my own government's best wishes and sincere hopes that we will shortly be able to resolve our... outstanding issues, with the United States."

He allowed himself a half-smile.

"Indeed," answered the President. "Well, everyone, although I'm obviously delighted to be able to chat with you today, this isn't just a social call," he said.

He looked to his side, then said, "Would you excuse me just for a second, please?"

Obligingly, the Air Force lieutenant turned off the audio link.

"I thought we were only going to have our *own* people on this call –" complained the American leader.

"That was understood to be the arrangement, sir," noted an aide. "I'm not sure what happened, but I'll have NASA look into it, sir," he added.

The wizened face of Fred McPherson suddenly appeared to the President's left, just out of camera view.

"I'd remind you, sir," he said, "That up there, we're not really in charge... *Cohen* is the guy who decides who's 'in' and who's 'out' for everything, whether it's cleaning out the space latrines or meeting the President of the United States. Did we ask him specifically just to have a link with Jacobson and his crew?"

"I think so," mentioned the aide.

"Well, I'd suggest that you double-check that," retorted McPherson. "I've known Cohen for ten years... I seriously doubt that he'd deliberately refuse such an order. Especially if he knew it came directly from the President."

"Okay, okay," motioned the President. "We'll have to resolve this later... I'll just have to do the best I can. Put them back on."

"Mr. President," interrupted the voice of the CIA Director, in as much of an elevated tone as this *apparatchik* was capable of mustering. "I don't think that's *advisable* – you might give away details that we don't want –"

"I'll be *fine*," grumbled the President.

"Put them *on*", he commanded.

The video-light again shone green.

"Sorry for the brief delay, there," said the President. "Just had to verify a few details, down here. May I continue?"

"Of course, sir," replied Cohen.

"Very good," started the President. "Now, as to the substance of our discussion today... first of all, I wanted to be the first one to have the privilege to inform you, that thanks to tireless efforts on the part of my Science Adviser, Fred McPherson, the Air Force, NASA and many others, we have managed to arrange a rescue-mission for the crew of ISS2, starting with yourselves as well as the other members of the Mars mission crew –"

On the video-screen, they saw Tanaka involuntarily grab Jacobson's arm, the trace of a tear in her eye.

"Oh God," she exclaimed. "It *can't* be true – can it? That means we're going to *live*. Thank you, Mr. President, thank you *so* much. From the bottom of our hearts."

"Thank you God," softly intoned White. "I *knew* y'all'd come through for us."

"That's – that's, *great* news, sir," added Jacobson. "Do you have any of the details? When, how – I mean, what kind of ship –"

"I'm going to leave that to the experts, Captain," replied the President. "Except that I can assure you, because I have received similar assurances, that we will eventually be able to evacuate *everyone* from your station, everyone who chooses to leave, that is. I have been told that this process won't happen overnight, because a number of different rockets and trips will be required, but in no more than a month or so, you'll all be home."

"We are all *tremendously* in your debt, sir," observed Cohen. "From what we had believed up until now, we thought the chances of our successful rescue would be very low. All I can say is... 'thank you'."

The President smiled.

"Now that we have that over with," he continued, "There's one *other* matter that I would like to discuss with you, and, well, this should be considered strictly 'off the record'. Can everyone who's present here today, commit to keeping the rest of our conversation confidential – strictly *not* to be disclosed to the news-media, should you be asked?"

A look of confusion, mixed with instant suspicion, appeared on the faces of several of those on the station.

"I... uhh... I don't see why not," half-stammered Cohen. "Such a request is somewhat... *irregular*, would you not say, sir, but personally I don't have a problem with keeping what you say confidential. But I must tell you that, as an officer of the Israel Defense Forces, if I were to receive a direct order from my own senior command, or my government, you have to understand –"

"Understood," agreed the American leader. "We all have to obey orders, don't we? What about the rest of you?"

The Chinese man stared at the camera, forcefully, for a second or two.

"Under these circumstances, sir," he officiously stated, "I believe that I have no choice but to excuse myself from the remainder of this discussion, since I am under standing orders from the People's Space Command to accurately report all events that occur here on the station, to them, on a continuous and prompt basis. May I be excused, Commander?"

He sent a glance to Cohen.

The Israeli nodded.

"You may leave, Li," he said.

The taikonaut gave a slight bow, grabbed a hand-hold and propelled himself out of the remote camera's field of vision.

"Okay," said the President, "Now that *that's* out of the way, let's get down to the point. Now, before I ask you what I'm going to ask, please keep in mind that I'm neither a rocket scientist like Fred," – he reflexively looked over his shoulder and gave a slight grin – "Nor do I presume to play one, even on TV, so I'll leave the evaluation of the math stuff to capable minds like his. Having said that, the question that I'm asking arises from a matter that even somebody as dumb as I, can understand from my high-school physics classes, that is, 'action-reaction', that kind of thing –"

Tanaka, her countenance immediately serious despite strenuous efforts to maintain a smile, tried to hide the foot-tap she gave Jacobson.

Uh-oh, she thought. *Here it comes*.

"So," the President went on, "I have been given to understand by the folks at NASA, also by those in the know at Air Force Space Command, that the fact that we're even having this conversation, what with your station being parked in an orbit around the Earth, well, that's left them kind of scratching their heads about how you accomplished it."

Y'all think? mused White, trying to avoid a grin.

"According to Fred and his rocket-engineer friends," inquired the U.S. leader, "The space-station had fired out its last booster-rockets some time ago and, to put it the way that Fred said it to me, 'they're like a car heading for a cliff at 100 miles per hour, and the brakes just failed'. Yet, *somehow*, you still managed to stop the station and park it into Earth orbit, instead of, well, flying right by us. I guess the bottom line here is... my people down here want to know, 'how'd you do it'?"

"I believe that we have already had a number of conversations about that, with the authorities at NASA, including Mr. McPherson himself," offered Cohen.

"Yes, that's right," responded the President.

"And?" countered Cohen.

"I have to tell you, Commander," demanded the President, "That they're not convinced that they have the entire story yet. So, what I'm here to do today, other than of course to give you the good news about the rescue, is to ask you, 'is there anything else that you'd care to add, to explain how you have managed to slow down your station and achieve Earth orbit'?"

"I'm afraid not, sir," evaded Cohen. "Oh – well, in fact there *is*, one other thing," he added.

Tanaka shot the man a furious glance.

Cohen's countenance grimaced as a pain, akin to a sinus headache, appeared from nowhere in his head, then went away as mysteriously as it had come.

"What I mean, Mr. President," prevaricated the Israeli, "Is, if you will recall, we *did*, thankfully, get a visit a day or so ago, from the three Soyuz-7G re-supply capsules that the Russian Federation was able send our way. The oxygen they delivered was absolutely vital, and... maybe the negative momentum caused by their docking with us, had some effect on the speed of our approach. Perhaps *that* would account for it. I just wish that these capsules could also be used to offload some of our crew back to Earth, but apparently we're too far away for this to be done safely."

The ISS2 participants could just see the President's head turn over his shoulder.

Someone behind him whispered something in his ear.

"Very well," said the American leader. "I'd like to address Captain Jacobson now, if I may."

"Certainly," complied Cohen.

"Yes, sir?" inquired Jacobson, neutrally.

"Captain," firmly demanded the President, "I'm sure you're aware of the chain of command that we're both part of?"

"Oh, *definitely*, sir," replied Jacobson, trying to sound polite.

"Then you're aware that if I give you a direct order, you're supposed to follow it to the best of your ability?" asked the President.

"And," he added with a slight pause, "That your failure to do so, might have... *serious* consequences?"

"That's my understanding of the rules, sir," confirmed Jacobson, staring straight forward.

"Okay, well, now that we have *that* made clear, I need to ask you basically the same thing as I asked our friend Mr. Cohen, a few seconds ago, Captain," said the President. "Are you aware of any event or mechanism that might account for the rapid deceleration of the space-station, from which you're now addressing me? If so, I'm *ordering* you to describe it briefly to myself, as well as to describe it in sufficient additional detail, to whomever I delegate that task, down here. You may go ahead."

The former Mars mission commander continued to silently stare forward, for second after second.

"Captain?" pressed the President.

"To answer your question as best I can, under the current circumstances, sir," offered Jacobson, "I would have to say two things. One, yes, I *am* aware of what has caused the... problematic trajectory results, that you speak of –"

"*Sam* –" plaintively exclaimed Tanaka.

Jacobson turned and motioned her silent with a 'hands-down' gesture.

"You may continue," ordered the U.S. leader.

"And two, sir," continued Jacobson, "Regarding the details of what I'm referring to, well, that's... that's... *complicated*, you see. As I said before, Mr. President, while I am very well aware of the chain of command and of my responsibilities as an Air Force officer, I'm concerned that premature disclosure of this information, particularly to the wrong parties, could have serious consequences, for which none of us is fully prepared at the present time. So, while I'm afraid that I cannot completely comply with your order as given to me here, I have resolved on an alternate plan of action that I'm hoping will still meet the objectives that you have stated."

"I hope you understand the consequences to yourself, for doing that," shot back the American leader.

"I do, sir," responded the ex-mission commander. "And I'm prepared to face them."

The President sat back in his chair, shaking his head.

"Well, let's *have* it," he grumbled.

"What I'm going to do, Mr. President," proposed Jacobson, speaking slowly and deliberately, "Is to describe what has been going up here, in full – but *only* to yourself, sir, and only in person, at whatever location you so designate on Earth, when my team and I get back there. At that time, I'll try to give you the details, although I should say in advance that you may find these rather... incomplete, considering that, well, I'm not really sure of what I'm talking about, anyway."

"*Really,*" coolly stated the President.

"I know it must be frustrating to hear me being so evasive, Mr. President," apologized Jacobson, "But there's a good reason for it, and you'll just have to wait until I can explain things. I'm hoping that when you hear the full story, you won't want to, please excuse the terminology, 'hang me from the nearest yard-arm', but that's a chance that I'm willing to take... no, that I *have* to take."

He looked up.

"That's about it, sir," he concluded.

"You know, Captain," grumbled the President, "I very much *do* have the right to do that, although I believe these days it's the firing squad. And for the record, you'd at least get a trial, beforehand."

He sat and thought for a second, then went on, "But look – supposing – *just* supposing, that I buy these excuses for what anybody in my position would consider to be gross insubordination on your part, Captain, why can't you just ask the other people up there to leave whatever room that you're in and just address me in private, over the link that we have going, right now? How would that be any different from what you're proposing?"

"I have my reasons, sir," countered Jacobson. "Including, but not limited to, the fact that everything that I say over a communications-link like this could theoretically be intercepted by anyone on ISS2, as well as by others on the ground – I have no reason to believe that's happening now, but in view of the sensitivity of this information, I'm afraid that it's simply too risky to take chances."

The President stared directly at the former Mars mission commander, through the camera, for a few long seconds.

"Alright," he allowed. "We'll do it *your* way. But I warn you, Captain, that this had better be damn *good*, worth waiting for. There are some big, I mean *really* big, things going on down here, that make it absolutely *essential* for us to know what has been happening up there, that is, the *whole* story, right from the start –"

"*Mr. President!*" shouted the aghast voice of the CIA director, from somewhere in the room. "Remember the rules under which we're working, that's *far* too much already! I *strongly* suggest that you just order this officer to –"

White stared knowingly at Tanaka and whispered, "Cherie, y'all thinkin' what I'm thinkin'?"

Tanaka nodded, trying to suppress a look of joy.

"It *has* to be," she whispered back. "But why wouldn't he just tell us that she –"

"Your objection is noted," remarked the President. "And over-ruled."

"But –" protested the CIA director.

"Over-*ruled!*" growled the U.S leader, his hand motioning 'shut up'.

"I can *assure* you, sir," stiffly added Jacobson, "That it very definitely *will* be worth the wait. Whether you'll like hearing it, and what you'll do with it, may be another matter."

"*I'll* be the judge of that," muttered the President. "But just for the record – I don't suppose any of the rest of you have anything to say, on this matter? Major White? Professor Tanaka?"

"With the greatest respect, Mr. President, sir," uneasily stammered White, "I think I'll let my commanding officer do the talkin' here. But, uhh, after Captain Jacobson's filled y'all in, I'd be happy to come 'n chat with you... I'm sure we'd have lots to talk about. *Sir.*"

He tried to fake a feeble grin.

"And that more or less goes for me, and, I suspect, Major Boyd, who couldn't be here today," echoed Tanaka. "Mr. President, you have to understand that as a scientist, it's the opposite of my normal way of doing business, to withhold information; but in *this* case, I believe that Captain Jacobson's plan of action is not just justified, but, in fact, it's *absolutely* necessary. I'd be willing to bet everything that I own that once he explains the details to you, that you'll see why we have had to insist on this level of confidentiality. I only hope that you'll decide wisely, once you're in the know, sir."

"You people certainly *do* know how to ratchet up the excitement, Professor," sarcastically commented the U.S. leader.

"So... Commander, do we have anything more to discuss, today?" he asked.

"I don't believe so, Mr. President," replied Cohen, politely. "Except for me to say again, 'thanks for the good news'. And... I have a feeling that all of this will be sorted out in due time, sir."

"I certainly hope so," retorted the President. "Because it isn't just your friend Captain Jacobson who will have some explaining to do, Commander... I'll have my own to do, the minute that my generals and scientists down here get told that they'll have to wait for the Captain's gems of knowledge, whatever these may be. This whole process is *highly* irregular; but however much I'd like to do so, I can't just send some MPs up there to throw selected Air Force staff in the brig until they talk, so I'll have to put up with it... until I don't have to. Until then, Commander."

"Until then, sir," agreed Cohen.

The transmission-light went to red.

Tucson

Bob's Slice Of Paradise

"*Finally*, we made it to Ricardo," announced Billings, with a palpable sigh of relief.

"I gotta tell you," he remarked, "I never thought I'd see this street – or this city – again, when I last set out from here. And judging from the traffic, which is not quite up to where it was before all the crap went down up there but there's enough of it... looks like things are getting back to normal."

He shook his head, reflectively.

"Never thought I'd see the day," he added.

"Y'all live on this 'Ricard-o Street', Bob?" inquired Claremont.

"Naw... I'm actually about three blocks off it," answered the salesman. "Don't really like the traffic-noise. But I'm still in Desert Palms Park. Wouldn't live *anywhere* else, for love or money."

"Why is that?" asked the 'Sari'-girl.

"We got it *all*, here, sister," explained Billings, "Sunshine, swimming-pools – well, okay, you can only fill 'em up once per year, unless you know somebody down at Town Hall to bump up your water-allowance, unfortunately I don't – but we got big-time shopping-malls, lots of parking space, nice big lots, and you can see the Catalina Hills from here, too. Oh, and I got a basement, too, unlike about ninety per cent of my neighbors, it's kind of on the small side, but it holds my wine collection quite nicely. My own little slice of paradise – that's the bottom line, my dear."

He swung the SUV expertly around a corner.

"The design of these dwellings is interesting," commented the newcomer. "They are all low and the roofs are all flat, like so many paving-stones. It is curious how these streets are arranged, and the decorations on them... the big palm-trees, all evenly spaced, and how they have set those rocks into cement, on the sides of the road. It reminds me of a place that I visited, many long years ago, ages, in fact, except for the cars and trucks, of course, there are *so* many of them, everywhere... but, Bob, did you not say that you are not a rich man?"

"Yeah," grunted Billings. "I do okay, well enough to be comfortable, I guess, but the minute I stop working, them old bills start piling up. Got no idea how I'm going to retire, if I ever do. But *rich*? Hardly. To be rich, you gotta be worth *billions*, and I don't mean one or two. What made you think I was rich? This car? Hate to disappoint you, girl, but I still got four years' payments to go on her, I'm afraid."

"Hmm," murmured the 'Sari'-girl. "It is just that where I come from, one would *have* to be rich to live in a place like this. The everyday folk would live in little huts, or worse, with many people at close quarters. Living in that way does not bother me, but it is hard on most others. There is nowhere to go, to be alone."

She stared out the window, through cheapish, dark glasses.

"One minute warning," interrupted the salesman. "Just two more corners and we're there. Jesus Christ, I can hardly *wait*. Oh, and by the way, I'm officially renouncing the cloth, if you don't mind. I guess I only got religion for the trip, right?"

He let out a hoarse laugh.

"The Lawd's not somethin' y'all can just pick up an' put down like a bottle of beer, y'all know, Bob," muttered Claremont. "No offense meant, y'all understand. We's awful grateful that y'all puttin' us up."

"None taken," responded Billings with a broad smile.

"God as a bottle of beer. Hey, I *like* that, you know," he chuckled. "Wonder if you get a quarter if you return Him to the recycle-center..."

Claremont tried hard not to glower, while her two children giggled.

"I hope that this 'God' of yours has a sense of humor," observed the fallen-girl, as if stating common knowledge. "I have run into quite a few deities who do not, to say the least; nor do their priests and devotees. They can be *very* dangerous if insulted. Whether or not they deserve it."

"Like *sure*, Miz Sari," joked the teenager. "Y'all *knows* there ain't no such thang."

Tommy looked up at the 'Sari'-girl and grinned, a gesture which she instantly returned with a motherly smile of her own.

"Do not be so certain of that, Melissa," pleasantly answered the newcomer. "Gods-a-plenty, have these eyes seen, over the ages."

"There it is!" joyfully exclaimed Billings.

"Number 21, here we are!" he announced. Then, not insincerely, he added, "Well, God, if you're listening, please just forget what I just said and let me say, 'Thanks a bunch for getting us home, Big Guy'."

The SUV pulled into an otherwise empty two-car driveway, located on the left-hand side of a 60s or 70s construction low-set, ranch-style suburban house, its sides decorated in typical Southwest stucco, with a large, boarded-up picture-window in the front and various newspapers, packages and magazines strewn aimlessly at the doorstep.

What might have been a landscaped front yard, now contained only artfully-arranged rocks and Japanese-style pebbles, since there remained naught but the dried-out husks of whatever plants and flowers had, at one time, graced the place.

The salesman stopped his car and slumped back in the seat, visibly relieved as if feeling a vast weight lifted from his shoulders.

He flipped the master door lock switch.

"We're *home*," he breathed, the traces of a tear in one eye. "We're *home*, thank God. I gotta tell you, there were times when I thought we'd never make it, *that's* for sure. Everybody out."

"Yayyy!" shouted at least two of the children, as they clambered rapidly out of the vehicle, racing up to the front door. Curtis gave it a mighty yank, only to be rewarded by an unceremonious pratfall as the resistance of an un-budging door overcame his own strength.

"Hey Mister Billings, it *locked!*" complained the boy.

"No shit, kid," replied Billings, as he strode forward and joined the Claremont boy at the front entrance. "Sorry, Whitney. Don't worry, I got the key here with me. Man, I'm two for two on the car and house front."

"Bit more dust on everything than I had expected," he commented, "But I was afraid that this place might get trashed, when I left, not that that would really have mattered –"

"Hey, Bob!" sounded an unfamiliar, female voice.

"Bob, that *you*?" it demanded.

Billings stepped back and looked around.

He scanned back and forth and saw a portly, past-middle-age but still apparently fit female, wearing a matronly summer dress and 50's-style sunglasses. The woman standing on the sun-dried remnants of a front lawn, two doors down from his own house, on the same side of the street.

"Beth? *Beth!*" exclaimed the salesman. "Great to see ya! Just got back from up north, over here. How've things been while I was away?"

The woman sauntered slowly over the intervening front yard until she was almost on Billings' own.

"Shitty, if you must know," she stated, in a friendly tone. "They only turned the power and the water back on yesterday, and then only at half allowance, or less – I can hardly get a trickle out of the damn shower, and my A/C just blows hot air."

"Well, that's not much different than it was... *before...*" grunted Billings.

"Yeah," allowed the woman. "You're lucky you got that land yacht of yours out of town before all the bad stuff started to happen, I got my truck ripped off by some punk kids the day before the comet was supposed to hit, cops eventually found it in the arroyo, total write-off. Marcie and Frank Johnson over on Calle Kuehn got their whole house trashed and robbed, and I ain't the *only* one to get a car lifted."

The 'Sari'-girl was about to ask what 'lifted' meant, but Beth ignored her and continued,

"There's a lot of talk that when the comet stuff was about to go down and they had pulled all the troops from everywhere, damn Mexicans came across the border in droves, ended up here stealin' *everything* that wasn't nailed down. Watch out for 'em, I heard some are holed up in houses around here that got abandoned at the same time, they come out at night doin' the old B&E thing... luckily I haven't seen any of 'em in Carlo's place, or yours. Well, at least the cops are patrolling here, again, better late than never."

The local woman looked over the group.

"So who're your friends?" she inquired.

"Oh, my *friends*, riiight," half-stammered Billings, trying to sound nonchalant.

"This here is Whitney Claremont and her two kids, Melissa and Curtis. The other boy is Tommy Stinging- Singing-, uhh, Tommy George, from one of the reserves up north. And the cute little lady here is Sari Tanak. She's, uhh, my friend."

"Very nice meeting you, Beth," spoke the fallen-girl, with a cheery smile and an odd, reflexive half-curtsy, adjusting her baseball-cap and sunglasses as she did, not that these were misaligned in any way, beforehand.

"I am Bob's *close* friend," she added.

Beth shot an envious glance at the newcomer, the kind that a woman past her prime bestows, in rueful acknowledgment of looks that she, herself, never really *did* have.

"*Bob*," she intoned, half-reproachingly.

Billings just smiled in devil-may-care fashion; but inwardly, he wanted to do a victory-dance.

"You too, Sari," said the local. "Oh, and by the way, I'm Beth Krutkowski, if you wanted to know. But, hey, Bob... you planning to start a youth hostel or something, here? Doesn't matter to me if you are, but they don't really *look* like your relatives, if you know what I mean."

She turned to address the others.

"Listen you all," she instructed, "Don't get your backs up, that I'm bothering poor old Bob like this. Around here we all kind of look out for each other, keep an eye out for people who don't *belong* in this neighborhood, can't be too careful, you know how it is –"

"Shore do," mumbled Claremont.

"No, they aren't my *folks*, and no, nothing like that, either," fumbled Billings. "My friends here are all just some people who I ran into at a... uhh... camp, up north, you might say. They needed a lift to somewhere where they could all catch their breath, make plans, get back to where they do belong."

"Oh," said Krutkowski.

"I don't know how much you heard about it down here," remarked the salesman, "But things up *there* are, well, pretty grim, there's no other way to put it. We had a *hell* of a time just getting across state lines, there's roadblocks filled with trigger-happy National Guard everywhere. Look, Beth – it's a long story, I'll fill you in on the details later, once we get unpacked and settled. Okay?"

"Okay," repeated the woman. "No problem. And listen, nice seein' you all down here – if any of you, or Bob, needs anything, just drop over to my place, knock on the door and say who you are, anything I got, you're welcome to borrow. They opened Park Place back up two days ago and I did some grocery-shoppin', had to pay for a damn cab to get there, shelves at the stores are still pretty bare but I got what I needed... I can spare a bit. You all have a nice day."

"You too," replied Billings.

Krutkowski turned and headed for her own house.

The salesman looked at the residence next to his. It was in considerably worse shape, with several windows broken and garbage strewn all over the front lawn and driveway.

"Beth!" he called.

The woman turned again to face him.

"What?" she shouted back.

"What's all this with Carlo's shack?" he asked. "Looks like the *crap* got kicked out of it, and he's not the type not to fix things. What gives?"

"Don't know," explained Krutkowski. "He and his wife and kids left for somewhere, three days before the comet was supposed to go down; he didn't say exactly where he was going but I think it was off east, St. Louis, maybe. Haven't heard hide nor hair of him, or them, since. As for the house, don't know, but I'd bet you good money it was the same damn kids that ripped off my truck, or maybe them wetbacks. This place was crawlin' with those little shitheads just before the Big Day, then they all just vanished when it looked like, 'surprise, surprise, we're all gonna be okay'. Did some damage, though, as you can see. I cleaned things up as best I could twice, but they came back each time, so I kinda gave up."

"Yeah," agreed Billings. "Can't blame you there – with the way things have been, you got to look out for yourself. Just glad they didn't hit *me*."

"Guess you're a lucky one," commented Krutkowski.

"Guess so," replied the salesman. "Thanks, Beth."

The woman waved, turned and headed back to her residence, eventually vanishing behind a door.

"Old friend of yours, Mister Sales Man?" asked Claremont, idly.

"Sort of," mentioned Billings. "More of an acquaintance, I'd say. But she's alright. I was closer to her before her husband passed away a few years ago... I used to go over to Paul and Beth's and do the poker thing each Saturday night, have a few beers."

He shrugged, philosophically. "*Those* were the days... but all things must pass, I guess."

"Yep," affirmed the black woman.

"Poker. A card game, based on bluffing one's opponents. Correct?" inquired the 'Sari'-girl.

"Um-hum," said Billings. "Used to play a quarter a point, but whoever won the jackpot for the night had to buy at least a twenty-four pack of beer for the next time. *Everybody* wins, that way."

His face wore a sad, far-off smile, in remembrance of less unsettled times.

The newcomer also looked to be tied up in thought for a moment, then she observed, "Hmm. Something tells me that I prefer the game called 'chess'."

"*Hate* it," countered the salesman. "Especially that damn 'Fools Mate', which happens to me about every time I give in and try that stupid game, again."

"Momma," interrupted Melissa, "When we gonna get to see our new house?"

"Ain't *our* house, child," corrected Claremont.

"My dear," shot back Billings, using his best W.C. Fields imitation as he sauntered over to the door and fumbled for a smart-key, busily pressing various buttons upon it, "My humble abode is yours, too, all of it, that is, except for the gun-rack and the liquor-cabinet. Oh, and except for those UV-Ray DVD discs in the plain white-box cassettes, on the top of the shelf in the living room. Not that *I* have anything against sharing those with you," – he revealed a cynical grin – "But I suspect that your mother might have a few things to say about their, ahem, content. If you know what I mean."

"Ahh, movie-pictures showing the arts of love and pleasure... right?" commented the 'Sari'-girl, catching on instantly. "But I would still like to review them, Bob, if it is oh-kay with you," she coltishly added. "I might learn some new techniques. There is always room for *improvement*, you know."

"Can't imagine how you could do better," leered Billings, winking at her, "But you're welcome to try."

"Lawd, it hard to raise kids th' proper way, 'round here, with all this trash-talk," complained Claremont.

Curtis giggled, but then lost track of the conversation as he barged through the now-open door. The other children raced through in short order, followed by a minor traffic jam amongst the adults, which was resolved by the 'Sari'-girl slipping through it as a fish slithers out of a tickler's grasp. The two boys went straight ahead, while Melissa headed down a side-corridor.

Billings dropped a suitcase on either side of himself, as he stood between the hallway and the living-room, studying the surroundings.

"Man," he observed, "I'm glad they didn't hit *me*, I've got a lot of stuff in here that would cost a ton of cash to replace, and that's assuming I'm working... don't know when I'll get back on track on that front. But all the stereo stuff and the paintings are all just like I left 'em."

He wiped a finger across a table-top.

"Whew," added Billings. "More dust in here than in the Sahara, and I haven't really been gone *that* long. Hope there isn't a busted window somewhere out back."

A voice called from further into the house, towards the kitchen.

"Hey, Mister Billings!" shouted Tommy.

"Yeah?" replied the salesman.

"Your back door is open," warned the boy. "So's the fridge."

"Shit!" cursed Billings.

"Maybe they *did* hit me," he growled, as he rapidly trotted back into the kitchen, followed by the fallen-girl and Claremont.

The three surveyed the scene. A foul smell – spoiled milk, perhaps – emanated from the open inside of a refrigerator which was otherwise nearly empty. Half-opened boxes of various foodstuffs were strewn all over the floor, as were at least three empty liquor-bottles.

The salesman slumped against a wall.

"God *damn*," he complained. "Looks like I wasn't so lucky, after all... that was my best gin, and my best Stolchi, as well. Looks like the little assholes had quite a party, at my expense. I hope they appreciated it."

Reluctantly, Billings started a half-hearted effort to mop up the worst of the spill from the fridge.

The 'Sari'-girl, for her part, was already hard at work, investigating the contents of the cupboards, having effortlessly jumped up on a kitchen counter.

"Y'all not s'posed to put yo' feet on there, girl," admonished Claremont. "Ain't, uhh, 'sanitary' to do that."

"The surface is dusty, anyway, Whitney," replied the newcomer. "And Bob, I have checked all four of these food-storage places and there does not appear to be much left... there are some spices, some – what *are* those again, oh yeah, 'coffee-filters' – and there is something that says, 'freeze-dried micro-wave dinner'; there are at least ten boxes of this last thing. That is strange... if whomever broke into your house wanted food, why would they not have taken these 'micro wave dinners', as well?"

Billings chuckled wearily, dragging a chair up to the kitchen table and sitting on it, paying no attention to the dust it deposited all over his back and the seat of his pants.

"My guess is," he explained, "They didn't have a microwave oven to carry around with them, to cook it with. So good for us, I *do* have one, as you can see over there, over the real stove. If it's working, we at least got something to eat, although I should warn you, it ain't *haute cuisine*, as they say."

The salesman shook his head, wiping his forehead with his hand.

"But oh, what I wouldn't give for a drink, right now," he muttered. "I'd even settle for warm Scotch."

"Well, maybe these ruffians did not take all of your, how do you say, 'booze', either, Bob," suggested the 'Sari'-girl. "You said that you keep that in the basement, right? I can go down there and check, if you would like. Where can I descend down there?"

Billings shrugged and pointed to a door in the kitchen, diagonally opposite the back one.

"I'm not betting any money, sister," he sighed.

The fallen-girl returned a goofy grin and then rapidly disappeared downstairs.

Claremont strode over to the door that she had entered. "Hey, girl," she exclaimed, "Y'all didn't turn on no lights, an' it near black as coal down there."

"Oh, sorry, I forgot to do that," came a voice from the near-total darkness at the bottom of the stairs, illuminated as it was only by a faint ray of light from a half-window at ground-level. "But it is alright. I can see perfectly well down here... in several different ways."

Billings shot a glance at Claremont and let out a bemused laugh.

The African-American woman shook her head.

"Yeah," she quietly stated. "*Ah* forgot, too."

The 'Sari'-girl's voice again issued from below.

"Fortune favors you, Bob," she announced. "There are quite a few bottles of this 'booze' still apparently unopened down here. Let us see... there is one that says 'Balls', another that says 'Dom Perig-non' and a third that says, 'Chivas Regal'. There are also a number of smaller ones that might serve only one or two drinks. Do you want me to bring any of them up there?"

"I'll never understand what goes through the minds of those punks," remarked the salesman, with a half-shake of his head. "They drain some of it but leave the really *good* stuff. Well, I'm not looking a gift horse in the mouth – Sari, drag up the Chivas, if you don't mind. I'll even share."

"Oh-kay," came back her voice, pleasant and even, as always.

After only another second or two, the newcomer appeared at the top of the stairs, holding an intricately-carved *faux*-crystal bottle with an elaborately-faceted stopper.

"Here it is," she demonstrated. "What does this stuff taste like, Bob? May I try some?"

"Certainly, my dear," replied a beaming Billings, wearing a cat-ate-the-canary look. "And as to how it *tastes*... well, 'the drink of the Gods' is how best I could describe it."

Claremont cackled.

"Y'all might need a little time to get used to it, there, girl," she cautioned.

"I take it that you drink this type of liquor all the time, too, then?" innocently asked the 'Sari'-girl.

"Wish ah did," answered the black woman. "But it a bit out of mah league back home. Best we can do there norm'lly is a six-pack of Bud or sometimes, bottle or two of Uncle Leroy's home-brew moonshine. Ain't had none of that for two year now, since the Man pick him up. But he gonna get out any day now. Least, that what *they* say."

The 'Sari'-girl laid a sympathetic hand on Claremont's own and, with a kind look, stated, "I pray that may soon be the case, Whitney. And if not... well, when I am more, uhh, *myself*...I will *see* to that... I *promise* you."

She arched an eyebrow, deliberately not paying attention to the guarded look on Claremont's face.

Billings arose and rummaged around in a cabinet, producing three half-sized glass cups, which he immediately deposited on the kitchen table.

"Hope you ladies aren't going to insist on Czech crystal," he joked.

"Back home we drink out of them plastic cups you get at th' burger-sto'," offered Claremont, with a shrug.

"Wouldn't be the first time *that's* been done around here," commented Billings, philosophically.

He quickly removed the stopper and expertly poured a double shot of whiskey into each of the three glasses.

"Care to join me?" he inquired.

"Oh, of *course*," confirmed the fallen-girl, as she pulled up a chair and rapidly doffed her baseball-cap and sunglasses.

Claremont sat down next to her.

God, she hasn't had a bath for a day or more, and that hair of hers sparkles like gold dust even though it's gray, silently thought Billings, as he shot a too-admiring glance at the alluring young thing across the table from him.

Better keep it to a couple of drinks, Bob, or who knows what you'll do, in front of Whitney or not, he mused.

Raising the first one to his lips, he gave the obligatory toast.

"Bottoms up," he said, and downed the liquid in one satisfied gulp.

Claremont did the same, taking perhaps a second longer.

"Shit, Bob," she exclaimed. "This *damn* good stuff. Seem like *ages* since ah had it. Don't know what y'all missin', 'till you get it again, ah guess."

The other two stared intently at the 'Sari'-girl.

"Well?" asked the salesman.

"Hmm... it does not seem to have killed either of you, so 'here goes', I guess," she answered.

Pouring a bit of the whiskey into her mouth, swizzling it around as if testing it for something-or-other, the newcomer knocked back a shot.

Suddenly, her eyes crossed involuntarily, giving her a goofy look that caused Claremont to laugh out loud, but the black woman's outburst was quickly silenced by a sub-second flash of dim light from the 'Sari'-girl's eyes.

"What the matter, girl," half-stammered the black woman. "80-proof whiskey not agree with y'all?"

"*120*-proof," corrected Billings.

"Uhh... no, it is... *fine*," countered the 'Sari'-girl. "I will even have some more, that is if you are willing to share more of this 'whiskey', Bob. It is just that it has quite a strong taste, for someone who is not used to it – but I become familiar with new kinds of food and drink pretty quickly."

She raised the glass in front of the other two and gave a cheerful smile.

"Let us try this, again," stated the newcomer, as she knocked back the remainder of what was in it.

This time, there was no obvious reaction.

"Laws," observed Claremont. "Y'all sure *do* get used to booze quick there, honey."

"Another round?" proposed Billings, although he was already busily pouring more Chivas Regal – twice what had been allocated a moment before, in fact – into each party-goer's cup.

"Sure!" enthusiastically responded the 'Sari'-girl. "This 'whiskey' of yours is really not that bad, when one becomes accustomed to it. It sort of reminds me of something that I used to drink, back at home..."

Her voice tailed off, as the hint of a sad look crossed her face.

"Uhh... *Bob*," cautioned Claremont, "Y'all think that such a good idea? Ah mean, maybe we oughtta just do one more an' call it a day at that. We... uhh...

don' want to get this young thang here too shit-faced – y'all know what ah mean, with what she can *do* –"

The black woman went silent in mid-sentence, looking at the fallen-girl, uncomfortably.

"Nothin' *personal*, girl," hastily added Claremont. "Just that this stuff sneak up, real fast... y'all end up doin' shit that y'all never *would* have, else-ways. Like endin' up in bed wid some slick who y'all hardly *knew*, day before..."

The 'Sari'-girl laughed bemusedly.

"Do not worry, Whitney," she counseled. "I will not become drunk, if that is what you are worrying about. I could drink Bob's whole *bottle* of whiskey, and all the other ones down in the basement as well, and I would not be, ah, how do you say, 'any the worse for wear'. Other than for having to pee a lot, I suppose."

She giggled, again.

"How do you figure that, Sari?" asked the salesman. "Draining even *one* bottle of this fine elixir, refreshing though it is, would put me under the table faster than you can say 'Jack be nimble', and I'd pay for it with one brutal hangover the next day, and I can hold my liquor better than most, if I do say so myself. I've only met one or two guys that can do better, and besides, you have – ahem – quite a bit less body mass than ol' Bob. If I were you, I'd go slow, girl. Whitney's not kidding about this stuff... it's to be respected. Savored and loved, but *respected*."

The salesman let out a belly-laugh as he shot a glance at the fallen-girl.

"Just like a good woman," he added.

A flash of too-sharp incisors, quickly suppressed, appeared as the 'Sari'-girl laughed out loud.

"I will take that as a compliment, my love," she replied. "But you do not understand how my body works. This is kind of hard to explain, but although I definitely *can* taste the alcohol in this drink, it does not affect my judgment, or my perceptive abilities, or my ability to think, or... *anything*, in fact. At least, it does not do that after the first second or so that I am exposed to this, or any other, drug or poison, for that matter. What you saw when I took the first sip was my body, uhh, 'neutralizing' the alcohol in your 'Chivas Regal' so that it cannot harm me."

She fell silent, for a second, then elaborated, "You know, sometimes I wish it were otherwise... so I could find out what it *feels* like to be 'drunk', or, what was that other word that Curtis told me about while we were back in the car, to be 'stoned', just once or twice. Ah, well, there are things that are out of reach for all of us, I suppose."

"It ain't all it cracked up to be, girl," commented Claremont. "'Specially the day after, when y'all wake up feelin' like death warmed over."

"Some things are worth the pain," observed Billings, with a wry smile.

This time, the fallen-girl beat him to the whiskey-bottle.

Imitating the salesman, she unstopped the container and quickly poured a double shot into each glass.

"Bottoms up," she announced, offering up a glass, while grinning like the Cheshire Cat.

The Follower

"Misha *tut*," stated the man behind the wheel, as he adjusted the seat to recline a bit more.

In pleasant, dispassionate Russian, he added, "I am using my 'hearing-aid' at this end, Alexi. Please confirm yours."

"Alexi here," replied a ghostly voice, also in Muscovite *russki eziek*. "My 'hearing-aid' is on, as well. We should be safe from interception, as long as we do not talk long enough for the NSA to break the encryption-key. I would recommend fifteen minutes or so, certainly no more than twenty. Moscow informs me, incidentally, that we should have a satellite up in the next three days... that will again free us from having to use the American communications-networks for these discussions."

"Fifteen minutes should be more than enough time," noted the man in the car. "Particularly as it is so blessed hot down here. I have had to turn off the engine, therefore the air-conditioning, and open the windows, because the American police in this city have some kind of law against 'idling' one's car; obviously I do not want to get arrested for doing that. So shall I proceed with my follow-on report?"

"*Pojowsta, spasiba*," responded the voice. "Are you in a safe location?"

"Yes, I am parked several blocks away from the house, more about that later." said the Russian.

"Proceed," ordered the SVR commander.

"Since the probable identification at the library," explained the man in the car, "I have been pursuing a late model Patriotic, silver and black, Arizona license-plate 892-BLB, at a discreet distance, although I have to admit that once or twice it looked like the man driving this vehicle may have been suspicious; on those occasions, I hung back further. This seemed to have worked because I have now followed the vehicle and its occupants to the city of Tucson, Arizona."

"Where, specifically?" asked the remote voice.

"They have stopped at a ranch-style house on the east side of the city in a neighborhood called 'Desert Palms'," said the agent. "I will send you the exact address later, Alexi, when I can safely get close enough to verify it, since the occupants of the car seem still to be inside the house. I could only observe them at long distance with my mini view-scope, but from the way in which they all behaved, it looks like the man who was driving the car is the owner of the house; or at least he is renting it, because he had the keys to open the door."

"Excellent work," commended the voice on the special cellphone. "Tell me, Misha, did you get any more details on the target?"

"Very little in the physical sense," replied the field-operative, "Because for most of the time, including when the group in this SUV arrived at the house, she has been wearing dark glasses and a red baseball-cap with a large letter 'A' on it, you should make a note of that for the benefit of the others. But there *was* one very interesting incident, when their group stopped by the side of the road, in the desert."

There was a slight pause, then, the voice directed, "Do go on."

"This is rather difficult to explain," stated the Russian, "But... the situation was, basically, that their group had parked the vehicle and they had all disembarked. I noticed that several of the children later went off a short distance into the desert, so maybe this was, how do the Americans call it, yes, a 'potty break'. The group was clustered around the side door of the SUV, and then... you see..."

"Misha?" requested the voice. "Are you still there?"

"Well, Commander," continued the man with the cellphone, "The target – the girl, I mean – she started *singing*. That is what happened."

"What is so unusual about that?" inquired the commander. "You are not making any sense."

"What is so *unusual*, you ask?" retorted the agent, with a rueful chuckle. "Alexi, she did not merely *sing*; no, sir, neither our mother tongue, nor English, nor any language spoken on this planet, can describe what I heard, no, what I *felt*, in my mind, because at the time, I was at least three kilometers away, so I could *not* really have heard it... could I? Such a song has never been heard by human beings, not in the elite Red Army chorus at the Bolshoi, not by those listening to the finest orchestra playing Beethoven or Tchaikovsky, not anywhere, *never*! I could not tell if it was just the target, or perhaps the entire group, that was singing; I think the former, though, because when the tune came to me, my eyes saw... colors, beautiful, shining colors all about the sky, my mind knew the secrets of the *universe* –"

"So you mean –" exclaimed the remote voice.

"Ah... curse it," protested the man in the car. "If only you could *understand*, Alexi! I am not ashamed to say, Commander, that tears came to my eyes, listening to this song, which was neither in English, nor in Russian, yet still, somehow, I understood it. I felt completely drained, emotionally, afterwards."

Faintly, the man could hear a gasp of recognition, over the cell connection.

"Indeed, Misha, I think that you have now made the final, positive confirmation that we have the correct target," observed the man called 'Alexi', "As this corresponds very closely with the observations made by Cosmonaut Chkalov, in his own reports to Star City. You have given us a *most* interesting report – of that there can be no doubt. Anything more?"

"No, Commander," replied the Russian. "Except, other than for continuous surveillance, does Headquarters have any new orders? The context here is, I believe that we are ahead of the Americans on this project; but our lead cannot last forever. If we are to act, we may have to do so, soon, but I have no idea what the ultimate outcome is to be."

"For the time being," ordered the remote voice, "You must lay low, keep the target and her group under observation, but do not attempt to make contact. We are pulling almost all our assets from around the continental United States, just leaving one or two in each area; the rest are on their way to assist you, but the first of them will probably not be there until two days from now, at the earliest. From our traffic-intercepts, Headquarters has concluded – no great surprise here, of course – that the American effort, while being directed from the highest levels, is poorly co-ordinated, with the various agencies involved competing with each other as opposed to working together."

Misha could not avoid a chuckle, upon hearing this.

"It also appears," continued the one called 'Alexi', "That the American government, or, at least, certain officials within it, has been compromised by one of their many religious sects, some of whom may be planning on a 'wet' operation against the target, for obscure theological reasons. If it appears that the target is about to be captured or killed, then you are authorized, even at the risk of your own life, to make contact and attempt to rescue her – but I have to stress that this course of action must be exercised only in the most extreme circumstances, if there is *absolutely* no other option."

"Understood," said the SVR agent.

"And you can also be sure of one other thing," the voice added.

"Which would be?" asked the other.

"You may now be the most important agent in the history of SVR, KGB and all that have gone before it, and before you, my friend. More important than Fuchs, Greenglass or Julius, or any of those on the Manhattan Project. A being who can shatter a *comet*... I do not have to explain why we cannot allow the Americans to obtain exclusive control over something like *that*."

"I will not fail you," replied the Russian, deadly serious, now. "Nor the Motherland. I *swear* it."

"We expect none less," said the voice.

"Misha out," said the man in the car, snapping shut the cover on his special cell-phone.

No Sparing Of The Rod

"Mommy... I'm *scared*," whimpered the little girl, nervously fidgeting with her pigtails.

"Where'd they take Daddy?" she asked, wiping the trace of a tear.

"I don't know, Trisha," consoled the mother while squeezing the child's shoulders closer to her own. "In the next room, or down the hall, maybe. But he'll be back in a few minutes, I'm sure..."

The harsh voice of a National Guardsman, or of a someone outfitted to look akin, sounded in the hall outside, behind the barred, locked metal door.

"No talking allowed, you understand?" ordered the man.

"Well, my children are *frightened*," countered the woman. "Haven't you ever had kids? Surely you must know how they'd feel, being subjected to all... *this*, with no warning or explanation. We have *rights*, you know."

"I have my orders, Ma'am, and they indicate that all of you are to remain silent, until told otherwise," growled the soldier. "Further violations of the rules may result in the children being removed from your room and kept separately. You've already been warned, so don't do anything you'll regret later."

He paused for a second, then added, "And let me correct you on one thing. Down here, you have *no* rights. None at all."

"Mommy –" the girl tried to start, but she was "shushed" by the mother's finger-to-lips gesture.

And so, they waited, minute after long minute, the three – suburban, average, white, previously smug, middle-class American mother, teenage daughter, school-age son and younger school-age daughter – in this bare, concrete walled-and-floored cell, their intimidated, uncomprehending visages starkly illuminated by a too-bright florescent bulb high above their heads.

Did it last twenty minutes or two hours?

How would they have known?

Silently, she cursed that these combat-fatigued men had "confiscated" her watch, cell-phone, wallet, and, indeed, everything she had, that would otherwise have connected her to the outside world or proved who she was.

But all things good and bad alike must come to an end, and eventually, they heard the "click" of a key turning in the door-lock.

Catherine suppressed a gasp at seeing her husband, or, rather, what remained of him. True, there were no bruises, there was no blood; but the man's body and face were sullen, bathed in sweat. His lips were puffy and there was a strange, uncomprehending stare to his eyes. He could barely stand, as the two camouflaged soldiers dragged him over to the bench, where he slumped, visibly struggling just to remain upright.

"What the hell have you *done* to him!" shrieked the woman. "He's as pale as a ghost! *Mark!*"

One soldier strode quickly over and roughly grabbed her arm, shaking her like a rag-doll.

"Shut the *fuck* up!" he bellowed. "And anyway, it's *your* turn. Get up!"

"My turn for *what?*" shouted the alarmed woman.

In front of the horrified stares of three children, the man threw Catherine to the floor. Her head hit the concrete, hard, and the warm feeling of blood met her fingers, as she probed her hair for the point of impact.

"Your turn to tell us the truth – to tell us what you *really* know," snarled the gendarme.

"*Mark!*" cried the wife, shooting a pleading glance to her husband's eyes.

But he just stayed in his dull isolation, mumbling something incomprehensible, although he was looking right at the scene.

"*Mark!*" she shrieked, as the men dragged her out the door.

Clang.

After a second, the terrified children heard a different, equally crude-sounding male voice.

"Keep your fucking little traps shut in there," admonished the soldier standing guard outside the door. "Because if your mother doesn't tell us something worthwhile, you'll all get plenty of chance to say your piece. *Plenty* of chance."

He let out a guttural laugh.

The children huddled together, a body's-space or so from their sweating, disoriented father, and shut their eyes, trying to make it go away.

Detour

"You got all the stuff off the SUV back in Salt Lake... right?" inquired the woman, not looking behind as she and the other two double-timed their pace towards the floodlit hangar from the plain-marked business-jet, its fold-down staircase already retracting.

"Uhh... yeah," huffed Boatman, sweating under the weight of two large duffel-bags, each bulging with the outlines of various pieces of electronic equipment.

"'Cept that I'd appreciate if I got a little *help* here, Agent Chu," he complained. "Or how 'bout you?"

The athletic-looking man behind the other two shook his head.

"Got all I can take already," he answered. "Change of clothes for three fine-looking young FBI-agents, plus... hell, I don't *know* what, but it's sure enough to fill up one bag, I can attest to that."

"We're almost there... see? There he is," indicated the Asian-American agent.

She waved to a limousine that had parked in the shadows, just inside the private aircraft-hangar about a hundred feet ahead.

"That's just *great*," managed the hulking, black man, as he tried to adjust the weight of the burden on his back to a different side, "But, I was meanin' to ask you, just where the hell *are* we, anyway?"

"I thought I told you in the plane," replied Chu. "Springfield, Illinois. The interviewees, a family named the 'Porters', are being kept in a secure location about ten miles outside the city limits, or so they tell me. Rumor is that the National Guard picked 'em up wandering aimlessly off the road, just over the state line – no car, no money, no ID – we only figured out who they were, with the bio-implants. They're in very rough shape... looks like somebody's already *gotten* to them, if you know what I mean. Apparently they can hardly talk at all."

"Ah, I see," knowingly remarked Boatman.

They were at the car now – an old-style North American boat of a vehicle, all black and chrome, with the obligatory tinted, but bullet-resistant, windows – and a smartly-dressed young man, outwardly very similar to the third agent in both looks and demeanor, stepped out, gave a half-salute and unlocked the doors.

Boatman gratefully let the duffel-bags drop from his grasp into the trunk, and grunted with recognition when the back end of the car compressed downward, until the shocks took over again. He swung around to the side, and again the vehicle gained some rear-axle traction, due to the man's own not inconsiderable weight.

"Yeah, okay," remarked the third agent, toward his boss. "But *why*? I got a chance to look at the profile on them while we were on the plane. They're just a white-bread family from Dearborn... nothing unusual on their file, not even porno checkouts or illegal music on the back-door scan of their computers. I checked the files on their kids, too – three of 'em – and they're all as Average American as apple pie, teenager got caught playing hooky one time but other than that... I mean, what can they possibly have to *do* with this case?"

The limousine came to life and it roared out of the hangar, traveling rapidly across the tarmac.

"Yeah," added the black man, finally able to somehow fit the seat belt around his waist, after plenty of trying every way that wouldn't work.

"It doesn't make any *sense*, Agent Chu," he said. "And you know, we had a hell of a good lead back there in Salt Lake – I mean, if I was the suspicious type, I'd say that somebody in one of the competin' agencies was tryin' to *deliberately* throw us off the trail. So *what* if nobody at the damn library saw where they went? I'd have flipped a coin and taken the Interstate that came up, heads or tails. Either way, we'd probably be a lot closer to them, when and if somebody else makes a positive ID on 'em."

Chu shook her head.

"Don't either of you ever bother to read the background-notes?" she complained. "*I* did, and I had the same two hours in the plane as the two of you."

"Was going to," offered the third agent, "But I kind of got side-tracked. NCAA's back on NeoNet, you know."

"Air-travel always puts me to sleep, you know that, Agent Chu," mentioned Boatman, sheepishly. "That and the wet bar. Damn... forgot my expense forms."

He grinned.

"Well then, let me fill you in, gentlemen," sighed the woman. "Since you're so up on your briefings, I'm sure this will just be review, right? Anyway. Here's what I've been told. Yes, they're as average as you can get, but this 'Porter' family, they *do* have one *very* interesting credential."

The car turned a corner and headed down a side-road, the gloom approaching from every direction as the sun slowly started to set.

"Which would be?" inquired the black man, arching an eyebrow.

"Remember that Tex-Mex restaurant that we dropped in on, right after we got on the case?" asked Chu, teasingly. "Up in Idaho, that is. The one just off the highway."

"Yeah," muttered the third agent. "How could I ever *forget?* Spent half an hour in the john after making the mistake of trying one of those greasy tacos they got there. And I grew up on the Mexican stuff – ate nothing but in high-school."

"Well, then," explained the FBI team-leader, "You probably sat very close to somewhere that had also accommodated a very famous... *being.*"

She took a long look out the window. "Come to think of it, *I* had to answer the call of nature there, too... there were two toilets... 50-50 that I used one that *she* did, too..."

"Whoa!" exclaimed Boatman. "What you *sayin'*?"

"Just this," answered the woman. "It seems that not more than a day or so before we stopped in, the 'Santa Esmerelda', as it's called, had a woebegone little stranger, like a hippie or a hobo, *et cetera*, wander in through their door, which Mrs. Catherine Porter, that's the mother of this family of course, in her infinite kindness, treated to a free continental breakfast. The mother described the girl as being disoriented, maybe in shock or something like that."

"You got *my* attention for sure, now," stated the black man.

Chu smiled.

She continued, "But here's the kicker: Our little hobo was wearing a badly beat-up, Air Force-issue uniform. Which," – the agent added, matter-of-factually – "*Precisely* matches one worn by a Professor Cherie Tanaka, Chief science-officer on the Mars landing space mission. You will recall, they had to give at least one of these to the alien, this 'Karéin-Mayréij', as she was wearing next to nothing when they dug her, or it, out of that tomb on Mars. And according to the people at the restaurant, the uniform that the hobo-girl was wearing, had tears, rips, burn-marks all over it... as if the person wearing it had been in a big crash with lots of fire."

"Oh boy," breathed the third agent.

"Oh, and one other thing," added the FBI field team-leader. "The restaurant staff didn't remember this one exactly, either, but we may have been wrong about her hair. They said something strange about 'she had granny hair', apparently it might not have been blond after all, despite the fact that the alien was clearly blond for the entire time that they had contact with her out on Mars and on Jacobson's space ships."

"Well," offered Boatman, "If I fell off a comet down to Earth and lived to tell about it, I bet *I'd* have a few gray hairs too."

"Holy *shit*," gasped the third agent. "If that ain't a positive ID, I don't know what would be."

"Then why the hell aren't we back in Idaho, trackin' her down?" growled Boatman. "This ain't *right*, Minnie! Somebody higher up is *tryin'* to steal the spotlight, here. What other possible reason is there for sending us a thousand miles from the scene of the crime?"

"And why the hell didn't that fuckin' restaurant-guy tell us about his little visitor, for God's sake?" added the other man.

"Don't know, to both questions," replied Chu. "But, if necessary, you'll get your chance to ask this guy, what's his name, yeah, 'Jiminez', that's it, personally. Also the waitress that did the tables at this place... apparently, she served our little Martian girl her first square meal here on Earth. Feds have both of them in custody in the same facility that the Porter family is being kept at, flew 'em there last night."

"Waste of time, in my opinion," muttered the third agent.

"Maybe, Will," answered the woman. "Maybe not. And by the way, as far as H.Q. knows, neither NSA, nor CIA, is aware of all these connections. Both the Porters and the restaurant staff are under FBI's exclusive control; the Director wants it kept that way, needless to say. Our official story to anyone else in the government, if it comes to that, is that we're just trying to 'contain any contamination that the detainees might have contracted, by coming into contact with the alien'. Who knows, it might even be true."

She leaned forward and addressed the driver.

"How far out are we?" she requested.

"Seven minutes or so," replied the third agent. "Bureau's got safe places like this all over, of course, but they picked this one for proximity to the airport. Just in case."

"Step on it, if you don't mind," demanded Boatman, with a round chuckle.

America Drops The Veil

Groggily, Billings stumbled towards the bedroom's private bathroom.

He fumbled for the light-switch, casting a glance over his shoulder in so doing.

"Sari? *Sari*? You there? Oh... never mind," he softly called.

Evidently, the fallen-girl was already up, as her side of the bed was unoccupied.

It took three tries to find the switch, which was more or less the number that it usually did. The fact was comforting.

Damn, it's good to be home, mused the salesman.

Mercifully, the tap worked when he hit the activator-button on the 'Cold' side of the faucet, although Billings noted that only half the expected flow came out, no matter how far up he turned the indicator.

He reached for his toothbrush.

Never saw her brush her teeth, he reflected. *But her breath is always nice. Not the* most *peculiar thing about her, I guess...*

He wearily moved the brush back and forth, each stroke offsetting just a tiny bit of the nasty hangover that he had somehow woken up with.

Well, okay, Billings allowed.

The morning-after crap, you should have seen coming... she warned *me that she could drink me under the table. But I cut off early.*

No, I didn't.

I should feel *a hell of a lot worse... damn, I must have finished off three-quarters of a bottle all by my lonesome... I should be in a hospital Emerg ward or some detox tank...*

But the truth is, it's actually not as bad as what I've felt before, with much less booze...

Odd... isn't it?

Bleary-eyed, Billings looked up at the mirror.

I'll shave later, he convinced himself, as he turned, grabbed a housecoat and shuffled off towards the kitchen.

"Momma, Curtis pushed me!" sounded the whine of the Claremont girl, from ahead.

"Curtis Ray, Melissa Arlene, y'all *behave* yourselves!" came back the voice of the mother. "We in 'nother man's house! Ah'll not be hearin' no more of this!"

Billings crossed a door threshold and beheld the three of them, sitting at the kitchen table.

The digital clock was showing ten, though that might not have been exactly the right time, since its NeoNet connection-light was blinking "Error".

"Guess I'm not the *only* one who slept in," he offered, looking at the black woman's uncharacteristically-frazzled hair.

"Y'all ain't the only one who had a bit too much of the good stuff, last night," ruefully answered Claremont. "Kids was up *way* before me. Only got up when they started yellin'. Don' help that it so *hot* already, y'all knows... makes 'em cranky. They used to it bein' warm in De-troit in th' summer, but not like this so early in the mornin'."

"I *tried* to turn on the A/C yesterday," explained the salesman, with a shrug. "No dice, as far as I can tell, I *think* it's still working, but that bloody remote-control box that they have it hooked up through must be still preventing it from firing up."

"Oh," muttered the black woman. "That too bad, Bob."

"Yeah," agreed Billings. "Knew a guy around here who could hot-wire it, so that you could still turn on the air and it would fake 'em out so that they thought it was still off, before the Big Bang that is, but I never wanted to try it after they put through that '20 years in the slammer for power theft' law... if I want to cool off I just get in the SUV and go hang out at a nice, air-conditioned bar somewhere, or, when they let me use water, I just take a cold shower. Kind of a fact of life around here, I'm afraid."

The salesman noticed three bowls of mush on the table. The woman was forcing intermittent mouthfuls of the stuff, but the other two bowls were just full of soggy mess, with Curtis and Melissa sitting stoically refusing to eat.

"Ain't no milk," remarked Claremont. "Found some cornflakes, but they don' like it too much, just with water."

"Don't y'all ever got no *milk* 'round here, Mister Billins'?" pleaded Melissa. "Looked all over but ain't even none of that powder stuff that we used to get from the food bank."

"And it ain't got no sugar on it," complained the Claremont boy.

"Things is tough all around," acerbically replied Billings. "And to answer your question, I just stocked up on booze – didn't figure there'd be much call for survival rations, when chances were that survival wasn't on the agenda. But never fear, kids, we'll be heading off to the mall as soon as I get organized around here... they got a supermarket there, although how much it will have in the way of food, I can't say. Look at the bright side of it; they can't have *less* than I got here, right? Try to put up with it for a few minutes. I'll even treat you to lunch at the food-court."

His eyes scanned to and fro.

"Where's Sari?" asked the salesman.

"Ah think she in th'other room with the Injun boy," mentioned Claremont. "Thought y'all already knew – kid started cryin' middle of the night, would have gone in there an' tried to settle him down myself, but yo' lady-friend beat me to it, she was there in bed with him before ah even got to the door. Y'all didn't notice she was gone?"

"No," replied Billings, "But by now I'm sure you'd be aware, her comings and goings are kind of... hard to follow, if you know what I mean."

Claremont nodded knowingly, looking straight forward.

"Well, I guess I'd better go and roust her out," muttered Billings.

He doubled back on his original route, took a turn down a side-hall and came to a room at the house's far left end.

The door was open, but only by a crack.

The salesman peered in, being immediately confronted by a scene that wouldn't have looked out of place in a Norman Rockwell painting, or perhaps in one of those feel-good movies that women can't get enough of and men can't stand more than a minute of.

The 'Sari'-girl was propped up by a pillow, semi-reclining against the headboard of the bed, while the Indian-boy's head lay peacefully sleeping across her waist.

Her face wore a look of serene satisfaction...of, *fulfillment.*

"Shh," admonished the newcomer, in a whisper. "It took me two hours to put him to sleep."

"What was he – oh, forget it," Billings whispered back.

He tried to back out and close the door, but while so doing, let out a most uncooperative 'creak'.

Lazily, the boy's eyes opened.

After a prolonged yawn, he looked up at the 'Sari'-girl with filial affection.

"Sorry... I guess I kinda fell asleep half way through the story, Miz Sari," he apologized.

"Not a problem," replied the fallen-girl, in a kind voice. "There is always another night, another time for stories that carry us from the land of here and now, to the far shores of mist and dreams. Maybe tonight, Tommy?"

The child grinned appreciatively.

"Tonight, for sure!" he responded, slowly arising. "Can we learn more about this, uhh... this 'passing the fire' thing?"

The newcomer nodded regally.

Forcing himself to ignore the implications, Billings addressed the boy.

"Trouble sleeping in a strange place, kid?" he asked.

"Yeah, I guess... Mister," answered Tommy. "Didn't mean to interrupt you and Miz Sari... I mean..."

"Don't worry about it," said the salesman. "Happens to me, too, especially on road trips, motels, that kind of thing. But you'll get over it. As long as there's no roaches under the bed. *Hate* it when that happens."

The boy laughed.

"Well," continued Billings, "I'd invite the two of you to breakfast, but Whitney tells me that there's no milk for the cornflakes, and apparently that doesn't agree with her kids' educated palates, so unless you want them dry, you'll have to wait until we head off to the mall and do a little shopping. How hungry are you?"

"What is a 'palate', Bob?" innocently inquired the 'Sari'-girl. "Is that like a big castle? It sounds like..."

Billings rolled his eyes.

"Yeah, I forgot you're not from... *around* here," he grunted. "It's like, what kinds of food, what tastes, appeal to you, and which ones don't."

"Oh, yeah. Sure. Like not eating cornflakes with whiskey on them, instead of milk?" replied the fallen-girl.

She shot a quick glance at Tommy, and then, without warning, the both of them broke out in paroxysms of laughter.

The salesman covered his eyes with his hand for a second and leaned back against the door, until the other two had enjoyed their little 'in' joke.

"Okay, team, if we're over *that*, now," he complained, trying not to sound overly sarcastic, "You might as well get dressed, get cleaned up to go outside, that is. I'm planning to get going in the next fifteen-twenty minutes, so if you want to tag along – you get the idea, right?"

"Um-humm," confirmed the 'Sari'-girl. "Except that... forgive me, Bob, I know that you are busy, but I wanted to mention something about that and it was never really the right time, you know what I mean? At least I do not *remember* having asked you..."

"About *what*?" asked Billings, hoping it wasn't anything that would singe the boy's tender young ears.

"What I wanted to say," said the newcomer, "Is, my, oh *my*, in your language, you people sure use this 'get' thing a lot... 'get ready', 'get going', 'get up', 'get sick', 'get well', 'get rich', 'get to bed', and so on. It took me quite a while to understand that it does not always mean that one is grabbing something, obtaining it – my language, and most of the other ones that I know, has no construct like this; when we want to describe something, we use the action-word that is really meant for the situation. You could even say it took me a long time to 'get used to Eng-lish'."

Again, she broke down in gales of laughter, accompanied by the boy, right on cue.

"I can see I'm not getting anywhere, here," sighed the salesman. "Oh, Christ, there's that 'get' again... look, I'll be out in the kitchen, okay?"

"We will get you there," giggled the 'Sari'-girl. "So I suppose that we should get dressed, Tommy... right?"

"I need a drink," said Billings, as he headed back for the kitchen.

The 'Sari'-girl shot him a stare of mock pity.

"On *second* thought..." he added.

The salesman shut the door behind him and noted, as he did, that the 'Sari'-girl and the boy were again roaring with laughter.

Come on, *Bob,* he thought to himself. *Don't be so lame as to get jealous over her spending some time with a kid. It's just the mothering thing, you know.*

Halfway down the corridor, he stopped and pondered a bit more.

But... she's how many Goddamn thousand years old? he thought.

How can she want to play Mommy again?

Then again, how could she want to, you-know-what, with yours truly?

Truth is, Bob, you don't have a clue *about what motivates her. Admit that to yourself.*

Of course, it's really no different from what it'd be with a normal chick... is it?

"Hey, Bob, is the waterfall – oh, sorry, I meant, the *shower* – is it working?" he heard from behind.

"Yeah," Billings called back. "Worked for me, this morning, anyway."

"Oh. Oh-kay – next time in there with you," came back the fallen-girl's cheery voice, immediately uplifting the man's spirits.

He half-heard something that she then said to the Indian-boy, who had started giggling again.

"I had to tell Tommy that this is something only grown-up people do," explained the 'Sari'-girl, peeking her head out of the doorway.

She stopped and thought for a second, then added, "Which sounds strange, to hear it coming from my mouth. It is not *my* way of doing things, but I guess I am a stranger here... right?"

Billings smiled obligingly.

"In a *nice* way, though. Meet you in the kitchen," he said. "Oh, and by the way, I un-boxed a new soap-on-a-rope and put fresh towels in the bathroom already. So you can dry yourself off, I mean."

Again, the 'Sari'-girl looked pensive.

"Hmm," she temporized. "I will leave that to you. The towels, I mean. What I usually do is just warm up – increase my body-temperature for a few seconds, the water then evaporates... remember from the motel, when you burned your finger, when you tried to touch me in the –"

Billings raised his finger to his mouth.

"Shh," he pleaded.

"Tommy is a very bright young man," countered the newcomer. "I think that there is little about this that he does not already know. Apparently there is not much privacy, on this 'reservation' that he comes from."

"Get cleaned up," demanded the salesman. "We're out of here in fifteen or so."

"Oh-kay, Bob," answered the 'Sari'-girl, as she slipped past him toward the bathroom.

Three or so seconds later, Billings heard the sound of a shower, or what passed for it with the half water pressure that had been imposed around here lately.

Shuffling into the living-room, the salesman scanned high and low and, after momentary "don't tell me they took *that*, too" panic, recalled that he had hidden the remote for the television inside a drawer in the book-cabinet.

Cleaning a fine film of dust from the screen of the beautiful, 70-inch next-generation nano-LED TV with the side of his arm, he did the same for the chesterfield, sat down, pressed the power-button and hoped for the best.

At first, Billings' heart dropped, as, although the sound of something powering up clearly sputtered in his ears, there was no sign of life at all on the screen.

A second later, he remembered that the damn thing's NeoNet connection was probably out – it couldn't call home, couldn't download the latest show schedule, nor could do any of the other behind-the-scenes viewing habits monitoring that, he had been so assured when he first connected up to Mojave Cable, were "just for statistical purposes".

Yeah, right, mused the salesman.

They're just looking in to make sure I'm not watching the wrong movies and to make sure they send me the right commercials.

Not that I really care.

But he knew from experience that the wizardry in this high-tech idiot box would eventually switch back to 'basic mode', whatever that was – Billings could never really tell the difference from what he got when the networking stuff was working – and it would give him something to watch.

Which, after two or three seconds, it mercifully did.

He felt the other side of the couch compress slightly and shot a glance to his right, seeing the Claremont boy having swiftly deposited himself alongside.

"What y'all gonna watch, Mister Billings?" asked Curtis. "Man, y'all got a *kickin'* TV! That *twice* the size of anythin' ah seen in our 'hood."

Billings shrugged.

"Glad you like it," he offered. "Got it half price from the Wal-Target across town, cashed in a favor from a guy I know there... free tiles for his patio. Hell of a time just getting it here, though... had to rent a U-Haul. I was thinking about reno'ing the basement, and I would have put down there so it would stay cool, but it was too big to fit down the stairs."

He flicked a few channels, up and down.

"Oh, and I was looking for the community channel, sometimes they have announcements on it, like about when we're going to get our full water and power turned back on, if ever. Doesn't seem to be up, today, though... ah, well, that one might be only with the NeoNet connection, and it's out. We might as well watch a ball-game until it's time to get going. Say, are your mother and sister ready?"

"Shore 'nuff," replied the boy. "Melissa, she brushin' she teeth again, after Momma made her eat all them cornflakes... she want to get th' taste out of her mouth."

"Don't you?" inquired Billings.

"Don't gots to," matter-of-factually answered Curtis. "Dumped half of 'em into Melissa's bowl when she ain't watchin', and dumped the rest into yo' flower garden when Momma went to the bathroom."

The salesman chuckled knowingly.

"You know, Curtis," he mentioned, "You aren't that different from yours truly, when I was your age. And *I* turned out okay, didn't I?"

The Claremont boy nodded, enthusiastically,

Happily, the next channel turned out to be a baseball-game – not MLB, just A-League – but certainly better than watching the infomercials that seemed to be on every second channel, these days.

"Damn straight," said Curtis, quickly moving his head back and forth in search of signs of his mother.

"Don' tell her ah said that bad word, though, okay, Mister Billins? Anyway, what ah means is... y'all turn out A-OK – y'all shacked up with *her*. That enough to make y'all *real* famous."

Nervously, Billings inquired, "Uhh... yeah, kid, but... why would just, you know, being with Sari make me *famous*? You think she's maybe a supermodel?"

Curtis giggled.

"She mo' super than *that*, Mister Billins. She *way* more. Momma told me not to ask or speak 'bout it, but ah already got it figured out by myself. Y'all in love with an *angel*, Mister Billings. Ain't no man ah *ever* heard 'bout, who got a lady like *that*. Make y'all real special, too... right?"

Damn kids, thought the salesman. *It's hard enough to keep my* own *trap shut.*

"That's... that's *right*, Curtis," prevaricated the salesman. "And your mother's got a very good point about us not discussing it, that is. See, the thing is, Curtis, that neither your mother nor I, believe that Sari really knows *who* she is. So we all owe it to her to give her some time, let her get settled. Then we'll work it out, all in good time. Okay?"

"Okay," agreed the boy. "But if it was me, ah'd tell *all* mah homies – ain't no way ah wouldn't, y'all know?"

Billings leaned forward, shaking his head.

"I know how you feel, son," he offered. "But some things are, well... kept secret for a good reason, I guess. I think this is one of them. Hey, look – base hit!"

Gratefully, the boy seemed to change the focus of his attention to the game, and so the two of them watched for another three or four minutes, until Curtis was called away by his mother.

"Come an' get yo' T-shirt, Curtis Ray," admonished Claremont. "Ain't been too much water in th' washin' machine, but somehow ah got the dirt out of it anyways."

Curtis got up and left.

"After I do that, I'm gonna see what y'all got in that shed out there, Mister Billins," was his parting comment.

"You break anything, your Momma buys it," warned Billings, to the boy's rapidly receding back. "You break *yourself*, don't blame ol' Bob."

Idly, Billings started flicking up the dial, as men are wont to do.

Wonder if it irritates her like it would a human-chick, he maliciously thought.

I'll have to try it on her and see.

The salesman skipped over two channels of infomercials, two more in some incomprehensible, fast-talking Spanish dialect – he knew only enough to order a *cerveca* or two, though it had been years since they had closed the Mexican border once and for all – and at least three more stations with various soap-operas and daytime talk-shows.

Finally, he hit KGUN, and one of their top-of-the-hour news-briefs.

"...And now, for today's world news summary," announced the blow-dried, nattily-dressed anchorman. "In a series of prepared statements, the President has declared that his next public news conference will be held in approximately two months, but, for the time being, he again reiterated his position that the 'Sword of Freedom' device, now credited with having been the decisive factor in the last-minute defeat of the 'Lucifer' comet, will neither be revealed, nor shared, with any foreign power."

Billings belched.

"Secretary of State Hyndman," stated the anchorman, "Has been dispatched to a top-level meeting with the EU, with a view to trying to find common ground on this issue, as well as to try to work out a common trans-Atlantic approach to the crisis in Pakistan. The parties are said to be far apart, however, and the Speaker of the European Parliament is quoted as saying that in view of the recent near overthrow of the Jordanian government by extremist Islamic elements, caution must be exercised to avoid further inflaming the situation."

The picture on the television changed to a jungle scene.

"The commander of U.S. expeditionary forces in Cuba announced today that he has every confidence that the corner has been turned in that conflict," proclaimed the news-reader. "Lieutenant-General Long also stated that insurgent activity in the southeastern half of the country has fallen to a three-year low, with the loss of only seventeen U.S. Army and GrayWar Corporation troops this week. However, the General denied rumors that the curfews currently in place in Havana and other large cities are about to be rescinded anytime soon; in his own words, 'As soon as these Commie-terrorist rebels realize that we're here in Cuba to stay, the minute that they do the smart thing and lay down their arms, then we'll let them come out at night, again.'"

I wonder if those cop-show re-runs are still on Channel 4589, idly thought Billings.

"This claim," droned on the announcer, "Was immediately contradicted by propaganda sites posted by the insurgents on NeoNet, and independent reports from battlefields in the Sierra Madre indicate that the insurgency is very much alive, with persistent reports that the rebels are receiving funding and weapons from the pro-terrorist, anti-American government in Brazil. The Secret Service and the National news-media Regulation Office, meanwhile, issued a joint press-release stating that they are investigating the origin of the insurgent NeoNet postings, and that any Americans found to have been involved, in the words of the two organizations, 'will be severely punished'."

The camera now panned to a different announcer, this one a Barbie-doll blond in a sequin-bedecked shirt.

"Turning to the domestic arena," she read, "The President contradicted persistent reports of unrest in Southern California, stating, in his words, that 'the only thing unusual about what's going on in Los Angeles, is that the Dodgers aren't leading their division', although he confirmed that communications with the L.A. metropolitan area may continue to be spotty for the next few weeks, due to stringent restrictions on the use of electricity. On the economic front, the Secretary of the Treasury spoke today in front of a Wall Street audience, and strenuously denied that the government is planning any deviation from its current, free-market policies..."

Billings flicked the channel up a few more places.

There was an old Roy Rogers western and some gardening-show, in which the host was doing his level best to convince the audience that "yes, you *can* grow a great back-yard floral-arrangement, on your existing water-ration".

Reluctantly, the salesman switched back to the news.

"In local news," intoned the female news-reader, "Governor Ratcliff has extended the emergency water and power regulations for another three months, subject to approval by the State Legislature, which informed political observers regard as likely. Despite this, the Governor, in a move that's being widely regarded as a pre-election good-will gesture, has announced the lifting of nightly curfews in Phoenix, Tucson and Chandler, with the rest of the cities due to follow as soon as order is fully restored."

Fuck – no A/C for months, thought an unhappy Billings.

"In a related announcement," continued the woman, "The State Board of Education has now set the first day for non-minority Arizona students to return to school, as May 15, although some local boards are said to be disputing this date, on the grounds that too little will remain of the school year for the move to be worthwhile."

Who cares, mused the salesman.

"Turning to the law-and-order beat," said the announcer, "Phoenix police went on a wild 25-minute car chase yesterday, eventually cornering three suspects in a stolen vehicle after an attempted carjacking. The pursuit ended in an off-road argicultural-complex in Laveen, where two of the criminals were shot and pronounced dead at the scene; the other is now in hospital, suffering from multiple bullet and hand-grenade injuries –"

Click.

A frustrated Billings made the damn thing shut up.

He looked up, past the TV, straight at the beaming figure of his personal angel, resplendent in new clothes, or, new *something*.

If a woman could look like a billion, not a million – *she*, did.

"What do you think, Bob?" earnestly asked the 'Sari'-girl.

"I went into the closet and looked for the clothes, like you suggested," she explained. "Many of them were, uhh, too large for me, but *these* ones – the shirt and blue jean leggings – they fit nicely. So do the 'sneakers', and this little carrying-bag fits quite comfortably around my shoulder. I tried on the, what do you call it, 'lip-stick', but it made my lips look like I had just eaten something far too spicy for my own good. Even without *that*... do I still look oh-kay?"

"*I'd* say," was all the salesman could muster.

"I tried out some of these 'dresses' that some of the women around here wear," added the fallen-girl, "But they just felt, I do not know exactly how to say this, *weird* – I am not accustomed to wearing something like that, which would flop over my face, if I were to do an up-and-over jump, or a flying-kick –"

"It's called a 'somersault'," noted Billings. "And don't bother to tell me why you'd need to do one of those moves. But... you look 'edible', my dear."

The 'Sari'-girl smiled appreciatively, with maybe the hint of a blush.

"Why, thank you, Bob," she replied. "So, I put on this 'bra-seer', like you asked me to, although it, too, feels kind of not to any useful purpose."

"It's so your boobs don't show through that pretty white shirt you've got on," pointed out the salesman. "I can personally attest, they can be awfully... *distracting*."

The newcomer showed an evil, sharp-toothed grin, as she was wont to do when she was, excited.

"You know that I sometimes feel what *you* feel, the perceptions and emotions of your mind," she stated. "Feed-back, you know. So, I will wear this 'bra-seer', however confining it may be. But not when we get home, oh-kay?"

Billings shrugged to the side and rolled his eyes in acknowledgment, trying to keep his mind from wandering in the wrong direction and taking certain parts of his anatomy merrily along with it for the ride.

A second later, he noted that the 'Sari'-girl was staring intently at the television, staring right past him, in fact.

"Bob," she requested, firmly and deliberately, "Re-enable the sound, if you please."

Focusing again on the screen, the instant that he hit the un-mute button, Billings realized what had caught her attention – a grim scene with four hooded figures, each one with a noose tied around the neck, standing beside the others on a platform.

The upper bodies of two of the condemned – evidently male, as they were taller than the other two – were rhythmically swaying slightly forward and back, as if doing repeated half-bows. Another hooded figure was resisting the captors, and both Billings and the fallen-girl could barely make out various Spanish-sounding curses coming from his direction, but the last one – a woman – just mutely stood there.

The platform was surrounded by uniformed men and a crowd of what resembled nothing so much as the average folk from one of those old TV game-shows.

"Sari," he warned, "You *really* don't want to watch this."

"Yes, I most certainly *do*," she countermanded, staring intently at the deadly goings-on. "Let your rulers now show me their way of mercy, Bob of Billings."

"Finally, tonight," stated the male TV announcer, as matter-of-factually as if describing a routine day on the stock-market, "Federal authorities have released the following footage this week's 'No Mercy For Perverts, Traitors, Criminals and Subversives' ceremony, with the death-sentence being carried out against four individuals – three men and one woman – for capital offenses against the United States."

The announcer picked up another reading-sheet and continued, "The most infamous of those executed, was the notorious Jorge Matarano Lopez, acknowledged second-in-command of the Houston branch of the *Maras* gang. Lopez was convicted under the No More Coddling of Immigrant Criminals, Gangsters and Parasites Act, of multiple charges of first- and second-degree murder, aggravated cross-race rape, running illegal inter-state dog-fighting, cock-fighting and rat-fighting rings, facilitating illegal immigration, criminal participation in a prohibited opposition group, trafficking in synthetic drug-compounds, pirated entertainment content and prohibited guided munitions, as well as felony evasion of the Tax Code, all of which are capital crimes."

"The other two men," intoned the news-reader, "Both disloyal minority members, were convicted in secret court of attempted Muslim subversion of the Armed Forces, in violation of the Keep America Free From Godless Islam Act. The nature of the crimes in which the woman was implicated, has not been released; however, one source has claimed that these include 'distributing 'day-after' contraceptives and inducing a miscarriage', contrary to the God's Human Life Begins At Conception Act."

The 'Sari'-girl looked as if she was going to ask a question, but, to Billings' relief, she held her silence, while watching the goings-on with laser-like precision.

"Final statements were taken from all of the condemned," said the announcer, "But these, too, have been withheld, due to profanity in the case of Mr. Lopez, because of federal regulations against the publication of Muslim propaganda in the case of the two other men, and for unspecified reasons in the case of the woman."

A voice-over sounded.

"Tensh-hut!" it bellowed, in a harsh, military tone, followed by "Proceed!"

Suddenly, the four figures dropped down, stopping abruptly with their heads, each now bent grotesquely forward, no more than a few inches above the platform upon which these wretched people had just taken their last mortal breaths.

All, that was, except for one, which still twitched back and forth, slightly.

A uniformed, masked soldier stepped briskly forward and gave this one recalcitrant figure, a mighty blow with something looking like an extra-large police baton, on the back of the head-shroud.

Instantly, this man, too, now totally lifeless, slumped forward. A trickle of blood poured out the front of the shroud, before the camera panned away.

"As you can see," dryly noted the announcer, "This particular execution did not proceed with one hundred per cent adherence to protocol, and the State Commissioner, who is authorized to carry out the process on behalf of the Federal government, has promised a full review of the preparation measures undertaken. Should a violation of process be determined, possible sanctions against those found negligent, include the loss of up to three days' worth of pay. The Commissioner's report is due in fourteen days, government sources stated."

Billings noticed Tommy's face staring at the 'Sari'-girl, whose own visage had taken on a weird façade, halfway between horror and anger.

"What are you looking at?" asked the boy.

The salesman quickly turned off the television.

"Oh, uhh... *nothing*, Tommy, dear," stuttered the newcomer. "Nothing at all. Listen, would you mind giving Bob and me a little, uhh, how do you say, 'privacy', for a few minutes? We have some... *adult* stuff to talk about."

"Sure," uneasily agreed the boy. "I'll just go out and see what Curtis and Melissa are doing outside, 'kay?"

"Oh-kay," replied the fallen-girl, forcing a smile.

When the Indian-boy was out of sight – and, presumably, out of earshot – the 'Sari'-girl turned to Billings and sent him a prosecutorial glance.

"I think that you said that this 'America' country of yours is a nice place, a, uhh, 'dem-aw-crassy', did you not, Bob?" she asked. "Where the rights of humans are respected?"

"Yeah... more or less," evaded Billings.

"Does what we just saw on your tele-vision, look much like a safe place, a nice place, to you?" she demanded.

"Compared to *what?*" argued the salesman. "Compared to those rathole Muslim countries across the pond – the Atlantic, I mean – where they hang kids by the *thousands* for messing up their Bible-lessons, or whatever they call that stupid holy book of theirs? Compared to the Chinese, who, if memory serves me right, have secret prisons on every street-corner? Compared to the Jews in the 'New Kingdom of Israel', who gave a couple million Arabs living there a one-way ticket to the deserts of Jordan and Egypt, at the point of a gun, a few years ago? My understanding is about two million got the 'don't forget to write' treatment, but only half of them were left after a few months out there without a canteen or sunscreen."

There was a thoroughly unnerving, angry look on the face of the fallen-girl, like that of a former ally who had turned one hundred per cent to the side of the enemy.

"I hate to break it to you, kid," continued Billings, "But this whole *world* is a pretty fucked-up place. I'd say that for all the crap that goes on here, we've got it better than most here in the Ew-Nighted States of America."

The 'Sari'-girl draped her achingly desirable figure across his sofa-chair.

"You are asking me to take that on faith, you know," she countered. "I did not like what I just saw, not the least little bit – four people whose short lives were just snuffed out right in front of our eyes, for stupid, trivial reasons. Perhaps the crimes of the 'gang-sta' *were* serious... but should a king slaughter a commoner, outside the fury and anger of war?"

Trying to avoid her stare, Billings shrugged.

"Maybe not, my dear, but it's par for the course, down here on this... *planet*," he offered. "Big boys beat up on the little 'uns. Been that way since the dawn of time... not much I could do about it, anyway."

"I should tell you, Bob," mentioned the fallen-girl, "That I have a very, *very* long memory, for things like this. And I find myself recalling seeing this scene, the powerful killing in public to rule by terror, that is, in many, how do you say, 'former lives'. Each time, it has been a warning signal that those who rule are *not* nice – that they may well be my *enemies*. If so... woe unto them."

Staring at him with a withering demeanor, she paused and then icily added, "That if they value the lives of the vulnerable so little, they should not expect their own to be treated any better, when someone far more... *powerful*, arrives."

"What do you want me to *say*, Sari?" pleaded Billings. "While we were driving together up north, I *tried* to clue you into what those idiots are all about; I wish you could have had a bit less of a gruesome demonstration of what they're capable of, when you get on the wrong side of them – thank God at least that the kids didn't get to see this – but look, whether or not I'm right about if my home and native land is any better than all the other ones, it's the only place we got... for better or worse, we're stuck here."

"Yeah," she muttered.

"I've learned to live with it, to know what the limits are," explained the salesman. "I think I told you, there was only one time where I really ended up Shit Creek with the government, and I was *damn* lucky to get out of it. Not an experience that I care to repeat. Beyond *that*, there's not much I can really do to change the situation. That's the way it is, I'm afraid."

The 'Sari'-girl looked down for a few long seconds, her eyes closed in contemplation.

Eventually, her glance again caught his own.

She offered, "'The way it is'... eh, Bob. Is that right?"

"You got it, babe," he replied, hoping to sound confident.

"Maybe," she remarked. "Maybe not. Perhaps... *change* is coming to this world."

Billings shrugged. "Speaking of 'change', can we change the subject?" he asked.

Finally, he got one of her trademark smiles, if only for a second or two.

"Oh-kay, Bob," she said. "I guess that last one is something that we will not fix today."

The newcomer pursed her lips.

"Listen, Bob," she asked, with a hint of worry in her voice. "Are you *sure* that this girl-friend of yours, will not mind that I have borrowed some of her clothes? I mean, in some cultures, what one wears is a very personal thing, one's clothes say what one's place is, in society... doing what I am doing, could be taken the wrong way..."

He shook his head.

"Don't worry about it at all," Billings counseled. "The truth is, I don't think she'll be back for them anytime soon. I tried to get Patty to go out on the last trip with me, the one on which we met at the camp, I mean, but she" – he drew a deep breath – "Elected instead to high-tail it off to her parents' place in Houston. She promised to call, but I never heard anything. Can't blame her, really; we had been together for a couple of years, but it wasn't *going* anywhere, if you know what I mean. I suppose I could have followed up with her, myself, but... I just hope that she's happy."

He fell silent.

Her hand was instantly over his, as she deposited herself next to Billings, where the Claremont boy had been.

"I know exactly how you feel, Bob," she mentioned. "I, too, have had to say 'goodbye' to many close friends and lovers, for various reasons. Sometimes willingly, sometimes not. I have done more of this than you will ever *know*, and it hurts me terribly, every time. *Every* time."

With the trace of a tear in her eye, she kissed his cheek.

Billings squeezed her hand appreciatively, then got up as quickly as his too-many-trade-show-booths legs would allow.

"Well, when you get *my* age," he quipped, "You gotta expect to lose a few here and there. Way life is, I'm afraid. Ready to go?"

The 'Sari'-girl giggled.

"I *had* to lead you out of the camp, did I not," she said, "So now it is *your* turn to lead me into this exciting world of 'Too-sawn' that you live in. I am ready."

"Whitney!" called the salesman. "Lock the back door... the Billings bus is leaving for the mall!"

Meet You In Bermuda

"I must say that I would rather be, how do you say in English, 'taking this flight home', with the rest of you," admitted Cosmonaut Sergei Chkalov, as he half-floated, half self-propelled himself through the corridor, towards the one remaining docking port on ISS2 that really worked reliably.

"You know," he continued, "When I was back in Russia, they trained candidates like me for the Mars mission, by making us do several tours on nuclear submarines, round-world trips without ever surfacing. After a few weeks down there, as you can imagine, it gets rather, 'stuffy' – I like the smell of *borscht*, but too much of a good thing... I have to confess, it is becoming a bit like that, up here."

Boyd slapped the man on the back, a friendly gesture.

"Sergei," he said, "To tell you the truth, I'm amazed that any of the rest of us have been able to put up with it, *this* long, either. Couldn't have done it without that rotgut Stolchi that you smuggled aboard. Damn pity that Chen had to pour the rest of it into the booster cocktail."

"As if y'all had anywhere else to go," commented Devon White. "May stink in here, but damn *cold* out there."

"Well, you don't have much longer to wait, or so I'm told," offered Jacobson, trying to maneuver his bulk so as to avoid the others, as all swam forward in the zero-G.

Hard enough using this stuff she taught us, just to move, he mused, *but when you get next to someone else who's using it... well, magnetic fields do the same thing, don't they?*

"Apparently in a week or so," added the former Mars Mission commander, the Russian Space Agency is sending the next one up to get you, Ariel, Alan and a couple other ones from ESA and so on. It's a tighter schedule than I would have thought, given the poor availability of spacecraft, but somebody down there is pulling a few strings, trying to smooth over a few little, ahem, political problems. At least that's how *I* read it."

"*Plus ça change*," muttered Cherie Tanaka, spinning quickly to out-pace and then face the rest of them.

"Yeah," replied White.

"Captain, any chance I can just stay up here? Suddenly it doesn't smell so bad..."

Jacobson wryly smiled.

"Berth's already booked, Devon," he pointed out. "And we got orders, remember?"

"Yeah," countered White, again. "*Orders*. Right."

"Ah, well," observed senior astronaut, "I'm sure that all will work out, in the grand scheme of things."

They were now at the airlock entrance.

"Listen," inquired Tanaka, "Since we might not have much time left together... I just wanted to ask, are all the rest of you, confident about your ability to *communicate*... you know, in the way we do?"

Five heads nodded, silently.

The woman's Eurasian eyebrows furrowed, slightly.

"I hear six people saying, 'yes'," Tanaka calmly noted.

"Thanks, Alan," she added. "Hmm. Thought I heard a *seventh*, for a while there. Let's hope, eh?"

Boyd shook his head.

"Man," he stated, "It's going to take me a *long* time to get used to this, Professor. You really think there's no chance that it's all going to just, I don't know, go 'poof', the minute we get back to good old *terra firma*?"

"The only thing that's going to go 'poof', Brent," replied Tanaka, "Are your muscles, when you get back to *real* gravity, after nearly a year of little bits of the fake stuff. And, despite your supplements, maybe your bones, too. So take it easy, everybody, oh-kay?"

"That was deliberate, wasn't it, Professor?" asked White.

"I guess," answered Tanaka, looking away, out the view-port.

The faces of Ariel Cohen and Alan Humber now appeared from around a corner.

The Englishman's cheery voice called out, "Time for you wankers to get going, unless that is you want yours truly to sneak in there while you're not looking."

"Or, to put it another way, Commander," mentioned Cohen, "I have positive confirm from Space Excursions Corporation's Shuttle *McAuliffe*, of airlock compression, they are good to go for egress."

He floated up to Jacobson.

That's funny, thought Boyd. *I didn't see him push off from anything.*

Neither did I, came a thought from White.

Congratulations, Ariel! sent Tanaka.

You sure left it to the last minute, to let us know.

The Israeli gave a Cheshire Cat smile, and if a bow could be detected in zero gravity, this was a bow.

"Well, I suppose it's time for our goodbyes," announced Jacobson. "Ariel, I assume we have five minutes? Listen, can someone disable the recorder?"

"Yeah," replied White. "Done that already. Kinda comes natural, after a few months doin' it back on the old ships, back from Mars."

Jacobson pivoted to address the others.

He spoke, "I'm not going to do the big speech thing, except to say that I don't think anyone could have anticipated what we were about to go through, when we all got into our seats on the *Eagle* and *Infinity*."

He fell silent for a second, with his eyes half-closed, then added, "And fine ships they *were*, let there be no doubt of that. I got to tell you guys, I miss them almost as much as I miss that *other* member of our crew, if you know what I mean."

"Maybe you *will* see them again," offered Boyd. "They're still up there, somewhere... as far as we know, but..."

"I know what you mean, Captain," remarked Chkalov. "*Infinity* was a part of me. So became *Eagle*, when I was in there with *her*. And if I had gone with the lifeboat mission, maybe –"

"Anyway," interrupted Jacobson, trying to change the subject, "We can't change the past, and even if we could, considering what *might* have been, things turned out pretty damn well, I think. What I really wanted to say, is that we have a unique fraternity, here; we all share a secret, or, rather, a whole treasure-chest of secrets, that we all have a duty to use, and reveal, wisely."

Several of the others nodded in agreement.

"The moment that we land down on Earth," continued the former Mars mission commander, "Human history is about to change, and I hope for the better, but we'll have our best chance of ensuring that if we work together – *if* we don't fall back into our old ways of doing things. I'm sure you all remember what she told us, about this thing getting out of control; I can tell everyone here that I intend to take that advice *very* seriously. Ariel, Alan, I'm making you a promise today, that as soon as I get settled down there, I'll start sending you guys regular messages via NeoNet, and I'll host a get-together where we can compare notes and help each other... move forward."

"Wonder if that's a birthday party for the new 'us', or a wake for the old 'us'," mused Humber.

"Either way," observed Tanaka, "It's a *different* 'us', wouldn't you say?"

"Aye, Professor," reflectively confirmed the Englishman. "That I would."

"I'll pay your way, if money's an issue, but we should agree, here and now, to meet somewhere, once we get back there," explained Jacobson. "You all know that I had to make a promise to my own chain of command to tell them, and I would expect that Ariel, Sergei, you might have to do the same, so... I guess what I'm getting at, is that if we decide to hold a party, and someone doesn't come, especially if we don't hear from them either, and there's no good excuse... we'll *know* that something is amiss, won't we?"

"You're assuming, Captain," commented Boyd, "That the Air Force isn't going to lock us up somewhere in Area 51 and slowly dissect us to find out what makes this wonderful new thing work, right?"

"Y'all have a way of sayin' that, Brent my man," half-joked White.

"In a way they *do* have a valid reason for keeping us well cooped-up for a while," observed Tanaka. "After all, we *were* on Mars."

"Major Boyd does, none the less, have a very valid point," noted Chkalov. "None of us can predict what the various national authorities are going to do, when they understand the magnitude of what has affected us. Perhaps more so for mine than even yours, Captain... the life of a single person, especially when the interests of the state are directly in question, has never counted for much in Russia. I believe that I told you, I have not yet told *them* – but I think that when your President is briefed, and he tells his subordinates, well... as you know, my country has never had much of a problem learning such things from, how do we say, 'unofficial channels'."

He smiled, modestly and added, "So even if I do not tell my own Space Command about these neat little tricks that the Storied Watcher taught me, the truth of it is bound to come out. We should all plan for that possibility."

"Precisely my point," replied Jacobson. "We should have our little get-together somewhere that's easy to get to; I'd suggest Miami, but –"

"You don't have to say it, Cap'n," interrupted Humber. "But for the record, Charlie and the kids would want to come, if for no other reason than to meet all of you, and..."

"Well then *I* will," countered Tanaka. "I've been catching up on what's been going on down there, lately, and frankly, it stinks; it's gotten substantially worse than when we left for Mars in the first place, and it was already bad then. Ever heard about the 'Undesirable Alien and Deviant Lifestyle Exclusion Act'? Alan probably wouldn't get past the airport, because of his, uhh, *relationship*, with his partner. For that matter, Sergei might not either, at least not without a lot of paperwork on the part of his government."

"Not that I'd *want* to," complained Humber, not trying to sound polite. "You Americans can take those old-time attitudes and stuff 'em, Professor – you can go ahead and exclude the rest of the world, if you like, it's *your* loss, not *ours*. No offense *intended*, of course."

"None to me," evenly replied Tanaka. "Can't speak for the idiots who are running things down there."

"'Undesirable Alien' act," muttered White, with a malicious smile. "Man, what I wouldn't give to have them try *that* on –"

"So," offered Jacobson, "I guess anywhere in the good old U.S. of A. is out, then. Ideas, anyone?"

"Russia would be about the same, as far as my good friend Alan is concerned," Chkalov philosophically noted. "You see, we seem to imitate everything that Americans do, although we have our fair share of good, home-grown Russian stupidity, as well."

"It should be somewhere central; somewhere that's easy for all of us to get to. Assuming, of course, that we're not just flying there all by ourselves, by that time," stated Boyd.

"I would like it to be somewhere warm," requested Chkalov.

"Well, I would have suggested Portugal, mates, but as there are more of you Yanks here than the rest of us, I suppose I *could* scrape up the plane fare to... Bermuda, maybe?" suggested Humber.

"Bermuda," answered White. "Yeah, Professor – I *like* that! Beaches... nightclubs... casinos... what y'all say, Captain?"

"You might change your mind if you got one look at me in Bermuda shorts," joked the former Mars mission commander.

"Oh, your legs aren't so bad, Sam," commented Tanaka.

A pained look by her former commander quickly ended this line of conversation.

"So..." proposed Boyd, "Bermuda, it is, then? Six months from now, say?"

"Why not?" asked White. "Give me some time to get my Earth legs back, chill out a bit, then catch the vapors down at the beach. Good for y'all as well?"

"Hopefully, yes," said Chkalov. "I just hope that my government does not send me on a tour talking to every school in the Federation. I must warn you that I heard rumors of something like that, last time that I was on the comm-link with Star City. A hazard of being a 'space-hero', I suppose."

Cohen spoke up.

"I am receiving a signal from the ship. Window closing in seven minutes... I think that it's time for you to go."

"Yeah," replied Jacobson, resignedly. "I guess it is."

"I guess," said Tanaka.

"Listen, Ariel," mentioned Jacobson, "I... uhh... on behalf of me and my crew, I... just wanted to tell you..."

The Mars mission leader obviously could not finish his statement; tough and experienced as he was, he seemed close to tears.

Boyd slapped a sympathetic hand on Jacobson's shoulder, and interjected, "I think what the Captain was trying to say, Commander, is that you've made this creaky old station one *hell* of a home for us, since we got here. We want you to know that we're very grateful for that. No astronaut – or cosmonaut – could have expected more."

Cohen nodded in acknowledgment.

"I can honestly say, Major," he replied, "That coming to have known all of you – and, for a brief time, that *other* one of your crew members – has been the most interesting and transforming experience of my life. You know how much every person on this station owes yourself and the other members of your expedition. May we meet again, soon."

Tanaka flew up and shook the Israeli's hand.

"May it be so," she implored.

Tanaka now embraced Humber.

"*Damn*, I'm going to miss you, Alan," she said, watching a globular tear float lazily from the side of her eye.

"Keep everything running up here, until we can get you back to Earth, okay?" she added.

"Promise, luv," answered the Englishman. "I got us *this* far; it'd be daft to let 'er fall apart now, wouldn't it?"

"Friends... no, *brothers* of mine... my last words to you up here will be, 'remember the pledge that you made'," pronounced Tanaka, addressing them all; and, for a second, her countenance seemed dazzling, dignified, glorious, in some indescribable way.

Then the hatch to the airlock between the station and the Shuttle opened. In a flash, she was into it and was gone.

"Was that a torch I saw passing?" quietly stated Cohen.

"Who can say?" offered Jacobson.

Boyd was next.

"I guess I'm not much on speeches, either," he stated, "So all I'll say is, 'I don't think the adventure is over yet, guys, not by a long-shot, so let's keep in touch. I'll see you soon."

Turning to Chkalov, he added, "And *you*, my friend."

Boyd, too, disappeared through the airlock.

White followed close behind.

"Sergei, my man," he started, giving the Russian a strong handshake with an instant, "We sure been through some *serious* shit together. Same with you two," – he gestured at Cohen and Humber – "Just maybe a little less serious.

Pensively, he added, "And somethin' tells me that Brent's bang-on; maybe it's not quite done with, man. So make sure to bring a couple jugs of that Stolchi with you when we do the Bermuda thang, you know?"

"And a jug of *borscht*," answered Chkalov, with a broad grin.

As White went through the hatch, they heard him quip, "Skip the *borscht*. Double the vodka."

Finally, it was Jacobson's turn.

"Sorry I got a little overwhelmed there, guys," he explained. "It's just that this scene reminds me of... *another* set of goodbyes, that my team and I had to say to someone else, I'm sure you know who, some time ago."

He looked around, up and down, east and west, right and left.

"I missed *Eagle* and *Infinity*, and now I'm going to miss *your* ship, too, Ariel," continued the former Mars mission commander. "I left a big chunk of *me* in those ships, and I'm doing so again with ISS2. I owe a huge debt to you, Alan and the rest of your fine crew. Take care of yourselves."

He shook a commanding finger at them.

"That's an *order*, you hear? The first and last one that you're going to get from me while I'm on ISS2."

Cohen saluted.

"Order understood and accepted," he replied. "See you in Bermuda, Captain; and may your trip home be a safe one."

Now, all that appeared to remain of the former Mars mission commander on ISS2, was his head, still peeking out the airlock.

He regarded Chkalov.

"Sergei," wondered Jacobson, "You think that we'll see space again?"

The Russian returned Jacobson a long look.

"Yes, I do," he answered. "But somehow, I do not think it will be as we last did. It will be... a *different* way."

"Until then," called Jacobson, as he slowly closed the hatch.

All those who had ever set foot on the Red Planet, were now away from Cohen's station.

The Israeli, the Englishman and the Russian stared back and forth at each other.

"I'm going to *miss* those wankers, you know," offered Humber. "And not just for all that they – you included, there mate – have taught us."

"Now we must learn from each other," remarked Chkalov.

Bemusedly, he added, "And I suppose that makes *me*, the 'teacher', as I have the most experience in our new craft. Ha! 'The blind lead the blind'... or is that not how the expression goes?"

Theodikas' voice was heard over the intercom.

"Excuse me, Commander Cohen," he announced, "I had the link to the egress-section shut off until now, but it's only thirty seconds until the Shuttle undocks. You should clear the area."

Cohen spoke into the wall media assembly.

"Understood, Mike," he confirmed. "Come on, you two... time to go."

They closed another hatch behind them.

Again, the intercom sounded.

"Shuttle McAuliffe now disengaged," stated Theodikas. "Five... four... three... two... one... engines firing. Checking... trajectory established. Systems nominal. ETA to Earth, forty-two minutes, sixteen seconds."

The sweet smell of Earth air, reflected Chkalov.

They will have that, soon.

Then, a half-second later, so thought the other two.

Strange Days At Park Place

"I do not think that I have ever been to a 'shopping-mall', before," commented the 'Sari'-girl, as she fiddled with her hair and watched the low-rise sights of suburban Tucson pass by Billings' SUV. "That is somewhere that one goes to, to buy things, correct? Like a marketplace, I mean."

"Laws," offered Melissa. "Y'all ain't never been to a mall? We even got 'em back home an' me and my friends go and hang there all the time."

"So you go shopping there?" replied the fallen-girl. "What kinds of things do you buy?"

"Not much," sheepishly admitted the Claremont girl. "Y'all gots to have lots of money an' me and mah homie girls ain't got that much. Mostly we just hangin' there, y'all know, chill out, 'specially in summer when it real hot outside, they got air-conditioning in them places. security-guards don' like it an' they shoo us along, but we just sneakin' back in, maybe buy a soda or some such thang, so they ain't got no 'scuse to get rid of us. It kinda like a game, Miz Sari."

"Well," interrupted Billings, "I'd advise you not to play too many games while you're inside Park Place, kids. They're a little strict in there – I heard it was to keep all the Mexicans out, one time – and, how would I say this, they're, uhh, not used to seeing people like *you*, wandering around in the mall. If you know what I mean... right, Whitney?"

"Right," confirmed Claremont.

She turned around to address the 'Sari'-girl. "What he mean is, 'they ain't lettin' no black folk in there'. Prolly nobody who ain't lily-white, that is."

"You know," observed the newcomer, "Bob, you, Whitney, your children, even my little friend Tommy, here," – she leaned over and gave the Indian-boy an affectionate kiss on the head – "Are all the same species, what is it called, '*Homo Sapiens*', that is... all that differs, is the color of your skin, perhaps that of your hair. People around here seem to attach a great deal of importance to these features, but I can assure you, there are places where... well..."

"Well... *what*?" inquired Tommy, looking up.

"Where... uhh... where there are a *lot* more differences between people, is what I meant to say," stuttered the 'Sari'-girl. "I guess that is just my clumsy way of saying, 'I am glad that I ended up looking like Bob, instead of waking up with green skin'."

She gave an evasive smile.

Curtis giggled. "You funny, Miz Sari," he said. "Only guy ah knows who look like *that*, is that big man on the can of peas that Momma make for us once 'n a while."

Claremont winced.

Billings just shrugged.

"Well, whether or not you have ambitions to be the next Jolly Green Giant," he cautioned, "Which, by the way, you'd have to do some quick growing to qualify for, just take my advice, don't go wandering off by yourself – that applies for *all* you kids, you hear? Those mall guards are *armed*, they got stun guns, too, and I'd bet you good money that they'd *love* to have a crack at some little black or Indian-boy that they think snuck in through the loading-dock door. We might get a few strange glances from the rest of the shoppers, but you all should be okay as long as you stick with me. Got that?"

"Yes sir," politely responded Melissa, followed a second later by the same thing from her brother.

"Got that," added the 'Sari'-girl.

The car rounded a corner.

"There she blows," announced Billings. "Hey, I guess there's a good side to comets, shortages of everything and roadblocks... lots of places to park – I bet I can get us within a block or so of the door."

Expertly, he maneuvered the SUV right, left and forward through the driving lanes that spread out two or three times larger than the shopping-mall in the middle of the lot.

The car shuddered to a halt.

"Everybody off the bus," commanded the salesman.

The six of them clambered out, resplendent in newly-washed clothes, although the 'Sari'-girl still proudly wore the baseball-cap with the large 'A' emblazoned on it. They strode forcefully toward the front gate, which was an arched thing, stuccoed in typical Southwest style.

Halfway in, they were confronted by a sealed glass door, extending all the way from the floor to the ceiling, with a card reader swipe slot on the side.

"Here goes," said Billings, as he retrieved a plastic credit-card like thing from his wallet. "Hope it's working."

"What is that?" inquired the 'fallen-girl.

"My access ID card for Park Place," replied the salesman. "You can't get into the mall without one, or most other shopping-malls these days, for that matter, but at least they set them all up on a common database a while ago, thank God, so I don't have to carry around fifty of the damn things like I used to do – at least when I shop in Tucson, that is."

He rapidly sent the mag-stripe edge of the card through the reader.

Mercifully, the door unlocked.

"Everybody through," ordered Billings. "Luckily they haven't figured out how to stop 'tailgating', with this thing."

The others rapidly complied and they all were now inside the mall, an upscale suburban shopping-center with lots of chrome and many, many places where one could waste money on overpriced clothes and other similar bric-à-brac.

Billings noted that there was less pedestrian traffic than he remembered from the good old days.

Turning to the 'Sari'-girl, he explained, "Of course, they ding my bank-account for a few cents every time I come and go – when they first started locking down the malls with these things, after the big gang-fights about five years back, they claimed it was 'to keep you safe' and 'to provide an enhanced shopping experience', but I figure all they're *really* doing is tracking you and figuring out how to jack up the prices when you visit a store that you'd be shopping in, anyway... no, I'm *sure* of it. Highway robbery, if you ask me, but it's the way of the world, I guess."

"Everything here seems to have to do with money," replied the newcomer, analytically. "I am surprised that I have not yet found a Temple where one can worship it."

"Ha, girl!" snorted Claremont. "Y'all just ain't lookin' in the right places. Y'all want a church for money, go to a bank. If y'all can *find* one, that is... 'round mah hood, they closed all of 'em down years ago, if'n y'all don' got a computer to do yo' bankin', y'all out of luck. Mah folk just use cash, or we trades one job for 'nother."

The 'Sari'-girl nodded mutely, in acknowledgment.

"Oh, *man*," exclaimed Melissa. "It *glorious* cool in here!"

"Real nice," added Tommy. "Better even than that car of yours, Mister Billings."

"I notice the difference in temperature, too," commented the 'Sari'-girl. "But it is not *nearly* so cold, as in some places where I have been."

Billings stopped and took a deep breath.

"Yeah," he mentioned. "Figures that they'd let the shopping-malls turn up the A/C, but cut off the rest of us. Oh well, we might as well enjoy it, while we can."

"So where are we going first, Bob?" asked the fallen-girl, enthusiasm bubbling in her voice. "Tommy told me that they sell, oh, how do you say it, yes, 'vid-ee-oh games' in one of the stores in here. You said that these were really amusing, fun to play, right?"

The Indian-boy nodded vigorously.

Billings motioned for calm.

"Definitely, maybe," he replied, "They're not really *my* cup of tea, but we'll see about it, if we pass by a games-store and there's one that isn't too hard on the pocketbook, just so you can have the wonderful experience of pretending you're some he-man with a gun, a rocket-launcher or God knows what else. Anyway, let's just wander around, for a while, if you don't mind... I haven't been in here since well before the funny stuff went down, and I'd like to see what's changed, what's in the store windows. Okay?"

"Oh-kay, chief," answered the fallen-girl, with a cutesy, mock-indulgent smile.

As the group walked slowly forward, Billings noted that the newcomer was intensively studying everyone who passed by, with overlong glances.

"Hey there," he cautioned, "I don't blame you for wanting to do a little people-watching – something that the best of us do, every so often – but it's not polite to *stare*, you know. Makes people feel weird."

"Oh, sorry," sheepishly replied the 'Sari'-girl. "It is just that there are so many different types of people here, and they are not all dressed at all the same... some are in these 'blue-jeans' that Melissa wears, while others seem to be in more confining, more formal clothes, like that man over there... what is the significance of the thing hanging from his neck? It looks a little large to be a pendant of office... and besides, it is made out of fabric... right? Why do so many of the men wear those? It does not look very comfortable, or very functional."

Billings rolled his eyes and patiently replied, "It's called a 'tie', my dear, and you're right, it basically doesn't do squat. A hold-over from a few hundred years ago, if memory serves me correctly."

"Odd," remarked the 'Sari'-girl. "Because the clothes that I am wearing – I mean, this track-suit, and the run-inng shoes, plus the attractive little red hat – they are all comfortable, maybe not that durable, I do not know, but it is just strange to see some people dressed so formally, while almost everybody else is wearing commoner-clothes. Oh, but look – see that group of people over there?"

She pointed excitedly to a very conservatively-garbed family, with the man and eldest son in a three-piece suit, while the women, heads bowed submissively toward the floor, all in 19th-Century long-dresses, were walking behind the males of the group.

"Sari, you shouldn't –" started Billings.

The salesman saw a look of contempt and disgust on the face of the patriarch of the group, who spat in the girl's direction, muttered something inaudible and then turned to lead his troupe rapidly off in the opposite direction.

"I kind of have the feeling that I offended them," admitted the newcomer. "That man called me a 'white whore who walks openly with niggers' – sorry, Whitney, Curtis, Melissa, but that is really what he said – I just do not *understand*. Honestly... what did I do wrong?"

"Ain't nothin' we ain't used to hearin' all the time," offered Claremont, laconically. "But all the same, thank y'all for not usin' it 'cept to 'splain what goin' on."

Mutely, the 'Sari'-girl nodded acknowledgment to the black woman.

"You'd best not be antagonizing those guys," warned Billings. "Although I don't blame you for being taken off-guard by them. They're from one of these nut-case Christian sects that have been springing up out in the gated communities around here for the last twenty years or so. They fly off the handle with very little provocation sometimes, and with the help of our enlightened Arizona state legislature, who they've infiltrated, co-opted or bought off, they now have the 'right' to beat the crap out of anybody who they think – correctly or otherwise – has 'insulted their womenfolk'... if you can believe that."

"Hmm," observed the fallen-girl. "Well, that is nothing new to me... many cultures are very protective, in this way. But it is strange to find such attitudes, in the middle of a society that has, uhh... the kinds of things that I was watching last night, on tel-ee-vision, you know?"

Curtis giggled, as the salesman went on, "Oh, and by the way, if you read any of their literature, they're the 'missionaries from the One True Lord, who's here to save us from the devil-worship of Islam'. You can't *reason* with these people... best off avoiding them, if you're smart."

"Uh-oh!" worriedly exclaimed the 'Sari'-girl. "Do not tell me that they are the same ones from the prison-camp to the north – Bob, what if they *recognize* us?"

"I wouldn't worry too much about that," reassured Billings. "I can understand how you'd have a hard time telling these guys apart from the ones in the Jesus Jail up in Idaho, but they're actually from a completely different group – they hate all the other fundamentalists almost as much as, maybe more than, the Muslims and us 'godless lib-rals'. Still, you're on the right track. The less attention, the better... right?"

"Right," unenthusiastically muttered the 'Sari'-girl.

On they marched, through several twists and turns, a long way down the marble-and-slate-floored main corridor of this latter-day temple to the Gods of Commerce. Though they had been in shopping-malls umpteen times before, the Claremont children 'oohed' and 'aahed' at the furnishings of the place, which was evidently on an order of magnitude more sophisticated than whatever they had been familiar with.

Curtis, who had been tarrying behind the group, gawking at the wares of the various shops, bolted over to a group of leather-bound waiting-chairs, arranged around the periphery of a decorative island.

He jumped up on one.

"Damn, Mister Billins," he shouted. "These is *real* palm-trees! Ain't never seen them growin' *inside* a mall, before!"

A second later, the boy felt the iron grip of a very large, blue-uniformed man on his shoulder.

"What're *you* doing here," growled the man. "You're not supposed to be in here, kid. You don't *belong*."

Out of nowhere, the 'Sari'-girl appeared at the man's side, even though a second before, she had been next to Billings.

"Curtis is with *us*," she tried to explain, pointing to the others. "With that man, and that woman – this little boy is her son, and the girl is her daughter. Please let him go."

The man stooped over and stared at the newcomer, not taking his hand from the Claremont boy's collarbone.

"This is a private, access-controlled mall, Miss," he retorted. "No little black boys supposed to be running around. He's got to get his dirty little ass *out* of here, and his sister and that little Mexican kid as well. Come on."

Roughly, the guard started to drag Curtis back toward the entrance.

Again, the 'Sari'-girl somehow appeared in the man's exit path, even though she stayed in everyone else's field of vision.

Looking determinedly at him – indeed, staring him deep in the eyes – she repeated with steely determination, "Let us be *friends*, sir. Let us be *good* friends, you and me... oh-kay? My friends are your friends, and they are *all* welcome here... right? No, Curtis will *not* be going – will he? Nor will Tommy, or Melissa, or Whitney... now, *will* they?"

There's that damn music again, thought Billings.

Far away, like a symphony carried over the ocean...

The mall-guard's grip loosened, reflexively, and he staggered back on his feet, like a drunk having had the last one too many. He shook his head, as if to clear the fog of slumber upon the first rays of morning.

"No... no, I guess... it'll be okay, then, Miss," he stammered. "Just... just keep them out of trouble, if you don't... mind?"

"Of course," the smiling 'Sari'-girl replied, "I promise that they will behave. Listen... would you mind telling the other guards not to bother my friends? On your radio-talking-thing, I mean."

"What?" asked the guard, still obviously disoriented. "Oh... yeah, sure. Here."

He pressed a button on a box attached to his belt, then grabbed the thing and held it to his lips. "Ainsworth to PP Security, general bulletin," he mumbled. "We got... we got a special group going through, white girl, white man, black woman and two black kids, one Mexican kid, too –"

"I'm not Mex –" complained Tommy, but he was shushed by the 'Sari'-girl holding her finger to lips.

"Was that the, uhh, 'fire'?" whispered the boy, to his erstwhile governess.

"Not *exactly*, son... but something similar," she replied, *sotto voce*. "I will explain it to you later... oh-kay?"

Tommy nodded, a slight smile on his face.

Billings approached the man.

"They're all with me, like our friend 'Sari' here, told you," mentioned the salesman. "We're... uhh... a *church* group, you see. Just stopped in to do a little grocery-shopping for our Sunday after-sermon get-together, get out of the heat, you know, nothing fancy."

"Hallelujah," grunted Claremont, rolling her eyes.

None but the 'Sari'-girl noticed the black woman's lips silently pleading with the Almighty, about forgiveness for the lie.

"Oh, certainly... sir," continued the guard, "PP Security, this group, the mixed one, I mean, they got special clearance, so don't bother 'em. Got that?"

"Rodge," answered a ghostly voice.

"Got it," echoed another.

"Clearance? *What*? Well, who *gives* a shit... I'm on break in fifteen anyway," came back a third.

"Okay," concluded the mall-guard, leaning back against a palm-tree, wiping his face with his hand. "You all can be on your way, now. Oh, and thanks for shopping at Park Place."

Painfully, he got up and staggered away down a side-corridor.

Now it was Billings' turn to do the grabbing. He took the 'Sari'-girl by the hand and sat her down in one of the expensively-upholstered leather chairs, after shooing Curtis from the other one.

The salesman sat down next to the newcomer.

"Sari," he admonished, calmly looking the fallen-girl straight in the face, "You got anything you want to explain to us?"

She looked away.

"No, Bob," she evaded. "Not really."

"Are you *sure*?" badgered Billings. "You got *anything* to explain to me? I think you know what I mean."

Accusingly, he glared at her.

Looking as if she was about to cry, the 'Sari'-girl just shook her head, staring icily forward.

"Come *on*, girl," mentioned Claremont. "Y'all just *looked* at that guy an' he give us a free pass to cruise 'round in here. Ah ain't never done half that good even when it cost me twenty dollar to make th' Man look the other way."

"Ah knows," interrupted Melissa. "She done *hypnotize* him. Ah seen it once on TV, this slick wave he watch, an' that other guy, he just –"

"I don't think Miz Sari wants to talk about it," countered Tommy.

"Here... get up," he added, offering his hand to the fallen-girl. The gesture was gratefully accepted and the newcomer got back to her feet.

"Listen, Whitney," requested the salesman, "Can you take the kids and go a bit ahead of us, please? I want to talk with Sari... *privately*, if you don't mind. We need ten minutes or so. Maybe fifteen."

"What? Oh, shore, Bob," knowingly replied the black woman. "Come on, y'all. Let them white-folk talk white stuff for a while. We go up aways, see if there anywhere we can get somethin' to eat."

"Not *too* far forward," cautioned Billings.

Claremont turned and nodded, then strode briskly ahead to catch up with the children, who were already ten meters out in front.

"Sari," Billings demanded, "Take my hand, please."

The fallen-girl complied, never looking except straight ahead.

"What I wanted to ask you, my dear," interrogated the salesman, slowly and deliberately, "Is... well... Whitney put it best. I'll put it more crudely. That was some fine mind-fuck you put on that goon back there... wasn't it?"

"Yeah," defensively breathed the 'Sari'-girl. "I suppose that it was."

"*Quite* a trick... isn't it?" pressed Billings, as they slowly walked down the corridor, the salesman keeping one eye on Claremont and the others all the while.

"Well what would you have had me *do*, Bob?" complained the newcomer. "Should I have had Curtis, or all of us, just *disappear*, in front of that man? As I understand it, doing that might bring undue attention, when we magically showed up again – right?"

"Right," answered Billings.

"Well then, Bob... what is your *problem?*" complained the fallen-girl.

"You *know* what my problem is," shot back the salesman. "Just think back to when we first met. Take your time... it'll come to you."

Abruptly, she threw down his grasp and turned to confront him, with the hint of a tear in her eye.

"Of what are you accusing me, Bob?" she half-shouted. "Of 'hypnotizing' *you?* Of bending your mind to my will, like I did with that man, back there?"

"*Yes*, damn it!" angrily retorted Billings. "What I saw back there, *scared* me, Sari – there's no other way to say it. I looked at that guy and thought, 'Christ, Bob, that's exactly how *you* must have looked, when you first ran into this chick – a stunned puppet on a string, a well-trained poodle on a leash... pick your unflattering comparison'."

He paused for a second, looking past her in fear and frustration, at being so far out of his comfort-zone.

Eventually, he added, "Sari, I'm just asking you to *level* with me, that's all. If our relationship is going to be at all worthwhile, you have to tell me the *truth*, girl. Did you use that hypnotic trick on *me*?"

Now it was her turn to hesitate.

Guiltily, she stared at him, hung her head and softly replied, "Yes, Bob... I *did*. I will not lie to you about this."

"*Why*?" countered the salesman. "It makes me *furious* to think that you took advantage of me, that way! *Why*, Sari?"

The newcomer looked ahead.

"We had better continue walking, Bob," she evaded. "They are moving out of eyesight."

"I'm not *that* stupid – don't change the subject!" growled Billings.

For a few long seconds, she just stood there, apparently lost in contemplation. Then she again spoke.

"Alright... and yes, Bob, you are *not* stupid, not at all," said the 'Sari'-girl, with a hint of that strange, entrancing music seeming to issue from the Muzak speakers in the ceiling, for a moment or two. "And you deserve an honest answer. If you take my hand and walk with me, man," she plaintively requested, "I will try to explain, as best I can. Will you take my hand, Bob. *Please?*"

A tear traced a path down her cheek.

"I'd *love* to," muttered the salesman, "But how the hell do I know that you're not using the same fucking thing on me, right *now*?"

"I am *not*," answered the fallen-girl. "Because if I *was*, you would just be my happy puppet-on-a-string, and I would not *let* you be angry with me. You would be oh, *so* agreeable. Just about everything that I would say, or ask, would make perfect sense – and you know what the really *scary* thing would be, Bob?"

Though her countenance was neutral, her tone was eerie, menacing.

"I'm scared enough," answered Billings. "But go ahead."

"You would know *exactly* what was happening... you would *think* that you were in complete control of your senses," replied the newcomer, reflectively, as if stating a fact that should be obvious. "You would not notice that the *slightest* thing was amiss. It is not crude mind-control; it is *much* more subtle than *that*. Far more difficult to detect, or defeat."

"Jesus H. *Christ*," breathed the salesman. "I hope you know how *threatening* that sounds. 'Terrifying' isn't too strong a word."

The 'Sari'-girl mutely nodded in the affirmative, looking abashed like a small child with her hand caught in the candy jar.

"Welcome to my world, Bob of Billings," she quietly observed. "A land of glorious wonders and deepest evils, of mighty powers and weirding perils... the likes of which, your kind cannot yet imagine."

Reluctantly, Billings got up and slowly extended his hand.

"Would it help to know," she remarked, "That I cannot do it to you, anymore? At least, I do not *believe* that I can."

"Makes about as much sense as *anything* does, with you, which is none at all," he complained. "Okay. But I want the *truth*, Sari... no evasions, no crap."

She smiled at him weakly and nodded, while clasping his hand.

For a second or two, his mind reeled with a kaleidoscope of strange thoughts and fantastic, impossible images; but these quickly faded, and he was, again, himself.

"No crap," she guaranteed. "And no 'mind-fucks', any more. I *promise*, on all that is dear to me."

They began walking slowly in the direction of Claremont and the children, who had stopped in a cross-corridor about fifty meters or so ahead.

"It is like this, Bob," started the fallen-girl, avoiding his glance as she spoke. "You already know about my little darkness-trick... right?"

"How could I ever *forget*," ruefully grunted Billings.

"This is another of them, one that I have used countless times to help me survive, when I wake up... somewhere *new*, where I am a stranger, all by myself," she explained. "I have many such tricks, ones that you and your people evidently can not do, *hundreds* of them, in fact, many far more powerful than anything that you have so far seen."

"Do us a favor and don't try any of them here and now," he demanded.

"Unfortunately, Bob," sighed the newcomer, "That will not be a problem... because... uhh... this is rather difficult to explain... I have tried and *tried*, but most of my, ahh, 'abilities', just are not *working*... that is the 'bottom line', I suppose. Oh, Bob, if you only *knew* how frustrating this situation is, to me – I feel like a cripple, a helpless, pale shadow of my former self –"

"Okay, okay... I *get* it," retorted the salesman. "And if *you* feel helpless, well, that's too bad, girl, try to imagine what it's like standing next to someone who maybe can take over your *mind*, any time she wants to. But what about this mind-fuck nonsense, anyway? I need to *know* what you did to me."

"Sorry, Bob, I sort of went off on, how do you say, a 'tangent', there," apologized the fallen-girl. "This particular skill is called *Unaìkh'l'é* in my language, and –"

"Ooo... what?" interrupted Billings.

"As closely as I can say it with the sounds that you use in Eng-lish, it would be 'oo-NAI-keh-el-AY'," explained the 'Sari'-girl. "It is a form of mental domination, 'hypnotism', I suppose you would say it that way in Eng-lish, but it does not translate very well."

"It sure as hell *works* pretty well, wouldn't you say?" countered the salesman.

"Yes, but Bob, this skill has many limitations," she continued. "For example, I must look right into my victim's eyes, I must have their undivided attention – which is why, incidentally, that it does not work through my dark-trick shadow – and they cannot suspect that I am trying to, how would you say, 'screw' around with their minds. If a victim's guard is up, if he or she already dislikes me or distrusts me, it is *much* more difficult to make it work... I have to use a lot more, uhh, *power*, for the mind-attack, and doing so can seriously hurt whomever I am trying to 'hypnotize'. If I try to force it on someone with a strong mind, if I try to impose my intellect into their own, and something goes *wrong*... it can... uhh... well, I am sure that you can imagine what might happen, then."

"I'd like not to think about that," observed Billings. "But why did you have to use it on *me*? What did *I* ever do to *you*, to deserve this kind of crap, Sari?"

"Do you really *want* the truth?" she replied, now looking at him earnestly.

"Yeah," answered the salesman, secretly dreading what he might hear.

"The truth *is*, Bob," she evenly stated, "I just needed to have a *friend*. The Gods of Fate brought you there to me, and you looked... you *smelled*, like a nice man, like a friendly person. You see, even in as weak a state as I was in, back then, I have a built-in ability to know if someone's motives are good or bad, if he or she is trustworthy, or not. You passed the test with, ahh, 'flighting colors'. That is all that there was to it... basically."

"Swell," muttered Billings. "Makes me feel real, *special*... convenient, at least."

He started to move away.

Again, the 'Sari'-girl broke contact and turned to confront the salesman.

"*Look*, Bob," she half-shouted with arms outstretched, palms-outward, and a pained, exasperated expression, "What do you *want* me to *say*? That I fell madly in love with you, at first *sight*? Sorry, man, considering where I have been, and the things that I have seen, if you only knew how *ridiculous* that sounds – it is not *you*, Bob... please try to *understand*! For the Gods' sakes, I woke up terribly hurt, all *alone*, in this completely strange place; I did not know where I was, hardly knew *who* I was – I still do not, really. I knew next to nothing about your culture – I had to have someone who I could trust, who could teach me how to get along, how to fit in. You did that *so* well. And I needed someone to..."

"To, *what*?" mumbled Billings, as he slowly shuffled forward, his feet feeling leaden with disappointment.

Her countenance lightening ever so slightly, the 'Sari'-girl laughed in half-contemptuous amusement.

"You *still* have not figured it out?" she inquired, incredulously.

"I'm afraid I'm not much up on riddles today," shot back the salesman.

You sound just like a dear friend who I know from somewhere, when you say that, she sent, hoping that his mind would take note.

"I needed someone to *love*, stupid!" argued the fallen-girl. "Just as much as I need air, water, food, sunlight and fire. Over more time than you will ever comprehend, I have learned through bitter experience, that having a mate – someone to hold and cherish – is just as important as these other things. *You* are that someone, Bob."

Billings shrugged and kept on his course.

"Why can you not just *accept* it, and be happy?" she pressed. "I would gladly accept the same, from yourself. Do you not remember me saying so, just after we escaped from those 'Jesus'-nuts in the camp, to the north?"

Billings motioned them to a stop.

"Now, *you* look!" he snarled. "I wouldn't pretend that I'll ever fully understand women – either the, uhh, 'normal' ones, or *you*, Sari.. but from what I hear, love isn't something that they can just turn on, or off, as they see fit. You make it sound like I was, I am, just some kind of *tool*... something that you happened to use, to get by."

The newcomer was about to say something, but Billings kept talking.

"Don't get me wrong, kid," he offered, in a brusque tone, "It's been a gas, but... I just don't *like* the way that we, ahem, got 'introduced' to each other. I'm sorry, but it just feels... phony. Maybe this little mesmerism-trick is how *you* do it, wherever *you* come from; but so far, it isn't how *we* do it, down here. At least, it's not how *I* do it."

The salesman had turned and was walking away from her, toward Claremont and the kids.

"Bob!" she cried.

"*Bob!*"

Quickly, she took hold of his hand, turning him again to face her.

"Please, Bob, *listen* to me," whimpered the 'Sari'-girl, panic palpable in her trembling voice. "Remember how I told you, that I can not *do* it to you, anymore?"

He nodded.

"Not that I *believe* you," he grumbled.

"What if I were to try it on you, again?" she stammered. "If you fought me off, if you knew that you successfully defended yourself... and then you still *felt* something, for me, that is... it would have to be real, not 'phony'... right?"

Billings looked down and shuffled his feet.

"Maybe," he replied. "For Christ's sake, Sari... how the hell would *I* know? This mumbo-jumbo stuff that you do – it's all way over my head. What if you end up pulling my strings like a puppet-master, all over again? I don't suppose you can appreciate how I might have a little problem with that?"

"Yes, I do," quietly acknowledged the fallen-girl. "And I promise that the second that I can tell that it is working... I will stop. But I do not think that will happen. *Believe* in yourself, Bob! You have power – great power – that you do not know about. I can help you to unlock it."

"Maybe it's locked up for a good *reason*," countered the salesman.

"Maybe it *is*," shot back the newcomer. "But if you stop now, you will never *know*... will you? Your life now comes to a fork in the road, Bob, one that ninety-nine point nine nine nine per cent of the people on this world will never be lucky enough to see; and I would have you choose the path that we can walk together –"

"Or," he interrupted, "I can just go back to being good ol' 'Bob Billings, Best Floor-Tile Sales Guy In Tucson, Arizona'... it's not much, but it's my *life*, you know? The only *sane* thing for me to do, you know, is walk away *fast*, right now –"

"And if you stop *now* – if you walk *away*," she pleaded with tear-filled eyes, slowly lowering herself to one knee, "*I* will have lost someone irreplaceable, too. I *will* survive – trust me on that, Bob, I always *do*, even in places where you would die, instantly – but it will *hurt*, being without you, it will hurt *so* much. Please – *please* stay, and be with me... for *me*, Bob... for *us*."

Billings stared at her, for a few, agonizing seconds.

You're way *out of your depth here, Bob*, his alarmed mind warned him.

Remember what it was like?

Remember?

Like your common sense just drained out your ears.

You would have jumped off a cliff, if she had asked you to.

What the fuck are you doing, *giving her another chance?*

Yes, her little crying-fit is breaking your heart... but how do you know that she isn't doing 'it' to you, right now?

If she was... how would you know?

"Yo, Bob!" he heard Claremont call, from far down the corridor. "Y'all tellin' her your life story, there? Kids is hungry, an' they got a food-court just down th' other way? Y'all comin'?"

"Just a minute or so, more!" shouted back the salesman.

He turned again to the 'Sari'-girl.

"Oh, eff it anyway," he groused. "Either I end up an angry old man in command of my senses, or a happy idiot. Not sure which is better, but let's get it over with. Do your worst."

Instantly, the fallen-girl's countenance changed from desperation to something else, relief mixed with professional concentration, perhaps.

She motioned to another pair of leather chairs.

"Sit down beside me," she requested.

Billings uneasily obliged.

"What I want you to do," she explained, "Is imagine that your mind is a tower, a castle – think of strong things, impregnable defenses... and, this is the thing that I hate to tell you, Bob, but it is necessary – start saying to yourself, 'she cannot be trusted, she is a bad person, she is trying to trick you'... things like that. The minute that you hear yourself agreeing with something that I tell you, say to yourself, 'it is a lie, get your fingers out of my head'. It will hurt to do this, the first time... but as I keep trying, it will become easier and easier. Are you ready?"

"No," retorted the salesman. "But go ahead."

The 'Sari'-girl moved her face uncomfortably close to the salesman's own, holding the palms of her hands against his cheeks.

Her beautiful, beckoning, beguiling green eyes were already drawing him in. Her face, always pretty, took on an unearthly, entrancing look, as if some kind of ethereal veil had been lifted, revealing a godly countenance below.

Instantly, Billings felt the sickening, bewitching feeling of her mind-trick – what the hell did she call it, anyway – starting to press against his consciousness. It was a feeling akin to, but far worse than, the haze of having over-slept by a few hours after too much booze.

You are my friend, cooed her thoughts, mingling with and polluting his own.

My nice friend... my pet.

Are you not?

No, came back the salesman.

You're not my friend. You're trying to lead me by the nose.

No friend of mine!

Billings felt a stabbing pain in his head, but it was followed, for the briefest of seconds, by a flash of euphoria.

Back off, bitch! he found himself thinking, although shame overcame him for the reaction.

He hoped she didn't hear that.

A different thought appeared in his mind, from the fallen-girl; but it was not like the probing, threatening ones that he had just experienced. Instead, it sounded more like a music instructor was giving spoken instructions *sotto voce*, all the while singing.

Good, she sent.

Now... we try the real thing.

A huge wave of stupefying, numbing commands, well-anticipated but nonetheless terrifying, now struck Billings' consciousness. Siren-like, they probed for the weak-spots, finding one after another.

Why fight? her cruel, overpowering intellect demanded.

You want *to give in, Bob.*

Admit it.

Desperately, Billings fought to keep in control, but he felt his grasp slipping. He struggled to keep his thoughts straight, to construct a phrase that made sense.

Is this what insanity feels like? he wondered.

Another voice in my head – for God's sake, way louder than my own – got to obey –

Again, she called, with each word more addictive than the last.

Be one with me.

Be my slave!

Get out of my head! Billings raged.

Get out!

Get out!

Anger, primal, irrational, flooded into his psyche.

I can't stop the tentacles of your mind, he sent to her.

But I can stop you.

Both of them, each through their own eyes, simultaneously through the other's, saw his arms shoot forward, his hands encircling the girl's midriff. He felt the flesh subsiding under his furious grasp, felt her ribs bending, felt the pain in like measure, as he inflicted it.

You fool, blazed an unfamiliar thought, not his own.

Wound me, you dare – my Fire will kill you!

His muscles flexed, then relaxed. He had somehow hurled the girl from her chair, sprawling her awkwardly on the white-shining tiled floor of the mall-corridor.

The fog of her mental attack evaporated the next second, and Billings came to his senses, only to see her slowly rising, hurt. She had her hand on her waist and moaned softly as she felt around her chest.

"Sari!" he shouted with alarm. "Oh, God, girl, I'm *sorry* – didn't *mean* to do that! Are you okay?"

Billings rushed over to the newcomer, who had now sat up fully. Compassionately, he enveloped her with his arms, holding his head next to hers.

"Oh-kay," she replied.

"Wow, Bob!" she added, "I suppose that I had forgotten how strong you can be... when you are angry. But I will be alright – they are just bruises. You are very lucky that I am the only one who was hurt, there... I am so foolish – I lost *control* of myself, if you had held on just a second or two more..."

Two elderly shoppers appeared, to Billings' right.

"Excuse me, Miss," interrupted one of them, "Is this man *hurting* you? You creep, there – you should be *ashamed* of yourself, assaulting a young thing like that! Miss, why don't we call Mall Security –"

"*Young* thing," muttered the 'Sari'-girl, propping her fore-body up by arms held palm-down out backward. "Ha! If you only *knew*... oh, but, thank you, sir, it is oh-kay... just, how do you say, 'a little misunderstanding', that is all. This man is my lover, my mate. All is well."

"Failure to come to a meeting of the minds... that's how I'd put it," grunted Billings.

"Are you *sure*, young lady?" demanded the old man, in the newcomer's direction.

"Sounds like one of those stories in the paper, where an abused woman is in denial, she can't defend herself against a brute like this man here –" castigated the old woman, in classic busybody style.

The 'Sari'-girl looked up and laughed, in a rueful tone.

"Cannot *defend* myself... ha ha," she quipped. "Mister, Madam, I appreciate your kind concerns, but... well, you could not be more mistaken, about *that*. I can assure you that many times, have I had to defend myself against far, far more formidable opponents than that this man... no offense meant there, Bob."

She rose back to her feet, saying, "Shall we go, then?"

Billings returned the smile.

"Let's," he agreed. "Save Whitey the trip back to figure out what the hell has been going on back here."

"Whitney!" called the salesman. "Take the kids and sit 'em down at the food-court. We'll be there in a minute."

Uneasily, the shopping couple moved away, extending a few suspicious stares as they went.

"So... does that mean I passed the test?" inquired Billings, as they started again toward the others.

"Take my hand," ordered the 'Sari'-girl.

He obliged.

"The answer is, 'yes'," she happily stated. "I assaulted your mind with everything that I had, Bob... and you lasted long enough to have disrupted my attack, if it had been a casual encounter. Your mind is *powerful* – I think that it is one of your innate blessings. In time, you will come to know how valuable that this is. And..."

"Yeah?" he answered, trying to ignore the raging headache that the encounter had inflicted on him.

With an enigmatic half-smile, she added, "The fortress of your mind is not just strong, Bob... it is now far past that of any... *human*..."

"What's *that* supposed to mean?" he challenged.

"Oh... nothingg," she chirped, in classic wife-or-girlfriend "change-the-subject" tone.

"Whatever," grumbled the salesman. "But, if you don't mind, that's not an experience that I care to repeat. Jesus, Sari, it was also the *weirdest* thing I've ever done. Did I tell you, I dropped some synth drugs one time, just to find out what it was like, you understand... but that was nothing like *this*. I knew that I had to resist you, but I didn't *want* to. One part of me wants to do it all over again, so I can give in, this time. If I tell you to, tell me I *don't* want to, and don't *let* me... okay?"

The newcomer looked up at him and smiled, affectionately.

"I will not hold you to that, Bob, because... well, because as yet, you understand so little of it," she said. "And there is something else, as well."

"Yeah?" he replied.

"Do you remember the first time that we mated?" she inquired. "You know, when I opened my legs and my woman-hole for your man-shaft, to be inside me, to fill me up so fully and completely?"

"You have a *way* of saying that," answered the salesman, trying to suppress a riot of lecherous thoughts that came to his mind out of left field. "But, yeah. How could I ever forget?"

"Remember how I told you, that when my saliva entered your mouth, it would bind us irreversibly?" asked the 'Sari'-girl.

"Something like that," muttered Billings. "And it sure *has*, on my side of the bed, at least. I seem to have lost some weight."

"Well, it is *true*," continued the fallen-girl. "Once I tasted your own, I *had* to be with you, to open up for you; I had as little choice as you did. I know that you people are kind of, uhh, *reserved* about discussing body secretions and fluids, but there is no other way to explain it... you see, each time that I take someone else's fluids inside me – I think that you know what I mean, Bob – I become, how would you say this, more 'at ease' here, more in tune with the environment... more *human*, maybe. I *adapt*."

"You seem to be adapting, uhh, just fine," observed the salesman.

"Well, I am pleased that you would think so," she said with a grin. "But now you need to pay very careful attention to what I will say next."

Billings stopped and looked her right in the eye.

"Yeah?" he said, guardedly.

"Bob," she quietly stated, "When I gift someone with my saliva, also with some of the other essences of my body – for example milk from my breasts – or maybe when I am just *around* a friend of a lover, for a period of time, I am not sure, exactly... it *changes* them. *Permanently*. Makes them stronger, smarter, healthier, and other things besides. I think that might be why you were able to so easily fend off my mind-fuck, Bob. As I said, I attacked your mind with all my powers, because... because..."

"Yes?" demanded Billings, arching an eyebrow.

"I am *ashamed*, Bob," she replied, quietly. "But I promised that I would not lie to you, so here it is. I attacked you as hard as I could, because something within me, *made* me do it, even though I promised that I would back off. I *had* to have you, I wanted you, *so* badly. Like I had no choice but to lie underneath you, take you inside me, when we kissed. What I am trying to say, Bob, is that I am bound to you. You have *power* over me."

"That's... uhh... *great*... I think," offered the salesman.

"Oh, give yourself some *credit*, man!" retorted the 'Sari'-girl, majestic exasperation sounding in her voice. "In former lives, kings and emperors, the great, powerful and famous, Gods and Demons, even, would have given *anything*, to be with me, as you are – people would bow down in awe, as I passed by. Poets would compose songs in my honor. You are in the presence of the *greatest* of my race, Bob Billings... meeting me is a *far* less likely event than winning all of your 'air-ee-zona State Lotteries', one after the other. Does that not mean *anything* to you?"

"I'll have to take your word for it... but I don't know how I'm better off because of it," replied Billings.

"Shortly," she obliquely stated, "You shall come to *understand* how much, ahh, 'better off', you are."

Then, he looked straight at her and stopped them both, for a second.

"Sari," he remarked, "You *know* that I love you, don't you?"

Earnestly, she stared back at him.

"Yes, I do," she affirmed, while wiping a tear. "And I know that your love is real, Bob Billings of Tucson, Arizona. And I, whomever I am, love *you*, too, without guile or mind-tricks. Even if it is falsely-planted, true love can still grow healthy and strong... if only we trust in it."

Her lips came fetchingly close to his own, but at the last minute, Billings' better senses warned him.

"Sari," he cautioned, "I'd love to, but with that damn spit of yours, in five seconds we'd be doing it right in front of the kids, the security-guards and the entire shopping population of the Park Place Mall, you know. rain-check?"

"For God's sake, Bob," protested the newcomer, "What is so important about the *weather*, right now? Talk about killing a nice mood..."

The salesman rolled his eyes.

"It's an *expression*, Sari. It means, 'promise to do something later'. As in, I promise we'll end up back in bed, together. I hope."

"Oh," sheepishly muttered the fallen-girl. "Sorry. Another one to remember, I suppose. I *hate* this stupid language of yours. It has far too many make-up phrases that do not mean what they say, until someone explains them to you."

Billings pulled her forward, again.

"I guess we had better catch up to them," he said.

"One other thing," mentioned the 'Sari'-girl, as they approached Claremont.

"Yeah?" asked the salesman.

"If I were you, Bob," she warned, "I would be *careful* about grabbing me like you did, back there – it is no problem if you are touching me with affection, or with sexual arousal, but if my mind perceives a physical assault, my body can react very... *forcefully*. It happens automatically – I must concentrate to deliberately prevent it, and if someone hurts me unexpectedly, I may not have enough time to suppress this natural reaction. I do not know if this ability is even working right now, but if it *is*... I just do not want to *hurt* you."

"I *told* you that I was sorry," he grumbled. "*My* mind wasn't working too well, remember? Anyway, what are you *talking* about? What are your ribs going to do, pop out and bite me?"

"No," she explained, evenly, "That is not what happens. It is more like an energy discharge. A 'short-circuit', is what I think you would call it. And when *that* trick comes back to me, it is *more* than powerful enough to burn your arms off... or worse."

"Swell," muttered Billings. "The human electric transformer-station. And I fell head and heels for you, didn't I?"

He sighed.

"half-right," answered the fallen-girl, flashing a goofy smile back at him. "About the 'transformer' part of it."

She stopped for a second.

"It's as new for me, as it is for you, Bob," she offered. "For someone like *me* – I think that you know what I mean – to be in love with someone like *you*. Somewhere, I have heard it wisely said, that love is one of the fundamental rules of the universe, no less than the rules of energy, matter, time and space... that love is found *everywhere,* if one just searches for it. That it can bind even those who are in fact far different, from each other. Is it not so?"

"Well, I've been looking for it in Tucson for about twenty years now, and until recently, it had eluded me," replied the salesman, with a wry grin.

They resumed walking and rounded a corner, to see Claremont and three bored-looking children draped in various odd positions over the bolted-down chairs and tables of an open concept food service area.

"Look at the bright side of it, Bob," cheerily added the 'Sari'-girl. "Just think of how much more *exciting* your life will be, making love with a 'transformer-station', every night. 'Sparks of passion' will fly everywhere."

She giggled.

"Gives a whole new meaning to the term, a 'real turn-on'... doesn't it?" sardonically answered Billings, as he led her in the direction of the others.

A Few Little Card-Tricks

"What y'all talkin' 'bout, there?" interrupted Claremont, now in earshot.

"Ah knows, Momma," chimed in Melissa. "They talkin' 'bout *adult* things."

"Shush," ordered the black woman.

"Ah'm hungry," added Curtis. "Momma, we gettin' some food?"

Claremont shot Billings a pained look.

"Look, Bob, ah *knows* we owes y'all already," she said, "But 'till ah can get somewhere to take out some money..."

"Don't worry about it," reassured the salesman. "Haven't seen an ATM around here, yet, but –"

"An ay-tee-what?" asked the fallen-girl, tugging on the man's shirt-sleeve.

"A banking-machine," explained Billings. "Somewhere that you can connect to a computer-network and access your bank, take out money."

"Ah," she replied. "How does one say it... yes – the mighty dollar bill, right?"

"Yeah," commented Claremont, "All the more mighty, if y'all ain't *got* none, girl."

The 'Sari'-girl wheeled and did a mock bow, accompanied with a cynical smile, in front of the black woman.

"In that respect," offered the newcomer, "You and I are then equally powerless, Whitney."

She turned to Billings, gave a fake curtsy and ruefully added, "See, Bob... the high and mighty 'Sari-The-Great-Something-Or-Other', without so much as two copper coins to call my own. Noble and exalted... am I not?"

"Been there *plenty* of times, sister," noted the salesman, with a shrug.

"Look, maybe they take debit," he suggested. "What does everybody want to eat? We'll try one of these places – worst that can happen is, it doesn't work."

"Ah wants pizza," instantly demanded Curtis.

"Me too – lots of pepp'roni 'n cheese," added Melissa.

"How about you, kid?" asked Billings of the Indian-boy.

"Don't feel like pizza right now," replied Tommy. "But, Mister Billings, there's a Chinese place next to the Pizza Deliciosa place... can I try some Chinese food? We used to get pizza all the time on the reserve, but we had to go into town for Chinese, so it was always a special treat."

"Doesn't matter to me one way or t'other," shrugged the salesman. "Comes down to who'll take my debit-card."

The 'Sari'-girl cruised over to the Indian-boy, taking his hand.

"I will have the same as Tommy," she requested. "Oh-kay?"

The boy looked up with affection glowing in his eyes.

"Okay!" he chirped.

"I'll try the pizza," said Billings. "Let's go."

The six of them walked rapidly over to the ordering-lineup for the pizza stand, although in fact there were only two other customers ahead of them.

Presently, a pimply-faced, bored-looking teenage boy addressed Billings.

"Take your order, Mister?" he lazily inquired.

"I hope so," responded the salesman. "I don't have much cash – I'd prefer debit, if you're taking it."

"Sort of," explained the boy. "Network's kinda screwed up – they said something about 'authentication down' when we asked them yesterday why people's cards weren't working, but later, this guy came by and said that if you don't try to charge more than 25 bucks'-worth, it'll go through."

"Will it?" demanded Billings.

"Did for somebody an hour ago... I think," offered the boy.

"I'll take that as a 'yes'," grunted the salesman.

"Okay – here's our order," he said, looking at the back-lit menu above the pizza ovens. "One number 3, large, one number 7, also large, make it extra cheese and sausage on the number 3 –"

Billings turned to the others.

"What you all want to drink?" he asked.

A babble of excited young voices came back at him, but somehow the salesman was able to make sense out of the cacophony.

"One High-Test Coke, one orange soda, and I'll have a coffee, large, cream and sugar, please," he continued. "Whitney, you having something to drink?"

"Coffee, ah guess. Jus' milk with it, please," responded the woman.

Billings could see the frustration of poverty in her eyes.

He turned to her and whispered, "Don't sweat it, for God's sake, Whitney – nobody's keeping score, after what we've been through. You want to pay me back, take my clothes downstairs and run 'em through the washing machine... *if*, we got any water to use in it, that is."

Claremont nodded, resignedly.

"That'll be twenty-two and fifteen," stated the boy. "Here's the machine."

The salesman fumbled for, and eventually found, his banking card, entered his PIN on the numeric keypad and ran the card through the reader.

After a second or two, the LCD display on the debit machine returned the message, "TRANSACTION FAILED : CODE 3592".

"Damn," cursed Billings. "I thought you said this thing was *working*...?"

"It is, Mister," answered the boy. "Must be your card. You got any money left on it?"

"Of *course* I do, kid," muttered the salesman. "Look, I didn't carry too much cash on me, today, so..."

"Not my problem, Mister," insolently replied the boy.

"Why do we not we try it again?" interrupted the 'Sari'-girl.

"I've never known that to help," said Billings. "But – what the H."

He re-entered his code and re-swiped the card through the machine.

Again, the display showed, "TRANSACTION FAILED : CODE 3592".

"I'm afraid it's pizza or nothing, folks," he sighed. "I got enough for what we bought here, but not enough for this and the Chinese stuff as well."

"Let me try it," requested the fallen-girl.

"Look, we tried it *twice*," argued Billings. "There's no point."

"Just let me try," demanded the newcomer.

"*Fine*," complained the salesman. "The rest of you go sit down and start eating. We'll be there in a second."

The Claremont clan headed for the chairs, while Tommy stayed by the 'Sari'-girl's side, looking up at her with filial affection.

"You mind if my girlfriend here gives it a shot?" inquired Billings, toward the pizza-boy.

The boy shrugged.

"Whatever, dude," he said. "Nobody behind you in the line, anyway. Listen, I just remembered, I gotta call my Dad so he can pick me up after my shift... can't afford the gas for my own car after they took away the ration for everybody under 19, bummer, you know? Phone's over at the other end of the stand, but don't leave without settling up... boss'll take it out of my pay, you know?"

"Oh, for *sure*," agreed Billings. "I'll have the change counted out before you get back."

The 'Sari-girl now advanced to the card-reader machine.

Her fingers played lightly over the keypad.

"My code's seven characters long," noted the salesman. "You memorized it after only *two* looks?"

The fallen-girl turned her head and gave him a cheerful, but somehow intimidating, look.

"I suppose that I have a talent for remembering such things, Bob," she remarked. "But do not worry – I promise that I will not use your card without permission."

She paused for a second, then added, "Of course, I *am* a woman, and I *am* in a 'shopping-mall', am I not? I should, ahh, 'play the part'... right?"

She giggled.

"I want the damn thing back the *second* you're done with it," countered Billings, with mock defensiveness.

"Tommy," counseled the 'Sari-girl, "Remember how I told you that I would teach you some of my tricks? Take my hand. Now... the first time, we will try it, just to see how it feels. When it talks on the wire, that is."

There was an odd tone in her voice, as she said this.

"'Sari'," protested Billings. "Is this really a good place –"

But the newcomer was already in full motion, one hand clasped around the Indian-boy's, her other whisking the debit-card through the machine.

The display showed the same error as before.

"Did you feel that?" she asked, bending over.

"Wow, *yeah!*" quickly answered an excited Tommy. "That was *neat* – it was like I could *see* – *feel* – the numbers in my –"

"That was me, showing you what the little pulses meant, when they are decoded," interrupted the 'Sari-girl.

Tommy nodded.

"And did you feel the flow, itself?" she inquired, as matter-of-factually as if explaining a sewing stitch.

"Yeah, sure did," replied the boy. "Like a song, or the ring of a phone."

"Anyway," interrupted Billings. "Are we done, folks?"

How the hell would she know how to do something like that... *didn't they say they dug her out of a stone tomb?* he mused, not particularly caring if she could read his thoughts.

"Now it is, how do you say, yes, 'for the money'," announced the fallen-girl, showing an oblique smirk to the salesman. "I will make the little numbers a bit stronger – more up to the up and more down to the down, for the little pulses on the wire. Let us see how *that* works, oh-kay?"

"Okay!" enthusiastically answered the Indian-boy.

She entered Billings' PIN in next to no time; then, staring intently at the machine, quickly ran the card through the reader.

"Hmm, hmm, hmm," she sang, just above the level of audibility.

The LCD flickered for a second, then displayed, "TRANSACTION ACCEPTED".

A second later, it spit out a printed transcript.

The 'Sari'-girl bent forward, over the serving-counter next to the pizza stand's point-of-sale register.

"Hey, young man, there," she called out. "I believe that we made your little reading-machine work, this time. Come and see!"

The boy looked up, then said into the phone receiver, "Listen, can you hold on for a sec? Got a customer... yeah, fine. Back in a sec."

He put down the phone and sauntered over to the register.

"See?" proudly remarked the 'Sari'-girl, showing the boy the machine and the bill.

"Wow... awesome," he replied. "Okay, well, then, I don't need any cash from you, Mister. Enjoy your pizza, dude."

The newcomer held the bill out in front of her, gesturing to the boy.

"Yes, lady?" he asked.

"Do you not you want it?" she innocently asked. "I did not want to take something that is not mine."

"What?" replied the boy, with confusion. "Oh, yeah... no, *you* take it, lady. It's yours... I mean, it's Mister whatever's, there. You never seen a debit-bill before?"

"I... uhh... oh, of *course,* I have," evaded the fallen-girl, posing coltishly. "I just do not *need* one, right now –"

"What she *means* is," said Billings, hastily jumping in, "We don't need the receipt. For expenses, that is. Not a business lunch, you know?"

"*Right,* dude," answered the boy, now staring at the 'Sari'-girl in new-found awe, as if he had just noticed her.

"Listen, lady... don't know exactly how to say this, don't want to get Mister whatever there mad, you know, but... man, you're *cute,* don't take that the wrong way, you know? You don't have a sister who isn't *with* anybody, maybe?"

"A sister," pensively mentioned the newcomer. "No, sorry... not that I know of, but I *have* heard rumors of a half-sister... it is a long story, different fathers, that kind of thing. If she is real, she would be very, *very* far away, by now... anyway, thank you for the compliment. You are 'cute', too – were I not, ahh, 'with' Bob here, I am sure that you and I could, how do you say, ahh, 'have some fun'."

She posed fetchingly for the boy, well aware of being undressed by his eyes.

"My lunch is getting cold," complained the salesman.

"Oh yeah, you *got* it, dude," apologized the pizza boy. "Oh, *shit* – Dad's still on the phone! You mind?"

"Not at all," insouciantly answered Billings.

"Have a nice day," said the boy, as he dashed to the other end of the pizza-stand, fumbling for the phone receiver.

"People become jealous quickly, in this culture," observed the 'Sari'-girl. "Not all are such – in other places, one has several partners, not always of the opposite –"

"Last I heard, only the *Mormons* get to do that, and this isn't Utah," interrupted Billings.

As he stuffed his paper money into his billfold and walked back toward the table where Claremont and her children were sitting, he noticed that an alarming amount of the pizza had already disappeared.

"You know, Sari," he cautioned, "You gotta be a little more *careful* about who you reveal your life story to. And you almost showed that 'trick' to the kid back there, if he had seen it, he might start asking *questions* – I know you *mean* well, but... well, he's just some kid serving pizza, you know?"

"Yeah," replied the fallen-girl. "Sorry, Bob... his question just caught me off-guard, I suppose – a sad thought from long ago, took hold of me. That happens, sometimes. And I hope that you have noticed, I do not need to use the little trick that we were discussing back down the corridor, to procure a favor. It is not that difficult to convince the opposite sex to do what one wants, if one knows how to ask... is it not?"

"*Tell* me," muttered Billings. "That's why I was – *am* – so pissed about it. All you have to do is strike that pose for me, girl, and you don't have to, uhh, do what we were talking about; I'm as helpless as a lovesick puppy. But I'm afraid it wouldn't work the same way if I tried it... you're a little more, uh, *photogenic* than I am, you know."

"*What* trick, Miz Sari?" asked Tommy.

"I will show you later," she said back to the boy, giving him an affectionate smile.

"As for the card-machine trick," she continued, speaking in Billings' direction, "You *do* know, that your body, too, works with little pulses of energy, in this case, manifested as electricity? Each human being has an aura of energy, every living thing does, in fact; so if I... uhh, *concentrate*, in the right way, I can see it around you. When you raise your arm, indeed, every time that you think a thought, well, oh-kay, there is more to it than just your mind, I will admit, but the point is, this is a trick that *you* can learn, too. You can make the power in your body, flow out of you, or in *to* you. Which is why I wanted Tommy to experience it."

"My Dad used to say, there's no better way to learn than by just doing something," observed the boy.

Billings stopped them just short of the others.

"*Look*, you two," he demanded, "I understand what Sari is saying, but as long as I'm in charge here, I'd really prefer for these 'lessons' only to happen in *private*, where nobody can see, you got that? Just *trust* me on this one – I know the authorities much better than either of you do, and I can personally attest, you *don't* want them to take an interest in you. Doing this kind of thing it in public is *dangerous*. You'll draw far too much attention to yourselves. And to me. Which is why I'd like it stopped, *pronto*."

"Yes, sir," reflexively agreed the Indian-boy.

"I know what you are saying, Bob, and I will try to be more... *careful*, next time," said the 'Sari'-girl, "But please try to appreciate... do you know what it is like, when you have a secret gift that you want to share, want to give to those who you love? It is very easy to become excited about the whole thing."

"Yeah," grumbled the salesman. "*Lots* of things are easy, or *seem* so, at first. About ninety per cent of them end up giving you a hangover, or worse."

"Like last night?" teased Tommy.

"Don't be *smart*, kid," grunted Billings.

The Indian-boy and the 'Sari'-girl had another giggle at Billings' expense.

"Listen, Bob," stated the newcomer, "Tommy and I are still hungry, and we do not have any money, so..."

The salesman had sat down with the Claremont troupe and had started to munch away at a slice of pizza, so the fallen-girl stooped down in front of him and sent him a pleading glance.

Billings rolled his eyes.

"*Fine*," he complained, "Here it is. Try this first, if they don't take it, then I'll dig up the cash."

He handed his debit-card to the 'Sari'-girl, who replied with an affectionate peck on the cheek, then whirled and led the Indian-boy at a rapid pace, toward the Chinese food serving-stall.

The two of them queued behind about three shoppers who had lined up ahead, but after two or three minutes in which Billings was, thankfully, able to wolf down another half-slice of pizza before Curtis got his greasy little paws on it, the salesman noticed that the 'Sari'-girl had turned and was pointing to him.

"Bob!" she shouted.

"Yeah?" replied Billings.

"They want your word of confirmation," she called.

"My *what?*" asked the salesman.

"Come over here," she requested.

"I *knew* this was going to happen," muttered Billings, as he got up.

"No shit," commented Claremont. "Y'all think they don' have no credit-cards, where *she* come from?" she joked, not looking up from her meal.

"Of *course* they don', Momma," chirped Melissa. "Lawd give them angels, anythin' they aks for. Don' gots to pay for nothin', 'cept maybe when they break a string on they harp."

Curtis almost spit out a mouthful of pizza, laughing as he heard this *bon mot*.

"What's the problem?" asked Billings, as he sauntered over to the Chinese food stall.

"Name on the card don't match her face, Mister," announced a teenage Hispanic girl, behind the serving-counter. "She don't look very much like a 'Robert K. Billings', if you know what I mean. Gotta get your go-ahead if you want to let her use your card, Mister."

"I do not look like a 'Robert Billings', you say?" sarcastically noted the 'Sari'-girl, showing a little too much sharp tooth as she smiled to reinforce the point.

"There's a lot of identity-theft going on," shrugged the salesman. "Each time they use a new chip to stop it, takes the crooks about a week to beat it, and back to Square One we go. Anyway, consider my permission given. Oh, wait... what's the charge, first?"

"Fifteen ninety-five," replied the serving-counter girl.

"Well, go ahead, I suppose, but that's a *lot* of food – what did you guys order, Peking Duck or something?" asked Billings.

"Tommy ordered, uhh, how do you say, 'sweet-and-sour chicken' and noodles, with a 'Pep-see' to drink," explained the fallen-girl. "I requested the vegetablian meal, no meat, that is, I think that I told you, Bob, I *can* eat meat but I really do not like to do so, and fried rice, and I asked for one of those 'Pep-see' things, too, because Tommy said that it was really sweet-tasting. Oh, look, *there* are our dinners – mmm... they smell great, do they not?"

"It's 'vegetarian', not 'vegetablian'," corrected Billings.

"Oh... oops," sheepishly replied the 'Sari'-girl.

She looked at the Hispanic girl.

"May I?" she asked.

The other girl nodded.

Expertly, the newcomer ran the debit-card through the reader.

"TRANSACTION ACCEPTED", appeared instantly.

Proudly, she handed the card back to the salesman.

"I believe that I have, how do you say, 'got the hang of this', Bob," she proudly stated. "It is a good system, if I do say. In other places, one has to carry around bags of coins. Doing that becomes tedious, after a while, and they give away one's location, if one moves too fast while carrying them."

"That went out a *long* time ago, around here," commented Billings. "Got too expensive to put the copper and silver into the coins. They tried making 'em out of plastic for a while, even had RFID chips in them, but it wasn't worth the effort... or so they said."

"Shall we eat?" proposed the 'Sari'-girl.

"I'm already done," said Billings, "So are they, almost. Man... that Curtis sure has an appetite. But you two go ahead."

The newcomer gave the salesman a quick peck on the cheek.

"Thank you, Bob," she earnestly intoned. "I want you to know that Tommy and I appreciate all that you have done for us. When I am able, I will repay you. I *promise* it."

She then led the Indian-boy rapidly over to the table with the others.

Billings, sort of groggy-headed from a combination of digestion and realization, slowly followed behind.

Ye Gods... and this is just 'her', in a shopping-mall, he silently reflected.

A half-second later, an impish, feminine smile, somehow impressed itself upon his mind.

Lunchtime Chat

As the 'Sari'-girl and the Indian-boy sat down, Claremont accosted them.

"Y'all shore took enough time to get yo' meal there, girl," she commented. "Round where ah comes from, y'all waste time like that, sometimes y'all don' get nothin' at all."

"I *could* have partaken of the pizza," evenly replied the 'Sari'-girl. "But you had that, uhh, 'pepper-oh-nee' on it, and I do not really enjoy eating the meat of animals. I do not like killing things, just to feed myself."

"Y'all ate lots of it when we was on the road," countered the black woman.

"Only what I had to, to stop the hunger-pains," answered the newcomer. "There is a difference between *trying* to live according to one's principles, Whitney, and doing so to the point where it no longer makes sense – that is, where one, or those who one loves, might end up starving. I have my principles, but I must occasionally bend them... I have to *compromise*, you know?"

"Sounds to yours truly that them's easy 'principles' to live by, what with y'all usin' them or not, when y'all likes," observed Claremont.

"Well, Momma," argued Melissa, "Don' the Bible say somethin' 'bout Jesus collectin' food on the Sabbath, when them priests tell Him that was 'gainst the rules? Y'all 'member? He say that it was okay, if y'all was hungry."

An odd look came over the 'Sari'-girl, as she regarded Melissa, straight on.

To the faint hum of ethereal music from somewhere, she said to the teenager, "Yes, Melissa, that is correct, I believe. At the library, I read about this 'Jesus', who I have come to know was a very important person – I also tried to look at some other religious books, but they would not let me access this 'Koran' of the Muslims; the lady at the desk said that it was 'illegal anti-Christian propaganda' and warned me that if I asked again, they might tell the police, so of course I apologized and promised not to do that."

"Been that way for years," noted the African-American woman. "Some damn terrorist thang went down Miami way befo' mah kids was born, ah heared it was some gangstas who done it, but they blamed them Muslims, came down on all of 'em *real* bad. Like, they cain't own no property or nothin', an' the guv'ment closed down all they churches 'n such. Too bad, but what ah thinks 'bout it don' make no difference... ah gots lots of problems on mah own, y'all understand?"

The fallen-girl looked off into the distance and quietly said, "Yeah... I have read about all *that*, too. These measures seem cruel, but it is difficult for me to know the truth of it, since I have never met any 'Muslims'... perhaps I will do so, someday. Odd, you know... I feel that I *have* met one of them... but I recall not where."

There was silence for a few seconds, then the newcomer continued, "Anyway, since we found Bob's car, I have taken some time to read the 'Bible'-book that has the story of your 'Jesus' in it. It is an interesting story, but it seems to be from very long ago... there does not seem to be anything in it, about what is going on today. I would have thought that this good magic, if there *is* such a thing, would still be here with you, I would have hoped for that..."

Her voice tailed off.

"Momma," whispered Curtis to Claremont, "How can she be an angel and not know 'bout Jesus?"

"Shush," whispered back the boy's mother. "That for *her* to deal with, not us."

"Yeah," mentioned the 'Sari'-girl, again staring off into space. "It is."

"Well, folks," interjected Billings, trying to preserve the last dregs of his coffee as he sipped, "Not that I want to change the subject from these profound issues... but, what's everyone want to do, once we're finished eating, here? Anywhere in particular that you want to go?"

"The bathroom," chirped Curtis.

"Don't let *me* stop you," cackled the salesman. "Don't know *where* you put all that. On second thought, don't tell me."

"Fine, y'all an' your sister go now, but don' hang 'round there too long, y'all hear... don' want the man gettin' on our case again," ordered Claremont. "Y'all knows they check them bathrooms every so often."

"Yes'm," answered the woman's two children.

"Come on, Curtis, washrooms just over there," exclaimed Melissa, pointing to a 'women / men' sign to one side of the food-court."

"I think that I would like to do some shopping," requested the 'Sari'-girl, between mouthfuls of Chinese vegetables and rice.

"Hmm... this food is not *that* bad, Bob, although there are a lot of un-natural substances in it," she added. "It reminds me of something that I used to eat, uhh, a long time ago."

"Glad you like it," replied Billings. "Although personally if I was to go for Chinese, I'd always pick the sweet-and-sour pork, as well as an egg-roll here and there. Used to eat a bit more of it until they came out with that 'Super-MSG' stuff a couple of years ago; they're all using it now, they claimed it was just fine but I dunno, I tend to stay away from chemicals whenever I can," he said.

"Bob," inquired the newcomer.

"Yes?" answered the salesman.

"You said that this was 'Chinese' food, right?" she asked. "Like from the country of China... correct?"

"Umm-humm," he forced, in between mouthfuls.

"That is on the other continent, right?" she questioned. "The big one, across the wide shining sea?"

"Across the Pacific Ocean, in fact," he explained. "I guess you'd call it a wide sea, for sure. It's about as far away from here as you can get."

"They have astronauts... people who go into space... do they not?" asked the fallen-girl. "The Chinese people, I mean."

"Yeah, so I hear," confirmed Billings. "They've got quite a rivalry going with good ol' Uncle Sam in that department, it actually almost got to the stage of us shooting down their satellites and them shooting down ours, at one point. Russians, European Union and the Indians, too... at least, they *did*, before the whole 'comet' thing went down. That's kind of reset the match up there – oh, sorry, girl. I forgot that's a *sensitive* subject with you."

His hand reached over to envelop hers.

Appreciatively, the 'Sari'-girl regarded him.

"Thanks, Bob," she said. "It is just that... well, that I have *memories* of meeting some of these 'astronauts' – I remember one who called himself 'Chinese', that is all. I guess that it must sound pretty stupid to you... right? Maybe they are all just dreams. Yes, that is what they must be. Just... *dreams*."

Her eyes had a weird, far-off look.

"Whatever they are," carefully commented Billings, "Your dreams and memories are safe with *me*, honey."

The fallen-girl just smiled warmly and demurely lowered her eyes.

After a few seconds, she again spoke.

"How much money can you ask to get out of that little plastic card, Bob?" she asked.

"More than enough for anything that I'll let *you* buy," replied Billings. "But what do you need, anyway?"

"Oh, I do not know... some new clothes, maybe, or... better still... is there somewhere in here that sells fabric?" mentioned the newcomer. "I have many years of experience at making my own garments. All that I need is a needle and some thread. Better still... do you know a place where one can buy thin metal, flexible metal, I mean, and some fine wire, anywhere in this 'Park Place' mall? Oh, and I will need a number of other things, for example, small gem-stones, com-pu-ter thinking-chips, certain kinds of plants and natural elements, like quartz or mica –"

"*Laws*, girl," exclaimed Claremont. "What y'all fixin' to do wid all *that*? They only usin' that stuff to do things like trick out they cars."

The 'Sari'-girl shot the black woman another one of her characteristic odd glances.

"To make clothes... and, uhh, equipment – needful things, I mean – for myself, of course," she replied.

"Well okay, but why make 'em out of out of metal 'n such?" demanded Claremont. "What's wrong with good ol' cotton, or maybe silk if y'all can get

Mr. Sales Man there to spring for it? Ah ain't seen *nobody* in no metal suits, 'cept maybe one of them guys who plays a knight from the olden days, on TV."

"Metal can withstand more heat and shock," matter-of-factually noted the fallen-girl. "And it transmits energy better... if one knows how to, ahh, 'improve' it."

Billings shrugged wearily and interjected, "I think they might carry some of that at the High-Kew Hardware and Outdoors store... according to the map back there, it's just down the corridor to the right, about half way. I used to shop there once in a while for fishing-gear, although I haven't done that for years since most of the good streams around here dried up, what with the global-warming stuff going on. But..."

"But?" asked the newcomer, right back.

"Well, it might cost a bit more than a meal at the food-court, you know," observed the salesman. "What do I *get*, for shelling out for this little hobby of yours?"

Coquettishly, the 'Sari'-girl batted her eyes and smiled cutely at the man.

"Oh... I am *sure* that I will find a way to pay you back, Bob," she chirped.

Tommy giggled.

"Look," complained Billings, scratching his head, "Are you sure that this isn't the same bloody thing that we were –"

"I *told* you," primly replied the fallen-girl, "It does not *work* on you, anymore. No, Bob – this is me doing it, how do you say, 'the hard way'. But I have had a long time in which to learn how to be, ahh, *persuasive*. Am I not so, Bob?"

"What y'all *talkin'* 'bout, Mister Billings –" started Melissa, returning from the direction of the washrooms with her brother in tow.

"Mister Billings was talkin' adult stuff," admonished Claremont.

"Oh, sorry, Momma," replied the black girl. "Jus' we got back here faster than ah thought we would, 'cuz we didn' have to fool them pay-for-use boxes that they got on the stalls, attendant said somethin' 'bout 'the Potty-Pay network bein' down' or somethin' like that."

"So... usually, one must to pay money, even to *pee*, around here," observed the 'Sari'-girl. "If one does not have any, and one, ahh, '*goes*', anyway, how do they charge more money to clean it up?"

"I'm sure they'll find a way," muttered Billings. "Anyway, about the shopping, I think it's a waste of money, frankly, but considering what I've already dropped on everything else so far, it's probably the least of my concerns. Let's go."

"Let us," echoed the 'Sari'-girl, hooking the salesman's arm in her own.

The two strode off down the corridor, the picture of marital, or, at least, relationship-wise contentment, with Claremont and the others tagging just behind.

A Bang For Bob's Buck

In a minute or two, the salesman and his troupe of hangers-on, had arrived at a large, multi-level combination hardware and outdoors-living department store.

"This it?" laconically asked the African-American woman.

"Yep," answered Billings. "Place you want, if it hasn't changed since I was last in here, is just up the escalator, ahead and a bit to the left."

"Curtis!" admonished Claremont, upon seeing her son charge ahead. The boy roared up to one of the side-shelves of the check-out lines.

"Yo Tommy, check this out!" he exclaimed. "water-gun, but it look jus' like a AK-90! That dread or what!"

The Indian-boy promptly followed Curtis to examine this amazing new thing.

"Melissa, go get yo' brother," ordered the black woman. "He *know* he not s'posed to grab thangs he can't pay for."

"Yes'm," replied the teenager, as she moved forward.

"Curtis!" she shouted.

"You wanted to know why I never had kids, Whitney?" rhetorically commented Billings, as he followed the Claremonts and the Indian-boy.

But as he and the 'Sari'-girl crossed the security-barrier just inside the store's outside periphery, an alarm went off, and the newcomer stopped in place.

"Did you feel that, Bob?" she inquired.

A split-second later, she corrected herself. "Oh, no, right... you would not have, *would* you..."

"*Excuse* me, Miss," interrupted a determined voice, from their left.

Turning, Billings and the fallen-girl saw that the voice belonged to a beefy, crew-cut store security-guard, evidently from a different company than the one that was charged with defending the rest of the mall, judging from his uniform.

"You set off the alarm," he warned. "May I search you, please? Please step back and spread your arms and legs."

"Look," protested Billings, "Sari and I were just walking in here – not the other way around. We couldn't *possibly* have stolen anything."

The 'Sari'-girl had moved back by a step or two, away from the store and toward the mall-corridor.

"You can go ahead, I suppose," she stated. "But Bob is quite right – I do not understand what is going on here... I have never been in this store in my life."

"The only way that you can set off this alarm, Miss," countered the guard, with officious determination in his voice, as he pulled out some kind of baton-like instrument, "Is to try to go across the security-barrier, with some contraband on you. Do you have any contraband on you today, Miss?"

"Contra-*what*?" perplexedly asked the newcomer, perplexedly. "Oh, yeah... I heard that word back when those police-men stopped us, on the highway..."

"Where'd *she* come from, Mister?" interjected the guard.

"You don't want to *know*," wearily muttered Billings.

Turning to the 'Sari'-girl, he explained, "It means, 'something illegal that you shouldn't have, or something that you've stolen'; the way they do this is they hide a tiny little micro-ID chip in the stuff that they sell here, and to turn it off you have to pay for the item at the counter, otherwise it goes apeshit when you try to get it out of the store."

"But this is a big waste of time," he continued, addressing the guard, who started now moving the baton up and down and all over the fallen-girl's body. "Like I said, we're coming *in*... not going *out*. Although if this takes much more time, we might just decide to take our business elsewhere."

Beep-beep-BEEP-BEEP-BEEP, went the probe. Lights flashed on and off, on its control panel.

The store-guard stepped back, furrowing his brow, as he tried to adjust the instrument.

He looked up at the 'Sari'-girl and her erstwhile boyfriend.

"Look... uhh... this is really weird, Miss," remarked the guard. "It says that you've got enough contraband to sink an ocean-liner on you, but... well, just *looking* at you, that doesn't make a lot of sense. Sorry about this, but the rules say that I've got to pat you down, or I can't let you in. May I pat you down to detect any contraband, Miss?"

The 'Sari'-girl shrugged, indifferently, although she shot a wink to Billings a second after.

"Watch where your hands go," grumbled the salesman.

The guard ran his hands up and down the fallen-girl's arms, then her midriff; then he knelt, moving them slowly, unprofessionally so, down each of her legs, one by one.

He started breathing heavily, with a faint sheen of sweat breaking on his brow.

What the hell are you doing now, thought Billings.

I hear that stupid rock music again, in my head... you could play it for me all night, but this isn't the place, isn't the time...

"That's *enough*," admonished the salesman. "No more groping my damn girlfriend, you *hear*?"

"Do not worry, Bob," answered the girl, as she bent down, staring the guard in the face with a look of bemusement and compassion rolled into one.

The guard had half-slumped in front of the two, his head hanging lazily as if he had had 'one too many', the night before.

"Young man," inquired the 'Sari'-girl, "How do you feel, right about now? Did you find what you were looking for?"

The guard slowly staggered to his feet.

"Uhh... what?" he stammered. "Oh... no, lady, no, I didn't, you're... you're good to go, I guess. Didn't find... anything."

"No," she corrected. "You *did* find something, you know, or, rather, *it* found *you*. Listen... may I give you some advice, Mister security-guard?"

By now, the man had mostly regained his composure.

"About... what?" he asked.

"If a stranger gives you a gift, for instance, the gift of better health," she quietly and purposefully explained, "Perhaps you should then do something *equally* good, for another stranger, in turn. You should do for others, as you would have them do for yourself."

Claremont shot a half-awed look at her daughter, who nodded back, suppressing a gasp.

"Momma," whispered Melissa, "She sayin' the 'zact same thang that –"

Again, the black woman nodded, her demeanor demanding "no more about this".

The guard regarded the fallen-girl, who was far more slightly built and at least a head shorter than himself, with scant comprehension.

"Yeah... good point, I guess," he acknowledged, still confused.

He motioned Billings and the 'Sari'-girl forward.

Again, the newcomer traversed the security-barrier, and again, the alarm sounded.

"Don't worry, Miss," mentioned the guard. "Must be... must be something wrong with the effing thing, again. You know, we just replaced it about six months ago, the sales guy from the alarm company said this one was the super-duper version, wouldn't *ever* screw up with false positives like the old one did. Sorry for the inconvenience."

"I'm in sales, myself," retorted Billings. "And let me give you a little *advice*... don't believe everything you hear from us guys. *Especially* around quota-time. May we go?"

"Oh, of *course*," agreed the guard. "You got a point there, Mister. Enjoy your shopping."

As they regrouped, with Claremont disentangling Curtis' reluctant little fingers from his new-found toys, Billings said under his breath to the 'Sari'-girl, "Listen – you didn't use that, you know, that *thing* we were talking about, back there, on him, did you?"

The fallen-girl shook her head.

"No," she half-whispered. "I only do *that*, when there is no other, easier way. *You* feel better, after touching me, do you not, Bob?" she pointed out. "Well, so did *he*. Maybe it will stay with him... maybe not. It is the way of things with me and has been so, since before I can remember. *Surely* there can be nothing wrong, with me helping people to have good health, to feel better about themselves?"

"In theory, no," countered the salesman, "But what if it draws... *attention*? You *know* that you may be endangering yourself – maybe all of us as well – by handing out these little 'gifts' here and there? Don't you remember that little incident back on the road? They may be looking for you already, you know."

Looking straight ahead, the 'Sari'-girl remarked, with absolute determination, "As for the risks to me, so be they; I am who I am and I will do what I am here to do. The time to change this manner of things passed me by, many, many years ago. And for the rest of you, being around me is a chance that you will all have to make your own decisions about."

"Seems we made that d'cision a ways back," mentioned Claremont, laconically. "But shore is never a dull minute with y'all 'round, girl."

The newcomer shot a friendly smile to the black woman.

"I will take that as a compliment, Whitney," she replied, "And I do *so* appreciate it."

They had reached the escalator in the center of the store, and Billings stood to its side and ushered them on, one by one.

"Been a while since ah was on one of *these*," commented Melissa. "Not since we went on our school trip to downtown De-troit."

"It smells of the only-one-air-element gas," stated the 'Sari'-girl. "Like what you breathe, but one of the little, uhh, 'particles', is missing."

"Y'all gots a chemistry-set, Miz Sari?" asked Curtis. "Ah had one back 'n th' hood and ah learned 'bout them atoms and molecules wid it, but then them po-lice men came an' took it away, they said ah was gonna use it to make bad things, like synth drugs, but it was a *lie*, all ah was gonna do was –"

"Never mind, boy," interrupted Claremont. "Past histr'y, anyways."

"My," observed the 'Sari'-girl, panning her view from right to left as the escalator lifted them high above the first floor, "Rarely have I seen so many things to buy, especially for the common-folk – look at that, there are shelves *overflowing* with wares, everything from lantern-lights to little boats! Bob, do you not find it exciting to see all this? You must shop here very often, just planning what to buy next, or wishing that you had more money."

"Nah," shrugged Billings. "I've got pretty much everything that I really need... I guess I might show up here a bit more often if I was still into the 'fishing' thing, but since the big droughts started happening about ten years back, there's nowhere to do that, close to here – you pretty much gotta go up into the mountains... couldn't justify the hassle, or the cost of filling up the SUV. I *did* buy a gas barbecue here a few years ago, but kinda stopped using it after they jacked up the price of gas to a hundred per tank... I can eat out at the restaurant every night for less – oh, here we are. Everybody off, watch your step."

"So where are we going, Mister Billings?" asked the Indian-boy.

"Straight ahead of you, off to the left, but I'm not sure how many aisles down it is," replied the salesman. "Just look for 'Home Repairs' – it'll be there. Although I have no idea what we're even *doing*, here."

"Leave that to me," requested the fallen-girl, already pacing out in front of the rest of the group. Her head darted bird-like to the side as she passed each aisle, until, three or four down to the left, she turned and disappeared behind a shelf containing buckets of drywall-cement.

"Don't get too far ahead!" exclaimed Billings.

He turned to Claremont.

"Just like a kid first time in a candy-shop," he muttered.

"Have some kids," snorted the black woman. "Y'all find out how bad it *really* get, in a *real* candy-store, 'specially if y'all ain't got no money, an' they already eaten it by time y'all catch up with 'em."

"Lucky for me, then," countered the salesman, "Because I don't have a lot of candy at home, and what I *do* have, is pretty well-hidden... gave it up long ago for the sake of the waistline. *Mostly* gave it up, that is."

He leaned forward.

"Sari? Sari!" he called.

"Down here, Bob," chirped the newcomer, now one corner ahead.

Before the rest of them got there, she appeared at the junction of the two aisles, with two decent-sized pieces of sheet-metal, a thick roll of fiberglass matting and various brass plumbing-fixtures deposited into a shopping-cart.

"These are not *exactly* the right kind of metal," she matter-of-factually remarked, "But perhaps I *can* work them into something usable, anyway. The flexible stuff is interesting, it smells like something with which I am familiar... *maybe*. Oh, and Bob, I could not find any wire or gem-stones," she added. "Do you know where there might be some?"

"Fishing- and hunting- gear section, maybe. Or home repairs," answered Billings. "For the wire, that is... got no idea about the gems... and no, I'm *not* buying you a ring. And you'll need to get some resin to harden that fiberglass that you've got on the roll. Look... materials like these have gotten quite expensive in the last little while – what the hell have you got in mind for it, again? Some little craft-project?"

"'Got', 'got' again," complained the 'Sari'-girl, as the group stopped around her. "You people sure use that word a *lot*."

She regarded them and explained, as if stating the obvious, "No, Bob, of course not – I would probably use clay or something like that, if I was to make you a sculpture... I never *was* very skilled at painting, even though I had who knows how many years of training in that art, now that I think upon it. To answer your question, I want to make some armor with this metal. Something to protect me... and to be an ark for my companion-spirits. If there is enough left over, I will make a piece or two for you, as well."

Claremont bellowed out a laugh.

"*Laws*," she chuckled, "Y'all gonna make like one of them knights in the olden days? Hate to burst yo' bubble, girl... but th' bad-guys don' use swords any more. Cheapest pistol in mah 'hood go through that stuff like knife through butter. It meant for roofin' your shack, not for stoppin' bullets."

"We shall *see*," serenely replied the fallen-girl, with an oddly-arched eyebrow.

"Well, the outdoors place is further down this main aisle, toward the far corner of this level," mentioned Billings. "Might as well get going. But it looks like I'm going to have to move the car around to the side entrance of the mall, to load all this crap that you're buying, Sari – I sure hope it's worth it."

"Look at the bright side of it, Bob," joked Claremont. "Even if'n it don' work out for yo' girlfriend, y'all can still fix yo' air-conditionin' vents wid it."

"Yeah," grunted the salesman, "That is if they ever let us turn it *on* again. They were already getting stupid about that before the Big Bang, and since then, I haven't been able to get that stupid little box they put on it to let us get a little relief."

He went behind the shopping-cart and started to push, trying to keep up with the 'Sari'-girl, who was already waltzing on ahead.

"Sari!" shouted the Indian-boy, as he pursued the newcomer. She had gone almost all the way to the far corner of the building, but had stopped in front of a glass case.

Huffing and puffing, the salesman and the rest of the troupe caught up.

"Man," he complained, "You sure *can* high-tail it when you want to, there girl."

The fallen-girl wheeled and turned to face him, with a puzzled look.

"High-tail?" she inquired. "Oh, yeah, wait, I, uhh, 'get it' – that is when I push up my 'pretty little butt'... right?"

"No," he corrected. "It means, 'to hurry' or 'to move fast'. And, for the record, yes, it *is* a cute little butt. Anyway, what are you so interested in – *oh*..."

They were now in the hunting-and-fishing department, and the 'Sari'-girl was staring intently at a vast array of guns – everything from small-caliber pistols to automatic rifles – arranged in wall-racks and in the showcase.

"Interested in a firearm for self-defense, Miss?" asked an overweight, middle-aged man who was evidently in charge of sales, from behind the counter.

"We've already *got* all the guns we need," countered Billings. "And then some."

The man, undressing the 'Sari'-girl with his eyes, went on, casting only a perfunctory glance at the salesman.

"But, if you *are* interested in picking up a gun, Miss," he blathered, "I don't blame you, what with all the low-lifes and wetbacks running around here, since law-and-order broke down a while ago and the border went unmanned. Can't be too careful... especially for a pretty one like yourself, I bet they'd *love* to get their greasy little hands on you..."

Claremont rolled her eyes.

"If y'all only *knowed*," she muttered to the gun-salesman. "Somehow ah don' think she need no gun, to defend herself."

"Tell me about these... 'guns'," requested the 'Sari'-girl, evenly. "Which one of these would you say is the most powerful? Which one does the most damage? Which one can fire the farthest and the fastest?"

"Yeah, *tell* us, mister!" chirped Curtis. "This stuff is neat! *All* them gangstas, dey packin', wid dey guns!"

"Boy," growled Claremont, "There nothin' 'neat', 'bout them. All they bring is misery. Y'all 'member what happen' to Uncle Tyrell, right on he front doorstep?"

"Yeah," quietly admitted the boy.

"We're just wasting *time* here, you know," complained Billings.

"Well, anyway, Miss, that's an easy question to answer – see that big black baby up there, top rack behind me?" continued the man, ignoring Billings and speaking with unsubtle, lip-smacking relish. "That there's the .50-caliber Amendment 2 Corporation M199 Devastator sniper-rifle, one shot in the chamber, six in the magazine, selectable squeeze bursts from one to three rounds, and it's got a real nice combo thermal night zoom sight, give you a rock-solid target lock at four miles, even with no moon out. Go straight through a Kevlar-II jacket at a mile and a half range."

"I take it, this 'Kev-lar' thing... that is strong armor, is it not?" questioned the 'Sari'-girl, her demeanor analytical and serious.

"Best you can get, legally," he replied. "Oh, but of course, that's with the special premium tungsten-cored ammo... might be a bit *big* for you to use, though, and it's got a kick like a mule with a bad attitude – now for a young thing like *you*, I'd suggest something like this little ol' Super-22 Mini handgun down here in the case, looks just like a Walther P-38 but light enough for a lady to use easily, got the latest composites in it, and won't cause you trouble at most metal-detector checkpoints.... like the one we got out front here, heh, heh."

"We know all *about* that damn thing, the metal-detector by the check-out lines, that is," grumbled Billings. "We managed to set it off quite nicely without a gun, a knife or a nail-file, thank you."

"How fast and far do their bullets fly, sir?" asked the fallen-girl, with mock innocence. "And how heavy are they? For both the big and the little guns, that is."

"Can't you look this up on the computer, at home, Sari?" protested Billings.

"I'm not sure, Miss," said the man with the guns. "Oh, wait a minute, yeah, *now* I remember... our distributor mentioned that for the big guy up there, those fifty-caliber rounds, at least the normal ones, they're about 3,000 feet per second or so, that's right after it leaves the gun, though, it's less at max range, which, as memory serves me, is about five miles. Much less for the Mini handgun, needless to say... it'll shoot clear across the parking-lot and hold a center, which is just excellent for such a small firearm, but I wouldn't go sniping with it. As to the weight, I don't even know, but here... check for yourself."

He handed a huge-looking rifle-bullet to the fallen-girl, who held it up in her fingers for a few seconds, intently staring at the lethal round. Then she handed back the bullet.

"I... *see*," she stated, her eyes staring vacantly past the man, as if she were calculating something in her head. "Interesting... soft-metal on the outside, hard-metal on the inside... that means, the impact-energy would be about... oh, never mind."

"Hey, you know," unctuously offered the gun-salesman, "It's nice to see somebody who's so interested in the details of this fine equipment – we don't usually get that from the ladies, mostly they just ask us, "will it stop a purse-snatcher, even if I just hit him in the back". I can assure you, incidentally, that even this little guy here definitely *can* do that, especially since they dropped that dumb-ass – oh, sorry, forgot for a second that I was addressin' a *lady* – law against hollow-points. By the way, our local NRA chapter has a special Ladies' Division, I'm sure that you'd be welcome –"

"Enn-Arr-Ay?" asked the 'Sari'-girl.

"A bunch of gun-nuts," interjected Billings.

He looked up at the man behind the counter, with poorly faked solicitude.

"No offense to the fine folk at the NRA, of course."

"How much?" mischievously inquired Tommy, his head barely high enough to be seen over the glass case. "Does it *cost*, I mean, Mister."

The man stooped over the counter. "Glad you asked, son!" he jovially replied. "Now, for the *big* gun, that might be a bit much to buy with your allowance, although the price *has* come down lately since they started mass production again after the freeze, you know, when they diverted all non-essential weapons production to that damn old comet project. It's about ten kilo-dollars, but for that price we'll throw in five boxes of the regular fifty-caliber ammo and one box of the nice special rounds, and two days' training on long-range shootin'... if you need it."

"Cool," giggled the Indian-boy, as the 'Sari'-girl sent him a bemused, motherly wink.

"For the handgun," went on the man at the counter, "We got that one, and most of the other ones in the case, on special all month – only three hundred excluding tax and license fee, which would come to about another fifty or so. Oh, and of course, for a small service-charge, we can spread the payments out over as much as two years, if you like. Helps the workin' man get what he, or she, needs to defend home and loved ones, you know."

"Hmm. Three hundred," said the newcomer, pursing her lips.

"Oh, sorry," he continued, "I forgot that with the special sale, you also get five boxes of high-impact .22 hollow-points and three whole days of 'how to shoot straight when you're scared' training, right here in the back of the store. I'd just need to see your internal passport or proof of citizenship, along with a major credit-card, to complete the sale – if it was *me*, I wouldn't bother with all that stuff, you know, I think it's a monumental waste of time, but with all the wetbacks sneakin' around these parts, if those 'Illegal Alien Enforcement' folk from INS get on my case for selling ... well, I'm sure you *understand*, right?"

Claremont braced herself on the glass case that enclosed the smaller guns, and tried desperately to avoid laughing out loud.

"Y'all gots *that* right," she managed. "Wouldn't want nobody who don', uhh, *belong* here, gettin' no *gun*."

"She belongs right *here*, Miz Claremont," argued Tommy, defensively coming to the 'Sari'-girl's aid and wrapping himself around her right leg, a gesture which she gratefully accepted.

"Ah knows, boy... ah *knows*," apologized the black woman. "Jus' a *joke*, that all."

"Hmm..." interrupted the newcomer. "Unfortunately I do not seem to have my, how do you say, 'pass-port' papers here with me today, and I will have to discuss the money-problem with my friend Bob, here, but thank you very much for the information, sir."

She paused for a second, turned to Billings and added, "Listen, Bob... this nice man has told me many valuable facts. Can you pay him a few dollars, please? I will make it up to you."

She cast the salesman another of her impossible-to-resist, begging looks.

"I'd *love* to," parried Billings, "But pay him for *what*? He's selling firearms, not cheap talk. Oh, and I'll add it to your bill with me, one way or another."

"Ah, don't worry, you two," counseled the man behind the counter. "We get a *lot* of tire-kickers through here, all the time. I'm on salary, not commission, anyway."

"Well, look," said Billings, "I'm in sales, too – at least when I'm working, which will be, I don't know when again, but to make all of this worth your while, why don't you give me a box of bullets, cheapest ones you got. I remember last time I was going to shoot at cans out in the desert – to impress my old girlfriend, you understand – I discovered that I couldn't find any bullets for my gun. As long as you take debit?"

"Sure do," answered the man, his countenance brightening slightly, "But for what kind of gun?"

".38, I think," replied Billings. "Got it second-hand off of a cop who I used to play poker with... his precinct was upgrading to those new Italian pistols and he put his old one up as collateral to cover a bet, but I had the better hand," he added, with a self-satisfied look. "How much just for the box of 'em?"

"Fifteen ninety-five, plus tax," said the gun-salesman. "Assuming it's a standard issue police snub-nose, which it probably is. That'll get you a box of 50 rounds, plus a coupon for half off on your next box, long as you buy 'em here. One of the cheaper weapons to provide ammo for. Only thing less are the .22s, like I wanted to sell your lady-friend there... unless, of course, you're one of the real *enthusiasts* like we get in our NRA meetings, they make their own; don't want to rely on a source that might run out, just when the going gets rough – some of them have got their own lead-smelters, gunpowder-mixin' gear... the works. I used to think they were carrying it a bit far, but then that ol' comet thing came along, and that certainly changed *my* mind."

He grinned unconvincingly. "Run your card through, sir?"

"Yeah, but it's been flaky today," commented Billings. "Here."

He handed his debit-card to the man behind the counter, but this time, miraculously, the transaction went smoothly, the moment that Billings entered his identity-code.

"There you are, Mister," said the man, as he deposited a sealed container of .38 caliber bullets on the top of the glass case. "And don't forget, there's a 30-

day guarantee on each and every round in this box, so what I'd recommend you do is fire off a couple of 'em right away... if you have any problems, just bring the box back and we'll replace it with a brand-new one, no questions asked."

"Swell," mordantly replied Billings. "So if it blows up in my hand, you'll give me a new box of bullets, but who gives me a new hand?"

"Hey, we do what we can do, sir," replied the gun-salesman, with mock cheerfulness. "Anything else I can do for you today?"

"Just one," requested the 'Sari'-girl, holding her index finger upward, pistol-like. "Oh-kay, maybe two. Tell me, sir... about these 'guns' – is it allowed for people to carry them around all the time? I have not yet seen any guns being kept in a gun-holder, you know, the kind that hangs off one's belt, except on the police-men, of course, although I have none the less detected quite a few being kept under various pieces of clothing..."

"And just how would you do *that*, Miss... you maybe got some X-Ray eyeglasses on you, somewhere?" bemusedly inquired the man.

"Not... *exactly*, about the glasses, that is," politely replied the newcomer, while Billings and Claremont cringed and the children giggled. "About the guns, well... I sort of *smell* them, one could say."

"It's the gunpowder," quickly intervened Billings. "She's got a nose like a *bloodhound*, you know. I can't even sneak a smoke and she'll know it a *mile* away."

"Oh, *right*," acknowledged the gun-salesman. "Knew a cop who could do that... damnedest thing, didn't matter *where* you'd hide your piece, but if you were packin', he'd know it, just by instinct. Actually, I heard of this several times before, the cops have these high-tech spy things that can detect metal under clothes at fifty feet, although of course that's why we sell so many of our special little .22's like this one here – composites, remember? Fakes 'em out every time."

He grinned insouciantly and patted the case, above where the handgun that he had tried to sell them, was resting.

"But as long as it's registered," he continued, "You're free to keep a hidden gun for self-defense, all over the great state of Arizona, most of the rest of the Southwest and the Southeast, as well... last I heard they were trying to get the same thing made national, but them damn Democrats were blocking it or something. Oh, sorry – you guys aren't *Democrats*, are you? If so, no offense. Our Democrats down here in Tucson, they're not so bad as the ones –"

God, this guy can *blather on*, thought Billings.

Still, I gotta admire his sales-technique.

Keep 'em talking... that's the first rule, isn't it?

"Bob, what is a 'Democrat'?" inquired the fallen-girl, pulling on Billings' shirt. "Are they, 'terrorists', 'enemies of America', or something like that?"

"*Something* like that," muttered the salesman, trying to suppress the urge to roll his eyes as he deliberately ignored the question. "Oh, and don't worry about it," he said to the man at the counter. "I'm not really very political, and as for Whitney, here, she isn't either... right?"

"Oh, no, Bob, ah ain't, neither," unenthusiastically echoed Claremont. "Ain't no politician every done *squat* for mah folk, be they Dem'crats, 'Publicans or whatever they is."

"So that's it, right?" demanded Billings. "Let's get going."

"Just one last thing," pleaded the 'Sari'-girl.

"You've got *one* minute, then I'm heading for the golf-gear section," countered Billings.

Turning to the man behind the counter, the newcomer asked, "Sir, you do not have any swords, fighting-axes or daggers for sale, do you? Especially, any that have been made with the special arts, so one can add one's spirit to them, give them a divine purpose, and so on?"

"For *Christ's* sake, Sari," complained Billings.

"You mean like a *magic* sword, Miss Sari?" asked Tommy, half-in-jest and half-in-awe.

The fallen-girl looked down at the boy.

"Yeah," she answered. "I suppose that this is the one time when I *will* allow that there is a place for 'magic', in my world."

The gun-salesman addressed Billings and said with a chuckle, "You know, Mister, if she's *your* girlfriend, I'd make sure to check her for concealed magic weapons, before bedtime, if you know what I mean – she sure has a healthy interest in fightin'-gear. Sounds like she just stepped out of one of them 'Magic and Monsters' shows that they play on cable, Saturday nights."

If only you knew, mused Billings, as he managed an even smile.

Wait until you find out, dear, appeared a thought in the salesman's mind.

"Thanks. I'll remember to do that," he sarcastically replied.

"For God's sake, Sari," he added, "Do you *see* any swords on the wall here? Those things went out with the Middle Ages, as soon as they invented gunpowder. It doesn't matter *what* kind of sword you've got – you're screwed, against somebody with a gun. Come on... let's get going."

"I love and respect you, Bob," shot back the 'Sari'-girl, "But you are *wrong* about that. The kind of hand-weapon that one has, very definitely *does* make a difference – a *big* one. I would rather have one of the great, old blades, at my side, than any or all of these 'guns' that you see up there. Can a 'gun' warn you and light your way against the darkest evil, shield you from a curse, or sing you a lullaby, when the day is done? Can it stand guard all by itself, lest you be surprised, while you repose?"

"Not to keep you here, Miss," interjected the counter-man, shaking his head in mirth, "But the only place where you're likely to find *that* kind of thing, the boring old non-enchanted kind, that is, is the Shogun Ninja Shop, they got all sorts of martial-arts gear down there, *shurikans, nunchuks*, Japanese swords and so on."

"Really," offered an instantly-interested fallen-girl. "Where does this, uhh, armorer and arms-maker, sell his wares?"

"Just around the corner from the downstairs entrance to the store that you're in now, Miss," explained the gun-salesman. "But a word to the wise, here... accordin' to the law, anything he sells is supposed to be dulled so it can't really do any damage – mild steel, that is; but I happen to know that if you slip ol' Bob Masamoto – he's the proprietor – a little extra cash when you pay for your sword, he'll make sure you get the real thing, nice and cold-tempered, hold a sharp edge *forever*... slice through a flak-jacket like it's made out of cardboard. You didn't hear that from *me*, you understand?"

"Oh, I understand," she politely replied. "Sho-Gun store, eh? Hmm, that is funny, you know... an armorer's shop, but it has the word 'gun' in it... well, I suppose it sort of makes sense, does it not?"

"That's Japanese for 'king', 'chief warlord', or something like that," counseled Billings, as he maneuvered the shopping-cart to bump the 'Sari'-girl in the direction he wanted to go. "Saw it on a Late Show movie a year or so ago."

"Ah, yet *another* language," observed the newcomer. "I am quite proficient at learning foreign tongues... but there *is* a limit to it."

She stopped and thought for a trice, then added, "Someone dear, someone latterly mighty, though she not yet know it... once taught me a few words of this 'Ja-pan-ees', you know."

The far-away look showed again on her face.

The fallen-girl wheeled and turned to face the gun salesman.

"Listen, sir," she concluded, while staring intently at him, "I must go now... but thank you very much for all the help."

For a second, the others experienced the same eerie feeling that they had some time ago in the car, creepy and other-worldly yet enlightening at the same time.

The store's Muzak system was playing 70's soft-rock, but that was not what sounded in the psyches of those in this place.

"Be of good health, sir," pronounced the 'Sari'-girl, "But remember... a weapon's soul can become evil, unless it is used for defending, in the cause of good".

As they proceeded down the corridor, Melissa looked behind her, and with a start, tugged on the 'Sari'-girl's shirt-sleeve.

"What y'all *do* to him, Miz Sari?" demanded the teenager. "He kinda leanin' on the show-case, like he sick or somethin'."

"He is not sick," knowingly explained the fallen-girl. "The opposite, in fact. I just sent him a blessing... that is all."

"Here we go *again*," complained Billings. "I suppose I'm *never* going to get you to stop... am I?"

The newcomer tightly grasped the salesman's hand.

"No, my love," she offered, looking reassuringly up at him. "Neither you, nor all the perils of this world; for this is *one* reason, for which I have come."

Curtis Ray Claremont whispered in Tommy's ear.

"Y'all *see*?" mentioned the African-American boy. "She an *an-gel*."

Never Single Spies, But In Battalions

The Russian fumbled for his cell-phone, almost dropping it as he tried to balance the thing with his left hand, all the while using the right to keep the mini-telescope-cum-hi-res-digital-camera perched in the window, trained on its target.

Somehow, cradling the phone now in the crook of his elbow, he managed to free one hand to wipe the sweat from his brow.

Silently, he cursed at the stupid Americans, who were evidently still unable to get enough electricity going to power the air-conditioning in this miserable little excuse of a rooming-house.

He had tried to get a plain old three-bladed fan going, but the damn thing had petered out after less than an hour, due to the pervasive power-rationing encountered everywhere, except for government offices and upscale shopping-centers.

That little experiment had put his real work, back by three hours' worth of battery-charging.

Not a lot of electricity back on yet in the Old Country, either, he remembered, *but at least one can dress for the cold.*

"Misha *tut*," he stuttered.

"Alexi *tut*," returned a faint voice from over the phone.

"Is your 'hearing-aid' working properly?" it said in Muscovite Russian.

"*Da, ne problema*," replied the spy.

"Report?" inquired the voice. "You can take a bit more time, now. Our experts have improved the algorithm, since we last spoke. They tell us that the Americans seem to have temporarily suspended, or at least reduced, their code-breaking efforts, on the network. We are not sure why, yet. Is your current location clean?"

"Checked both manually and with the sensors," answered the Russian. "So I do not think that we need to worry about those things. I am all set up now... at first, I had some strange looks from the old woman who rents out the rooms in this house – maybe, my American accent is perhaps not as perfect as I had thought – but she needed the money more than she needed to check my papers."

"Yes, yes, okay," interrupted the voice. "We had no doubt that you would get settled, but what of the target? And the others?"

"Just back from what appears to have been an shopping-expedition," explained the spy, stooping to peer through the eye-piece of the telescope. "They have unpacked their groceries and what appear to be some building-materials about ten minutes ago."

"Good," stated the man in Moscow.

"I am a bit less than a kilometer away from the bungalow in which the target, the man, the black woman and the children, seem to be staying," continued the Russian in the rented-room. "Incidentally, Alexi, my room is on the corner of this house, so if I move the scope, I can get a clear field of view on both the front driveway and back-yard of the residence. I already have dozens of clear pictures, which I will upload after this discussion. The only shortcoming is that the dish-microphone is still picking up a great deal of interference – I can only get a clear recording of their conversations by running the raw input through the computer and isolating the necessary wave-forms."

"Could the Americans be doing electronic jamming in the area?" asked the remote voice, with a trace of worry. "If so, that might mean that they are also aware of the target's presence."

"I do not believe so," countered the spy, "Because if they were doing this, I would have recognized the interference-patterns. The whole exercise has been taking longer than I expected, due to the electricity-rationing that has been going on around here. I have to stop and re-charge my computer every so often... there is not enough wall-current to run the laptop without using the battery. And, frankly, with the heat in here, I am thankful that it has not yet completely failed – the fan in the computer cannot be cooling it very much."

"You could not get any closer? We wanted *real-time* relay of these conversations, if you recall," complained the voice.

"Not safely," answered the Russian. "As it was, I had enough trouble finding a room at all... most of the dwellings around here are single-family homes. I suppose that I *could* have moved into one of the many abandoned houses in the area, but there probably would be no electricity at all in these, and the risk would be high, if the owners returned. I could also try to drop a bug into the target's residence... but I did not want to try that without prior authorization from Headquarters."

"I will check," said the man at the other end. "Until the higher-ups give permission, we will have to use your existing method. Observations so far?"

"As you can appreciate, I can only draw indirect conclusions from this distance," explained the spy. "But it *has* certainly been interesting, so far. Most of the conversations that I have been able to synthesize through the computer have been about mundane affairs, 'what are we having for lunch', 'boy is it hot today', that kind of thing... however, I have come to recognize the target's voice with little difficulty; it is alluring, musical, in a way that is hard to describe – the waveform is unique and complex, with many sounds that are out of normal human hearing-range, and there are some other characteristics to it that as yet I cannot explain."

"I will make a note of that," remarked the other. "Since the Americans may also be able to distinguish this characteristic. But tell me, has there not been anything that would tell us more about the target's situation, or about her motives?"

"The only substantive conversation that I have heard her participate in," answered the man in the room, "Was about the group's short-term plans; this man – yes, 'Robert', or 'Bob', 'Billings' is his name, I confirmed that via the up-link with Headquarters – was saying that he had to get back to work, bills are piling up, *et cetera*, and the target – oh, how did I possibly forget to mention, Alexi, she seems to be going by the name of 'Sar-ee', 'Seer-ee' or something like that – she replied that she would like to help this man wherever he is working, he apparently is a salesman of some kind. Any additional information that you can dig up on him would help; as you know, I have to be careful about connecting to the American NeoNet, there are interception points everywhere..."

"Well," offered the voice, "It is still early days, in this project, you know. Other operations have sometimes taken *years*, before we obtained any really useful intelligence... although I fear we may not have anything like that amount of time, in this case. I will have the file pulled on this 'Billings" immediately and send it to you by phone, soon. As to the target... what is she doing right now?"

"Hmm, let me see," mumbled the Russian, as he again squinted against the eye-piece.

"She – actually, all of them... sorry, *not* all of them, I do not see the black woman – they are lined up, the target on one side and the rest of them on another, they are engaging in some kind of physical exercise... wait, not just simple exercises, it seems more like dancing... whoa! Look at *that!* And *that*, too! It is *amazing!*"

"See *what*?" instantly shot back the Moscow voice.

"No," excitedly corrected the spy, "It is *not* dancing – on second thought, it looks more like some type of martial-arts, judo, Mu Tau, Kung-Fu, *et cetera* – and the target, she crouched down and then jumped above shoulder-height, of the man, that is, and that has to be the better part of two meters off ground-level, and what is more, she did a very quick 360-degree turn in mid-air, along with a kick. I have only seen things like *that* in the movies, up to now. *No* human being that I know, not even the best-trained Olympic athlete, could perform *that* kind of maneuver, not from a standing start."

"Fascinating," started the Muscovite, but he was interrupted by more on-the -ground reporting from his field-operative.

"Oh, and this 'Billings'," elaborated Misha, "He punched at a fairly thick wooden board and put his fist right *through* it – is it only my imagination, or did I see a brief flash of light, when he did that? He seems to be swearing and holding his one hand with the other... you know, Alexi, I was only able to break dense objects with my hands, after two years of training... wait... she is now gesturing to the man and the children... one of them is performing a jump... impressive, not as high as her, but still... *okay*, now here comes the salesman... ha, he just fell on his backside."

"Amazing," said the voice from Russia.

There was a slight pause, then the man on the phone mentioned, "Listen, Misha, we have Agents Katya and Oleg on their way; they will establish contact with you, very soon. I know that you said that your room was clean, but what is your assessment of the counter-intelligence situation? Any signs of possible compromise?"

"Negative," replied the spy. "If our American friends are on my trail – or that of the target – they are either very good, or, more likely in my opinion, they are just not here in the first place. You must be aware, Alexi, that we do not even have adequate local law-enforcement in this area, and, from what I see on the local news, not in much of the rest of the country, either. I have overhead conversations – one while standing in line to get a sandwich at a restaurant, yesterday – saying that matters are out of control in the southern California area, and the situation is apparently not much better towards the southern border with Mexico."

"Yes," agreed the Muscovite, "We can confirm that, from this end. Apparently the FBI is very concerned that the 'gangsters' are almost in a position to completely take over the city of Los Angeles, for example. Also, many of the American state governments have closed their borders with other states, which is something that you need be aware of, should you have to relocate in a hurry."

"The point is," continued Misha, "That the American authorities have their hands full with just basic law-and-order... remember, this is a society where every second person has a machine-gun in his hall closet, a pistol in his pocket and a grenade under his bed. If they are closing in on to me, or on our friend 'Sar-ee', there is certainly no evidence of that... at least not now."

"That is good," commented the voice, "But do not take it for granted. For things can change at any time, and Headquarters may not have a chance to inform you immediately when we see a threat. Understood?"

There was silence, accompanied by pensive breathing... followed by a muffled curse and the sound of something being dropped.

"Misha? Misha!" sounded the alarmed cell-phone voice. "Respond, please!"

After an agonizing few seconds more, the field-operative spoke again.

"Sorry about that," he managed. "I was just looking through the telescope again, you know, observing these martial-arts lessons that seem to be going on over there –"

"And...?" demanded the voice from Moscow.

"All of a sudden," explained the spy, "*She* – the target, that is – turned around and stared. At *me*. *She was looking right at me, Alexi*. I felt frozen, unnerved, and – this is hard to describe – I *felt* something, a random thought, as if I was being, ah, how to say this, 'observed', myself. No, *not* a thought. More like a musical eighth-note. It only lasted for a split-second, but it was *most* disconcerting. Then, I am sorry, I suppose that I somewhat panicked; I yanked the telescope out of the window and lost hold of it. However, it is still intact. I am now sitting against the wall, with no line of sight to the window."

Now it was Moscow's turn to sit and reflect.

After two or three seconds, and the hint of an oath having been sworn, the voice came back.

"What does this *mean*, do you think?" it asked.

"I think," offered the man in the Tucson room, speaking deliberately, "That I am not the *only* one doing the 'observing' today. Alexi, she was *aware* of me. Do not ask me how, but I saw it in her eyes – or, maybe, I *felt* it, in my mind. She was *aware* of me, from nearly a *kilometer* away. How the *hell* could she –"

Another Russian curse sounded, remotely.

"You will have to leave this place, *immediately*, you know," the voice interrupted. "If there is the *slightest* chance that she will come looking for you –"

"I know the procedure; I am already starting to pack," shot back the spy, using his one free hand to draw the window-blinds and then frantically start throwing items into his suitcase. "I will call you again when I have established a new observation-post. Tell the other Agents to hold off, until I have a permanent place."

"Understood," countered the cell-voice. "Although, how do we know, that the same thing will not happen, once you set up the scope, in the new location?"

"We do not," answered Agent Misha. "We are stalking this being, perhaps the CIA and FBI are, too, in their own clumsy way; but... what if the hunted, becomes the huntress?"

"Explain," demanded the other.

"Ah, Alexi, I should have *foreseen* this," sighed the man in the room. "That episode in the desert, when they had stopped the car... if you had been there, you would understand... I have been reading and re-reading the report given to Headquarters by Cosmonaut Chkalov, over the last few days. If what he says is even half-true, we are, how do the Americans say it, 'way out of our depth', here. This is a being that has probably survived and defeated a *thousand* nations such as ours, or such as that of the Americans. Who knows *what* abilities that she has, to turn against us, should we get too close or antagonize her. This really *is* unknown territory, for all of us. None of the familiar rules apply."

"We certainly know that," replied the man in Russia, "However, it does not change our duty. I, too, wish that we were just following some anti-Russian traitor or defector, like the last three we had to make 'disappear', at least *then* we would know what is and is not safe to do... but in *this* case, I am afraid that we will have to learn as we go."

"And I should go, now," requested the field-operative.

"Yes, you should," agreed the voice over the cell-phone. "Good luck. Call as soon as you can do so safely."

"*Do Sviedanya*, Alexi," concluded Misha.

He snapped his cell-phone shut, trying to remember where he had put his hat.

Ten minutes after a fruitless and frustrating conversation with that stupid bumpkin that the President had so ill-advisedly picked to be a political adviser, the colorless monotone of the CIA director's voice sounded on the special triple-secured voice link, its data packets scrambled so many ways that a minor cryptographic miracle occurred with each syllable.

"South-West Office? Do I have the South-West Office?" he stated. "This is Top Dog, ID value is Anthill 456, Geranium 89, Torus 3A."

"Affirmative. ID value Sunny Sky, ID value Quorum 08K, Fox 300, Velvet 1F44," came back a voice. "Childress here. I've been told this is the Director. Quite an honor, sir. What's the occasion?"

"Red Rover came over," said the man in Langley, coolly. "We now have a positive fix. And in it's in *your* backyard, Mr. Childress."

There was a pause, accompanied by a gasp.

"My *God*," inveighed the man in Las Vegas."

After a second more, he requested, "What are the orders, sir?"

"Field team, four or more, direct observation – for now," instructed the Director. "Details will follow on this line after our conversation, but so far, it appears to be staying with a 'Robert Billings', a floor and tile salesman, in a bungalow in the Desert Palms suburb of Tucson."

"Got that," said Childress, taking notes.

"Unfortunately," explained the Director, "Our really high-resolution satellites are still non-operational, but we do have a second-tier one on synchronous track now, and so far it has given us a good shot of this 'Billings' individual, as as of a black woman and at least two juveniles also at this location... we're not exactly sure what the relationship is between all of these people and the alien, but we're running facial and morphological database-scans on all of them right now. Results are inconclusive, we're going to have to get good close-ups of those within the house with less of a slant angle than we're getting from the satellite."

"Anything from the telecom channels?" inquired the man in Las Vegas. "Radiation-signatures?"

"Their computer seems to be off, right now," replied the CIA headmaster. "We have the television viewing scans, but they're showin' mostly sports-games. There has been only one phone call – apparently to the house-owner's place of business, we're sending a team down there to watch that location, too – and the moment when another call pops up, we'll pipe it right into your mobile command-post. Right now we're out of range on the radiation sampling, but be of no doubt, we have a *high* level of confidence that we have a positive ID on the creature. In the meantime, assemble your team and get them down to the location, as soon as possible."

"You *bet*, sir," agreed the field-agent. "Standard deep-cover protocols?"

"Confirmed, with one very important factor," stated the Director. "This is a Level Zero Minus One Agency operation. *Exclusively* an Agency project– there is to be *no* interaction with, nor release of information to – *any* other entity, including but not limited to FBI, DIA, Homeland Security, the military, or anyone else. No matter *what* they say. You are to avoid compromise by any third-party, and you are authorized to use *all* necessary means, including wet-operations, to ensure that. cover-story, if anyone asks, is that this is a top-priority stake-out of a suspected drug-lab – run by turncoat foreign assets – and thus it is out of jurisdiction for anyone but us."

"Got that, sir," said Childress. "I assume that we are talking about Level Zero Minus One protocols, sir?"

"We most *definitely* are," said the man in Langley.

"Sir," asked the agent, "Just so that we know what the local threat surface is, does it appear that the Agency is first-to-field, here?"

"We have verified that we are first-to-field, and right now, the Agency is using standard disinformation processes to ensure that the other government organizations do not pick up the trail," explained the Director, neutrally, as if reading from a cooking-recipe. "The usual stuff, decoy-stories like the one I told you, red-herring data-traffic on easily-compromised channels, that sort of thing. I should caution you and your team, however, that this is an unusual situation and we are not sure how long we can keep the curtain up."

"And if we can't, sir? What are the orders, in that case?" requested Childress.

"If we get evidence that the alien's location is about to become known to some other department, and if we cannot capture it in such a way that the Agency alone will know of that fact, zero-residue termination *may* be required," instructed the Director. "We'd consider that to be a last resort, in view of the creature's possible utility to the Agency. But for now, the orders are to observe and follow only, until capture can be effected without *any* chance of inadvertent disclosure. Oh, and... obviously, you'll also have to 'disappear' all of the alien's fellow-travelers – that is, the salesman, the black woman, the children, anyone else in the immediate vicinity, and so on... but those shouldn't be much of a challenge, I would imagine. Standard cover-story there, 'they were involved in subversive activities'... that kind of thing, right?"

"Right. But, sir," pressed the field-agent, "Given that capture is the preferred option, other than the standard snatch-and-grab with immobilizing spray, does Headquarters have a suggested methodology? Since the onset of this program, my agents and I have been reviewing the relevant files, and we're concerned that there may be a high risk to such an undertaking. We know next to *nothing* about the being's capabilities, but if they're anything like what was displayed while she was with the Mars-expedition –"

"We have reason to believe," smoothly stated the Director, "That these abilities, if they ever really existed as they were portrayed on the Mars mission, have been significantly... *degraded*. Having said that, when and if you are given direction to effect a sequestration, muscle-neutralizing restraint-protocol will be in effect at all times, and there is to be no physical contact at all with the alien, except the minimum needed to capture it in the first place. It is to be kept *completely* isolated."

"Copy," said Childress.

"After capture is effected," the Director went on, "A mobile command-post will be remotely issued auto-nav directions to an off-map airfield, and from there, the target will be airlifted to one of our special extra-territorial holding-facilities. Of course, I can't tell you where *that* is, but suffice it to say that there won't be any media or inter-governmental problems, once she – *it* – gets there."

"On the termination front... I'm aware that I have discretion as to tools," asked the Vegas man, "But is there a suggested methodology?"

"That's still under review up here, as well," noted the Director, "Right now, the thinking is that Compound 1856 via homing-dart would be optimal, in that case we would still at least have the corpse for later examination. The problem there is the being's apparently corrosive blood – we're reasonably sure that the composites in the projectiles will stand up long enough to deliver the necessary dose, but we have no idea if it will work past that point. If the darts aren't effective, or if the situation involves a risk of extra-Agency interference, after conventional silenced low-caliber rounds, use the Type D thermic-DU charges, follow up with high-concentration hydrochloric vapor-charges to neutralize any remaining DNA or proteins. We're already working on cover-stories to deal with any media issues that may arise."

"Got that," acknowledged the field-agent. "Any other orders, sir?"

"No," stated the Director.

There was a short delay, then he added, "Actually, there *is* one thing. I'm sure that you know what the Zero Minus One protocols require for you and your team, should anything go *wrong*, Agent Childress?"

"You don't have to remind *me*, sir," stiffly replied the man in Las Vegas. "We all know the rules, and we've all taken a pledge to follow them... even if it comes to... *that*. You have my word."

"The Agency expects no less, and will ensure that we get it," concluded the man in Langley. "If it's of any interest... the same rules apply to me, and I have issued orders that should I ever fail to conform to them, the same sanctions will apply."

"Understood. I'll be going, now, sir... okay?" requested the field-agent, as he cut the connection.

"Top Dog out," confirmed the Director.

Childress leaned back in his chair and stared blankly at the ceiling, for a few seconds.

Does it feel good to be a Man In Black? he pondered.

Squashing A Bug

It was getting on dusk, and the large, black SUV with out-of-state plates, its windows tinted so deeply that a casual observer would have wondered how anyone could see out from inside, leisurely cruised down the Desert Palms street, turning a corner.

In perhaps a minute, it had passed two or three suburban bungalows that had seen better days, with boarded-up windows that evidently had not stopped the various ne'er-do-wells in this vicinity from enjoying a night or two, inside.

About halfway between the street that it had just turned down and the next T-junction a few hundred meters further forward, the vehicle slowed, coming almost but not quite to a full stop.

A small hatch no larger than a baseball, discreetly located just above the step-board on the SUV's side, slid open.

There was a faint 'pop', and – if you had been looking closely – you would have seen something resembling nothing so much as a stone-colored *thing*, about the size of a silver dollar, shoot across the lawn of the house just to the side of the car, coming to rest among all the small stones that formed what passed as the front lawn.

The little something-or-other didn't look out of place, at all.

But nobody *was* there to observe this quiet operation, and the SUV slowly picked up speed, turning right at the next street. From there, it sped away to who-knows-where.

"Parcel successfully delivered," announced the man inside the vehicle, into a microphone.

Inside the nondescript suburban bungalow, a more-than-a-girl-creature stopped, momentarily, arching an eyebrow. She closed her eyes, as if trying to recall a memory from somewhere.

"Sari?" asked the salesman, turning to regard her serenely pretty face.

"It is nothing, Bob," she smoothly replied. "It is taken care of."

Fire Of Mighty Shiva

"This meeting will come to order," commanded the President.

Obediently, the small-talk ended and all eyes were on the Commander-In-Chief, his neatly-cut gray mane and immaculate business-suit making him look all the more, the captain of industry.

"Where's Cesar?" asked the annoyed U.S. leader.

"Oh, sorry, Mr. President – I neglected to update you on that," quickly replied White House Chief of Staff Jerry Kaysten. "Director Ochoa sent his apologies to me about an hour ago. He's tied up on a critical law-enforcement security matter – had to fly down to Chicago for something, but he promised that he'll be at the next meeting with us all here. He also asked me to mention that the Southern California gang-clearance operation will be ready to commence, as of tomorrow... although, we're *critically* short of troops – we can expect significant casualties."

"What about the mercs?" asked the Vice-President. "Why can't we use a few of *them?*"

"They're already a third of our boots on the ground down there, sir," interjected a medal-bedecked general. "GrayWar Corporation, America Fights Incorporated, SecureArms Inc., *et cetera* – they're all heavily-committed elsewhere, for example in Cuba, where things haven't been going too well lately – and since we passed the laws discouraging recruiting minorities into the land forces, they're drawing from the same limited pool of available mainstream manpower that the regular Army is. You may remember that last year, before the comet, that is, we loosened the rules on recruiting foreigners into the 'soldiers-for-hire' business... but even there, the background checks are taking quite a long time, I'm afraid."

"*Great,*" muttered the President.

He looked around, then turned to his Chief of Staff.

"Horn?" he asked.

"Also in transit," stated Kaysten. "He said he should be in Washington tonight... he'll call when he gets here."

"A *lot* of things are evidently going on that are more important than a little old President of the United States," sardonically observed the President. "Well, can you get through to Horn and tell him to call our friends in the Senate so they can work something out with the Faith Foundation?"

"Sure, Mr. President... but what's *that* all about?" inquired Kaysten, with his trademark, annoyingly-pleasant hint-of-a-smile.

"I got a message from the Republican caucus yesterday afternoon and there's a bunch of stuff in that 'America Is Christian Act' that I can't go for," complained the President. "I mean – pardon the pun – for God's sake, what is all this nonsense about them 'needing the right to search the houses of the rich as well as those of the poor, for blasphemous literature'? It was bad *enough* when they blackmailed us into having the religious loyalty-oaths for the Armed Forces. But *this* is going too far."

"*I'll* say," echoed the Vice-President. "If Billy-boy's Jesus-nuts want to go rummaging through the pantries of the ghetto-folk, that's fine – they don't get to vote, anyway, and they don't have any money to send our way. The minute that the Bible-bangers try this in the mansions of *my* people, there'll be *hell* to pay. And no pardon for the French."

A few politely giggled.

"I'll get right *on* that, sir," sighed the harried Chief of Staff, busily tapping notes into his mobile communicator, all the while.

"That having been said, we'll start with the economy," announced the President. "Bob... how's Wall Street taking the news?"

"Not well," replied the Treasury Secretary, "But we made it plain to them that they don't have much of a choice in the matter."

"They've *already* started moving deposits out to China, India and Brazil, you know," complained the Vice-President. "As if those bloodsuckers need any *more* of our money. I *told* you that when you interfere with private enterprise, people are going to go behind your back. It's basic human nature – greed, that is. We should be *encouraging* it... not trying to stop it."

"But do you think the situation is manageable?" requested the President, addressing the Treasury Secretary.

"For the time being, the answer is 'yes'," answered the man. "My own guess is that we're okay for about six weeks or so; after that, we're going to *have* to level with them about what's going on."

"Well, that's better than having about six days, or six hours – either of which I was fully expecting to hear," philosophically offered the President.

"Oh... and by the way, the Democrats have agreed not to filibuster the enabling-legislation... sorry, I forgot to mention that," added the Treasury Secretary.

"Good," idly mused the U.S. leader. "Listen – e've got a Council of Economic Advisers meeting later today anyway, so maybe we had better just get right to the State Department stuff, okay?"

"Okay," replied the ever-obedient Treasury Secretary.

"Jacob?" asked the President.

An elderly, inconspicuously Jewish man, taking off his *pince-nez* glasses as he spoke, turned his gaze to the CIA director.

"Should I tell him... or do you want to?" asked the Secretary of State.

The man's tone oddly restrained.

"Mr. President," spoke the CIA director, seizing the cue, "Regarding the situation with the unaccounted-for, ex-Pakistani nuclear weapons, I'm afraid that we have a developing crisis situation. Before I go any further, however, I need to remind everyone in this room that this is a *strict* 'need-to-know' situation. The Agency can and will take preventative measures to ensure that anything I say from this point forward, will not be repeated, without my express, prior, *written* authorization. Is that clear?"

A dozen or so faces mutely and grimly nodded.

"At 19:50 hours local time yesterday evening," slowly and methodically continued the director, "The Algerian Secret Service received a telephoned threat – of course, delivered via a throw-away cell-phone – of what was described as 'what the Muslim Salvation League has in store for the filthy Crusader-Zionist infidels who violate Muslim virgins in America and Europe'. Initially, the Algerians didn't take this very seriously, since they get threats of this kind periodically, but this particular one claimed to be about, ahem, a nuclear bomb, and it was very precise about the details of the weapon."

The monotone of the CIA director went on, matter-of-factually, "At approximately 21:30 hours Algiers time, one of our deep-space early-warning satellites – you may recall, these are part of the network that is stationed in long geosynchronous orbits, and thus weren't subject to disruption by the 'Lucifer' comet – detected a medium kiloton range nuclear explosion, probably a single-stage fission bomb, at a point near the eastern end of the Ahaggar highlands near the south-eastern part of Algeria."

He hit a touch-screen button on a device that outwardly looked like a mobile communicator, and the room darkened; he hit a second, and an overhead picture of what looked like an ugly, black pock-mark on an otherwise serenely sand-gray desert, appeared on the wall at the front of the room.

"Here is an *Aurora-II* shot of the blast site," he noted, "The yield, which is estimated to be between 90 and 180 kilotons, is consistent with what we would expect of a miniaturized Pakistani Pu-238 missile warhead."

Gasps issued from several places around the table, followed by a quick remonstration by the President for 'silence'.

"The region of the detonation is, luckily, I suppose, largely uninhabited," explained the CIA director, "But it was clearly visible and audible in the district capital, which happens to be named Tamanrasset. The Agency believes that we have a window of no more than a day or so, before some form of computer media starts to show up on the extra-U.S. NeoNet depicting this event. We have, of course, implemented filters on our domestic NeoNet to purge any such references... but as you will appreciate our capabilities in this area are not one hundred per cent effective, and here again, the rumors are bound to start surfacing fairly soon."

"General?" demanded the President, of Anderson, who had been sitting quietly in the background. "Why am I hearing this from CIA and not the Air Force?"

"You put them in charge of the deep-space detection-array, when the Pakistan nuke situation started melting down, sir... don't you remember?" peevishly answered the Air Force general.

"Ah, yes... right," acknowledged the President.

"It fucking *figures*," growled the Vice-President. "We fire off each and every one of *ours*, against the comet, and who's the only one with a nuke to use? The goddamn camel-kissers!"

The CIA director looked up, doffing his glasses slightly. "Not *every* one of ours, sir," he smoothly contradicted. "But, in any event, Mr. President... I'm sure that you can appreciate the implications of this event."

"No *kidding*," replied the U.S. leader, as the color slowly returned to his face. "Not that we had completely failed to foresee this day."

The President turned to face Anderson.

"Harry," he pressed, "I thought somebody said that they – the Pakis, that is – had *controls* – locks, on these things. That even if the Muslim League got their hands on 'em, they couldn't fire them... at least not reliably."

"That's indeed what we were *told*," remarked Anderson, his hands folded on the table in front.

"Mr. President," interrupted the Secretary of State, "There's more, that has come in through our diplomatic channels. Following, or maybe at the same time as the detonation, my counterparts in Israel, the United Kingdom, France and India have all started to receive credible threats to the effect of 'you're next, unless', and as you might imagine, these governments are in a state of near panic trying to figure out what their next steps should be. They're trying to come up with some kind of a unified response."

"Unless *what?*" requested the American leader.

"It's the standard Muslim Salvation League laundry-list," commented the Secretary of State, leaning back in his chair, his glance darting occasionally from person to person as he spoke. "For the Israelis, it's 'withdraw from all lands occupied by Zionism since 1948 and send the Jews back to wherever they were in 1900'; for the Brits and the French, it's 'immediately replace your legal systems with *Sharia* law, and ensure that only Muslims are allowed to serve in the government'; and for the Indians, it's 'tear down the 21 Hindu temples built on the bones of Muslims and surrender all your nuclear weapons to our brethren in Pakistan, lest your cities burn in Allah's righteous fire'."

"Sounds fair," Kaysten tried to joke; but his grin was quickly erased by the stony faces to be seen in every direction.

"Oh, yeah," elaborated Hyndman and they want the British and the French to require all women to wear the *hijab* – that's the thing that covers women head to toe, for those of you who aren't up on these kinds of things – and they want the Indians to hand over Kashmir and most of western India, to the Pakistanis... I forgot to mention those."

"They want the Jews to all get out of Palestine?" grunted the Vice-President. "Who's going to take over there, afterwards – the *Italians*, maybe? Don't these bagheads remember that the Arabs all got the 'ethnic cleanse thing' out of Israel, a few year ago?"

There was a modest little 'beep-beep' sound, and an admiral reached for his mobile communicator.

"Yeah, Halford here," he stated, *sotto voce.*

"I have to take this, sir," the admiral mentioned, as he got up and decamped to one corner of the room.

"You can't blame them for not thinking big," offered the Treasury Secretary, to substantial amounts of nervous laughter.

"Listen, Jacob," hesitatingly requested the President, "I'm almost afraid to ask this, but... well... why haven't *we* received one of these threats, yet?"

"Yeah – they hate *us*, almost as much as they hate the Jews," unhelpfully added the Vice-President.

"I'll take that as a compliment," coolly offered the Secretary of State. "The truth is, we don't know. There are various theories, but –"

Uncharacteristically, the CIA director broke in, saying, "One possibility, sir, is that the Muslim Salvation League has not yet been able to pre-position a device in the continental United States. It would make sense that it would take them more time to do so, simply because of the geographical distance from where these weapons originated – namely, Pakistan – to here, compared to, say, Europe or India, and –"

"*My God,*" gasped the admiral, his face turning white. "Is that *confirmed*? Yes, of course. The second you get it in position, pipe the scan right into the room here. I'll tell him. Halford out."

"Kyle?" demanded a worried President.

Halford advanced until he was halfway to the seat that he had previously occupied, but he stopped in mid-stride and addressed the group, all as one.

"Mr. President," stammered the admiral, not hiding his shock, "We have a report from a Navy stealth-cruiser on patrol in the Arabian Sea, just off the western coast of India. There has been a nuclear detonation, apparently in or near downtown Mumbai. The commander says that the scene is... *horrific*. In his own words, 'it's a fire that goes on to forever'. They're intercepting chaotic Indian communications-traffic... but as you can imagine, there's little sense to it –"

"Ye *gods*," muttered the Secretary of State, hanging his head. "So it starts. I wonder if, when they first did the Manhattan Project, they'd have gone through with it if they had known that people like *this*, were going to eventually get their hands on a bomb."

"You can't unmake history," observed Anderson.

"Excuse me, sir," interrupted the White House Chief of Staff. "We've got a feed from Indian state television."

"On screen," ordered a grim-faced U.S. leader.

A large LCD screen appeared where the picture of the Saharan blast had formerly been displayed, and, a second later, a gasp arose involuntarily from several in the room.

The scene on the monitor appeared to be shot from a hand-held camcorder or other consumer-level video-camera, with repeated jostles and bumps as the cameraman was trotting rapidly in reverse from a scene reminiscent of a Dantean nightmare. In the distance, a dark, almost black pillar of smoke and fire shot straight up from the ground, as far up as the field of view could capture.

Heavily-accented English, panicked almost to the point of incomprehensibility, tried to explain the situation.

"Viewers, this is Rajiv Dal of Maharashtra Broadcasting, coming to you live," announced the voice-over. "Ohh, a scene of horror, total horror, the fire of mighty Shiva herself on the land... we are running away now because the fire is leaping from house to house... nothing can stop it, and we are at least fifteen kilometers away from where the bomb went off... in our relay-station here in Thane City we had a feed from the downtown office, we saw a bright flash, then the feed went off the air... two or three seconds the windows all shattered, people were cut into ribbons... we heard loud explosions from both airports on the Peninsula, and two big airliners crashed on either side of us about ten seconds after the... the... initial blast, oh my... what? What's that? Yes, I'm... okay. Okay.

Hard to breathe, you can see all the smoke... have to find a basement where there is good air..."

The room fell silent as the Chief of Staff turned down the volume, although they could still see the transmission coming in from India as the poor cameraman tried to keep the lens focused on the funeral pyre of downtown Mumbai, all the while running for his life.

"Mr. President," ominously noted Anderson, "There can be no reasonable doubt now that these guys mean *business*... and, that they have the capability to make good on their threats. In these circumstances, sir, I don't think it's prudent for you – or the National Security Council – to remain here in Washington, even in the bunker. I'd prefer a standing airborne deployment aboard Air Force One, but you would have the option of Camp David or the Woods Lodge, as long as we can do continuous security sweeps of the perimeter."

Cupping his hand, the President whispered to the Chief of Staff. "Get the copters ready – and make sure that you pick up my family as well, you got that?"

Kaysten nodded and rapidly headed off to the corner of the room, rapidly entering numbers into a mobile communicator.

"Umm humm," mumbled the Admiral, again speaking softly into own portable phone-computer.

"Okay, you got that now?" he whispered. "Right. Yeah, channel C-In-C-One. Put it through."

Halford turned to the President.

"Live feed from cruiser U.S.S. *Boise*, sir," he said. "She's approximately twenty kilometers off Mumbai harbor to the southwest, but she's got the image-intensifier going."

At first, the picture that overlaid the first one looked like nothing at all; it was seemingly a random combination of flickering red-orange lights interspersed within an ebon-black background. Then, the cruiser's crew must have zoomed out, revealing the charred foundations of what had, not an hour before, been one of the world's most cosmopolitan port cities, with the first hint of anything more than a completely leveled skyscraper appearing no closer than six or seven kilometers from what must have been Ground Zero.

A pall of dark gray smoke, akin to a devil's perverted version of a monsoon-cloud, floated a few thousand feet over the scene, and the blackened, scarred hulls of capsized ocean-liners and supertankers bobbed aimlessly in various places in and around Mumbai harbor.

Nowhere in the field of vision, was there the slightest hint of life.

Little flakes of gray ash were falling in front of the cruiser's camera, lightly impacting on the bosom of the sea.

"We've got audio from the *Boise*, sir," announced Halford. "From the radius of total destruction, they're estimating that this was a *big* one – 220 kilotons at least, possibly as much as 350 – which would make it considerably larger than the 'warning shot' that the League set off in the desert. Looks like it may have been salted or boosted, too – the *Boise* is picking up rapidly increasing radiation levels, more than you'd expect from a standard fission bomb. It's certainly not supergrade Pu-238... which might make its signature a bit easier to track. If that's any consolation."

"This is rather perplexing, I'm afraid," observed the CIA director, his tone as unflappable as ever. "Mr. President, I'm just trying to resolve in my own mind, why they would do this so quickly after setting off the Saharan warning blast; it doesn't make *sense*, at least if they're trying to achieve some kind of concrete objective. They haven't given the Indian government any time to implement the agenda that was first communicated by the League, nor have they even given the Indians enough time to acknowledge receipt of the demands. Admittedly, the actions of the Muslim Salvation League have, in the past, been occasionally erratic... but this seems uncharacteristic even for *them*."

"They're a bunch of fucking baghead *lunatics* – what don't you understand about *that*, for Christ's sake!" shouted the Vice-President. "The idea of making sense probably doesn't have a translation in that stupid A-rab language of theirs."

"We're *all* feeling the strain, George," admonished the President, "But let's try to keep it on the level here. We've got to think straight and think fast about what comes next. Which is – ?"

"We have done computer-simulations on what might happen in a 'loose nukes' scenario with this assumption in mind," explained the CIA director, "And the results are, uhh, not very reassuring."

"How could that be worse than what we're seeing on the feed from the *Boise*, right now?" asked Halford.

"Basically, Admiral," dispassionately replied the CIA director, "Our simulation implies that we might be facing what could best be described as a 'nuclear suicide-bomb arms-race', with the hard-core cadres of each of these groups – that is, those of them that have managed to both obtain an ex-Pakistani device, as well as the technical know-how to detonate it – vying with each other to see who can take the greatest number of 'infidels', along with himself. In practical terms, this would mean that at this very moment, nuclear suicide-bombings are being planned for various urban targets around the world."

"It's only a theory, you know," argued the Secretary of State, his voice almost a whimper. "I *have* to believe that *nobody* would be insane enough to seriously consider something as nihilistic as *that*. Islam would be forever discredited, in the eyes of the world."

"Since the President has asked me to be polite," growled the Vice-President, "I won't respond to that. But you *know* what I'd say, if I could."

"Maybe it's *already* started," observed Anderson. "We're seeing it right on the screen, in front of us."

The President sat, stony-faced, for many long seconds, as he weighed the options again and again.

Finally, he came back to life.

"It's obvious," he commented, "That we can't run the *slightest* risk of, God forbid, something like *this*," – he pointed at the screen – "Happening to an *American* city."

"Effective immediately, and continuing for the next six months, or until we get total control of what's coming in," ordered the President, "We're going to seal the borders – and yes, that *does* mean *everything*, air-travel, trucking, rail, sea travel, shipping, tourism... the *works*. If it gets here via a pipeline, like the oil from Mexico, that's fine; if it comes here on a tanker, a truck, a ship or a plane, that's *not* fine. Domestic air-travel will still be allowed; foreign air-travel, for *any* reason except by specific authorization by Homeland Security, will be prohibited. Anderson, I want a 24-hour standing combat air patrol over every major city, with "shoot to kill" orders for any unidentified aircraft that looks like it's heading to a city."

The white-haired Air Force general gravely nodded and whispered something to a subordinate.

"For the Army and Guard," the President went on, looking in the directions of General Blanshard and Admiral Halford, "I want roadblocks on every Interstate route in to a major city, with spot inspections of *every* vehicle – and get that order back to Ochoa, FBI will work with Homeland Security and CIA to start rounding up *anyone* who looks the slightest bit suspicious."

A crew-cut, bull-headed man in a green U.S. Army uniform responded, "Yes, Mr. President, *sir*."

He began to write with an electronic stylus, on to a thin-tablet computer.

"Kyle," demanded the U.S. leader, while pointing to the admiral, "Pull back as much of the Navy as you possibly can spare, and put it on continuous patrol with the Coast Guard, off the Eastern and Western seaboards, plus around the populated parts of Alaska and Hawaii... oh, and Puerto Rico too, if you can. Ships and aircraft are to be stopped no less than twenty miles off the coast, and anything that twice refuses an order to stop, to be inspected or turned back, is to be *immediately* destroyed, on my personal authority. No exceptions."

"Given the amount of sea-traffic and our available resources," noted Halford, "That's going to be difficult, Mr. President... don't forget that we have almost no Coast Guard *left*, after the last round of domestic budget-cuts; but Navy won't let you down, sir... you have my personal commitment."

"I expect nothing less – and that goes for all of you," commanded the President.

"Jesus H. *Christ*," exclaimed the Vice-President, "I understand what you're thinking... but are you aware of what's going to happen if you try to seriously go *through* with this? My business-pals won't be able to take their vacations down South –"

"Florida's *lovely* this time of year," grunted the President, with a wave of his hand.

"We can't *do* it, Mr. President!" protested the Treasury Secretary. "The economy will *collapse* – quickly. We can't run this country without imports, of everything from oil to iron ore to water. We're already tottering on the edge of a full-scale depression, as it is. With all due respect, sir... it's *insanity*!"

"Maybe," mused the President. "I know there'll be some hard times, resulting from this. Better *that*, than what I'm seeing on the feed from Mumbai."

"Sir," interjected the CIA director, "I sympathize with your objective, and of course CIA will attempt to help enforce it to the degree we are given latitude to act, but I should point out that the terrorists would still have many viable avenues of attack, even if we were to seal off the United States in the manner you are suggesting."

"What do you mean?" asked the American leader.

"Well, they could simply wheel a bomb up to a border crossing with Canada or Mexico... preferably one in close proximity to a major American urban center," remarked the director. "Next to Detroit, for example, or to San Diego... they could either detonate it right there, or smuggle it across the international border, exploding the device if they were about to be caught. The problem here is that for these situations where we don't have exclusive jurisdiction, we have to rely on the local authorities to –"

"Keep a very close eye on what's going on with the Canadians and Mexicans within 50 miles of their border with us," commanded the President, "And tell them that the *second* we detect anything in the least bit suspicious anywhere within that zone, we're going to blow it to Kingdom Come – no warnings, *no* second chances. Either they do *their* job in keeping America safe, or we'll do it *for* them, and damn the consequences."

"Mr. President, I don't think you appreciate what this will do to our relationship with the Canadians and the Mexicans, we need to negotiate a –" pleaded the Secretary of State.

"Jacob," retorted the U.S. leader, "You can do this privately with them if you want... but the order stands as I just outlined it. We've got to make our dear friends to the north and south aware that *this* time, Uncle Sam isn't playing around – and we're not going to take 'no' or 'maybe', for an answer. The survival of this Republic is at stake – and if they're interested, they should know that their *own* survival is, as well."

"That's true... but Treasury has a point," argued the Vice-President. "As much as I'd like to shut the doors on the rest of the effing world, we might be doing the damn A-rabs' work *for* them... we're running the risk of an economic disaster of *historic* proportions. We need *time* to read the riot-act to all these other countries, make 'em adjust their way of doing business to what suits us –"

"You're assuming that they *will* 'adjust their way of doing business'," countered Hyndman. "I'd make no such assumption. Look, Mr. President... with all due respect, we *need* to work with our allies on this one – even if we manage to dodge the bullet, or I guess the bomb, and they get one of *their* cities blown up, well, that's going to be almost as bad, in the long-run –"

"No it isn't," shot back the Vice-President. "It won't be *Americans* being turned into an overdone microwave dinner, it'll be somebody else. I'll drink to that."

"For God's sake, George, don't you have a humane bone in your *body –*" started the Secretary of State.

"*Enough!*" exclaimed the President. "The order stands, as I said it a few minutes ago. Look, all of you... I'm very well aware of the likely consequences, both economic and otherwise – but as President, I have a constitutional duty to safeguard the lives of American citizens, and that duty comes first, above all others."

He paused for a second or two, then went on, "I want Treasury and State, all other departments too, to do the best they can under the circumstances, try to explain our predicament to anyone who asks... but you need to communicate firmly to them that there will be *no* backtracking on this order. If and when we track down each and every *one* of those goddamn Pakistani bombs and melt them down into fuel for our reactors, *then* we'll talk about re-opening the borders, but until then, we're battening down the hatches... that's how it's going to be. Any questions?"

With a mixture of shock, exasperation and resignation, all present, shook their heads.

Finally one of them spoke up.

"Mr. President," asked Kaysten, "What're we going to tell the people?"

"The truth," calmly replied the U.S. leader.

"Are you *sure*, sir?" pressed the Chief of Staff. "You might get mass panic."

A heretofore silent Cabinet-secretary spoke up from the far end of the table.

"You *will* get mass panic," she said.

"That's certainly a possibility," acknowledged the President. "And if it had been just the bomb in the desert, we *might* have been able to do our standard baffegab dance with the press, but this thing in Mumbai... no, *that* one's going to be impossible to explain away – not worth the effort to try. I'll prepare an address to the nation, for delivery tomorrow night."

"Understood," said the Chief of Staff.

"Well," sighed the President, "This has been one 'H' of a meeting – that's for sure; I walked in here expecting just the usual economic-crisis, and I'll be walking out trying to deal with nuclear terrorism – and *that*, after the comet stuff. You know... when I decided to run for this job, I had been expecting just the usual problems, race-riots, declining standards of living, complaints by the Europeans and the Third World... those would have been easy. I've been asking myself, 'what next'."

"We live in interesting times," offered Anderson.

"No kidding," muttered the U.S. leader. "Anyway... I had better get on the helicopter; our next meeting will probably be on Air Force One. Is there anything else?"

"Just one thing," added the Air Force general. "About Project Red Rover... I wish I had more definitive news, but, according to Director Ochoa, with whom I spoke yesterday, they've managed to track the alien as far as a library at Salt Lake City... the 'good news' is, they have some video-surveillance footage which we think is a positive ID on her, or it – looks for all the world just like one of those cute little models they have on the Disney News Channel. Except that her hair looked different from what we had in the records, from the Mars mission. Assuming, of course, that the footage really *is* of the right person."

"Figures," grunted the Vice-President. "What's the newest one's name – oh, yeah, now I remember – little Miss Blaine Maine... only with green skin and vampire teeth."

"Unfortunately," continued Anderson, "The trail has gone cold, past that point. We're stopping and inspecting all vehicles on the Interstates and side roads, within a 250-mile radius of Salt Lake, paying special attention to anything remotely resembling the SUV that someone at the Library thought that they saw her leaving in... but so far we're zero for 10 or so – there were two on the highway east that looked promising and one that was apparently stopped by a State Trooper patrol going south, but the alien female was nowhere to be seen in either case."

"Are you following up?" absent-mindedly asked the President, as he stood up and started packing up his leather-bound portfolio case.

"Certainly," confirmed the senior Air Force general. "But we're encountering difficulties in the data-bank searches for the individuals to whom ownership of all the SUV's inspected, are registered. A few of the names seem to have been disappeared, or else, the records are unavailable. But we're working with FBI and the Secret Service to try to trace them down. Oh, and the Mars mission astronauts are all back in Houston, now, and they're being debriefed, but with your permission, sir, I'd like to move them to somewhere more... *secure*. Given the new situation, you understand."

"Well... good," mentioned the President, now fully packed up and ready to go. "You have my authorization – and start arrangements for me to meet this Jacobson guy, I have a few things that I need to discuss with him."

"Sir?" queried Anderson. "As I said, we're already de-briefing not only *him*, but the others as well..."

"Just what I *said*, Harry," the U.S. leader demanded. "You have your orders. I'd *love* to spend more time on this subject, team – but as you've all probably already figured out, I'm a lot more worried right now about a *real* threat from *real* Muslim extremists, who really *have* a bomb and who are ready to use it, than I am the theoretical threat of some half-fictional alien-girl."

He looked quickly at the CIA director.

"Anything from your end?" asked the President.

"Negative, sir," replied the Director, with a saturnine half-smile. "Except that we're doing our level best to help the rest of those on the project, of course."

"Good, well, keep me informed," concluded the President. "Meeting adjourned."

With a worried, weary look on his face, he headed toward life on the run.

We're On To You

"*Da, da, ya khochu govoryet po-Alexi,*" stammered the Russian, into his "special" mobile communicator.

"*Pojowsta. Spasiba,*" he added, looking over his shoulder, first to the left, then to the right.

"*Alexi tut,*" came back a Muscovite voice. "Misha – where are you?" it demanded. "We were not expecting a call until you were fully established –?"

"I have just set up," replied the spy, in hushed Russian. "In a motel, as it turns out – unfortunately this one has a good view only of the back-yard, only bits and pieces of the street in front. I have something *very* important to tell you."

"Yes?" stated the voice at the other end. "And... is your 'hearing-aid' working?"

"Yes, showing secure," answered Misha. "I am walking outside the motel, as I have not yet had time to do a sweep of my room. Listen, Alexi, I was calibrating the scope... I figured that now would be a good time to do that, it is almost dark and none of the subjects are outside the house, so there would be less of a chance like the incident that made me move."

"And?" asked the voice.

"By pure happenstance, a few minutes ago, I obtained a clear shot of a large, black sport-utility vehicle, standard Secret Service and FBI domestic issue, cruising up the street," explained the Russian. "It made only one pass, but seems to have slowed in front of the target's residence – I cannot confirm this with one hundred per cent certitude, because as I mentioned I could not see the SUV while it was behind the house – but if I am right, this pattern is consistent with CIA and FBI tactical assessment protocols. There has been very little other traffic over the course of the day, incidentally."

A Slavic curse echoed over the airwaves.

"Damn!" inveighed the Muscovite. "It looks like the Americans are ahead of schedule. We had figured that we had at least two or three days – maybe as much as a week – until their domestic security-forces picked up the trail. Misha, this is good work on your part, if not good news. We will have to rapidly re-adjust our plans, now. Is there any chance that they found their way to the target, by trailing yourself?"

"Negative," the spy quickly answered. "I have been very careful and have been watching at all times – including now – for signs of a shadow, and I have been moving continuously since we started this conversation, to throw off any parabolic microphones that they might have set up around here. In any event, even if they *had* been on my tail, unless they have been able to break the security on our link, I would remind you that I have never been close enough to the target's place of residence to give away its exact location. No, Alexi, I think the Americans did this themselves... and that surprises me. Perhaps we underestimated them, this time."

"Perhaps," came back the voice from Russia. "After all, they surely know the importance of this mission. Even *Americans* can accomplish things, if they throw enough resources at them. As for this side of the operation, I will escalate your new information to the highest levels within the Kremlin, immediately. The President may have to make some quick decisions if the situation deteriorates."

"So what are my new instructions?" asked Misha.

"For no... continuous observation, only," said the man at the other end. "Do not get too close, unless it looks like a capture-operation is imminent. In that case, you know the protocol."

"Alexi," inquired the field-operative, as he walked around a corner and sat down on a crate next to the rear entrance of a restaurant, "In the event that I must intervene... do we have any human assets within the American intelligence-agencies that I could count on to, how would you say, 'muddle things up a little'?"

"Obviously, we have our deep-cover operatives," stated the Muscovite, matter-of-factually. "But do not count on their help. We are willing to sacrifice every one of our assets for this project; but there is no point in doing so, if they cannot materially affect the outcome."

"So, it is up to myself – is that what you are saying?" asked the man with the mobile communicator.

"For at least the next few days... unfortunately... yes," confirmed the voice from Moscow.

"I understand," noted the agent. "And I will not fail."

"*Do Sviedanya, moi droog,*" came back the remote voice.

Then, there was naught but static.

Bedtime Revelations

It was still very dark outside.

None the less, Billings sat up and noticed that the room already had a soft light illuminating it, as the fallen-girl had turned the lamp on her side of the bed up to its lowest setting, which set out about as much illumination as a child's night-light.

How the hell can she read in this darkness? he wondered.

Reluctantly, the salesman picked up one of the detective-novels that he kept by his side of the bed and fumbled for the switch on the lamp over the side-table.

Reading this stuff never really dealt with insomnia; but it was certainly better than just trying, and failing, to get back to sleep.

He *would* have considered one of the pills in the bathroom drug-cabinet, were it not for the several shots of Jack Daniels he had knocked back a few hours before.

I'm feeling 20 years younger than I did before I met her, he thought.

But even then, *it was a dodgy idea mixing booze and pills.*

The 'Sari'-girl was already propped up by a pillow, her eyes washing rapidly back and forth across the content of a copy of *Timeweek* magazine.

From the number of pages remaining, it looked like she didn't have much more to go before she'd have to grab another of the dusty periodicals stuffed into the magazine-holder on the bed's left side. The pile of those journals, now duly cleaned and perused, was already impressively large.

There was also a box of chocolates, with at least three of them gone, on the lamp-table beside the newcomer.

"Already up, I see," commented Billings, trying to keep his voice down so as not to wake up Claremont or the kids.

"Umm-hmm," she replied, not taking her eyes off the magazine.

Now fully awake, he asked, "Mind if I turn my light up? I don't know how you manage to read *anything* with that little light – even with my glasses, it's all a blur."

"Looks fine to me," she insouciantly replied. "I am quite at home in the dark... or had you not noticed? And anyway... soon, Bob, you will not need those 'glasses', and the night will reveal many more secrets to your eyes. This blessing *will* come to pass – trust me."

"Sorry I *asked*," complained the salesman.

"Umm-hmm," murmured the 'Sari'-girl.

"What time is it?" he asked.

"Oh, never mind," he added, seeing the digital display of the clothes-bureau-top clock showing "2:30 A.M.".

"You were kind of late coming to bed," observed the salesman.

"Yeah," she answered. "I was busy down in the basement."

"Doing what?" he inquired.

"Hmm, what is the word that one would use for it... ah, yes, I guess that you would call it, 'metallurgy'... but that is not *exactly* what I was doing," remarked the 'Sari'-girl, all the while paging back and forth through the magazines, as if she was doing some kind of research project.

"Uhh... *right*," said Billings.

I hate being ignored, thought Billings.

Especially by her.

"I am *not* ignoring you, dear Bob," she instantly offered, still looking at the magazine and not regarding him. "It is just that I have *much* to learn, and we already... *you know*, once tonight. Did you want to do that, again? Will it help you get back to sleep? Sometimes it does for me."

"Did I mention that I *hate* people reading my mind?" he grumbled. "Or eating my Belgian chocolates – you gotta get 'em special, you know, after they passed that 'Hershey Protection Act', some years back – they're the ones that I left for... oh, never mind. Go ahead. They look a hell of a lot better on *you*, than they'd look on *me*."

"Sorr-eee," chirped the fallen-girl, sounding perfectly like a wife or steady girlfriend, having well and truly settled into the nest.

Billings rolled his eyes, hoping that she could see.

His eyes now as used to the light as they'd ever be, he looked her over more carefully.

God, she looks even cuter than before, he mused. *If that's possible.*

But what's changed?

"I see you found the hair-coloring formula that my old girlfriend had squirreled away in the bathroom," mentioned Billings, trying for some small-talk. "I like it. That salt-and-pepper thing made you look a bit exotic."

"'Hair-coloring'?" absentmindedly mumbled the newcomer.

"Do not be *silly*," she added. "Like, a paint for the hair? I do not think that such a thing would work on me."

Lie about it if you want, thought the salesman. *But blonds have more fun.*

"Oh, the... uhh... *change* in it – *now* I understand what you mean," she stated. "Well, it *does* that every so often, you know. It is a sign that I am, uhh, 'coming back'."

"Riight," he muttered, not wanting to know what she meant.

For the next hour or so, Billings tried to dive into the plot of the novel, while the 'Sari'-girl serenely read on, methodically going through magazine after magazine, occasionally returning to one or the other, as would someone trying to cross-reference some group of ancient texts.

Finally, she put the last copy of *Timeweek* back in its holder.

She looked straight forward, avoiding Billings' glance, and said, "Bob?"

"Yeah," replied the salesman. "What is it?"

"There's something that I must tell you," she announced.

"Go ahead," he requested.

She looked down.

"It *should* be easier for me to explain this," started the fallen-girl, "For something tells me that I have had to do so, many times in the past, but... this time, it is... *difficult*. Perhaps that is because I love you so, and I do not want to say anything that might make you distrust me."

"As if there's anything that you could say now, that would do *that*," Billings stated. "After all the weird stuff that I've seen, already."

"At the risk of sounding funny, Bob," she evenly stated, "It... uhh... becomes even, 'weirder'. Is that a 'real' word, in Eng-lish?"

"Yeah, I think it is," he replied. "What do you mean?"

Now, you got me a bit worried, girl, he thought.

"It is like this, Bob," she offered. "You know when we were outside today, practicing our *Vrùn-Ch'é* exercises? When I was trying to teach a little of that skill to yourself and the children?"

"Yeah," he sheepishly acknowledged. "When I got reminded that I'm no 'Kung-Fu master of death' – the hard way, that is. How could I *forget*."

"Ha," came back a girlish half-laugh, "Do not underestimate yourself, Bob... *that* art, requires *time*, to develop. Many years, even for myself. But it is like a fire – it will grow gradually, over time, if you just practice a bit; I was quite impressed with the progress that you have made in a short time. The spark has been lit in you, and in the others."

Billings just stared at her, waiting for the other shoe to drop.

"Did you notice how at one point, I stopped and looked at something far away, over the fence?" she inquired.

"Sure – remember, we asked, 'what's going on', 'what do you see', and so on, and you just said, 'oh... nothing'?" answered the salesman.

"I did not want to alarm Whitney or the children, so I said a, uhh, 'little white lie', is that not the expression... I did not *see* anything – not as you would understand what it means to 'see', that is," explained the 'Sari'-girl. "But, I *did* sense a threat – there was someone – a man, I think – watching us. For a second, I perceived his mind, and the pattern of his thinking was not in Eng-lish; no, it was some other language, one that I have heard before... but I do not remember where."

"*Shit!*" cursed Billings. "That means they're *on* to us, we gotta – wait a minute... you said, 'not in English'? Doesn't add up – if the Feds are on our trail, they wouldn't –"

"Calm *down*, Bob," she requested. "I am as well aware as you of the possibility that someone is following us... although I do not completely understand why. If they were right outside, I would know it, and we would not be sitting comfortably in this bed – I can assure you of *that*."

Oh, come on, *girl, use those brains of yours*, he silently thought.

And I don't care if you heard that.

"Anyway, Bob," continued the fallen-girl, "There is a larger, much more important meaning to what happened this afternoon. This man, whomever he was, was quite far away, and it was my, uhh, I do not know how to say this in your language, I guess the best translation would be, 'warning-sense', that alerted me to the man's observing us –"

"Warning-whaa?" stammered Billings, with mock surprise.

"This is another ability that has saved my life, untold times, through the ages," she remarked. "If there is danger – a trap – someone who means me ill – I *always* know of it, maybe not with as much time as I would like... but with *enough* time to defend myself. In all the time that I can remember, I have *never* been 'surprised'... at least not in a harmful way. And that this skill is back with me, *that* means..."

Now, the 'Sari'-girl turned to look him straight in the face.

There was a dim glow in her eyes.

Not the kind of glow of which lovers speak; not the metaphysical kind. No, this was *real* luminescence, eerie and intimidating in a way that he had only ever seen in cheap science-fiction movies, as if her eyeballs were back-lit by some improbable watch-hand. The glint of unnaturally-sharp teeth only made the effect that much worse.

But *damn!* She still looked beautiful, alluring, even more so than before, if such a thing was possible in the face of the fear that crept in at the edges of his consciousness.

Reflexively, Billings moved backwards toward the edge of the bed, away from her.

"Are you *afraid* of me, Bob?" she asked, and the salesman didn't know if the words were plaintive or menacing.

"That would have to be a 'yes'," he nervously confirmed. "For *God's* sake, Sari – your *eyes* –"

"Yeah," remarked the newcomer, with a shrug. "I can see that you are illuminated by them... if this is of any interest, the glow does not affect my ability to see at all. But it would be more, uhh, 'atmospheric', if you turned off all the lights. Then it would be just my eye-light – like one of your 'night-lights', to reassure children like Tommy. He told me that he was afraid of the dark."

"Don't mind if I don't take you up on that," he tried to joke.

"Listen, Sari," continued Billings, "Like I said... things have been more than a bit weird on your side of the bed since I first met you – but, this is *really* pushing the limit, if you know what I mean. I hate to say this, and I know how it's going to sound, but... well..."

She just arched an eyebrow at him, as if already knowing what he was about to say.

"It's just that you're looking quite a bit less... *human*," he observed.

"I *know*," she quietly replied.

"And," said the newcomer, drawing a breath, "I am afraid that you are correct about that, Bob. I told you that I would not lie to you, anymore – oh-kay, I hope that not telling you about the man watching us does not, uhh, *count*, there – and that I will not deceive you about *this*."

"I'm afraid I'm not going to like the answer that I'm likely to get," commented the salesman, "But... what the hell is going on, Sari?"

"I think the best way to say this," explained the fallen-girl, slowly and deliberately like a parent does when tutoring a child, "Is that I am... *changing*, into who I really am; no – let me re-phrase that. I am changing *back* into who I always *have* been. The thing is, Bob, that... ah, curses, it is just *so* challenging to describe this in Eng-lish, where you see one person called 'Sari Tanak', that is not the whole story, far from it, in fact. I am *many* people, all at once."

"You mean you're, uhh, 'schizoid'?" asked Billings.

"Heavens no, Bob!" she answered with an exasperated sigh, "There is the 'Sari' who you know, a human, oh-kay, *nearly* human female who loves you dearly – and who wants you to keep loving her, above all else..."

Uh-oh, mused the salesman.

There's that Celtic-rock music again, in the back of my head...

Keep it together, Bob...

"But there is also *another* 'Sari'," continued the newcomer, "No, *not* 'Sari', wrong name altogether – I wish that I remembered what my *true* name is, but I am *strong*, powerful, so very, *very* powerful, mighty far above and beyond the understanding of human beings – I fly across the sky, with a sparkling mantle of gold and white fire blazing all around, I do great things, vanquish the Demons of Hell, scatter their armies... and to answer your next question – no, I am *not* human, I am *far* different from your people, as different as you are from... uhh... I know how this may sound, but as different as you would be from a fish or an insect."

"Really," gulped the salesman.

"A few days ago, this was all just a dream," she noted, "But now I know that it is *real*, Bob. And it is coming back. *I*, am coming back."

For a few seconds, neither of them spoke.

Then she remarked, "I know that hearing this must be a little frightening for you... oh-kay, maybe a *lot* frightening."

The 'Sari'-girl regarded Billings, apparently in earnest kindness, and asked, "Do you remember when I tried to show you a little of my 'mind-fuck trick', back at the shopping-mall? When our minds saw each others' thoughts, I mean?"

"Yeah," replied the salesman. "Nine-point-nine on the bad dreams scale – *that's* for sure. But I *apologized* for whacking you silly... remember?"

"I know, and apology accepted – but why did you *do* that, Bob?" she pressed. "What kind of feeling made you do it?"

Trying to avoid re-awakening bad memories, but failing, Billings retorted, "Not sure, really – it was that I felt that I was losing the fight... you remember it was a test of wills, if we could put it that way, and – and – well –"

"Just come out and *say* it, Bob," she counseled. "I already know what you are thinking, anyway."

"Sari," he pleaded, "Please don't take this the wrong way, but it's just that what I saw – no, *felt* – in my head was strange beyond strange, weird in a terrifying way, like one of those nightmares where nothing's as it should be, where you're falling over and over, in a crazy house of totally unfamiliar shapes, patterns and nowhere to go to get your bearings. Pardon the pun, but it was like I knew I was 'in over my head'. It felt... uhh... *alien*. Like I said, I mean that in a nice way."

"Yeah, I *bet* that it did," she offered, "Because what you were experiencing there, was a glimpse of the surface of the *other* 'me', the greater, 'me', along with how I perceive and remember places where your people will not be able to safely go for many, many years, yet... maybe, never. And I do not blame you, since I am totally unlike you, in that way; I can appreciate how touching this knowledge, with your own mind not properly prepared, might be disconcerting and frightening."

"I'm finding a *lot* of things 'kind of scary', right about now," mentioned Billings.

"Right now, Bob, you *can not* comprehend this other side of me," elaborated the fallen-girl. "I wish that there was a better way for me to say this, because it sounds insulting in your language, but my other self is... uhh... just too far *above* you. If it helps any to know this, the... uhh... 'other' Sari, is too far above, for *me* – that is, the 'almost-human' Sari – to fully comprehend, either. And *both* of me are looking at you, speaking to you, right now. My thoughts – how I perceive the world – these work on many different levels, simultaneously. Pretty cool, eh, Bob?"

"You have a talent for understatement," evaded the salesman. "I felt like I was about to go stark raving mad, if I spent so much as another five *seconds* dealing with that weirdo stuff. How can you possibly *handle* it – having your mind crammed with these thoughts, I mean – all the time?"

"It is what is natural for me," she answered, matter-of-factually. "I can try to explain it, if you want... should I?"

"Go ahead," he requested.

"Imagine," proposed the fallen-girl, "That you are in the countryside, looking over a river, at the mountains far behind. The rational, analytical part of your mind would see such a scene in terms of science; for example you would know that the water is made up of one little breathing-gas atom and two of the light-gas atoms, you could tell a folding-up mountain from a volcano, you could distinguish the rain-clouds from the wispy white ones high in the sky, and so on. There is much joy and contentment in being able to perceive these facts, to know that you have a deep understanding of how the river and the environment works, that a fish or animal would never have – even though it lives out its entire life in that place."

"With you so far," he observed. "So?"

"So," she elaborated, "At the same time, the humane, philosophical side of your mind would appreciate the scene just for its beauty, the sense of natural rhythm within, the amazing intricacy and interdependence of living-things, and so on. Perhaps you would even feel the hand of God, however you believe in Him, Her or It – and there is *another* concept that humans will have to come to understand, on a whole different level – all around you. One can smell a flower and understand that the lovely perfume within it, is really there to help the plant reproduce; but this would not prevent you from just accepting the scent as a thing of pleasure. Your own mind can incorporate all these ideas at the same time; it is up to *you* to decide which ones you will concentrate upon and use, at any time. *My* mind works the same way, only on a... uhh... somewhat more *complex*, level..."

The 'Sari'-girl stopped and stared pensively out into space, as if pondering the right thing to say.

"But in time," she softly and kindly spoke, "Maybe you *will* begin to understand, to perceive things as I do, as does the greater part of me, that is, to share some of these other... uhh... *higher*, thoughts and feelings. I want to help you do that, Bob, I *really* do. It is perhaps the greatest gift that I have to give. I can show you *wondrous* things and I can teach you wisdom that you could never learn in a *thousand* human lifetimes. I can help you to see and understand the world like you never have before... like it really *is*, Bob. You do not *know* what you are missing – and that makes me really sad."

"That's, uhh, *wonderful*," apprehensively stammered Billings, hoping that she couldn't see the sweat on his brow.

"Feeling hot, Bob? Need a cool face-cloth?" she teased.

"Forgot that it's hard to keep secrets from you," he evaded. "I'm okay, though."

He lied.

"Let me show you something," continued the 'Sari'-girl, as she emptied a pillow out of its case.

She scrunched the thing up into about the size of a hand-towel, and, for a split-second while she did, the glow in her eyes waxed perceptibly.

"Here," she suggested, with an evilly-arched eyebrow. "Try it."

Trepidation warning him at any contact with her, now, Billings nervously accepted the gift, but upon contact, he instantly dropped it.

"*Jesus*, Sari," he protested, "It's fucking *freezing*!"

"Yep," answered the newcomer, like a housewife explaining a new cookie-recipe. "And in a few weeks, a month or two at the most, if I want to, I will be able to make it *so* cold that the little molecules within it – or in anything that I want to affect in this way – will stop moving altogether. It will be as cold as the deepest Hells of the Unending Dark, so deathly cold that touching it will freeze your hand into ice-cubes –"

"Just about *did*," interrupted the salesman, holding his one hand in the other to try to make the ache go away.

"Later on, I will not have to touch it at all," elaborated the fallen-girl. "I will just gaze at something nearby; and if I want to destroy it utterly, or make it burst into a fire so hot that nothing will remain... that will happen. *Everything* around me will blaze so hot that it will burn you to approach me, and the invisible little-particle-shine will surround me, bringing a silent and terrible death to any living thing that means me harm. I will move, or, destroy things – really *big* things – with nothing but a thought. Only another of my kind – and there are very few of these, none at all anywhere near this planet, as far as I can tell – might be able to stop me. *Maybe* they could stop me... but I would not bet on it. Several have tried. None have succeeded. That is a *good* thing – because I want to *help* people... not hurt them or rule them."

"You don't *say*," breathed an incredulous Billings.

"How does knowing that, make you feel?" she inquired.

"Terrified, if you want to know the truth," he replied.

"I know," she quietly acknowledged. "You have good reason to be... this is both my blessing and my curse. To be so great as to have no equal – but to be so great that one is feared, rather than loved. I cannot do anything to change it, and – I must be honest with you – Bob, I probably *would* not change it, even if I could. It is part of who I *am*. No... let me correct that. It *is* who I am, as much as your face or brain makes up who *you* really are."

"Well, where does *that* leave us?" shot back Billings, half-dreading, half-desiring the expected response. "Is this how a, oh – the hell with it, let's not kid ourselves, shall we – how a Martian chick gives somebody the old 'this is it for us' speech?"

"This is 'it'?" asked the 'Sari'-girl. "This is, *what?*"

His shoulders slumping, the salesman answered, "Forgot that you're still learning the lingo. It means, 'are you saying that you don't want to stay with me, anymore'?"

With a tear slowly making its way down her cheek – the effect was truly bizarre, lit as it was by the glow of this improbable creature's alien eyes – she replied, "*No*, Bob... not by the light of a thousand suns, do I want to leave you! And," – she managed a weak laugh – "That goes for *all* of us, on this side of the bed, man."

"That's, uhh, reassuring," offered Billings. "Always nice to have a vote and make it unanimous. Even if afterwards."

The fallen-girl held up her hand in a mock vote.

"We all vote for the Bob of Billings, sir," she joked.

Reluctantly, inwardly wondering if he should be vaulting for the door at this point, the salesman uneasily let his back again find the pillows and bed-board.

"*Look*, Bob," she stated, herself regaining her previous position next to him, "Let us be honest with each other... you are – how would one say – 'hitched up' with a, yes, I might as well say it, too, an *alien* being who is down here on Earth for who knows *what* reason, and this female – well, *that* part of her is 'human' enough, would you not agree – is very soon going to develop weirding powers that have, I believe, never been seen before on your planet... although I will reserve judgment on *that* point, since I have been reading some books of legends and religion that say... but, *anyway*. You and Whitney thought that I had not guessed your suspicions about me? Do not blame yourselves about my having figured it out. Being perceptive about my surroundings, and about how I am being perceived by others, is a skill that I have had for a *very* long time."

The 'Sari'-girl reached to her side and fetched the candy-box, holding it in front of the salesman.

"Chocolate?" she insouciantly asked, popping one into her own mouth and happily munching away.

A song comes to mind, he mused.

That old one by, who was it, now, oh yeah, they were called 'OMC', I think...

"We were, uhh, trying to figure out how to break it to you," offered Billings. "We were afraid that confronting you with it might be traumatic... or something."

Not knowing at all what to do, he reluctantly selected a butter pecan swirl.

"'*Traumatic*'?" contemptuously laughed the 'Sari'-girl, throwing her head back in obvious bemusement. "Compared to *what*? Maybe, to the 'trauma' of waking up on a completely alien planet, unarmed, completely without any of one's usual abilities and without either friends, or anywhere to *find* a friend? How about not knowing if some huge beast would show up around the next tree, ready to eat me? *You* should try doing something like that – I am sure that you would appreciate my position, a little more, if you did."

Well, at least we're leveling with one another, thought Billings.

Where that gets us, I don't know.

"I will spare you the need to think of something clever to say," continued the newcomer, "Meanwhile... good old Bob K. Billings, Junior, is sitting next to that same Martian creature – uhh, by the way, Bob, I do not remember where I am from, but it is not from *there*, that I can say for *sure* – and is trying to figure out what he should do next. Does that sound correct, so far?"

"Hate to say it, but, 'yes'," muttered the salesman. "Boy, you sure make it sound like a magazine-article."

The 'Sari'-girl gave a friendly shrug, accompanied with arched eyebrows and lips, as if this was all old hat to her.

"What is the matter... do I not look like one of those, er, 'space-aliens' from those movies you have on the little com-puter memory-cards in the living-room?" she teased. "Not quite what you had expected? No slimy tentacles or extra limbs, underneath my 'cute human-chick suit'?"

"None that I *know* of," quipped Billings, hoping – though he knew it was probably futile – that she couldn't hear the fear in his voice.

"What is it that I am supposed to say, there is a line..." mentioned the fallen-girl. "Oh, yeah, Tommy told me when he showed me one of the science-fiction books that you have in our bedroom, *now* I remember... 'take me to your leader'... is that not it? On second thought, do *not* take me to your leader – I kind of like it right *here*. From what you tell me, your leader is not that nice a person, is he?"

She giggled at this *bon mot*.

"Well, I gotta say," admitted the salesman. "You're a hell of a good facsimile of a real human-girl – except for the eyes, and... the... uh... *teeth*."

She turned to look him straight on, and, in an instant, four frighteningly-sharp incisors extended, glistening malevolently.

"You mean *these*?" she inquired, feigning innocence, while pointing a shapely index finger at one of her fangs.

Involuntarily, Billings flinched away.

"You'd do Count Dracula proud with those things, you know," he offered.

"Hmm," commented the 'Sari'-girl, "He was a 'vam-pire' – right? I remember skimming over a reference to those things, on your com-puter network, back at the library. An evil supernatural being, who is supposed to gain life by sucking blood out of humans – is that not correct?"

"Uhh... yeah," nervously confirmed the salesman. "That's the general idea. Oh, and he was supposed to be able to fly and he could become invisible. So... you're, uhh, two for three... the teeth and the disappearing-act, that is. Thankfully, I haven't seen you flying on a broomstick... yet."

"Flying, eh?" she neutrally replied. "Just give me *time* on that one, Bob... just give me *time*, until you see me soaring past those fighter-planes of which your 'America' empire seems to be so proud. And what is the idea with the broomstick? Oh... *right*. Witches, evil magic-women – *now* I understand."

Billings sat and listened.

"Well, do not worry about me doing any of *that*, with a broom, or with these," noted the newcomer, while the fangs retracted to what would look more or less like a normal set of incisors. "I do *not* drink blood – ugh! What a *thought*... almost as revolting a habit as those 'nice juicy red steaks' that you seem to enjoy. But... we *are* being honest with each other, Bob... are we not?"

"Hopefully," he grimaced.

"I would appreciate it, if you do not repeat this to anyone else, unless I tell you ahead of time that it is oh-kay," she went on, "So I thought that I should let you know, you would not want to be bitten with these in-and-out hiding teeth. As I said, I do *not* drink blood... *but...*"

"But... what?" he demanded. "As if I really want to *know*."

"Normally these teeth just do what your own do – that is, slice and chew food," explained the 'Sari'-girl, "But if I concentrate and force this ability to manifest itself, my four sharp teeth become poisonous – they inject an organic venom which shuts down the nervous-system of most creatures. It kills within seconds to minutes, depending on how big my victim is."

The salesman's face started to take on a pale color, upon hearing this.

"The idea of doing that to any living being makes me sick to my stomach, as you say," she quickly added. "Oh... and I do not know how a bite from my fangs would affect the people of your world – I obviously do not want to experiment on anyone who I do not want to hurt, and that is basically *everyone*, right now – but I suspect that it would be just as effective here, as elsewhere. I can also force *other* body-fluids into my teeth, and... ah, it is so hard to remember, but something tells me that they do... *different* things, that is – not all of them are bad for you..."

"Jesus H. Christ," muttered Billings. "And I've been – I had your tongue right inside my –"

"Ah, yes, what is the human expression for what you're thinking right now, Bob my love?" she maliciously noted. "Yes, I remember now. There is this alien creature, with poisoned fangs which can kill with one bite, in the bed next to you, and you have been, how would one say, 'fucking her brains out', exchanging body-fluids all over the place, since you met her. Did I guess right?"

"At least you have a sense of humor about it," was all he could think of to say.

"I guess the 'space-aliens' with whom you are familiar, do not have sexual relations with humans and do not laugh at their jokes, eh, Bob?" she teased.

"Well, for the record," explained the fallen-girl, "It took me a while to appreciate what you think is funny – like how people here interact with each other in everyday life, your humor sometimes has a cruel edge that was challenging for me to become accustomed to – but I *love* hearing your jokes. Not only can they be amusing, but they are a great way to understand how your people see the world – what they think is important and so on."

"And," she coquettishly added, "Regarding what you have been doing to her... this 'space-alien' would be *very* pleased to keep doing that, as much as you are able. Remember, one part of me – a big and important part – is just like a human woman. When our bodies give each other pleasure, as I told you some time ago, it helps me adapt... but that is not the *main* reason why I want to do it."

She showed him a gentle smile.

"You know, Sari," observed Billings, "This is all a *hell* of a lot for an average Joe like yours truly to take in, all at one time. Where does this all leave us?"

"That is a good question," acknowledged the 'Sari'-girl. "You see... I have lately been doing some thinking about some things that you said to Whitney, the children and I, while we were all driving in your ess-you-vee. In particular, about what you told us regarding 'the Man', the government of this 'United States' country that we all seem to find ourselves living in."

"'I'm from the government and I'm here to help you'," commented the salesman. "That what you mean?"

"Yeah," she stated, again staring philosophically straight ahead. "I guess that I should mention, when I first... *landed* here, I had been seriously considering the possibility of just, how do you say, 'turning myself in', to the authorities of your country. I figured that just who I am, might have led them to treat me nicely, give me social status, money, authority and so on. Maybe I would even be famous!"

"Until they put you in a zoo somewhere, the minute they get their hands on you," Billings warned.

She nodded and continued, "But later – when I observed how the henchmen of this government of yours *really* behave – as well as when I did that research in the big city-library, back up the multi-lane road – well, *that*, along with the personal experiences that you and Whitney told me, changed my mind."

She fell silent for a second and then stated, "Most of the people who I have so far met here – yourself and the others in our car included – have been nice to me, and I would like to melt in with them, be one of the common people, learn their ways, truly know their dreams, hopes and fears... even if doing that takes many years. What I know of your people is only what little I have seen with my own eyes, plus book- and com-pu-ter-reading. To fully understand a society, how people think and feel, that always takes much longer... it takes *being* one of them."

"Maybe so," offered the salesman, "But it ain't much to write home about... wherever 'home' *is* for you, Sari. I mean, you've seen how I live, and most folks around here are actually worse off. Does that matter to you?"

"*Sure* it does," confirmed the newcomer, "And thus it has always been, whenever I have found myself in a new place; but, I fear, your government may not want me to be among the common-folk, because from what I have been able to read so far, the rulers of your world are very competitive, always looking for some way to uhh, how do you say, 'get the upper hand' over each other. They may want to capture me, try to compel me to do their bidding. Or maybe they just want to be *rid* of me. Does that sound like something that they might do, Bob? After all... you know them far better than I do."

"Unfortunately, my dear Martian-or-whatever-you are girl," replied Billings, "It sounds *exactly* like what they'd do. Maybe what they're planning to do, right *now*, as we speak. That guy spying on you this afternoon, is just the icing on the cake – Sari, we *gotta* get out of here! If we hang around in my house, it's only a matter of time until the guys in the combat gear come crashing through the windows."

"Bob," she kindly remarked, turning to face him, "You *know* that I cannot endanger you, Whitney and the children, by my presence. To see any of you harmed or killed... I am afraid of what I might do, if *that* happened. I suppose that I can be rather... *moody*, is that not the word... and you would *not* want to see me if I was truly angry. If ever the occasion arises where you have to explain that to this 'U.S. government', you have my permission to do so."

"I'll take your word on that," said Billings. "So... what are you saying?"

"What I am saying," stated the fallen-girl, calmly and slowly, "Is that at the first sign of trouble – if danger should confront us – you muct remove Whitney and the children, as far away from me as possible. They might be exposed to a great deal of danger, if they were too close to me when, ah, how did Curtis say it, yes, 'when the shit goes down'. Many of my defenses are somewhat, ahh, *indiscriminate* – not a good idea to be too close, you know?"

"I can just *imagine*," mordantly answered the salesman.

"No, you can not – and you would not want to," she contradicted, sounding duly menacing, "But regardless... it would be much more difficult for me to properly defend myself, if all of you might be in the line-of-fire. On the other hand, I cannot protect you from this government of yours, if you are off by yourselves. It is a serious dilemma."

"I thought you said you didn't want to leave me," protested Billings, trying to hide the despair building in his voice. "Or leave *us*."

The Angel Brings Fire Book 2 : Doubt Me Not

"I do not," answered the newcomer. "And I *will* not... at least, not permanently. Did I leave you to defend yourselves, when we were back at the, uhh, 'Jesus Jail' place?"

"Only for a while," retorted the salesman, "But that was *completely* different... I mean, *those* guys were just some bunch of religious nuts playing 'concentration-camp for amateurs'. What we're talking about now, is the *whole fucking U.S. Army*, plus the CIA, the Men In Black, the Navy SEALs and God knows who else. Those buggers *don't* play around, and you *don't* get second chances with them; I can assure you that unlike those idiots up north, the CIA *doesn't* miss when *they* start firing."

"Really?" she interjected.

"Sari, it would be *suicide* to stand up and fight them, and double, triple suicide to come back to try to 'rescue' somebody that they had captured," pressed Billings. "And even if you managed to sneak in somewhere, they'd probably just set off an atomic bomb and blow *everything* to Kingdom Come, rather than let you get away with it. Surely *that* isn't what you're thinking of?"

"If it comes to that, yes, Bob... that is *exactly* what I am thinking of," she offered, with steely determination. "I may have to temporarily leave and hide, not only because I am as yet quite weak – I can easily defeat small numbers of assailants right now, however a full army, I am not so confident about – but also because to fully realize my war-powers, I must, uhh... *prepare* some things... and doing so takes substantial time and effort, which cannot be undertaken if I am in captivity. But doubt me not! If you are captured, I *will* free you, or force our enemies to free you – and in the interim, you, Whitney and the children must be strong... you *are* strong now, Bob, in ways that you do not yet understand. Plural 'you'. Eng-lish is annoying, in that I must *say* that, to be clear. Why do you not have a word for 'more than one of you', 'you'? Most every other language does, you know."

"For Christ's sake – who cares about how many words there are for 'you', girl... and I won't *let* you do any such thing," he argued. "Besides, weren't you listening? I *told* you, girl – if I'm right about this, and being a pessimist I usually am – you'd be up against the entire military and spook resources of this little old rock's biggest, baddest country. I don't care who you think you are, Sari; but it's crazy, you'll be *killed*. And I don't want that to happen. I really... don't."

"I will, uhh, 'get by', Bob," she counseled. "I always *have*, you know."

"Sari, I'm saying this not just because I'm stupid in love with you," he added. "You have a *responsibility* not to get snuffed out, down here. One of us miserable little humans gets whacked – well, that's too bad, but there are about twenty billion more of us to take the next place in line. *You* end up on the wrong end of a missile... *that*, would be a *huge* loss to science. I'm not much of up on the subject, but even *I* know what a tragedy that would be. You can't take the chance, girl!"

"Bob," she countered, her eyes flashing *Fire* while her weirding-music waxed in his psyche, "I am very well aware of my importance, and in fact you are understating it, but you – and they – had better *understand* this next part, very well. When my strength fully returns – and that day is not far off, now – your government, all of its army-men, guns and other weapons of war, *will not stand a chance against me.*"

"Oh, come *on*," he complained. "You've got some tricks, that I'll attest to, but you're just one person. Even Superman –"

The 'Sari'-girl cut him off, waving a finger in the air with majestic certitude.

"I am almost certain they have never had to deal with my kind... and I can assure you that their first encounter on the field of battle will not be a pleasant one. You want an example of what I will do to them? Let me tell you about just *one* of my arts, dear Bob... try to imagine one of those micro-wave ovens that everyone around here uses to heat up food – except ten thousand, maybe a hundred thousand, times more powerful, with its door open to let the little short energy particles out..."

A malevolent grin, complete with evilly-sharp teeth, showed on her face, as Billings nervously wiped his brow.

"Oh, and by the way," she elaborated, "It is really *amazing* what kind of information that one can access on that 'Neo-Net' of yours, not only exactly how the guns and bullets and fighter-planes and missiles work, but also how they make those 'thermo-nuclear' bombs... what elements go into their construction, that is. I have paid close attention to all of this information. There was even an estimate of how many of these bombs that your government, and the other ones, have left – and that is apparently not too many of them, after the incident with the... the... *comet*. I would have thought that knowledge of that kind would be carefully concealed."

"It is... or it's supposed to be," noted the salesman. "They can track you down if you search for that kind of stuff."

"Well, they did not do a very good job," remarked the 'Sari'-girl. "And I guess they *would* be tracking me down, whether or not I inquired into these subjects, would they not? In any event... I do not *want* to hurt anyone – please believe me, that would be the *last* thing that I would want to have happen – but I *will not* be imprisoned... and I *will* protect my friends."

"Including, uhh, yours truly?" asked Billings.

"Of *course*," she confirmed, laying a warm, friendly hand over his own.

"It would be very foolish of your government to act aggressively toward me, or toward you, Curtis, Whitney, Melissa or, *especially*, Tommy," explained the fallen-girl. "If they want to talk with me – reason with me – that path would lead to mutual benefit and understanding, and I will not actively resist, as long as I – and all of you – am treated with respect. The other, will lead swiftly to their *total* destruction. If ever you fall into their captivity... will you tell them that, for me?"

"Damn straight," stated the salesman.

First fucking time in my life that I've got the big guns on my *side*, he reflected with relish, trying and failing to suppress a mental swagger.

"I will take that as a 'yes'," she replied, with a girlish laugh.

Both a godlike alien and the cutest little girlfriend who's ever graced my bed, mused Billings.

And I'm scared for – by – both of them.

"Oh, come *on*, Bob," she offered. "It may not come to all that. I am giving you the, how do you say, 'worst-case' here, because it is prudent to plan for it. Perhaps all that they will do, is send you an 'ee-mail' saying, 'We would like to have a chat with Sari at the local restaurant'. If I am so important to them, and if they are wise, they will want to be friends. At least – that is what I *hope* will happen."

"I wish I could say I *believed* that," warned the salesman. "But given their past pattern of behavior, it's far more likely that they'll just come in with guns a-blazin'."

"Then," coolly mentioned the 'Sari'-girl, "They will learn why *not* to do that, a second time. *If*, that is, any are left alive, to tell the tale. I *might* be lenient and let one or two escape, so that they can inform the others of what will happen if they are foolish enough to confront me again."

"Why do you have to talk to them at *all*?" protested Billings. "Why don't we just run away, together? You've got that hide-me trick... they'd *never* catch us! Sure, it makes sense! Leave the place to Whitney and the kids, leave her the deed and the keys – hell, I wouldn't mind losing all of it for good, Sari, if... if... I can just *be* with you. I don't care if I'm saying this because of your famous Martian mind-fuck, or that amyl-nitrate spit of yours, or just because you're *you*. You're all I can think about... and I just can't *bear* the idea of being away from you."

He stopped for a second, ashamed at the outburst.

"There... I've *said* it," he muttered.

"Bob, *Bob*," she kindly and compassionately answered, instantly upon him with a warm embrace, "I accept your love gladly – but we both must think with our minds here... not with our hearts. I know enough of the technology of your world to realize that if we did that, we would always be running... always be hiding. We *could* go somewhere far out into the wilderness, and there – it *is* true – they would have little chance of ever finding us... as a matter of fact, man, in time, we could flee to places entirely off this planet – and yes, you *would* adapt to and survive even in these, using arts that you do not yet know that you have."

"There was a song called 'Fly Me To The Moon', you know," he tried to joke, "But I never thought..."

"However," continued the fallen-girl, "This would be a hard and meager existence... you would be away from the, how do you say, 'comforts of home', for all your life – and merely *surviving*, I can personally attest, is a much different concept from being able to lead an enjoyable life. And if ever we returned to try to be part of your society, the tracking-things and spies that your government have everywhere, would *surely* find us. I would fight them off, flee with you from place to place... but sooner or later, something would go wrong and one of us, maybe both of us, might be hurt past my ability to heal us back again. I can not – I *will not* – take the chance of that happening, and I *will* not leave Tommy forever by himself. Besides, there is *another* reason... a more important one."

"What could *that* be?" inquired a crestfallen Billings.

She looked down for a second, then again regarded the man, straight on.

"I am here for a *purpose*, Bob," she quietly explained. "One that I do not yet fully comprehend; but it is a purpose that I know exists, just as much as you are here beside me. It is my duty and my destiny to complete it, whatever it might be. Running off with you will just postpone the inevitable."

"Are you *sure?*" demanded the salesman, in equally subdued tone.

With wide, doe eyes, the 'Sari'-girl nodded an affirmative reply.

"How do you know that you haven't already *done* it?" he argued. "Or that it isn't just, 'shack up with Bob Billings from Tucson, Arizona'?"

After how you got here, he thought, *what are you supposed to do for an encore?*

"I just... *know*," she replied. "And it may not be a single thing. Sometimes, I must stay for years, ages..."

He stared at her, wondering if he should come out and just *say* it.

"You know," observed Billings, "There's something else about all this, that I've got to get off my chest. Curtis, Melissa and Tommy think you're an... *angel*. Even Whitney has been wondering about that."

He paused, then added, "Any truth to the rumor?"

"We are being honest with each other... are we not?" she calmly responded.

Now it was his turn to nod "yes".

"The truth is, Bob," she said, measuredly, "I do not *know*. Sometimes, I – the greater side of 'me', I mean – I *feel* things – thoughts in my head, a little voice saying, 'Sari, this is the path that you must take', 'you are straying now, turn back', and so on – messages that I cannot explain... and I pride myself in *always* knowing about what is really going on, about who is talking to me, who is *thinking* to me. I do not always do what the voices request, but the, uhh, *weird* thing is, when I do not, I feel *terribly* guilty afterwards; it just feels like all the energy has been drained from me, even though I know that it has not.... it is *most* peculiar. And it is *very* unsettling."

After a short pause, the 'Sari'-girl remarked, "This 'angel' idea – I mean, 'a supernatural being, sent by God, to do His bidding' – it is rather, uhh, 'challenging', if you know what I mean? If that is what I am, I do not feel anywhere *near* up to the task. Are these 'angels' not supposed to be perfect? You know, 'always get things right, the first time'? Every so often I make a mistake, and when I do, the results can be... *disastrous*."

Suddenly, her face had a distant, thunderstruck look, as if captured by an unsought, suppressed memory.

"The results can be... *terrible*, in fact," she quietly stated, hanging her head. "More terrible than you would ever want to *know*, Bob."

A tear formed in one eye.

"Maybe you're just a *fallen* angel," interjected the salesman, trying to cheer her up. "Which would make you a real hazard to be around – if I remember my lessons from Sunday-school, God really has it in for them. To say nothing of what He's going to do to yours truly, when He finds out that I've been bopping one of His elect from heaven, almost every night of the week. If *that* ain't a sin, and probably a mortal one to boot, I don't know what *would* be."

Visibly relieved, the 'Sari'-girl tossed back her just-a-shade-off-golden hair, smiled warmly and gave a friendly giggle.

"This 'sin' thing that I hear about all the time – it is no more than a stupid *human* idea invented by the priests, to make people feel guilty about doing what comes naturally... it cannot be something imposed by the Divine," she declared. "Why would a deity who loves you, be angry with you all the time, if He made you in His own image? It makes no sense at all!"

She stopped and pondered for a second, then added, "If there really *is* a God, and I really *am* one of His angels, I am sure that what we have been doing – that is, giving each other pleasure, as mortal man does for mortal woman and back again – is part of the plan. And if I am ever called to account for my actions, or yours... I will testify on your behalf. As long as you will vouch for *me*, Bob Billings."

Again, she smiled, with an expression of regal beauty and serenity that could have made dust of a heart of stone.

Billings longingly looked at her.

I never thought I could be so in love with anyone, he realized.

For a few seconds, the two stared dreamily at each other, savoring the moment.

"Listen, Sari," he mentioned, trying to change the subject, "There's something else that just came to mind. Namely, we've been doing a *lot* of talking, tonight... what if... I mean, I've heard stories of them having bugs, listening devices, I mean, things that can let them overhear what you're saying, from miles away. If they've been recording this conversation –"

"You mean with something like the little spying-device that they dropped on your front lawn late this afternoon, or with the other that they dropped on the roof just after we went to bed?" remarked the 'Sari'-girl, feigning surprise. "Or did you not hear the small flying-machine that deposited the second one? Actually I do not blame you for missing *that* one; I almost overlooked it myself... it was as silent as a night-bird gliding through the forest."

"Uhh... yeah, those'd do," muttered the salesman.

He bent his neck to face the ceiling and spoke, rather too loudly, "I hope you dickheads in the CIA got that. Make sure the President knows, I say he's an horse's ass, too."

"Shh – you will wake the children!" counseled the fallen-girl. "Those little spy-gadgets are like most of these electrical-powered things that you have in this very advanced society of yours. They have quite a unique – uhh, how would I say this – 'aura', that is, the way that they, uhh, 'smell', when I turn on the energy-smelling sense... which mostly I do not, as it becomes confusing, although I make it a habit to do it every so often; something new, something unexpected... well, *that* stands out like a bright purple coin in a bag of gold."

"But what if they're listening right now –" he protested.

"I am afraid that your, uhh, 'spooks' will not be hearing much of interest, tonight," explained the newcomer. "You see, these little spying-things seem to send their information back to wherever it is meant to go, with radio-energy waves, yes, *that* is what you call these, is it not? All that one need do, is to radiate a few of the same thing, matching the pattern, of course, and it the 'real' ones become all jumbled-up, you understand? Oh... I am sorry, Bob, this must be kind of hard for you to grasp, I should have realized that it is not something that you can do yourself... *yet*."

"No, I 'get it', perfectly," indicated Billings, shaking his head and rolling his eyes. "The human – okay, Martian – radio-jammer. In bed, right next to me. Ye Gods, what's *next*? Don't tell me, let me guess. Can you turn off all those effing 3D video cell-phones, next time we're at the movie-theater?"

"Probably," noted the 'Sari'-girl, with a bemused laugh. "You might find it interesting to know that I am actually happy to put these particular senses and abilities, to some useful purpose. Most places where I go, there are no, uhh, waves, to 'smell'; it is like a gray nothingness, because these other places do not have electric-machines, or com-pu-ters, or anything like that... all they *do* have, is my nemesis, accursed magic. Ah, different times... different challenges, I suppose."

"So what do we do now?" demanded the salesman. "I have to tell you, girl, after all *that*, if I had any chance of getting back to sleep before, it's long gone now – I'd just worry myself awake again. Might as well get up and try to do some paperwork. For the store, that is."

"Oh, do not do *that*," she pleaded. "The night is still long. And I would be *lonely*, here in this bed, all by myself."

She patted the spot on the bed, right next to her.

Her wide eyes, now no longer glowing except psychically, stared at him.

"I am not using my weirding skills now, Bob," she cooed. "But if you come and lay with me, you shall experience gentle arts that will release us both, to the dream-world."

Like a moth to a flame, Billings dropped all pretense of common sense and shuffled over to meet the 'Sari'-girl, in the middle of the bed.

"Sari," he wearily inquired, "Just in case... I hope you can jam their damn video-cameras, too."

"Poof," she replied, with a wry grin and a wave of her hand.

A New Title For Sari

"What troubles you so, Tommy?" asked a concerned-sounding 'Sari'-girl, as she turned on the lamp on the bedside dresser, side-saddled on to the Indian-boy's cot and ran her hand gently over his hair.

"Nothing, I guess, Miss Sari," answered the boy, his eyes down-turned.

"I heard you crying," she remarked. "Did you have a bad dream, maybe?"

"Maybe," mumbled Tommy.

Taking hold of the boy's hand, the 'Sari'-girl shot him an earnest, knowing stare, noting with interest that by now he seemed quite used to the experience.

"Tommy," she demanded, "I have a certain gift that lets me know when people are not telling me the truth... or the whole truth. Is there something that you want to talk about?"

"No," he evaded.

"*Really* 'no'?" she pressed. "That sounds more like 'yes' to me."

The boy fell silent for a second or two, pondering what to do.

Finally, he said, "Miss Sari... if I tell you something, and it's a secret, will you promise not to tell *anyone* else?"

"Of course," responded the fallen-girl.

"*Promise?*" repeated the child. "I *especially* don't want Curtis to know."

"I promise," committed a smiling 'Sari'-girl, making a strange gesture, with her hands almost in fists, except for the thumbs, which she crossed together. "On the Shadow of the Two Suns."

"That's silly," protested Tommy. "There's only one Sun."

"Around *here*, that is correct," she remarked. "But there are other places, where it is not. Anyway – what were you going to tell me?"

"Well..." he started, then hesitated, as if not knowing what to say next.

"Tommy," gently counseled the 'Sari'-girl, "Do not be afraid to tell me your secret, and do not be worried if it is something of which you are ashamed, like peeing your bed while you are sleeping, for example. I have had many, *many* years of experience with children – it is very unlikely that whatever you are hiding inside, will be new to me. I promise that I will never judge you by it, or say that you are a bad person."

"I guess I should just *tell* you, then," he muttered. "Remember how I said, when we were back up North, I mean, about how much I missed my Mom and my Dad?"

"Umm-humm," confirmed the newcomer.

"The truth is," confessed Tommy, forcing every word out slowly and with difficulty, "I don't *have* a Mom or a Dad, Miss Sari. Well, at least, I don't *think* that I have. Back on the reserve, before I... uhh... ran away, I used to live with my uncle on my mother's side – I got stuck with him when Mom went off... *somewhere*. That all happened when I was really little."

"Ahh," knowingly murmured the fallen-girl, with a slight nod of the head.

"I hardly even remember what Mom looks like," continued the boy, "Except for one picture that I had back at my uncle's place. My Dad, I never knew a lot about *him*, either, but he's dead now... he used to drink a lot, and one day he got into a car-crash. And I don't get along too well with my uncle. *He* drinks a lot, too. He throws things at me when he's had too much... which is most of the time. I guess I shouldn't feel too bad about that, 'cause he does it to his own kids, too."

The 'Sari'-girl squeezed his hand and slid up next to the boy, embracing him.

"I understand, now," she compassionately half-whispered.

"I didn't *mean* to lie to anyone!" whimpered Tommy, his voice rising perceptibly. "It's just that when Curtis, then you, ran into me up at that camp, I was afraid that you'd leave me all by myself with those bad people, on account of not wanting to be stuck with me when you found out that I didn't have family to go home to. They beat me up even *worse* than my uncle *ever* did."

"Your fears were unjustified," replied the fallen-girl. "I would *never* have left you just because of *that*. If I had known how badly they had treated you –"

"You didn't *want* to take me along, anyway – remember?" accused the boy.

Nonplussed, the 'Sari'-girl stared at him for a second, hung her head and then admitted, "Tommy... I cannot lie about that... I was, uhh, *new* here, at that time. I was making decisions too quickly and did not realize how much I would come to like you. I am very sorry."

"It's okay," he said, simply.

"I sure owe Curtis a lot for his little trick to force me to take you along," she commented. And if it is of any interest – make sure not to tell Curtis this, by the way, I can just *see* the face that he would make at me, if he found out – he is the *only* one who's been able to outsmart me like that, in a long, long time. Many very powerful people, and others, have tried and failed, where he succeeded."

The 'Sari'-girl looked away, deep in thought, while trying to hide a tear.

"That's about it," offered Tommy. "Sorry I woke you up, Miss Sari."

She turned to face him and unapologetically wiped the tracks of dampness from her cheeks.

"Tommy," she quietly requested, "I have something that I want to ask you."

"Sure," replied the boy.

"And it will be oh-kay, if the answer is 'no'," added the newcomer.

"Sure," he repeated.

"Tommy," she started, with an uncertain tone, most unlike her, "When you said what you just did – about your family, that is – I, how do you say, 'got to thinking', about you... about me... about *us*."

"What do you mean?" he asked.

"I guess what I am trying to say," she explained, "Is that you and I are the same, in one very important way : we are both out here, alone... I mean, neither one of us has a family to love us, to care for us. Whitney has Curtis and Melissa, and Bob... well, he does not really *need* a family – at least that is what he tells *me*. I *surely* know what it is like to be by myself, to forever be watching from the outside, looking at other people who have a place where they can go and always be welcome, where people will love them for who they *are*, without judgment or threat of having to be alone again."

After a slight pause, she appended, "Being all alone, uhh, 'sucks', does it not?"

"Yeah," sighed Tommy. "You got *that* right. The truth is, I don't mind the reserve and most of the people who live there, but I don't want to go back to my uncle's place. Things would just be the way they were before. He really doesn't want me there with him... but I got nowhere else to *go*, Miss Sari."

"So..." offered the fallen-girl.

"So... *what?*" inquired the boy.

"Do you think that maybe... you and I, could be a *family*, together, Tommy?" she proposed, the same tentativeness and defensiveness unhidden in her tone. "I could be your Mom, and you could be my... *son*. I could look after you – watch you grow, try to protect you from trouble, teach you the lessons of life and all *sorts* of other things – beyond. Does that sound like something that you would consider doing?"

Again, Tommy stopped and pondered.

Then he commented, "I don't know... doesn't it take, like, a signed piece of paper from the government, or something like that?"

"Maybe those *are* the rules, around here," countered the 'Sari'-girl. "But they are not *my* rules – and they do not have to be yours, either. What I believe is, what we feel in *here*," – she held a hand over where her heart would have been, had she been akin to the boy – "*That*, is what would make us a family. Tommy, do you feel anything like that... for... *me?*"

Mutely, the Indian-boy nodded approval.

"Tommy," she continued while again wiping a tear, trying to balance elation at the boy's statement against her fear of rejection, "There is one more thing – something very important – that we have to discuss. I need to be sure that you know, about... *me*. Do you know what I am talking about?"

"I think so," he answered.

The fallen-girl looked deep into his eyes, disciplining her mind to ensure that no weirding arts would take hold of his young intellect.

"Son," she remarked, "I am not... from *around* here... you know? I am *different* from you and Bob and Whitney and Melissa and Curtis and from *everyone* else here, on the Earth. Like my teeth, for example. I guess that you have seen them, when they are... uhh... *out?*"

"Uh-huhh," he confirmed, nodding seriously.

The crestfallen newcomer slumped back a bit.

"So much for my fine tricks of trying to hide who I am," she muttered. "Oh-kay, then."

"Tommy," she instructed, "Look here. At my mouth."

Slowly, four carnivore-like fangs issued malevolently forth from her upper and lower jaw.

"Touch them," requested the 'Sari'-girl, moving her head down and toward the boy, within his reach. "Just be careful with the pointed ends. They are... uhh... *sharp*."

More in fascination than in fear, the Indian-boy carefully extended one hand and ran it over two of these strange teeth, one on the top and another below it.

"Are those, like... *vampire* teeth, Miss Sari?" he asked, again more in curiosity than trepidation.

"For sucking out people's blood, you mean?" she patiently responded.

"Yeah," replied Tommy.

"No way!" retorted the fallen-girl. "Ugh... I hate even *thinking* about it. I do not even like eating cooked meat... remember?"

"Well then what do you *have* them for?" pressed the boy. "What's the point of having sharp teeth like a dog or a lion, if you don't use them to bite things with?"

"If I tell you the answer to that," negotiated the 'Sari'-girl, "Can you promise to keep it a secret and not tell *anyone* else, swear on your heart?"

"Uh-huhh," he enthusiastically agreed.

"I *can* bite with them, Tommy," she disclosed, as gently as she could figure how to do. "And when I do that, I can make a poison come out of them, if I want to. It is a venom more potent than that of your 'cobras' or 'rattlesnakes'."

"Worse than a tiger-snake?" he quickly pressed, with typical little-boy-and-scary-things fascination. "Because they're even worse than a cobra, I read about them in school, one bite from a tiger-snake can kill an *elephant* –"

The 'Sari'-girl hung her head and, fangs still very evident, laughed, ruefully.

"How would I *know*, young man?" she stated, with a low chuckle. "I am not in the habit of running around, idly biting innocent living creatures and seeing if they die in three minutes, or ten. I want to help people *live* – not help them die."

She stopped for a few seconds, eying him wistfully.

"Tommy," she nervously inquired, as, the point having been made, the newcomer retracted her teeth, "Does knowing that, make you afraid of me? Does it make you think twice about me being your... 'Mom'?"

"At first... it kind of did," confessed the boy. "Because I never met an *alien* before. I mean, on TV, they're all big and mean and scary and they never *love* anybody – you know? But you're *different*, Miss Sari. Aliens on TV and in the movies... they're never lonely. Like *me*, I mean."

He paused for a second, then asked, "Are *you* lonely too, Miss Sari?"

Now, she couldn't suppress the tears.

"Yes," whimpered the fallen-girl, "Yes, I am. *Help* me, Tommy. I am *so very* lonely. I need someone to *love*."

Tommy held out a hand, then positioned himself under her breast.

"*Mommy*," whispered the boy, his eyes contentedly shut.

"Oh, *Tommy*," she breathed, while weeping openly and holding him tight. "Thank you *so* much. You have no *idea* how much having a little one to call my own... to *love*, means to me..."

The child said nothing, but he snuggled even deeper into her grateful embrace.

Looking out into space, the fallen-girl elaborated, "Son, I should warn you... life with me will not be simple, and it will not always be easy; being with me will change you in ways that even *I* cannot undo... but when you grow to age, you will be as a god among men, more cunning and powerful than any who yet walk the upon this world. I will give you wisdom and arts, that *no-one* here on Earth has ever known, and I will defend you against all the perils of this world, with my very *life*, if needs be. Yet... Tommy... can you trust me as your... *mother*?"

"Sure," he replied, smiling in instant filial respect. "You *aren't* like everyone else, Miss Sari. I know that. We *all* know that. But I'm not scared of you, or of how well you'll take care of me. You've already done a lot better than anybody else I've ever had as a parent. You and Mister Billings, that is."

"Then I have done *something* right," she surmised, still beaming.

"And it is just 'Sari', from now on. You do not have to call me 'Mommy', in front of the others."

The young-looking woman paused for a second or two, then added,

"But Gods mark me now, I do *so* love to hear it, my beloved... *son*," she whispered, hugging and crying.

Brother, Prepare Thy Martyrs

"Brother Harold!" exclaimed the younger, taller man, after naught but a perfunctory knock on the office door, prior to barging in. "An update!"

"You *know* I don't like being interrupted," growled the second man, quickly depositing the pill bottle in a drawer and then turning around in his swivel chair to face forward across the sturdy oak desk. "And... you aren't wearing your tie."

"Sorry, sir," replied the first man, flushing slightly. "But this is so important that I *knew* you'd need to see it immediately."

"We'll *see*," said the second man. "Out with it, then."

"Praise the Lord, we have a positive trace on the Devil-Girl, sir," excitedly announced the first man. "One of our deep-cover operatives inside CIA, has sent in all the information we need to track it down and deal with it."

"More!" commanded the second man, standing now, with his fore-body propped up over the desk by flattened palms. "How did we find out about this?"

"Our operative noticed a 'top-priority alert' from the Agency, directing their best domestic wet-operations team down to Tucson," explained the younger man. "The alert also contained a request for some unusual equipment, like a radiation-proof van, as well as for data mining centered on everything that they could find on a group of suspects that exactly corresponded to the profiles we identified from the compound in Idaho."

"*Interesting*," offered the older man, his leather face revealing the slightest trace of a smile.

"Here are the details," added the first man. "It's staying at a suburban house in Tucson, Arizona, along with a white man, name apparently 'Robert Billings' – he's apparently a home-furnishings salesman or something like that – and a nigger woman and her two nigger kids, one's a female teenager, the other's a school-age boy... there's also a wetback Mexican boy, we're not sure *who* this last one belongs to."

"Do you have an address?" demanded the second man.

"Yes," confirmed the first. "I don't have it handy but we know *exactly* where the group is hiding out."

"How did the Agency track the creature down? Do we know?" inquired the older man.

"We're not completely sure, sir," noted the younger man. "Maybe some of their own deep-cover people – they have almost as many of them as we do. Possibly they used some kind of technology, or perhaps computer-checking."

"If this came in from our people in the Palace, then that means that the government itself *must* know," observed the second man, standing up fully now and pacing nervously around the desk. "Along with the military. Have we intercepted any of their other communications? Do we know what they're planning?"

"Unfortunately not, revered Brother Harold," answered the first man. "We haven't seen anything yet that would suggest that the military, or other government agencies, have caught wind of this situation, but it's clear that the CIA, at least, knows what I just told you, sir. Our problem is that our source is actually back at D.C., not in Tucson, so we don't have anyone close to the action... there's no visibility on day-to-day operations, other than for the bulletin that I mentioned a second ago."

The second man paused, reflecting deep thought, for several seconds.

"We've got to act quickly, Brother Martin," he instructed. "I *know* how the Agency and the military think – after all, I was in the U.S. Army myself for the better part of twenty years – and there's a good chance that they'll try to capture this accursed spawn of Satan, try to analyze it, study it, maybe even try to *reason* with it... instead of doing God's will and sending it back to Hell, where it belongs. If they're successful in capturing it, they may take it somewhere where we can't get at it. I want you to contact all those who have signed up to the Martyr's List for the South-West Realm, and let them know that the hour when they can see the Lord, is almost at hand."

"God be *praised*," intoned the younger man. "But if the government is also planning something, at this house in Tucson, I mean, Brother, their operation will probably be well-guarded. They may even evacuate the entire area. How could our martyrs get close enough –"

The other man held up his hand, ordering silence.

"That's why we'll send some spies ahead of the martyrs, to scout out the situation and see how and when we can best strike," he ordered. "Also to assess the Devil-Girl's capabilities and defenses, as well as those of the government. We've got quite a few down there in Phoenix and Tucson... right?"

"Yep," noted the first man. "Dozens. I believe that one of them even lives only two or three streets away from where this particular house is located."

"Excellent!" exclaimed the older man. "I want you to start selecting names, Brother Martin, and except for this one operative, who needs to start observations immediately, make sure that you pick only the most intelligent and discreet – we *can't* afford to be discovered, now, when we are *so* close."

"I'm taking notes," muttered the younger man; and indeed he was.

"Now... we're gonna need at least one or two additional field-workers in place in no more than twelve hours, preferably eight if we can do it," instructed the Christian leader. "If a capture-operation appears to be imminent, we'll have to send in the martyrs right away, regardless of the circumstances; but failing that, our assumption should be that we'll deal with the Devil-Girl in no more than two days from now. Any more of a delay might give the government too much time to get organized and spirit the creature away. You understand?"

"As God is my witness," eagerly replied the first man.

He turned and was about to head for the door, but was again ordered to attention.

"Oh... and one last thing," requested the second man. "What of the situation in, uhh, Illinois, I believe it is?"

"Well, as you'll recall, sir," responded the younger man. "We had this family under our control – the one from Idaho, that is, they were among the first to be contaminated by contact with the Devil-Girl – we were trying to extract the same information that has, God be Praised, fallen into our possession by other means. The FBI showed up all of a sudden, and luckily, we were able to evacuate without having any of the faithful lost or, worse, captured."

"Well, of course, they would be of no further use to us, anyway," opined the second man. "In view of the news that we've just received. But tell me, did we get anything of interest out of these... 'Porters'?"

"Unfortunately we didn't have as much time as we needed," apologized the first man, "We weren't able to extract much that was useful. They *were* able to confirm beyond a doubt that it *was* the Accursed One, although they didn't understand what they were dealing with. The husband and wife, weren't... *cooperating*, so we had to use punition and the chemical cocktail, to get their tongues moving. When the FBI showed up, the woman was already almost gone, but we didn't have time to terminate the man and offspring. I'm aware that this was a serious oversight, sir, and I'm following up to ensure that next time, we don't leave anyone alive to talk to the authorities."

"Make sure that whomever was in charge of that operation, gets whipped within an inch of his life, so he remembers not to be so lenient, next time," commanded the second man.

"I hear and obey, sir," echoed the first man, standing stiffly to attention. "And by the Blood of the Lamb, I will *not* fail you, nor will I fail the Lord."

"Then go, and Godspeed to you," commanded the elder, staring intently at the crucifix on his neck-chain, as his understudy hurried out the door.

Back By Dinner-Time

The radio in the salesman's kitchen had been droning on in the background, playing comfortable country-rock, until a government announcement about some sort of 'overseas terrorist catastrophe' combined with new economic rules, interrupted the pleasant down-home tone and beat; but, being in no mood for distractions from today's plan, Billings located the remote and clicked the boring drivel into its deserved "off" position.

"I was *listening* to that!" protested the 'Sari'-girl. "They were saying something about a big bomb going off somewhere – terrible loss of life – and 'you cannot take your mon-ee out of' –"

"Ah, we'll catch it on the evening news on TV," stated Billings. "I don't like to hear *anything* depressing before work. Gets me in the wrong mood."

Casually dismissing his weirdo girlfriend's exasperated demeanor, he turned to address Claremont.

"Whitney," he half-joked, as, with an impact that no doubt would have shattered a dozen lesser chairs, he fell contentedly backward into his favorite dining-room seat, "I'm extending my invitation to you and the kids about staying here, indefinitely. That was simply the *best* home-cooked breakfast that I've had in I don't know *how* long."

"Glad y'all likes it," replied Claremont, managing a faint smile. "After all, they just a few pancakes, 'an that bacon we bought when we stopped at the Mini Mart. Tell y'all the truth, it mighty nice to have these supplies to cook wid... back home, we *always* scroungin' for this or that."

"Why does *everything* that anybody eats around here, have dead animals in it?" pouted the 'Sari'-girl. "I *will* admit that it tasted oh-kay, but... well, this is an *advanced* society. I would have thought that slaughtering living-things – living, breathing things, I mean – would have been considered crude and backward, some time ago."

"We eat whatever we get our hands on, girl," retorted Claremont. "When y'all come from where we do, y'all ain't too fussy 'bout what's on the table, else y'all be goin' hungry quite a bit of the time."

"Yo, Sari, what's a 'crude and backward', that some kinda oil well?" teased Curtis, as he was still finishing off a mouthful.

"What 'bout them poor carrots 'n corn that y'all eat without sayin' nothin' bout it?" joked Melissa. "*They* got feelin's, too, Miz Sari!"

The 'Sari'-girl stuck out her tongue at the boy, maliciously, gaining a giggle simultaneously with Claremont's baleful stare of admonishment at her son.

"So what we doing today, Mister Billings?" asked Tommy.

"*We*, aren't doing anything, young man," amicably replied the salesman. "*I*, on the other hand, am heading off to the office – where I work, that is, for those of you who aren't familiar with the concept – so I can figure out how to start picking up the pieces of my stressed financial situation. The phone number and e-mail address for Tucson Floor and Tile are on a piece of paper stuck on the fridge-door, by the way."

Several pairs of eyes turned to the refrigerator and indeed, the information was plainly there.

"Oh, but you're all welcome to hang around here, of course," added Billings, "As long as you stay away from, 'a', my booze, 'b', my gun collection and, uhh, 'c', that would be my 'special' movie disc collection, the one locked away in the top shelf of the living-room cabinet. Listen, Whitney... you need anything, before I go?"

"Don' think so, Bob," replied Claremont. "Ain't no point in givin' me no money – ah don' have nowhere in walkin'-distance to spend it in, anyways. But, what we 'sposed to do 'round here... just sit an' watch TV?"

"If you want," solicitously allowed the salesman. "By the way, I'd stay away from the front window and not show your face too much in the front yard, if I were you. They're, uhh, not used to seeing people like you and your kids – Tommy either, for that matter – around here. Beth is fine about it, but there's no need to draw undue *attention*... right?"

The black woman shrugged.

"Ah's a bit s'prised that the Man ain't showed up already," she remarked, "But ah gets y'all, Bob – so back-yard only, y'all hear? Well, guess ah can try to clean up a bit... pay y'all back as best ah can."

"That go for all of us... right?" she added, shooting a commanding glance at Curtis and Melissa.

"Works for me," said Billings. "And as for dinner..."

"Don' worry, ah'll get somethin' for y'all. When y'all wants it for? Five or so?" asked Claremont.

"Five-thirty or sixish would be better," replied the salesman. "I might just give up on all of it after an hour or two, especially if Hugo – that's the boss, incidentally – isn't back yet, but more likely, I'll get stuck there trying to sort out all the backed-up paperwork. Bloody secretaries all packed up and left two weeks before the comet thing... we were *months* behind, when I went off myself."

"*I* could cook something, too," interjected the 'Sari'-girl. "I have a lot of experience in making appealing-tasting foods."

"Don't tell me, let me guess – all with fascinating combinations of herbs, spices, fruits and vegetables, full stop," quipped Billings.

"Yeah, that is more or less 'it', Bob," answered the newcomer. "Oh, and cakes, pastries, candy, too. What do you want me to *say*? It is what I am skilled at. In the food department, that is. Did you know that I have cooked the finest of meals, for kings, emperors and high-priests?"

"Which ones?" inquired Curtis, but he was quickly quieted by his mother.

"No offense, but I'll pass," evaded the salesman. "Whitney, you remember those very expensive steaks we bought on the way home yesterday?"

"Shore 'nuff," replied Claremont. "Ah's good with the barbecue. Mind y'all, we ain't got none of this fancy-pants pro-pane stuff back in the 'hood, on account of them tellin' us that it 'gainst the law for 'minorities' to have it or some such nonsense... so we just gotta use charcoal or what gets left over from our firewood... but ah'll figure it out. Y'all be ready for dinner 'round six. How y'all like me to cook it?"

"Medium rare to rare," happily responded Billings. "And all you got to do is turn on the gas, then hit the red button on the side of the barbecue. No more than five minutes per side – not a *second* more."

"Got it," confirmed the black woman.

"Well, if I am not allowed to show you my cooking-skills," complained the 'Sari'-girl, "Then, may I go to your workplace with you, Bob? Maybe I could help there. If Whitney will clean up things for you here, perhaps I could do the same there."

The salesman pondered for a moment, then asked, "Are you, uhh, *sure* that's a good idea? Wouldn't it be a little, uhh, *safer* for you to just hang around here?"

"Oh, I will be quite safe, wherever I go," replied the fallen-girl, shooting a subtext stare at the salesman. "But, Whitney, I would advise you to keep the front door locked. What was it that the man at the motel said, a few days ago? Oh, yes, *now* I remember – 'cannot be too careful, you know'."

"Ah'll be sure to do that," laconically replied Claremont. "An' if y'all had spent some time in *mah* 'hood... well, y'all would know that ain't the *half* of it, girl."

"I guess I don't have a choice, then," muttered Billings.

"Nope," cheerily stated the newcomer. "Besides, I would like to get out and see things a bit... 'build up the old knowledge base', you know what I mean, Bob?"

"And *how*," unenthusiastically replied the salesman, while Claremont arched an eyebrow.

"Oh-kay... give me a minute or two to don some new clothes," requested the fallen-girl. "I do not believe that you would want me to go out to this workplace of yours, in these 'pajamas'... right?"

"*I* would," noted Billings. "The *boss*, well, he's a bit of a stick-in-the-mud about that kind of thing. Bastard even makes me wear a tie."

"*One* of these days, I will figure out what you mean, when you use all these funny expressions," complained the 'Sari'-girl, as she disappeared down the hall corridor, darting through the door to the bedroom that she and Billings shared.

"Bob," asked the black woman, "There anything y'all want to bring me up to date on?"

Billings made a "come hither" gesture with his index finger.

Claremont obliged, moving out of the children's earshot.

"Yeah?" she mouthed, *sotto voce*.

"She and I had a little talk, last night," whispered Billings. "Whitney, she... *knows*. About who – *what* – she is, that is. That, and a whole hell of a lot more. She's known for quite a long time, in fact."

"Oh, *really*," mumbled Claremont, looking out of the corner of her eye to see if the children were trying their usual nosy tricks; but the three of them seemed busy alternately finishing the last bits of breakfast and making faces at each other.

"Look, I don't have a lot of time here, I'll fill you in on the details when we get back, when the kids aren't around, that is – but there are two things that I should mention, before I head off," quietly explained the salesman. "One, if there's any, uhh, *trouble* – you know what I mean – she asked that you get yourself, and the kids, away somewhere where you won't be too close to her... the basement should do nicely."

The black woman stared intently at Billings as he spoke, giving him a nod of acknowledgement.

"And two, she, uhh, filled me in on who she *really* is... and what she's capable of," he added.

"Do ah wants to *know*, Bob?" asked Claremont.

"Probably not," replied the salesman. "It's pretty... uhh... *overwhelming*, let's just put it that way. Remember how I told you that we're kind of out of our depth, in having her tagging along?"

"Umm-hmm," confirmed the woman.

"I was wrong," mused Billings. "We're not just a *little* out of our depth – we're as 'out', as 'out' can *be*, my dear. You have *no* idea. We're living with a being, who can – or so she says – blow things up, just by *looking* at them. I don't want to think about what might happen if the government comes after her, and we get caught in the middle."

"Listen, Bob," asked a worried Claremont, "Y'all sayin' we really *is* in *danger*, bein' 'round her?"

"Not as long as you're in the basement, when the bombs and rockets start flying," observed the salesman, as neutrally as he was able.

"Ah... *see*," offered Claremont.

"Hey Bob," came a familiar voice, "What do you think of *this*? Would they let me in your office?"

He half-turned a head and saw the 'Sari'-girl, who had ditched her usual easy-living outdoors garb of sweatshirt and track pants for a petite blue blouse –

to Billing's private disappointment and relief at the same time, finally with a bra underneath – along with stretch jeans, white, semi-casual naval canvas sneakers, and a different baseball-cap than the one with the 'A' on it.

Her face wore a mischievous smile, as if she enjoyed pushing his limits.

I wonder if the ghost of Marilyn Monroe can see how far out in left field we had to go, to find someone who could finally best her, thought the salesman.

"Whoo-oo!" exclaimed Claremont. "Girl, y'all shore ain't too bad... for a *white* chick, ah means," she added, with more than a hint of jealousy.

"I will take that as a compliment – thank you," replied the newcomer, with a self-satisfied grin.

"Now if I could only get you to wear some earrings or something like that," joked Billings. "You'd knock 'em dead."

A bemused smile came to the fallen-girl's face.

"Yeah, but Bob," she noted, "I think that I *told* you about that... correct? You know, about the, uhh, blood?"

"Oh, yeah," acknowledged the salesman.

"What y'all mean, Miz Sari?" asked Melissa.

"Oh, it was just about the little decorative rings that you sometimes wear, Melissa," answered the newcomer. "Like, you have these little holes drilled in your ear, so you can attach these 'earrings', right?"

"Yeah," said the teenager. "An' some of the kids in mah 'hood got 'em in they nose, and... it hurt somethin' *fierce* when Momma first pierce them for me, but she say that it somethin' that all us girls gotta do, sometime... right, Momma?"

"Yes, child," uneasily confirmed the black woman.

"All I meant was just that doing that – drilling a hole in my ear, that is – well, it would not work for me," explained the 'Sari'-girl.

"What do you mean, Sari?" asked Tommy, as he looked affectionately up at the newcomer. "You mean it would hurt too much?"

"No, Tommy dear," she replied, bending over and giving him a kiss on the head. "It is just that, uhh... they – the earrings, I mean – they would, uhh, *melt*. If you could push something sharp through, to make a hole in the first place. Which you could *not*, because –"

Tommy laughed out loud.

"You're funny, you know," he said.

Claremont and Billings shot an uneasy stare at each other, then at the newcomer.

Now the fallen-girl crouched down to address the Indian-boy straight to his face. Her demeanor was serious.

"Tommy," she counseled, so quietly as to be almost inaudible to the rest in the room, "This is another one of the things that you will learn about me, and it is very important that you pay attention, because my arts now grow also in yourself. Even on this day, you are more noble and mighty than any other young man of your age; but you must learn how to control your powers, so that they do not control *you*. I will start teaching you, very soon. Do you understand, dear son?"

"*Sure* I do," he disingenuously answered with a grin, while vigorously nodding. "I can't *wait* to start my lessons... *Mom*."

She quickly wiped a tear, kissed his cheek and embraced the boy, then again stood up.

"And speaking of that," announced the 'Sari'-girl, "Bob, should we maybe embark on our trip? Off to where you work, I mean."

"An excellent idea," confirmed Billings, standing as he spoke, while adjusting his tie.

All of a sudden, a darker look came over the newcomer's face, and she stepped backward, into the hallway just past the kitchen.

She motioned to Billings, then to Claremont.

"Listen," she requested, "May I speak with both of you for a second, please?"

As elegantly as they could muster, the salesman and the black woman walked over, their backs to the Melissa, Tommy and Curtis.

"Yeah?" asked Billings.

The 'Sari'-girl sent him a pensive glance.

"Bob," she stated, "I just had a warning-thought. I need your opinion on something. Yours too, Whitney."

"'Bout what?" inquired the black woman.

"I am, uhh, a little *worried*, that is all," offered the fallen-girl. "About going off with you, Bob. Do you think that it is *safe* for me to leave the rest of them, I mean, you, Whitney, and the children, back here at the house?"

"Ah don' get y'all, girl," replied Claremont. "Ah lived mah whole *life* without y'all 'round me an' mah kids, and we been okay in a 'hood that's a *lot* rougher than this one. What y'all so spooked 'bout?"

"Bob, do you remember what I told you last night?" reminded the 'Sari'-girl.

The salesman nodded.

"*That*... is what I am worried about. Whitney, last night I told Bob the truth, about... *me*. About who I am, and what that means, in the long term. I will explain it to you, too, when I have a chance to do so privately... but for now, what is important is, I am not sure that I like the idea of going off with Bob, so that I cannot be here to protect you, Melissa, Curtis and Tommy. Bob, *must* you go off to work, today? Could you not postpone this duty for a day or two, if I asked you nicely?"

Claremont stared hard, first at the newcomer, then at Billings.

"'Fraid not," argued the salesman. "Hugo was quite insistent. And besides, you and I both know, even if I did, we'd just be putting off the inevitable – we can't all stick around together, *all* the time. As much as I'd *like* to, you understand."

"Look, Sari," offered the black woman, intermittently looking down and nervously shuffling her feet, "Y'all knows ah *likes* y'all, girl – but y'all gots to *level* wid Bob 'n me, 'bout all this stuff. Ah don' know if we safer with y'all here wid us or off sellin' floor-tiles wid ol' Bob here... but ah gots to keep mah kids an' Tommy out of harm's way, y'all understand?"

"Whitney," softly explained the 'Sari'-girl, "I wish that I had a good answer for you. I honestly do not know *what* I should do, as Bob's mind really *is* set on driving off to this 'job' of his. Like I said, I will fill you in on the details, as much as I know them myself, a little later... for now, I will just say, I think you already *know* that I am not, uhh, exactly what I seem to be –"

"No shit, girl... or *whatever* y'all is," replied Claremont, the trace of a rueful grin on her face.

The fallen-girl extended a quick embrace to the black woman, then remarked, "The last thing that I would ever want, is for either yourself or the children, to be hurt, on account of me. If – Gods forbid – it ever looked like something like *that* was about to happen, I want you to warn whomever is threatening you, that they had better leave you alone. Please *promise* me you will do that."

Claremont let out an amused laugh.

"Or *what*, girl?" she inquired. "Y'all maybe gonna make them disappear into that ol' hidey-trick of yours?"

The 'Sari'-girl unleashed an unnerving, steely stare at the black woman, stopping the latter instantly in her tracks.

"*Something* like that," she stated, evenly. "But *much* less pleasant, I assure you. I am unfortunately kind of, uhh, *weak*, right now; however, very soon, my greater arts will return. When that happens, you will have nothing to fear from anyone on this planet, while I am around."

"Y'all ain't even gots no *gun*," managed Claremont. "The Man, he gots lots, y'all knows. So do them gangstas."

"I do not *need* a 'gun'," proudly countered the fallen-girl. "And I am not afraid of these 'guns', either."

"Sari, girl, ah loves y'all, the kids all does too, but y'all talkin' *shit* there," argued the black woman. "*Y'all* promise *me* that y'all ain't gonna argue with no 'salt rifle, when it pointed in yo' di'rection –"

"Look," interjected Billings, "I gotta get going, but, Whitney, if you're smart, you'll accept what she's saying – like I said, you have *no* idea. I have to admit that I'm not a totally disinterested party in this discussion; but after thinking about it for awhile it's probably better that Sari goes with me, after all. Only one person, well, two if you count Hugo, I guess, would be, uhh, at risk, that way... and let's not assume the worst, okay? Things are going to be *fine*... just... *fine*."

"Yeah," mused the 'Sari'-girl. "Fine... just *fine*. I hope that you are right, Bob. Ah, you know me – always calculating the risk, always trying to plan ahead. Maybe that is a fault; but it is a habit learned, how would one say, 'the hard way', over many long years."

"It's no fault," reassured the salesman. "Let's go."

"Oh-kay," she responded, although the two other adults could see that the fallen-girl was conflicted over the decision.

The newcomer hurried over to Tommy, giving the boy a quick kiss on the head and a tight, seconds-long hug.

"Tommy," she requested, "I do not *have* to go with Bob, you know... I could stay here with you, if you want."

"Don't worry, I'll be okay," replied the Indian-boy, smiling affectionately up at her. "I told Curtis that I'd show him how we make a slingshot, back on the reserve. Back there, I can take out a beer bottle at sixty feet, with one of those."

"Do me a *favor* and make sure that you aim away from my windows, kid," ordered Billings.

"Least it ain't no gun he gots," commented Claremont.

"Yes, sir," promised Tommy.

"I will return, soon," said the 'Sari'-girl, to the boy, with another kiss.

Then she bent down and privately whispered, "And *remember*, dear son – remember what I told you about the Flame that binds us, the one to the other. Keep it close to your heart, and it will defend you in the darkest of times... and if you need me, call my name, over and over again... oh-kay?"

The Indian-boy nodded with a serious look on his face, a gesture that was rewarded with a final hug.

The fallen-girl and the salesman headed for the door, with Billings snatching a briefcase as he went forth, but as they exited the house, Claremont heard the newcomer's voice mentioning, "Let me see that 'license' of yours, Bob... if I can talk to the little electric thing on my credit-card, maybe I can talk to the one on your license-card, too."

The fallen-girl turned to regard those who were staying in the house.

"Be safe," she exclaimed, in their direction. "I will be return with Bob... or, when I am called for."

"Just don't try *that* nonsense with my point-of-sale system... okay?" was the last thing that Claremont heard, as the front door swung shut.

Four Rare Birds In A Cage

With a more alarming shudder than the President was expecting, Air Force One landed; the 747-variant came slowly to a stop.

"We're down, sir," announced the pilot, over the intercom. "Sorry for the shaking going on there. This airstrip's quite a bit shorter than what we're normally used to, so I had to use both the thrust-reversers and maximum brake. Stairway is already deploying, so you can get off as soon as you want."

The President nodded, even though he knew the pilot couldn't see.

"Let's get this over with," he said to Anderson.

"Can't wait," replied McPherson, his face looking less tired than normal. "When I get to touch them... only then, I'll *know* it was all real."

As the three appeared at the door, their eyes were confronted by a forest scene, dark-green redwoods, or some such species equally imposing. The only sign of civilization apparent anywhere, other than the runway on which they had just precariously landed, was a nondescript building, about the size of perhaps a double-level car dealership; this was windowless, concrete-gray, standing starkly by itself in the forest, ringed by a high measure of razor-wire fence.

As he navigated the last of the steps down to the tarmac and headed forward, flanked by SWAT-bedecked gendarmes as well as black-suited, sunglassed Secret Service staff and more than a few regular U.S. Marine guards, the President inquired, "So you've got them all in there?"

Walking at a brisk pace toward the building, Anderson explained, "All the Americans are here, Mr. President – that is, specifically, Jacobson, White, Boyd and Tanaka, although I had better warn you, the Professor is not in a very good mood, she's been complaining to everyone within earshot about 'you have no right to drag me out here against my will' and nonsense like that."

"Heh," interrupted McPherson. "That's Cherie Tanaka, all right."

"Well, after all, she's a civilian... I guess she's not used to taking orders," noted the general. "The only other member of the Mars crew is the Russian – Chkalov – and he's apparently now back in Moscow; the Russians somehow scraped up a launcher and a spare *Progress-7* module to get him back to his own country. They put quite a high priority in doing that as soon as they found out that we were getting the others down to the U.S.. The Intelligence boys are trying to figure out what they know... if anything."

"Hopefully," offered the President, as they came up to the faint outline of a door in the front of the building, "Soon, *we'll* know what the hell is going on here, as well. Lieutenant?"

"Sir," responded a tough-looking young Marine.

He put his hand on a completely nondescript part of the outside wall, and instantly, a keypad appeared alongside.

The Marine entered a combination, then shot a look at one of the Secret Service agents, who also entered a long sequence of keystrokes.

Whoosh.

The outline of the door clarified, then a corresponding chunk of this concrete-stuff moved slightly back, then disappeared into something on one side. A brightly-lit corridor extended inside.

"*Impressive,*" remarked the President.

"The latest," confirmed Anderson. "Whole building is 'stealthed' against detection by satellite surveillance, as well as lock-on by any form of guidance, IR, radar, magnetic interferometry... the *works*. Zero RF-emission and a whole bunch of other tricks."

"Listen," asked the President, "You're *sure* that you've checked them for, uhh, any little Martian bugs that they might have carried back? I mean, that *is* the reason why you've got them way out here in the boondocks, right?"

"Tests for pathogens, radiation poisoning, the works – all came up completely negative," explained McPherson. "And anyway... remember that they spent *months* on ISS2, with no apparent ill effect on anyone else. The only thing that's somewhat unusual is that Tanaka's blood pH is elevated, almost to the point where we'd expect it to start causing cardiovascular issues or soft tissue degradation... but it doesn't seem to be having any ill effect on her. White's is up a bit, too, but less than Tanaka's. We're re-testing in case this was just an equipment-failure."

"So there's no risk?" demanded the President.

"Actually, I'd say you'd have a far greater chance of getting sick, by simply going to the local shopping-mall or swimming-pool," countered McPherson. "Truth is, all four of them are in rip-roarin' good health, considerably better even than what we have recorded when they set out from Earth a while ago; as yet, we don't have a good explanation for this, but no, I wouldn't worry about it, Mr. President, if I were you."

"Swell," replied the President. "That means *you* go in first."

"Nothing would please me more," agreed McPherson, with a laugh.

He turned to the Marine.

"May we enter?" he asked.

"Honor guard will lead, sir," replied the soldier, snapping his fingers.

At this gesture, the Marine was joined by two others, who formed a mini-phalanx in front. They marched down the corridor.

"I guess that means 'yes'," joked McPherson.

"Mr. President?" requested Anderson, palm up to indicate "go ahead".

McPherson went forth, with the general and President following close behind and the Marines in front and the rest of the extensive protective troupe in the rear.

The trip was not a long one, and it ended with a double-paned high-impact Plexiglas door, again locked by some kind of sophisticated biometric authentication-system, which was duly unlocked, this time by a member of the Secret Service.

"We're in," stated Anderson. "Which one did you want to speak with, first, sir?"

"I'd like to see all of them together," requested the President.

"Sir," protested the general, "I don't think that's advisable. Didn't you say that you were going to discuss this with Jacobson, privately? As you know, I didn't like the idea of *that*, either, but still worse, you in there with *all* of them –"

"I gave the man my word," countered the President. "Besides, I'm meeting with three staff of the U.S. Air Force, plus one civilian professor, not with the chief gangster of the Craps, or Cripes, or whatever the hell they call themselves. As long as they're not carrying some lethal germs with them, I'll be alright."

Anderson did not reply. Instead, he nodded to one of the Marines, who touched a wall-panel button.

Instantly, an inner area, complete with sleeping-bunks, a translucently-hidden commode and various furnishings, surrounded by the same high-impact transparent plastic that made up the door, came into view directly in front of them, where, a second before, all that had appeared to be there was a concrete wall. Inside this inner sanctum, were three strapping military men – an older white one, a younger white one and a younger black one, accompanied by an almond-eyed, shapely Eurasian woman. All were dressed in standard-issue Air Force leisure uniforms.

"Okay," directed the President. "Open the door. You can sit here and watch, but I promised them that I wouldn't allow recordings."

"Very well," sighed Anderson.

Another previously-invisible portal opened and the President strode through it. A half-second later, there was no door.

Three Air Force astronauts instantly came to attention.

"At ease, gentlemen," counseled the President.

He extended a hand to the eldest man. "Commander Jacobson, it's a pleasure to finally meet you in person," he started.

Shaking his hand, Jacobson replied, "The pleasure is mutual, sir."

Devon White now shone one of his trademark smiles.

"It's good to be home, sir," mentioned the African-American astronaut. "Meeting y'all was the last thing I set out to do for my son – he's back in L.A., you know. Now I can tell him that yours truly met the President."

"Glad to oblige, Major White," replied the U.S. leader.

"Mr. President," offered Boyd, shaking the man's hand vigorously.

"Major Boyd," courteously replied the President.

"I don't want to be impolite, Mr. President sir," remarked the woman, as she reluctantly extended her hand. "But, we're all expecting some answers as to why we've all been taken here on such short notice. I had been hoping on some shore leave – we've all been away for *so* long, now – and instead, the *minute* we get back to Earth, they load us out to here, at gunpoint. Not much of a welcome, wouldn't you say, sir?"

"May I sit down?" evaded the American leader, pointing to a chair next to a meeting-table.

"Of course," agreed Jacobson, motioning to the others to do so as well.

The former commander of the Mars mission sat down across from the President, directly facing his Commander-In-Chief.

"Mr. President," started Jacobson, "As I said, it's a great honor to meet you in person, but... wasn't it our arrangement, that you and I would be speaking, uhh, *privately?*"

"We can still do that," answered the President, "But first, I have some news that I thought you should all know. Just to set the stage for our discussions."

"And *that* would be – ?" inquired Boyd.

"I'll make this brief and to the point," stated the U.S. leader, "Because, basically, we don't have many facts available to us. So here it is. Remember that alien being that you brought back to life on Mars, gentlemen? And, ladies?"

"You *mean* –" gasped White, anticipation reverberating through his voice.

"The bottom line is," continued the President, "We have almost irrefutable evidence, that the alien, this 'Karéin-Mayréij' of yours, has landed on Earth. In the northwestern United States, to be precise. And –"

"Thank you, Dear Lord, for answering our prayers," whispered White, his head bowed, a tear coming to his eye. "We never doubted you, Lord."

For their parts, Boyd and Jacobson just sat there, staring silently and introspectively into space.

"Oh God – she's *alive!*" cried Tanaka, joyously, her eyes flashing. "Where *is* she? *How* is she? When can we go see her?"

"Wait... *wait*," cautioned the President, gesturing for order. "If I knew that, I'd be far better off than I am now. All we know for *sure*, is that shortly after the comet incident, she seems to have... uhh... crash-landed, for the lack of a better term, somewhere in the Rocky Mountain foothills, in Idaho."

"Was she hurt?" pressed Boyd. "Can't we at least give her a *call* –"

Again, the American leader motioned for the floor.

"As you can imagine," he pointed out, "The government had a lot of other problems to deal with around then – things *still* aren't back to normal down here, not by a long-shot – and we lost her trail, initially. Then, several days later, we got what we think is a positive ID of her, in a library in Salt Lake City, but again, we lost track of her, after that. We simply don't *know* where she is right now – or why she's making herself so difficult to contact. That's the truth. I have no reason to mislead you on this topic."

"Are you *sure* it's the truth?" demanded Tanaka, fixing the man in a laser-like stare.

"I'm leveling with you," stated the U.S. leader, "One hundred per cent, because we *need* your cooperation in this matter."

Now the former Mars mission science-officer commented, "If we take you at your word, sir... this doesn't add up. Why would she run around like that, intentionally trying to avoid detection? Several times, she said that she came to *serve* humankind – I'd have thought that she'd go right *to* you, or maybe to the United Nations or something like that – after all, she spoke directly with yourself, when we were back on the *Infinity*... remember? Who would she be hiding from?"

"Maybe she's just sick of the old 'saving-the-world' schtick," offered Boyd. "Can't blame her if she is. That was one H of a big bang that she pulled off –"

"Without which," added Jacobson, "None of us would be here, talking about this, you know."

"That's... *another* thing," requested the President. "I'd like you not to express that opinion to anyone outside this room – *especially* not to the media. Doing so could cause problems for some of our foreign-policy initiatives."

"You mean that big lie you're spreading about this so-called 'Sword of Freedom' thing?" contemptuously shot back Tanaka. "We all heard the announcement. If it's of any interest, every single person with whom we discussed the subject, knows that it's nonsense. They *know* who saved the Earth. They saw it with their own eyes, and felt it in their hearts. We *all* did."

"Professor," retorted the President, "With all due respect, I'd suggest that you leave the management of the United States to those of us who were elected to do so, and I'll leave management of *your* affairs, to yourself. We have a lot of very good reasons why we are promoting the 'Sword of Freedom' story, and besides, I don't need to justify these to those of you further down the chain of command. So if we could get back to business –"

"Yes, sir," interrupted White. "Like, with all due respect – *sir* – when are we gettin' out of here?"

"That will depend," stated the President, with icy precision, "On how much cooperation I get out of all of you."

"So exactly what do you want us to 'cooperate' *on*, sir?" asked Boyd.

"You can start by telling me *exactly* what happened up there," demanded the American leader. "With the alien, I mean. We know perfectly well that you're holding back a great deal of information, and, with the new development that I just explained to you, as well as several other very serious issues that have unfortunately occurred since, we now don't have the luxury of playing games, any more."

"With however much respect that's due, sir," countered Tanaka, "I've already *told* you all I have to say."

"It's too bad that you feel that way," officiously noted the President. "That's probably not going to help your situation, you know."

"Mr. President," Jacobson broke in, "Perhaps it's time for you and I to have that little private conversation that I had promised you?"

"By all means," replied the President.

"Sam, you're making a *huge* mistake," warned Tanaka. "We have no idea what they'll *do*, if –"

"I *understand*, Cherie," acknowledged Jacobson. "But we've been over this before, I'm an Air Force officer, and I have to respect the chain of command – the President has a right to know. And use common *sense*, for God's sake... it's inevitable that it's going to leak out eventually, anyway. Far better for it to be explained here, now, to the right people, than for it to just get out completely without control."

"Well, you've certainly got my attention, now," commented the President. "One minor amendment to our arrangement, if you don't mind... I presume you know Fred McPherson? Would you mind if he was to be here, when we discuss this matter? I have a feeling that the Secret Service will have a problem with me being completely alone with one other person."

Jacobson sat and thought for a second or two and then replied, "I don't like last-minute surprises, but... Fred, eh? Well, it's okay, I suppose... I mean, he'd be the first person that you'd turn to, to verify things. I *know* Fred – he's not a bad guy. Sure, bring him in. But nobody else... okay?"

"Agreed," confirmed the U.S. leader.

He raised his hand, and the instant-door appeared in the far wall.

"Ah, the *hell* with it," growled Tanaka. "Fine, have it *your* way, Sam. I think this is a *very* bad idea, but I'll stay, if only to ensure that you get the facts right."

Suddenly, a thought that all somehow knew had the sound of Tanaka's psyche, reverberated in the minds of Jacobson, Boyd and White.

Meet me half-way, it pleaded. *Tell them about all our new skills, except this one, oh-kay?*

"Thanks for the vote of confidence," mentioned Jacobson.

He shot a glance at Boyd and White, who both shrugged.

"I'm with Cherie on this, Captain," stated White, "But considerin' that if my C-In-C tells me to spill the beans, and I BS him, I'll probably end up in some brig that's a hell of a lot worse than *this* one... so as long as I'm welcome, I guess I'm stayin'."

He looked up at the President. "I hope y'all like what you're gonna hear, sir," he cautioned.

Boyd shrugged again and rolled his eyes.

"So much for party solidarity," he muttered. "At least Sergei only has one mind to make up."

The face of a Marine guard appeared in the doorway. "Sir!" he shouted.

"Send in McPherson," commanded the President. "Then do whatever you have to do to make these walls back into something like a wall, instead of a window. That you can't see through, I mean."

"Sir?" asked the guard. "If we do *that*, we can't see if something is going wrong in there. I don't think –"

"That's an *order*," retorted the President. "I'll be alright, but if you don't hear from me – I'll knock three times on that invisible door-thing you're in the middle of, now – in a half hour, you can come in here and find out where they put my body. Understood?"

"Understood, sir," uneasily confirmed the Marine. He saluted and shouted something in the opposite direction.

"Chill out, sir," suggested White. "Ain't nothin' like *that* going to happen. It's happy news. Least, I *think* it is."

The wizened, slightly stooped figure of the President's Science Adviser appeared in the doorway.

"Hi, all you Martians," announced McPherson, with a broad grin, as he sauntered into the room, with the door vanishing behind him.

A second or two later, the walls were again as opaque as concrete.

Tanaka jumped up and hurried over to the Science Advisor, enveloping the man in a tight hug.

"My God, Fred – I thought I'd never get to do *this* again," she breathed. "What with all that went on..."

Beaming, McPherson answered, "Neither did I; nor did I think that I'd ever get to hold someone who's touched a real alien."

With a far-off look in her eyes, Tanaka softly remarked, "Fred – if you thought *that* was the *piece de resistance*... wait 'till you hear what's coming."

McPherson shot the woman a look both quizzical and knowing, all at once.

"I guess I shouldn't disrupt the party, any more," he stated, sitting down and shaking a few hands. "Mr. President – thanks for inviting me in."

"No problem, Fred," replied the President. "I hope that we're going to find out something worthwhile."

He regarded Jacobson.

"Okay, Commander," directed the President. "Your turn."

Jacobson got up, starting to pace slowly around the table.

"First of all, Mr. President, I think I should re-iterate, just for Fred's benefit, that our arrangement was that this information would stay with yourself," started the former Mars mission commander. "Now that Fred's here, for reasons that will shortly become obvious, I just wanted to say, that we're counting on you to exercise discretion with how, or if, you reveal what I'm about to tell you."

Both the President and McPherson nodded.

"Okay," acknowledged Jacobson. "So, here it is. As you know, for an extended period during the return trip from Mars, Majors Boyd and White, Professor Tanaka, myself, and also Sergei Chkalov, were in close proximity to Karéin-Mayréij, the 'Storied Watcher', as she called herself, after we inadvertently freed her from the tomb on Mars in which she was, uhh, 'sleeping', and after she stowed away on the *Eagle* when we lifted off from that planet. This wasn't a dream, it wasn't a trick, it was *real*... and in the short time that we had with her, Karéin became as good a friend as anyone here will ever have."

"She *wasn't* just a friend, as Sam well knows," interjected Tanaka. "She was so much *more* than that, so much more in ways that I don't think anybody except us could ever really appreciate. She was – *is*, thank God – our guide, our teacher, and, yes, she's Earth's guardian-angel, who opened our eyes to knowledge, wisdom and power that the human race might take ten thousand generations to come across, by itself –"

"You know, Professor," counter-interrupted the President, "You sound a lot like some brainwashed cult believer, when you say that... are you *sure* that this 'Storied Watcher' being, hasn't... *influenced* you, in some inappropriate way?"

"Don't be *ridiculous*," the former Mars science-officer shot back, her Eurasian eyes narrowing with thinly-disguised contempt. "Every member of our mission team, including myself, is *fully* in control of our senses, and what I just said is eminently rational; sorry to disappoint you, Mr. President, there's no mind control going on here –"

"*Really*," commented the American leader.

"But I *will* allow you this," offered Tanaka. "Seeing Karéin over a video link, and having a little light conversation with her in that manner, is a far inferior experience, compared to actually being in her presence, *living* with her... *touching* her. I'm telling you this not only to answer your question and allay your fears, but also to prepare you for what you're likely to feel, if you end up seeing her in person. It can be quite an intimidating experience."

"I can personally attest to what the Professor's sayin'," added White. "Pardon the French, Mr. President, but she ain't shittin' y'all about that. Karéin's really polite and all, but she's on a whole different *level*... if y'all know what I mean."

"As can I," reflectively observed Boyd. "As the others from our mission know, I have a somewhat... *deeper* understanding of Karéin than many of you, and I guess the best way to put it is, what you see of her, is only scratching the surface of what she *really* is, *who* she really is... kind of like an iceberg, except that for her, 99 per cent is under the surface. When you get a clear glimpse of it, as I did, it's thrilling, exhilarating, fascinating... but also... terrifying. You get a feeling of being way out of your depth, in over your head... pick the analogy that you want."

"Cherie," inquired McPherson, "We're all aware, that Karéin had a fascinating background and that she had priceless insight into the universe, exobiology and so on; but, because of the 'Lucifer' threat, she had to leave us before she had a chance to explain very much. Is it *that*, you're referring to?"

Tanaka was about to reply, but she was one-upped by her former commander.

"No," countered Jacobson, shaking his head. "Not by a long-shot. You see, Fred, she didn't just teach us. She... *changed* us... *improved* us."

The President warily demanded, "Just what do you *mean*, Commander Jacobson?"

"Just what I *said*, sir," replied the former Mars mission commander. "She bestowed upon us some of her... uhh... 'gifts', I guess that's how you would say it. Here is the truth: *we have inherited some of her alien-powers*."

"My *God*," gasped McPherson. "Then she *did* infect you in some way –"

"Whoa, Fred," cautioned Tanaka. "You're leaping to conclusions, here. First of all, it's not biological – not as far as we've been able to tell, anyway; what she did, we think, is drench us in this *Amaiish* stuff – otherwise known as 'The *Fire*', that seems to be the closest English translation of '*Amaiish*' – and somehow it kind of 'stuck' to us. We gained these 'gifts' via a ceremony – a very solemn and purposeful one, by the way – in which she had us all participate. Since then, we've been steadily working on our new abilities, practicing them whenever we could do so discreetly; Karéin told us that they work just like any other normal talent... 'practice makes perfect' as it were."

"Except that she's had a few hundred thousand more years in which to learn 'em," observed White, "Than we have."

"There's also the 'talent' thing," noted Boyd. "As in *her* case, 'lots and lots'. As in *our* case, 'little to none'.""

"Okay... *fine*," muttered the Professor, obviously not wanting to speak, but feeling compelled to. "If the rest of you are so eager to spill the beans, then I suppose I had better fill them in on the scientific facts involved, before they start looking at us like we had green skin and tentacles."

"While we were back on ISS2," she explained, "I conducted a few preliminary experiments on how these new abilities work; that is, I tried to detect and analyze physiological, neurological and psychological state-changes that might be associated with their exercise, although since we had to keep the lid on all of this, I wasn't able to get a lot of good research done. But the results that we *were* able to get, even under these constrained circumstances, were extremely interesting."

"I want to know *everything* about it," demanded a fascinated McPherson.

"Basically, when someone like Sam, Devon, Brent or I activates one of these alien-powers," mentioned Tanaka, "It seems to energize parts of the human brain that – to the best of my knowledge, and I'll admit out front that I'm not a neurosurgeon – as of yet, don't seem to have a well-known association with any known physiological or neurological function. It's almost as if we're using parts of the brain that have been lying dormant for perhaps millions of years, just waiting for the right... I don't know what, to 'unlock' them, to flip the 'on' switch, as it were."

"And that's not all... here's the *really* weird part," she continued. "Depending on what abilities are activated and how much mental exertion we have to expend to get them to have whatever effect we're trying to achieve, I was able to observe surges of this *Amaiish* energy that seems to be powering our new 'gifts', traveling all over our central nervous-systems. The nearest analogy that I could give you to what this looks like, is, 'being lit up like a Christmas tree, from the inside out'. What's scary about it is, if my measurements are correct, the energy levels involved here are *frighteningly* high... so much so that they'd be instantly lethal to a normal human being –"

"*Incredible*," gasped McPherson.

Tanaka smiled at the White House Science Advisor and observed, "But somehow, not only doesn't it hurt, but to tell you the truth, it feels... *wonderful*, when you use this power. So much so, that we have to be careful not to overdo it. She warned us about that – apparently, letting *Amaiish* run wild before you really know how to control it, is *not* a good idea."

"Kinda like we been turned into a walkin' ten thousand amp battery, and it feels way too good to ground the circuit," added White. "Another one that yours truly can personally attest to."

"Tell me," inquired the President, leaning back in his chair, "Exactly what *are* these new abilities, Commander? What do they allow you to do?"

"Yeah," quipped McPherson. "Can I send you up to the Moon without a space-suit, now?"

"Not if you want me to give you a live report from the surface," answered Jacobson, with a grin. "But let me give you a demonstration of what we *can* do."

He shot a quick stare first toward the President, then toward McPherson, then to a point midway between the two.

"Going up," announced the former Mars mission commander.

He gestured with his palms upward, as if lifting some imaginary object, and as he did, an ethereally-faint electric-rock back-beat started to play, somewhere off in the distance.

Slowly, the chairs containing the President and Science Adviser began to float upward.

"Say, Mister President... what floor was it that y'all said you wanted to stop at?" joked White, as the two chairs were almost about to clear the table-top.

"That will be *enough*," nervously ordered the U.S. leader.

"You should have seen the first couple of times that she tested *us* to see if this *Amaiish* stuff was working properly," commented Boyd. "If you thought being hoisted a meter or so in the air was bad, well..."

"Oh, sorry, we didn't know that you gentlemen were afraid of heights," teased Tanaka, as Jacobson gently guided the two men down to a safe landing on the floor.

"Incidentally, that was how we slowed ISS2," she proudly disclosed. "It's far too large an object for us to manipulate like Sam just did to the two of you, of course, but if you remember your physics, even a small force, applied consistently over a long period of time, can have a significant effect. Luckily for us, not to say everybody else on the station... it worked."

"Telekinesis," gasped McPherson. "I never thought I'd see the day... God, this is going to keep us scientists going for the next hundred years!"

"Yep," smugly confirmed Tanaka. "And a few thousand more for the other ones. Fred, you have *no* idea! This is the next stage in the evolution of the human species – it's what we need, to travel to the nearest stars and beyond. It's a gift of *incalculable* value!"

"Mr. President, she's right – this is a development of *huge* importance," excitedly added McPherson. "I'm almost afraid to ask... what *else* is there?"

"Well," explained Jacobson, "All of us have been experiencing heightened powers of perception... this one's more difficult to describe... it's not just that our eyesight's better, or that our hearing and other senses are back to 100 per cent. It's like, we're, I don't know, more *aware* of what's going on, better able to sense other people's moods even before they say something, and... and..."

"And what?" pressed McPherson.

"This is also going to sound crazy, but I'm starting to understand what Karéin meant, when she used to say to us, 'that thing over there, it looks hotter than everything else'," replied the former Mars mission commander.

"You mean you're seeing in the infra-red?" asked an astonished McPherson.

"I guess so," confirmed Jacobson. "A bit into the UV spectrum, too, I think. I first noticed that when they took us out of the plane, on the way into this lovely little, uhh, hotel; it happened to be at night-time and we were outside. The forest looked... *different,* somehow. I saw more detail, even though something intuitively told me that it was almost pitch-black, to the normal, unaided eye."

"I know this is going to sound like a stupid question," inquired McPherson, "But what does it *look* like? Doesn't it make using your eyes, confusing, tiring, maybe?"

"Just like Sam said," interjected Tanaka, "It looks... *different,* that's all. Not worse, not hard to take in, just different, better – *wonderful,* in fact. When Karéin first explained that she could do this, like you, now, we had no frame of reference – how do you explain color to someone who only sees in black and white?"

She looked at McPherson, with a kind, affectionate stare that Boyd, White and Jacobson had seen somewhere else, before.

"Fred," she elaborated, "I hope that some day, you, and everyone else, will be able to experience this. I really *do*... it's not fair that only a few of us have been given these gifts, that only a few of us have – *literally* – had our eyes opened to how intricate and beautiful the world really is. You don't *know* what you're missing."

The President shot a suspicious and distrustful look at McPherson, who tried not to respond.

"So we've got enhanced perception, being able to see like a thermal-imaging scope with your own eyes, and telekinesis," he stated. "Is that the *whole* list, Commander?"

He's sizing us up, came a thought from Tanaka.

I'm from the government and I'm here to help you... remember, Sam?

"No," cautiously answered Jacobson. "All of us have developed an ability to heal wounds at an unnaturally rapid pace, and we also seem to be somewhat resistant to elemental energy – cold, fire, electricity, that kind of thing – where a normal person would get a burn from, say, snuffing out a candle with his or her hand, while we *do* feel it, when the *Amaiish* kicks in, you get a pleasant feeling, as if the heat, cold or current is being, uhh, sucked into your body. I'd compare the experience with psychotropic drugs, but it isn't really a good analogy... the truth is, none of us have ever felt anything like it, before."

The President had the former Mars commander locked in an unforgiving stare, while Jacobson kept explaining.

"I should point out that the progression of these abilities varies between different members of the crew, for reasons that we don't understand," noted Jacobson. "For example, I seem to be pretty good at getting hurt but not having much of a scar to show for it afterwards – not the one I'd have picked if I had a choice in the matter – but that's the way it goes... the abilities vary from person to person. The bottom line here, Mr. President, Fred, is that we're learning this as we go. I wish we had better answers for you... but that's about it."

"Commander," demanded the U.S. leader, "If you were directed to do so by myself, would you be able to teach this ability to someone else? Say, one of my Secret Service personnel?"

After a second or two of uncomfortable silence, Boyd spoke up.

"With all due respect, sir, " he offered, "I don't think that'd be possible."

"What do you mean?" countered the President.

"Well," stated the ex-astronaut, "Apart from the fact that Karéin specifically told us *not* give the knowledge of this '*Fire*', to anyone that she hadn't personally approved, the truth is... we don't know how to *do* it. We gained these abilities as a result of having participated in the ceremony that was mentioned earlier, and as near as we were able to tell, without both this ceremony, and Karéin's physical presence, apparently it's, uhh, almost *impossible* for another human to start using these powers."

"'*Almost*', Major?" retorted the American leader. "That doesn't sound like a one hundred per cent 'no', to me. How could it hurt to try?"

"Sir," defensively replied Boyd, "Putting on my scientist's-hat, particularly considering the unusual and poorly understood nature of what we're dealing with here, I have to allow for the possibility that there *is* some other way – just like I have to allow for the possibility that you could make some isotope of water, that wouldn't be wet. That doesn't mean that such an outcome is likely, or that attempting it would be worth the effort."

"*Really,*" sarcastically shot back the President.

"As far as I can tell, sir," responded Boyd, in a flat monotone.

The U.S. leader cast a suspicious glance at McPherson, who, to Tanaka's relief, didn't take the bait.

"Well, we'll *see* about that,' commented the President. "In any event, there's something else that I wanted to discuss with you folks."

"Sir?" asked Jacobson.

"Specifically," remarked the President, "Although it's good to see four, uhh, loyal Americans, being among the first to develop these amazing new abilities, I need to know if there's anyone *else* to whom the alien imparted these, uhh, 'gifts'. It's very important for us to understand if we have an 'exclusive' here, or if there are other players in the game."

"I hate to disappoint you, Mr. President," broke in Tanaka, "But there definitely *is* one other – as if Fred hadn't already guessed, Sergei Chkalov is very much a member of our new little family. This shouldn't be a surprise when you consider that he was actually the first person to come into, ahem, close personal contact with Karéin, after she stowed away on the *Eagle*."

"That's true," confirmed McPherson.

"*Damn!*" cursed the President, grim-faced.

He turned to the Science Adviser.

"Is that the cosmonaut who the Russians just transported back to Moscow?" he asked.

McPherson nodded.

"The one who I told you about, outside," he confirmed.

The American leader momentarily hung his head, wiping his brow in frustration.

"There goes our monopoly, Fred," he complained. "Neither the Joint Chiefs nor the intelligence community, are going to *like* hearing that. It's going to complicate our plans for – anyway..."

He turned to Jacobson.

"Commander," accused the President, "Did you *have* to let Chkalov in on your little secret, there? Didn't it occur to you that the alien's abilities could have a *significant* impact on the military balance of power, and that if they were going to be bestowed upon humans, that her little 'gifts' should only be given to people within your own chain of command?"

Tanaka rolled her eyes, and was about to say something highly uncomplimentary, but she was beaten to the punch by Devon White.

"Mr. President, sir... I don't want to talk out of turn, but y'all ain't *understandin'* what went on, up there," interjected the black ex-astronaut. "What I'm tryin' to say, sir, is that neither the Captain, nor any of us, had much of a say on all this – it was up to our friend the 'Angel', and I don't think she'd have thought much of us tryin' to tell her who could or couldn't put their hat in the ring, you know? We had our hands full with just, uhh, *relatin'* to her... the *last* thing we needed to do, was go pickin' fights with her. And, for the record, sir, I think y'all should know, that she really didn't want to play favorites, either with us up there, or with everybody else down here."

"Major White is telling you the truth, here," added Boyd. "And consider also that apart from the fact that she was – *is* – just as close to Sergei as she is to the rest of us, at the time, all of us had no idea whether there'd even *be* an Earth left in a few weeks. In circumstances like those, it seemed pretty pointless to be worrying about who might or might not get some kind of a military advantage... not that we ever really thought of *Amaiish* in that context, anyway."

"You spoke with her, yourself, Mr. President," noted McPherson. "None of this should be completely unexpected."

Again, the President leaned back in his chair, his eyes washing over each of Jacobson's former crew-members with barely-disguised suspicion.

"You know," he slowly mentioned, "Even if I were to agree with that version of those events – and I *don't* – I would remind you that this business about Chkalov, and yourselves, being granted these special abilities, was known to you substantially in advance of the time when you all, the Russian included, were scheduled to leave the space-station for Earth. Your reluctance to tell me all of this, at that point, Mr. Jacobson," – he paused for maximum effect – "Deprived both me and your superior officers, of the ability to prevent the egress of this 'Chkalov' guy, back to Russia. In so doing, you have needlessly handed over a potentially vital military secret to an unfriendly foreign power. I'm sure you're aware that there will likely be *consequences*, for this."

"*Sir*," started Jacobson, but this time, he was cut off by Tanaka.

"Oh, spare us the self-righteous posturing!" growled the woman, her voice rising in anger. "Even if Sam, or I, or anybody, *had* told you about this – what the hell could you have done to stop Sergei from leaving ISS2, anyway? I'd remind *you*, sir, that the station's not even under *partial* U.S. control... three-quarters of the damn thing was built by the Europeans, the Russians and the Chinese. Ariel Cohen doesn't answer to you, Mr. President; and as a matter of fact, most of ISS2's crew doesn't, either. If you had 'ordered' them not to let Sergei go back to Russia, they'd have told you to go stuff yourself. Which is what *we* should have done, when you demanded that we tell you what we've just told you, about Karéin's gift to humanity – I can see that you mean to use it, in the exact way that she warned us *not* to use it."

"Are you *quite* finished, Professor?" condescendingly replied the U.S. leader.

A glowering Tanaka just stared at the politician.

"To answer your question," the President flatly stated, "If it *was* a question, that you were asking... we could have made a diplomatic request to the Israeli government, to detain the Russian; my Secretary of State has told me that we have a few chits to cash in with them, if memory serves me correctly. Failing that, perhaps we would have, undertaken... *preventative* measures. But, unfortunately, I guess neither of those options are any longer open to us."

Tanaka shot a stare at Jacobson, as well as toward Boyd and White.

"Didn't I *tell* you, *this* was what was going to happen?" she icily hissed. "He's talking about *killing* Sergei, lest this precious 'secret' get leaked from the mighty United States of America, to the other 95 per cent of the world! Thank God you kept your mouth shut, Sam."

"Now, *now*, Cherie, I don't think that the President meant –" stammered McPherson.

"You can all think whatever you want," retorted the American leader. "But as Commander Jacobson should be abundantly aware, as Commander-in-Chief, my primary duty is to protect the United States from any *possible* threat, and, to quote another one of my advisers, 'we have to worry about capabilities... not intentions'. It's most unfortunate that this new capability has, due to someone's negligence, been released to a foreign power, over whom we have little control."

He turned to Jacobson and demanded, "Tell me, Commander... did it cross your mind, what might happen if, say, Chkalov was to teach even one or two of these powers, to a Russian SVR assassination squad, or, worse, a terrorist? What would you be doing differently, if you were in my shoes?"

"Sir," stiffly replied the former Mars mission commander, looking away from the man, "I'd probably start, by being a little more understanding, with the four Americans in front of you, all of whom definitely *do* have these abilities, already, and all of whom have honestly tried to make the right call as they saw it, given the circumstances at the time."

"Let me second that," echoed Boyd. "Mr. President, all three of myself, Commander Jacobson and Major White, are loyal members of the Armed

Forces, and none of us would ever knowingly do something that might endanger the United States."

The President said nothing, so Boyd went on, "Cherie is maybe being a little abrupt, but we all know her well enough to know that *she* wouldn't do anything disloyal or hazardous, either. As for Sergei... well, yes, it's true that he doesn't answer to you, and remember, incidentally, that he was under the Captain's chain of command only during the Mars mission itself. You'll just have to take our word for it, sir, he'd never willingly allow his powers to be used as a weapon by Russia against us – or against anyone else, for that matter."

"What if it's 'unwillingly', then, Major?" queried the U.S. leader. "What am I supposed to do, then?"

"I know this is kind of hard for you to understand, sir," said the ex-astronaut, "But Karéin went far out of her way to make us all promise to be... *responsible*, with *Amaiish* and the abilities that it enables. She wanted us to 'set an example', sir. We all have a strong moral commitment not to let her down, in this respect."

"It's *more* than that," added White, quietly. "Screwin' 'round with this stuff, usin' it as a weapon for fun and profit, goin' back on what she asked us to do... it's like tryin' to outsmart an *angel*, Mr. President, sir. I'm not really that much into religion, not that I'd admit to, anyways, but... well, from where I sit, it's kind of like makin' faces at the minister at a wedding or a funeral... kind of likely to get God mad at you, y'all understand?"

"You're not making a lot of sense, Major White," offered the President, indifferently. "This is about *power*... not religion."

"Well, like I said, sir... it's not that easy to understand. I didn't expect you to," muttered White.

The door that was not a door, now opened, with the face of the same, combat-bedecked Marine guard, evident within it.

"Sir," came his voice, "The half-hour is up. Are you alright?"

"Fine," replied the President.

"What are my orders, sir?" requested the soldier.

"For now," said the President, standing as he spoke, "Just let Mr. McPherson and I out, and ensure that our guests here, are kept... *comfortable*. Oh, and give them a non-NeoNet television, with all 128,000 channels – domestic, incoming-signal only, if you don't mind. No need to have their minds polluted by all that Islamic stuff that seems to be coming off the cables, these days."

A look of alarm overtook Tanaka.

"I thought we were getting *out* of here!" she protested.

"Yeah," echoed White. "A *lot* of us did. Like, my wife, son and daughter."

"Why... *certainly*," unctuously replied the President, looking straight at Tanaka. "In good time, Professor."

"What's *that* supposed to mean?" angrily shot back the former Mars science-officer. "An hour? A day? A month? A *year*? *Never*?"

"It means, Madam," countered the American leader, "Whatever I *say* that it means, when I *say* that it means it. But let me put it another way, so we can both be clear."

"Right now, unfortunately," he explained, "I have in front of me, four former astronauts – I'll use the term loosely, Ms. Tanaka, out of courtesy to yourself – who have suffered the effects of close, long-term exposure to an extremely powerful alien being of unknown origins, motivations and – ahem – whereabouts. These individuals have demonstrated access to unusual abilities that may or may not have affected their rational judgment, not to mention their loyalty as U.S. citizens, and which may or may not be further transmissible, either voluntarily or otherwise. I *also* don't know if these new-found 'alien-powers' are going to remain at their current, rather modest level... or if they're going to transform you into something that the government of the United States is so far completely unprepared to deal with."

There was a stony silence.

"Say, Fred," inquired the President, with mock uncertainty, "From a purely *scientific* point of view, is there anything that I've just said, that doesn't sound plausible?"

"Mr. President," answered McPherson, forcing the words out, "For the record, I think that you're going about this all the wrong way, but... no. I have to admit that viewed just on the facts, you *do* have a case."

He looked plaintively up, at Tanaka.

"Sorry, Cherie," he stammered. "I *know* it's hard on you all – but you've got to look at this from his perspective. He's responsible for the whole *country*, you know. And there's some very serious stuff going on, out there, currently. Too many crises as it is –"

"I had thought *better* of you, Fred," spat back the woman. "Obviously my trust was unwarranted."

"Cherie –" he tried to plead; but again, the President spoke.

"So the bottom line, ladies and gentlemen," continued the President, in a lecturing-tone like a teacher lecturing a recalcitrant class of schoolchildren, "Is that the more you cöoperate – that is, the faster we learn what we need to know – then, the faster it will be for you to all get out. For your own sakes, I'd suggest that you go out of your way to help us understand what's happened to you, as well as how this, uhh, *Amaiish* stuff works. Once we're certain that releasing you won't cause a risk to the public... then, of course, you'll be free to go."

"Mr. President, sir," argued White, "I'd like to go on the record as registerin' a strong protest against this course of action, but, sir, can't y'all at least let us get on the video with our friends and folk back home? They *got* to be wonderin' where we are... I told my family that I was gonna be home in a few days. They're gonna be worried *sick* – they'll think somethin's *happened*, if y'all know what I mean."

"I'm afraid that won't be possible, Major White," officiously denied the President. "This project is under a *complete* communications blackout. We can't take the chance of the news leaking. We'll prepare an appropriate cover-story, to give your families some... *closure*, in this matter."

You son of a bitch! raged the mind of Cherie Tanaka, over those of her three companions.

I bet I could kill you with only a thought –

What did she say, Cherie, retorted the thoughts of White and Jacobson, simultaneously.

"...And remember your pledges..."

Fuming, Tanaka, her lips pursed in disgust, stared at the President.

After a few seconds, she was able to say,"And *I'd* like to state something, for the record, about this 'alien' – otherwise known as our dear friend – who you're obviously pursuing. If I were you, Mr. President, I'd be very, *very* careful about how you approach her and about how you treat her. If you try the same nonsense with *her*, as you're doing with *us* here and now... well, all I can say is, 'I hope you've brought along a cigar-box, because that'll be all that's *left* of you, once she's finished with you'."

"Should I interpret that as a *threat*, Professor?" asked the President, with open contempt.

"I'd call it an objective warning," retorted the former science-officer. "*We*, are basically... uhh... helpless, to resist you. *She*, I can assure you, is anything *but*. Do with it whatever you choose."

"Mr. President," stated Boyd, "I think Cherie is being a bit melodramatic about this – Karéin is, for the most part, a very level-headed and rational being, *but...*"

"But... *what?*" inquired the U.S. leader.

"But," jumped in White, "I think what Brent's tryin' to say, sir, is that Superman's a nice guy, too, but y'all know how the song goes, 'you don't tug on Superman's cape'. Point is, Karéin's the most reasonable person yours truly ever met... but even *she* probably has a limit that y'all shouldn't push her past. She's pretty loyal to her friends and from what we've seen, she don't like seein' them put in harm's way. I think the Professor's exaggeratin', but as some friendly advice, I'd try just *talkin'* to Angel Lady, if y'all want to start up a relationship. Tryin' to force the issue would be a really *bad* idea, sir."

"I'm sure we'll take that into due consideration," smoothly replied the President.

"Sir," spoke Jacobson, "As an Air Force officer, I will of course carry out these orders, to the best of my ability, as I would expect Majors White and Boyd to do. But I would like to add my own protest to that of Major White. In my professional opinion, this course of action – that is, keeping us in captivity, for an indefinite period – is likely to prove *highly* counterproductive."

"Your comments are noted, Commander," dryly answered the President.

"I'll do my duty," added Boyd, looking at the President with a resentful stare. "But the Commander speaks for all of us, I believe. While I will faithfully execute any orders consistent with the Uniform Military Code of Justice, I also want to state for the record that I do *not* approve of this situation... not least because it's unfair and unnecessary for the government to mislead my family about what's happened to me. My wife Laura and my kids don't *deserve* this, sir."

"Sometimes, Major Boyd, measures like this are – regrettably – necessary," countered the American leader. "Too many of the facts about this situation, as yet aren't fully understood. That's why I'm taking this one step at a time."

"At *our* expense," hissed Tanaka. "This is *outrageous* – not to mention, illegal. You didn't even bother to ask for our permission."

"Sorry you feel that way, Professor," observed the President. "But what's legal, is what I *say* is legal – things have been that way ever since the first quarter of this century... or hadn't you read your history books? Presumably you'll have a different perspective, in a day or a week... or two. Fred – time to go, I believe."

Somehow, two or three burly Marine-guards quickly entered the enclosure, upon these words. McPherson and the President wheeled, and turned for the door.

But the Science Adviser tarried at the portal, turning around once more, shooting a sad look of regret and remorse, toward the four.

"Be seeing you soon... I hope," he said, too low for human ears to hear.

Even An Angel Needs A Job

"I still think that you should have stopped back there," protested the 'Sari'-girl, her head still looking at the passenger-side rear-view mirror in the forlorn hope of seeing more of the anarchic scene that they had just rushed past. "There were people who had no guns – wounded, bleeding, all around. Maybe I could have helped some of them."

Billings shrugged.

"I *should* have just *flown* back to help them," complained the newcomer, pounding her clenched fist on the hand-rest. "Curse me – I am *still* so weak, so dependent on others –"

A flash of something jarring and musical echoed through Billings' mind.

"You still have a *lot* to learn about getting around, in downtown U.S. A.," he grimly remarked, over top of the SUV's purring engine. "You *don't* get between two groups of gangstas who're in the middle of a shoot-out... in fact, you get your ass out of there, as quickly as possible, if you know what's good for you."

The fallen-girl was staring straight ahead, arms crossed defensively in front of her.

"Anyway," continued the salesman, "Didn't you hear the sirens? The cops are on the way, and they'll add even *more* firepower to the party... I guess you weren't around when they passed that 'Police License to Kill' law a few years back... were you? They don't have to read you your rights anymore – they just have to *think* they see you committing a crime, and they get to open up from a hundred feet... no questions asked. Knew a guy down in Taos who got offed that way, two years ago; he forgot his keys and the cops thought he was trying to jack his own car. Hell of a thing... I had to attend his funeral..."

"No, I was, uhh, asleep then; so I am not that familiar with these thousands of arbitrary laws that you seem to have dictating every aspect of your life, in this 'America' empire," answered the 'Sari'-girl. "There are *so* many of them, and they so often conflict with each other, that one might as well just try to act on one's instincts, and hope for the best."

"We're just lucky that none of those rounds that they were spraying all over Hell's half acre hit *us*," noted Billings. "Before the Big Thing went down, we had at least 30 people killed in Tucson in exactly that way last year – that is, stray bullets. The ammo they're using these days can go right *through* a car door, even a special armored one like I got with the options package on this crate. That is, if they aren't using rocket-launchers – which they frequently are."

"Their bullets do not scare *me*," she defiantly muttered. "And as for the rockets... I just need another few days, Bob."

"Another reason why I should be scared of you?" demanded the salesman.

A moment later, he realized how he had sounded.

"Sorry," Billings hastily apologized. "That came out wrong."

The 'Sari'-girl reached over and squeezed his hand.

"Apology accepted," she affectionately replied. "And it is *very* possible to love someone, but to still be afraid of them – or of what they are capable of doing – at the same time. Life is a story with many twists and turns, never a nice, straight line – who is the 'good guy', who is the 'bad guy'... sometimes there is neither the one or the other; there is just a lot of both, all mixed up. And anyway, Bob, there is an even *more* important reason why 'being afraid of someone', does not make a lot of sense, here. Want to guess?"

"I'm almost afraid to ask," he muttered, "But *do* enlighten me."

"Simple," explained the newcomer. "You fear me, because of these weirding arts, to which I have access. But soon enough, dear Bob... some of these, will come to *you*, as well. At that point, you will no longer be... *human*. So you might as well be afraid of yourself, as you are of me."

"I don't suppose I get a say in all of this," he complained. "What if I don't *want* to be a space-alien?"

"No... and no," she replied. "What has begun, cannot be stopped; but if it is any consolation, all that you will, uhh, become, is a better *man*, Bob; not some slimy, multi-limbed monster."

She paused for a second or two for comic effect, then mischievously added with an arched eyebrow, "At least, I do not *believe* that you will grow any more eyes, teeth, organs or extremities. Ah, but time will tell... will it not, my love?"

Billings sighed, rolled his eyes and offered, "Sorry I asked... *if* I asked."

They made one final turn into a wide, almost deserted parking-lot.

"Wish there was more distance between here, and that altercation back there," remarked the salesman. "Hopefully, the cops will catch all the buggers before they get anywhere closer to our nice little floor-tile operation. Let's get out of here and in to the store... shall we?"

They both clambered out.

"Now *listen*, girl," instructed Billings, as he clicked the remote-control on the SUV to lock the vehicle, looking reflexively backwards to ensure that the anti-theft man-trap light was activated.

A nice jolt from the battery when the pricks try to use one of those 'any-car' keys – that oughtta teach them a lesson, he mused.

I wonder if the gangsters know about the knockout-dart in the driver's side door-frame. Good thing Whitney and Melissa didn't trigger it...

I will have to try that... all that energy! By now it would probably feel really good – did I mention that I have learned how to deal with the back-and-forth power-particle flow? appeared an unrequited idea, in his head, followed by,

Sorr-ee... you told me not to, and I am trying *not to, Bob – but when you stop and concentrate on a thought like that, it is like you are* broadcasting *it... the urge to send you one back is hard to resist...*

"That one over there," he directed, pointing to a nondescript door in Unit #15 of a very nondescript industrial strip-mall, simultaneously shooting the 'Sari'-girl a dirty look.

She didn't bite, and only smiled pleasantly back at him.

"It looks like a modest place," she observed, trying to be polite. "Which is a good thing. I think that I told you, Bob – my sympathies are much more with common-folk like Whitney and yourself, than with kings and nobles. I have spent much time with both types of people... and after a while it is challenging to tolerate the pretenses of the rich and powerful. Even if they *mean* well, or if they *think* that they have virtue on their side."

"Good to hear that," he replied. "And incidentally, we pull several million a year through that little place, thank you very much. Cash-flow, my dear... cash-flow! *That's* what it's all about."

"If you say so," answered the 'Sari'-girl, noticing that the salesman was doing up his tie, expertly re-looping it back upon itself to make a nice tight knot at the top.

"Bob," she inquired, "I have seen many men around here – for example the one at the Park Place Mall – wearing those 'tie'-things... but it looks rather uncomfortable. Everybody else is mostly dressed in easy-to-wear clothes. What is the point of these 'ties'? What function do they serve? Like, maybe they tell people what God you worship?"

"It's the required dress-code for business," explained Billings. "For men, I mean – a while back, a few of the more professional women used to wear 'em too; but that was before the 'back to Christian America' thing took hold in the country about twenty years ago. After *that*, if you were a chick and you tried to show up at a business-meeting in a suit – as opposed to a nice, feminine skirt – you started to get a lot of unpleasant looks. It would mark you as, uhh, a 'dyke'... and *that* kind of thing has been illegal since I was a kid."

"I care not for these stupid sexual prohibitions, and I do not like these 'skirts'," she interjected. "They are rather confining... for example it is difficult to do martial-arts maneuvers like a back-flip, without the skirt falling right down over one's head. And if they identify one as being in a lower caste –"

"Hate to break it to you, my dear," remarked the salesman, "But *these* days, if you're a woman, or a minority, and you try to get above a certain level in big business or the government, you're in for a frustrating experience. By the way, the 'tie' thing has got nothing to do with religion – lots of Jews wear 'em, and I guess the Muslims could, too, if it was legal for them to show their faces above ground. They really don't serve *any* function... and yeah, they *do* get confining, especially when it's 130 degrees in the shade and it's a long walk from your air-conditioned office to your air-conditioned car... but you sort of get used to them. You can get used to a lot, you know."

"Well," she mentioned, "I have seen places with standards of dress that make these 'ties' of yours, look pretty tame."

"So here's the idea," spoke Billings, trying to change the subject, as they started the long walk across the parking-lot, in the precise middle of which he had stationed the SUV, "Hugo's usually not very big on the whole nepotism thing, so –"

"Nepo... what?" asked the 'Sari'-girl.

"Nepotism," answered the salesman. "It means hiring family or friends for a position at work, or in the government, that ordinarily, you'd have to hire a stranger to fill."

The fallen-girl now wore a puzzled look.

"I am not sure that I understand, Bob," she responded. "Why would one *not* offer a job first to people who one knows, loves and trusts? How could having someone with no loyalty to you, working beside you, be any better?"

"Just the way that capitalism works, or is *supposed* to work," replied Billings. "The idea is that if it's family or friends, they're difficult to fire, so they don't work as hard, being as they know that they didn't get hired on their merits, in the first place –"

"Why is being able to, uhh, 'fire' someone the most important consideration in hiring them?" countered the 'Sari'-girl. "I mean... if you are already thinking of, uhh, 'getting rid of them', when you first give them a job – how does that make sense? Would everything not work better if you spent your time thinking of how you can make them happy where they work, so there is no *need* to 'fire' them, in the first place?"

"*Look*," protested an exasperated Billings, stopping momentarily to wipe his brow in the hot Arizona sun, silently cursing his strange girlfriend's complete lack of sweat, "I can see that you're coming at this from a different perspective, Sari – but you gotta *believe* me, that's just the way things *work* around here... so you'll have to try to get used to it."

"Yeah... sure," she unenthusiastically replied.

"And anyway," the salesman went on, "What I originally wanted to tell you is, although Hugo doesn't much like nepotism, I don't think he'll have a lot of choice about it right now... couple of weeks before the comet business, the two girls we had doing reception and order-desk, ran off back home, and in my brief chat with him last night, Hugo mentioned that he hasn't heard hide nor hair of them since. So as long as you don't mouth off to him and don't scare off any customers that wander in – I don't think there'll be a lot, by the way, we don't usually get that many walk-ins, which is why I'm driving around so much doing sales-calls – you should be fine."

"So... you want me to, uhh, sell things for you, Bob?" she inquired.

"No... you don't have to explain how wonderful all our floor-tiles and custom-kitchen sets are; I've been in this business for years, and every so often even *I* get into trouble doing that," instructed Billings. "Just ask the customers to wait and then hand them off to either Hugo or myself."

Impulsively, the fallen-girl gave him the same mock salute that he had seen in bed, a night ago.

"Yes *sir*, sir!" she intoned, with a silly grin.

"Oh, and... try to keep the *teeth*... you know..." warned the salesman.

"Oops," she apologized, and Billings was interested to see that even *this* mysterious creature, sometimes showed a hint of a blush.

Makes you seem more... human, he thought.

That's a good *thing*.

"They were not, uhh... *out*, were they? I did not think that they were..." she abashedly stammered.

"No – they weren't," counseled the salesman, "But even when you aren't doing the Dracula-act with them, you still have a real Colgate smile... so just try to keep it under control – okay?"

"Oh-kay," quickly replied the 'Sari'-girl. "But what is a 'Colgate', Bob?"

"Toothpaste," he explained. "You know, what you use to clean your teeth with."

"Ah, that soapy-and-sweet-tasting stuff in your bathroom," she observed. "I thought it was a kind of candy, at first, you know; but then, a memory of having seen it before from somewhere, came back to me... strange, huh? I guess that is something else to which I will need to become accustomed."

"*Right*," answered Billings, fighting an urge to roll his eyes.

They had reached the door.

The salesman reached for his key-chain, and was fumbling for the right one, but the newcomer interrupted him.

"It is open, Bob," she pointed. "There is already someone in there. One person, only."

"Must be Hugo," replied Billings. "But how did you know – we've got it soundproofed – oh, never mind," he muttered, as he pushed the door open to reveal a small front waiting-area, with another door separating it from the main showroom.

In the middle of the second wall containing the second door, was a bank-teller style secretarial-station with a high-impact Plexiglas window set into the wall, and only a few inches of open space between the bottom of this and the desk counter extending into the waiting-area. The walls in the front area were bedecked by pictorial depictions of various types of floor-tiles and kitchen-accessories, but there were also two reasonably attractive paintings of Southwest desert landscapes.

Billings pointed to the pictures.

"Got those on distress sale, when they closed all those auto-dealerships," he proudly disclosed. "Only paid a tenth of the asking-price."

"They are pretty," she commented. "The Earth and its scenery are very beautiful. But I am curious... how much did the artist want, at first?"

"One hundred and ten for the first one, one-fifty for the bigger one," answered the salesman.

He got another cute, but more controlled, grin, from the fallen-girl, this time.

"I could have used your skills in the marketplace, where people sell food, wine and other needful things, a few lifetimes ago," she remarked, with a far-away look in her eyes. "I have good bargaining-skills, but I also have a bad habit of getting the best price by giving the other person 'the stare' – I think you know what I mean."

"Do I *ever*," retorted Billings. "And we'll have none of *that* here, mind you," he commanded, wagging a finger at her.

"Understood, my love," agreed the 'Sari'-girl, with a slight bow of the head.

A moment later, the door opened, revealing the head and shoulders of another man, also dressed in a business-suit. He was a rotund, bald, clean-shaven guy with bulging eyes behind rather thick glasses, a good half-foot shorter than Billings and probably ten or more years older.

"Hey, Bob, nice to see you – *oh*," greeted the man, his gaze falling on the 'Sari'-girl.

"Who's *this*?" he asked. "Your daughter? But, uhh, didn't you tell me that she was only, uhh, how old *was* it, now –"

"Nice to see you, too, Hugo," replied Billings, as the man opened the door fully and stood in the entranceway. "Oh, and it's a son, by my ex-wife... remember? As for Sari here, she's definitely *not* my daughter. She's my, ahem, girlfriend. Sari, this is Hugo Szabo... the boss."

"Your – *what*?" inquired Szabo. "Hey, but what happened to that other girl, the one from... oh, never mind. Nice to meet you, Miss, Miss –"

"Tanak," politely responded the newcomer. "It is an honor to meet my lover's, uhh, 'boss', too, sir."

"It's '*boyfriend*', for Christ's sake – not 'lover'," whispered Billings, hoping that Szabo couldn't hear.

Oops, came back a quick thought.

But Bob – you are much more than a 'friend' –

Billings tried to smile, but it came out as a wince.

"Sari's from, uhh, overseas," he prevaricated. "She's still trying to learn the lingo, if you know what I mean."

"Oh... no problem," answered Szabo. "None of my bees-wax, anyway, Bob. But listen, guy – we got some stuff to go over today, before we get any calls or walk-ins. You got a minute?"

"Sure," agreed the salesman, "But first, Hugo, I got kind of a favor to ask of you."

"Yeah?" said the manager.

"Well, see, here's the thing," Billings started. "Sari's staying with me for the time being, and it's kind of *boring* for her just hanging around the house – I mean, she's already watched all the movies and whatnot –"

You liar! she thought to him.

I wanted to watch the special ones on the little com-puter chips that you have stashed away – the ones with the arts of love on them – but Whitney and the kids were always around.

He shook it off.

"So... I was wondering if she maybe could lend a hand to us here," ventured the salesman. "I mean, since Sue and Marlene took off for parts unknown, we could sure use the help."

Szabo stood in front of the two, sizing up the fallen-girl.

"Whew... certainly good-looking enough for front-desk," he remarked. "And at least she ain't no Hispanic dame... shouldn't attract too much attention from the Immo cops."

"Thank you, sir," she replied, with a polite bow of her head.

"But... look, Bob – we don't even know if those other two are on their way back, right now," argued Szabo. "Listen, kid... you got your papers? Authorization to work, *et cetera*?"

The 'Sari'-girl shot Billings an alarmed look.

"Bob, please do not tell me that there is yet *another* little card or slip of paper, above and beyond the driving-license thing, involved here!" she whined.

"What can I *say*," grunted the salesman, shrugging his shoulders. "That's what you get for showing up... *unannounced*, if you know what I mean."

"Okay, okay – let's skip that for a minute," interrupted Szabo. "Look, Miss... uhh... Miss 'Tanak' – you got any front-office experience? You know, secretarial, exec-assistant, contact-list, e-mail correspondence, taking sales-calls, dealing with the public... that kinda thing?"

"Hmm..." answered the fallen-girl. "I would have to say, 'not really', to the first few of those duties; but Bob has explained most of them to me in some depth, and I am skilled at learning and retaining new duties – you can test me on that, if you like. Gor example, I have already figured out how the, uhh, Neo-Net thing works. Oh, but as to dealing with *people*, understanding what they like, what they are afraid of, and so on – well, I have many, *many* long years of experience in doing that."

"You don't *look* that old, if you don't mind me saying," offered the manager.

"I am, ahem, somewhat older than I appear to be," evenly replied the newcomer.

Billings masked a mordant chuckle with a feigned cough.

"Well... we'll *see* about being able to handle the job," said Szabo. "Listen, kid... how much money you lookin' for?"

"Money?" shot back the 'Sari'-girl, with a 'deer-in-the-headlights' look.

"Oh, yes... *money!*" she hastily added, with a nervous half-smile. "My, *my* – how *could* I have forgotten about that... sorr-ee, Mr. Szabo, I suppose that I had just been concentrating on what I would do first, to help your fine company... to sell more of these, uhh, floor-tiles, I mean –"

"All I can offer you to start is about twenty per hour," interrupted the manager. "Ever since they dropped the minimum-wages, I can't very well offer a lot more than the competition – gotta keep them old costs down, you know?"

Twenty per hour, she sent to Billings' unwilling, resisting brain.

Is that good?

"That would be *great*, Hugo," he stated. "Especially for somebody like Sari, who's still learning the ropes."

"Bob, I'm goin' *way* out on a limb for you, here," warned Szabo. "But as long as it's under the table, I'm okay with it – we'll write it up as 'restocking expenses after recent disruption' or something like that... *capiche*? Mind you, if either of them other two show up, I'm afraid I'm going to have to offer them back their old positions – like, what if they were to get mad, go in and talk to the *authorities*, you know what I mean – so I want both you and your young Miss here to be ready for that, if it happens. No hard feelin's in that case... okay?"

"Oh, no 'hard feelings', *never*, sir," responded the newcomer, with an unctuously polite smile.

"Oh, and don't be thinking that this is some kind of 'time off with pay' thing, by the way," added the manager. "It's great that you're hangin' out with Bob – more power to both of you – but that gets you *diddly-squat* around here... you pull your weight, you'll be fine; you don't, well, it's gonna be 'hasta la vista, baby', you got that?"

'Diddly' – *'Hasta la'...* what? she again intruded into his psyche.

Oh, never mind... it was in that imaginative old movie about the killer mechanical men from the future... was it not?

Your people have so many of these 'alternative futures' in your entertainment, it is challenging for me to keep reality separated from fiction...

"Oh... for *sure*," happily chirped the 'Sari'-girl. "I am glad to be given a chance to try something new, for as long as it lasts. And if your regular employees come back here and want their jobs back, do not worry about *that*, Mr. Szabo. Just between the three of us – if I look back on the last month or so of my life, I can tell you, I have had many more, ahh... *stressful*, things happen to me. So I will take this situation as it comes. I will not be upset if you must replace me with somebody who is better at all these 'secretary'-type duties."

"Then we understand each other," stated Szabo, with a mild smile and a hand-wave. "And as a bit of friendly advice... remember, dear, 'the customer's *king*', around here – as long as they're buying product, if they want us to vacuum out their car or sing 'Smoke Gets In Your Eyes' at their kid's Bar Mitzvah, that's what we're gonna *do*, you know?"

"Certainly," she replied. "I like singing, too. People have told me that I am quite good at it."

What is a 'Bar Mitsva'? Is that some kind of booze-drinking party? she sent to Billings.

Never mind... tell me later...

"Anyway, why don't I show you to the front-desk and get you settled, so that Bob and I can go into the back and talk shop for a while," asked the manager. "Sound like a plan?"

"Perfect," agreed the 'Sari'-girl.

"Okay," acknowledged Szabo. "Now follow me around the corner, here," – he pulled out a modestly-padded office-chair at the secretarial-station, behind the Plexiglas barrier – "Here's where we'll have you sit. Bob... you want to give her the five-minute tour? Then meet me in my office – we got some *talkin'* to do. We're a month and a half behind quota, and yes, I *do* know about that little problem we had a few weeks back... but, hey, we're still here to live to tell, right, so we gotta get back to sellin', know what I mean?"

"You *got* it, big guy," answered Billings, not hiding his relief at the impending return to normalcy. "But... isn't it a bit *hot* in here, Hugo, or is that my imagination? Doesn't much matter to me, you know, but the walk-ins might not like it."

"Damn A/C's on allocation, again," complained Szabo. "They told us that business would be exempt, but it's all BS, as usual. What did you *expect* from the government? I *have* set up only every second spotlight, I *haven't* turned up the kilns and we're only gonna to use the video-displays when we got a real customer in here. But look at the bright side – we at least got *water*. Which is more than we had just before... *you* know."

"Yeah... swell," acknowledged the salesman.

The manager waved and headed off to the back of the interior space, which was much larger than the waiting-area, with a steel-beam and corrugated-metal ceiling considerably higher than the ante-room. It was replete with shadowy, half-lit displays of ceramic tiles, custom-kitchen mini-showrooms and sample driveways.

There were also a few large-screen, flex-panel TV-screens, but these were all dark and lifeless. Dimly visible in the far end of the warehouse-cum-showroom was what must have been a loading-dock and overhead retractable door.

"It *is* rather lonely in here," observed the 'Sari'-girl, as she hopped backwards, up into the secretarial-chair. "Will you be around to talk with, Bob?"

"Not for a while," noted Billings. "I can see that Hugo's back on the old quota-warpath... didn't expect him to be ramping up *this* soon after the event, but then, I guess that's what's made him top divisional manager for the Southwest, three years running. Anyway... we gotta make this quick, because I need to get back to Hugo's office before he thinks up some bright idea like sending me out on the road again."

"Go ahead," requested the fallen-girl.

"Now *this*, over here, this is the headset – see, you just loop this little part over your ear, so you can hear what the other person is saying, and this little button thing clips on to your blouse, like so," – he affixed something no larger than a dime, to the newcomer's blouse, trying hard not to look at what was fetchingly out of reach, just below the fabric – "And then you can walk anywhere you want around here; as a matter of fact you can go to the far end of the parking-lot, and it'll still connect with what comes in over the phone," explained Billings.

Her eyes were busily washing over everything in the area – to what end, the salesman wasn't quite sure.

"This push-button over here answers an incoming call, which you'll know of by a ringing tone and a light flashing, here," he continued. "This one, puts the caller on 'hold' – oh, by the way, *that* means, they just sit there on the line, listening to crappy music, while you answer someone else – just hit the button corresponding to their line to reconnect them and talk to them again. Last but not least... if you hold down the button corresponding to the caller's line, and hold down this one, at the same time, it sends them to 'voice-mail' – that's a recording service where they can leave a message by just talking."

"Got it," she pledged.

"You *sure*?" asked Billings, perturbed by her look of serene confidence. "This can be pretty complicated stuff... we had to let two girls go, because they took too long to figure out how it works. Kids had valid university-degrees, too. Shows you the crap they're teaching in the schools, these days."

"Bob," remarked the 'Sari'-girl, "This is, uhh, how do you say, 'kid's play', for me. I have learned how to operate technical-things that are *much* more complicated, all by myself. For example, there was one that, hmm – hard to remember exactly where or when this was – I had to figure out a bunch of key-presses to open this little round door, that went from the one to the other, but it was not so difficult... ah, I suppose that I am wasting your time telling you this... sorr-ee."

She winced, coltishly.

"No problem," uneasily replied the salesman. "Listen... you need a walk-through on the e-mail terminal? It's actually easier than the one that I showed you at home, because we have this guy come and get the, uhh, what did he call it, yeah, the 'bad programs from NeoNet', off it, every two weeks or so... I couldn't be bothered with my home terminal. Anyway... you don't even have to enter a name or secret code to get this one to work – it's all set up and ready to go. You just put your finger on the screen, here," – he reached over her and pointed to an icon on the flat-screen – "And up it comes. Here... *you* try."

"Oh-kay," said the fallen-girl, pointing to the same spot; but instantly, the images on the screen shimmered and broke up in a radial pattern around the tip of her finger.

"Curses!" she complained. "I forgot about that. Let me try it again."

With a look of concentration, she repeated the gesture, and this time, the message composition window appeared front and clear, before her.

"You know how to use the keyboard?" inquired Billings.

"Yep," she cheerily affirmed.

"So you're okay?" he asked.

"Just *fine*," she promised, then stopped and thought for a second, and added, more seriously, "Listen, Bob... there *is* just one little thing."

"Yeah?" said the salesman.

"Remember how I told you about, uhh, 'screwing around' with those little electronic-spying-things that the government-men dropped around our house, the other day?" she asked. "You know... the ones that I found and shut off for good, a few hours later?"

"Umm-hmm," confirmed Billings.

"I just thought that I should mention," cautioned the fallen-girl, "If you and Hugo want to keep using your 'cell' com-pu-ters – the little mobile ones that you talk into, I mean – I cannot just block the 'bad' electronic devices... I have to block *all* of them."

"What do you mean?" pressed the salesman. "I thought that –"

"This is kind of hard to describe," she tried to explain, "But they all have their own specific little, uhh, 'color' that transmits and receives signals, and it is very difficult for me just to turn off, say, those using green, as opposed to, say, turquoise. To do that would require a great deal of concentration... which is very distracting, like having to play a musical instrument all day, while one is trying to do everything else, at the same time."

"I... see," offered Billings.

"What I am trying to say, Bob," pointed out the newcomer, "Is that I cannot fully protect this place from being spied on, in the way that I could at home. *If* you want to be able to use your phones, that is."

"That's a chance that we'll have to take, I guess," answered the salesman.

"Just wanted you to know," she concluded. "Well, now that *that*, is settled... Bob, should you not go back there to talk with Hugo? I would not want to cause you any problems with your, uhh, boss, you know."

"Right... yeah, I'd better be going," agreed Billings, looking over his shoulder at the 'Sari'-girl, as he headed to the back of the showroom.

He did a double-take, as he saw her teenager-figure silhouetted by what looked for all the world like a golden aura, suffusing the secretarial-station with a warm, ethereal glow.

Maybe he even saw a halo, out of the corner of his eye.

Must just be the light from the waiting-room behind her, he tried to tell himself.

The Best-Laid Plans...

"Are they ready?" demanded a waspish-looking, middle-aged white woman with a beehive-hairdo, peering through her dark sunglasses into the half-rolled-down passenger-side window of a nondescript '25 Malibu, as she tapped a silver button on her lapel.

"Not really," warned the crew-cut, red-haired man in the car, the sweat showing slightly on the exposed part of his right arm, all the while slowly staining his short-sleeved, white Sunday shirt. "We've got a *problem* – just found out from the Brothers who are watching the house."

"What?" asked the woman.

"Looks like it left the place about five minutes ago, in a black SUV being driven by the guy that the Brothers back home told us about," explained the man.

"Why didn't they strike right then and there?" protested the woman.

"Not sure," he replied. "The target and this man got into the vehicle very quickly and then just drove off, before anyone had a chance to react."

"Is anyone following them?" pressed the woman. "This isn't going to look good to the Master. Not good at *all!*"

"We *couldn't* go straight after them – remember, the instructions were to give no warning at all, either to the target, or to the authorities," argued the man. "And we're getting reports that someone else, possibly the government, is now after them – our Brothers mentioned another black SUV, with dark-tinted windows, following the Devil-Girl's vehicle, at a discreet distance. But we put out an urgent appeal, and – God be praised – we have a tentative sighting of the same SUV going south on Houghton. We've got three cars full of believers looking for them everywhere and anywhere in the south-east part of the city."

"Well, you had better pray that they find the target, and *quickly*," admonished the woman. "But even if we have faith in *that* – faith's the key, Brother – I'm still very worried. The chosen martyrs, the ones who have had the instruction and who have made their final peace with the Lord... they're all *here*, by the house, I mean, not down there."

"I know," acknowledged the man, "But there *are* some down there, remember. It was always the plan in case of an escape –"

"They're not *trained* – not nearly as well as the ones we have at the main site," the woman pointed out. "We all admire their willingness to make sacrifice... but they'll be far too easy for the Devil-girl, or the authorities, to recognize and intercept. The Master will *not* be in a forgiving mood, if this doesn't work out. I'm just a woman lay-believer – I can only ask, not decide – but I'm tempted to call the Temple and suggest that we leave it for another day or two. We *can't* risk failure, here."

"I hear you, Sister," answered the man, wiping his brow, "But we just have to pray and trust in our Father God, now. If Almighty Jesus wants us to succeed, we will. Otherwise we won't. That's about all there is *to* it, I'm afraid. Not *everyone* gets into Heaven, you know."

The woman leaned back against the car, her shoulders slumped in worry and disappointment.

"His will be done," she managed.

Doubt Me Not (Finale)

"How are things going so far?" called Billings, half-afraid of hearing the answer, while approaching the 'Sari'-girl from behind.

To no surprise, she had obviously heard – or otherwise perceived – his advance from far off, as she wheeled in her chair to face him, while the salesman was still a good twenty feet away.

"Good," she cheerily replied. "I was hungry, so I found one of those small soup-cups that were stored in one of the cabinets near the little refrigerator and short-wave oven, so I added some water to it and heated it... very tasty. You are lucky that you have such good food always at your disposal. I also had some of that insta-coffee, from the glass jar. Rather strong taste, but still nice. Did you want me to warm a cup up for you, Bob?"

The microwave has been on the fritz... and we haven't had hot running water around here, since the comet, silently reflected Billings.

"No, it's okay – I was planning on taking a short break in a few minutes to get some from the McBuck's around the corner," he answered.

"After you showed me how to greet people as they come in – I mean, the 'Missus' this and the 'Mister' that, along with the other titles," continued the fallen-girl, "It did not take long to figure out how to do that correctly, and I enjoy talking to people... I always learn something new with each one. Hey, Bob, of the three that I sent back there to meet with Hugo and yourself, did you manage to sell them anything? Oh... and what about the two phone-calls that I transferred to your mobile talking-box?"

"Nah... didn't get anything from any of those," said Billings, as he walked up to be beside her. "But that's kind of par for the course – I'll save you the trouble, that's an expression from the game of golf, by the way – it means, 'about what we'd expect'."

"Ah," she replied, with a friendly nod.

"The first two walk-in guys were just tire-kickers – uhh, what I mean is, they weren't seriously interested in buying," explained the salesman, "But that dame from Oro Valley – you know, the one with the thick classes and the yellow polka-dot dress – she might be back, said she was pricing out some alternatives... well, we sell on *value*, not lowest cost... one of the phone-calls was from a contractor... we might get something there, the other guy from a few minutes ago, the one you said asked for me specifically, he just hung up the second I answered – damn crank-callers, wasting my time."

"That *is* odd," remarked the newcomer, with a strange, guarded tone. "I forgot to tell you... I received just such a call, a few minutes before that one – it was a man, and he just dropped the line – that is how you say it, right – when he had heard me..."

Her voice trailed off for a second, and there was a pensive look on her face as her eyes scanned right and left, up and down.

"I am a little worried... about Tommy, that is," she added.

"Ah, he'll be okay – we're in one of the safest neighborhoods in Tucson back there," reassured the salesman. "And, by the way, after you've been in sales for a while, you start to get a feeling for who's going to buy and who's not, you know. After all... things are still pretty unsettled, after all the nonsense of a few weeks ago. When people get back to building patios and driveways, we'll start moving some product – I'm sure of it."

"It is *more* than just a 'feeling', Bob,' knowingly counseled the 'Sari'-girl. "And it is *more* than just becoming familiar with your customers' mannerisms or their, uhh, 'body-language'. I think this 'sales sense' that you have, is kind of like the way we share thoughts, you and I... what you are picking up is actually your customers' thoughts – the ones that they believe to be private – only you have not developed the ability as fully as I have."

She gave him a kind, hopeful look.

"If I am right, Bob," she added, "It means that your people are not so different from me, after all. You are finding your own way to where I am at... and you will get there eventually, whether or not I am here to help."

"Girl, you *always* make my day," responded Billings, with a grin. "I keep telling all the new guys that there's a little magic in being a good salesman, but they –"

Another voice now sounded. It was Szabo.

"Hey, Bob!" he shouted from the shadowy back of the showroom, "Call for you – some broad callin' herself 'Whitney' – thick ghetto accent. Sure sounds mad, or upset, or whatever – says she's *gotta* talk to you right away. She your housekeeper, or somethin' like that? Wanna take it back here?"

"Nah – send it through to my mobile," requested Billings.

"Something is not *right*," warned an alarmed 'Sari'-girl. "Outside here, I mean."

"Yeah?" spoke the salesman, worry now infecting his voice. "Funny, I asked her not to call, unless it was –"

His phone sounded out its kitschy ring-tone, a few semi-chords from that old Pink Floyd song about "it's a hit".

"Hello?" he started.

"Yeah? Whitney? That you? *What*?" he gasped, his jaw dropping. "They're *what*? Holy – yes, I'll tell her, but for God's sake, get them down to the –"

"Bob – *Bob!*" sounded the far-away voice of Claremont, over the cell-phone. "Tell Sari we *tried –*"

He could hear the numbing Muzak over the showroom's speakers, alright, but now there was *another* tune going through his head, its entrancing, yet ominous, Celtic-electric-rock beat starting to rise in psychic volume.

The 'Sari'-girl leaped down from the chair, all of a sudden, her hands slowly clenching into fists.

Somehow, the cell-phone shot out of his hand, flying over to the newcomer's own, more quickly than the best fastball in the World Series.

"Whitney!" she cried. "No, I *know*, I am *sorr-ee*, oh Gods, *so* sorr-ee – no time for that – woman, shut up and *listen!* Behind the gun-cabinet – yellow, gold color, maybe, handles on the right and left, on the inside – Whitney? *Whitney! Speak to me*! Mercy save – oh-kay, now listen *very* carefully... the big metal-sheet – stay underneath it, make sure that you all hold hands, keep them held together – you are *strong*, dear friend, more than you know... call on the *power*, call on *me*, and I will come, I will find you – *what*? No time to explain, just *do* it, for God's sake! *Whitney!!!*"

Her hands trembling, the fallen-girl handed the phone back to Billings.

"No signal," she lamented, through tears.

"*Bob*," she exclaimed, "Something is going on outside – a man is yelling 'stop right now or we'll' –"

A sound like firecrackers detonating, echoed against the outside walls of the industrial unit.

BOOM!

Something shockingly *loud*, like thunder from a bolt just outside one's bedroom window, reverberated outside.

"*Down!*" shrieked the newcomer, as she hurtled at the salesman and, in a diving tackle worthy of the best wrestlers on the Full-Contact Channel, bowled him completely over.

His eyes, at least, were able to move enough to see that there was, in fact... *nothing*, to see.

That old coal-black cape, he started to think, but his reminiscing was abruptly cut short by an unfamiliar crashing, impacting sound, like being behind a wall that something had hit hard, on the opposite side.

After no more than a half-second, there was naught but silence, broken only by the occasional 'creakk' of what sounded like wood or metal collapsing.

"Jesus H. *Christ*," angrily muttered Billings. "Not *this* again. What the hell –"

He rolled halfway over and saw that the 'Sari'-girl behind and on top of him had risen to her knees, with her arms, fists again clenched, at about a 60-degree angle from her body.

Which had something looking very like charges of static electricity, complete with an acrid, pungent ozone-smell to complement it, shooting all the way up and down her trunk, dangerously close to his legs, still pinned under the girl's own. Smaller discharges of the same energy silhouetted the girl's eyes, which were glowing a bright, ominous blue.

The music was stirring, pounding... exciting.

"You know, the *last* time we were in this position," he tried to weakly joke, but she held her finger up to her lips in the 'shh' gesture.

The whole situation was totally ludicrous, Billings realized.

I'm being told to shut up by a glowing, lightening-enveloped alien that graced my bed, not a night before.

What else *is new today, Bob, old boy?*

"I am hearing voices, more shots, more violence, going on, outside," whispered the fallen-girl. "They are saying something about 'agents down'. And we are pinned under a *lot* of wreckage – I am using all my strength just to avoid having us crushed by it. Damn them, anyway! I *must* go back to protect Tommy –"

"Shit," cursed the salesman. "How much is 'a lot'?"

"At least a few thousand of your 'pounds' of it, or more," she answered, then let out a rueful laugh, *sotto voce*. "Good exercise for me, I suppose."

"What's this electric-crap?" stammered Billings. "It's spreading all *over* you. Can't you stop it? I don't make a good rechargeable-battery, in case you hadn't noticed."

The 'Sari'-girl bent down over him, her arms now bent at the elbows, braced on her belt, her beautiful face and pouting lips tantalizingly close to his own.

Ordinarily, Billings wouldn't have been able to control himself, but the creature's weirdly glowing eyes put him off by just enough.

"Bob, my love," she quietly explained, "I am now a big step further down the path to who I really *am;* this is my energy, my power, the essence of my being, that you are seeing... that you are *feeling*. Be of no doubt – it *can* kill others... but it will not hurt you, Whitney or the kids. The opposite, in fact : it can keep you alive, when you would otherwise be dead. And I mean to see you and my friends stay *alive*, man."

Now even Billings could hear a shouting commotion, somewhere in the direction of the parking-lot.

With a sad, knowing tone, she continued, "They are *coming* for me, Bob; and that means you and I do not have much more time together. I owe you something to remember me by – something to thank you for the beautiful love that you have given me. You are ready for my gift, which is the nobility and fortitude of my ancestors. Behold how I give it to you."

The fallen-girl's hands – now glowing with the same short-circuit scary-stuff that was still darting over her body – reached quickly to each side of his head, cupping his ears, and as she did so, Billings heard ethereal music, halfway between a Beethoven symphony and the best of Led Zeppelin, ricocheting through his brain.

"Sari, I don't think I *can*," he protested; but his voice was silenced by a bewildering kaleidoscope of insane thoughts, every bit as alien and incomprehensible as the ones he had felt back at the Park Place Mall. But this time, they were somehow reassuring – not scary at all – as they raced through his mind.

A warm glow, like what you get from the best Scotch but a thousand-fold more potent, enveloped him from head to toe.

The Peace of God, something told him, as he fought an overpowering urge to curl up and go to sleep.

The newcomer looked at Billings with an affectionate, satisfied stare.

"If our paths must part... I beg you to use this gift wisely, Bob Billings of Tucson, Arizona," she whispered. "Use it to survive the unimaginable... to live through what cannot be endured. I empower you to bless Whitney, Melissa, Curtis and Tommy, as I have gifted yourself. Teach them also to hold fast, until I return, as I surely *will*."

"Don't *go!*" he pleaded, only half-believing himself, as he regarded the 'Sari'-girl, whose demeanor was now neither that that of a fetching young woman, nor of an alien; she now looked resplendent in a way that Billings had never seen, or understood before.

She looked like a *goddess*.

Not so far off toward the parking-lot, a voice shouted out, "Secure the perimeter! Are there any more of them out there? Report! What's that damn *music!* Turn it off, it's fuckin' up the audio –"

There was another explosion, this time, further off. The structure of the building groaned, as the concussion of this second blast impacted.

"I cannot risk it," she softly argued, as if coming to an unwillingly-reached conclusion. "They want to *kill* me, Bob; and if they fail *this* time, they will just keep using more and more powerful weapons. I can only protect myself by using all my skills... but until your own gifts fully mature, you and the others will be in great danger if you remain around me. Remember what I told you about the microwave oven?"

"I don't *care*," he desperately retorted, but then he thought again, and muttered, "You're going to do *that* to them now? For Christ's sake, Sari – that's *murder!* Not that I give a shit about *them* – but they'll hang me on live TV –"

"I only take life as an absolute last resort, and I suffer each time when I do," she coolly replied. "But I *can* and *will* kill... *especially* those who threaten my kin. Be sure to tell them that. And anyway, I cannot handle the nuclear-bombs...

yet. I will barely be able to defend myself – maybe not even *that* – if I tarry here too long. We must away from here... I think that I can...”

The 'Sari'-girl closed her eyes, concentrating intensely, and Billings felt a surge of... he didn't know what, going right through him, followed rapidly by the sounds of things rattling, falling crashing.

“I am throwing it off,” she confidently announced. “Yeah, oh-kay – that is all of it. We should be able to leave now – I will drop the cloak, so that we can both see.”

The special darkness vanished, and with a mixture of amazement and horror, the salesman looked out over a huge pile of debris, at whose bottom he was now standing, along with the 'Sari'-girl.

Evidently, part of the ceiling had collapsed over top of them, and the rest of the showroom was in ruins. Though the only light was now coming in through the hole in the ceiling, he could see that the whole place looked like it was about to cave in, any minute.

“My *God*,” he gasped. “*Hugo!*”

Billings turned to look at the fallen-girl, whose eyes and body now looked what passed for normal, for her. “We've got to see if he's okay... Jesus, Sari, you threw off all *that*? With just a *shrug*?”

It must have been several tons. Or more.

“Wait until it is an ocean-liner ship that I lift above my head,” she answered, matter-of-factly, with an insouciant half-smile.

“That's all of them, accounted for,” crackled a voice from outside. “Facility surrounded. Medic! *Medic!*”

“Why can't you just *surrender* to them?” pleaded the salesman, as he tried to clamber over the mounds of shattered drywall, jagged pieces of rent sheet-metal and smashed wood-trim. “White flag, hands up in the air where we can see them... that kind of thing?”

“Hold up,” called out another voice. “Special team ETA – three minutes.”

“And what if I step out the door and walk right into one of their, uhh, tank-rockets, mini-atom-bombs or death-ray guns, and it kills you in the same shot?” she countered. “Or what if they put me in a car and then blow it up with an airplane missile?”

“Yeah,” reluctantly admitted Billings.

“A few seconds ago,” explained the fallen-girl, “Your government showed me all that I need to *know*, about how much they value life... and I did not survive all these ages uncounted, by being *stupid*, Bob. I *think* that my force-screen can stop their little bullets – that is a chance that I must take – but I *believe* what you told me about your wonderful American government... they may have weapons that I cannot yet defeat. I *must* sneak away and hide, until my powers fully return. Then I can negotiate with them from strength... not weakness.”

“Which leaves me... *where*?” asked the heartbroken salesman.

She came up to him and warmly embraced him.

Staring compassionately into the man's tear-filled eyes, she counseled, "It leaves you right *here,* my love. It is *me* who they want... not you. Go and help Hugo – I can sense that he is hurt, though not fatally. When the government-men come in, do not resist; but tell them that you, and everyone who have helped me, are under my protection. Tell them nothing else about me – except, not to hurt you."

"Or else... *what?*" he demanded.

"Or else," she replied, dead-serious, with the eyes aglow again, "There will be, how do you say it, yes, *hell* to pay. Be of no doubt, I *will* come back for you and the others – I pray that they are oh-kay, right now – and if I find any of you harmed on account of being with me, all of *this*," – she made a sweeping gesture with her arms – "Will look like a *model* of order, compared with what I will do to whoever may hurt you, Whitney, or the kids. And since he was kind and offered me a job... that goes for Hugo, too."

She paused for a second, then added, "*Especially*, it goes for Tommy. Tell them that if they do cruelty to my son, *I will lay this 'America' of yours, in ruins.* Do you understand what I said, Bob?"

"And you *wonder* why I was a little scared of you, a while ago," remarked the salesman. "Or why they want to put you in a cage."

"You are not stupid, either, Bob," she knowingly mentioned. "You distrust me – good for you! For the record... it does not mean that I love you, any the less. I want a mate who is not afraid to tell me what he thinks is right and wrong... not a puppet."

She extended a hand and helped him over the last pile of debris.

They now stood beneath a jagged hole in what was left of the former roof of the building, sunlight streaming down, illuminating the darkness inside.

"I'm sure that these threats of yours will get their attention – but not in a way that'll be good for yours truly," noted Billings, his eyes darting from place to place for signs of black-suited intruders.

To his alarm, he heard the sound of many trampling boots, outside.

For a penultimate time, another one of those from-elsewhere thoughts invaded his mind.

Call to them, Bob, she requested.

Tell them that you surrender.

The hell of it is, he pondered,

I'm almost getting used to this texting-without-a-phone stuff.

And I'm almost used to you, *by now, my beloved Sari.*

Through you, this utterly-forgettable sales-guy from Tucson, Arizona, has – if only for a few brief but glorious days – been a 'somebody'.

Thank you so much... for the good times.

"Two civilians in here, one hurt – unarmed!" shouted Billings. "We surrender! We need medical assistance!"

"On your knees, assholes – hands on the back of your head!" yelled the outside voice. "One false move, you're *dead* – got that?"

Reluctantly, the salesman complied, staring straight ahead.

"Welcome to the standard position for us lucky citizens of today's U.S. of A.", he muttered.

He felt a kiss on his cheek; and for a second, that weirdo moist stuff in it almost made him lose control, as he had scant days earlier.

All cruel empires fall, his mind perceived. *If by the Fire of my being... that will be their decision.*

Think of me each night, man; and I will be with you in the Land of Dreams, to give you peace. You will be strong – much more than you know – if you believe *in the greatness that now waxes within you.*

And remember – call my name out loud – chant it as a prayer – and this will lead me to where you are.

I love you, Bob K. Billings of Tucson, Arizona, and I will *return...*

Doubt me not!

There was a 'whoosh' sound – no, in fact it was *two* sounds, like that – and then the rattle of a can dropping somewhere, along with the slightest hint of light feet landing on what was left of the roof.

Girl... you make a hell of a kangaroo, thought Billings, a wan smile coming to his face.

Goodbye, my love! he mused, just before the gas blanked his mind.

Don't miss Book Three of *The Angel Brings Fire...*

Angel and The Empire